The New Granta Book of the

AMERICAN
SHORT STORY

The New Granta Book of the

AMERICAN
SHORT STORY

EDITED AND INTRODUCED BY

RICHARD FORD

Granta Books

London

Granta Publications, 2/3 Hanover Yard,
Noel Road, London N1 8BE

First published in Great Britain by
Granta Books, 2007

A CIP catalogue record for this book is
available from the British Library.

1 3 5 7 9 10 8 6 4 2

ISBN 978-1-86207-847-5

Typeset by M Rules
Printed and bound in Great Britain by
William Clowes Ltd, Beccles, Suffolk

CONTENTS

INTRODUCTION

Short stories by nature are daring little instruments and almost always represent commensurate daring in their makers. For one thing, short stories want to give us something big but want to do it in precious little time and space. For another, they succeed by willfully falsifying many of the observable qualities of the lived life they draw upon. They also leave out a lot of life and try to make us not worry about it. They often do funny things with time—things we know can't be done, *really*—but then make us go along with that. They persuade us that the human-being-like characters they show us can be significantly known on the strength of rather slight exposure; and they make us believe that entire lives can change (turn on a dime) on account of one little manufactured moment of clear-sightedness. You could say, based on this evidence, that the most fundamental character trait of short stories, other than their shortness, would seem to be audacity. More than even the sestina, short stories are the high-wire act of literature, the man keeping all those pretty plates up and spinning on skinny sticks.

Of course, short stories do many of the same things that the 'longer forms' do, and frankly (we all know this) not always as well. Novels foreshorten life. Novels aver that characters have important interior selves and reveal them to us. Novels offer epiphanies. Novels have artful beginnings, middles and ends, and can certainly be shapely. Novels make characters talk and cavort about. Novels can be sudden, pleasurably manipulative and blatant about their nature as artifice. They're generally just longer. They're a different sort of performance— but similar to the short story in their function and devices. Each is linear and made of words, each aims to please and aspires to beauty. Each enacts a kind of narrative and wants to make the reader pay closer attention to life before returning him to it renewed and better aware of what the writer deems important. Novels can be and often are daring and audacious. They just have more 'assets'. If they try for more, risk more (and they usually do), they also come equipped with more: more characters, more settings, more activities, more words, more chances to be good. In this way they're a more various and self-forgiving form. A novel with a defective structure, a wrong opening movement, a dead end, or a fractured end part can still be a novel and may—on balance—be good (think of *Tender is the Night*, *The Sound and the Fury*, *The Sheltering Sky*). But if a short story suffers these aesthetic flaws, it risks being nothing at all. A minor aesthetic nullity.

With the short story having so many of these formal features in common with its larger relative, what distinguishes it, what confers its basic self (and what's so good about it) seems to be linked to its brevity and to its bravura quality, its daring and (again) its audacity, to how it makes much of little, and to how it wields its authority as— to borrow from Auden—a 'verbal artifact', lacking for the most part the supportive, fulfilling and camouflaging furnishment of a novel. Being the slightly discomforting/intensely pleasing aesthetic agents they are, short stories are often good on the strength of sheer nerve.

Not everyone adores or has adored short stories. Walter Benjamin *said* he liked them—at least the ones you can tell out loud. Yet he wrote in his essay 'The Story Teller,' in a slightly exasperated tone, 'We no longer work at things that can't be abbreviated.' The poet Howard Nemerov, who wrote plenty of things that were short, drew the line at short stories. He wrote in a kind of overheated dismay, 'That so much of our experience or the stereotype which passes for it should be dealt with by means of the short story is perhaps the symptom not unnoticeable elsewhere in the public domain of an unlovely cynicism about human character.'

Historically, young American writers who come to publishers carrying books of stories are either subjected to stern treatment, or are taken on with the bullying insistence that a novel's to come. The same Eudora Welty who wrote that 'all serious daring starts from within' was made to prove that claim early in her writing life when New York publishers in the 1930s declined her first virtuoso collection *The Wide Net* because she wouldn't knuckle down or under to writing a novel. She just didn't want to. Nearly five decades later, when I myself was lurking around *Esquire* magazine—this was the middle 1980s—and publishing an occasional short story, the editor-in-chief-of-the-moment told me over dinner one night (at Elaine's, where else?) that he wouldn't publish short stories *at all* in *Esquire* (publisher of Hemingway, Fitzgerald, Capote, Flannery O'Connor, Carver, Bellow, Roth, Updike, Salter, Beattie) if he could find something else to wedge in between the ads. Short stories, I guessed—when you priced them out—were cheaper than pictures or more 'new journalism.'

What it is that short stories uniquely *do* in the exercise of their audacious authority seems worth considering, especially since most all of art—sculpture, painting, music, even dance—can be viewed as being, at least in part, about the exercise of authority. The sculptor takes a shapeless gob of clay or an apparently pointless hunk of I-beam and gets busy exerting on it. The painter squeezes the paint tube, lays on the color, etc., etc. The writer, for her part, exerts herself on otherwise unorganized language, creates utterances that provisionally subordinate our concerns to hers and— as we're induced to read on— draws us away from what we think toward what *she* thinks. And once we've, so to speak, surrendered in this way (a giving-in to authority which in itself can be thrilling, pleasurable, cathartic and more) she tries in all the strenuous, guileful and felicitous ways fiction can act upon us to authorize our response to every single thing she makes happen.

'Really, universally, relations stop nowhere . . . the exquisite problem of the artist is eternally to draw, by a geometry of his own, the circle within which they shall happily appear to do so.' Henry James, here, is commenting on art's abstracting-coercing relation to lived life when performed by the hand of the artist. James's 'geometry of his own' is the restrictive, importance-making exercise of (in the case of writing fiction) the writer's authority—as expressed by such authorial decisions as how much of this character to reveal, when to end a scene, where to commence the story and where to stop it. When John Cheever's narrator, at the astonishing conclusion of his brief but harrowing story 'Reunion' bluntly tells us, 'And that was the last time I saw my father . . .' we readers feel the story's 'geometry' fiercely close down. We have known Cheever's two people—a father and son—for only a page or two and not well, we think. Can it really be, though, that the son *never* sees his father again—ever? We would surely wonder about this in real life and demand to know more—require a novel to explain it all. But the story doesn't entertain doubt and neither do we. Relations in life may, indeed, stop nowhere. But in the hot alembic of the story's manufacture they do. Cheever's story, published in *The New Yorker* in 1962, is a model of short-story virtue, focus and conciseness. In fewer than a thousand words we visit Grand Central station twice, enter and depart three distinct midtown eateries. Cocktails are consumed, harsh, assaultive even hilarious words are exchanged, tempers burn hot, dismay turns toxic. A callow son's hopes for resuscitating the love of his father are summarily ruined, following which a vital part of life is over for ever. _

Only, life's not like that—we say again. At least ours isn't—we hope. Yet within Cheever's great authority something of life we couldn't know any other way and that can't be truly paraphrased is shaped into indisputable truth for which the story is the only testament and evidence. Moreover, this ferocity and concentration of the story's formal resources (its formal brevity, dramatic emphasis, word choice, sudden closure) are aesthetic features we readers like being close to, and submit to with pleasure—if only because these events aren't really happening to us. And while saying this much may not tell us precisely *why* 'Reunion' is so dazzling, it begins to suggest importantly *how*. And our awareness of this *how* may please us, too.

Nothing, in fact, may tell us definitively why any story is excellent. Cheever's story is about a father and a son in an instant of defining, galvanizing crisis—the dramatic and moral values are thus set up high (always a help). The scene and settings are recognizable, vivid and deftly limned. It's extremely funny, albeit in a hateful sort of way. A risibly mean and pathetic drunk is given his (to us) satisfying comeuppance, while a sweet-seeming, impressionable son survives to tell the tale. Bliss is once again moved revealingly into the orbit of bale, all of it delivered inside a streamlined little verbal torpedo that explodes upon us almost before we know it.

That's, of course, not exactly *it*. What's *it* is the story's interconnected, amalgamated, shapely and irreducible self— embodying, representing, acquainting and connecting us to something crucial about life that doesn't even exist as intelligence (or didn't) except in these specific terms and by no other authority than this. Cheever was a great writer—full stop, as the English so enjoy saying. And his story, with all its foreshortenings, daring spatial and temporal improbabilities, drastic economies and subordinations cannot finally be assayed, but simply *is*.

'Real-life improbability rendered fictively plausible by authorial main force inside a small space of words' may be one provisional, exploded description of a good short story and part of the source of its pleasing torque. (We like experiencing the implausible made plausible as fiction; how else explain the American presidency?) Donald Barthelme's classic story 'Me and Miss Mandible', in which an insurance adjuster is returned to the sixth grade after counseling a claimant to sue the insurer, could certainly make you subscribe to such a definition. Mary Gaitskill's nervy, roguish story, 'A Romantic Weekend', sets two questing, comically-inept young sexual masochists off on their first 'date'—improbably, to our nation's capitol. Things get started wrong for the 'lovers', get wrong-er, get *very* wrong (and funny), get messy, painful, get hopeless, then strangely and quickly transmute, on the strength of Gaitskill's imagination, into something like amity and empathy, before a lost weekend's nearly rescued and the characters go safely home. Balanced on great timing, wit, intelligence, humanity and conciseness, 'A Romantic Weekend' pivots on Gaitskill's ability—in the galvanizing force-field of art fastened to an apt form—to draw strength from improbability and brevity, and from the author's will to transform both into something probable and indeed into something close to love's first pulse beats.

I'm not attempting to pronounce a formula here: that all great short stories rely on something screwy and far-fetched being made 'fetched' by a writer's imaginative muscle and canniness. Sometimes that happens. Nothing improbable happens, however, in Chekhov's elegant 'The Lady with the Dog', the all-time short-story gold standard, in which a rather dull married man encounters a rather aimless married woman in a Crimean seaside resort consecrated for exactly these casually furtive rendezvous. The two commence a tepid affair, then dutifully trudge home to separate cities and lives, only to be drawn again to each other's tenderness for reasons that seem eminently ordinary (they're bored, they're willing, and they're able), following which re-coupling, a complex and predictably desultory future is quietly acknowledged and acceded to. And there the story, in what seems both an undramatic but also oddly pressurized fashion, ends.

There's no flashy audacity here—unless you care to say (and, of course, I do) that Chekhov's act of magisterial authority is in *choosing* and then *forcing* these rather sallow, nearly featureless beings and prosaic behaviors onto our notice as formal constituents and moral integers of a short story. The story—and it's as good as any of us will ever read—is full of fine, nuanced, writerly precisions, skewering verbal and dramatic ironies, great if concisely set emphases, and the pathos of human frailty half-enlivened by sex. But the first great authoritative leap is in the *imagining*—in Chekhov's daring to imagine what a great story could conceivably (perhaps improbably) be about.

Bharati Mukherjee's quietly superb story 'The Management of Grief', is similarly empowered by acts subtle, unobvious but predisposing authorial choice—Mukherjee's intuition that a great story can be made from what might go unrecognized in other people's fiction as well as in life. A jet airplane full of passengers has exploded and crashed into the sea off Ireland—all lives apparently lost. Back home in Toronto, surviving family members—Indo-Canadians, preoccupied by the routine but uneasy chores of multi-cultural assimilation (house warmings, kids' lives, sports, trips to the mall, prayers), are sent reeling into grief, shock and loss. Mrs Bhave—Mukherjee's focal character and narrator—is anguished no less than her neighbors. But Mrs Bhave, who's lost her husband and two sons to the crash, is by nature a 'pillar', who experiences loss within a 'terrible calm' that permits her to assist friends, counsel aged strangers, view grisly death photos of crash victims and somehow resist doing away with herself from the sheer accumulation of awfulness. Mukherjee's narrative manner and dramatic atmosphere in this extraordinary story is also Mrs Bhave's personal demeanor of strained but oceanic equability, in which horror, the mundane, even the most hopeful of 'cosmic consolations' are viewed as facets of a vast, interconnected human drama-on-earth which we who remain are charged to make the most of or be lost. Grief is managed but ingeniously brought into an unexpected fictive context that invites us to see all of life within its walls.

I fall short of touching this story's great subtleties, its bracing concisions in time and setting, its verbal felicity and grace notes. But let me just say that the story's premise—how a grief-diminished, capable but regular-seeming woman quietly manages her life's greatest burden and test and eventually survives and goes on—becomes almost preternaturally powerful for *not* directly exploiting the most obvious dramatic values available (the furious crash, the wailing, the general ghastliness), but by staying within the quieter human eddy. Like Chekhov's, Mukherjee's instinct—her pre-eminent act of authority—is to sense that here, where smaller dramas might seem to wait

inconspicuous, lies much that's large and important when seized by
the divining force of daring artistic notice.

Once you begin to think that writing fiction is all about writers exerting
authority upon readers, pretty soon the evidence starts to pop up
everywhere—like those Disneyesque cartoon drawings from my youth,
depicting apparently vacant forest scenes in which the spectator is
asked to 'find the cow in this picture'. First, I find no cow. Then I find
one cow staring enigmatically back at me. But then before long I find
cows, cows and nothing *but* cows, and I can't see the woods anymore—
for the cows.

Writers exercising authority is, of course, not *the thing* fiction is all
about, nor the key to what makes short stories great. Great stories are
congeries of plan, vigor, will and application, but also of luck and error
and intuition and even, God knows, sudden inspiration for all of which
there is no key, and in the midst of which things often just happen—a
fact that should make us like stories even better for their life-mimicking
knack of seeming to come out of nowhere (like those bovines), thereby
fortifying our faith in art and life's mystery. Back in 1992, in the
Introduction to the first *Granta Book of the American Short Story*, I quoted
Ford Madox Ford to the point that the general effect of fiction should be
the 'effect life has on mankind'. For decades I'd thought the elder Ford's
precept was just a throat-clearing Edwardian *profundo* predicated on
life's being murky and heavily 'meaningful' like Edwardian furniture,
and was predicated also on humanity's fly-in-the-bottle efforts to make
life get clearer toward its end. However, if you go on thinking about
boilerplate truths, they sometimes (though not always) begin to seem
even truer. So that I've started to think that Ford might indeed have
believed that well, yes, life *is* all these indistinct gray-toned things, but
it's also (as his own novels attest) mercurial in the extreme, unobvious,
coercive, shocking, and capable of confronting us with *the new* using
means that make existence itself revelatory and even appealing. Stories,
he would say, should be that way, too.

To perform these great mimetic feats by which art and life have
similar effects, short stories (and novels, too) almost always contain
small and large, glaringly obvious and also barely observable exertions
of their writers' authority. By authority I mean, roughly speaking, a
writer's determination, variously enacted, to assume provisional

command of a reader's attention and volition, thereby overcoming the reader's resistance and engaging his credulity for the purpose of interposing some scheme the writer imagines to be worth both his and the reader's time and trouble.

The mere act of writing a story *at all* and proffering it into a mental 'space' some citizen might be otherwise happy to fill with the Wednesday-night fights or a '64 Chateau Montrose, always constitutes an act of presumptuous and first-principle authority, and necessarily anticipates all the fictive demands to follow. (This is the privileged tap on the would-be reader's shoulder that many young writers take as their due, but that many older writers grow to feel—by dint of time spent reading—is an act of imposition whose harsh demands ought to be weighed in strict moral terms and ultimately rewarded.)

This first conceptual act of authority ('I've dreamed up a story—for somebody') pretty quickly, however, materializes into the actual story itself and its first significant gesture, excluding the title. 'My mother swore we'd never live in a boarding house again, but circumstances did not allow her to keep this promise . . .' begins, almost lamentingly, Tobias Wolff's wonderful story 'Firelight'. I myself once began a story with what I believed to be the brash and irresistible sentence—because I thought brash was good—'This is not a happy story, I warn you.' But Wolff's calmer, meditative, not the least bit brash or obviously audacious first sentence takes command of the reader's attention at least as well as mine did, and probably more shrewdly and promisingly.

Certainly there's no black-letter law for how to overcome the reader's preoccupations elsewhere, and thus to allow the writer his specific authoritative intentions. 'When in doubt have a man walk through a door holding a gun,' Raymond Chandler famously suggested as a possible strategy. Which is fine if you want to do that and are willing to sacrifice any other plans you might have. But what if you, like Wolff, have something else in mind that doesn't involve men with guns and that still seems important? *Something* has to persuade us readers that we're being confronted with a force (a mind, a promising competence, a storage of words, an appealing imagination) that has *something* for us that we need, will be better for and possibly renewed by. This initial gesture implying the good promise of the story's waiting self, represents one aspect and one bit of evidence of a story's authority. Wolff's deft, understated, almost mannerly first sentence lets us know imposing things: (1) the story's about the speaker's mother and his relation to her—so it's probably important; (2) apparently the story involves hard times—so we're possibly empathetic; (3) strong wishes are engaged but don't finally succeed—one of life's signature dramas; (4) the narrator's competent authority as a teller is expressed by an ability to be concise, clear and direct—longed-for qualities when it comes to talking truly about life, which is what the story apparently means to do. It's daring, but it's daring that comes from within.

And not that *everything* has to take place with the very first scratch on the page—as happens say, in Denis Johnson's story 'Work' which begins, 'I'd been staying at the Holiday Inn with my girlfriend, honestly the most beautiful woman I'd ever known, for three days under a phony name, shooting heroin.' This is an opening that would thrill Chandler, and thrills me. But we can agree that authoritative gestures come in soft as well as loud volume levels. 'In the car on the way south,' begins Richard Bausch's grave story of family mourning 'Ancient History', 'after hours of quiet between them, of only the rattle and static of the radio, she began to talk about growing up so close to Washington: how it was to have all the shrines of Democracy as part of one's daily idea of home; she had taken it all for granted, of course. "But your father was always a tourist in his own city," she said. "It really excited him. That's why we spent our honeymoon there. Everybody thought we'd got tickets to travel, and we weren't fifteen minutes from home . . ."'

Somewhere, however, near to the story's beginning an opportunity for the writer to take control must by some means be seized. And unless I'm the most easily distractible reader in the world and everybody else is way more patient, this opportunity seems precious.

'For years,' Deborah Eisenberg's story 'The Custodian' begins, 'after Isobel left town (was sent from town, to live with an aunt in San Francisco) Lynnie would sometimes see her at a distance, crossing the street or turning a corner. But just as Lynnie started after her Isobel would vanish, having been replaced by a substitute, some long-legged stranger with pale floaty hair. And while Lynnie might have been just as happy, by and large, not to see Isobel, at those moments she was felled by a terrible sorrow, as though somewhere a messenger searching for her had been waylaid, or was lost.'

What, in fact, proclaims Eisenberg's and her story's authority in this rather talkative, unassuming first paragraph? It really isn't so hard to see: (1) confidence inspired by Eisenberg's (or her narrator's) word choices—'floaty', 'felled' (not *struck*, nor *overcome*, not *seized*), and even by the character's unusual name—'Lynnie'; (2) the narrator's self-actualizing impulse to interrupt her own first sentence with a sudden, apparently needed, parenthesis; (3) the ambiguity of Lynnie's ability to 'see' and then not to 'see' Isobel being cast as a minor but enticing mystery (Isobel's 'disappearance'); (4) the writer/narrator's paragraph-capping resort to dramatic, amplifying, illuminating metaphor (simile, really) '. . . *as though* somewhere a messenger searching for her had been waylaid, or was lost'; and, finally, (5) the imaginative connection, the authoritative pushing-out of the entire experience to assert its capacity to provoke 'terrible sorrow'.

All these seemingly smallish elements, conveyed within Eisenberg's measured sentences, accumulate to cause the reader perhaps not even consciously to 'cooperate', as Virginia Woolf put it, but to submit at least provisionally to the story's intentions—after which we and Eisenberg and 'The Custodian' are off and going to paragraph two and beyond.

Having preached ardently about stories' openings, it seems natural now to speak about stories' endings as manifestations of writerly authority. James's pronouncement about relations stopping nowhere except via some writer's peculiar 'geometry' applies—in my view— most discernibly to stories' endings and to their character as artifice dependent solely on when and how the writer wants to draw a halt to things. Unlike beginnings, which seem to possess duties instantly pertinent to the story that follows—duties that can be performed in any variety of ways but rarely ignored—endings have no such responsible duties. Stories can 'close', they can 'dovetail', they can recapitulate what's gone on up until then, they can end then start then stop again, guns can go off. Or they can simply quit and let everybody go home, which is often how I feel about the stirring stories of Edward P. Jones. Jones frequently just seems to quit when *he's* finished with what *he* deems important, never mind other internal niceties. Yet no matter how the reader may feel personally about which strategy the writer employs, by how satisfying the ending is or isn't, the ending *is* the end of the story, and the reader at some level of notice realizes and concedes it's the writer's authority that's caused it (not that the crippled kid's dog has come home, or whether Eddie's divorce is finalized, or that they at last took the bandages off and Myrna can see again). All readers with any inkling of sensitivity about stories realize, whether the writer has stuck his landing and scored a ten or has left his readers leaning and agape, that the writer could always write more if he chose to, could go on making things up, except that due to the gaugeable effects created by stopping just here, he chooses not to. In terms of authority, in terms of daring, in terms of audacity and nerve, endings are nearly always the most conspicuous form of artifice in short stories. They are, in fact, often the part that makes shortness a distinct and palpable feature. The stories in this collection bring off their endings in all manner of wondrous ways, and importantly so, in as much as the ending comprises the last words the reader has with the writer, so that any writer might reasonably want to calculate them. But in terms of what's at stake—with the entire story having already gone by—the ending, at least structurally, is also the part the reader is likely to experience most sensibly and be most tolerant of, whether he approves of it or not. A good friend of mine, who is a distinguished editor of fiction, vociferously disputes this last dictum, arguing that endings are the formal feature in short stories that writers are least likely to get right, and for this reason are the parts in stories he is *least* tolerant of, and are often the cause of stories being sent back where they came from. My view is, however (and I'm taking the last word here), that the paramount task of any story writer (or librettist or sonneteer or novelist) is to induce the reader to read *all* of his story— this being well before we get into matters of goodness or likeability. Thus, if I can write my story well enough to get you to its end, you the reader will be likely to read whatever I write next, almost no matter what it is. (This, admittedly, is a bare-bones version of what a successful story might be, though it is also one that allows the writer his fullest freedom all the way to the very end of the very last line.)

Middles, however are another matter. Most short stories—except for those little novelty acts variously called Sudden Stories or Instant Fiction, and that I can never read to the end because of their iron-clad promise of toxic slightness—most stories mostly take place in what we might call their middles, in what's written between their crucial, artful beginnings and their geometric, non-negotiable endings. It's here, in the murky middle—in the dicey second act and onward, where the woolliest of woolly life issues come under scrutiny—that the air can sigh out of the dramatic balloon, and for this reason where the fundamental business of writing fiction must exhibit the incontestable authority and writerly daring that make the experience of reading the story full and intense and sustainable.

Emerson, in 'Self Reliance', wrote that 'Power ceases in the instant of repose; it resides in the moment of transition from a past to a new state, in the shooting of the gulf.' Emerson might have been describing one of the signal attributes of almost all high-quality short stories: the fierce authority expressed by choosing—to choose this word and leave that one out, to subordinate that line, clause or scene to something deemed more important; to cease and then move on concisely, or else to linger, push, dedicate more language. Power, Emerson believed, is what's gained in these critical choosings. And in fiction it's the persuasive power the story takes on and that the reader experiences from the authoritative election of this word rather than that one, to describe that character's interior, to make this line be dialogue rather than narrative, to end this scene here and commence that one there. This power drawn from good election is part of the story's potent capacity to command our attention and to assure us that while there's blessedly, dismayingly, more to life than we can ever say—a sensation felt most acutely in stories' middle parts—it is specifically by these choices that something crucial *within* life is illumined as nowhere else and put on radiant, consequential display.

Cheever's story 'Reunion' comes vividly to mind again when contemplating *middles* and how they're managed by writerly authority. 'Reunion' gives us New York in a nutshell: Grand Central twice, many cocktails, a few acerbic New Yorkerish words uttered, one or two heartbreaking ones, and out of the story's deftly managed body somehow erupts a life suddenly changed in a way no one could've imagined. Raymond Carver's perfect little masterpiece, 'Are These the Actual Miles?' (from the first *Granta* collection) is equally exhibitable. In 1,500 or so well-quarried words and a few savagely supervised little narrative increments, an entire dark night of the soul is traversed: a wife is alienated; a man gets drunk and despondent; terrible, irrevocable words are spoken; a marriage edges nearer the abyss; the same man who's suffered so is casually dishonored in his driveway by a used-car salesman he's never even met. Plus a convertible gets sold.

In any story's significant elections—for details, for more words, for tropes, for stopping and starting again—the reader (by reading) is caused to submit to the writer's authorizing 'eye', and the story is enabled to offer what readers come to serious fiction expecting: transport out of our private moments, affirmation of the world's mysterious thereness, contact with and recognition of the *new* and felicitous where those had seemed unlikely, a renewed faith in language, and in writing's capacity to exact trust in return for pleasure and illumination.

This passage from Kevin Canty's 'Blue Boy' displays all these virtues of choice and authority by seizing what might easily have been a depressurized spot in the story's middle, and holding us poised until its details can be pushed by Canty to heretofore unimagined but incontrovertible truth:

Kenny stood in the kitchen door, next to the winter coats, men's and women's woolen overcoats hanging on their pegs like abandoned persons. In the dead of summer these coats seemed exotic as sponge divers' outfits. There was a man's good gray overcoat hanging on the rack, a husband's coat. Kenny felt an obscure jealousy, as if he were married to Mrs. Jordan, as if the child sleeping under the water had been their own child, born into the air again. On an impulse, Kenny put his hand into the pocket of the overcoat, a soft solid pocket meant for a bigger hand than his, and brought out a passcard for the Washington subway, a white cotton handkerchief, a scrap of gum wrapper and seven dollars, two singles and a five. Kenny kept the money and the passcard and stuffed the handkerchief back into the coat pocket, the yellow gum wrapper fluttering to the floor in his hurry. Now this ordinary hallway felt dangerous, as if it had suddenly been raised fifty feet off the ground, so that walking it required care.

So vivid in Canty's remarkable interior paragraph is the writer's muscular choice to write *more* rather than less, to urge himself into the no-man's land beyond where any sentence might stop, but where the

next sentence could be the best he will ever write. Poised on his chosen
details and images—coats as '. . . exotic as sponge divers' outfits . . . a
solid pocket meant for a bigger hand . . . a scrap of gum wrapper and
seven dollars, two singles and a five . . .' Canty authorizes and enlivens
the unknown and furnishes it with language that risks saying (all the
way out to the 'danger' at the passage's end) what hasn't been said
before.

Think again of Deborah Eisenberg's opening paragraph (though
already pressing into the heart of the story); but think of it without the
daring push, the resolve to write more that reaches the metaphor of the
last sentence. Or imagine this paragraph toward the end of 'Firelight',
if Tobias Wolff hadn't pressed us and himself forward for one more
deal-clenching sentence:

> He lost me there, and I went back to looking at the flames. Dr.
> Avery rumbled on. He had been quiet before, but once he got
> started he didn't stop, and I wouldn't have wanted him to. The
> sound of his voice made me drowsy with assurance, like the
> drone of a car engine when you're lying on the backseat, going
> home from a long trip.

We can't know, from the settled evidence of a story, what was its actual
path into existence. But we can see what lay ahead for Wolff as he
wrote this passage and elected for one more utterance. What he gained
is the fresh, defining connection that joins a boy's remembered
drowsiness to a sense of assurance, and (by implication) to a happier
picture of childhood than the real world would ever offer.

Finally, imagine this glorious paragraph of Elizabeth Spencer's from
the inner workings of 'Ship Island', but without the commanding leap,
the choice to push beyond a description of mundane southern
bathroom decor, toward a consummate peroration on the moral
character of human kind:

> The Skeltons' bathroom was all pale blue and white, with
> handsome jars of rose bath salts and big fat scented bars of rosy
> soap. The lights came on impressively and the fixtures were
> heavy, yet somehow it all looked dead. It came to Nancy that she
> had really been wondering about just what would be in this sort

of bathroom ever since she had seen those boys, with maybe Rob among them, playing tennis while she jumped on a trampoline. Surely the place had the air of an inner shrine, but what was there to see? The tops of all the bottles fitted firmly tight, and the soap in the tub was dry. Somebody had picked it all out—that was the point—judging the soap and bath salts just the way they judged outsiders, business, real estate, politics. Nancy's father made judgments, too. Once, he argued all evening that Hitler was a well-meaning man; another time, he said the world was ready for communism.

Why stress authority in fiction when there's so much more to talk about? For instance, the cold, suffocating hands of the American writing-program industry on our faltering national literary 'product'; or the sad decline of the traditional story form—bested again by stories of yet another 'new stylistic moment'; or the future of the graphic novel or story, now that Chekhov and Cheever have got stale. One reason might be that given the stylistically and intellectually diverse work that follows in this volume, the exertion of writerly authority may be the only defining acts these stories perform both brilliantly *and mutually*— getting their artifices up and going, determining what *can actually become* a story, authorizing what's more important than what, which details in a character's 'life' to include, which to leave unimagined, what to make a character 'think', how to suppress the reader's doubt about the streamlined, un-lifelike nature of the short-story form itself, devising ways to authorize readers' responses to every sensuous detail, every concise transition, every extravagance in language, every ending.

Admittedly *authority* is just one keyhole glimpse into the basic nature of stories. Still, it is by a story's willingness and ability to take command and husband our attention that it gets us to the last word of the last sentence. Most writers, as I've already suggested, would say that if they just can perform that little miracle then their story can be said to 'work'.

And there might be other reasons to think on authority's importance. In his memoir *Experience*, the novelist Martin Amis wrote that as readers we always have a 'conversation', (possibly even an argument), with any piece of literary fiction, of which this collection is composed. Rhetorically speaking, this is serious fiction's nature, and serious fiction means to make it be our nature. And it is generally in stories' most exigent parts, the parts where the story's authority acts on us strenuously—suppresses our doubt, challenges us with words put newly and well, with unexpected events, with its choices—that this vital conversation takes up: 'Can it be,' we implicitly ask as we read, 'that such a father would behave in such a way toward his son?' The story— Cheever's 'Reunion'—contends it can. 'Is it logical that an ordinary bathroom's ordinary contents would give rise to moral inquiry?' 'Is this the proper place for a story to begin? To finish? To stop and start again?' 'Is this *really* the consequence of *that*?' 'From the quiet, un-notable self-ministrations of a heart-broken mother and wife can the quintessence of grief be revealed and ourselves consoled?' 'Can this even be a great story?' Whether we experience it frontally or subliminally, this is the challenge to *our* readerly authority that great fiction presents, the conversation it wants to have with us. When we read and go forward, we engage this conversation, and by submitting to it we admit the story's authority and let ourselves in for literature's great miracle of renewal and awareness.

Of course, as I've also already stated (probably too often), one of reading's unique pleasures can arise precisely from acts of submission, from consigning our attention to a promising *other*—a writer. Years ago, as a young and slow-going reader in Mississippi, I first registered this very pleasure—the pleasure of co-operation with the story's authority—and began just faintly to realize how good it might be to provide such an experience to a stranger. This co-operation set me on the way to a writing life. And possibly, now, some other young reader will read the stories that follow here, register the pleasure I did, notice the stories' authority, the longing it can provoke and satisfy, and find a vocation.

These days, contemporary short-story writing in America, as the stories here exemplify, presents many colorations and flourishes and strategies of verisimilitude and conceptions of what a story might be. And these variations regularly appear side by side in the same publications, seeking the same readers, finding the same advocates. I noted this fact in the Introduction to the first *Granta* collection in 1992. I concluded, probably hopefully then, that a state of what I called 'unsettlement' existed among Americans who wrote and read fiction, unsettlement about how to transcend the short story form in order to make it better. Unsettlement seemed good, fertile, challenging. And the state of aesthetic affairs that it denoted seemed a positive consequence of another state of affairs that had existed when I was a kid writer, in the late sixties and early seventies, a time when writing short stories and fiction in general felt like a cultural movement loosely organized into often antipathetic, sometimes rivalrous 'camps' or 'schools' and reader cohorts. 'Anti-story' experimenters made claims about newness, kept different company from traditionalists (like me), who were said by our detractors to be 'sleepy'. Inaccurately named minimalists were uneasy in the sixties about magical realists. John Gardner roostered with William Gass and Stanley Elkin. People wrote position papers, took tough stands. One knew where one's self (and one's readers) resided, whether or not one was very pleased to reside there.

In 2007—post 9/11, post-Katrina, mid-George-Bush-II, mid-Gulf war II, mid-oil crisis, early-eco disaster—when we Americans, with good reason, sense that our country is on the brink of even more ominously large events, it seems to me that very little aesthetic ruckus is audible within our cultural conversation about fiction, and that we are distant from any legitimate and new aesthetic movement there. Maybe I'm just older and notice less. Or perhaps in this period of lessened readership for serious fiction, when magazines are fewer and great publishing houses are apparently less interested, it just may be that *all* imaginative writing feels experimental, so that there's less cause to argue about 'audience issues', and only time to concentrate on the fundamental artistic one—on doing it. It's appealing to believe we could actually be living in a fictively liberated moment in America, just as some of us always wanted, when literary-historical antitheses have harmonized into florid diversity and co-existence. Only it doesn't feel very plausible—in fact, it feels complacent—to say so. Much more likely, that in a time of noisy, terrifying and extremely plausible world political turmoil, when 'the news' in all its compromised forms and conveyances threatens to become our modern novel, and when our high-speed sensation of *event* occurs faster than we can transact it imaginatively—more likely that wonderful American fiction may simply be not very adept at capturing headlines.

Not that I sense story-writing or fiction in general to have suffered a decline in excellence in America, only a fall-off in its public relations campaign. A bravura story by Barry Hannah, Julie Orringer or Matt Klam written the day before yesterday stands up quite well beside one written by John Cheever or Eudora Welty fifty years ago. If I didn't believe that, I wouldn't be writing this now and handing over these stories. And surely no one can argue that a need for great fiction isn't present in this atmosphere saturated by the news and the perfidies of politics. When Emerson wrote in the mid-nineteenth century—in his own version of 'Experience'—that 'nature doesn't like to be observed,' he was only acknowledging that the imagination can bring us news about our natures that the other news organs can't and never will, and that what literature tells is vital to our survival.

As was true in the first volume, in the stories chosen here I have carelessly eschewed pseudo-critical considerations of periodicity, and am not identifying 2007 to be 'a moment', as Virginia Woolf did when she wrote, 'On or about December, 1910, human character changed.' I haven't felt a need to represent every ethnic group in the American quilt. I have again played rather fast and loose with 'American', relative to this book's title, since I have even less evidence than I had a decade ago that upon our shrinking globe American stories are fated to be stylistically, thematically, generically different from another nationality's. For that reason, if a writer claims to be American and writes in English, I've let down the citizenship barrier. I have also not championed imaginative literature's porousness to history, or its indifference, so that there's no '9/11' story in this volume—though there *is* a majestic story partly about Aids by Dennis McFarland. And, needless to say, 'The Artificial Nigger' has a distinctly politically incorrect title. But these matters would always be beside my point—mine being the story's excellence. My certain belief is that literature always reflects its times either clearly or opaquely whether it wants to or not. In any case these concerns are, to me, extra-literary and the rightful province of those pale heroes of the extra-literary—the critics.

A reader of this volume will notice that these collected stories represent work by fourteen American writers who were included, albeit with different stories, in the first Granta volume, and that the remainder are by writers possibly new to many short-story enthusiasts, and also some stories by writers who're not so new. My design has been a simple one: to present and encourage the work of the young, to refresh the readership of significant writers absent from the first volume, and finally to honor those American writers, Updike, Beattie, Cheever, Welty, Oates, Williams, Wolff, Boyle, Bausch and others whose work continues to renew itself and to make a significant and lasting contribution to our literature.

My tastes, of course, have been at work. Duchamps noted that taste can be the enemy of art. He felt taste promoted dull redundancy. And I completely agree and have therefore tried hard to avoid dull redundancy. Still, there lurks the uneasiness of the anthologizer, the worry that he's missed something or someone momentous and that his tastes are not wholesome and broad at all, but narrow and timid, and have led him unwittingly to writing he finds easy to take. I'm sure I've missed good stories and good writers in my endeavors not to, and for those errors I'm sorry.

In purely generic terms—where writers are the authorities—I have sought to exclude no story because of what its writer imagined a story *could be* or could contain (since I don't know what a story might be until I read it—an anticipation which, I guess, is part of the pleasure), and have tried to entertain stories on their own terms, excluding them only when they didn't seem good enough. Relatedly, if a writer says his is a short story, and it doesn't patently seem *not* to be one (because it's too long, for instance, to be considered 'short'), then I've been ready to agree it's a short story, whether I'd have written it that way myself or not. Likewise with a piece of fiction that's too 'short' and by that economy inconsequential, I might agree that here was a short story, only not a very good short story.

I've also, years back, jettisoned most of those old 'instructive' rules of thumb, the ones you can learn in school and that seek to define short stories for the amateur practitioner: don't start stories with dialogue ('We won't know who's talking, and all meaning comes from character'); keep the point of view 'consistent', observe temporal and spatial unities, don't kill off characters in stories since death is only as important as the life that ends, and in stories not enough life is ever portrayed. All that's fine - until it isn't. Until it gets in the way of daring. Once, years ago, my pal Ray Carver sent me a 'framed' story he'd just written. A 'framed' story is one in which the narrator tells a story *within* a larger story, thus 'framing' it. *Heart of Darkness* is an example, as is Sherwood Anderson's wonderful 'I Want to Know Why.'

Ray's story ended without the 'framed' interior story being brought to an end so that the outer story could neatly enclose it. This was the rule (I thought): in a framed story the interior story *is supposed* to conclude, before the outside (framing) story ends, thus allowing the past's important significations to radiate neatly 'out' to the fictive present and beyond. I don't know why I thought that. Probably some teacher who couldn't write a lick 'taught' it to me. But I tried to be helpful and point out this defect to Ray, who told me he didn't care at all if the frame got closed, that his was a very good story, which was all he asked from life. I never afterward felt very good about that story, and occasionally would remind Ray of the unfinished 'frame'. And he, having never developed an appetite for dissent, never showed me another story in manuscript as long as he lived, but also never failed to telephone me when that particular story, 'The Calm', won one award and prize after another, and to remind me that the frame still wasn't closed.

V.S. Pritchett wrote that short stories were 'exquisitely difficult' things to make. Though by that I don't think he meant that they were such difficult things to 'put together', since we've all read bad ones that were put together rather neatly. Rather, I believe Pritchett meant that they were difficult things—the great ones, anyway—to *imagine*, in the way Chekhov imagined 'The Lady with the Dog', or in the way that imagining time is more difficult than making a clock tick. One task asks for skill, the other for serious daring of the sort Pritchett understood and could perform splendidly, as could his great friend Miss Welty from the rich turbulence of her 'sheltered life'. I think of her now, gone from us—Pritchett, too, and Carver—having left so much of excellence. Their great spirits and incomparable stories spell out so well for us where daring starts and where it leads, and exactly why it is the pure and indispensable and thrilling call that brings us all to stories.

Richard Ford
February 16, 2007

LADIES IN SPRING

Eudora Welty

The pair moved through that gray landscape as though no one would see them—dressed alike in overalls and faded coats, one big, one little, one black-headed, one tow-headed, father and son. Each carried a cane fishing pole over his shoulder, and Dewey carried the bucket in his other hand. It was a soft, gray, changeable day overhead—the first like that, here in the month of March.

Just a quarter of an hour before, Dewey riding to school in the school bus had spotted his father walking right down the road, the poles on his shoulder—two poles. Dewey skimmed around the schoolhouse door, and when his father came walking through Royals, he was waiting at the tree by the post office.

'Scoot. Get on back in the schoolhouse. You been told,' said his father.

In a way, Dewey would have liked to obey that: Miss Pruitt had promised to read them about *Excalibur*. What had made her go and pick today?

'But I can see you're bound to come,' said his father. 'Only we ain't going to catch us no fish, because there ain't no water left to catch 'em in.'

'The river!'

'All but dry.'

'You been many times already?'

'Son, this is my first time this year. Might as well keep still about it at home.'

The sky moved, soft and wet and gray, but the ground underfoot was powder dry. Where an old sycamore had blown over the spring before, there was turned up a tough round wall of roots and clay all white, like the moon on the ground. The river had not backed up into the old backing places. Vines, leafless and yet abundant and soft, covered the trees and thickets as if rainclouds had been dropped down from the sky over them. The swamp looked gray and endless as pictures in the Bible; wherever Dewey turned, the world held perfectly still for moments at a time—then a heron would pump through.

'Papa, what's that lady doing?'

'Why, I believe that's Miss Hattie Purcell on foot ahead.'

'Is she supposed to be way out here?'

'Miss Hattie calls herself a rainmaker, son. She could be at it. We sure can use the rain. She's most generally on hand at the post office.'

'I know now.' He opened his mouth.

'Don't be so apt to holler,' said his father. 'We may can keep to the rear of her, if we try good.'

The back of Miss Hattie rose up a little steep place, her black hat sharp above the trees. She was ahead of them by a distance no longer than the street of Royals. Her black coat was a roomy winter one and hung down in the back to her ankles, when it didn't catch on things. She was carrying, like a rolling pin, a long furled umbrella, and moved straight forward in some kind of personal zigzag of a walk—it would be hard to pass *her*.

Now Miss Hattie dipped out of sight into a gully.

'Miss Hattie's making a beeline, ain't she,' said Dewey's father. 'Look at her go. Let's you and me take us a plain *path*.'

But as they came near the river in a little while, Dewey pointed his finger. Fairly close, through the trees, they saw a big strong purse with a handle on it like a suitcase, set down on the winter leaves. Another quiet step and they could see Miss Hattie. There on the ground, with her knees drawn up the least bit, skirt to her ankles, coat spread around her like a rug, hat over her brow, steel glasses in her hand, sat Miss Hattie Purcell, bringing rain. She did not even see them.

Miss Hattie brought rain by sitting a vigil of the necessary duration beside the nearest body of water, as everybody knew. She made no more sound at it than a man fishing. But something about the way Miss Hattie's comfort shoes showed their tips below her skirt and carried a dust of the dry woods on them made her look as though she'd be there forever: longer than they would.

His father made a sign to Dewey, and they got around Miss Hattie there and went on.

'This is where I had in mind the whole time,' he said.

It was where there was an old, unrailed, concrete bridge across the Little Muscadine. A good jump—an impossible jump—separated the bridge from land, for the Old Road—overgrown, but still coming through the trees this far—fell away into a sandy ravine when it got to the river. The bridge stood out there high on its single foot, like a table in the water.

There was a sign, 'Cross at Own Risk,' and a plank limber as a hammock laid across to the bridge floor. Dewey ran the plank, ran the bridge's length, and gave a cry—it was an island.

The bearded trees hung in a ring around it all, the Little Muscadine without a sound threaded through the sand among fallen trees, and the two fishermen sat on the bridge, halfway across, baited their hooks from the can of worms taken out of a pocket, and hung their poles over the side.

They didn't catch anything, sure enough.

About noon, Dewey and his father stopped fishing and went into a lunch of biscuits and jelly the father took out of another pocket.

'This bridge don't belong to nobody,' his father said, then. 'It's just going begging. It's a wonder somebody don't stretch a tent over this good floor and live here, high and dry. You could have it clean to yourself. Know you could?'

'Me?' asked Dewey.

His father faintly smiled and ate a biscuit before he said, 'You'd have to ask your ma about it first.'

'There's another one!' said Dewey.

Another lady had dared to invade this place. Over the water and through the trees, on the same side of the river they'd come from, her face shone clear as a lantern light in nighttime. She'd found them.

'Blackie?' she called, and a white arm was lifted too. The sound was like the dove-call of April or May, and it carried as unsurely as something she had tried to throw them across that airy distance.

Blackie was his father's name, but he didn't answer. He sat just as he was, out in the open of the bridge, both knees pointed up blue, a biscuit with a bite gone out of it in his hand.

Then the lady turned around and disappeared into the trees.

Dewey could easily think she had gone off to die. Or if she hadn't, she would have had to die there. It was such a complaint she sent over, it was so sorrowful. And about what but death would ladies, anywhere, ever speak with such soft voices—then turn and run? Before

she'd gone, the lady's face had been white and still as magic behind the
trembling willow boughs that were the only bright-touched thing.

'I think she's gone,' said Dewey, getting to his feet.

Turtles now lay on logs sticking up out of the low water, with their
small heads raised. An old log was papped with baby turtles. Dewey
counted fourteen, seven up one side and seven down the other. Just
waiting for rain, said his father. On a giant log was a giant turtle, gray-
tailed, the size of a dishpan, set at a laughable angle there, safe from
everybody and everything.

With lunch over, they still didn't catch anything. And then the lady
looked through the willow boughs again, in nearly the same place. She
was giving them another chance.

She cupped her hands to her silent lips. She meant 'Blackie!'

'Blackie!' There it was.

'You hold still,' said his father. 'She ain't calling you.'

Nobody could hold so still as a man named Blackie.

That mysterious lady never breathed anything but the one word,
and so softly then that it was all the word could do to travel over the
water; still his father never said anything back, until she disappeared.
Then he said, 'Blackie yourself.'

He didn't even bait his hook or say any longer what he would do to
the fish if they didn't hurry up and change their minds. Yet when
nothing came up on the hook, he looked down at his own son like a
stranger cast away on this bridge from the long ago, before it got cut
off from land.

Dewey baited his hook, and the first thing he knew he'd caught a
fish.

'What is it, what is it?' he shouted.

'You got you a little goggle-eye there, son.'

Dewey, dancing with it—it was six inches long and jumping on the
hook—hugged his father's neck and said, 'Well—ready to go?'

'No ... Best not to stay either too long or too little-bit. I favor
tarrying awhile,' said his father.

Dewey sat back down, and gazed up at his father's solemn side-
face—then followed the look his father shot across the river like a
fishing line of great length, one that took hold.

Across the river the lady looked out for the third time. She was
almost out of the willows now, on the sand. She put the little shells of

her hands up to her throat. What did that mean? It was the way she'd pull her collar together if she'd been given a coat around her. It was about to rain. She knew as well as they did that people were looking at her hard; but she must not feel it, Dewey felt, or surely people would have to draw their looks away, and not fasten her there. She didn't have even one word to say, this time.

The bay tree that began moving and sighing over her head was the tall slender one Dewey had picked as his marker. With its head in a stroke of sun, it nodded like a silver flower. There was a little gentle thunder, and Dewey knew that her eyes shut, as well as he would know even in his sleep when his mother put down the windows in their house if a rain was coming. That way, she stood there and waited. And Dewey's father—whose sweat Dewey took a deep breath of as he stood up beside him—believed that the one *that* lady waited for was never coming over the bridge to her side, any more than she would come to his.

Then, with a little sound like a mouse somewhere in the world, a scratch, then a patter like many mice racing—and then at last the splash on Dewey's cheek—it simply began raining. Dewey looked all around—the river was dancing.

'Run now, son! Run for cover! It's fixing to pour down! I'll be right behind you!' shouted his father, running right past him and then jumping over the side of the bridge. Arms and legs spread wide as surprise itself he did a grand leap to the sand. But instead of sheltering under the bridge, he kept going, and was running up the bank now, toward Royals. Dewey resigned himself to go the same way. As for the lady, if she was still where they left her, about to disappear perhaps, she was getting wet.

They ran under the sounding trees and vines. It came down in earnest, feeling warm and cool together, a real spring shower.

'Trot under here!' called a pre-emptory voice.

'Miss Hattie! Forgot she was anywhere near,' said Dewey's father, falling back. 'Now we got to be nice to *her*.'

'Good evening, Lavelle.'

At that name, Dewey fell back, but his father went on. Maybe he was getting used to being called, today, and it didn't make any difference what name he got, by now.

Something as big as a sail came out through the brambles.

'Did you hear me?' said Miss Hattie—there she stood. 'Get you both under this umbrella. I'm going straight back to town, and I'll take you with me. Can't take your fishing poles, unless you drag 'em.'

'Yes'm,' they said, and got under.

Starting forward, Miss Hattie held her own umbrella, a man with her or not, branches of trees coming or not, and the harder the rain fell the more energetically she held to the handle. There were little cowlicks of damp standing up all around the black fur of her collar. Her spectacles were on her nose, and both windows had drops all over them like pearls. Miss Hattie's coat tapered up like one tent, and the umbrella spread down like another one. They marched abreast or single file, as the lay of the land allowed, but always politely close together under the umbrella, either despising paths or taking a path so fragrant and newly slick it didn't seem familiar. But there was an almost forgotten landmark of early morning, boarded twin towers of a colored church, set back closet-like in the hanging moss. Dewey thought he knew where he was. Suddenly frogs from everywhere let loose on the world, as if they'd been wound up.

In no time, Miss Hattie brought them to the edge of the woods. Next they were at the gravel road and walking down the middle of it. The turn was coming where Royals could be seen spread out from Baptist church to schoolhouse.

Dewey, keeping watch around Miss Hattie's skirt, saw the lady appear in the distance behind them, running like a ghost across the road in the shining rain—shining, for the sun had looked through.

'The Devil is beating his wife,' said Miss Hattie in a professional voice.

There ran the figure that the rain sheathed in a spinning cocoon of light—as if it ran in peril. It was cutting across Mr. Jep Royal's yard, where the Royals were all sitting inside the house and some cows as black as blackbirds came close and watched her go.

'Look at that, to the side,' said Miss Hattie suddenly. 'Who's that, young eyes?'

Dewey looked shyly under her forward sleeve and asked his father, 'Reckon it's the lady?'

'Well, *call* her,' said Miss Hattie. 'Whoever she is, she can trot under this umbrella just as easy as we can. It's good size.'

'La-dy!'

That was Dewey, hollering.

They stood and waited for the lady to come across the pasture, though his father looked very black, trapped under the umbrella. Had Miss Hattie looked at him, that showed what his name was and how he got it.

But the lady, now opposite, in a whole field of falling light, was all but standing still. Starting here, starting there, wavering, retreating, she made no headway at all. Then abruptly she disappeared into the Royals' pear orchard—this time for good.

'Maybe somebody new has escaped from the lunatic asylum,' said Miss Hattie. 'March.'

On they went in the rain.

Opal Purcell slipped sideways through the elderberry bushes at the creek bank, with both hands laid, like a hat, on top of her head, and waited for them.

'Why, it's only my own niece,' said Miss Hattie. 'Trot under here, Opal. How do you like this rain?'

'Hey, Aunt Hat. Hey,' said Opal to Dewey.

She was grown. Sometimes she waited on people in the Seed & Feed. She was plump as ever. She didn't look far enough around her aunt to speak to his father.

Miss Hattie touched Opal on the head. 'Has it rained that much?' she said in a gratified way.

'I thought I saw you in the post office, Aunt Hat,' objected Opal.

'I expect you did. I had the mail to tie up. I'm a fast worker when the case demands.'

They were all compelled, of course, to keep up with Miss Hattie and stay with her and be company all the way back to town. Her black cotton umbrella lacked very little of being big enough for four, but it lacked some. Dewey gave Opal his place.

He marched ahead of them, still in step with his father, but out in the open rain, with his fish now let up high on its pole behind him. He felt the welcome plastering down of his hair on his forehead, and the relentless way the raindrops hit and bounced on him.

Opal Purcell had a look, to Dewey, as if she didn't know whether she was getting wet or not. It was his father's fishing look. And Miss Hattie's rainmaking look. He was the only one—out here in the rain itself—that didn't have it.

Like a pretty lady's hand, to tilt his face up a little and make him smile, deep satisfaction, almost love came down and touched him.

'Miss Hattie,' he turned walking and said over his shoulder, 'I caught me a goggle-eye perch back yonder, see him? I wish I could give him to you—for your supper!'

'You good and wet, honey?' she said back, marching there in the middle.

The brightest thing in Royals—rain was the loudest, on all the tin roofs—was the empty school bus drawn up under the shed of the filling station. The movie house, high up on its posts, was magnesia-bottle blue. Three red hens waited on the porch. Dewey's and Opal's eyes together looked out of their corners at the 'Coming Saturday' poster of the charging white horse. But Miss Hattie didn't dismiss them at the movie house.

They passed the Baptist church getting red as a rose, and the Methodist church getting streaky. In the middle of the first crossing, the water tank stood and they walked under; water from its bottom, black and cold as ice, fell a drop for each head as always. And they passed along the gin, which alone would sleep the spring out. All around were the well-known ditches and little gullies; there were the chinaberry trees, and some Negroes and some dogs underneath them; but it all looked like some different place to Dewey—not Royals. There was a line of faces under the roof of the long store porch, but they looked, white and black, like the faces of new people. Nevertheless, all spoke to Miss Hattie, Blackie, Opal, and Dewey by name; and from their umbrella—out in the middle of the road, where it was coming down hardest—Miss Hattie did the speaking back.

'It's the beginning!' she called. 'I'd a heap rather see it come this way than in torrents!'

'We're real proud of you, Miss Hattie!'

'You're still a credit to Royals, Miss Hattie!'

'Don't you drown yourself out there!'

'Oh, I won't,' said Miss Hattie.

At the bank corner, small spotty pigs belonging to nobody, with snouts as long as corncobs, raced out in a company like clowns with the Circus, and ran with Dewey and Miss Hattie and all, for the rest of the way. There was one more block, and that was where the post office

was. Also the Seed & Feed, and the schoolhouse beyond, and the Stave
Mill Road; and also home was that way.

'Well, good-by, everybody,' said Miss Hattie, arrived at the post
office tree.

Dewey's father—the darkest Coker of the family, much darker than
Uncle Lavelle, who had run off a long time ago, by Dewey's
reckoning—bowed himself out backwards from under the umbrella
and straightened up in the rain.

'Much obliged for the favor, Miss Hattie,' he said. With a quiet hand
he turned over his fishing pole to Dewey, and was gone.

'Thank you, ma'am, I enjoyed myself,' said Dewey.

'You're wet as a drowned rat,' said Miss Hattie admiringly.

Up beyond, the schoolhouse grew dim behind its silver yard. The
bell mounted at the gate was making the sound of a bucket filling.

'I'll leave you with the umbrella, Opal. Opal, run home,' said Miss
Hattie, pointing her finger at Opal's chest, 'and put down the south
windows, and bring in the quilts and dry them out again before the
fire. I can't tell you why I forgot clean about my own windows. You
might stand on a chair and find a real pretty quart of snapbeans and
put them on with that little piece of meat out of the safe. Run now.
Where've you been?'

'Nowheres.—Hunting poke salad,' said Opal, making a little face
twice. She had wet cheeks, and there was a blue violet in her dress,
hanging down from a buttonhole, and no coat on her back of any kind.

'Then dry yourself,' said Miss Hattie. *'What's that?'*

'It's the train whistle,' said Dewey.

Far down, the mail train crossed the three long trestles over Little
Muscadine swamp like knocking three knocks at the door, and blew its
whistle again through the rain.

Miss Hattie never let her powers interfere with mail time, or mail
time interfere with her powers. She had everything worked out. She
pulled open the door of her automobile, right there. There on the back
seat was her mail sack, ready to go.

Miss Hattie lived next door—where Opal had now gone inside—
and only used her car between here and the station; it stayed under the
post office tree. Some day old Opal was going to take that car, and ride
away. Miss Hattie climbed up inside.

The car roared and took a leap out into the rain. At the corner it turned, looking two stories high, swinging wide as Miss Hattie banked her curve, with a lean of her whole self deep to the right. She made it. Then she sped on the diagonal to the bottom of the hill and pulled up at the station just in time for Mr. Frierson to run out in his suspenders and hand the mail as the train rushed through. It hooked the old sack and flung off the new to Royals.

The rain slacked just a little on Miss Hattie while she hauled the mail uphill. Dewey stamped up the post office runway by her side to help her carry it in—the post office used to be a stable. He held the door open, they went inside, and the rain slammed down behind them.

'Dewey Coker?'

'Ma'am?'

'Why aren't you in school?'

In a sudden moment she dropped the sack and rubbed his head—just any old way—with something out of her purse; it might have been a dinner napkin. He rubbed cornbread crumbs as sharp as rocks out of his eye. Across the road, while this drying was happening, a wonderful white mule that had gotten into the cemetery and rolled himself around till he was green and white like a marble monument, got up to his feet and shivered and shook the raindrops everywhere.

'I may can still go,' he said dreamily. '*Excalibur*—'

'Nonsense! Don't you see that rain?' cried Miss Hattie. 'You'll stay here in this post office till I tell you.'

The post office inside was a long bare room that looked and smelled like a covered bridge, with only a little light at the other end where Miss Hattie's window was. Dewey had never stayed inside here more than a minute at a time, in his life.

'You make yourself at home,' said Miss Hattie, and disappeared into the back.

Dewey stood the poles by the front door and kept his fish in his hand on the bit of line, while Miss Hattie put up the mail. After she had put it all up as she saw fit, then she gave it out: pretty soon here came everybody. There was a lot of conversation through the window.

'Sure is a treat, Miss Hattie! Only wish it didn't have to stop.'

'It looks like a gully washer to me, Miss Hat!'

And someone leaned down and said to Dewey, 'Hi, Dewey! I saw you! And what was *you* up to this evening?'

'It's a beginning,' was all Miss Hattie would say. 'I'll go back out there tomorrow, if I have the time, and if I live and don't nothing happen, and do some more on it. But depends on the size of the mail.'

After everybody had shed their old letters and papers on the floor and tracked out, there would have been silence everywhere but for the bombardment on the roof. Miss Hattie still didn't come out of her little room back there, of which Dewey could see nothing but the reared-back honeycomb of her desk with nine letters in the holes.

Out here, motes danced lazily as summer flies in the running green light of the cracks in the walls. The hole of a missing stovepipe high up was blocked with a bouquet of old newspapers, yellow as roses. It was a little chilly. It smelled of rain, of fish, of pocket money and pockets. Whether the lonely dangling light was turned on or off it was hard to see. Its bulb hung down fierce in a little mask like a biting dog.

On the high table against the wall there was an ink well and a pen, as in a school desk, and an old yellow blotter limp as biscuit dough. Reaching tall, he rounded up the pen and with a great deal of the ink drew a picture on the blotter. He drew his fish. He gave it an eye and then mailed it through the slot to Miss Hattie.

Presently he hung his chin on the little ledge to her window, to see if she got it.

Miss Hattie was asleep in her rocking chair. She was sitting up with her head inclined, beside her little gas stove. She had laid away her hat, and there was a good weight to her hair, which was shaped and colored like the school bell. She looked noble, as if waiting to have the headsman chop off her head. All was quietness itself. For the rain had stopped. The only sound was the peeping of baby chicks from the parcel post at her feet.

'Can I go now?' he hollered.

'Mercy!' she exclaimed at once. 'Did it bite? Nothing for you today! Who's that? I wasn't asleep! Whose face is that smiling at me? For pity's sakes!' She jumped up and shook her dress—some leaves fell out. Then she came to the window and said through it, 'You want to go leave me? Run then! Because if you dream it's stopped, child, I won't be surprised a bit if it don't turn around and come back.'

At that moment the post office shook with thunder, as if horses ran right through it.

Miss Hattie came to the door behind him. He slid down the runway with all he had. She remained there looking out, nodding a bit and speaking a few words to herself. All she had to say to him was 'Trot!'

It was already coming down again, with the sound of making up for the lapse that had just happened. As Dewey began to run, he caught a glimpse of a patchwork quilt going like a camel through the yard next door toward Miss Hattie's house. He supposed Opal was under it. Fifteen years later it occurred to him it had very likely been Opal in the woods.

Just in time, he caught and climbed inside the rolling school bus with the children in it, and rode home after all with the others, a sort of hero.

After the bus put him down, he ran cutting across under the charred pines. The big sky-blue violets his mother loved were blooming, wet as cheeks. Pear trees were all but in bloom under the purple sky. Branches were being jogged with the rush and commotion of birds. The Cokers' patch of mustard that had gone to seed shone like gold from here. Dewey ran under the last drops, through the hooraying mud of the pasture, and saw the corrugations of their roof shining across it like a fresh pan of cornbread sticks. His father was off at a distance, on his knees—back at mending the fences. Minnie Lee, Sue, and Annie Bess were ready for Dewey and came flocking from the door, with the baby behind on all fours. None of them could hope to waylay him.

His mother stood in the back lot. Behind her, blue and white, her morning wash hung to the ground, as wet as clouds. She stood with a switch extended most strictly over the head of the silky calf that drank from the old brown cow—as though this evening she knighted it.

'Whose calf will that be? Mine?' he cried out to her. It was to make her turn, but this time, he thought, her answer would be yes.

'You have to ask your pa, son.'

'Why do you always tell me the same thing? *Mama!*'

Arm straight before him, he extended toward her dear face his fish—still shining a little, held up by its tail, its eye and its mouth as agape as any big fish's. She turned.

'Get away from me!' she shrieked. 'You and your pa! Both of you get the sight of you clear away!' She struck with her little green switch, fanning drops of milk and light. 'Get in the house. Oh! If I haven't had enough out of you!'

*

Days passed—it rained some more, sometimes in the night—before Dewey had time to go back and visit the bridge. He didn't take his fishing pole, he just went to see about it. The sky had cleared in the evening, after school and the work at home were done with.

The river was up. It covered the sandbars and from the bridge he could no longer remember exactly how the driftwood had lain—only its upper horns stuck out of the water, where parades of brown bubbles were passing down. The gasping turtles had all dived under. The water must now be swimming with fish of all sizes and kinds.

Dewey walked the old plank back, there being no sand to drop down to. Then he visited above the bridge and wandered around in new places. They were drenched and sweet. The big fragrant bay was his marker.

He stood in the light of birdleg-pink leaves, yellow flower vines, and scattered white blooms each crushed under its drop of water as under a stone, the maples red as cinnamon drops and the falling, thready nets of willows, and heard the lonesomest sound in creation, an unknown bird singing through the very moment when he was the one that listened to it. Across the Little Muscadine the golden soldier-tassels of distant oaks filled with light, and there the clear sun dropped.

Before he got out of the river woods, it was nearly first-dark. The sky was pink and blue. The great moon had slid up in it, but not yet taken light, like the little plum tree that had sprung out in flower below. At that mysterious colored church, the one with the two towers and the two privies to the rear, that stood all in darkness, a new friend sat straight up on the top church step. Head to one side, little red tongue hanging out, it was a little black dog, his whole self shaking and alive from tip to tip. He might be part of the church, that was the way he acted. On the other hand, there was no telling where he might have come from.

Yet he had something familiar about him too. He had a look on his little pointed face—for all he was black; and was it he, or she?—that reminded Dewey of Miss Hattie Purcell, when she stood in the door of the post office looking out at the rain she'd brought and remarking to the world at large: 'Well, I'd say that's right persnickety.'

REUNION

John Cheever

The last time I saw my father was in Grand Central Station. I was going from my grandmother's in the Adirondacks to a cottage on the Cape that my mother had rented, and I wrote my father that I would be in New York between trains for an hour and a half, and asked if we could have lunch together. His secretary wrote to say that he would meet me at the information booth at noon, and at twelve o'clock sharp I saw him coming through the crowd. He was a stranger to me—my mother divorced him three years ago and I hadn't been with him since—but as soon as I saw him I felt that he was my father, my flesh and blood, my future and my doom. I knew that when I was grown I would be something like him; I would have to plan my campaigns within his limitations. He was a big, good-looking man, and I was terribly happy to see him again. He struck me on the back and shook my hand. 'Hi, Charlie,' he said. 'Hi, boy. I'd like to take you up to my club, but it's in the Sixties, and if you have to catch an early train I guess we'd better get something to eat around here.' He put his arm around me, and I smelled my father the way my mother sniffs a rose. It was a rich compound of whiskey, after-shave lotion, shoe polish, woolens, and the rankness of a mature male. I hoped that someone would see us together. I wished that we could be photographed. I wanted some record of our having been together.

We went out of the station and up a side street to a restaurant. It was still early, and the place was empty. The bartender was quarreling with a delivery boy, and there was one very old waiter in a red coat down by the kitchen door. We sat down, and my father hailed the waiter in a loud voice. '*Kellner!*' he shouted. '*Garçon! Cameriere! You!*' His boisterousness in the empty restaurant seemed out of place. 'Could we have a little service here!' he shouted. 'Chop-chop.' Then he clapped his hands. This caught the waiter's attention, and he shuffled over to our table.

'Were you clapping your hands at me?' he asked.

'Calm down, calm down, *sommelier*,' my father said. 'If it isn't too much to ask of you—if it wouldn't be too much above and beyond the call of duty, we would like a couple of Beefeater Gibsons.'

'I don't like to be clapped at,' the waiter said.

'I should have brought my whistle,' my father said. 'I have a whistle that is audible only to the ears of old waiters. Now, take out your little pad and your little pencil and see if you can get this straight: two Beefeater Gibsons. Repeat after me: two Beefeater Gibsons.'

'I think you'd better go somewhere else,' the waiter said quietly.

'That,' said my father, 'is one of the most brilliant suggestions I have ever heard. Come on, Charlie, let's get the hell out of here.'

I followed my father out of that restaurant into another. He was not so boisterous this time. Our drinks came, and he cross-questioned me about the baseball season. He then struck the edge of his empty glass with his knife and began shouting again. *'Garçon! Kellner! Cameriere! You!* Could we trouble you to bring us two more of the same.'

'How old is the boy?' the waiter asked.

'That,' my father said, 'is none of your God-damned business.'

'I'm sorry, sir,' the waiter said, 'but I won't serve the boy another drink.'

'Well, I have some news for you,' my father said. 'I have some very interesting news for you. This doesn't happen to be the only restaurant in New York. They've opened another on the corner. Come on, Charlie.'

He paid the bill, and I followed him out of that restaurant into another. Here the waiters wore pink jackets like hunting coats, and there was a lot of horse tack on the walls. We sat down, and my father began to shout again. 'Master of the hounds! Tallyhoo and all that sort of thing. We'd like a little something in the way of a stirrup cup. Namely, two Bibson Geefeaters.'

'Two Bibson Geefeaters?' the waiter asked, smiling.

'You know damned well what I want,' my father said angrily. 'I want two Beefeater Gibsons, and make it snappy. Things have changed in jolly old England. So my friend the duke tells me. Let's see what England can produce in the way of a cocktail.'

'This isn't England,' the waiter said.

'Don't argue with me,' my father said. 'Just do as you're told.'

'I just thought you might like to know where you are,' the waiter said.

'If there is one thing I cannot tolerate,' my father said, 'it is an impudent domestic. Come on, Charlie.'

The fourth place we went to was Italian. '*Buon giorno,*' my father said. '*Per favore, possiamo avere due cocktail americani, forti, forti. Molto gin, poco vermut.*'

'I don't understand Italian,' the waiter said.

'Oh, come off it,' my father said. 'You understand Italian, and you know damned well you do. *Vogliamo due cocktail americani. Subito.*'

The waiter left us and spoke with the captain, who came over to our table and said, 'I'm sorry, sir, but this table is reserved.'

'All right,' my father said. 'Get us another table.'

'All the tables are reserved,' the captain said.

'I get it,' my father said. 'You don't desire our patronage. Is that it? Well, the hell with you. *Vada all' inferno.* Let's go, Charlie.'

'I have to get my train,' I said.

'I'm sorry, sonny,' my father said. 'I'm terribly sorry.' He put his arm around me and pressed me against him. 'I'll walk you back to the station. If there had only been time to go up to my club.'

'That's all right, Daddy,' I said.

'I'll get you a paper,' he said. 'I'll get you a paper to read on the train.'

Then he went up to a newsstand and said, 'Kind sir, will you be good enough to favor me with one of your God-damned, no-good, ten-cent afternoon papers?' The clerk turned away from him and stared at a magazine cover. 'Is it asking too much, kind sir,' my father said, 'is it asking too much for you to sell me one of your disgusting specimens of yellow journalism?'

'I have to go, Daddy,' I said. 'It's late.'

'Now, just wait a second, sonny,' he said. 'Just wait a second. I want to get a rise out of this chap.'

'Goodbye, Daddy,' I said, and I went down the stairs and got my train, and that was the last time I saw my father.

SHIP ISLAND: THE STORY OF A MERMAID

Elizabeth Spencer

The French book was lying open on a corner of the dining room table, between the floor lamp and the window. The floor lamp, which had come with the house, had a cover made of green glass, with a fringe. The French book must have lain just that way for two months. Nancy, coming in from the beach, tried not to look at it. It reminded her of how much she had meant to accomplish during the summer, of the strong sense of intent, something like refinement, with which she had chosen just that spot for studying. It was out of hearing of the conversations with the neighbors that went on every evening out on the side porch, it had window light in the daytime and lamplight at night, it had a small, slanting view of the beach, and it drew a breeze. The pencils were still there, still sharp, and the exercise, broken off. She sometimes stopped to read it over. 'The soldiers of the emperor were crossing the bridge: *Les soldats de l'empereur traversaient le pont*. The officer has already knocked at the gate: *L'officier a déjà frappé*—' She could not have finished that sentence now if she had sat right down and tried.

Nancy could no longer find herself in relation to the girl who had sought out such a good place to study, had sharpened the pencils and opened the book and sat down to bend over it. What she did know was how—just now, when she had been down at the beach, across the boulevard—the sand scuffed beneath her step and shells lay strewn about, chipped and disorderly, near the water's edge. Some shells were empty; some, with damp drying down their backs, went for short walks. Far out, a long white shelf of cloud indicated a distance no gull could dream of gaining, though the gulls spun tirelessly up, dazzling in the white light that comes just as morning vanishes. A troop of pelicans sat like curiously caned knobs on the tops of a long series of wooden piles, which were spaced out at intervals in the water. The piles were what was left of a private pier blown away by a hurricane some years ago.

Nancy had been alone on the beach. Behind her, the boulevard glittered in the morning sun and the season's traffic rocked by the long curve of the shore in clumps that seemed to burst, then speed on. She stood looking outward at the high straight distant shelf of cloud. The islands were out there, plainly visible. The walls of the old Civil War fort on the nearest one of them, the one with the lighthouse—Ship Island—were plain today as well. She had been out there once this summer with Rob Acklen, out there on the island, where the reeds grew in the wild white sand, and the water teemed so thick with seaweed that only crazy people would have tried to swim in it. The gulf had rushed white and strong through all the seaweed, frothing up the beach. On the beach, the froth turned brown, the color of softly moving crawfish claws. In the boat coming home through the sunset that day, a boy standing up in the pilothouse played 'Over the Waves' on his harmonica. Rob Acklen had put his jacket around Nancy's shoulders—she had never thought to bring a sweater. The jacket swallowed her; it smelled more like Rob than he did. The boat moved, the breeze blew, the sea swelled, all to the lilt of the music. The twenty-five members of the Laurel, Mississippi, First Baptist Church Adult Bible Class, who had come out with them on the excursion boat, and to whom Rob and Nancy had yet to introduce themselves, had stopped giggling and making their silly jokes. They were tired, and stood in a huddle like sheep; they were shaped like sheep as well, with little shoulders and wide bottoms—it was somehow sad. Nancy and Rob, young and trim, stood side by side near the bow, like figureheads of the boat, hearing the music and watching the thick prow butt the swell, which the sunset had stained a deep red. Nancy felt for certain that this was the happiest she had ever been.

Alone on the sand this morning, she had spread out her beach towel and stood for a moment looking up the beach, way up, past a grove of live oaks to where Rob Acklen's house was visible. He would be standing in the kitchen, in loafers and a dirty white shirt and an old pair of shorts, drinking cold beer from the refrigerator right out of the can. He would eat lunch with his mother and sister, read the paper and write a letter, then dress and drive into town to help his father in the office, going right past Nancy's house along the boulevard. Around three, he would call her up. He did this every day. His name was Fitzrobert Conroy Acklen—one of those full-blown Confederate names. Everybody liked him, and more than a few—a general mixture of every color, size, age, sex, and religion—would say when he passed by, 'I declare, I just love that boy.' So he was bound to have a lot of nicknames: 'Fitz' or 'Bobbie' or 'Cousin' or 'Son'—he answered to almost anything. He was the kind of boy people have high, undefined hopes for. He had first seen Nancy Lewis one morning when he came by her house to make an insurance call for his father.

Breaking off her French—could it have been the sentence about 'l'officier'?—she had gone out to see who it was. She was expecting Mrs. Nattier, their neighbor, who had skinny white freckled legs she never shaved and whose husband, 'off' somewhere, was thought not to be doing well; or Mrs. Nattier's little boy Bernard, who thought it was fun to hide around corners after dark and jump out saying nothing more original than 'Boo!' (once, he had screamed 'Raw head and bloody bones!' but Nancy was sure somebody had told him to); or one of the neighbor ladies in the back—old Mrs. Poultney, whom they rented from and who walked with a cane, or Miss Henriette Dupré, who was so devout she didn't even have to go to confession before weekday Communion and whose hands, always tucked up in the sleeves of her sack, were as cold as church candles, and to think of them touching you was like rabbits skipping over your grave on dark rainy nights in winter up in the lonely wet-leaf-covered hills. Or else it was somebody wanting to be paid something. Nancy had opened the door and looked up, and there, instead of a dozen other people, was Rob Acklen.

Not that she knew his name. She had seen boys like him down on the coast, ever since her family had moved there from Little Rock back in the spring. She had seen them playing tennis on the courts back of the hotel, where she sometimes went to jump on the trampoline. She believed that the hotel people thought she was on the staff in some sort of way, as she was about the right age for that—just a year or so beyond high school but hardly old enough to work in town. The weather was already getting hot, and the season was falling off. When she passed the courts, going and coming, she saw the boys out of the corner of her eye. Were they really so much taller than the boys up where they had moved from, up in Arkansas? They were lankier and a lot more casual. They were more assured. To Nancy, whose family was in debt and whose father, in one job after another, was always doing something wrong, the boys playing tennis had that wonderful remoteness of creatures to be admired on the screen, or those seen in whiskey ads, standing near the bar of a country club and sleekly talking about things she could not begin to imagine. But now here was one, in a heavy tan cotton suit and a light blue shirt with a buttoned-down collar and dark tie, standing on her own front porch and smiling at her.

Yet when Rob called Nancy for a date, a day or two later, she didn't have to be told that he did it partly because he liked to do nice things for people. He obviously liked to be considerate and kind, because the first time he saw her he said, 'I guess you don't know many people yet?'

'No, because Daddy just got transferred,' she said—'transferred' being her mother's word for it; fired was what it was. She gave him a Coke and talked to him awhile, standing around in the house, which unaccountably continued to be empty. She said she didn't know a thing about insurance.

Now, still on the beach, Nancy Lewis sat down in the middle of her beach towel and began to rub suntan lotion on her neck and shoulders. Looking down the other way, away from Rob's house and toward the yacht club, she saw a man standing alone on the sand. She had not noticed him before. He was facing out toward the gulf and staring fixedly at the horizon. He was wearing shorts and a shirt made out of red bandanna, with the tail out—a stout young man with black hair.

Just then, without warning, it began to rain. There were no clouds one could see in the overhead dazzle, but it rained anyway; the drops fell in huge discs, marking the sand, and splashing on Nancy's skin. Each drop seemed enough to fill a Dixie cup. At first, Nancy did not know what the stinging sensation was; then she knew the rain was burning her. It was scalding hot! Strange, outlandish, but also painful, was how she found it. She jumped up and began to flinch and twist away, trying to escape, and a moment later she had snatched up her beach towel and flung it around her shoulders. But the large hot drops kept falling, and there was no escape from them. She started rubbing her cheek and forehead and felt that she might blister all over; then, since it kept on and on and was all so inexplicable, she grabbed her lotion and ran up the beach and out of the sand and back across the boulevard. Once in her own front yard, under the scraggy trees, she felt the rain no longer, and looked back curiously into the dazzle beyond the boulevard.

'I thought you meant to stay for a while,' her mother said. 'Was it too hot? Anybody would be crazy to go out there now. There's never anybody out there at this time of day.'

'It was all right,' said Nancy, 'but it started raining. I never felt anything like it. The rain was so hot it burned me. Look. My face—' She ran to look in the mirror. Sure enough, her face and shoulders looked splotched. It might blister. I might be scarred for life, she thought—one of those dramatic phrases left over from high school.

Nancy's mother, Mrs. Lewis, was a discouraged lady whose silky, blondish-gray hair was always slipping loose and tagging out around her face. She would not try to improve herself and talked a lot in company about her family; two of her uncles had been professors simultaneously at the University of North Carolina. One of them had written a book on phonetics. Mrs. Lewis seldom found anyone who had heard of them, or of the book, either. Some people asked what phonetics were, and others did not ask anything at all.

Mrs. Lewis now said to her daughter, 'You just got too much sun.'

'No, it was the rain. It was really scalding hot.'

'I never heard of such a thing,' her mother said. 'Out of a clear sky.'

'I can't help that,' Nancy said. 'I guess I ought to know.'

Mrs. Lewis took on the kind of look she had when she would open the handkerchief drawer of a dresser and see two used, slightly bent carpet nails, some Scotch Tape melted together, an old receipt, an unanswered letter announcing a cousin's wedding, some scratched negatives saved for someone but never developed, some dusty foreign coins, a bank deposit book from a town they lived in during the summer before Nancy was born, and an old telegram whose contents, forgotten, no one would dare now to explore, for it would say something awful but absolutely true.

'I wish you wouldn't speak to me like that,' Mrs. Lewis said. 'All I know is, it certainly didn't rain here.'

Nancy wandered away, into the dining room. She felt bad about everything—about quarreling with her mother, about not getting a suntan, about wasting her time all summer with Rob Acklen and not learning any French. She went and took a long cool bath in the big old bathroom, where the bathtub had ball-and-claw feet painted mustard yellow and the single light bulb on the long cord dropped down one mile from the stratosphere.

What the Lewises found in a rented house was always outclassed by what they brought into it. Nancy's father, for instance, had a china donkey that bared its teeth in a great big grin. Written on one side was 'If you really want to look like me' and on the other 'Just keep right on talking.' Her father loved the donkey and its message, and always put it on the living room table of whatever house they were in. When he got a drink before dinner each evening he would wander back with glass in hand and look the donkey over. 'That's pretty good,' he would say just before he took the first swallow. Nancy had often longed to break the donkey, by accident—that's what she would say, that it had all been an accident—but she couldn't get over the feeling that if she did, worse things than the Lewises had ever imagined would happen to them. That donkey would let in a flood of trouble, that she knew.

After Nancy got out of the tub and dried, she rubbed Jergens Lotion on all the splotches the rain had made. Then she ate a peanut-butter sandwich and more shrimp salad left over from supper the night before, and drank a cold Coke. Now and then, eating, she would go look in the mirror. By the time Rob Acklen called up, the red marks had all but disappeared.

That night, riding down to Biloxi with Rob, Nancy confided that the catalogue of people she disliked, headed by Bernard Nattier, included every single person—Miss Henriette Dupré, Mrs. Poultney, and Mrs. Nattier, and Mr. Nattier, too, when he was at home—that she had to be with these days. It even included, she was sad to say, her mother and father. If Bernard Nattier had to be mean—and it was clear he did have to—why did he have to be so corny? He put wads of wet, chewed bubble gum in her purses—that was the most original thing he ever did. Otherwise, it was just live crawfish in her bed or crabs in her shoes; anybody could think of that. And when he stole, he took things *she* wanted, nothing simple, like money—she could have forgiven him for that—but cigarettes, lipstick, and ashtrays she had stolen herself here and there. If she locked her door, he got in through the window; if she locked the window, she suffocated. Not only that, but he would crawl out from under the bed. His eyes were slightly crossed and he knew how to turn the lids back on themselves so that it looked like blood, and then he would chase her. He was browned to the color of dirt all over and he smelled like salt mud the sun had dried. He wore black tennis shoes laced too tight at the ankles and from sunup till way past dark he never thought of anything but what to do to Nancy, and she would have liked to kill him.

She made Rob Acklen laugh. She amused him. He didn't take anything Nancy Lewis could say at all to heart, but, as if she was something he had found on the beach and was teaching to talk, he, with his Phi Beta Kappa key and his good level head and his wonderful prospects, found everything she told about herself cute, funny, absurd. He did remark that he had such feelings himself from time to time—that he would occasionally get crazy mad at one of his parents or the other, and that he once planned his sister's murder down to the last razor slash. But he laughed again, and his chewing gum popped amiably in his jaws. When she told him about the hot rain, he said he didn't believe it. He said, 'Aw,' which was what a boy like Rob Acklen said when he didn't believe something. The top of his old white Mercury convertible was down and the wind rushed past like an endless bolt of raw silk being drawn against Nancy's cheek.

In the ladies' room mirror at the Beach View, where they stopped to eat, she saw the bright quality of her eyes, as though she had been drinking. Her skirts rustled in the narrow room; a porous white disc of deodorant hung on a hook, fuming the air. Her eyes, though blue, looked startlingly dark in her pale skin, for though she tried hard all the time, she never seemed to tan. All the sun did, as her mother was always pointing out, was bleach her hair three shades lighter; a little more and it would be almost white. Out on the island that day, out on Ship Island, she had drifted in the water like seaweed, with the tide combing her limbs and hair, tugging her through lengths of fuzzy water growth. She had lain flat on her face with her arms stretched before her, experiencing the curious lift the water's motion gave to the tentacles of weed, wondering whether she liked it or not. Did something alive clamber the small of her back? Did something wishful grope the spiral of her ear? Rob had caught her wrist hard and waked her—waked was what he did, though to sleep in the water is not possible. He said he thought she had been there too long. 'Nobody can keep their face in the water that long,' was what he said.

'I did,' said Nancy.

Rob's brow had been blistered a little, she recalled, for that had been back early in the summer, soon after they had met—but the changes the sun made on him went without particular attention. The seasons here were old ground to him. He said that the island was new, however—or at least forgotten. He said he had never been there but once, and that many years ago, on a Boy Scout picnic. Soon they were exploring the fort, reading the dates off the metal signs whose letters glowed so smoothly in the sun, and the brief summaries of what those little boys, little military-academy boys turned into soldiers, had endured. Not old enough to fill up the name of soldier, or of prisoner, either, which is what they were—not old enough to shave, Nancy bet—still, they had died there, miserably far from home, and had been buried in the sand. There was a lot more. Rob would have been glad to read all about it, but she wasn't interested. What they knew already was plenty, just about those boys. A bright, worried lizard ran out of a hot rubble of brick. They came out of the fort and walked alone together eastward toward the dunes, now skirting near the shore that faced the sound and now wandering south, where they could hear or sometimes glimpse the gulf. They were overlooked all the way by an old white lighthouse. From far away behind, the twenty-five members of the adult Bible class could be overheard playing a silly, shrill Sunday-school game. It came across the ruins of the fort and the sad story of the dead soldiers like something that had happened long ago that you could not quite remember having joined in. On the beach to their right, toward the gulf, a flock of sandpipers with blinding-white breasts stepped pecking along the water's edge, and on the inner beach, toward the sound, a wrecked sailboat with a broken mast lay half buried in the sand.

Rob kept teasing her along, pulling at the soft wool strings of her bathing suit, which knotted at the nape and again under her shoulder blades, worrying loose the damp hair that she had carefully slicked back and pinned. 'There isn't anybody in that house,' he assured her, some minutes later, having explored most of that part of the island and almost as much of Nancy as well, having almost, but not quite—his arms around her—coaxed and caressed her down to ground level in a clump of reeds. 'There hasn't been in years and years,' he said, encouraging her.

'It's only those picnic people,' she said, holding off, for the reeds would not have concealed a medium-sized mouse. They had been to look at the sailboat and thought about climbing inside (kissing closely, they had almost fallen right over into it), but it did have a rotten tin can in the bottom and smelled, so here they were back out in the dunes.

'They've got to drink all those Coca-Colas,' Rob said, 'and give out all those prizes, and anyway—'

She never learned anyway what, but it didn't matter. Maybe she began to make up for all that the poor little soldiers had missed out on, in the way of making love. The island's very spine, a warm reach of thin ground, came smoothly up into the arch of her back; and it was at least halfway the day itself, with its fair, wide-open eyes, that she went over to. She felt somewhat historical afterward, as though they had themselves added one more mark to all those that place remembered.

Having played all the games and given out the prizes, having eaten all the homemade cookies and drunk the case of soft drinks just getting warm, and gone sight-seeing through the fort, the Bible class was now coming, too, crying 'Yoohoo!' to explore the island. They discovered Rob hurling shells and bits of rock into the surf, while Nancy, scavenging a little distance away, tugged up out of the sand a shell so extraordinary it was worth showing around. It was purple, pink, and violet inside—a palace of colors; the king of the oysters had no doubt lived there. When she held it shyly out to them, they cried 'Look!' and 'Ooo!' so there was no need for talking to them much at all, and in the meantime the evening softened, the water glowed, the glare dissolved. Far out, there were other islands one could see now, and beyond those must be many more. They had been there all along.

Going home, Nancy gave the wonderful shell to the boy who stood in the pilothouse playing 'Over the Waves.' She glanced back as they walked off up the pier and saw him look at the shell, try it for weight, and then throw it in the water, leaning far back on his arm and putting a good spin on the throw, the way boys like to do—the way Rob Acklen himself had been doing, too, just that afternoon.

'Why did you do that?' Rob had demanded. He was frowning; he looked angry. He had thought they should keep the shell—to remember, she supposed.

'For the music,' she explained.

'But it was ours,' he said. When she didn't answer, he said again, 'Why did you, Nancy?'

But still she didn't answer.

When Nancy returned to their table at the Beach View, having put her lipstick back straight after eating fish, Rob was paying the check. 'Why not believe me?' she asked him. 'It was true. The rain was hot as fire. I thought I would be scarred for life.'

It was still broad daylight, not even twilight. In the bright, air-conditioned restaurant, the light from the water glazed flatly against the broad picture windows, the chandeliers, and the glasses. It was the hour when mirrors reflect nothing and bars look tired. The restaurant was a boozy, cheap sort of place with a black-lined gambling hall in the back, but everyone went there because the food was good.

'You're just like Mama,' she said. 'You think I made it up.'

Rob said, teasing, 'I didn't say that. I just said I didn't believe it.' He loved getting her caught in some sort of logic she couldn't get out of. When he opened the door for her, she got a good sidelong view of his longish, firm face and saw the way his somewhat fine brows arched up with one or two bright reddish hairs in among the dark ones; his hair was that way, too, when the sun hit it. Maybe, if nobody had told him, he wouldn't have known it; he seemed not to notice so very much about himself. Having the confidence of people who don't worry much, his grin could snare her instantly—a glance alone could make her feel how lucky she was he'd ever noticed her. But it didn't do at all to think about him now. It would be ages before they made it through the evening and back, retracing the way and then turning off to the bayou, and even then, there would be those mosquitoes.

Bayou love-making suited Rob just fine; he was one of those people mosquitoes didn't bite. They certainly bit Nancy. They were huge and silent, and the minute the car stopped they would even come and sit upon her eyelids, if she closed her eyes, a dozen to each tender arc of flesh. They would gather on her face, around her nose and mouth. Clothlike, like rags and tatters, like large dry ashes of burnt cloth, they came in lazy droves, in fleets, sailing on the air. They were never in any hurry, being everywhere at once and always ready to bite. Nancy had been known to jump all the way out of the car and go stamping across the grass like a calf. She grew sulky and despairing and stood on one leg at a time in the moonlight, slapping at her ankles, while Rob leaned his chin on the doorframe and watched her with his affectionate, total interest.

Nancy, riddled and stinging with beads of actual blood briar-pointed here and there upon her, longed to be almost anywhere else—she especially longed for New Orleans. She always talked about it, although, never having been there, she had to say the things that other people said—food and jazz in the French Quarter, beer and crabs out on Lake Pontchartrain. Rob said vaguely they would go sometime. But she could tell that things were wrong for him at this point. 'The food's just as good around here,' he said.

'Oh, Rob!' She knew it wasn't so. She could feel that city, hanging just over the horizon from them scarcely fifty miles away, like some swollen bronze moon, at once brilliant and shadowy and drenched in every sort of amplified smell. Rob was stroking her hair, and in time his repeated, gentle touch gained her attention. It seemed to tell what he liked—girls all spanking clean, with scrubbed fingernails, wearing shoes still damp with white shoe polish. Even a fresh gardenia stuck in their hair wouldn't be too much for him. There would be all sorts of differences, to him, between Ship Island and the French Quarter, but she did not have much idea just what they were. Nancy took all this in, out of his hand on her head. She decided she had better not talk any more about New Orleans. She wriggled around, looking out over his shoulder, through the moonlight, toward where the pitch-black surface of the bayou water showed in patches through the trees. The trees were awful, hung with great spooky gray tatters of Spanish moss. Nancy was reminded of the house she and her family were living in; it had recently occurred to her that the peculiar smell it had must come from some Spanish moss that had got sealed in behind the paneling, between the walls. The moss was alive in there and growing, and that was where she was going to seal Bernard Nattier up someday, for him to see how it felt. She had tried to kill him once, by filling her purse with rocks and oyster shells—the roughest she could find. She had read somewhere that this weapon was effective for ladies in case of attack. But he had ducked when she swung the purse at him, and she had only gone spinning round and round, falling at last into a camellia tree, which had scratched her . . .

'The Skeltons said for us to stop by there for a drink,' Rob told her. They were driving again, and the car was back on the boulevard, in the still surprising daylight. 'What did you say?' he asked her.

'Nothing.'

'You just don't want to go?'

'No, I don't much want to go.'

'Well, then, we won't stay long.'

The Skelton house was right on the water, with a second-story, glassed-in, air-conditioned living room looking out over the sound. The sofas and chairs were covered with gold-and-white striped satin, and the room was full of Rob's friends. Lorna Skelton, who had been Rob's girl the summer before and who dressed so beautifully, was handing drinks round and saying, 'So which is your favorite bayou, Rob?' She had a sort of fake 'good sport' tone of voice and wanted to appear ready for anything. (Being so determined to be nice around Nancy, she was going to fall right over backward one day.)

'Do I have to have a favorite?' Rob asked. 'They all look good to me. Full of slime and alligators.'

'I should have asked Nancy.'

'They're all full of mosquitoes,' said Nancy, hoping that was O.K. for an answer. She thought that virgins were awful people.

'Trapped, boy!' Turner Carmichael said to Rob, and banged him on the shoulder. Turner wanted to be a writer, so he thought it was all right to tell people about themselves. 'Women will be your downfall, Acklen. Nancy, honey, you haven't spoken to the general.'

Old General Skelton, Lorna's grandfather, sat in the corner of the living room near the mantel, drinking a scotch highball. You had to shout at him.

'How's the election going, General?' Turner asked.

'Election? Election? What election? Oh, the election! Well—' He lowered his voice, confidentially. As with most deaf people, his tone went to extremes. 'There's no question of it. The one we want is the one we know. Know Houghman's father. Knew his grandfather. His stand is the same, identical one that we are all accustomed to. On every subject—this race thing especially. Very dangerous now. Extremely touchy. But Houghman—absolute! Never experiment, never question, never turn back. These are perilous times.'

'Yes, sir,' said Turner, nodding in an earnestly false way, which was better than the earnestly impressed way a younger boy at the general's elbow shouted, 'General Skelton, that's just what my daddy says!'

'Oh yes,' said the old man, sipping scotch. 'Oh yes, it's true. And you, missy?' he thundered suddenly at Nancy, making her jump. 'Are you just visiting here?'

'Why, Granddaddy,' Lorna explained, joining them, 'Nancy lives here now. You know Nancy.'

'Then why isn't she tan?' the old man continued. 'Why so pale and wan, fair nymph?'

'Were you a nymph?' Turner asked. 'All this time?'

'For me I'm dark,' Nancy explained. But this awkward way of putting it proved more than General Skelton could hear, even after three shoutings.

Turner Carmichael said, 'We used to have this crazy colored girl who went around saying, "I'se really white, 'cause all my chillun is,"' and of course *that* was what General Skelton picked to hear. 'Party's getting rough,' he complained.

'Granddaddy,' Lorna cried, giggling, 'you don't understand!'

'Don't I?' said the old gentleman. 'Well, maybe I don't.'

'Here, Nancy, come help me,' said Lorna, leading her guest toward the kitchen.

On the way, Nancy heard Rob ask Turner, 'Just where did you have this colored girl, did you say?'

'Don't be a dope. I said she worked for us.'

'Aren't they a scream?' Lorna said, dragging a quart bottle of soda out of the refrigerator. 'I thank God every night Granddaddy's deaf. You know, he was in the First World War and killed I don't know how many Germans, and he still can't stand to hear what he calls loose talk before a lady.'

'I thought he was in the Civil War,' said Nancy, and then of course she knew that that was the wrong thing and that Lorna, who just for an instant gave her a glance less than polite, was not going to forget it. The fact was, Nancy had never thought till that minute which war General Skelton had been in. She hadn't thought because she didn't care.

It had grown dark by now, and through the kitchen windows Nancy could see that the moon had risen—a moon in the clumsy stage, swelling between three-quarters and full, yet pouring out light on the water. Its rays were bursting against the long breakwater of concrete slabs, the remains of what the hurricane had shattered.

After saying such a fool thing, Nancy felt she could not stay in that kitchen another minute with Lorna, so she asked where she could go comb her hair. Lorna showed her down a hallway, kindly switching the lights on.

The Skeltons' bathroom was all pale blue and white, with handsome

jars of rose bath salts and big fat scented bars of rosy soap. The lights
came on impressively and the fixtures were heavy, yet somehow it all
looked dead. It came to Nancy that she had really been wondering
about just what would be in this sort of bathroom ever since she had
seen those boys, with maybe Rob among them, playing tennis while
she jumped on the trampoline. Surely the place had the air of an inner
shrine, but what was there to see? The tops of all the bottles fitted
firmly tight, and the soap in the tub was dry. Somebody had picked it
all out—that was the point—judging soap and bath salts just the way
they judged outsiders, business, real estate, politics. Nancy's father
made judgments, too. Once, he argued all evening that Hitler was a
well-meaning man; another time, he said the world was ready for
communism. You could tell he was judging wrong, because he didn't
have a bathroom like this one. Nancy's face in the mirror resembled a
flower in a room that was too warm.

When she went out again, they had started dancing a little—a sort
of friendly shifting around before the big glass windows overlooking
the sound. General Skelton's chair was empty; he was gone. Down
below, Lorna's parents could be heard coming in; her mother called
upstairs. Her father appeared and shook hands all around. Mrs.
Skelton soon followed him. He was wearing a white jacket, and she
had on a silver cocktail dress with silver shoes. They looked like people
in magazines. Mrs. Skelton held a crystal platter of things to eat in one
hand, with a lace handkerchief pressed between the flesh and the glass
in an inevitable sort of way.

In a moment, when the faces, talking and eating, the music, the talk,
and the dancing swam to a still point before Nancy's eyes, she said,
'You must all come to my house next week. We'll have a party.'

A silence fell. Everyone knew where Nancy lived, in that cluster of
old run-down houses the boulevard swept by. They knew that her
house, especially, needed paint outside and furniture inside. Her
daddy drank too much, and through her dress they could perhaps
clearly discern the pin that held her slip together. Maybe, since they
knew everything, they could look right through the walls of the house
and see her daddy's donkey.

'Sure we will,' said Rob Acklen at once. 'I think that would be grand.'

'Sure we will, Nancy,' said Lorna Skelton, who was such a good
sport and who was not seeing Rob this summer.

'A party?' said Turner Carmichael, and swallowed a whole anchovy. 'Can I come, too?'

Oh, dear Lord, Nancy was wondering, what made me say it? Then she was on the stairs with her knees shaking, leaving the party, leaving with Rob to go down to Biloxi, where the two of them always went, and hearing the right things said to her and Rob, and smiling back at the right things but longing to jump off into the dark as if it were water. The dark, with the moon mixed in with it, seemed to her like good deep water to go off in.

She might have known that in the Marine Room of the Buena Vista down in Biloxi, they would run into more friends of Rob's. They always ran into somebody, and she might have known. These particular ones had already arrived and were even waiting for Rob, being somewhat bored in the process. It wasn't that Rob was so bright and witty, but he listened and liked everybody; he saw them the way they liked to be seen. So then they would go on to new heights, outdoing themselves, coming to believe how marvelous they really were. Two fraternity brothers of his were there tonight. They were sitting at a table with their dates—two tiny girls with tiny voices, like mosquitoes. They at once asked Nancy where she went to college, but before she could reply and give it away that her school so far had been only a cow college up in Arkansas and that she had gone there because her daddy couldn't afford anywhere else, Rob broke in and answered for her. 'She's been in a finishing school in Little Rock,' he said, 'but I'm trying to talk her into going to the university.'

Then the girls and their dates all four spoke together. They said, 'Great!'

'Now watch,' said one of the little girls, whose name was Teenie. 'Cootie's getting out that little ole rush book.'

Sure enough, the tiniest little notebook came out of the little cream silk bag of the other girl, who was called Cootie, and in it Nancy's name and address were written down with a sliver of a gold pencil. The whole routine was a fake, but a kind fake, as long as Rob was there. The minute those two got her into the ladies' room it would turn into another thing altogether; that she knew. Nancy knew all about mosquitoes. They'll sting me till I crumple up and die, she thought, and what will they ever care? So, when the three of them did leave the table, she stopped to straighten the strap of her shoe at the door to the ladies' room and let them go on through, talking on and on to one another about Rush Week. Then she went down a corridor and around a corner and down a short flight of steps. She ran down a long basement hallway where the service quarters were, past linen closets and cases of soft drinks, and, turning another corner and trying a door above a stairway, she came out, as she thought she would, in a night-club place called the Fishnet, far away in the wing. It was a good place to hide; she and Rob had been there often. I can make up some sort of story later, she thought, and crept up on the last bar stool. Up above the bar, New Orleans-style (or so they said), a man was pumping tunes out of an electric organ. He wore rings on his chubby fingers and kept a handkerchief near him to mop his brow and to swab his triple chins with between songs. He waved his hand at Nancy. 'Where's Rob, honey?' he asked.

She smiled but didn't answer. She kept her head back in the shadows. She wished only to be like another glass in the sparkling row of glasses lined up before the big gleam of mirrors and under the play of lights. What made me say that about a party? she kept wondering. To some people it would be nothing, nothing. But not to her. She fumbled in her bag for a cigarette. Inadvertently, she drank from a glass near her hand. The man sitting next to her smiled at her. 'I didn't want it anyway,' he said.

'Oh, I didn't mean—' she began. 'I'll order one.' Did you pay now? She rummaged in her bag.

But the man said, 'What'll it be?' and ordered for her. 'Come on now, take it easy,' he said. 'What's your name?'

'Nothing,' she said, by accident.

She had meant to say Nancy, but the man seemed to think it was funny. 'Nothing what?' he asked. 'Or is it by any chance Miss Nothing? I used to know a large family of Nothings, over in Mobile.'

'Oh, I meant to say Nancy.'

'Nancy Nothing. Is that it?'

Another teaser, she thought. She looked away from his eyes, which glittered like metal, and what she saw across the room made her uncertainties vanish. She felt her whole self settle and calm itself. The man she had seen that morning on the beach wearing a red bandanna shirt and shorts was standing near the back of the Fishnet, looking on.

Now he was wearing a white dinner jacket and a black tie, with a red cummerbund over his large stomach, but he was unmistakably the same man. At that moment, he positively seemed to Nancy to be her own identity. She jumped up and left the teasing man at the bar and crossed the room.

'Remember me?' she said. 'I saw you on the beach this morning.'

'Sure I do. You ran off when it started to rain. I had to run, too.'

'Why did you?' Nancy asked, growing happier every minute.

'Because the rain was so hot it burnt me. If I could roll up my sleeve, I'd show you the blisters on my arm.'

'I believe you. I had some, too, but they went away.' She smiled, and the man smiled back. The feeling was that they would be friends forever.

'Listen,' the man said after a while. 'There's a fellow here you've got to meet now. He's out on the veranda, because it's too hot in here. Anyway, he gets tired just with me. Now you come on.'

Nancy Lewis was always conscious of what she had left behind her. She knew that right now her parents and old Mrs. Poultney, with her rent collector's jaw, and Miss Henriette Dupré, with her religious calf eyes, and the Nattiers, mother and son, were all sitting on the back porch in the half-light, passing the bottle of 6-12 around, and probably right now discussing the fact that Nancy was out with Rob again. She knew that when her mother thought of Rob her heart turned beautiful and radiant as a sea shell on a spring night. Her father, both at home and at his office, took his daughter's going out with Rob as excuse for saying something disagreeable about Rob's father, who was a big insurance man. There was always some talk about how Mr. Acklen had trickily got out of the bulk of his hurricane-damage payments, the same as all the other insurance men had done. Nancy's mother was probably responding to such a charge at this moment. 'Now, you don't know that's true,' she would say. But old Mrs. Poultney would say she knew it was true with *her* insurance company (implying that she knew but wouldn't say about the Acklen Company, too). Half the house she was renting to the Lewises had blown right off it—all one wing—and the upstairs bathroom was ripped in two, and you could see the wallpapered walls of all the rooms, and the bathtub, with its pipes still attached, had got blown into the telephone wires. If Mrs. Poultney had got what insurance money had been coming to her, she would have torn down this house and built a new one. And Mrs. Nattier would say that there was something terrible to her about seeing wallpapered rooms exposed that way. And Miss Henriette Dupré would say that the Dupré house had come through it all ab-so-lootly intact, meaning that the Duprés had been foresighted enough to get some sort of special heavenly insurance, and she would be just longing to embark on explaining how they came by it, and she would, too, given a tenth of a chance. And all the time this went on, Nancy could see into the Acklens' house just as clearly—see the Acklens sitting inside their sheltered game room after dinner, bathed in those soft bug-repellent lights. And what were the Acklens saying (along with their kind of talk about their kind of money) but that they certainly hoped Rob wasn't serious about that girl? Nothing had to matter if he wasn't serious . . . Nancy could circle around all of them in her mind. She could peer into windows, overhearing; it was the only way she could look at people. No human in the whole human world seemed to her exactly made for her to stand in front of and look squarely in the eye, the way she could look Bernard Nattier in the eye (he not being human either) before taking careful aim to be sure not to miss him with a purseful of rocks and oyster shells, or the way she could look this big man in the red cummerbund in the eye, being convinced already that he was what her daddy called a 'natural.' Her daddy liked to come across people he could call that, because it made him feel superior.

As the big man steered her through the crowded room, threading among the tables, going out toward the veranda, he was telling her his life story all along the way. It seemed that his father was a terribly rich Yankee who paid him not to stay at home. He had been in love with a policeman's daughter from Pittsburgh, but his father broke it up. He was still in love with her and always would be. It was the way he was; he couldn't help being faithful, could he? His name was Alfred, but everybody called him Bub. The fellow his father paid to drive him around was right down there, he said, as they stepped through the door and out on the veranda.

Nancy looked down the length of the veranda, which ran along the side of the hotel, and there was a man sitting on a bench. He had on a white jacket and was staring straight ahead, smoking. The highway curled around the hotel grounds, following the curve of the shore, and the cars came glimmering past, one by one, sometimes with lights on inside, sometimes spilling radio music that trailed up in long waves and met the electric-organ music coming out of the bar. Nancy and Bub walked toward the man. Bub counseled her gently, 'His name is Dennis.' Some people in full evening dress were coming up the divided walk before the hotel, past the canna lilies blooming deeply red under the high, powerful lights, where the bugs coned in long footless whirlpools. The people were drunk and laughing.

'Hi, Dennis,' Bub said. The way he said it, trying to sound confident, told her that he was scared of Dennis.

Dennis's head snapped up and around. He was an erect, strong, square-cut man, not very tall. He had put water on his light brown hair when he combed it, so that it streaked light and dark and light again and looked like wood. He had cold eyes, which did not express anything—just the opposite of Rob Acklen's.

'What you got there?' he asked Bub.

'I met her this morning on the beach,' Bub said.

'Been holding out on me?'

'Nothing like that,' said Bub. 'I just now saw her again.'

The man called Dennis got up and thumbed his cigarette into the shrubbery. Then he carefully set his heels together and bowed. It was all a sort of joke on how he thought people here behaved. 'Would you care to dance?' he inquired.

Dancing there on the veranda, Nancy noticed at once that he had a tense, strong wrist that bent back and forth like something manufactured out of steel. She also noticed that he was making her do whatever it was he called dancing; he was good at that. The music coming out of the Fishnet poured through the windows and around them. Dennis was possibly even thirty years old. He kept talking the whole time. 'I guess he's told you everything, even about the policeman's daughter. He tells everybody everything, right in the first two minutes. I don't know if it's true, but how can you tell? If it wasn't true when it happened, it is now.' He spun her fast as a top, then slung her out about ten feet—she thought she would certainly sail right on out over the railing and maybe never stop till she landed in the gulf, or perhaps go splat on the highway—but he got her back on the beat and finished up the thought, saying, 'Know what I mean?'

'I guess so,' Nancy said, and the music stopped.

The three of them sat down together on the bench.

'What do we do now?' Dennis asked.

'Let's ask her,' said Bub. He was more and more delighted with Nancy. He had been tremendously encouraged when Dennis took to her.

'You ask her,' Dennis said.

'Listen, Nancy,' Bub said. 'Now, listen. Let me just tell you. There's so much money—that's the first thing to know. You've got no idea how much money there is. Really crazy. It's something, actually, that nobody knows—'

'If anybody knew,' said Dennis, 'they might have to tell the government.'

'Anyway, my stepmother on this yacht in Florida, her own telephone—by radio, you know—she'd be crazy to meet you. My dad is likely off somewhere, but maybe not. And there's this plane down at Palm Beach, pilot and all, with nothing to do but go to the beach every day, just to pass away the time, and if he's not there for any reason, me and Dennis can fly just as good as we can drive. There's Alaska, Beirut—would you like to go to Beirut? I've always wanted to. There's anything you say.'

'See that Cad out there?' said Dennis. 'The yellow one with the black leather upholstery? That's his. I drive.'

'So all you got to do,' Bub told her, 'is wish. Now, wait—now, think. It's important!' He all but held his hand over her mouth, as if playing a child's game, until finally he said, 'Now! What would you like to do most in the world?'

'Go to New Orleans,' said Nancy at once, 'and eat some wonderful food.'

'It's a good idea,' said Dennis. 'This dump is getting on my nerves. I get bored most of the time anyway, but today I'm bored silly.'

'So wait here!' Nancy said. 'So wait right here!'

She ran off to get Rob. She had all sorts of plans in her head.

But Rob was all taken up. There were now more of his friends. The Marine Room was full of people just like him, lounging around two big tables shoved together, with about a million 7-Up bottles and soda bottles and glasses before them, and girls spangled among them, all silver, gold, and white. It was as if while Nancy was gone they had moved into mirrors to multiply themselves. They were talking to themselves about things she couldn't join in, any more than you can dance without feet. Somebody was going into politics, somebody was getting married to a girl who trained horses, somebody was just back from Europe. The two little mosquito girls weren't saying anything much any more; they had their little chins glued to their little palms. When anybody mentioned the university, it sounded like a small country the people right there were running *in absentia* to suit themselves. Last year's Maid of Cotton was there, and so, it turned out, was the girl horse trainer—tall, with a sheaf of upswept brown hair fastened with a glittering pin; she sat like the mast of a ship, smiling and talking about horses. Did she know personally every horse in the Southern states?

Rob scarcely looked up when he pulled Nancy in. 'Where you been? What you want to drink?' He was having another good evening. He seemed to be sitting up above the rest, as though presiding, but this was not actually so; only his fondness for every face he saw before him made him appear to be raised a little, as if on a special chair.

And, later on, it seemed to Nancy that she herself had been, among them, like a person who wasn't a person—another order of creature passing among or even through them. Was it just that nothing, nobody, could really distract them when they got wrapped up in themselves?

'I met some people who want to meet you,' she whispered to Rob. 'Come on out with me.'

'O.K.,' he said. 'In a minute. Are they from around here?'

'Come on, come on,' she urged. 'Come on out.'

'In a minute,' he said. 'I will in a minute,' he promised.

Then someone noticed her pulling at his sleeve, and she thought she heard Lorna Skelton laugh.

She went racing back to Bub and Dennis, who were waiting for her so docilely they seemed to be the soul of goodness, and she said, 'I'll just ride around for a while, because I've never been in a Cadillac before.' So they rode around and came back and sat for a while under the huge brilliant overhead lights before the hotel, where the bugs spiraled down. They did everything she said. She could make them do anything. They went to three different places, for instance, to find her some Dentyne, and when they found it they bought her a whole carton of it.

The bugs did a jagged frantic dance, trying to climb high enough to kill themselves, and occasionally a big one crashed with a harsh dry sound against the pavement. Nancy remembered dancing in the open air, and the rough salt feel of the air whipping against her skin as she spun fast against the air's drift. From behind she heard the resonant, constant whisper of the gulf. She looked toward the hotel doors and thought that if Rob came through she would hop out of the car right away, but he didn't come. A man she knew passed by, and she just all of a sudden said, 'Tell Rob I'll be back in a minute,' and he, without even looking up said, 'O.K., Nancy,' just like it really was O.K., so she said what the motor was saying, quiet but right there, and definitely running just under the splendid skin of the car, 'Let's go on for a little while.'

'Nancy, I think you're the sweetest girl I ever saw,' said Bub, and they drove off.

She rode between them, on the front seat of the Cadillac. The top was down and the moon spilled over them as they rode, skimming gently but powerfully along the shore and the sound, like a strong rapid cloud traveling west. Nancy watched the point where the moon actually met the water. It was moving and still at once. She thought that it was glorious, in a messy sort of way. She would have liked to poke her head up out of the water right there. She could feel the water pouring back through her white-blond hair, her face slathering over with moonlight.

'If it hadn't been for that crazy rain,' Bub kept saying, 'I wouldn't have met her.'

'Oh, shut up about that goofy rain,' said Dennis.

'It was like being spit on from above,' said Nancy.

The needle crept up to eighty or more, and when they had left the sound and were driving through the swamp, Nancy shivered. They wrapped her in a lap robe from the back seat and turned the radio up loud.

It was since she got back, since she got back home from New Orleans, that her mother did not put on the thin voile afternoon dress any more and serve iced tea to the neighbors on the back porch. Just yesterday, having nothing to do in the hot silence but hear the traffic stream by on the boulevard, and not wanting a suntan, and being certain the telephone would not ring, Nancy had taken some lemonade over to

Bernard Nattier, who was sick in bed with the mumps. He and his mother had one room between them over at Mrs. Poultney's house, and they had stacks of magazines—the *Ladies' Home Journal*, *McCall's*, *Life*, and *Time*—piled along the walls. Bernard lay on a bunk bed pushed up under the window, in all the close heat, with no breeze able to come in at all. His face was puffed out and his eyes feverish. 'I brought you some lemonade,' said Nancy, but he said he couldn't drink it because it hurt his gums. Then he smiled at her, or tried to— it must have hurt even to do that, and it certainly made him look silly, like a cartoon of himself, but it was sweet.

'I love you, Nancy,' he said, most irresponsibly.

She thought she would cry. She had honestly tried to kill him with those rocks and oyster shells. He knew that very well, and he, from the moment he had seen her, had set out to make her life one long torment, so where could it come from, a smile like that, and what he said? She didn't know. From the fever, maybe. She said she loved him, too.

Then, it was last night, just the night before, that her father had got drunk and made speeches beginning, 'To think that a daughter of mine . . .' Nancy had sat through it all crouched in the shadows on the stair landing, in the very spot where the moss or old seaweed back of the paneling smelled the strongest and dankest, and thought of her mother upstairs, lying, clothed, straight out on the bed in the dark, with a headache and no cover on and maybe the roof above her melted away. Nancy looked down to where her father was marching up to the donkey that said, 'If you really want to look like me—Just keep right on talking,' and was picking it up and throwing it down, right on the floor. She cried out, before she knew it—'Oh!'—seeing him do the very thing she had so often meant to do herself. Why had he? Why? Because the whiskey had run out on him? Or because he had got too much of it again? Or from trying to get in one good lick at everything there was? Or because the advice he loved so much seemed now being offered to him?

But the donkey did not break. It lay there, far down in the tricky shadows; Nancy could see it lying there, looking back over its shoulder with its big red grinning mouth, and teeth like piano keys, still saying the same thing, naturally. Her father was tilting uncertainly down toward it, unable, without falling flat on his face, to reach it. This made a problem for him, and he stood thinking it all over, taking every aspect of it well into account, even though the donkey gave the impression that not even with a sledgehammer would it be broken, and lay as if on some deep distant sea floor, toward which all the sediment of life was drifting, drifting, forever slowly down . . .

Beirut! It was the first time she had remembered it. They had said they would take her there, Dennis and Bub, and then she had forgotten to ask, so why think of it right now, on the street uptown, just when she saw Rob Acklen coming along? She would have to see him sometime, she guessed, but what did Beirut have to do with it?

'Nancy Lewis,' he said pleasantly, 'you ran out on me. Why did you act like that? I was always nice to you.'

'I told them to tell you,' she said. 'I just went to ride around for a while.'

'Oh, I got the word, all right. About fifty different people saw you drive off in that Cadillac. Now about a hundred claim to have. Seems like everybody saw those two characters but me. What did you do it for?'

'I didn't like those Skeltons, all those people you know. I didn't like those sorority girls, that Teenie and Cootie. You knew I didn't, but you always took me where they were just the same.'

'But the point is,' said Rob Acklen, 'I thought you liked me.'

'Well, I did,' said Nancy Lewis, as though it all had happened a hundred years ago. 'Well, I did like you just fine.'

They were still talking on the street. There had been the tail of a storm that morning, and the palms were blowing. There was a sense of them streaming like green flags above the low town.

Rob took Nancy to the drugstore and sat at a booth with her. He ordered her a fountain Coke and himself a cup of coffee. 'What's happened to you?' he asked her.

She realized then, from what he was looking at, that something she had only half noticed was certainly there to be seen—her skin, all around the edges of her white blouse, was badly bruised and marked, and there was the purplish mark on her cheekbone she had more or less powdered over, along with the angry streak on her neck.

'You look like you fell through a cotton gin,' Rob Acklen continued, in his friendly way. 'You're not going to say the rain over in New Orleans is just scalding hot, are you?'

'I didn't say anything,' she returned.

'Maybe the mosquitoes come pretty big over there,' he suggested. 'They wear boxing gloves, for one thing, and, for another—'

'Oh, stop it, Rob,' she said, and wished she was anywhere else.

It had all stemmed from the moment down in the French Quarter, over late drinks somewhere, when Dennis had got nasty enough with Bub to get rid of him, so that all of Dennis's attention from that point onward had gone exclusively to Nancy. This particular attention was relentless and direct, for Dennis was about as removed from any sort of affection and kindness as a human could be. Maybe it had all got boiled out of him; maybe he had never had much to get rid of. What he had to say to her was nothing she hadn't heard before, nothing she hadn't already been given more or less to understand from mosquitoes, people, life-in-general, and the rain out of the sky. It was just that he said it in a final sort of way—that was all.

'I was in a wreck,' said Nancy.

'Nobody killed, I hope,' said Rob.

She looked vaguely across at Rob Acklen with pretty, dark blue eyes that seemed to be squinting to see through shifting lights down in the deep sea; for in looking at him, in spite of all he could do, she caught a glimmering impression of herself, of what he thought of her, of how soft her voice always was, her face like a warm flower.

'I was doing my best to be nice to you. Why wasn't that enough?'

'I don't know,' she said.

'None of those people you didn't like were out to get you. They were all my friends.'

When he spoke in this handsome, sincere, and democratic way, she had to agree; she had to say she guessed that was right.

Then he said, 'I was having such a good summer. I imagined you were, too,' and she thought, He's coming down deeper and deeper, but one thing is certain—if he gets down as far as I am, he'll drown.

'You better go,' she told him, because he had said he was on his way up to Shreveport on business for his father. And because Bub and Dennis were back; she'd seen them drift by in the car twice, once on the boulevard and once in town, silenter than cloud, Bub in the back, with his knees propped up, reading a magazine.

'I'll be going in a minute,' he said.

'You just didn't realize I'd ever go running off like that,' Nancy said, winding a damp Coca-Cola straw around her finger.

'Was it the party, the one you said you wanted to give? You didn't have to feel—'

'I don't remember any party,' she said quickly.

Her mother lay with the roof gone, hands folded. Nancy felt that people's mothers, like wallpapered walls after a hurricane, should not be exposed. Her father at last successfully reached the donkey, but he fell in the middle of the rug, while Nancy, on the stair landing, smelling seaweed, asked herself how a murderous child with swollen jaws happened to mention love, if love is not a fever, and the storm-driven sea struck the open reef and went roaring skyward, splashing a tattered gull that clutched at the blast—but if we will all go there immediately it is safe in the Dupré house, because they have this holy candle. There are hidden bone-cold lairs no one knows of, in rock beneath the sea. She shook her bone-white hair.

Rob's whole sensitive face tightened harshly for saying what had to come next, and she thought for a while he wasn't going to make it, but he did. 'To hell with it. To absolute hell with it then.' He looked stricken, as though he had managed nothing but damaging himself.

'I guess it's just the way I am,' Nancy murmured. 'I just run off sometimes.'

Her voice faded in a deepening glimmer where the human breath is snatched clean away and there are only bubbles, iridescent and pure. When she dove again, they rose in a curving track behind her.

FRIENDS

Grace Paley

To put us at our ease, to quiet our hearts as she lay dying, our dear friend Selena said, Life, after all, has not been an unrelieved horror—you know, I *did* have many wonderful years with her.

She pointed to a child who leaned out of a portrait on the wall—long brown hair, white pinafore, head and shoulders forward.

Eagerness, said Susan. Ann closed her eyes.

On the same wall three little girls were photographed in a schoolyard. They were in furious discussion; they were holding hands. Right in the middle of the coffee table, framed, in autumn colors, a handsome young woman of eighteen sat on an enormous horse—aloof, disinterested, a rider. One night this young woman, Selena's child, was found in a rooming house in a distant city, dead. The police called. They said, Do you have a daughter named Abby?

And with *him*, too, our friend Selena said. We had good times, Max and I. You know that.

There were no photographs of *him*. He was married to another woman and had a new, stalwart girl of about six, to whom no harm would ever come, her mother believed.

Our dear Selena had gotten out of bed. Heavily but with a comic dance, she soft-shoed to the bathroom, singing, 'Those were the days, my friend . . .'

Later that evening, Ann, Susan, and I were enduring our five-hour train ride to home. After one hour of silence and one hour of coffee and the sandwiches Selena had given us (she actually stood, leaned her big soft excavated body against the kitchen table to make those sandwiches), Ann said, Well, we'll never see *her* again.

Who says? Anyway, listen, said Susan. Think of it. Abby isn't the only kid who died. What about that great guy, remember Bill Dalrymple—he was a non-cooperator or a deserter? And Bob Simon. They were killed in automobile accidents. Matthew, Jeannie, Mike. Remember Al Lurie—he was murdered on Sixth Street—and that little kid Brenda, who O.D.'d on your roof, Ann? The tendency, I suppose, is to forget. You people don't remember them.

What do you mean, 'you people'? Ann asked. You're talking to *us*.

I began to apologize for not knowing them all. Most of them were older than my kids, I said.

Of course, the child Abby was exactly in my time of knowing and in all my places of paying attention—the park, the school, our street. But oh! It's true! Selena's Abby was not the only one of that beloved generation of our children murdered by cars, lost to war, to drugs, to madness.

Selena's main problem, Ann said—you know, she didn't tell the truth.

What?

A few hot human truthful words are powerful enough, Ann thinks, to steam all God's chemical mistakes and society's slimy lies out of her life. We all believe in that power, my friends and I, but sometimes . . . the heat.

Anyway, I always thought Selena had told us a lot. For instance, we knew she was an orphan. There were six, seven other children. She was the youngest. She was forty-two years old before someone informed her that her mother had *not* died in childbirthing her. It was some terrible sickness. And she had lived close to her mother's body—at her breast, in fact—until she was eight months old. Whew! said Selena. What a relief! I'd always felt I was the one who'd killed her.

Your family stinks, we told her. They really held you up for grief.

Oh, people, she said. Forget it. They did a lot of nice things for me too. Me and Abby. Forget it. Who has the time?

That's what I mean, said Ann. Selena should have gone after them with an ax.

More information: Selena's two sisters brought her to a Home. They were ashamed that at sixteen and nineteen they could not take care of her. They kept hugging her. They were sure she'd cry. They took her to her room—not a room, a dormitory with about eight beds. This is your bed, Lena. This is your table for your things. This little drawer is for your toothbrush. All for me? she asked. No one else can use it? Only me. That's all? Artie can't come? Franky can't come? Right?

Believe me, Selena said, those were happy days at the Home.

Facts, said Ann, just facts. Not necessarily the *truth*.

I don't think it's right to complain about the character of the dying or start hustling all their motives into the spotlight like that. Isn't it amazing enough, the bravery of that private inclusive intentional community?

It wouldn't help not to be brave, said Selena. You'll see.

She wanted to get back to bed. Susan moved to help her.

Thanks, our Selena said, leaning on another person for the first time in her entire life. The trouble is, when I stand, it hurts me here all down my back. Nothing they can do about it. All the chemotherapy. No more chemistry left in me to therapeut. Ha! Did you know before I came to New York and met you I used to work in that hospital? I was supervisor in gynecology. Nursing. They were my friends, the doctors. They weren't so snotty then. David Clark, big surgeon. He couldn't look at me last week. He kept saying, Lena . . . Lena . . . Like that. We were in North Africa the same year—'44, I think. I told him, Davy, I've been around a long enough time. I haven't missed too much. He knows it. But I didn't want to make him look at me. Ugh, my damn feet are a pain in the neck.

Recent research, said Susan, tells us that it's the neck that's a pain in the feet.

Always something new, said Selena, our dear friend.

On the way back to the bed, she stopped at her desk. There were about twenty snapshots scattered across it—the baby, the child, the young woman. Here, she said to me, take this one. It's a shot of Abby and your Richard in front of the school—third grade? What a day! The show those kids put on! What a bunch of kids! What's Richard doing now?

Oh, who knows? Horsing around someplace. Spain. These days, it's Spain. Who knows where he is? They're all the same.

Why did I say that? I knew exactly where he was. He writes. In fact, he found a broken phone and was able to call every day for a week— mostly to give orders to his brother but also to say, Are you O.K., Ma? How's your new boyfriend, did he smile yet?

The kids, they're all the same, I said.

It was only politeness, I think, not to pour my boy's light, noisy face into that dark afternoon. Richard used to say in his early mean teens, You'd sell us down the river to keep Selena happy and innocent. It's true. Whenever Selena would say, I don't know, Abby has some peculiar friends, I'd answer for stupid comfort, You should see Richard's.

Still, he's in Spain, Selena said. At least you know that. It's probably interesting. He'll learn a lot. Richard is a wonderful boy, Faith. He acts like a wise guy but he's not. You know the night Abby died, when the police called me and told me? That was my first night's sleep in two years. I *knew* where she was.

Selena said this very matter-of-factly—just offering a few informative sentences.

But Ann, listening, said, Oh!—she called out to us all, Oh!—and began to sob. Her straightforwardness had become an arrow and gone right into her own heart.

Then a deep tear-drying breath: I want a picture too, she said.

Yes. Yes, wait, I have one here someplace. Abby and Judy and that Spanish kid Victor. Where is it? Ah. Here!

Three nine-year-old children sat high on that long-armed sycamore in the park, dangling their legs on someone's patient head—smooth dark hair, parted in the middle. Was that head Kitty's?

Our dear friend laughed. Another great day, she said. Wasn't it? I remember you two sizing up the men. I *had* one at the time—I thought. Some joke. Here, take it. I have two copies. But you ought to get it enlarged. When this you see, remember me. Ha-ha. Well, girls—excuse me, I mean ladies—it's time for me to rest.

She took Susan's arm and continued that awful walk to her bed.

We didn't move. We had a long journey ahead of us and had expected a little more comforting before we set off.

No, she said. You'll only miss the express. I'm not in much pain. I've got lots of painkiller. See?

The tabletop was full of little bottles.

I just want to lie down and think of Abby.

It was true, the local could cost us an extra two hours at least. I looked at Ann. It had been hard for her to come at all. Still, we couldn't move. We stood there before Selena in a row. Three old friends. Selena pressed her lips together, ordered her eyes into cold distance.

I know that face. Once, years ago, when the children were children, it had been placed modestly in front of J. Hoffner, the principal of the elementary school.

He'd said, No! Without training you cannot tutor these kids. There are real problems. You have to know *how to teach.*

Our P.T.A. had decided to offer some one-to-one tutorial help for the Spanish kids, who were stuck in crowded classrooms with exhausted teachers among little middle-class achievers. He had said, in a written communication to show seriousness and then in personal confrontation to *prove* seriousness, that he could not allow it. And the board of ed itself had said no. (All this no-ness was to lead to some terrible events in the schools and neighborhoods of our poor yes-requiring city.) But most of the women in our P.T.A. were independent—by necessity and disposition. We were, in fact, the soft-speaking tough souls of anarchy.

I had Fridays off that year. At about 11 a.m. I'd bypass the principal's office and run up to the fourth floor. I'd take Robert Figueroa to the end of the hall, and we'd work away at storytelling for about twenty minutes. Then we would write the beautiful letters of the alphabet invented by smart foreigners long ago to fool time and distance.

That day, Selena and her stubborn face remained in the office for at least two hours. Finally, Mr. Hoffner, besieged, said that because she was a nurse, she would be allowed to help out by taking the littlest children to the modern difficult toilet. Some of them, he said, had just come from the barbarous hills beyond Maricao. Selena said O.K., she'd do that. In the toilet she taught the little girls which way to wipe, as she had taught her own little girl a couple of years earlier. At three o'clock she brought them home for cookies and milk. The children of that year ate cookies in her kitchen until the end of the sixth grade.

Now, what did we learn in that year of my Friday afternoons off? The following. Though the world cannot be changed by talking to one child at a time, it may at least be known.

Anyway, Selena placed into our eyes for long remembrance that useful stubborn face. She said, No. Listen to me, you people. Please. I don't have lots of time. What I want . . . I want to lie down and think about Abby. Nothing special. Just think about her, you know.

In the train Susan fell asleep immediately. She woke up from time to time, because the speed of the new wheels and the resistance of the old track gave us some terrible jolts. Once, she opened her eyes wide and said, You know, Ann's right. You don't get sick like that for nothing. I mean, she didn't even mention him.

Why should she? She hasn't even seen him, I said. Susan, you still have him-itis, the dread disease of females.

Yeah? And you don't? Anyway, he *was* around quite a bit. He was there every day, nearly, when the kid died.

Abby. I didn't like to hear 'the kid.' I wanted to say 'Abby' the way I've said 'Selena'—so those names can take thickness and strength and fall back into the world with their weight.

Abby, you know, was a wonderful child. She was in Richard's classes every class till high school. Good-hearted little girl from the beginning, noticeably kind—for a kid, I mean. Smart.

That's true, said Ann, very kind. She'd give away Selena's last shirt. Oh yes, they were all wonderful little girls and wonderful little boys.

Chrissy *is* wonderful, Susan said.

She *is*, I said.

Middle kids aren't supposed to be, but she is. She put herself through college— I didn't have a cent—and now she has this fellowship. And, you know, she never did take any crap from boys. She's something.

Ann went swaying up the aisle to the bathroom. First she said, Oh, all of them—just wohunderful.

I loved Selena, Susan said, but she never talked to me enough. Maybe she talked to you women more, about things. Men.

Then Susan fell asleep.

Ann sat down opposite me. She looked straight into my eyes with a narrow squint. It often connotes accusation.

Be careful—you're wrecking your laugh lines, I said.

Screw you, she said. You're kidding around. Do you realize I don't know where Mickey is? You know, you've been lucky. You always have been. Since you were a little kid. Papa and Mama's darling.

As is usual in conversations, I said a couple of things out loud and kept a few structured remarks for interior mulling and righteousness. I thought: She's never even met my folks. I thought: What a rotten thing to say. Luck—isn't it something like an insult?

I said, Annie, I'm only forty-eight. There's lots of time for me to be totally wrecked—if I live, I mean.

Then I tried to knock wood, but we were sitting in plush and leaning on plastic. Wood! I shouted. Please, some wood! Anybody here have a matchstick?

Oh, shut up, she said. Anyway, death doesn't count.

I tried to think of a couple of sorrows as irreversible as death. But truthfully nothing in my life can compare to hers: a son, a boy of fifteen, who disappears before your very eyes into a darkness or a light behind his own, from which neither hugging nor hitting can bring him. If you shout, Come back, come back, he won't come. Mickey, Mickey, Mickey, we once screamed, as though he were twenty miles away instead of right in front of us in a kitchen chair; but he refused to return. And when he did, twelve hours later, he left immediately for California.

Well, some bad things have happened in my life, I said.

What? You were born a woman? Is that it?

She was, of course, mocking me this time, referring to an old discussion about feminism and Judaism. Actually, on the prism of isms, both of those do have to be looked at together once in a while.

Well, I said, my mother died a couple of years ago and I still feel it. I think *Ma* sometimes and I lose my breath. I miss her. You understand that. Your mother's seventy-six. You have to admit it's nice still having her.

She's very sick, Ann said. Half the time she's out of it.

I decided not to describe my mother's death. I could have done so and made Ann even more miserable. But I thought I'd save that for her next attack on me. These constrictions of her spirit were coming closer and closer together. Probably a great enmity was about to be born.

Susan's eyes opened. The death or dying of someone near or dear often makes people irritable, she stated. (She's been taking a course in relationships *and* interrelationships.) The real name of my seminar is Skills: Personal Friendship and Community. It's a very good course despite your snide remarks.

While we talked, a number of cities passed us, going in the opposite direction. I had tried to look at New London through the dusk of the windows. Now I was missing New Haven. The conductor explained, smiling: Lady, if the windows were clean, half of you'd be dead. The tracks are lined with sharpshooters.

Do you believe that? I hate people to talk that way.

He may be exaggerating, Susan said, but don't wash the window.

A man leaned across the aisle. Ladies, he said, I do believe it. According to what I hear of this part of the country, it don't seem unplausible.

Susan turned to see if he was worth engaging in political dialogue.

You've forgotten Selena already, Ann said. All of us have. Then you'll make this nice memorial service for her and everyone will stand up and say a few words and then we'll forget her again—for good. What'll you say at the memorial, Faith?

It's not right to talk like that. She's not dead yet, Annie.

Yes, she is, said Ann.

We discovered the next day that give or take an hour or two, Ann had been correct. It was a combination—David Clark, surgeon, said—of being sick unto real death and having a tabletop full of little bottles.

Now, why are you taking all those hormones? Susan had asked Selena a couple of years earlier. They were visiting New Orleans. It was Mardi Gras.

Oh, they're mostly vitamins, Selena said. Besides, I want to be young and beautiful. She made a joking pirouette.

Susan said, That's absolutely ridiculous.

But Susan's seven or eight years younger than Selena. What did she know? Because: People *do* want to be young and beautiful. When they meet in the street, male or female, if they're getting older they look at each other's face a little ashamed. It's clear they want to say, Excuse me, I didn't mean to draw attention to mortality and gravity all at once. I didn't want to remind you, my dear friend, of our coming eviction, first from liveliness, then from life. To which, most of the time, the friend's eyes will courteously reply, My dear, it's nothing at all. I hardly noticed.

Luckily, I learned recently how to get out of that deep well of melancholy. Anyone can do it. You grab at roots of the littlest future, sometimes just stubs of conversation. Though some believe you miss a great deal of depth by not sinking down down down.

Susan, I asked, you still seeing Ed Flores?

Went back to his wife.

Lucky she didn't kill you, said Ann. I'd never fool around with a Spanish guy. They all have tough ladies back in the barrio.

No, said Susan, she's unusual. I met her at a meeting. We had an amazing talk. Luisa is a very fine woman. She's one of the office-worker organizers I told you about. She only needs him two more years, she says. Because the kids—they're girls—need to be watched a little in their neighborhood. The neighborhood is definitely not good. He's a good father but not such a great husband.

I'd call that a word to the wise.

Well, you know me—I don't want a husband. I like a male person around. I hate to do without. Anyway, listen to this. She, Luisa, whispers in my ear the other day, she whispers, Suzie, in two years you still want him, I promise you, you got him. Really, I may still want him then. He's only about forty-five now. Still got a lot of spunk. I'll have my degree in two years. Chrissy will be out of the house.

Two years! In two years we'll all be dead, said Ann.

I know she didn't mean all of us. She meant Mickey. That boy of hers would surely be killed in one of the drugstores or whorehouses of Chicago, New Orleans, San Francisco. I'm in a big beautiful city, he said when he called last month. Makes New York look like a garbage tank.

Mickey! Where?

Ha-ha, he said, and hung up.

Soon he'd be picked up for vagrancy, dealing, small thievery, or simply screaming dirty words at night under a citizen's window. Then Ann would fly to the town or not fly to the town to disentangle him, depending on a confluence of financial reality and psychiatric advice.

How *is* Mickey? Selena had said. In fact, that was her first sentence when we came, solemn and embarrassed, into her sunny front room that was full of the light and shadow of windy courtyard trees. We said, each in her own way, How are you feeling, Selena? She said, O.K., first things first. Let's talk about important things. How's Richard? How's Tonto? How's John? How's Chrissy? How's Judy? How's Mickey?

I don't want to talk about Mickey, said Ann.

Oh, let's talk about him, talk about him, Selena said, taking Ann's hand. Let's all think before it's too late. How did it start? Oh, for godsake talk about him.

Susan and I were smart enough to keep our mouths shut.

Nobody knows, nobody knows anything. Why? Where? Everybody has an idea, theories, and writes articles. Nobody knows.

Ann said this sternly. She didn't whine. She wouldn't lean too far into Selena's softness, but listening to Selena speak Mickey's name, she could sit in her chair more easily. I watched. It was interesting. Ann breathed deeply in and out the way we've learned in our Thursday-night yoga class. She was able to rest her body a little bit.

We were riding the rails of the trough called Park-Avenue-in-the-Bronx. Susan had turned from us to talk to the man across the aisle. She was explaining that the war in Vietnam was not yet over and would not be, as far as she was concerned, until we repaired the dikes we'd bombed and paid for some of the hopeless ecological damage. He didn't see it that way. Fifty thousand American lives, our own boys—we'd paid, he said. He asked us if we agreed with Susan. Every word, we said.

You don't look like hippies. He laughed. Then his face changed. As the resident face-reader, I decided he was thinking: Adventure. He may have hit a mother lode of late counterculture in three opinionated left-wing ladies. That was the nice part of his face. The other part was the sly out-of-town-husband-in-New-York look.

I'd like to see you again, he said to Susan.

Oh? Well, come to dinner day after tomorrow. Only two of my kids will be home. You ought to have at least one decent meal in New York.

Kids? His face thought it over. Thanks. Sure, he said. I'll come.

Ann muttered, She's impossible. She did it again.

Oh, Susan's O.K., I said. She's just right in there. Isn't that good?

This is a long ride, said Ann.

Then we were in the darkness that precedes Grand Central.

We're irritable, Susan explained to her new pal. We're angry with our friend Selena for dying. The reason is, we want her to be present when we're dying. We all require a mother or mother-surrogate to fix our pillows on that final occasion, and we were counting on her to be that person.

I know just what you mean, he said. You'd like to have someone around. A little fuss, maybe.

Something like that. Right, Faith?

It always takes me a minute to slide under the style of her public-address system. I agreed. Yes.

The train stopped hard, in a grinding agony of opposing technologies.

Right. Wrong. Who cares? Ann said. She didn't have to die. She really wrecked everything.

Oh, Annie, I said.

Shut up, will you? Both of you, said Ann, nearly breaking our knees as she jammed past us and out of the train.

Then Susan, like a New York hostess, began to tell that man all our private troubles—the mistake of the World Trade Center, Westway, the decay of the South Bronx, the rage in Williamsburg. She rose with him on the escalator, gabbing into evening friendship and, hopefully, a happy night.

At home Anthony, my youngest son, said, Hello, you just missed Richard. He's in Paris now. He had to call collect.

Collect? From Paris?

He saw my sad face and made one of the herb teas used by his peer group to calm their overwrought natures. He does want to improve my pretty good health and spirits. His friends have a book that says a person should, if properly nutritioned, live forever. He wants me to give it a try. He also believes that the human race, its brains and good looks, will end in his time.

At about 11:30 he went out to live the pleasures of his eighteen-year-old nighttime life.

At 3 a.m. he found me washing the floors and making little apartment repairs.

More tea, Mom? he asked. He sat down to keep me company. O.K., Faith. I know you feel terrible. But how come Selena never realized about Abby?

Anthony, what the hell do I realize about you?

Come on, you had to be blind. I was just a little kid, and I saw. Honest to God, Ma.

Listen, Tonto. Basically Abby was O.K. She was. You don't know yet what their times can do to a person.

Here she goes with her goody-goodies—everything is so groovy wonderful far-out terrific. Next thing, you'll say people are darling and the world is so nice and round that Union Carbide will never blow it up.

I have never said anything as hopeful as that. And why to all our knowledge of that sad day did Tonto at 3 a.m. have to add the fact of the world?

The next night Max called from North Carolina. How's Selena? I'm flying up, he said. I have one early-morning appointment. Then I'm canceling everything.

At 7 a.m. Annie called. I had barely brushed my morning teeth. It was hard, she said. The whole damn thing. I don't mean Selena. All of us. In the train. None of you seemed real to me.

Real? Reality, huh? Listen, how about coming over for breakfast?— I don't have to get going until after nine. I have this neat sourdough rye?

No, she said. Oh Christ, no. No!

I remember Ann's eyes and the hat she wore the day we first looked at each other. Our babies had just stepped howling out of the sandbox on their new walking legs. We picked them up. Over their sandy heads we smiled. I think a bond was sealed then, at least as useful as the vow we'd all sworn with husbands to whom we're no longer married. Hindsight, usually looked down upon, is probably as valuable as foresight, since it does include a few facts.

Meanwhile, Anthony's world—poor, dense, defenseless thing—rolls round and round. Living and dying are fastened to its surface and stuffed into its softer parts.

He was right to call my attention to its suffering and danger. He was right to harass my responsible nature. But I was right to invent for my friends and our children a report on these private deaths and the condition of our lifelong attachments.

THE ARTIFICIAL NIGGER

Flannery O'Connor

Mr. Head awakened to discover that the room was full of moonlight. He sat up and stared at the floor boards—the color of silver—and then at the ticking on his pillow, which might have been brocade, and after a second, he saw half of the moon five feet away in his shaving mirror, paused as if it were waiting for his permission to enter. It rolled forward and cast a dignifying light on everything. The straight chair against the wall looked stiff and attentive as if it were awaiting an order and Mr. Head's trousers, hanging to the back of it, had an almost noble air, like the garment some great man had just flung to his servant; but the face on the moon was a grave one. It gazed across the room and out the window where it floated over the horse stall and appeared to contemplate itself with the look of a young man who sees his old age before him.

Mr. Head could have said to it that age was a choice blessing and that only with years does a man enter into that calm understanding of life that makes him a suitable guide for the young. This, at least, had been his own experience.

He sat up and grasped the iron posts at the foot of his bed and raised himself until he could see the face on the alarm clock which sat on an overturned bucket beside the chair. The hour was two in the morning. The alarm on the clock did not work but he was not dependent on any mechanical means to awaken him. Sixty years had not dulled his responses; his physical reactions, like his moral ones, were guided by his will and strong character, and these could be seen plainly in his features. He had a long tube-like face with a long rounded open jaw and a long depressed nose. His eyes were alert but quiet, and in the miraculous moonlight they had a look of composure and of ancient wisdom as if they belonged to one of the great guides of men. He might have been Vergil summoned in the middle of the night to go to Dante, or better, Raphael, awakened by a blast of God's light to fly to the side of Tobias. The only dark spot in the room was Nelson's pallet, underneath the shadow of the window.

Nelson was hunched over on his side, his knees under his chin and his heels under his bottom. His new suit and hat were in the boxes that they had been sent in and these were on the floor at the foot of the pallet where he could get his hands on them as soon as he woke up. The slop jar, out of the shadow and made snow-white in the moonlight, appeared to stand guard over him like a small personal angel. Mr. Head lay back down, feeling entirely confident that he could carry out the moral mission of the coming day. He meant to be up before Nelson and to have the breakfast cooking by the time he awakened. The boy was always irked when Mr. Head was the first up. They would have to leave the house at four to get to the railroad junction by five-thirty. The train was to stop for them at five forty-five and they had to be there on time for this train was stopping merely to accommodate them.

This would be the boy's first trip to the city though he claimed it would be his second because he had been born there. Mr. Head had tried to point out to him that when he was born he didn't have the intelligence to determine his whereabouts but this had made no impression on the child at all and he continued to insist that this was to be his second trip. It would be Mr. Head's third trip. Nelson had said, 'I will've already been there twict and I ain't but ten.'

Mr. Head had contradicted him.

'If you ain't been there in fifteen years, how you know you'll be able to find your way about?' Nelson had asked. 'How you know it hasn't changed some?'

'Have you ever,' Mr. Head had asked, 'seen me lost?'

Nelson certainly had not but he was a child who was never satisfied until he had given an impudent answer and he replied, 'It's nowhere around here to get lost at.'

'The day is going to come,' Mr. Head prophesied, 'when you'll find you ain't as smart as you think you are.' He had been thinking about this trip for several months but it was for the most part in moral terms that he conceived it. It was to be a lesson that the boy would never forget. He was to find out from it that he had no cause for pride merely because he had been born in a city. He was to find out that the city is not a great place. Mr. Head meant him to see everything there is to see in a city so that he would be content to stay at home for the rest of his life. He fell asleep thinking how the boy would at last find out that he was not as smart as he thought he was.

He was awakened at three-thirty by the smell of fatback frying and he leaped off his cot. The pallet was empty and the clothes boxes had been thrown open. He put on his trousers and ran into the other room. The boy had a corn pone on cooking and had fried the meat. He was sitting in the half-dark at the table, drinking cold coffee out of a can. He had on his new suit and his new gray hat pulled low over his eyes. It was too big for him but they had ordered it a size large because they expected his head to grow. He didn't say anything but his entire figure suggested satisfaction at having arisen before Mr. Head.

Mr. Head went to the stove and brought the meat to the table in the skillet. 'It's no hurry,' he said. 'You'll get there soon enough and it's no guarantee you'll like it when you do neither,' and he sat down across from the boy whose hat teetered back slowly to reveal a fiercely expressionless face, very much the same shape as the old man's. They were grandfather and grandson but they looked enough alike to be brothers and brothers not too far apart in age, for Mr. Head had a youthful expression by daylight, while the boy's look was ancient, as if he knew everything already and would be pleased to forget it.

Mr. Head had once had a wife and daughter and when the wife died, the daughter ran away and returned after an interval with Nelson. Then one morning, without getting out of bed, she died and left Mr. Head with sole care of the year-old child. He had made the mistake of telling Nelson that he had been born in Atlanta. If he hadn't told him that, Nelson couldn't have insisted that this was going to be his second trip.

'You may not like it a bit,' Mr. Head continued. 'It'll be full of niggers.'

The boy made a face as if he could handle a nigger.

'All right,' Mr. Head said. 'You ain't ever seen a nigger.'

'You wasn't up very early,' Nelson said.

'You ain't ever seen a nigger,' Mr. Head repeated. 'There hasn't been a nigger in this county since we run that one out twelve years ago and that was before you were born.' He looked at the boy as if he were daring him to say he had ever seen a Negro.

'How you know I never saw a nigger when I lived there before?' Nelson asked. 'I probably saw a lot of niggers.'

'If you seen one you didn't know what he was,' Mr. Head said, completely exasperated. 'A six-month-old child don't know a nigger from anybody else.'

'I reckon I'll know a nigger if I see one,' the boy said and got up and straightened his slick sharply creased gray hat and went outside to the privy.

They reached the junction some time before the train was due to arrive and stood about two feet from the first set of tracks. Mr. Head carried a paper sack with some biscuits and a can of sardines in it for their lunch. A coarse-looking orange-colored sun coming up behind the east range of mountains was making the sky a dull red behind them, but in front of them it was still gray and they faced a gray transparent moon, hardly stronger than a thumbprint and completely without light. A small tin switch box and a black fuel tank were all there was to mark the place as a junction; the tracks were double and did not converge again until they were hidden behind the bends at either end of the clearing. Trains passing appeared to emerge from a tunnel of trees and, hit for a second by the cold sky, vanish terrified into the woods again. Mr. Head had had to make special arrangements with the ticket agent to have this train stop and he was secretly afraid it would not, in which case, he knew Nelson would say, 'I never thought no train was going to stop for you.' Under the useless morning moon the tracks looked white and fragile. Both the old man and the child stared ahead as if they were awaiting an apparition.

Then suddenly, before Mr. Head could make up his mind to turn back, there was a deep warning bleat and the train appeared, gliding very slowly, almost silently around the bend of trees about two hundred yards down the track, with one yellow front light shining. Mr. Head was still not certain it would stop and he felt it would make an even bigger idiot of him if it went by slowly. Both he and Nelson, however, were prepared to ignore the train if it passed them.

The engine charged by, filling their noses with the smell of hot metal and then the second coach came to a stop exactly where they were standing. A conductor with the face of an ancient bloated bulldog was on the step as if he expected them, though he did not look as if it mattered one way or the other to him if they got on or not. 'To the right,' he said.

Their entry took only a fraction of a second and the train was already speeding on as they entered the quiet car. Most of the travelers were still sleeping, some with their heads hanging off the chair arms, some stretched across two seats, and some sprawled out with their feet in the aisle. Mr. Head saw two unoccupied seats and pushed Nelson toward them. 'Get in there by the winder,' he said in his normal voice which was very loud at this hour of the morning. 'Nobody cares if you sit there because it's nobody in it. Sit right there.'

'I heard you,' the boy muttered. 'It's no use in you yelling,' and he sat down and turned his head to the glass. There he saw a pale ghost-like face scowling at him beneath the brim of a pale ghost-like hat. His grandfather, looking quickly too, saw a different ghost, pale but grinning, under a black hat.

Mr. Head sat down and settled himself and took out his ticket and started reading aloud everything that was printed on it. People began to stir. Several woke up and stared at him. 'Take off your hat,' he said to Nelson and took off his own and put it on his knee. He had a small amount of white hair that had turned tobacco-colored over the years and this lay flat across the back of his head. The front of his head was bald and creased. Nelson took off his hat and put it on his knee and they waited for the conductor to come ask for their tickets.

The man across the aisle from them was spread out over two seats, his feet propped on the window and his head jutting into the aisle. He had on a light blue suit and a yellow shirt unbuttoned at the neck. His eyes had just opened and Mr. Head was ready to introduce himself when the conductor came up from behind and growled, 'Tickets.'

When the conductor had gone, Mr. Head gave Nelson the return half of his ticket and said, 'Now put that in your pocket and don't lose it or you'll have to stay in the city.'

'Maybe I will,' Nelson said as if this were a reasonable suggestion.

Mr. Head ignored him. 'First time this boy has ever been on a train,' he explained to the man across the aisle, who was sitting up now on the edge of his seat with both feet on the floor.

Nelson jerked his hat on again and turned angrily to the window.

'He's never seen anything before,' Mr. Head continued. 'Ignorant as the day he was born, but I mean for him to get his fill once and for all.'

The boy leaned forward, across his grandfather and toward the stranger. 'I was born in the city,' he said. 'I was born there. This is my second trip.' He said it in a high positive voice but the man across the aisle didn't look as if he understood. There were heavy purple circles under his eyes.

Mr. Head reached across the aisle and tapped him on the arm. 'The thing to do with a boy,' he said sagely, 'is to show him all it is to show. Don't hold nothing back.'

'Yeah,' the man said. He gazed down at his swollen feet and lifted the left one about ten inches from the floor. After a minute he put it down and lifted the other. All through the car people began to get up and move about and yawn and stretch. Separate voices could be heard here and there and then a general hum. Suddenly Mr. Head's serene expression changed. His mouth almost closed and a light, fierce and cautious both, came into his eyes. He was looking down the length of the car. Without turning, he caught Nelson by the arm and pulled him forward. 'Look,' he said.

A huge coffee-colored man was coming slowly forward. He had on a light suit and a yellow satin tie with a ruby pin in it. One of his hands rested on his stomach which rode majestically under his buttoned coat, and in the other he held the head of a black walking stick that he picked up and set down with a deliberate outward motion each time he took a step. He was proceeding very slowly, his large brown eyes gazing over the heads of the passengers. He had a small white mustache and white crinkly hair. Behind him there were two young women, both coffee-colored, one in a yellow dress and one in a green. Their progress was kept at the rate of his and they chatted in low throaty voices as they followed him.

Mr. Head's grip was tightening insistently on Nelson's arm. As the procession passed them, the light from a sapphire ring on the brown hand that picked up the cane reflected in Mr. Head's eye, but he did not look up nor did the tremendous man look at him. The group proceeded up the rest of the aisle and out of the car. Mr. Head's grip on Nelson's arm loosened. 'What was that?' he asked.

'A man,' the boy said and gave him an indignant look as if he were tired of having his intelligence insulted.

'What kind of a man?' Mr. Head persisted, his voice expressionless.

'A fat man,' Nelson said. He was beginning to feel that he had better be cautious.

'You don't know what kind?' Mr. Head said in a final tone.

'An old man,' the boy said and had a sudden foreboding that he was not going to enjoy the day.

'That was a nigger,' Mr. Head said and sat back.

Nelson jumped up on the seat and stood looking backward to the end of the car but the Negro had gone.

'I'd of thought you'd know a nigger since you seen so many when you was in the city on your first visit,' Mr. Head continued. 'That's his first nigger,' he said to the man across the aisle.

The boy slid down into the seat. 'You said they were black,' he said in an angry voice. 'You never said they were tan. How do you expect me to know anything when you don't tell me right?'

'You're just ignorant is all,' Mr. Head said and he got up and moved over in the vacant seat by the man across the aisle.

Nelson turned backward again and looked where the Negro had disappeared. He felt that the Negro had deliberately walked down the aisle in order to make a fool of him and he hated him with a fierce raw fresh hate; and also, he understood now why his grandfather disliked them. He looked toward the window and the face there seemed to suggest that he might be inadequate to the day's exactions. He wondered if he would even recognize the city when they came to it.

After he had told several stories, Mr. Head realized that the man he was talking to was asleep and he got up and suggested to Nelson that they walk over the train and see the parts of it. He particularly wanted the boy to see the toilet so they went first to the men's room and examined the plumbing. Mr. Head demonstrated the ice-water cooler as if he had invented it and showed Nelson the bowl with the single spigot where the travelers brushed their teeth. They went through several cars and came to the diner.

This was the most elegant car in the train. It was painted a rich egg-yellow and had a wine-colored carpet on the floor. There were wide windows over the tables and great spaces of the rolling view were caught in miniature in the sides of the coffee pots and in the glasses. Three very black Negroes in white suits and aprons were running up and down the aisle, swinging trays and bowing and bending over the travelers eating breakfast. One of them rushed up to Mr. Head and Nelson and said, holding up two fingers, 'Space for two!' but Mr. Head replied in a loud voice, 'We eaten before we left!'

The waiter wore large brown spectacles that increased the size of his eye whites. 'Stan' aside then please,' he said with an airy wave of the arm as if he were brushing aside flies.

Neither Nelson nor Mr. Head moved a fraction of an inch. 'Look,' Mr. Head said.

The near corner of the diner, containing two tables, was set off from the rest by a saffron-colored curtain. One table was set but empty but at the other, facing them, his back to the drape, sat the tremendous Negro. He was speaking in a soft voice to the two women while he buttered a muffin. He had a heavy sad face and his neck bulged over his white collar on either side. 'They rope them off,' Mr. Head explained. Then he said, 'Let's go see the kitchen,' and they walked the length of the diner but the black waiter was coming fast behind them.

'Passengers are not allowed in the kitchen!' he said in a haughty voice. 'Passengers are NOT allowed in the kitchen!'

Mr. Head stopped where he was and turned. 'And there's good reason for that,' he shouted into the Negro's chest, 'because the cockroaches would run the passengers out!'

All the travelers laughed and Mr. Head and Nelson walked out, grinning. Mr. Head was known at home for his quick wit and Nelson felt a sudden keen pride in him. He realized the old man would be his only support in the strange place they were approaching. He would be entirely alone in the world if he were ever lost from his grandfather. A terrible excitement shook him and he wanted to take hold of Mr. Head's coat and hold on like a child.

As they went back to their seats they could see through the passing windows that the countryside was becoming speckled with small houses and shacks and that a highway ran alongside the train. Cars sped by on it, very small and fast. Nelson felt that there was less breath in the air than there had been thirty minutes ago. The man across the aisle had left and there was no one near for Mr. Head to hold a conversation with so he looked out the window, through his own reflection, and read aloud the names of the buildings they were passing. 'The Dixie Chemical Corp!' he announced. 'Southern Maid Flour! Dixie Doors! Southern Belle Cotton Products! Patty's Peanut Butter! Southern Mammy Cane Syrup!'

'Hush up!' Nelson hissed.

All over the car people were beginning to get up and take their luggage off the overhead racks. Women were putting on their coats and hats. The conductor stuck his head in the car and snarled,

'Firstoppppmry,' and Nelson lunged out of his sitting position, trembling. Mr. Head pushed him down by the shoulder.

'Keep your seat,' he said in dignified tones. 'The first stop is on the edge of town. The second stop is at the main railroad station.' He had come by this knowledge on his first trip when he had got off at the first stop and had had to pay a man fifteen cents to take him into the heart of town. Nelson sat back down, very pale. For the first time in his life, he understood that his grandfather was indispensable to him.

The train stopped and let off a few passengers and glided on as if it had never ceased moving. Outside, behind rows of brown rickety houses, a line of blue buildings stood up, and beyond them a pale rose-gray sky faded away to nothing. The train moved into the railroad yard. Looking down, Nelson saw lines and lines of silver tracks multiplying and criss-crossing. Then before he could start counting them, the face in the window started out at him, gray but distinct, and he looked the other way. The train was in the station. Both he and Mr. Head jumped up and ran to the door. Neither noticed that they had left the paper sack with the lunch in it on the seat.

They walked stiffly through the small station and came out of a heavy door into the squall of traffic. Crowds were hurrying to work. Nelson didn't know where to look. Mr. Head leaned against the side of the building and glared in front of him.

Finally Nelson said, 'Well, how do you see what all it is to see?'

Mr. Head didn't answer. Then as if the sight of people passing had given him the clue, he said, 'You walk,' and started off down the street. Nelson followed, steadying his hat. So many sights and sounds were flooding in on him that for the first block he hardly knew what he was seeing. At the second corner, Mr. Head turned and looked behind him at the station they had left, a putty-colored terminal with a concrete dome on top. He thought that if he could keep the dome always in sight, he would be able to get back in the afternoon to catch the train again.

As they walked along, Nelson began to distinguish details and take note of the store windows, jammed with every kind of equipment— hardware, drygoods, chicken feed, liquor. They passed one that Mr. Head called his particular attention to where you walked in and sat on a chair with your feet upon two rests and let a Negro polish your shoes. They walked slowly and stopped and stood at the entrances so he could see what went on in each place but they did not go into any of them. Mr. Head was determined not to go into any city store because on his first trip here, he had got lost in a large one and had found his way out only after many people had insulted him.

They came in the middle of the next block to a store that had a weighing machine in front of it and they both in turn stepped up on it and put in a penny and received a ticket. Mr. Head's ticket said, 'You weigh 120 pounds. You are upright and brave and all your friends admire you.' He put the ticket in his pocket, surprised that the machine should have got his character correct but his weight wrong, for he had weighed on a grain scale not long before and knew he weighed 110. Nelson's ticket said, 'You weigh 98 pounds. You have a great destiny ahead of you but beware of dark women.' Nelson did not know any women and he weighed only 68 pounds but Mr. Head pointed out that the machine had probably printed the number upside down, meaning the 9 for a 6.

They walked on and at the end of five blocks the dome of the terminal sank out of sight and Mr. Head turned to the left. Nelson could have stood in front of every store window for an hour if there had not been another more interesting one next to it. Suddenly he said, 'I was born here!' Mr. Head turned and looked at him with horror. There was a sweaty brightness about his face. 'This is where I come from!' he said.

Mr. Head was appalled. He saw the moment had come for drastic action. 'Lemme show you one thing you ain't seen yet,' he said and took him to the corner where there was a sewer entrance. 'Squat down,' he said, 'and stick you head in there,' and he held the back of the boy's coat while he got down and put his head in the sewer. He drew it back quickly, hearing a gurgling in the depths under the sidewalk. Then Mr. Head explained the sewer system, how the entire city was underlined with it, how it contained all the drainage and was full of rats and how a man could slide into it and be sucked along down endless pitchblack tunnels. At any minute any man in the city might be sucked into the sewer and never heard from again. He described it so well that Nelson was for some seconds shaken. He connected the sewer passages with the entrance to hell and understood for the first time how the world was put together in its lower parts. He drew away from the curb.

Then he said, 'Yes, but you can stay away from the holes,' and his face took on that stubborn look that was so exasperating to his grandfather. 'This is where I come from!' he said.

Mr. Head was dismayed but he only muttered, 'You'll get your fill,' and they walked on. At the end of two more blocks he turned to the left, feeling that he was circling the dome; and he was correct for in a half-hour they passed in front of the railroad station again. At first Nelson did not notice that he was seeing the same stores twice but when they passed the one where you put your feet on the rests while the Negro polished your shoes, he perceived that they were walking in a circle.

'We done been here!' he shouted. 'I don't believe you know where you're at!'

'The direction just slipped my mind for a minute,' Mr. Head said and they turned down a different street. He still did not intend to let the dome get too far away and after two blocks in their new direction, he turned to the left. This street contained two- and three-story wooden dwellings. Anyone passing on the sidewalk could see into the rooms and Mr. Head, glancing through one window, saw a woman lying on an iron bed, looking out, with a sheet pulled over her. Her knowing expression shook him. A fierce-looking boy on a bicycle came driving down out of nowhere and he had to jump to the side to keep from being hit. 'It's nothing to them if they knock you down,' he said. 'You better keep closer to me.'

They walked on for some time on streets like this before he remembered to turn again. The houses they were passing now were all unpainted and the wood in them looked rotten; the street between was narrower. Nelson saw a colored man. Then another. Then another. 'Niggers live in these houses,' he observed.

'Well come on and we'll go somewheres else,' Mr. Head said. 'We didn't come to look at niggers,' and they turned down another street but they continued to see Negroes everywhere. Nelson's skin began to prickle and they stepped along at a faster pace in order to leave the neighborhood as soon as possible. There were colored men in their undershirts standing in the doors and colored women rocking on the sagging porches. Colored children played in the gutters and stopped what they were doing to look at them. Before long they began to pass rows of stores with colored customers in them but they didn't pause at the entrances of these. Black eyes in black faces were watching them from every direction. 'Yes,' Mr. Head said, 'this is where you were born—right here with all these niggers.'

Nelson scowled. 'I think you done got us lost,' he said.

Mr. Head swung around sharply and looked for the dome. It was nowhere in sight. 'I ain't got us lost either,' he said. 'You're just tired of walking.'

'I ain't tired, I'm hungry,' Nelson said. 'Give me a biscuit.'

They discovered then that they had lost the lunch.

'You were the one holding the sack,' Nelson said. 'I would have kepaholt of it.'

'If you want to direct this trip, I'll go on by myself and leave you right here,' Mr, Head said and was pleased to see the boy turn white. However, he realized they were lost and drifting farther every minute from the station. He was hungry himself and beginning to be thirsty and since they had been in the colored neighborhood, they had both begun to sweat. Nelson had on his shoes and he was unaccustomed to them. The concrete sidewalks were very hard. They both wanted to find a place to sit down but this was impossible and they kept on walking, the boy muttering under his breath, 'First you lost the sack and then you lost the way,' and Mr. Head growling from time to time, 'Anybody wants to be from this nigger heaven can be from it!'

By now the sun was well forward in the sky. The odor of dinners cooking drifted out to them. The Negroes were all at their doors to see them pass. 'Whyn't you ast one of these niggers the way?' Nelson said. 'You got us lost.'

'This is where you were born,' Mr. Head said. 'You can ast one yourself if you want to.'

Nelson was afraid of the colored men and he didn't want to be laughed at by the colored children. Up ahead he saw a large colored woman leaning in a doorway that opened onto the sidewalk. Her hair stood straight out from her head for about four inches all around and she was resting on bare brown feet that turned pink at the sides. She had on a pink dress that showed her exact shape. As they came abreast of her, she lazily lifted one hand to her head and her fingers disappeared into her hair.

Nelson stopped. He felt his breath drawn up by the woman's dark eyes. 'How do you get back to town?' he said in a voice that did not sound like his own.

After a minute she said, 'You in town now,' in a rich low tone that made Nelson feel as if a cool spray had been turned on him.

'How do you get back to the train?' he said in the same reed-like voice.

'You can catch you a car,' she said.

He understood she was making fun of him but he was too paralyzed even to scowl. He stood drinking in every detail of her. His eyes traveled up from her great knees to her forehead and then made a triangular path from the glistening sweat on her neck down and across her tremendous bosom and over her bare arm back to where her fingers lay hidden in her hair. He suddenly wanted her to reach down and pick him up and draw him against her and then he wanted to feel her breath on his face. He wanted to look down and down into her eyes while she held him tighter and tighter. He had never had such a feeling before. He felt as if he were reeling down through a pitchblack tunnel.

'You can go a block down yonder and catch you a car take you to the railroad station, Sugarpie,' she said.

Nelson would have collapsed at her feet if Mr. Head had not pulled him roughly away. 'You act like you don't have any sense!' the old man growled.

They hurried down the street and Nelson did not look back at the woman. He pushed his hat sharply forward over his face which was already burning with shame. The sneering ghost he had seen in the train window and all the foreboding feelings he had on the way returned to him and he remembered that his ticket from the scale had said to beware of dark women and that his grandfather's had said he was upright and brave. He took hold of the old man's hand, a sign of dependence that he seldom showed.

They headed down the street toward the car tracks where a long yellow rattling trolley was coming. Mr. Head had never boarded a streetcar and he let that one pass. Nelson was silent. From time to time his mouth trembled slightly but his grandfather, occupied with his own problems, paid him no attention. They stood on the corner and neither looked at the Negroes who were passing, going about their business just as if they had been white, except that most of them stopped and eyed Mr. Head and Nelson. It occurred to Mr. Head that since the streetcar ran on tracks, they could simply follow the tracks. He gave Nelson a slight push and explained that they would follow the tracks on into the railroad station, walking, and they set off.

Presently to their great relief they began to see white people again and Nelson sat down on the sidewalk against the wall of a building. 'I got to rest myself some,' he said. 'You lost the sack and the direction. You can just wait on me to rest myself.'

'There's the tracks in front of us,' Mr. Head said. 'All we got to do is keep them in sight and you could have remembered the sack as good as me. This is where you were born. This is your old home town. This is your second trip. You ought to know how to do,' and he squatted down and continued in this vein but the boy, easing his burning feet out of his shoes, did not answer.

'And standing there grinning like a chim-pan-zee while a nigger woman gives you direction. Great Gawd!' Mr. Head said.

'I never said I was nothing but born here,' the boy said in a shaky voice. 'I never said I would or wouldn't like it. I never said I wanted to come. I only said I was born here and I never had nothing to do with that. I want to go home. I never wanted to come in the first place. It was all your big idea. How you know you ain't following the tracks in the wrong direction?'

This last had occurred to Mr. Head too. 'All these people are white,' he said.

'We ain't passed here before,' Nelson said. This was a neighborhood of brick buildings that might have been lived in or might not. A few empty automobiles were parked along the curb and there was an occasional passerby. The heat of the pavement came up through Nelson's thin suit. His eyelids began to droop, and after a few minutes his head tilted forward. His shoulders twitched once or twice and then he fell over on his side and lay sprawled in an exhausted fit of sleep.

Mr. Head watched him silently. He was very tired himself but they could not both sleep at the same time and he could not have slept anyway because he did not know where he was. In a few minutes Nelson would wake up, refreshed by his sleep and very cocky, and would begin complaining that he had lost the sack and the way. You'd have a mighty sorry time if I wasn't here, Mr. Head thought; and then another idea occurred to him. He looked at the sprawled figure for several minutes; presently he stood up. He justified what he was going to do on the grounds that it is sometimes necessary to teach a child a lesson he won't forget, particularly when the child is always reasserting his position with some new impudence. He walked without a sound to the corner about twenty feet away and sat down on a covered garbage can in the alley where he could look out and watch Nelson wake up alone.

The boy was dozing fitfully, half conscious of vague noises and black forms moving up from some dark part of him into the light. His face worked in his sleep and he had pulled his knees up under his chin. The sun shed a dull dry light on the narrow street; everything looked like exactly what it was. After a while Mr. Head, hunched like an old monkey on the garbage can lid, decided that if Nelson didn't wake up soon, he would make a loud noise by hamming his foot against the can. He looked at his watch and discovered that it was two o'clock. Their train left at six and the possibility of missing it was too awful for him to think of. He kicked his foot backwards on the can and a hollow boom reverberated in the alley.

Nelson shot up onto his feet with a shout. He looked where his grandfather should have been and stared. He seemed to whirl several times and then, picking up his feet and throwing his head back, he dashed down the street like a wild maddened pony. Mr. Head jumped off the can and galloped after but the child was almost out of sight. He saw a streak of gray disappearing diagonally a block ahead. He ran as fast as he could, looking both ways down every intersection, but without sight of him again. Then as he passed the third intersection, completely winded, he saw about half a block down the street a scene that stopped him altogether. He crouched behind a trash box to watch and get his bearings.

Nelson was sitting with both legs spread out and by his side lay an elderly woman, screaming. Groceries were scattered about the sidewalk. A crowd of women had already gathered to see justice done and Mr. Head distinctly heard the old woman on the pavement shout, 'You've broken my ankle and your daddy'll pay for it! Every nickel! Police! Police!' Several of the women were plucking at Nelson's shoulder but the boy seemed too dazed to get up.

Something forced Mr. Head from behind the trash box and forward, but only at a creeping pace. He had never in his life been accosted by a policeman. The women were milling around Nelson as if they might suddenly all dive on him at once and tear him to pieces, and the old woman continued to scream that her ankle was broken and to call for an officer. Mr. Head came on so slowly that he could have been taking a backward step after each forward one, but when he was about ten feet away, Nelson saw him and sprang. The child caught him around the hips and clung panting against him.

The women all turned on Mr. Head. The injured one sat up and shouted, 'You sir! You'll pay every penny of my doctor's bill that your boy has caused. He's a juve-nile deliquent! Where is an officer? Somebody take this man's name and address!'

Mr. Head was trying to detach Nelson's ringers from the flesh in the back of his legs. The old man's head had lowered itself into his collar like a turtle's; his eyes were glazed with fear and caution.

'Your boy has broken my ankle!' the old woman shouted. 'Police!'

Mr. Head sensed the approach of the policeman from behind. He stared straight ahead at the women who were massed in their fury like a solid wall to block his escape, 'This is not my boy,' he said. 'I never seen him before.'

He felt Nelson's ringers fall out of his flesh.

The women dropped back, staring at him with horror, as if they were so repulsed by a man who would deny his own image and likeness that they could not bear to lay hands on him. Mr. Head walked on, through a space they silently cleared, and left Nelson behind. Ahead of him he saw nothing but a hollow tunnel that had once been the street.

The boy remained standing where he was, his neck craned forward and his hands hanging by his sides. His hat was jammed on his head so that there were no longer any creases in it. The injured woman got up and shook her fist at him and the others gave him pitying looks, but he didn't notice any of them. There was no policeman in sight.

In a minute he began to move mechanically, making no effort to catch up with his grandfather but merely following at about twenty paces. They walked on for five blocks in this way. Mr. Head's shoulders were sagging and his neck hung forward at such an angle that it was not visible from behind. He was afraid to turn his head. Finally he cut a short hopeful glance over his shoulder. Twenty feet behind him, he saw two small eyes piercing into his back like pitchfork prongs.

The boy was not of a forgiving nature but this was the first time he had ever had anything to forgive. Mr. Head had never disgraced himself before. After two more blocks, he turned and called over his shoulder in a high desperately gay voice, 'Let's us go get us a Co' Cola somewheres!'

Nelson, with a dignity he had never shown before, turned and stood with his back to his grandfather.

Mr. Head began to feel the depth of his denial. His face as they walked on became all hollows and bare ridges. He saw nothing they were passing but he perceived that they had lost the car tracks. There was no dome to be seen anywhere and the afternoon was advancing. He knew that if dark overtook them in the city, they would be beaten and robbed. The speed of God's justice was only what he expected for himself, but he could not stand to think that his sins would be visited upon Nelson and that even now, he was leading the boy to his doom.

They continued to walk on block after block through an endless section of small brick houses until Mr. Head almost fell over a water spigot sticking up about six inches off the edge of a grass plot. He had not had a drink of water since early morning but he felt he did not deserve it now. Then he thought that Nelson would be thirsty and they would both drink and be brought together. He squatted down and put his mouth to the nozzle and turned a cold stream of water into his throat. Then he called out in the high desperate voice, 'Come on and getcher some water!'

This time the child stared through him for nearly sixty seconds. Mr. Head got up and walked on as if he had drunk poison. Nelson, though he had not had water since some he had drunk out of a paper cup on the train, passed by the spigot, disdaining to drink where his grandfather had. When Mr. Head realized this, he lost all hope. His face in the waning afternoon light looked ravaged and abandoned. He could feel the boy's steady hate, traveling at an even pace behind him and he knew that (if by some miracle they escaped being murdered in the city) it would continue just that way for the rest of his life. He knew that now he was wandering into a black strange place where nothing was like it had ever been before, a long old age without respect and an end that would be welcome because it would be the end.

As for Nelson, his mind had frozen around his grandfather's treachery as if he were trying to preserve it intact to present at the final judgment. He walked without looking to one side or the other, but every now and then his mouth would twitch and this was as when he felt, from some remote place inside himself, a black mysterious form reach up as if it would melt his frozen vision in one hot grasp.

The sun dropped down behind a row of houses and hardly noticing, they passed into an elegant suburban section where mansions were set back from the road by lawns with birdbaths on them. Here everything was entirely deserted. For blocks they didn't pass even a dog. The big white houses were like partially submerged icebergs in the distance. There were no sidewalks, only drives, and these wound around and around in endless ridiculous circles. Nelson made no move to come nearer to Mr. Head. The old man felt that if he saw a sewer entrance he would drop down into it and let himself be carried away; and he could imagine the boy standing by, watching with only a slight interest, while he disappeared.

A loud bark jarred him to attention and he looked up to see a fat man approaching with two bulldogs. He waved both arms like someone shipwrecked on a desert island. 'I'm lost!' he called. 'I'm lost and can't find my way and me and this boy have got to catch this train and I can't find the station. Oh Gawd I'm lost! Oh hep me Gawd I'm lost!'

The man, who was bald-headed and had on golf knickers, asked him what train he was trying to catch and Mr. Head began to get out his tickets, trembling so violently he could hardly hold them. Nelson had come up to within fifteen feet and stood watching.

'Well,' the fat man said, giving him back the tickets, 'you won't have time to get back to town to make this but you can catch it at the suburb stop. That's three blocks from here,' and he began explaining how to get there.

Mr. Head stared as if he were slowly returning from the dead and when the man had finished and gone off with the dogs jumping at his heels, he turned to Nelson and said breathlessly, 'We're going to get home!'

The child was standing about ten feet away, his face bloodless under the gray hat. His eyes were triumphantly cold. There was no light in them, no feeling, no interest. He was merely there, a small figure, waiting. Home was nothing to him.

Mr. Head turned slowly. He felt he knew now what time would be like without seasons and what heat would be like without light and what man would be like without salvation. He didn't care if he never made the train and if it had not been for what suddenly caught his attention, like a cry out of the gathering dusk, he might have forgotten there was a station to go to.

He had not walked five hundred yards down the road when he saw, within reach of him, the plaster figure of a Negro sitting bent over on a low yellow brick fence that curved around a wide lawn. The Negro was about Nelson's size and he was pitched forward at an unsteady angle because the putty that held him to the wall had cracked. One of his eyes was entirely white and he held a piece of brown watermelon.

Mr. Head stood looking at him silently until Nelson stopped at a little distance. Then as the two of them stood there, Mr. Head breathed, 'An artificial nigger!'

It was not possible to tell if the artificial Negro were meant to be young or old; he looked too miserable to be either. He was meant to look happy because his mouth was stretched up at the corners but the chipped eye and the angle he was cocked at gave him a wild look of misery instead.

'An artificial nigger!' Nelson repeated in Mr. Head's exact tone. The two of them stood there with their necks forward at almost the same angle and their shoulders curved in almost exactly the same way and their hands trembling identically in their pockets. Mr. Head looked like an ancient child and Nelson like a miniature old man. They stood gazing at the artificial Negro as if they were faced with some great mystery, some monument to another's victory that brought them together in their common defeat. They could both feel it dissolving their differences like an action of mercy. Mr. Head had never known before what mercy felt like because he had been too good to deserve any, but he felt he knew now. He looked at Nelson and understood that he must say something to the child to show that he was still wise and in the look the boy returned he saw a hungry need for that assurance. Nelson's eyes seemed to implore him to explain once and for all the mystery of existence.

Mr. Head opened his lips to make a lofty statement and heard himself say, 'They ain't got enough real ones here. They got to have an artificial one.'

After a second, the boy nodded with a strange shivering about his mouth, and said, 'Let's go home before we get ourselves lost again.'

Their train glided into the suburb stop just as they reached the station and they boarded it together, and ten minutes before it was due to arrive at the junction, they went to the door and stood ready to jump off if it did not stop; but it did, just as the moon, restored to its full splendor, sprang from a cloud and flooded the clearing with light. As they stepped off, the sage grass was shivering gently in shades of silver and the clinkers under their feet glittered with a fresh black light. The treetops, fencing the junction like the protecting walls of a garden, were darker than the sky which was hung with gigantic white clouds illuminated like lanterns.

Mr. Head stood very still and felt the action of mercy touch him again but this time he knew that there were no words in the world that could name it. He understood that it grew out of agony, which is not denied to any man and which is given in strange ways to children. He understood it was all a man could carry into death to give his Maker and he suddenly burned with shame that he had so little of it to take with him. He stood appalled, judging himself with the thoroughness of God, while the action of mercy covered his pride like a flame and consumed it. He had never thought himself a great sinner before but he saw now that his true depravity had been hidden from him lest it cause him despair. He realized that he was forgiven for sins from the beginning of time, when he had conceived in his own heart the sin of Adam, until the present, when he had denied poor Nelson. He saw that no sin was too monstrous for him to claim as his own, and since God loved in proportion as He forgave, he felt ready at that instant to enter Paradise.

Nelson, composing his expression under the shadow of his hat brim, watched him with a mixture of fatigue and suspicion, but as the train glided past them and disappeared like a frightened serpent into the woods, even his face lightened and he muttered, 'I'm glad I've went once, but I'll never go back again!'

OH, JOSEPH, I'M SO TIRED

Richard Yates

When Franklin D. Roosevelt was President-elect there must have been sculptors all over America who wanted a chance to model his head from life, but my mother had connections. One of her closest friends and neighbors, in the Greenwich Village courtyard where we lived, was an amiable man named Howard Whitman who had recently lost his job as a reporter on the *New York Post*. And one of Howard's former colleagues from the *Post* was now employed in the press office of Roosevelt's New York headquarters. That would make it easy for her to get in—or, as she said, to get an entrée—and she was confident she could take it from there. She was confident about everything she did in those days, but it never quite disguised a terrible need for support and approval on every side.

She wasn't a very good sculptor. She had been working at it for only three years, since breaking up her marriage to my father, and there was still something stiff and amateurish about her pieces. Before the Roosevelt project her specialty had been 'garden figures'—a life-size little boy whose legs turned into the legs of a goat at the knees and another who knelt among ferns to play the pipes of Pan; little girls who trailed chains of daisies from their upraised arms or walked beside a spread-winged goose. These fanciful children, in plaster painted green to simulate weathered bronze, were arranged on homemade wooden pedestals to loom around her studio and to leave a cleared space in the middle for the modeling stand that held whatever she was working on in clay.

Her idea was that any number of rich people, all of them gracious and aristocratic, would soon discover her: they would want her sculpture to decorate their landscaped gardens, and they would want to make her their friend for life. In the meantime, a little nationwide publicity as the first woman sculptor to 'do' the President-elect certainly wouldn't hurt her career.

And, if nothing else, she had a good studio. It was, in fact, the best of all the studios she would have in the rest of her life. There were six or eight old houses facing our side of the courtyard, with their backs to Bedford Street, and ours was probably the showplace of the row because the front room on its ground floor was two stories high. You went down a broad set of brick steps to the tall front windows and the front door; then you were in the high, wide, light-flooded studio. It was big enough to serve as a living room too, and so along with the green garden children it contained all the living-room furniture from the house we'd lived in with my father in the suburban town of Hastings-on-Hudson, where I was born. A second-floor balcony ran along the far end of the studio, with two small bedrooms and a tiny bathroom tucked away upstairs; beneath that, where the ground floor continued through to the Bedford Street side, lay the only part of the apartment that might let you know we didn't have much money. The ceiling was very low and it was always dark in there; the small windows looked out underneath an iron sidewalk grating, and the bottom of that street cavity was thick with strewn garbage. Our roach-infested kitchen was barely big enough for a stove and sink that were never clean, and for a brown wooden icebox with its dark, ever-melting block of ice; the rest of that area was our dining room, and not even the amplitude of the old Hastings dining-room table could brighten it. But our Majestic radio was in there too, and that made it a cozy place for my sister Edith and me: we liked the children's programs that came on in the late afternoons.

We had just turned off the radio one day when we went out into the studio and found our mother discussing the Roosevelt project with Howard Whitman. It was the first we'd heard of it, and we must have interrupted her with too many questions because she said 'Edith? Billy? That's enough, now. I'll tell you all about this later. Run out in the garden and play.'

She always called the courtyard 'the garden,' though nothing grew there except a few stunted city trees and a patch of grass that never had a chance to spread. Mostly it was bald earth, interrupted here and there by brick paving, lightly powdered with soot and scattered with the droppings of dogs and cats. It may have been six or eight houses long, but it was only two houses wide, which gave it a hemmed-in, cheerless look; its only point of interest was a dilapidated marble fountain, not much bigger than a birdbath, which stood near our house. The original idea of the fountain was that water would drip evenly from around the rim of its upper tier and tinkle into its lower basin, but age had unsettled it; the water spilled in a single ropy stream from the only inch of the upper tier's rim that stayed clean. The lower basin was deep enough to soak your feet in on a hot day, but there wasn't much pleasure in that because the underwater part of the marble was coated with brown scum.

My sister and I found things to do in the courtyard every day, for all of the two years we lived there, but that was only because Edith was an imaginative child. She was eleven at the time of the Roosevelt project, and I was seven.

'Daddy?' she asked in our father's office uptown one afternoon. 'Have you heard Mommy's doing a head of President Roosevelt?'

'Oh?' He was rummaging in his desk, looking for something he'd said we might like.

'She's going to take his measurements and stuff here in New York,' Edith said, 'and then after the Inauguration, when the sculpture's done, she's going to take it to Washington and present it to him in the White House.' Edith often told one of our parents about the other's more virtuous activities; it was part of her long, hopeless effort to bring them back together. Many years later she told me she thought she had never recovered, and never would, from the shock of their breakup: she said Hastings-on-Hudson remained the happiest time of her life, and that made me envious because I could scarcely remember it at all.

'Well,' my father said. 'That's really something, isn't it.' Then he found what he'd been looking for in the desk and said, 'Here we go; what do you think of these?' They were two fragile perforated sheets of what looked like postage stamps, each stamp bearing the insignia of an electric light bulb in vivid white against a yellow background, and the words 'More light.'

My father's office was one of many small cubicles on the twenty-third floor of the General Electric building. He was an assistant regional sales manager in what was then called the Mazda Lamp Division—a modest job, but good enough to have allowed him to rent into a town like Hastings-on-Hudson in better times—and these 'More light' stamps were souvenirs of a recent sales convention. We told him the stamps were neat—and they were—but expressed some doubt as to what we might do with them.

'Oh, they're just for decoration,' he said. 'I thought you could paste them into your schoolbooks, or—you know—whatever you want. Ready to go?' And he carefully folded the sheets of stamps and put them in his inside pocket for safekeeping on the way home.

Between the subway exit and the courtyard, somewhere in the West Village, we always walked past a vacant lot where men stood huddled around weak fires built of broken fruit crates and trash, some of them warming tin cans of food held by coat-hanger wire over the flames. 'Don't stare,' my father had said the first time. 'All those men are out of work, and they're hungry.'

'Daddy?' Edith inquired. 'Do you think Roosevelt's good?'

'Sure I do.'

'Do you think all the Democrats are good?'

'Well, most of 'em, sure.'

Much later I would learn that my father had participated in local Democratic Party politics for years. He had served some of his political friends—men my mother described as dreadful little Irish people from Tammany Hall—by helping them to establish Mazda Lamp distributorships in various parts of the city. And he loved their social gatherings, at which he was always asked to sing.

'Well, of course, you're too young to remember Daddy's singing,' Edith said to me once after his death in 1942.

'No, I'm not; I remember.'

'But I mean really remember,' she said. 'He had the most beautiful tenor voice I've ever heard. Remember "Danny Boy"?'

'Sure.'

'Ah, God, that was something,' she said, closing her eyes. 'That was really—that was really something.'

When we got back to the courtyard that afternoon, and back into the studio, Edith and I watched our parents say hello to each other. We always watched that closely, hoping they might drift into conversation and sit down together and find things to laugh about, but they never did. And it was even less likely than usual that day because my mother had a guest—a woman named Sloane Cabot who was her best friend in the courtyard, and who greeted my father with a little rush of false, fiirtatious enthusiasm.

'How've you been, Sloane?' he said. Then he turned back to his former wife and said 'Helen? I hear you're planning to make a bust of Roosevelt.'

'Well, not a bust,' she said. 'A head. I think it'll be more effective if I cut it off at the neck.'

'Well, good. That's fine. Good luck with it. Okay, then.' He gave his whole attention to Edith and me. 'Okay. See you soon. How about a hug?'

And those hugs of his, the climax of his visitation rights, were unforgettable. One at a time we would be swept up and pressed hard into the smells of linen and whiskey and tobacco; the warm rasp of his jaw would graze one cheek and there would be a quick moist kiss near the ear; then he'd let us go.

He was almost all the way out of the courtyard, almost out in the street, when Edith and I went racing after him.

'Daddy! Daddy! You forgot the stamps!'

He stopped and turned around, and that was when we saw he was crying. He tried to hide it—he put his face nearly into his armpit as if that might help him search his inside pocket—but there is no way to disguise the awful bloat and pucker of a face in tears.

'Here,' he said. 'Here you go.' And he gave us the least convincing smile I had ever seen. It would be good to report that we stayed and talked to him—that we hugged him again—but we were too embarrassed for that. We took the stamps and ran home without looking back.

'Oh, aren't you excited, Helen?' Sloane Cabot was saying. 'To be meeting him, and talking to him and everything, in front of all those reporters?'

'Well, of course,' my mother said, 'but the important thing is to get the measurements right. I hope there won't be a lot of photographers and silly interruptions.'

Sloane Cabot was some years younger than my mother, and strikingly pretty in a style often portrayed in what I think are called Art Deco illustrations of that period: straight dark bangs, big eyes, and a big mouth. She too was a divorced mother, though her former husband had vanished long ago and was referred to only as 'that bastard' or 'that cowardly son of a bitch.' Her only child was a boy of Edith's age named John, whom Edith and I liked enormously.

The two women had met within days of our moving into the courtyard, and their friendship was sealed when my mother solved the problem of John's schooling. She knew a Hastings-on-Hudson family who would appreciate the money earned from taking in a boarder, so John went up there to live and go to school, and came home only on weekends. The arrangement cost more than Sloane could comfortably afford, but she managed to make ends meet and was forever grateful.

Sloane worked in the Wall Street district as a private secretary. She talked a lot about how she hated her job and her boss, but the good part was that her boss was often out of town for extended periods: that gave her time to use the office typewriter in pursuit of her life's ambition, which was to write scripts for the radio.

She once confided to my mother that she'd made up both of her names: 'Sloane' because it sounded masculine, the kind of name a woman alone might need for making her way in the world, and 'Cabot' because— well, because it had a touch of class. Was there anything wrong with that?

'Oh, Helen,' she said. 'This is going to be wonderful for you. If you get the publicity—if the papers pick it up, and the newsreels—you'll be one of the most interesting personalities in America.'

Five or six people were gathered in the studio on the day my mother came home from her first visit with the President-elect.

'Will somebody get me a drink?' she asked, looking around in mock helplessness. 'Then I'll tell you all about it.'

And with the drink in her hand, with her eyes as wide as a child's, she told us how a door had opened and two big men had brought him in.

'Big men,' she insisted. 'Young, strong men, holding him up under the arms, and you could see how they were straining. Then you saw this *foot* come out, with these awful metal braces on the shoe, and then the *other* foot. And he was sweating, and he was panting for breath, and his face was—I don't know—all bright and tense and horrible.' She shuddered.

'Well,' Howard Whitman said, looking uneasy, 'he can't help being crippled, Helen.'

'Howard,' she said impatiently, 'I'm only trying to tell you how *ugly* it was.' And that seemed to carry a certain weight. If she was an authority on beauty—on how a little boy might kneel among ferns to play the pipes of Pan, for example—then surely she had earned her credentials as an authority on ugliness.

'Anyway,' she went on, 'they got him into a chair, and he wiped most of the sweat off his face with a handkerchief—he was still out of breath—and after a while he started talking to some of the other men there; I couldn't follow that part of it. Then finally he turned to me with this smile of his. Honestly, I don't know if I can describe that smile. It isn't something you can see in the newsreels; you have to be there. His eyes don't change at all, but the corners of his mouth go up as if they're being pulled by puppet strings. It's a frightening smile. It makes you think: This could be a dangerous man. This could be an evil man. Well anyway, we started talking, and I spoke right up to him. I said "I didn't vote for you, Mr. President." I said "I'm a good Republican and I voted for President Hoover." He said "Why are you here, then?" or something like that, and I said "Because you have a very interesting head." So he gave me the smile again and he said "What's interesting about it?" And I said "I like the bumps on it."'

By then she must have assumed that every reporter in the room was writing in his notebook, while the photographers got their flashbulbs ready; tomorrow's papers might easily read:

GAL SCULPTOR TWITS FDR
ABOUT 'BUMPS' ON HEAD

At the end of her preliminary chat with him she got down to business, which was to measure different parts of his head with her calipers. I knew how that felt: the cold, trembling points of those clay-encrusted calipers had tickled and poked me all over during the times I'd served as model for her fey little woodland boys.

But not a single flashbulb went off while she took and recorded the measurements, and nobody asked her any questions; after a few nervous words of thanks and goodbye she was out in the corridor again among all the hopeless, craning people who couldn't get in. It must have been a bad disappointment, and I imagine she tried to make up for it by planning the triumphant way she'd tell us about it when she got home.

'Helen?' Howard Whitman inquired, after most of the other visitors had gone. 'Why'd you tell him you didn't vote for him?'

'Well, because it's true. I *am* a good Republican; you know that.'

She was a storekeeper's daughter from a small town in Ohio; she had probably grown up hearing the phrase 'good Republican' as an index of respectability and clean clothes. And maybe she had come to relax her standards of respectability, maybe she didn't even care much about clean clothes anymore, but 'good Republican' was worth clinging to. It would be helpful when she met the customers for her garden figures, the people whose low, courteous voices would welcome her into their lives and who would almost certainly turn out to be Republicans too.

'I believe in the aristocracy!' she often cried, trying to make herself heard above the rumble of voices when her guests were discussing communism, and they seldom paid her any attention. They liked her well enough: she gave parties with plenty of liquor, and she was an agreeable hostess if only because of her touching eagerness to please; but in any talk of politics she was like a shrill, exasperating child. She believed in the aristocracy.

She believed in God, too, or at least in the ceremony of St. Luke's Episcopal Church, which she attended once or twice a year. And she believed in Eric Nicholson, the handsome middle-aged Englishman who was her lover. He had something to do with the American end of a British chain of foundries: his company cast ornamental objects into bronze and lead. The cupolas of college and high-school buildings all over the East, the lead-casement windows for Tudor-style homes in places like Scarsdale and Bronxville—these were some of the things Eric Nicholson's firm had accomplished. He was always self-deprecating about his business, but ruddy and glowing with its success.

My mother had met him the year before, when she'd sought help in having one of her garden figures cast into bronze, to be 'placed on consignment' with some garden-sculpture gallery from which it would never be sold. Eric Nicholson had persuaded her that lead would be almost as nice as bronze and much cheaper; then he'd asked her out to dinner, and that evening changed our lives.

Mr. Nicholson rarely spoke to my sister or me, and I think we were both frightened of him, but he overwhelmed us with gifts. At first they were mostly books— a volume of cartoons from *Punch*, a partial set of Dickens, a book called *England in Tudor Times* containing tissue-covered color plates that Edith liked. But in the summer of 1933, when our father arranged for us to spend two weeks with our mother at a small lake in New Jersey, Mr. Nicholson's gifts became a cornucopia of sporting goods. He gave Edith a steel fishing rod with a reel so intricate that none of us could have figured it out even if we'd known how to fish, a wicker creel for carrying the fish she would never catch, and a sheathed hunting knife to be worn at her waist. He gave me a short axe whose head was encased in a leather holster and strapped to my belt— I guess this was for cutting firewood to cook the fish—and a cumbersome net with a handle that hung from an elastic shoulder strap, in case I should be called upon to wade in and help Edith land a tricky one. There was nothing to do in that New Jersey village except take walks, or what my mother called good hikes; and every day, as we plodded out through the insect-humming weeds in the sun, we wore our full regalia of useless equipment.

That same summer Mr. Nicholson gave me a three-year subscription to *Field and Stream*, and I think that impenetrable magazine was the least appropriate of all his gifts because it kept coming in the mail for such a long, long time after everything else had changed for us: after we'd moved out of New York to Scarsdale, where Mr. Nicholson had found a house with a low rent, and after he had abandoned my mother in that house—with no warning—to return to England and to the wife from whom he'd never really been divorced.

But all that came later; I want to go back to the time between Franklin D. Roosevelt's election and his Inauguration, when his head was slowly taking shape on my mother's modeling stand.

Her original plan had been to make it life-size, or larger than life-size, but Mr. Nicholson urged her to scale it down for economy in the casting, and so she made it only six or seven inches high. He persuaded her too, for the second time since he'd known her, that lead would be almost as nice as bronze.

She had always said she didn't mind at all if Edith and I watched her work, but we had never much wanted to; now it was a little more interesting because we could watch her sift through many photographs of Roosevelt cut from newspapers until she found one that would help her execute a subtle plane of cheek or brow.

But most of our day was taken up with school. John Cabot might go to school in Hastings-on-Hudson, for which Edith would always yearn, but we had what even Edith admitted was the next best thing: we went to school in our bedroom.

During the previous year my mother had enrolled us in the public school down the street, but she'd begun to regret it when we came home with lice in our hair. Then one day Edith came home accused of having stolen a boy's coat, and that was too much. She withdrew us both, in defiance of the city truant officer, and pleaded with my father to help her meet the cost of a private school. He refused. The rent she paid and the bills she ran up were already taxing him far beyond the terms of the divorce agreement; he was in debt; surely she must realize he was lucky even to have a job. Would she ever learn to be reasonable?

It was Howard Whitman who broke the deadlock. He knew of an inexpensive, fully accredited mail-order service called The Calvert School, intended mainly for the homes of children who were invalids. The Calvert School furnished weekly supplies of books and materials and study plans; all she would need was someone in the house to administer the program and to serve as a tutor. And someone like Bart Kampen would be ideal for the job.

'The skinny fellow?' she asked. 'The Jewish boy from Holland or wherever it is?'

'He's very well educated, Helen,' Howard told her. 'And he speaks fluent English, and he'd be very conscientious. And he could certainly use the money.'

We were delighted to learn that Bart Kampen would be our tutor. With the exception of Howard himself, Bart was probably our favorite among the adults around the courtyard. He was twenty-eight or so, young enough so that his ears could still turn red when he was teased by children; we had found that out in teasing him once or twice about such matters as that his socks didn't match. He was tall and very thin and seemed always to look startled except when he was comforted enough to smile. He was a violinist, a Dutch Jew who had emigrated the year before in the hope of joining a symphony orchestra, and eventually of launching a concert career. But the symphonies weren't hiring then, nor were lesser orchestras, so Bart had gone without work for a long time. He lived alone in a room on Seventh Avenue, not far from the courtyard, and people who liked him used to worry that he might not have enough. to eat. He owned two suits, both cut in a way that must have been stylish in the Netherlands at the time: stiff, heavily padded shoulders and a nipped-in waist; they would probably have looked better on someone with a little more meat on his bones. In shirtsleeves, with the cuffs rolled back, his hairy wrists and forearms looked even more fragile than you might have expected, but his long hands were shapely and strong enough to suggest authority on the violin.

'I'll leave it entirely up to you, Bart,' my mother said when he asked if she had any instructions for our tutoring. 'I know you'll do wonders with them.'

A small table was moved into our bedroom, under the window, and three chairs placed around it. Bart sat in the middle so that he could divide his time equally between Edith and me. Big, clean, heavy brown envelopes arrived in the mail from The Calvert School once a week, and when Bart slid their fascinating contents onto the table it was like settling down to begin a game.

Edith was in the fifth grade that year—her part of the table was given over to incomprehensible talk about English and History and Social Studies—and I was in the first. I spent my mornings asking Bart to help me puzzle out the very opening moves of an education.

'Take your time, Billy,' he would say. 'Don't get impatient with this. Once you have it you'll see how easy it is, and then you'll be ready for the next thing.'

At eleven each morning we would take a break. We'd go downstairs and out to the part of the courtyard that had a little grass. Bart would carefully lay his folded coat on the sidelines, turn back his shirt cuffs, and present himself as ready to give what he called airplane rides. Taking us one at a time, he would grasp one wrist and one ankle; then he'd whirl us off our feet and around and around, with himself as the pivot, until the courtyard and the buildings and the city and the world were lost in the dizzying blur of our flight.

After the airplane rides we would hurry down the steps into the studio, where we'd usually find that my mother had set out a tray bearing three tall glasses of cold Ovaltine, sometimes with cookies on the side and sometimes not. I once overheard her telling Sloane Cabot she thought the Ovaltine must be Bart's first nourishment of the day— and I think she was probably right, if only because of the way his hand would tremble in reaching for his glass. Sometimes she'd forget to prepare the tray and we'd crowd into the kitchen and fix it ourselves; I can never see a jar of Ovaltine on a grocery shelf without remembering those times. Then it was back upstairs to school again.

And during that year, by coaxing and prodding and telling me not to get impatient, Bart Kampen taught me to read.

It was an excellent opportunity for showing off. I would pull books down from my mother's shelves—mostly books that were the gifts of Mr. Nicholson—and try to impress her by reading mangled sentences aloud. 'That's wonderful, dear,' she would say. 'You've really learned to read, haven't you.'

Soon a white and yellow 'More light' stamp was affixed to every page of my Calvert First Grade Reader, proving I had mastered it, and others were accumulating at a slower rate in my arithmetic workbook. Still other stamps were fastened to the wall beside my place at the school table, arranged in a proud little white and yellow thumb-smudged column that rose as high as I could reach.

'You shouldn't have put your stamps on the wall,' Edith said.

'Why?'

'Well, because they'll be hard to take off.'

'Who's going to take them off?'

That small room of ours, with its double function of sleep and learning, stands more clearly in my memory than any other part of our home. Someone should probably have told my mother that a girl and boy of our ages ought to have separate rooms, but that never occurred to me until much later. Our cots were set foot-to-foot against the wall, leaving just enough space to pass alongside them to the school table, and we had some good conversations as we lay waiting for sleep at night. The one I remember best was the time Edith told me about the sound of the city.

'I don't mean just the loud noises,' she said, 'like the siren going by just now, or those car doors slamming, or all the laughing and shouting down the street; that's just close-up stuff. I'm talking about something else. Because you see there are millions and millions of people in New York—more people than you can possibly imagine, ever—and most of them are doing something that makes a sound. Maybe talking, or playing the radio, maybe closing doors, maybe putting their forks down on their plates if they're having dinner, or dropping their shoes if they're going to bed—and because there are so many of them, all those little sounds add up and come together in a kind of hum. But it's so faint—so very, very faint— that you can't hear it unless you listen very carefully for a long time.'

'Can you hear it?' I asked her.

'Sometimes. I listen every night, but I can only hear it sometimes. Other times I fall asleep. Let's be quiet now, and just listen. See if you can hear it, Billy.'

And I tried hard, closing my eyes as if that would help, opening my mouth to minimize the sound of my breathing, but in the end I had to tell her I'd failed. 'How about you?' I asked.

'Oh, I heard it,' she said. 'Just for a few seconds, but I heard it. You'll hear it too, if you keep trying. And it's worth waiting for. When you hear it, you're hearing the whole city of New York.'

The high point of our week was Friday afternoon, when John Cabot came home from Hastings. He exuded health and normality; he brought fresh suburban air into our bohemian lives. He even transformed his mother's small apartment, while he was there, into an enviable place of rest between vigorous encounters with the world. He subscribed to both *Boys' Life* and *Open Road for Boys*, and these seemed to me to be wonderful things to have in your house, if only for the illustrations. John dressed in the same heroic way as the boys shown in those magazines, corduroy knickers with ribbed stockings pulled taut over his muscular calves. He talked a lot about the Hastings high-school football team, for which he planned to try out as soon as he was old enough, and about Hastings friends whose names and personalities grew almost as familiar to us as if they were friends of our own. He taught us invigorating new ways to speak, like saying 'What's the diff?' instead of 'What's the difference?' And he was better even than Edith at finding new things to do in the courtyard.

You could buy goldfish for ten or fifteen cents apiece in Woolworth's then, and one day we brought home three of them to keep in the fountain. We sprinkled the water with more Woolworth's granulated fish food than they could possibly need, and we named them after ourselves: 'John,' 'Edith,' and 'Billy.' For a week or two Edith and I would run to the fountain every morning, before Bart came for school, to make sure they were still alive and to see if they had enough food, and to watch them.

'Have you noticed how much bigger Billy's getting?' Edith asked me. 'He's huge. He's almost as big as John and Edith now. He'll probably be bigger than both of them.'

Then one weekend when John was home he called our attention to how quickly the fish could turn and move. 'They have better reflexes than humans,' he explained. 'When they see a shadow in the water, or anything that looks like danger, they get away faster than you can blink. Watch.' And he sank one hand into the water to make a grab for the fish named Edith, but she evaded him and fled. 'See that?' he asked. 'How's that for speed? Know something? I bet you could shoot an arrow in there, and they'd get away in time. Wait.' To prove his point he ran to his mother's apartment and came back with the handsome bow and arrow he had made at summer camp (going to camp every summer was another admirable thing about John); then he knelt at the rim of the fountain like the picture of an archer, his bow steady in one strong hand and the feathered end of his arrow tight against the bowstring in the other. He was taking aim at the fish named Billy. 'Now, the velocity of this arrow,' he said in a voice weakened by his effort, 'is probably more than a car going eighty miles an hour. It's probably more like an airplane, or maybe even more than that. Okay; watch.'

The fish named Billy was suddenly floating dead on the surface, on his side, impaled a quarter of the way up the arrow with parts of his pink guts dribbled along the shaft.

I was too old to cry, but something had to be done about the shock and rage and grief that filled me as I ran from the fountain, heading blindly for home, and halfway there I came upon my mother. She stood looking very clean, wearing a new coat and dress I'd never seen before and fastened to the arm of Mr. Nicholson. They were either just going out or just coming in—I didn't care which—and Mr. Nicholson frowned at me (he had told me more than once that boys of my age went to boarding school in England), but I didn't care about that either. I bent my head into her waist and didn't stop crying until long after I'd felt her hands stroking my back, until after she had assured me that goldfish didn't cost much and I'd have another one soon, and that John was sorry for the thoughtless thing he'd done. I had discovered, or rediscovered, that crying is a pleasure—that it can be a pleasure beyond all reckoning if your head is pressed in your mother's waist and her hands are on your back, and if she happens to be wearing clean clothes.

There were other pleasures. We had a good Christmas Eve in our house that year, or at least it was good at first. My father was there, which obliged Mr. Nicholson to stay away, and it was nice to see how relaxed he was among my mother's friends. He was shy, but they seemed to like him. He got along especially well with Bart Kampen.

Howard Whitman's daughter Molly, a sweet-natured girl of about my age, had come in from Tarrytown to spend the holidays with him, and there were several other children whom we knew but rarely saw. John looked very mature that night in a dark coat and tie, plainly aware of his social responsibilities as the oldest boy.

After a while, with no plan, the party drifted back into the dining-room area and staged an impromptu vaudeville. Howard started it: he brought the tall stool from my mother's modeling stand and sat his daughter on it, facing the audience. He folded back the opening of a brown paper bag two or three times and fitted it onto her head; then he took off his suit coat and draped it around her backwards, up to the chin; he went behind her, crouched out of sight, and worked his hands through the coatsleeves so that when they emerged they appeared to be hers. And the sight of a smiling little girl in a paper-bag hat, waving and gesturing with huge, expressive hands, was enough to make everyone laugh. The big hands wiped her eyes and stroked her chin and pushed her hair behind her ears; then they elaborately thumbed her nose at us.

Next came Sloane Cabot. She sat very straight on the stool with her heels hooked over the rungs in such a way as to show her good legs to their best advantage, but her first act didn't go over.

'Well,' she began, 'I was at work today—you know my office is on the fortieth floor—when I happened to glance up from my typewriter and saw this big old man sort of crouched on the ledge outside the window, with a white beard and a funny red suit. So I ran to the window and opened it and said "Are you all right?" Well, it was Santa Claus, and he said "Of course I'm all right; I'm used to high places. But listen, miss: can you direct me to number seventy-five Bedford Street?"'

There was more, but our embarrassed looks must have told her we knew we were being condescended to; as soon as she'd found a way to finish it she did so quickly. Then, after a thoughtful pause, she tried something else that turned out to be much better.

'Have you children ever heard the story of the first Christmas?' she asked. 'When Jesus was born?' And she began to tell it in the kind of hushed, dramatic voice she must have hoped might be used by the narrators of her more serious radio plays.

'. . . And there were still many miles to go before they reached Bethlehem,' she said, 'and it was a cold night. Now, Mary knew she would very soon have a baby. She even knew, because an angel had told her, that her baby might one day be the saviour of all mankind. But she was only a young girl'—here Sloane's eyes glistened, as if they might be filling with tears—'and the traveling had exhausted her. She was bruised by the jolting gait of the donkey and she ached all over, and she thought they'd never, ever get there, and all she could say was "Oh, Joseph, I'm so tired."'

The story went on through the rejection at the inn, and the birth in the stable, and the manger, and the animals, and the arrival of the three kings; when it was over we clapped a long time because Sloane had told it so well.

'Daddy?' Edith asked. 'Will you sing for us?'

'Oh, well, thanks, honey,' he said, 'but no; I really need a piano for that. Thanks anyway.'

The final performer of the evening was Bart Kampen, persuaded by popular demand to go home and get his violin. There was no surprise in discovering that he played like a professional, like something you might easily hear on the radio; the enjoyment came from watching how his thin face frowned over the chin rest, empty of all emotion except concern that the sound be right. We were proud of him.

Some time after my father left a good many other adults began to arrive, most of them strangers to me, looking as though they'd already been to several other parties that night. It was very late, or rather very early Christmas morning, when I looked into the kitchen and saw Sloane standing close to a bald man I didn't know. He held a trembling drink in one hand and slowly massaged her shoulder with the other; she seemed to be shrinking back against the old wooden icebox. Sloane had a way of smiling that allowed little wisps of cigarette smoke to escape from between her almost-closed lips while she looked you up and down, and she was doing that. Then the man put his drink on top of the icebox and took her in his arms, and I couldn't see her face anymore.

Another man, in a rumpled brown suit, lay unconscious on the dining-room floor. I walked around him and went into the studio,

where a good-looking young woman stood weeping wretchedly and
three men kept getting in each other's way as they tried to comfort her.
Then I saw that one of the men was Bart, and I watched while he
outlasted the other two and turned the girl away toward the door. He
put his arm around her and she nestled her head in his shoulder; that
was how they left the house.

Edith looked jaded in her wrinkled party dress. She was reclining in
our old Hastings-on-Hudson easy chair with her head tipped back and
her legs flung out over both the chair's arms, and John sat cross-legged
on the floor near one of her dangling feet. They seemed to have been
talking about something that didn't interest either of them much, and
the talk petered out altogether when I sat on the floor to join them.

'Billy,' she said, 'do you realize what time it is?'

'What's the diff?' I said.

'You should've been in bed hours ago. Come on. Let's go up.'

'I don't feel like it.'

'Well,' she said, 'I'm going up, anyway,' and she got laboriously out
of the chair and walked away into the crowd.

John turned to me and narrowed his eyes unpleasantly. 'Know
something?' he said. 'When she was in the chair that way I could see
everything.'

'Huh?'

'I could see everything. I could see the crack, and the hair. She's
beginning to get hair.'

I had observed these features of my sister many times—in the
bathtub, or when she was changing her clothes—and hadn't found
them especially remarkable; even so, I understood at once how
remarkable they must have been for him. If only he had smiled in a
bashful way we might have laughed together like a couple of regular
fellows out of *Open Road for Boys*, but his face was still set in that
disdainful look.

'I kept looking and looking,' he said, 'and I had to keep her talking
so she wouldn't catch on, but I was doing fine until you had to come
over and ruin it.'

Was I supposed to apologize? That didn't seem right, but nothing
else seemed right either. All I did was look at the floor.

When I finally got to bed there was scarcely time for trying to hear
the elusive sound of the city—I had found that a good way to keep

from thinking of anything else—when my mother came blundering in.
She'd had too much to drink and wanted to lie down, but instead of
going to her own room she got into bed with me. 'Oh,' she said. 'Oh,
my boy. Oh, my boy.' It was a narrow cot and there was no way to
make room for her; then suddenly she retched, bolted to her feet, and
ran for the bathroom, where I heard her vomiting. And when I moved
over into the part of the bed she had occupied my face recoiled quickly,
but not quite in time, from the slick mouthful of puke she had left on
her side of the pillow.

For a month or so that winter we didn't see much of Sloane because
she said she was 'working on something big. Something really big.'
When it was finished she brought it to the studio, looking tired but
prettier than ever, and shyly asked if she could read it aloud.

'Wonderful,' my mother said. 'What's it about?'

'That's the best part. It's about us. All of us. Listen.'

Bart had gone for the day and Edith was out in the courtyard by
herself—she often played by herself—so there was nobody for an
audience but my mother and me. We sat on the sofa and Sloane
arranged herself on the tall stool, just as she'd done for telling the
Bethlehem story.

'There is an enchanted courtyard in Greenwich Village,' she read.
'It's only a narrow patch of brick and green among the irregular shapes
of very old houses, but what makes it enchanted is that the people who
live in it, or near it, have come to form an enchanted circle of friends.

'None of them have enough money and some are quite poor, but
they believe in the future; they believe in each other, and in themselves.

'There is Howard, once a top reporter on a metropolitan daily
newspaper. Everyone knows Howard will soon scale the journalistic
heights again, and in the meantime he serves as the wise and
humorous sage of the courtyard.

'There is Bart, a young violinist clearly destined for virtuosity on the
concert stage, who just for the present must graciously accept all lunch
and dinner invitations in order to survive.

'And there is Helen, a sculptor whose charming works will someday
grace the finest gardens in America, and whose studio is the favorite
gathering place for members of the circle.'

There was more like that, introducing other characters, and toward
the end she got around to the children. She described my sister as 'a

lanky, dreamy tomboy,' which was odd—I had never thought of Edith that way—and she called me 'a sad-eyed, seven-year-old philosopher,' which was wholly baffling. When the introduction was over she paused a few seconds for dramatic effect and then went into the opening episode of the series, or what I suppose would be called the 'pilot.'

I couldn't follow the story very well—it seemed to be mostly an excuse for bringing each character up to the microphone for a few lines apiece—and before long I was listening only to see if there would be any lines for the character based on me. And there were, in a way. She announced my name—'Billy'—but then instead of speaking she put her mouth through a terrible series of contortions, accompanied by funny little bursts of sound, and by the time the words came out I didn't care what they were. It was true that I stuttered badly—I wouldn't get over it for five or six more years—but I hadn't expected anyone to put it on the radio.

'Oh, Sloane, that's marvelous,' my mother said when the reading was over. 'That's really exciting.'

And Sloane was carefully stacking her typed pages in the way she'd probably been taught to do in secretarial school, blushing and smiling with pride. 'Well,' she said, 'it probably needs work, but I do think it's got a lot of potential.'

'It's perfect,' my mother said. 'Just the way it is.'

Sloane mailed the script to a radio producer and he mailed it back with a letter typed by some radio secretary, explaining that her material had too limited an appeal to be commercial. The radio public was not yet ready, he said, for a story of Greenwich Village life.

Then it was March. The new President promised that the only thing we had to fear was fear itself, and soon after that his head came packed in wood and excelsior from Mr. Nicholson's foundry.

It was a fairly good likeness. She had caught the famous lift of the chin—it might not have looked like him at all if she hadn't—and everyone told her it was fine. What nobody said was that her original plan had been right, and Mr. Nicholson shouldn't have interfered: it was too small. It didn't look heroic. If you could have hollowed it out and put a slot in the top, it might have made a serviceable bank for loose change.

The foundry had burnished the lead until it shone almost silver in the highlights, and they'd mounted it on a sturdy little base of heavy black plastic. They had sent back three copies: one for the White House presentation, one to keep for exhibition purposes, and an extra one. But the extra one soon toppled to the floor and was badly damaged—the nose mashed almost into the chin—and my mother might have burst into tears if Howard Whitman hadn't made everyone laugh by saying it was now a good portrait of Vice President Garner.

Charlie Hines, Howard's old friend from the *Post* who was now a minor member of the White House staff, made an appointment for my mother with the President late on a weekday morning. She arranged for Sloane to spend the night with Edith and me; then she took an evening train down to Washington, carrying the sculpture in a cardboard box, and stayed at one of the less expensive Washington hotels. In the morning she met Charlie Hines in some crowded White House anteroom, where I guess they disposed of the cardboard box, and he took her to the waiting room outside the Oval Office. He sat with her as she held the naked head in her lap, and when their turn came he escorted her in to the President's desk for the presentation. It didn't take long. There were no reporters and no photographers.

Afterwards Charlie Hines took her out to lunch, probably because he'd promised Howard Whitman to do so. I imagine it wasn't a first-class restaurant, more likely some bustling, no-nonsense place favored by the working press, and I imagine they had trouble making conversation until they settled on Howard, and on what a shame it was that he was still out of work.

'No, but do you know Howard's friend Bart Kampen?' Charlie asked. 'The young Dutchman? The violinist?'

'Yes, certainly,' she said. 'I know Bart.'

'Well, Jesus, there's *one* story with a happy ending, right? Have you heard about that? Last time I saw Bart he said "Charlie, the Depression's over for me," and he told me he'd found some rich, dumb, crazy woman who's paying him to tutor her kids.'

I can picture how she looked riding the long, slow train back to New York that afternoon. She must have sat staring straight ahead or out the dirty window, seeing nothing, her eyes round and her face held in a soft shape of hurt. Her adventure with Franklin D. Roosevelt had come to nothing. There would be no photographs or interviews or feature articles, no thrilling moments of newsreel coverage; strangers would never know of how she'd come from a small Ohio town, or of how she'd nurtured her talent through the brave, difficult, one-woman journey that had brought her to the attention of the world. It wasn't fair.

All she had to look forward to now was her romance with Eric Nicholson, and I think she may have known even then that it was faltering—his final desertion came the next fall.

She was forty-one, an age when even romantics must admit that youth is gone, and she had nothing to show for the years but a studio crowded with green plaster statues that nobody would buy. She believed in the aristocracy, but there was no reason to suppose the aristocracy would ever believe in her.

And every time she thought of what Charlie Hines had said about Bart Kampen—oh, how hateful; oh, how hateful—the humiliation came back in wave on wave, in merciless rhythm to the clatter of the train.

She made a brave show of her homecoming, though nobody was there to greet her but Sloane and Edith and me. Sloane had fed us, and she said 'There's a plate for you in the oven, Helen,' but my mother said she'd rather just have a drink instead. She was then at the onset of a long battle with alcohol that she would ultimately lose; it must have seemed bracing that night to decide on a drink instead of dinner. Then she told us 'all about' her trip to Washington, managing to make it sound like a success. She talked of how thrilling it was to be actually inside the White House; she repeated whatever small, courteous thing it was that President Roosevelt had said to her on receiving the head. And she had brought back souvenirs: a handful of note-size White House stationery for Edith, and a well-used briar pipe for me. She explained that she'd seen a very distinguished-looking man smoking the pipe in the waiting room outside the Oval Office; when his name was called he had knocked it out quickly into an ashtray and left it there as he hurried inside. She had waited until she was sure no one was looking; then she'd taken the pipe from the ashtray and put it in her purse. 'Because I knew he must have been somebody important,' she said. 'He could easily have been a member of the Cabinet, or something like that. Anyway, I thought you'd have a lot of fun with it.' But I didn't. It was too heavy to hold in my teeth and it tasted terrible when I sucked on it; besides, I kept wondering what the man must

have thought when he came out of the President's office and found it
gone.

Sloane went home after a while, and my mother sat drinking alone
at the dining-room table. I think she hoped Howard Whitman or some
of her other friends might drop in, but nobody did. It was almost our
bedtime when she looked up and said 'Edith? Run out in the garden
and see if you can find Bart.'

He had recently bought a pair of bright tan shoes with crepe soles.
I saw those shoes trip rapidly down the dark brick steps beyond the
windows—he seemed scarcely to touch each step in his buoyancy—
and then I saw him come smiling into the studio, with Edith closing the
door behind him. 'Helen!' he said. 'You're back!'

She acknowledged that she was back. Then she got up from the
table and slowly advanced on him, and Edith and I began to realize we
were in for something bad.

'Bart,' she said, 'I had lunch with Charlie Hines in Washington
today.'

'Oh?'

'And we had a very interesting talk. He seems to know you very
well.'

'Oh, not really; we've met a few times at Howard's, but we're not
really—'

'And he said you'd told him the Depression was over for you
because you'd found some rich, dumb, crazy woman who was paying
you to tutor her kids. Don't interrupt me.'

But Bart clearly had no intention of interrupting her. He was backing
away from her in his soundless shoes, retreating past one stiff green
garden child after another. His face looked startled and pink.

'I'm not a rich woman, Bart,' she said, bearing down on him. 'And
I'm not dumb. And I'm not crazy. And I can recognize ingratitude and
disloyalty and sheer, rotten viciousness and *lies* when they're thrown
in my face.'

My sister and I were halfway up the stairs, jostling each other in our
need to hide before the worst part came. The worst part of these things
always came at the end, after she'd lost all control and gone on
shouting anyway.

'I want you to get out of my house, Bart,' she said. 'And I don't ever
want to see you again. And I want to tell you something. All my life

I've hated people who say "Some of my best friends are Jews." Because *none* of my friends are Jews, or ever will be. Do you understand me? *None* of my friends are Jews, or ever will be.'

The studio was quiet after that. Without speaking, avoiding each other's eyes, Edith and I got into our pajamas and into bed. But it wasn't more than a few minutes before the house began to ring with our mother's raging voice all over again, as if Bart had somehow been brought back and made to take his punishment twice.

'. . . And I said *"None* of my friends are Jews, or ever will be . . ."'

She was on the telephone, giving Sloane Cabot the highlights of the scene, and it was clear that Sloane would take her side and comfort her. Sloane might know how the Virgin Mary felt on the way to Bethlehem, but she also knew how to play my stutter for laughs. In a case like this she would quickly see where her allegiance lay, and it wouldn't cost her much to drop Bart Kampen from her enchanted circle.

When the telephone call came to an end at last there was silence downstairs until we heard her working with the ice pick in the icebox: she was making herself another drink.

There would be no more school in our room. We would probably never see Bart again—or if we ever did, he would probably not want to see us. But our mother was ours; we were hers; and we lived with that knowledge as we lay listening for the faint, faint sound of millions.

ME AND MISS MANDIBLE

Donald Barthelme

13 September

Miss Mandible wants to make love to me but she hesitates because I am officially a child; I am, according to the records, according to the gradebook on her desk, according to the card index in the principal's office, eleven years old. There is a misconception here, one that I haven't quite managed to get cleared up yet. I am in fact thirty-five, I've been in the Army, I am six feet one, I have hair in the appropriate places, my voice is a baritone, I know very well what to do with Miss Mandible if she ever makes up her mind.

In the meantime we are studying common fractions. I could, of course, answer all the questions, or at least most of them (there are things I don't remember). But I prefer to sit in this too-small seat with the desktop cramping my thighs and examine the life around me. There are thirty-two in the class, which is launched every morning with the pledge of allegiance to the flag. My own allegiance, at the moment, is divided between Miss Mandible and Sue Ann Brownly, who sits across the aisle from me all day long and is, like Miss Mandible, a fool for love. Of the two I prefer, today, Sue Ann; although between eleven and eleven and a half (she refuses to reveal her exact age) she is clearly a woman, with a woman's disguised aggression and a woman's peculiar contradictions. Strangely neither she nor any of the other children seem to see any incongruity in my presence here.

15 September

Happily our geography text, which contains maps of all the principal land-masses of the world, is large enough to conceal my clandestine journal-keeping, accomplished in an ordinary black composition book. Every day I must wait until Geography to put down such thoughts as I may have had during the morning about my situation and my fellows. I have tried writing at other times and it does not work. Either the teacher is walking up and down the aisles (during this period, luckily, she sticks close to the map rack in the front of the room) or Bobby Vanderbilt, who sits behind me, is punching me in the kidneys and wanting to know what I am doing. Vanderbilt, I have found out from certain desultory conversations on the playground, is hung up on sports cars, a veteran consumer of *Road & Track*. This explains the continual roaring sounds which seem to emanate from his desk; he is reproducing a record album called *Sounds of Sebring*.

19 September

Only I, at times (only at times), understand that somehow a mistake has been made, that I am in a place where I don't belong. It may be that Miss Mandible a1so knows this, at some level but for reasons not fully understood by me she is going along with the game. When I was first assigned to this room I wanted to protest, the error seemed obvious, the stupidest principal could have seen it; but I have come to believe it was deliberate, that I have been betrayed again.

Now it seems to make little difference. This life-role is as interesting as my former life-role, which was that of a claims adjuster for the Great Northern Insurance Company, a position which compelled me to spend my time amid the debris of our civilization: rumpled fenders, roofless sheds, gutted warehouses, smashed arms and legs. After ten years of this one has a tendency to see the world as a vast junkyard, looking at a man and seeing only his (potentially) mangled parts, entering a house only to trace the path of the inevitable fire. Therefore when I was installed here, although I knew an error had been made, I countenanced it, I was shrewd; I was aware that there might well be some kind of advantage to be gained from what seemed a disaster. The role of The Adjuster teaches one much.

22 September

I am being solicited for the volleyball team. I decline, refusing to take unfair profit from my height.

23 September

Every morning the roll is called: Bestvina, Bokenfohr, Broan, Brownly, Cone, Coyle, Crecelius, Darin, Durbin, Geiger, Guiswite, Heckler, Jacobs, Kleinschmidt, Lay, Logan, Masei, Mitgang, Pfeilsticker. It is like the litany chanted in the dim miserable dawns of Texas by the cadre sergeant of our basic training company.

In the Army, too, I was ever so slightly awry. It took me a fantastically long time to realize what the others grasped almost at once: that much of what we were doing was absolutely pointless, to no purpose. I kept wondering why. Then something happened that proposed a new question. One day we were commanded to whitewash, from the ground to the topmost leaves, all of the trees in our training area. The corporal who relayed the order was nervous and apologetic. Later an off-duty captain sauntered by and watched us white-splashed and totally weary, strung out among the freakish shapes we had created. He walked away swearing. I understood the principle (orders are orders), but I wondered: Who decides?

29 September

Sue Ann is a wonder. Yesterday she viciously kicked my ankle for not paying attention when she was attempting to pass me a note during History. It is swollen still. But Miss Mandible was watching me, there was nothing I could do. Oddly enough Sue Ann reminds me of the wife I had in my former role, while Miss Mandible seems to be a child. She watches me constantly, trying to keep sexual significance out of her look; I am afraid the other children have noticed. I have already heard, on that ghostly frequency that is the medium of classroom communication, the words *'Teacher's pet!'*

2 October

Sometimes I speculate on the exact nature of the conspiracy which brought me here. At times I believe it was instigated by my wife of former days, whose name was . . . I am only pretending to forget. I know her name very well, as well as I know the name of my former motor oil (Quaker State) or my old Army serial number (US 54109268).

Her name was Brenda, and the conversation I recall best, the one which makes me suspicious now, took place on the day we parted. 'You have the soul of a whore,' I said on that occasion, stating nothing less than literal, unvarnished fact. 'You,' she replied, 'are a pimp, a poop, and a child. I am leaving you forever and I trust that without me you will perish of your own inadequacies. Which are considerable.'

I squirm in my seat at the memory of this conversation, and Sue Ann watches me with malign compassion. She has noticed the discrepancy between the size of my desk and my own size, but apparently sees it only as a token of my glamour, my dark man-of-the-world-ness.

7 October

Once I tiptoed up to Miss Mandible's desk (when there was no one else in the room) and examined its surface. Miss Mandible is a clean-desk teacher, I discovered. There was nothing except her gradebook (the one in which I exist as a sixth-grader) and a text, which was open at a page headed *Making the Processes Meaningful*. I read: 'Many pupils enjoy working fractions when they understand what they are doing. They have confidence in their ability to take the right steps and to obtain correct answers. However, to give the subject full social significance, it is necessary that many realistic situations requiring the processes be found. Many interesting and lifelike problems involving the use of fractions should be solved . . .'

8 October

I am not irritated by the feeling of having been through all this before. Things are done differently now. The children, moreover, are in some ways different from those who accompanied me on my first voyage through the elementary schools: '*They have confidence in their ability to take the right steps and to obtain correct answers.*' This is surely true. When Bobby Vanderbilt, who sits behind me and has the great tactical advantage of being able to maneuver in my disproportionate shadow, wishes to bust a classmate in the mouth he first asks Miss Mandible to lower the blind, saying that the sun hurts his eyes. When she does so, *bip!* My generation would never have been able to con authority so easily.

13 October

It may be that on my first trip through the schools I was too much umder the impression that what the authorities (who decides?) had ordained for me was right and proper, that I confused authority with life itself. My path was not particularly of my own choosing. My career stretched out in front of me like a paper chase, and my role was to pick up the clues. When I got out of school, the first time, I felt that this estimate was substantially correct, and eagerly entered the hunt. I found clues abundant: diplomas, membership cards, campaign buttons, a marriage license, insurance forms, discharge papers, tax returns, Certificates of Merit. They seemed to prove, at the very least, that I was *in the running*. But that was before my tragic mistake on the Mrs. Anton Bichek claim.

I misread a clue. Do not misunderstand me: it was a tragedy only from the point of view of the authorities. I conceived that it was my duty to obtain satisfaction for the injured, for this elderly lady (not even one of our policyholders but a claimant against Big Ben Transfer & Storage, Inc.) from the company. The settlement was $165,000; the claim, I still believe, was just. But without my encouragement Mrs. Bichek would never have had the self-love to prize her injury so highly. The company paid, but its faith in me, in my efficacy in the role, was broken. Henry Goodykind, the district manager, expressed this thought in a few not altogether unsympathetic words, and told me at the same time that I was to have a new role. The next thing I knew I was here, at Horace Greeley Elementary, under the lubricious eye of Miss Mandible.

17 October

Today we are to have a fire drill. I know this because I am a Fire Marshal, not only for our room but for the entire right wing of the second floor. This distinction, which was awarded shortly after my arrival, is interpreted by some as another mark of my somewhat dubious relations with our teacher. My armband, which is red and decorated with white felt letters reading FIRE, sits on the little shelf under my desk, next to the brown paper bag containing the lunch I carefully make for myse]f each morning. One of the advantages of packing my own lunch (I have no one to pack it for me) is that I am able to fill it with things I enjoy. The peanut butter sandwiches that my mother made in my former existence, many years ago, have been banished in favor of ham and cheese. I have found that my diet has mysteriously adjusted to my new situation; I no longer drink, for instance, and when I smoke, it is in the boys' john, like everybody else. When school is out I hardly smoke at all. It is only in the matter of sex that I feel my own true age; this is apparently something that, once learned, can never be forgotten. I live in fear that Miss Mandible will one day keep me after school, and when we are alone, create a compromising situation. To avoid this I have become a model pupil: another reason for the pronounced dislike I have encountered in certain quarters. But I cannot deny that I am singed by those long glances from the vicinity of the chalkboard; Miss Mandible is in many ways, notably about the bust, a very tasty piece.

24 October

There are isolated challenges to my largeness, to my dimly realized position in the class as Gulliver. Most of my classmates are polite about this matter, as they would be if I had only one eye, or wasted, metal-wrapped legs. I am viewed as a mutation of some sort but essentially a peer. However Harry Broan, whose father has made himself rich manufacturing the Broan Bathroom Vent (with which Harry is frequently reproached; he is always being asked how things are in Ventsville), today inquired if I wanted to fight. An interested group of his followers had gathered to observe this suicidal undertaking. I replied that I didn't feel quite up to it, for which he was obviously grateful. We are now friends forever. He has given me to understand privately that he can get me all the bathroom vents I will ever need, at a ridiculously modest figure.

25 October

'Many interesting and lifelike problems involving the use of fractions should be solved . . .' The theorists fail to realize that everything that is either interesting or lifelike in the classroom proceeds from what they would probably call interpersonal relations: Sue Ann Brownly kicking me in the ankle. How lifelike, how womanlike, is her tender solicitude after the deed! Her pride in my newly acquired limp is transparent; everyone knows that she has set her mark upon me, that it is a victory in her unequal struggle with Miss Mandible for my great, overgrown heart. Even Miss Mandible knows, and counters in perhaps the only way she can, with sarcasm. 'Are you wounded, Joseph?' Conflagrations smolder behind her eyelids, yearning for the Fire Marshal clouds her eyes. I mumble that I have bumped my leg.

30 October

I return again and again to the problem of my future.

4 November

The underground circulating library has brought me a copy of *Movie-TV Secrets*, the multicolor cover blazoned with the headline 'Debbie's Date Insults Liz!' It is a gift from Frankie Randolph, a rather plain girl who until today has had not one word for me, passed on via Bobby Vanderbilt. I nod and smile over my shoulder in acknowledgment; Frankie hides her head under her desk. I have seen these magazines being passed around among the girls (sometimes one of the boys will condescend to inspect a particularly lurid cover). Miss Mandible confiscates them whenever she finds one. I leaf through *Movie-TV Secrets* and get an eyeful. 'The exclusive picture on these pages isn't what it seems. We know how it looks and we know what the gossipers will do. So in the interests of a nice guy, we're publishing the facts first. Here's what really happened!' The picture shows a rising young movie idol in bed, pajama-ed and bleary-eyed, while an equally blowzy young woman looks startled beside him. I am happy to know that the picture is not really what it seems; it seems to be nothing less than divorce evidence.

What do these hipless eleven-year-olds think when they come across, in the same magazine, the full-page ad for Maurice de Paree, which features 'Hip Helpers' or what appear to be padded rumps? ('A real undercover agent that adds appeal to those hips and derriere, both!') If they cannot decipher the language the illustrations leave nothing to the imagination. 'Drive him frantic . . .' the copy continues.

Perhaps this explains Bobby Vanderbilt's preoccupation with Lancias and Maseratis; it is a defense against being driven frantic.

Sue Ann has observed Frankie Randolph's overture, and catching my eye, she pulls from her satchel no less than seventeen of these magazines, thrusting them at me as if to prove that anything any of her rivals has to offer, she can top. I shuffle through them quickly, noting the broad editorial perspective:

'Debbie's Kids Are Crying'
'Eddie Asks Debbie: Will You . . .?'
'The Nightmares Liz Has About Eddie!'
'The Things Debbie Can Tell About Eddie'
'The Private Life of Eddie and Liz'
'Debbie Gets Her Man Back?'
'A New Life for Liz'
'Love Is a Tricky Affair'
'Eddie's Taylor-Made Love Nest'
'How Liz Made a Man of Eddie'
'Are They Planning to Live Together?'
'Isn't It Time to Stop Kicking Debbie Around?'
'Debbie's Dilemma'
'Eddie Becomes a Father Again'
'Is Debbie Planning to Re-wed?'
'Can Liz Fulfill Herself?'
'Why Debbie Is Sick of Hollywood'

Who are these people, Debbie, Eddie, Liz, and how did they get themselves in such a terrible predicament? Sue Ann knows, I am sure; it is obvious that she has been studying their history as a guide to what she may expect when she is suddenly freed from this drab, flat classroom.

I am angry and I shove the magazines back at her with not even a whisper of thanks.

5 November

The sixth grade at Horace Greeley Elementary is a furnace of love, love, love. Today it is raining, but inside the air is heavy and tense with passion. Sue Ann is absent; I suspect that yesterday's exchange has driven her to her bed. Guilt hangs about me. She is not responsible, I know, for what she reads, for the models proposed to her by a venal publishing industry; I should not have been so harsh. Perhaps it is only the flu.

Nowhere have I encountered an atmosphere as charged with aborted sexuality as this. Miss Mandible is helpless; nothing goes right today. Amos Darin has been found drawing a dirty picture in the cloakroom. Sad and inaccurate, it was offered not as a sign of something else but as an act of love in itself. It has excited even those who have not seen it, even those who saw but understood only that it was dirty. The room buzzes with imperfectly comprehended titillation. Amos stands by the door, waiting to be taken to the principal's office. He wavers between fear and enjoyment of his temporary celebrity. From time to time Miss Mandible looks at me reproachfully, as if blaming me for the uproar. But I did not create this atmosphere, I am caught in it like all the others.

8 November

Everything is promised my classmates and I, most of all the future. We accept the outrageous assurances without blinking.

9 November

I have finally found the nerve to petition for a larger desk. At recess I can hardly walk; my legs do not wish to uncoil themselves. Miss Mandible says she will take it up with the custodian. She is worried about the excellence of my themes. Have I, she asks, been receiving help? For an instant I am on the brink of telling her my story. Something, however, warns me not to attempt it. Here I am safe, I have a place; I do not wish to entrust myself once more to the whimsy of authority. I resolve to make my themes less excellent in the future.

11 November

A ruined marriage, a ruined adjusting career, a grim interlude in the Army when I was almost not a person. This is the sum of my existence to date, a dismal total. Small wonder that re-education seemed my only hope. It is clear even to me that I need reworking in some fundamental way. How efficient is the society that provides thus for the salvage of its clinkers!

Plucked from my unexamined life among other pleasant, desperate, money-making young Americans, thrown backward in space and time, I am beginning to understand how I went wrong, how we all go wrong. (Although this was far from the intention of those who sent me here; they require only that I *get right*.)

14 November

The distinction between children and adults, while probably useful for some purposes, is at bottom a specious one, I feel. There are only individual egos, crazy for love.

15 November

The custodian has informed Miss Mandible that our desks are all the correct size for sixth-graders, as specified by the Board of Estimate and furnished the schools by the Nu-Art Educational Supply Corporation of Englewood, California. He has pointed out that if the desk size is correct, then the pupil size must be incorrect. Miss Mandible, who has already arrived at this conclusion, refuses to press the matter further. I think I know why. An appeal to the administration might result in my removal from the class, in a transfer to some sort of setup for 'exceptional children.' This would be a disaster of the first magnitude. To sit in a room with child geniuses (or, more likely, children who are 'retarded') would shrivel me in a week. Let my experience here be that of the common run, I say; let me be, please God, typical.

20 November

We read signs as promises. Miss Mandible understands by my great height, by my resonant vowels, that I will one day carry her off to bed. Sue Ann interprets these same signs to mean that I am unique among her male acquaintances, therefore most desirable, therefore her special property as is everything that is Most Desirable. If neither of these propositions work out then life has broken faith with them.

I myself, in my former existence, read the company motto ('Here to Help in Time of Need') as a description of the duty of the adjuster, drastically mislocating the company's deepest concerns. I believed that because I had obtained a wife who was made up of wife-signs (beauty, charm, softness, perfume, cookery) I had found love. Brenda, reading the same signs that have now misled Miss Mandible and Sue Ann Brownly, felt she had been promised that she would never be bored again. All of us, Miss Mandible, Sue Ann, myself, Brenda, Mr. Goodykind, still believe that the American flag betokens a kind of general righteousness.

But I say, looking about me in this incubator of future citizens, that signs are signs, and that some of them are lies. This is the great discovery of my time here.

23 November

It may be that my experience as a child will save me after all. If only I can remain quietly in this classroom, making my notes while Napoleon plods through Russia in the droning voice of Harry Broan, reading aloud from our History text. All of the mysteries that perplexed me as an adult have their origins here, and one by one I am numbering them, exposing their roots.

2 December

Miss Mandible will refuse to permit me to remain ungrown. Her hands rest on my shoulders too warmly, and for too long.

7 December

It is the pledges that this place makes to me, pledges that cannot be redeemed, that confuse me later and make me feel I am not *getting anywhere*. Everything is presented as the result of some knowable process; if I wish to arrive at four I get there by way of two and two. If I wish to burn Moscow the route I must travel has already been marked out by another visitor. If, like Bobby Vanderbilt, I yearn for the wheel of the Lancia 2.4-liter coupé, I have only to go through the appropriate process, that is, get the money. And if it is money itself that

I desire, I have only to make it. All of these goals are equally beautiful in the sight of the Board of Estimate; the proof is all around us, in the no-nonsense ugliness of this steel and glass building, in the straightline matter-of-factness with which Miss Mandible handles some of our less reputable wars. Who points out that arrangements sometimes slip, that errors are made, that signs are misread? *'They have confidence in their ability to take the right steps and to obtain correct answers.'* I take the right steps, obtain correct answers, and my wife leaves me for another man.

8 December

My enlightenment is proceeding wonderfully.

9 December

Disaster once again. Tomorrow I am to be sent to a doctor, for observation. Sue Ann Brownly caught Miss Mandible and me in the cloakroom, during recess, and immediately threw a fit. For a moment I thought she was actually going to choke. She ran out of the room weeping, straight for the principal's office, certain now which of us was Debbie, which Eddie, which Liz. I am sorry to be the cause of her disillusionment, but I know that she will recover. Miss Mandible is ruined but fulfilled. Although she will be charged with contributing to the delinquency of a minor, she seems at peace: *her* promise has been kept. She knows now that everything she has been told about life, about America, is true.

I have tried to convince the school authorities that I am a minor only in a very special sense, that I am in fact mostly to blame—but it does no good. They are as dense as ever. My contemporaries are astounded that I present myself as anything other than an innocent victim. Like the Old Guard marching through the Russian drifts, the class marches to the conclusion that truth is punishment.

Bobby Vanderbilt has given me his copy of *Sounds of Sebring*, in farewell.

NATURAL COLOR

John Updike

Frank saw her more than a block away, in the town where he had come to live, where Maggie had no business to be, and he no expectation of seeing her. Something about the way she held her head, as if she were marvelling at the icicled eaves of the downtown shops, sparked recognition. Or perhaps it was the way the low winter sun caught the red of her hair, so it glinted like a signal. His wife used to doubt aloud that the color was natural, and he had had to repress the argument that if Maggie dyed it she dyed her pubic hair to match. It was true, Maggie considered her hair a glory. When she let it down, the sheaves of it became an enveloping, entangling third presence in the bed, and when it was pinned up, as it was today, her head looked large and her neck poignantly thin, at its cocky tilt.

She was with a man—a man taller than she, though she was herself tall. He moved beside her with a bearlike protective shuffle, half sideways, so as not to miss a word she was tossing out, her naked hands gesturing in the February sun. Frank remembered her face whitened by shock and wet with tears. Each word he reluctantly pulled from himself had been a blow deepening her pallor, driving her deeper into defeat. 'I can't swing it,' he had said, with both their households in turmoil and the town around them scandalized.

'You mean,' she said, her face furrowed, her upper lip tense in her effort to have utter clarity at this moment, 'you want to go back?'

'I don't want to, exactly, but I think I should.'

'Then go, Frank. Go, darling. It makes it simpler for me, in a way.'

He had thought that a lovely, pathetic bit of female bravado, an attempt to match rejection with rejection, but in fact she had carried through with her divorce, whereas he had kept his family intact and had moved to another town. That was more than twenty years ago. The children he had decided not to leave had eventually grown up and left home. The wife he had clung to had maintained a self-preserving detachment, which as they together advanced into middle age became a decided distance, maintained with dry humor and an impervious dignity. He had opted for a wife, and a wife she was, no less or more.

As for Maggie, she had recovered; she had a companion, and at a distance looked smart, in a puffy pea-green parka and black pants that made her legs appear theatrically long. Shocked by the spark glinting from her hair, Frank ducked into the nearest door, that of the drugstore, to spare himself the impact of a confrontation, of introductions and chatter. It was somehow an attack on him, to have her striding about so boldly in his town.

While he roamed the drugstore aisles as if looking for a magic medication or a perfect birthday card, he slowly filled with fury at her, for going on beyond him and making a life. Sexual jealousy of a wholly unreasonable sort raged in him as he blindly stalked between the cold tablets and the skin lotions, the sleeping pills and stomach-acid neutralizers. He skimmed the array of condoms, displayed, in this progressive, AIDS-wary age, like a rack of many-colored candies, each showing on the box a shadowy man and woman bending their heads conspiratorially close. It occurred to him, as his blood pounded, that sex has very little to do with kindness. He had been rough with Maggie, cruel, in the heat of their affair. It had been his first, but not hers. She had told him in the front seat of his car, with that serious, concentrating stare of hers, 'That time when Sam and I were separated, I was an absolute whore. I'd sleep with *any*body.'

The sweeping solemnity of the confession would have made him smile, had he not been awed by the grandeur of her promiscuity as he tried to imagine it. She seemed to swell in size, there beside him in the front seat of his Ford station wagon, parked on a dead-end lane between towns. That early-spring meeting, hurriedly arranged by phone, was like an interview, she in winter tweeds from shopping in Boston, he in his business suit. He didn't ask for details. She volunteered a ski instructor in Vermont, a scuba instructor in the Caribbean—handsome, carefree young fishers of women. She didn't say if she had slept with any of their neighbors, but he imagined some, and thus his heart was hardened before their own affair had begun. He was obliged to sleep with her now. It was a kind of race, in which he had fallen dangerously behind. The men she had slept with were each still in her, a kind of investment, generating interest while he had been chastely admiring her from afar. Part of Frank's gift to her was the

heightened value that his innocence had assigned her. Because she was
so experienced, they were never quite equal. She ran risks, coming to
him, the same risks he did, of discovery and a disrupted family, but he
considered her marriage too damaged already to grieve for, whereas
his own was enhanced by his betrayal, his wife and children rendered
precious in their vulnerability. Returning to them, damp and panting
from his sins, he nearly wept at their sweet ignorance. Yet he couldn't
stop. He led Maggie on, addicted to her and careless of their fate, until
the time came to disentangle his fate from hers. She herself had said it:
'You're *hard* on me, Frank.'

He thought she might mean just the vigor of his lovemaking. They
were both in a sweat, in her sunny bed with its view of a horse-farm
riding ring, and she, underneath him, was doubly drenched. They had
begun seeing each other in April; they were discovered and cut off
before autumnal weather arrived. He remembered her in bright cotton
frocks, animated at parties afloat in summer lightness, all her
animation secretly directed at him. She was warm with Ann, his wife,
and he was hearty with Sam, her husband, though even here there was
inequality. She seemed genuinely to like Ann and, when with Frank,
would wonder aloud how he could ever think of leaving his lovely
wife. Each tryst, on the other hand, strengthened his impression that
Sam—big, red-faced, his heavy head lowered with clumsy,
shortsighted menace—was unworthy of her, and her remaining in her
marriage was a sign of weakness, a meek acceptance of daily pollution.

'You have anything better to offer?' Maggie had once challenged
him, having pinched her lips together and decided to take the leap. Her
eyes in this moment of daring had been round, like a child's.

He felt attenuated, strained, answering weakly, 'You know I'd love
to be your husband. If I weren't already somebody else's.'

'The beautiful prisoner,' she said, gazing off as if suddenly bored. 'I
do think we should stop seeing each other.'

'Oh my God, no. I'll die.'

'Well, it's killing me. You're not being mature. When a gentleman
has had his fun with a lady, he takes his leave.'

He hated it when she pulled sexual rank on him. He wanted to learn
but not to be instructed. 'Is that how Sam would act?'

'Sam's not so bad as you think,' she said, brushing away, with a
sudden awkward hiding motion, tears that had started to her eyes,

sprung by some image touched within the tense works of this suspended situation.

'Good in bed,' Frank suggested, hating the two of them. In bed: this very bed, with its view of trim stables and fenced pastures.

She ignored the jealous probe. She said, reflecting, 'He has a sense of me that's not entirely off. In his coarse way, he has manners.'

'And I don't?'

'Frank,' she exclaimed in an exasperation that still let the tears stand in her eyes. 'Why does everything always have to come back to you?'

'Because,' he could have answered, 'you have made me love myself.' But there were many things he could have said to Maggie, before communications between them suddenly ceased, Sam blundering in with bullish fury and lawyerly threats, Ann receding with a beautiful wounded pride. Frank found himself Maggie's enemy, having failed to become her husband.

In the freezing winter and raw spring before he and his family had moved from that town to this one, six miles distant, there was a long social season in which they all continued to rotate in each other's vicinity. Sam moved to a bachelor rental in yet another town, three miles away— not so far as to be out of reach of sympathetic gestures from their large communal acquaintance. Frank and Ann hunkered down in embattled, recriminatory renewal of their vows, mixed with spells of humorous weariness. And Maggie found herself marooned in her big house with the two children, an eight-year-old girl and a six-year-old boy. Their formerly shared friends, forced to choose among these explosive elements, opted for the intact couple over the separated one. Sam, though his face seemed redder than ever and his eyes were narrowed as if his face had been pummelled, established himself as willing to co-exist in the same room with Frank, and even to exchange a few forced courtesies. But Ann fled the one occasion, the annual Christmas-carol sing in the historical-society mansion, where Maggie had dared appear. Maggie showed up late, in a dazzling sequined long-sleeved green top and a long scarlet velvet skirt. Frank smiled at the audacity of the outfit; Ann gave a whimper and whirled from the room, straight down the hallway, hung with old daguerreotypes, toward the front door, prized for its exemplary Federalist moldings and fine leaded fanlight. Chasing her out with their coats into the cold, Frank said, 'That was a cruel thing to do.'

'Not as cruel as trying to steal my husband.'

'That isn't what she tried.'

'Well, what did she try? Fucking as a spiritual exercise?'

'Please, Ann. People are looking out of the windows.' Though in fact the choruses of 'Good King Wenceslas' rolled obliviously out the tall windows onto the snowy sidewalk. The town had seen worse spats than theirs, including a Unitarian-Congregationalist church schism in the 1820s. 'Put on your coat,' he said stiffly, and led her by the arm to where their car was parked, the station wagon in which Maggie had solemnly told him she had been an absolute whore, but whose interior now was awash in the childish odor of candy-bar crumbs and spilled milkshakes. In truth, the marriage had in the short run fattened on the affair: Ann was impressed that he had made a conquest of the spectacular Maggie, and Frank was moved by his cool wife's flare of jealous passion. It was as if Maggie, in her bereft, ostracized state, were a prize they had jointly dragged home. 'If you can't hold it together in public,' he told her, 'it means she can't go anywhere where you're apt to be.'

'We're *try*ing to get out of town, we've got realtors coming out of our *ears*,' Ann said with comical vehemence. 'I'm *damned* if I'm going to take the children out of school before it ends in May. They're heartbroken we're moving in any case.' As the car heater warmed, drowning in its gases the sour-milkshake scent, and the rumpled blocks of the old town rolled by, she conceded, 'I'm sorry. That was not a good-sport thing to do. But just seeing her physically, after talking about her for weeks and weeks, it came over me how you'd seen her . . . how you knew every . . . and she looked so great, actually, in that grotesque outfit.' Ann went on, 'Pale and tense, but it's taken a few pounds off her. Wish I could say the same.'

He reached over and squeezed her plump thigh through the thickness of her winter coat. 'Different styles,' he said, obliquely bragging. They were united, it seemed to him, in admiration of Maggie—two suppliants bowed beneath a natural force. Though rapprochement on such a basis was bound to decay, for a time it made for a conspiratorial closeness.

In the meantime, Maggie was crossed off party lists. She pursued her daily duties in majestic isolation, visited by only a few gossip-hungry women and oddball men sensing an opportunity. Frank was divided between acquiescence in her exclusion—her power over him, the grandeur she had for him, left no room for pity—and an impossible wish to reunite, to say the words to her that would lift them above it all and put them back in bed together. More experienced than he, she knew there were no such words. A few months after the Christmas-carol sing, the town fathers sponsored an Easter-egg hunt on the sloping common, this side of the cemetery. In the milling about, while parents chased after frantic, scooting children on the muddy brown grass, he managed to sidle up to Maggie, in her familiar spring tweeds. She gave him an unamused stare and said to him, as if the words had been stored up, 'Your wife has ruined my social life. And my children's. Sam is furious.'

Such a petty and specific grievance seemed astonishingly unworthy of them and their love. Startled, Frank said, 'Ann doesn't scheme. She just lets things happen.' As if, after all this silence between them, they had met to debate his wife's character. Maggie turned away. Sick with the rejection, he admired the breadth of her shoulders and the wealth of her hair, done up in a burnished, glistening French twist.

To a tourist travelling through, one New England town looks much like another—white spire, green common, struggling little downtown—but they have considerable economic and spiritual differences, and their citizens know what they are. Frank and Ann had, after a six-month struggle with real-estate agents, moved to a town where the property lines were marked by walls and hedges and No Trespassing signs. The friends they slowly made were generally older than they, a number of them widowed or retired. The lives, the winterized summer houses, the grounds maintained by lawn services were all in a state of finish. The town they had moved from had been a work in progress, with crooked streets laid out by Puritan footsteps and boundary lines marked by lost boulders and legendary trees whose stumps had rotted to nothing. The young householders had tried to do their own maintenance, leaving ladders leaning against porch roofs and two sides of a house unpainted until next summer. The yards were hard-used by packs of children; there was a constant coming and going of Saturday-afternoon tennis or touch football turning into drinks before everyone rushed home to shower and shave for that night's dinner party. You lived in other people's houses as much as you could; there was an ache to being in your own, a nagging unsuppressible suspicion that happiness was elsewhere. Driving back from taking the babysitter home, Frank would pass darkened houses where husbands he knew were lying in bed, head to murmuring head, with wives he coveted.

Out of this weave of promiscuous friendship, this confusedly domestic scrimmage, Maggie had emerged, touching his hip with hers as they stood side by side at a lawn party's busy, linen-clad bar, or exclaiming, in an involuntary, almost fainting little-girl voice, 'Oh, don't go!' when he and Ann stood up at last to leave a dinner party that she and Sam had given. And when, at one of the suburban balls with which the needs of charity dotted the calendar, his turn came to dance with Maggie, they nestled as close as the sanction of alcohol allowed, and at the end she gave his hand a sharp, stern, quite sober squeeze. It took very clear signals to burn through his fog of shyness and connubial inertia, but she had enough expertise to know that, once ignited, he would blaze.

How gentle and patient, in retrospect, her initiation of him had been. Their meetings took place mostly in her house, because Sam worked in Boston and Ann didn't. Frank remembered, rounding the rack of condoms into a realm of packaged antihistamine capsules, how the driveway of her house, which sat on the edge of town, next to a horse farm and riding stable, was hidden behind a tilting tall stockade-style fence and a mass of overgrown lilacs. Sam would talk of replacing the fence and pruning the lilacs but didn't do it that summer. Approaching, Frank needed to slow for the hairpin turn into the driveway; it was a dangerous moment when his car might have been recognized on the road—several of their friends' children took riding lessons—and he would hold his breath as, half hidden behind the great straggly lilacs, he would glide across the crackling gravel and into the garage. Maggie would have swung up the garage door for him, which took some strength in this era before electronic controls. She would be waiting for him behind the connecting door into the kitchen, in a bathing suit or less. His eyes would still be adjusting from sunlight. She would bound into his arms like a long, smooth, shivering puppy. He stared at the Sudafed and Contac, his whole body swollen by a stupid indignation at having lost all that.

*

At last, making a few distracted purchases by way of paying for the shelter, he dared leave the drugstore. He looked down the street and saw with relief that the vista of icicled shops held no red glint. Heart pounding, as if he were being pursued by an enemy, he made his way to his car and returned to his house. It was a weather-tight box, a well-built tract house on a two-acre square of land. The foundation-masking shrubs newly planted when they moved in now looked overgrown, crowding the brick steps and front windows. In the kitchen, Ann, in her tan loden coat, was unpacking bags of groceries into the refrigerator; her face as she turned to him wore a slant expression, brimming with wary mischief. 'I saw an old friend of yours in the Stop & Shop.' The giant bright supermarket was part of a mall that had arisen in the farm country, slowly going under to development, between the town they had left and the town where they lived.

'Who?' he asked, though from the peculiar liveliness of her expression he had already guessed.

'Maggie Linsford. Or whatever her name is now.' Maggie had taken back her maiden name after her divorce from Sam, and Ann could never be bothered to remember it.

'Chase,' Frank said. 'Unless she's remarried.'

'She wouldn't do that to you. What's in that bag in your hand?'

'Razor blades. Sudafed. And I got you some of that perfumed French bath gel you like. "*Dorlotez-vous*," the label says.'

'How sweet and silly of you. I have scads of it. Don't you want to hear about Maggie?'

'Sure.'

'She was with this man, she introduced him, in that rather grand way she has, as "my friend." He reminded me of Sam—big and red-faced and take-charge.'

'Good.'

'Frank, don't look so sick. You're thinking back twenty-five years.'

'No, I was thinking about "take-charge." I guess he was. Did she seem pleasant?'

'Oh, effusive. I always liked her, until you came between us. And she me, no?'

He wondered. At the height of their affair their spouses had seemed small and pathetic beneath them, like field mice under a hawk, virtually too small to discuss. 'Sure,' he said 'She admired you very much. She couldn't understand what I saw in her.'

'Don't be sarcastic. You're no fun, Frank. I bring you this goodie, and you look constipated.'

'What did the two of you discuss, effusively?'

'Oh, winter. Food. The appallingness of malls. Apparently a new one is going in on the land of the old riding stable next to that place she had with Sam. She complained there wasn't any gluten-free flour or low-fat cookies in the whole supermarket—maybe she's trying to slim down her beefy friend—and I told her we had a new health-food store just open up here, a charming idealistic girl we were all trying to give business to. She said she'd drive right over. If you were hanging out in the drugstore, I'm surprised you didn't see her.'

He saw he must confess; there was no evading feminine intuition. 'I did. I saw this flash of red hair down below the post office, and ducked into the drugstore rather than talk to her.'

'Frank dear, how silly again. She would have been nothing but pleasant, I'm sure.'

'I didn't like the look of the thug she was with.'

'If she had been alone, would you have gone up to her?'

'I doubt it.'

Ann put the last package into the refrigerator and closed the door, hard enough so that a magnet in the shape of a pineapple fell to the floor. She didn't pick it up. 'Your reacting so skittishly doesn't speak very well for us.'

Infidelity, he reflected, widens a couple's erotic field at first, but leaves it weaker and frazzled in the end. Like a mind-expanding drug, it destroys cells. He told Ann, 'I felt nothing. I felt repelled.'

'A "flash of red hair"—I'll say. She's dyeing it an impossible color these days.'

'You always said she dyed it.'

'And she always did. Certainly now.'

'I don't think so. Not Maggie.'

'Oh, you poor thing, her hair would be as gray as yours and mine if she didn't dye it. She looked cheap, cheap and whorish, which is something I couldn't have honestly said before. You were smart not to allow yourself a look up close.'

'You bitch. I know Maggie's hair better than you do.' Ann froze, not certain from his expression whether or not he would come forward and strike her; but she was safe, he was not even seeing her. The woman he did see, stepping naked toward him across a sun-striped carpet, was the one who, as long as he loved her, he must hate.

THE HALF-SKINNED STEER

Annie Proulx

In the long unfurling of his life, from tight-wound kid hustler in a wool suit riding the train out of Cheyenne to geriatric limper in this spooled-out year, Mero had kicked down thoughts of the place where he began, a so-called ranch on strange ground at the south hinge of the Big Horns. He'd got himself out of there in 1936, had gone to a war and come back, married and married again (and again), made money in boilers and air-duct cleaning and smart investments, retired, got into local politics and out again without scandal, never circled back to see the old man and Rollo bankrupt and ruined because he knew they were.

They called it a ranch and it had been, but one day the old man said it was impossible to run cows in such tough country where they fell off cliffs, disappeared into sink-holes, gave up large numbers of calves to marauding lions, where hay couldn't grow but leafy spurge and Canada thistle throve, and the wind packed enough sand to scour windshields opaque. The old man wangled a job delivering mail, but looked guilty fumbling bills into his neighbors' mailboxes.

Mero and Rollo saw the mail route as a defection from the work of the ranch, work that fell on them. The breeding herd was down to eighty-two and a cow wasn't worth more than fifteen dollars, but they kept mending fence, whittling ears and scorching hides, hauling cows out of mudholes and hunting lions in the hope that sooner or later the old man would move to Ten Sleep with his woman and his bottle and they could, as had their grandmother Olive when Jacob Corn disappointed her, pull the place taut. That bird didn't fly and Mero wound up sixty years later as an octogenarian vegetarian widower pumping an Exercycle in the living room of a colonial house in Woolfoot, Massachusetts.

One of those damp mornings the nail-driving telephone voice of a woman said she was Louise, Tick's wife, and summoned him back to Wyoming. He didn't know who she was, who Tick was, until she said, Tick Corn, your brother Rollo's son, and that Rollo had passed on, killed by a waspy emu though prostate cancer was waiting its chance. Yes, she said, you bet Rollo still owned the ranch. Half of it anyway. Me and Tick, she said, we been pretty much running it the last ten years.

An emu? Did he hear right?

Yes, she said. Well, of course you didn't know. You heard of Down Under Wyoming?

He had not. And thought, what kind of name was Tick? He recalled the bloated grey insects pulled off the dogs. This tick probably thought he was going to get the whole damn ranch and bloat up on it. He said, what the hell was this about an emu? Were they all crazy out there?

That's what the ranch was now, she said, Down Under Wyoming. Rollo'd sold the place way back when to the Girl Scouts, but one of the girls was dragged off by a lion and the G.S.A. sold out to the Banner ranch next door who ran cattle on it for a few years, then unloaded it on a rich Australian businessman who started Down Under Wyoming but it was too much long-distance work and he'd had bad luck with his manager, a feller from Idaho with a pawnshop rodeo buckle, so he'd looked up Rollo and offered to swap him a half-interest if he'd run the place. That was back in 1978. The place had done real well. Course we're not open now, she said, it's winter and there's no tourists. Poor Rollo was helping Tick move the emus to another building when one of them turned on a dime and come right for him with its big razor claws. Emus is bad for claws.

I know, he said. He watched the nature programs on television.

She shouted as though the telephone lines were down all across the country, Tick got your number off the computer. Rollo always said he was going to get in touch. He wanted you to see how things turned out. He tried to fight it off with his cane but it laid him open from belly to breakfast.

Maybe, he thought, things hadn't finished turning out. Impatient with this game he said he would be at the funeral. No point talking about flights and meeting him at the airport, he told her, he didn't fly, a bad experience years ago with hail, the plane had looked like a waffle iron when it landed. He intended to drive. Of course he knew how far it was. Had a damn fine car, Cadillac, always drove Cadillacs, Gislaved tires, interstate highways, excellent driver, never had an accident in his life knock on wood, four days, he would be there by Saturday afternoon. He heard the amazement in her voice, knew she was plotting his age, figuring he had to be eighty-three, a year or so older than Rollo, figuring he must be dotting around on a cane too, drooling the tiny days away, she was probably touching her own faded hair. He flexed his muscular arms, bent his knees, thought he could dodge an emu. He would see his brother dropped in a red Wyoming hole. That event could jerk him back; the dazzled rope of lightning against the cloud is not the downward bolt, but the compelled upstroke through the heated ether.

He had pulled away at the sudden point when it seemed the old man's girlfriend—now he couldn't remember her name—had jumped the track, Rollo goggling at her bloody bitten fingers, nails chewed to the quick, neck veins like wires, the outer forearms shaded with hairs, and the cigarette glowing, smoke curling up, making her wink her bulged mustang eyes, a teller of tales of hard deeds and mayhem. The old man's hair was falling out, Mero was twenty-three and Rollo twenty and she played them all like a deck of cards. If you admired horses you'd go for her with her arched neck and horsy buttocks, so high and haunchy you'd want to clap her on the rear. The wind bellowed around the house, driving crystals of snow through the cracks of the warped log door and all of them in the kitchen seemed charged with some intensity of purpose. She'd balanced that broad butt on the edge of the dog food chest, looking at the old man and Rollo, now and then rolling her glossy eyes over at Mero, square teeth nipping a rim of nail, sucking the welling blood, drawing on her cigarette.

The old man drank his Everclear stirred with a peeled willow stick for the bitter taste. The image of him came sharp in Mero's mind as he stood at the hall closet contemplating his hats; should he bring one for the funeral? The old man had had the damnedest curl to his hat brim, a tight roll on the right where his doffing or donning hand gripped it and a wavering downslope on the left like a shed roof. You could recognize him two miles away. He wore it at the table listening to the woman's stories about Tin Head, steadily emptying his glass until he was nine-times-nine drunk, his gangstery face loosening, the crushed rodeo nose and scar-crossed eyebrows, the stub ear dissolving as he drank. Now he must be dead fifty years or more, buried in the mailman sweater.

*

The girlfriend started a story, yeah, there was this guy named Tin Head down around Dubois when my dad was a kid. Had a little ranch, some horses, cows, kids, a wife. But there was something funny about him. He had a metal plate in his head from falling down some cement steps.

Plenty of guys has them, said Rollo in a challenging way.

She shook her head. Not like his. His was made out of galvy and it eat at his brain.

The old man held up the bottle of Everclear, raised his eyebrows at her: Well, darlin?

She nodded, took the glass from him and knocked it back in one swallow. Oh, that's not gonna slow *me* down, she said.

Mero expected her to neigh.

So what then, said Rollo, picking at the horse shit under his boot heel. What about Tin Head and his galvanized skull-plate?

I heard it this way, she said. She held out her glass for another shot of Everclear and the old man poured it and she went on.

Mero had thrashed all that ancient night, dreamed of horse breeding or hoarse breathing, whether the act of sex or bloody, cut-throat gasps he didn't know. The next morning he woke up drenched in stinking sweat, looked at the ceiling and said aloud, it could go on like this for some time. He meant cows and weather as much as anything, and what might be his chances two or three states over in any direction. In Woolfoot, riding the Exercycle, he thought the truth was somewhat different: he'd wanted a woman of his own without scrounging the old man's leftovers.

What he wanted to know now, tires spanking the tar-filled road cracks and potholes, funeral homburg sliding on the backseat, was if Rollo had got the girlfriend away from the old man, thrown a saddle on her and ridden off into the sunset?

The interstate, crippled by orange pylons, forced traffic into single lanes, broke his expectation of making good time. His Cadillac, boxed between semis with hissing air brakes, snuffled huge rear tires, framed a looming Peterbilt in the back window. His thoughts clogged as if a comb working through his mind had stuck against a snarl. When the traffic eased and he tried to cover some ground the highway patrol pulled him over. The cop, a pimpled, mustached specimen with mismatched eyes, asked his name, where he was going. For the minute he couldn't think what he was doing there. The cop's tongue dapped at the scraggy mustache while he scribbled.

Funeral, he said suddenly. Going to my brother's funeral.

Well you take it easy, Gramps, or they'll be doing one for you.

You're a little polecat, aren't you, he said, staring at the ticket, at the pathetic handwriting, but the mustache was a mile gone, peeling through the traffic as Mero had peeled out of the ranch road that long time ago, squinting through the abraded windshield. He might have made a more graceful exit but urgency had struck him as a blow on the humerus sends a ringing jolt up the arm. He believed it was the horse-haunched woman leaning against the chest and Rollo fixed on her, the old man swilling Everclear and not noticing or, if noticing, not caring, that had worked in him like a key in an ignition. She had long grey-streaked braids, Rollo could use them for reins.

Yah, she said, in her low and convincing liar's voice. I'll tell you, on Tin Head's ranch things went wrong. Chickens changed color overnight, calves was born with three legs, his kids was piebald and his wife always crying for blue dishes. Tin Head never finished nothing he started, quit halfway through a job every time. Even his pants was half-buttoned so his wienie hung out. He was a mess with the galvy plate eating at his brain and his ranch and his family was a mess. But, she said. They had to eat, didn't they, just like anybody else?

I hope they eat pies better than the ones you make, said Rollo, who didn't like the mouthful of pits that came with the chokecherries.

His interest in women began a few days after the old man had said, take this guy up and show him them Indan drawrings, jerking his head at the stranger. Mero had been eleven or twelve at the time, no older. They rode along the creek and put up a pair of mallards who flew downstream and then suddenly reappeared, pursued by a goshawk who struck the drake with a sound like a handclap. The duck tumbled through the trees and into deadfall trash and the hawk shot as swiftly away as it had come.

They climbed through the stony landscape, limestone beds eroded by wind into fantastic furniture, stale gnawed breadcrusts, tumbled bones, stacks of dirty folded blankets, bleached crab claws and dog teeth. He tethered the horses in the shade of a stand of limber pine and led the anthropologist up through the stiff-branched mountain mahogany to the overhang. Above them reared corroded cliffs brilliant with orange lichen, pitted with holes and ledges darkened by millennia of raptor feces.

The anthropologist moved back and forth scrutinizing the stone gallery of red and black drawings: bison skulls, a line of mountain sheep, warriors carrying lances, a turkey stepping into a snare, a stick man upside-down dead and falling, red ochre hands, violent figures with rakes on their heads that he said were feather headdresses, a great red bear dancing forward on its hind legs, concentric circles and crosses and latticework. He copied the drawings in his notebook, saying rubba-dubba a few times.

That's the sun, said the anthropologist who resembled an unfinished drawing himself, pointing at an archery target, ramming his pencil into the air as though tapping gnats. That's an atlatl and that's a dragonfly. There we go. You know what this is; and he touched a cloven oval, rubbing the cleft with his dusty fingers. He got down on his hands and knees, pointed out more, a few dozen.

A horseshoe?

A horseshoe! The anthropologist laughed. No boy, it's a vulva. That's what all of these are. You don't know what that is, do you? You go to school on Monday and look it up in the dictionary.

It's a symbol, he said. You know what a symbol is?

Yes, said Mero, who had seen them clapped together in the high school marching band. The anthropologist laughed and told him he had a great future, gave him a dollar for showing him the place. Listen, kid, the Indians did it just like anybody else, he said.

He had looked the word up in the school dictionary, slammed the book closed in embarrassment, but the image was fixed for him (with the brassy background sound of a military march), blunt ochre tracing on stone, and no fleshy examples ever conquered his belief in the subterranean stony structure of female genitalia, the pubic bone a proof, except for the old man's girlfriend whom he imagined down on all fours, entered from behind and whinnying like a mare, a thing not of geology but flesh.

*

Thursday night, balked by detours and construction, he was on the outskirts of Des Moines and no farther. In the cinderblock motel room he set the alarm but his own stertorous breathing woke him before it rang. He was up at five-fifteen, eyes aflame, peering through the vinyl drapes at his snow-hazed car flashing blue under the motel sign SLEEP SLEEP. In the bathroom he mixed the packet of instant motel coffee and drank it black without ersatz sugar or chemical cream. He wanted the caffeine. The roots of his mind felt withered and punky.

A cold morning, light snow slanting down: he unlocked the Cadillac, started it and curved into the vein of traffic, all semis, double- and triple-trailers. In the headlights' red glare he missed the westbound ramp and got into torn-up muddy streets, swung right and right again, using the motel's SLEEP sign as a landmark, but he was on the wrong side of the interstate and the sign belonged to a different motel.

Another mudholed lane took him into a traffic circle of commuters sucking coffee from insulated cups, pastries sliding on dashboards. Halfway around the hoop he spied the interstate entrance ramp, veered for it, collided with a panel truck emblazoned STOP SMOKING! HYPNOSIS THAT WORKS!, was rammed from behind by a stretch limo, the limo in its turn rear-ended by a yawning hydroblast operator in a company pickup.

He saw little of this, pressed into his seat by the air bag, his mouth full of a rubbery, dusty taste, eyeglasses cutting into his nose. His first thought was to blame Iowa and those who lived in it. There were a few round spots of blood on his shirt cuff.

A star-spangled Band-Aid over his nose, he watched his crumpled car, pouring dark fluids onto the highway, towed away behind a wrecker. A taxi took him, his suitcase, the homburg funeral hat, in the other direction to Posse Motors where lax salesmen drifted like disorbited satellites and where he bought a secondhand Cadillac, black like the wreck, but three years older and the upholstery not cream leather but sun-faded velour. He had the good tires from the wreck brought over and mounted. He could do that if he liked, buy cars like packs of cigarettes and smoke them up. He didn't care for the way it handled out on the highway, throwing itself abruptly aside when he twitched the wheel and he guessed it might have a bent frame. Damn, he'd buy another for the return trip. He could do what he wanted.

He was half an hour past Kearney, Nebraska, when the full moon rose, an absurd visage balanced in his rearview mirror, above it a curled wig of a cloud, filamented edges like platinum hairs. He felt his swollen nose, palped his chin, tender from the stun of the air bag. Before he slept that night he swallowed a glass of hot tap water enlivened with whiskey, crawled into the damp bed. He had eaten nothing all day yet his stomach coiled at the thought of road food.

He dreamed that he was in the ranch house but all the furniture had been removed from the rooms and in the yard troops in dirty white uniforms fought. The concussive reports of huge guns were breaking the window glass and forcing the floorboards apart so that he had to walk on the joists and below the disintegrating floors he saw galvanized tubs filled with dark, coagulated fluid.

On Saturday morning, with four hundred miles in front of him, he swallowed a few bites of scorched eggs, potatoes painted with canned *salsa verde*, a cup of yellow coffee, left no tip, got on the road. The food was not what he wanted. His breakfast habit was two glasses of mineral water, six cloves of garlic, a pear. The sky to the west hulked sullen, behind him smears of tinselly orange shot through with blinding streaks. The thick rim of sun bulged against the horizon.

He crossed the state line, hit Cheyenne for the second time in sixty years. There was neon, traffic and concrete, but he knew the place, a railroad town that had been up and down. That other time he had been painfully hungry, had gone into the restaurant in the Union Pacific station although he was not used to restaurants and ordered a steak, but when the woman brought it and he cut into the meat the blood spread across the white plate and he couldn't help it, he saw the beast, mouth agape in mute bawling, saw the comic aspects of his revulsion as well, a cattleman gone wrong.

Now he parked in front of a phone booth, locked the car although he stood only seven feet away, and telephoned the number Tick's wife had given him. The ruined car had had a phone. Her voice roared out of the earpiece.

We didn't hear so we wondered if you changed your mind.

No, he said, I'll be there late this afternoon. I'm in Cheyenne now.

The wind's blowing pretty hard. They're saying it could maybe snow. In the mountains. Her voice sounded doubtful.

I'll keep an eye on it, he said.

He was out of town and running north in a few minutes.

The country poured open on each side, reduced the Cadillac to a finger-snap. Nothing had changed, not a goddamn thing, the empty pale place and its roaring wind, the distant antelope as tiny as mice, landforms shaped true to the past. He felt himself slip back, the calm of eighty-three years sheeted off him like water, replaced by a young man's scalding anger at a fool world and the fools in it. What a damn hard time it had been to hit the road. You don't know what it was like, he told his ex-wives until they said they did know, he'd pounded it into their ears two hundred times, the poor youth on the street holding up a sign asking for work, and the job with the furnace man, *yatata yatata ya.* Thirty miles out of Cheyenne he saw the first billboard, DOWN UNDER WYOMING, *Western Fun the Western Way*, over a blown-up photograph of kangaroos hopping through the sagebrush and a blond child grinning in a manic imitation of pleasure. A diagonal banner warned, *Open May 31.*

So what, Rollo had said to the old man's girlfriend, what about that Mr. Tin Head? Looking at her, not just her face, but up and down, eyes moving over her like an iron over a shirt and the old man in his mailman's sweater and lopsided hat tasting his Everclear and not noticing or not caring, getting up every now and then to lurch onto the porch and water the weeds. When he left the room the tension ebbed and they were only ordinary people to whom nothing happened. Rollo looked away from the woman, leaned down to scratch the dog's ears, saying, Snarleyow Snapper, and the woman brought a dish to the sink and ran water on it, yawning. When the old man came back to his chair, the Everclear like sweet oil in his glass, glances resharpened and inflections of voice again carried complex messages.

Well well, she said, tossing her braids back, every year Tin Head butchers one of his steers, and that's what they'd eat all winter long, boiled, fried, smoked, fricasseed, burned and raw. So one time he's out there by the barn and he hits the steer a good one with the axe and it drops stun down. He ties up the back legs, hoists it up and sticks it, shoves the tub under to catch the blood. When it's bled out pretty good he lets it down and starts skinning it, starts with the head, cuts back of the poll down past the eye to the nose, peels the hide back. He don't cut the head off but keeps on skinning, dewclaws to hock up the inside of the thigh and then to the cod and down the middle of the belly to brisket to tail. Now he's ready to start siding, working that tough old skin off. But siding is hard work— (the old man nodded)— and he gets the hide off about halfway and starts thinking about dinner. So he leaves the steer half-skinned there on the ground and he goes into the kitchen, but first he cuts out the tongue which is his favorite dish all cooked up and eat cold with Mrs. Tin Head's mustard in a forget-me-not teacup. Sets it on the ground and goes in to dinner. Dinner is chicken and dumplins, one of them changed-color chickens started out white and ended up blue, yessir, blue as your old daddy's eyes.

She was a total liar. The old man's eyes were murk brown.

Onto the high plains sifted the fine snow, delicately clouding the air, a rare dust, beautiful, he thought, silk gauze, but there was muscle in the wind rocking the heavy car, a great pulsing artery of the jet stream swooping down from the sky to touch the earth. Plumes of smoke rose hundreds of feet into the air, elegant fountains and twisting snow devils, shapes of veiled Arab women and ghost riders dissolving in white fume. The snow snakes writhing across the asphalt straightened into rods. He was driving in a rushing river of cold whiteout foam. He could see nothing, trod on the brake, the wind buffeting the car, a bitter, hard-flung dust hissing over metal and glass. The car shuddered. And as suddenly as it had risen the wind dropped and the road was clear; he could see a long, empty mile.

How do you know when there's enough of anything? What trips the lever that snaps up the STOP sign? What electrical currents fizz and crackle in the brain to shape the decision to quit a place? He had listened to her damn story and the dice had rolled. For years he believed he had left without hard reason and suffered for it. But he'd learned from television nature programs that it had been time for him to find his own territory and his own woman. How many women were out there! He had married three or four of them and sampled plenty.

With the lapping subtlety of incoming tide the shape of the ranch began to gather in his mind; he could recall the intimate fences he'd made, taut wire and perfect corners, the draws and rock outcrops, the watercourse valley steepening, cliffs like bones with shreds of meat on them rising and rising, and the stream plunging suddenly underground, disappearing into subterranean darkness of blind fish, shooting out of the mountain ten miles west on a neighbor's place, but leaving their ranch some badland red country as dry as a cracker, steep canyons with high caves suited to lions. He and Rollo had shot two early in that winter close to the overhang with the painted vulvas. There were good caves up there from a lion's point of view.

He traveled against curdled sky. In the last sixty miles the snow began again. He climbed out of Buffalo. Pallid flakes as distant from each other as galaxies flew past, then more and in ten minutes he was crawling at twenty miles an hour, the windshield wipers thumping like a stick dragged down the stairs.

The light was falling out of the day when he reached the pass, the blunt mountains lost in snow, the greasy hairpin turns ahead. He drove slowly and steadily in a low gear; he had not forgotten how to drive a winter mountain. But the wind was up again, rocking and slapping the car, blotting out all but whipping snow and he was sweating with the anxiety of keeping to the road, dizzy with the altitude. Twelve more miles, sliding and buffeted, before he reached Ten Sleep where streetlights glowed in revolving circles like Van Gogh's sun. There had not been electricity when he left the place. In those days there were seventeen black, lightless miles between the town and the ranch, and now the long arch of years compressed into that distance. His headlights picked up a sign: 20 MILES TO DOWN UNDER WYOMING. Emus and bison leered above the letters.

He turned onto the snowy road marked with a single set of tracks, faint but still discernible, the heater fan whirring, the radio silent, all beyond the headlights blurred. Yet everything was as it had been, the shape of the road achingly familiar, sentinel rocks looming as they had in his youth. There was an eerie dream quality in seeing the deserted Farrier place leaning east as it had leaned sixty years ago, the Banner ranch gate, where the companionable tracks he had been following turned off, the gate ghostly in the snow but still flying its wrought iron flag, unmarked by the injuries of weather, and the taut five-strand fences and dim shifting forms of cattle. Next would come the road to their ranch, a left-hand turn just over the crest of a rise. He was running now on the unmarked road through great darkness.

*

Winking at Rollo the girlfriend said, yes, she had said, yes sir, Tin Head eats half his dinner and then he has to take a little nap. After a while he wakes up again and goes outside stretching his arms and yawning, says, guess I'll finish skinning out that steer. But the steer ain't there. It's gone. Only the tongue, laying on the ground all covered with dirt and straw, and the tub of blood and the dog licking at it.

It was her voice that drew you in, that low, twangy voice, wouldn't matter if she was saying the alphabet, what you heard was the rustle of hay. She could make you smell the smoke from an unlit fire.

How could he not recognize the turnoff to the ranch? It was so clear and sharp in his mind: the dusty crimp of the corner, the low section where the snow drifted, the run where willows slapped the side of the truck. He went a mile, watching for it, but the turn didn't come up, then watched for the Bob Kitchen place two miles beyond, but the distance unrolled and there was nothing. He made a three-point turn and backtracked. Rollo must have given up the old entrance road, for it wasn't there. The Kitchen place was gone to fire or wind. If he didn't find the turn it was no great loss; back to Ten Sleep and scout a motel. But he hated to quit when he was close enough to spit, hated to retrace black miles on a bad night when he was maybe twenty minutes away from the ranch.

He drove very slowly, following his tracks, and the ranch entrance appeared on the right although the gate was gone and the sign down. That was why he'd missed it, that and a clump of sagebrush that obscured the gap.

He turned in, feeling a little triumph. But the road under the snow was rough and got rougher until he was bucking along over boulders and slanted rock and knew wherever he was it was not right.

He couldn't turn around on the narrow track and began backing gingerly, the window down, craning his stiff neck, staring into the redness cast by the taillights. The car's right rear tire rolled up over a boulder, slid and sank into a quaggy hole. The tires spun in the snow, but he got no purchase.

I'll sit here, he said aloud. I'll sit here until it's light and then walk down to the Banner place and ask for a cup of coffee. I'll be cold but I won't freeze to death. It played like a joke the way he imagined it with Bob Banner opening the door and saying, why, it's Mero, come

on in and have some java and a hot biscuit, before he remembered that
Bob Banner would have to be 120 years old to play that role. He was
maybe three miles from Banner's gate, and the Banner ranch house
was another seven miles beyond the gate. Say a ten-mile hike at
altitude in a snowstorm. On the other hand he had half a tank of gas.
He could run the car for a while, then turn it off, start it again all
through the night. It was bad luck, but that's all. The trick was
patience.

He dozed half an hour in the wind-rocked car, woke shivering and
cramped. He wanted to lie down. He thought perhaps he could put a
flat rock under the goddamn tire. Never say die, he said, feeling
around the passenger-side floor for the flashlight in his emergency bag,
then remembering the wrecked car towed away, the flares and car
phone and AAA card and flashlight and matches and candle and
Power Bars and bottle of water still in it, and probably now in the
damn tow-driver's damn wife's car. He might get a good enough look
anyway in the snow-reflected light. He put on his gloves and the heavy
overcoat, got out and locked the car, sidled around to the rear, bent
down. The taillights lit the snow beneath the rear of the car like a fresh
bloodstain. There was a cradle-sized depression eaten out by the
spinning tire. Two or three flat ones might get him out, or small round
ones, he was not going to insist on the perfect stone. The wind tore at
him, the snow was certainly drifting up. He began to shuffle on the
road, feeling with his feet for rocks he could move, the car's even
throbbing promising motion and escape. The wind was sharp and his
ears ached. His wool cap was in the damn emergency bag.

My lord, she continued, Tin Head is just startled to pieces when he
don't see that steer. He thinks somebody, some neighbor don't like him,
plenty of them, come and stole it. He looks around for tire marks or
footprints but there's nothing except old cow tracks. He puts his hand
up to his eyes and stares away. Nothing in the north, the south, the
east, but way over there in the west on the side of the mountain he sees
something moving stiff and slow, stumbling along. It looks raw and it's
got something bunchy and wet hanging down over its hindquarters.
Yah, it was the steer, never making no sound. And just then it stops and
it looks back. And all that distance Tin Head can see the raw meat of
the head and the shoulder muscles and the empty mouth without no

tongue open wide and its red eyes glaring at him, pure teetotal hate like arrows coming at him, and he knows he is done for and all of his kids and their kids is done for, and that his wife is done for and that every one of her blue dishes has got to break, and the dog that licked the blood is done for, and the house where they lived has to blow away or burn up and every fly or mouse in it.

There was a silence and she added, that's it. And it all went against him, too.

That's it? said Rollo. That's all there is to it?

Yet he knew he was on the ranch, he felt it and he knew this road, too. It was not the main ranch road but some lower entrance he could not quite recollect that cut in below the river. Now he remembered that the main entrance gate was on a side road that branched off well before the Banner place. He found a good stone, another, wondering which track this could be; the map of the ranch in his memory was not as bright now, but scuffed and obliterated as though trodden. The remembered gates collapsed, fences wavered, while the badland features swelled into massive prominence. The cliffs bulged into the sky, lions snarled, the river corkscrewed through a stone hole at a tremendous rate and boulders cascaded from the heights. Beyond the barbwire something moved.

He grasped the car door handle. It was locked. Inside by the dashboard glow, he could see the gleam of the keys in the ignition where he'd left them to keep the car running. It was almost funny. He picked up a big two-handed rock and smashed it on the driver's-side window, slipped his arm in through the hole, into the delicious warmth of the car, a contortionist's reach, twisting behind the steering wheel and down, and had he not kept limber with exercise and nut cutlets and green leafy vegetables he never could have reached the keys. His fingers grazed and then grasped the keys and he had them. This is how they sort the men out from the boys, he said aloud. As his fingers closed on the keys he glanced at the passenger door. The lock button stood high. And even had it been locked as well, why had he strained to reach the keys when he had only to lift the lock button on the driver's side? Cursing, he pulled out the rubber floor mats and arranged them over the stones, stumbled around the car once more. He was dizzy, tremendously thirsty and hungry, opened his mouth to snowflakes. He had eaten nothing for two days but the burned eggs that morning. He could eat a dozen burned eggs now.

The snow roared through the broken window. He put the car in reverse and slowly trod the gas. The car lurched and steadied in the track and once more he was twisting his neck, backing in the red glare, twenty feet, thirty, but slipping and spinning; there was too much snow. He was backing up an incline that had seemed level on the way in but showed itself now as a remorselessly long hill studded with rocks and deep in snow. His incoming tracks twisted like rope. He forced out another twenty feet spinning the tires until they smoked, and the rear wheels slewed sideways off the track and into a two-foot ditch, the engine died and that was it. It was almost a relief to have reached this point where the celestial fingernails were poised to nip his thread. He dismissed the ten-mile distance to the Banner place: it might not be that far, or maybe they had pulled the ranch closer to the main road. A truck might come by. Shoes slipping, coat buttoned awry, he might find the mythical Grand Hotel in the sagebrush.

On the main road his tire tracks showed as a faint pattern in the pearly apricot light from the risen moon, winking behind roiling clouds of snow. His blurred shadow strengthened whenever the wind eased. Then the violent country showed itself, the cliffs rearing at the moon, the snow smoking off the prairie like steam, the white flank of the ranch slashed with fence cuts, the sagebrush glittering and along the creek black tangles of willow bunched like dead hair. There were cattle in the field beside the road, their plumed breaths catching the moony glow like comic strip dialogue balloons.

He walked against the wind, his shoes filled with snow, feeling as easy to tear as a man cut from paper. As he walked he noticed one from the herd inside the fence was keeping pace with him. He walked more slowly and the animal lagged. He stopped and turned. It stopped as well, huffing vapor, regarding him, a strip of snow on its back like a linen runner. It tossed its head and in the howling, wintry light he saw he'd been wrong again, that the half-skinned steer's red eye had been watching for him all this time.

KILLINGS

Andre Dubus

On the August morning when Matt Fowler buried his youngest son, Frank, who had lived for twenty-one years, eight months, and four days, Matt's older son, Steve, turned to him as the family left the grave and walked between their friends, and said: 'I should kill him.' He was twenty-eight, his brown hair starting to thin in front where he used to have a cowlick. He bit his lower lip, wiped his eyes, then said it again. Ruth's arm linked with Matt's, tightened; he looked at her. Beneath her eyes there was swelling from the three days she had suffered. At the limousine Matt stopped and looked back at the grave, the casket, and the Congregationalist minister who he thought had probably had a difficult job with the eulogy though he hadn't seemed to, and the old funeral director who was saying something to the six young pallbearers. The grave was on a hill and overlooked the Merrimack, which he could not see from where he stood; he looked at the opposite bank, at the apple orchard with its symmetrically planted trees going up a hill.

Next day Steve drove with his wife back to Baltimore where he managed the branch office of a bank, and Cathleen, the middle child, drove with her husband back to Syracuse. They had left the grandchildren with friends. A month after the funeral Matt played poker at Willis Trottier's because Ruth, who knew this was the second time he had been invited, told him to go, he couldn't sit home with her for the rest of her life, she was all right. After the game Willis went outside to tell everyone goodnight and, when the others had driven away, he walked with Matt to his car. Willis was a short, silver-haired man who had opened a diner after World War II, his trade then mostly very early breakfast, which he cooked, and then lunch for the men who worked at the leather and shoe factories. He now owned a large restaurant.

'He walks the Goddamn streets,' Matt said.

'I know. He was in my place last night, at the bar. With a girl.'

'I don't see him. I'm in the store all the time. Ruth sees him. She sees him too much. She was at Sunnyhurst today getting cigarettes and aspirin, and there he was. She can't even go out for cigarettes and aspirin. It's killing her.'

'Come back in for a drink.'

Matt looked at his watch. Ruth would be asleep. He walked with Willis back into the house, pausing at the steps to look at the starlit sky. It was a cool summer night; he thought vaguely of the Red Sox, did not even know if they were at home tonight; since it happened he had not been able to think about any of the small pleasures he believed he had earned, as he had earned also what was shattered now forever: the quietly harried and quietly pleasurable days of fatherhood. They went inside. Willis's wife, Martha, had gone to bed hours ago, in the rear of the large house which was rigged with burglar and fire alarms. They went downstairs to the game room: the television set suspended from the ceiling, the pool table, the poker table with beer cans, cards, chips, filled ashtrays, and the six chairs where Matt and his friends had sat, the friends picking up the old banter as though he had only been away on vacation; but he could see the affection and courtesy in their eyes. Willis went behind the bar and mixed them each a Scotch and soda; he stayed behind the bar and looked at Matt sitting on the stool.

'How often have you thought about it?' Willis said.

'Every day since he got out. I didn't think about bail. I thought I wouldn't have to worry about him for years. She sees him all the time. It makes her cry.'

'He was in my place a long time last night. He'll be back.'

'Maybe he won't.'

'The band. He likes the band.'

'What's he doing now?'

'He's tending bar up to Hampton Beach. For a friend. Ever notice even the worst bastard always has friends? He couldn't get work in town. It's just tourists and kids up to Hampton. Nobody knows him. If they do, they don't care. They drink what he mixes.'

'Nobody tells me about him.'

'I hate him, Matt. My boys went to school with him. He was the same then. Know what he'll do? Five at the most. Remember that woman about seven years ago? Shot her husband and dropped him off the bridge in the Merrimack with a hundred pound sack of cement and said all the way through it that nobody helped her. Know where she is now? She's in Lawrence now, a secretary. And whoever helped her, where the hell is he?'

'I've got a .38 I've had for years. I take it to the store now. I tell Ruth it's for the night deposits. I tell her things have changed: we got junkies here now too. Lots of people without jobs. She knows though.'

'What does she know?'

'She knows I started carrying it after the first time she saw him in town. She knows it's in case I see him, and there's some kind of a situation—'

He stopped, looked at Willis, and finished his drink. Willis mixed him another.

'What kind of a situation?'

'Where he did something to me. Where I could get away with it.'

'How does Ruth feel about that?'

'She doesn't know.'

'You said she does, she's got it figured out.'

He thought of her that afternoon: when she went into Sunnyhurst, Strout was waiting at the counter while the clerk bagged the things he had bought; she turned down an aisle and looked at soup cans until he left.

'Ruth would shoot him herself, if she thought she could hit him.'

'You got a permit?'

'No.'

'I do. You could get a year for that.'

'Maybe I'll get one. Or maybe I won't. Maybe I'll just stop bringing it to the store.'

Richard Strout was twenty-six years old, a high school athlete, football scholarship to the University of Massachusetts where he lasted for almost two semesters before quitting in advance of the final grades that would have forced him not to return. People then said: Dickie can do the work; he just doesn't want to. He came home and did construction work for his father but refused his father's offer to learn the business; his two older brothers had learned it, so that Strout and Sons trucks going about town, and signs on construction sites, now slashed wounds into Matt Fowler's life. Then Richard married a young girl and became a bartender, his salary and tips augmented and perhaps sometimes matched by his father, who also posted his bond. So his friends, his enemies (he had those: fist fights or, more often, boys and then young men who had not fought him when they thought they should have), and those who simply knew him by face and name, had a series of images of him which they recalled when they heard of the killing: the high school running back, the young drunk in bars, the oblivious hard-hatted young man eating lunch at a counter, the bartender who could perhaps be called courteous but not more than that: as he tended bar, his dark eyes and dark, wide-jawed face appeared less sullen, near blank.

One night he beat Frank. Frank was living at home and waiting for September, for graduate school in economics, and working as a lifeguard at Salisbury Beach, where he met Mary Ann Strout, in her first month of separation. She spent most days at the beach with her two sons. Before ten o'clock one night Frank came home; he had driven to the hospital first, and he walked into the living room with stitches over his right eye and both lips bright and swollen.

'I'm all right,' he said, when Matt and Ruth stood up, and Matt turned off the television, letting Ruth get to him first: the tall, muscled but slender suntanned boy. Frank tried to smile at them but couldn't because of his lips.

'It was her husband, wasn't it?' Ruth said.

'Ex,' Frank said. 'He dropped in.'

Matt gently held Frank's jaw and turned his face to the light, looked at the stitches, the blood under the white of the eye, the bruised flesh.

'Press charges,' Matt said.

'No.'

'What's to stop him from doing it again? Did you hit him at all? Enough so he won't want to next time?'

'I don't think I touched him.'

'So what are you going to do?'

'Take karate,' Frank said, and tried again to smile.

'That's not the problem,' Ruth said.

'You know you like her,' Frank said.

'I like a lot of people. What about the boys? Did they see it?'

'They were asleep.'

'Did you leave her alone with him?'

'He left first. She was yelling at him. I believe she had a skillet in her hand.'

'Oh for God's sake,' Ruth said.

Matt had been dealing with that too: at the dinner table on evenings when Frank wasn't home, was eating with Mary Ann; or, on the other nights—and Frank was with her every night—he talked with Ruth while they watched television, or lay in bed with the windows open and he smelled the night air and imagined, with both pride and muted sorrow, Frank in Mary Ann's arms. Ruth didn't like it because Mary Ann was in the process of divorce, because she had two children, because she was four years older than Frank, and finally—she told this in bed, where she had during all of their marriage told him of her deepest feelings: of love, of passion, of fears about one of the children, of pain Matt had caused her or she had caused him—she was against it because of what she had heard: that the marriage had gone bad early, and for most of it Richard and Mary Ann had both played around.

'That can't be true,' Matt said. 'Strout wouldn't have stood for it.'

'Maybe he loves her.'

'He's too hot-tempered. He couldn't have taken that.'

But Matt knew Strout had taken it, for he had heard the stories too. He wondered who had told them to Ruth; and he felt vaguely annoyed and isolated: living with her for thirty-one years and still not knowing what she talked about with her friends. On these summer nights he did not so much argue with her as try to comfort her, but finally there was no difference between the two: she had concrete objections, which he tried to overcome. And in his attempt to do this, he neglected his own objections, which were the same as hers, so that as he spoke to her he felt as disembodied as he sometimes did in the store when he helped a man choose a blouse or dress or piece of costume jewelry for his wife.

'The divorce doesn't mean anything,' he said. 'She was young and maybe she liked his looks and then after a while she realized she was living with a bastard. I see it as a positive thing.'

'She's not divorced yet.'

'It's the same thing. Massachusetts has crazy laws, that's all. Her age is no problem. What's it matter when she was born? And that other business: even if it's true, which it probably isn't, it's got nothing to do with Frank, it's in the past. And the kids are no problem. She's been married six years; she ought to have kids. Frank likes them. He plays with them. And he's not going to marry her anyway, so it's not a problem of money.'

'Then what's he doing with her?'

'She probably loves him, Ruth. Girls always have. Why can't we just leave it at that?'

'He got home at six o'clock Tuesday morning.'

'I didn't know you knew. I've already talked to him about it.'

Which he had: since he believed almost nothing he told Ruth, he went to Frank with what he believed. The night before, he had followed Frank to the car after dinner.

'You wouldn't make much of a burglar,' he said.

'How's that?'

Matt was looking up at him; Frank was six feet tall, an inch and a half taller than Matt, who had been proud when Frank at seventeen outgrew him; he had only felt uncomfortable when he had to reprimand or caution him. He touched Frank's bicep, thought of the young taut passionate body, believed he could sense the desire, and again he felt the pride and sorrow and envy too, not knowing whether he was envious of Frank or Mary Ann.

'When you came in yesterday morning, I woke up. One of these mornings your mother will. And I'm the one who'll have to talk to her. She won't interfere with you. Okay? I know it means—' But he stopped, thinking: I know it means getting up and leaving that suntanned girl and going sleepy to the car, I know—

'Okay,' Frank said, and touched Matt's shoulder and got into the car.

There had been other talks, but the only long one was their first one: a night driving to Fenway Park, Matt having ordered the tickets so they could talk, and knowing when Frank said yes, he would go, that he knew the talk was coming too. It took them forty minutes to get to Boston, and they talked about Mary Ann until they joined the city traffic along the Charles River, blue in the late sun. Frank told him all the things that Matt would later pretend to believe when he told them to Ruth.

'It seems like a lot for a young guy to take on,' Matt finally said.

'Sometimes it is. But she's worth it.'

'Are you thinking about getting married?'

'We haven't talked about it. She can't for over a year. I've got school.'

'I *do* like her,' Matt said.

He did. Some evenings, when the long summer sun was still low in the sky, Frank brought her home; they came into the house smelling of

suntan lotion and the sea, and Matt gave them gin and tonics and
started the charcoal in the backyard, and looked at Mary Ann in the
lawn chair: long and very light brown hair (Matt thinking that twenty
years ago she would have dyed it blonde), and the long brown legs he
loved to look at; her face was pretty; she had probably never in her
adult life gone unnoticed into a public place. It was in her wide brown
eyes that she looked older than Frank; after a few drinks Matt thought
what he saw in her eyes was something erotic, testament to the rumors
about her; but he knew it wasn't that, or all that: she had, very young,
been through a sort of pain that his children, and he and Ruth, had
been spared. In the moments of his recognizing that pain, he wanted
to tenderly touch her hair, wanted with some gesture to give her solace
and hope. And he would glance at Frank, and hope they would love
each other, hope Frank would soothe that pain in her heart, take it from
her eyes; and her divorce, her age, and her children did not matter at
all. On the first two evenings she did not bring her boys, and then Ruth
asked her to bring them next time. In bed that night Ruth said, 'She
hasn't brought them because she's embarrassed. She shouldn't feel
embarrassed.'

Richard Strout shot Frank in front of the boys. They were sitting on the
living room floor watching television, Frank sitting on the couch, and
Mary Ann just returning from the kitchen with a tray of sandwiches.
Strout came in the front door and shot Frank twice in the chest and
once in the face with a 9 mm. automatic. Then he looked at the boys
and Mary Ann, and went home to wait for the police.

It seemed to Matt that from the time Mary Ann called weeping to
tell him until now, a Saturday night in September, sitting in the car with
Willis, parked beside Strout's car, waiting for the bar to close, that he
had not so much moved through his life as wandered through it, his
spirit like a dazed body bumping into furniture and corners. He had
always been a fearful father: when his children were young, at the start
of each summer he thought of them drowning in a pond or the sea, and
he was relieved when he came home in the evenings and they were
there; usually that relief was his only acknowledgment of his fear,
which he never spoke of, and which he controlled within his heart. As
he had when they were very young and all of them in turn, Cathleen
too, were drawn to the high oak in the backyard, and had to climb it.

Smiling, he watched them, imagining the fall: and he was poised to catch the small body before it hit the earth. Or his legs were poised; his hands were in his pockets or his arms were folded and, for the child looking down, he appeared relaxed and confident while his heart beat with the two words he wanted to call out but did not: *Don't fall*. In winter he was less afraid: he made sure the ice would hold him before they skated, and he brought or sent them to places where they could sled without ending in the street. So he and his children had survived their childhood, and he only worried about them when he knew they were driving a long distance, and then he lost Frank in a way no father expected to lose his son, and he felt that all the fears he had borne while they were growing up, and all the grief he had been afraid of, had backed up like a huge wave and struck him on the beach and swept him out to sea. Each day he felt the same and when he was able to forget how he felt, when he was able to force himself not to feel that way, the eyes of his clerks and customers defeated him. He wished those eyes were oblivious, even cold; he felt he was withering in their tenderness. And beneath his listless wandering, every day in his soul he shot Richard Strout in the face; while Ruth, going about town on errands, kept seeing him. And at nights in bed she would hold Matt and cry, or sometimes she was silent and Matt would touch her tightening arm, her clenched fist.

As his own right fist was now, squeezing the butt of the revolver, the last of the drinkers having left the bar, talking to each other, going to their separate cars which were in the lot in front of the bar, out of Matt's vision. He heard their voices, their cars, and then the ocean again, across the street. The tide was in and sometimes it smacked the sea wall. Through the windshield he looked at the dark red side wall of the bar, and then to his left, past Willis, at Strout's car, and through its windows he could see the now-emptied parking lot, the road, the sea wall. He could smell the sea.

The front door of the bar opened and closed again and Willis looked at Matt then at the corner of the building; when Strout came around it alone Matt got out of the car, giving up the hope he had kept all night (and for the past week) that Strout would come out with friends, and Willis would simply drive away; thinking: *All right then. All right*; and he went around the front of Willis's car, and at Strout's he stopped and aimed over the hood at Strout's blue shirt ten feet away. Willis was aiming too, crouched on Matt's left, his elbow resting on the hood.

'Mr. Fowler,' Strout said. He looked at each of them, and at the guns. 'Mr. Trottier.'

Then Matt, watching the parking lot and the road, walked quickly between the car and the building and stood behind Strout. He took one leather glove from his pocket and put it on his left hand.

'Don't talk. Unlock the front and back and get in.'

Strout unlocked the front door, reached in and unlocked the back, then got in, and Matt slid into the back seat, closed the door with his gloved hand, and touched Strout's head once with the muzzle.

'It's cocked. Drive to your house.'

When Strout looked over his shoulder to back the car, Matt aimed at his temple and did not look at his eyes.

'Drive slowly,' he said. 'Don't try to get stopped.'

They drove across the empty front lot and onto the road, Willis's headlights shining into the car; then back through town, the sea wall on the left hiding the beach, though far out Matt could see the ocean; he uncocked the revolver; on the right were the places, most with their neon signs off, that did so much business in summer: the lounges and cafés and pizza houses, the street itself empty of traffic, the way he and Willis had known it would be when they decided to take Strout at the bar rather than knock on his door at two o'clock one morning and risk that one insomniac neighbor. Matt had not told Willis he was afraid he could not be alone with Strout for very long, smell his smells, feel the presence of his flesh, hear his voice, and then shoot him. They left the beach town and then were on the high bridge over the channel: to the left the smacking curling white at the breakwater and beyond that the dark sea and the full moon, and down to his right the small fishing boats bobbing at anchor in the cove. When they left the bridge, the sea was blocked by abandoned beach cottages, and Matt's left hand was sweating in the glove. Out here in the dark in the car he believed Ruth knew. Willis had come to his house at eleven and asked if he wanted a nightcap; Matt went to the bedroom for his wallet, put the gloves in one trouser pocket and the .38 in the other and went back to the living room, his hand in his pocket covering the bulge of the cool cylinder pressed against his fingers, the butt against his palm. When Ruth said goodnight she looked at his face, and he felt she could see in his eyes the gun, and the night he was going to. But he knew he couldn't trust what he saw. Willis's wife had taken her sleeping pill, which gave her eight hours—the reason, Willis had told Matt, he had the alarms installed, for nights when he was late at the restaurant—and when it was all done and Willis got home he would leave ice and a trace of Scotch and soda in two glasses in the game room and tell Martha in the morning that he had left the restaurant early and brought Matt home for a drink.

'He was making it with my wife.' Strout's voice was careful, not pleading.

Matt pressed the muzzle against Strout's head, pressed it harder than he wanted to, feeling through the gun Strout's head flinching and moving forward; then he lowered the gun to his lap.

'Don't talk,' he said.

Strout did not speak again. They turned west, drove past the Dairy Queen closed until spring, and the two lobster restaurants that faced each other and were crowded all summer and were now also closed, onto the short bridge crossing the tidal stream, and over the engine Matt could hear through his open window the water rushing inland under the bridge; looking to his left he saw its swift moonlit current going back into the marsh which, leaving the bridge, they entered: the salt marsh stretching out on both sides, the grass tall in patches but mostly low and leaning earthward as though windblown, a large dark rock sitting as though it rested on nothing but itself, and shallow pools reflecting the bright moon.

Beyond the marsh they drove through woods, Matt thinking now of the hole he and Willis had dug last Sunday afternoon after telling their wives they were going to Fenway Park. They listened to the game on a transistor radio, but heard none of it as they dug into the soft earth on the knoll they had chosen because elms and maples sheltered it. Already some leaves had fallen. When the hole was deep enough they covered it and the piled earth with dead branches, then cleaned their shoes and pants and went to a resuurant farther up in New Hampshire where they ate sandwiches and drank beer and watched the rest of the game on television. Looking at the back of Strout's head he thought of Frank's grave; he had not been back to it; but he would go before winter, and its second burial of snow.

He thought of Frank sitting on the couch and perhaps talking to the children as they watched television, imagined him feeling young and strong, still warmed from the sun at the beach, and feeling loved, hearing Mary Ann moving about in the kitchen, hearing her walking into the living room; maybe he looked up at her and maybe she said something, looking at him over the tray of sandwiches, smiling at him, saying something the way women do when they offer food as a gift, then the front door opening and this son of a bitch coming in and Frank seeing that he meant the gun in his hand, this son of a bitch and his gun the last person and thing Frank saw on earth.

When they drove into town the streets were nearly empty: a few slow cars, a policeman walking his beat past the darkened fronts of stores. Strout and Matt both glanced at him as they drove by. They were on the main street, and all the stoplights were blinking yellow. Willis and Matt had talked about that too: the lights changed at midnight, so there would be no place Strout had to stop and where he might try to run. Strout turned down the block where he lived and Willis's headlights were no longer with Matt in the back seat. They had planned that too, had decided it was best for just the one car to go to the house, and again Matt had said nothing about his fear of being alone with Strout, especially in his house: a duplex, dark as all the houses on the street were, the street itself lit at the corner of each block. As Strout turned into the driveway Matt thought of the one insomniac neighbor, thought of some man or woman sitting alone in the dark living room, watching the all-night channel from Boston. When Strout stopped the car near the front of the house, Matt said: 'Drive it to the back.'

He touched Strout's head with the muzzle.

'You wouldn't have it cocked, would you? For when I put on the brakes.'

Matt cocked it, and said: 'It is now.'

Strout waited a moment; then he eased the car forward, the engine doing little more than idling, and as they approached the garage he gently braked. Matt opened the door, then took off the glove and put it in his pocket. He stepped out and shut the door with his hip and said: 'All right.'

Strout looked at the gun, then got out, and Matt followed him across the grass, and as Strout unlocked the door Matt looked quickly at the row of small backyards on either side, and scattered tall trees, some evergreens, others not, and he thought of the red and yellow leaves on the trees over the hole, saw them falling soon, probably in two weeks, dropping slowly, covering. Strout stepped into the kitchen.

'Turn on the light.'

Strout reached to the wall switch, and in the light Matt looked at his wide back, the dark blue shirt, the white belt, the red plaid pants.

'Where's your suitcase?'

'My suitcase?'

'Where is it.'

'In the bedroom closet.'

'That's where we're going then. When we get to a door you stop and turn on the light.'

They crossed the kitchen, Matt glancing at the sink and stove and refrigerator: no dishes in the sink or even the dish rack beside it, no grease splashings on the stove, the refrigrator door clean and white. He did not want to look at any more but he looked quickly at all he could see: in the living room magazines and newspapers in a wicker basket, clean ashtrays, a record player, the records shelved next to it, then down the hall where, near the bedroom door, hung a color photograph of Mary Ann and the two boys sitting on a lawn—there was no house in the picture—Mary Ann smiling at the camera or Strout or whoever held the camera, smiling as she had on Matt's lawn this summer while he waited for the charcoal and they all talked and he looked at her brown legs and at Frank touching her arm, her shoulder, her hair; he moved down the hall with her smile in his mind, wondering: was that when they were both playing around and she was smiling like that at him and they were happy, even sometimes, making it worth it? He recalled her eyes, the pain in them, and he was conscious of the circles of love he was touching with the hand that held the revolver so tightly now as Strout stopped at the door at the end of the hall.

'There's no wall switch.'

'Where's the light?'

'By the bed.'

'Let's go.'

Matt stayed a pace behind, then Strout leaned over and the room was lighted: the bed, a double one, was neatly made; the ashtray on the bedside table clean, the bureau top dustless, and no photographs; probably so the girl—who *was* she?—would not have to see Mary Ann in the bedroom she believed was theirs. But because Matt was a father and a husband, though never an ex-husband, he knew (and did not want to know) that this bedroom had never been theirs alone. Strout turned around; Matt looked at his lips, his wide jaw, and thought of Frank's doomed and fearful eyes looking up from the couch.

'Where's Mr. Trottier?'

'He's waiting. Pack clothes for warm weather.'

'What's going on?'

'You're jumping bail.'

'Mr. Fowler—'

He pointed the cocked revolver at Strout's face. The barrel trembled but not much, not as much as he had expected. Strout went to the closet and got the suitcase from the floor and opened it on the bed. As he went to the bureau, he said: 'He was making it with my wife. I'd go pick up my kids and he'd be there. Sometimes he spent the night. My boys told me.'

He did not look at Matt as he spoke. He opened the top drawer and Matt stepped closer so he could see Strout's hands: underwear and socks, the socks rolled, the underwear folded and stacked. He took them back to the bed, arranged them neatly in the suitcase, then from the closet he was taking shirts and trousers and a jacket; he laid them on the bed and Matt followed him to the bathroom and watched from the door while he packed his shaving kit; watched in the bedroom as he folded and packed those things a person accumulated and that became part of him so that at times in the store Matt felt he was selling more than clothes.

'I wanted to try to get together with her again.' He was bent over the suitcase. 'I couldn't even talk to her. He was always with her. I'm going to jail for it; if I ever get out I'll be an old man. Isn't that enough?'

'You're not going to jail.'

Strout closed the suitcase and faced Matt, looking at the gun. Matt went to his rear, so Strout was between him and the lighted hall; then using his handkerchief he turned off the lamp and said: 'Let's go.'

They went down the hall, Matt looking again at the photograph, and through the living room and kitchen, Matt turning off the lights and talking, frightened that he was talking, that he was telling this lie he had not planned: 'It's the trial. We can't go through that, my wife and me. So you're leaving. We've got you a ticket, and a job. A friend of Mr. Trottier's. Out west. My wife keeps seeing you. We can't have that anymore.'

Matt turned out the kitchen light and put the handkerchief in his pocket, and they went down the two brick steps and across the lawn. Strout put the suitcase on the floor of the back seat, then got into the front seat and Matt got in the back and put on his glove and shut the door.

'They'll catch me. They'll check passenger lists.'

'We didn't use your name.'

'They'll figure that out too. You think I wouldn't have done it myself if it was that easy?'

He backed into the street, Matt looking down the gun barrel but not at the profiled face beyond it.

'You were alone,' Matt said. 'We've got it worked out.'

'There's no planes this time of night, Mr. Fowler.'

'Go back through town. Then north on 125.'

They came to the corner and turned, and now Willis's headlights were in the car with Matt.

'Why north, Mr. Fowler?'

'Somebody's going to keep you for a while. They'll take you to the airport.' He uncocked the hammer and lowered the revolver to his lap and said wearily: 'No more talking.'

As they drove back through town, Matt's body sagged, going limp with his spirit and its new and false bond with Strout, the hope his lie had given Strout. He had grown up in this town whose streets had become places of apprehension and pain for Ruth as she drove and walked, doing what she had to do; and for him too, if only in his mind as he worked and chatted six days a week in his store; he wondered now if his lie would have worked, if sending Strout away would have been enough; but then he knew that just thinking of Strout in Montana or whatever place lay at the end of the lie he had told, thinking of him walking the streets there, loving a girl there (who *was* she?) would be enough to slowly rot the rest of his days. And Ruth's. Again he was certain that she knew, that she was waiting for him.

They were in New Hampshire now, on the narrow highway, passing the shopping center at the state line, and then houses and small stores and sandwich shops. There were few cars on the road. After ten minutes he raised his trembling hand, touched Strout's neck with the gun, and said: 'Turn in up here. At the dirt road.'

Strout flicked on the indicator and slowed.

'Mr. Fowler?'

'They're waiting here.'

Strout turned very slowly, easing his neck away from the gun. In the moonlight the road was light brown, lighter and yellowed where the headlights shone; weeds and a few trees grew on either side of it, and ahead of them were the woods.

'There's nothing back here, Mr. Fowler.'

'It's for your car. You don't think we'd leave it at the airport, do you?'

He watched Strout's large, big-knuckled hands tighten on the wheel, saw Frank's face that night: not the stitches and bruised eye and swollen lips, but his own hand gently touching Frank's jaw, turning his wounds to the light. They rounded a bend in the road and were out of sight of the highway: tall trees all around them now, hiding the moon. When they reached the abandoned gravel pit on the left, the bare flat earth and steep pale embankment behind it, and the black crowns of trees at its top, Matt said: 'Stop here.'

Strout stopped but did not turn off the engine. Matt pressed the gun hard against his neck, and he straightened in the seat and looked in the rearview mirror, Matt's eyes meeting his in the glass for an instant before looking at the hair at the end of the gun barrel.

'Turn it off.'

Strout did, then held the wheel with two hands, and looked in the mirror.

'I'll do twenty years, Mr. Fowler; at least. I'll be forty-six years old.'

'That's nine years younger than I am,' Matt said, and got out and took off the glove and kicked the door shut. He aimed at Strout's ear and pulled back the hammer. Willis's headlights were off and Matt heard him walking on the soft thin layer of dust, the hard earth beneath it. Strout opened the door, sat for a moment in the interior light, then stepped out onto the road. Now his face was pleading. Matt did not look at his eyes, but he could see it in the lips.

'Just get the suitcase. They're right up the road.'

Willis was beside him now, to his left. Strout looked at both guns. Then he opened the back door, leaned in, and with a jerk brought the suitcase out. He was turning to face them when Matt said: 'Just walk up the road. Just ahead.'

Strout turned to walk, the suitcase in his right hand, and Matt and Willis followed; as Strout cleared the front of his car he dropped the suitcase and, ducking, took one step that was the beginning of a sprint to his right. The gun kicked in Matt's hand, and the explosion of the shot surrounded him, isolated him in a nimbus of sound that cut him off from all his time, all his history, isolated him standing absolutely still on the dirt road with the gun in his hand, looking down at Richard Strout squirming on his belly, kicking one leg behind him, pushing himself forward, toward the woods. Then Matt went to him and shot him once in the back of the head.

Driving south to Boston, wearing both gloves now, staying in the middle lane and looking often in the rearview mirror at Willis's headlights, he relived the suitcase dropping, the quick dip and turn of Strout's back, and the kick of the gun, the sound of the shot. When he walked to Strout, he still existed within the first shot, still trembled and breathed with it. The second shot and the burial seemed to be happening to someone else, someone he was watching. He and Willis each held an arm and pulled Strout face-down off the road and into the woods, his bouncing sliding belt white under the trees where it was so dark that when they stopped at the top of the knoll, panting and sweating, Matt could not see where Strout's blue shirt ended and the earth began. They pulled off the branches then dragged Strout to the edge of the hole and went behind him and lifted his legs and pushed him in. They stood still for a moment. The woods were quiet save for their breathing, and Matt remembered hearing the movements of birds and small animals after the first shot. Or maybe he had not heard them. Willis went down to the road. Matt could see him clearly out on the tan dirt, could see the glint of Strout's car and, beyond the road, the gravel pit. Willis came back up the knoll with the suitcase. He dropped it in the hole and took off his gloves and they went down to his car for the spades. They worked quietly. Sometimes they paused to listen to the woods. When they were finished Willis turned on his flashlight and they covered the earth with leaves and branches and then went down to the spot in front of the car, and while Matt held the light Willis crouched and sprinkled dust on the blood, backing up till he reached the grass and leaves, then he used leaves until they had worked up to the grave again. They did not stop. They walked around the grave and through the woods, using the light on the ground, looking up through the trees to where they ended at the lake. Neither of them spoke above the sounds of their heavy and clumsy strides through low brush and over fallen branches. Then they reached it: wide and dark, lapping softly at the bank, pine needles smooth under Matt's feet, moonlight on the lake, a small island near its middle, with black, tall evergreens. He took out the gun and threw for the island: taking two steps back on the pine needles, striding with the throw and going to one knee as he followed through, looking up to see the dark shapeless object arcing downward, splashing.

They left Strout's car in Boston, in front of an apartment building on Commonwealth Avenue. When they got back to town Willis drove slowly over the bridge and Matt threw the keys into the Merrimack. The sky was turning light. Willis let him out a block from his house, and walking home he listened for sounds from the houses he passed. They were quiet. A light was on in his living room. He turned it off and undressed in there, and went softly toward the bedroom; in the hall he smelled the smoke, and he stood in the bedroom doorway and looked at the orange of her cigarette in the dark. The curtains were closed. He went to the closet and put his shoes on the floor and felt for a hanger.

'Did you do it?' she said.

He went down the hall to the bathroom and in the dark he washed his hands and face. Then he went to her, lay on his back, and pulled the sheet up to his throat.

'Are you all right?' she said.

'I think so.'

Now she touched him, lying on her side, her hand on his belly, his thigh.

'Tell me,' she said.

He started from the beginning, in the parking lot at the bar; but soon with his eyes closed and Ruth petting him, he spoke of Strout's house: the order, the woman presence, the picture on the wall.

'The way she was smiling,' he said.

'What about it?'

'I don't know. Did you ever see Strout's girl? When you saw him in town?'

'No.'

'I wonder who she was.'

Then he thought: *not was: is. Sleeping now she is his girl.* He opened his eyes, then closed them again. There was more light beyond the curtains. With Ruth now he left Strout's house and told again his lie to Strout, gave him again that hope that Strout must have for a while believed, else he would have to believe only the gun pointed at him for the last two hours of his life. And with Ruth he saw again the dropping suitcase, the darting move to the right: and he told of the first shot, feeling her hand on him but his heart isolated still, beating on the road still in that explosion like thunder. He told her the rest, but the words had no images for him, he did not see himself doing what the words said he had done; the only saw himself on that road.

'We can't tell the other kids,' she said. 'It'll hurt them, thinking he got away. But we mustn't.'

'No.'

She was holding him, wanting him, and he wished he could make love with her but he could not. He saw Frank and Mary Ann making love in her bed, their eyes closed, their bodies brown and smelling of the sea; the other girl was faceless, bodiless, but he felt her sleeping now; and he saw Frank and Strout, their faces alive; he saw red and yellow leaves falling to earth, then snow: falling and freezing and falling; and holding Ruth, his cheek touching her breast, he shuddered with a sob that he kept silent in his heart.

HELPING

Robert Stone

One gray November day, Elliot went to Boston for the afternoon. The wet streets seemed cold and lonely. He sensed a broken promise in the city's elegance and verve. Old hopes tormented him like phantom limbs, but he did not drink. He had joined Alcoholics Anonymous fifteen months before.

Christmas came. childless, a festival of regret. His wife went to Mass and cooked a turkey. Sober, Elliot walked in the woods.

In January, blizzards swept down from the Arctic until the weather became too cold for snow. The Shawmut Valley grew quiet and crystalline. In the white silences, Elliot could hear the boards of his house contract and feel a shrinking in his bones. Each dusk, starveling deer came out of the wooded swamp behind the house to graze his orchard for whatever raccoons had uncovered and left behind. At night he lay beside his sleeping wife listening to the baying of dog packs running them down in the deep moonshadowed snow.

Day in, day out, he was sober. At times it was almost stimulating. But he could not shake off the sensations he had felt in Boston. In his mind's eye he could see dead leaves rattling along brick gutters and savor that day's desperation. The brief outing had undermined him.

Sober, however, he remained, until the day a man named Blankenship came into his office at the state hospital for counseling. Blankenship had red hair, a brutal face and a sneaking manner. He was a sponger and petty thief whom Elliot had seen a number of times before.

'I been having this dream,' Blankenship announced loudly. His voice was not pleasant. His skin was unwholesome. Every time he got arrested the court sent him to the psychiatrists and the psychiatrists, who spoke little English, sent him to Elliot.

Blankenship had joined the army after his first burglary but had never served east of the Rhine. After a few months in Wiesbaden, he had been discharged for reasons of unsuitability, but he told everyone he was a veteran of the Vietnam War. He went about in a tiger suit. Elliot had had enough of him.

'Dreams are boring,' Elliot told him.

Blankenship was outraged. 'Whaddaya mean?' he demanded.

During counseling sessions Elliot usually moved his chair into the middle of the room in order to seem accessible to his clients. Now he stayed securely behind his desk. He did not care to seem accessible to Blankenship. 'What I said, Mr. Blankenship. Other people's dreams are boring. Didn't you ever hear that?'

'Boring?' Blankenship frowned. He seemed unable to imagine a meaning for the word.

Elliot picked up a pencil and set its point quivering on his desktop blotter. He gazed into his client's slack-jawed face. The Blankenship family made their way through life as strolling litigants, and young Blankenship's specialty was slipping on ice cubes. Hauled off the pavement, he would hassle the doctors in Emergency for pain pills and hurry to a law clinic. The Blankenships had threatened suit against half the property owners in the southern part of the state. What they could not extort at law they stole. But even the Blankenship family had abandoned Blankenship. His last visit to the hospital had been subsequent to an arrest for lifting a case of hot-dog rolls from Woolworth's. He lived in a Goodwill depository bin in Wyndham.

'Now I suppose you want to tell me your dream. Is that right, Mr. Blankenship?'

Blankenship looked left and right like a dog surrendering eye contact. 'Don't you want to hear it?' he asked humbly.

Elliot was unmoved. 'Tell me something, Blankenship. Was your dream about Vietnam?'

At the mention of the word 'Vietnam,' Blankenship customarily broke into a broad smile. Now he looked guilty and guarded. He shrugged. 'Ya.'

'How come you have dreams about that place, Blankenship? You were never there.'

'Whaddaya mean?' Blankenship began to say, but Elliot cut him off.

'You were never there, my man. You never saw the goddamn place. You have no business dreaming about it! You better cut it out!'

He had raised his voice to the extent that the secretary outside his open door paused at her computer.

'Lemme alone,' Blankenship said fearfully. 'Some doctor you are.'

'It's all right,' Elliot assured him. 'I'm not a doctor.'

'Everybody's on my case,' Blankenship said. His moods were volatile. He began to weep.

Elliot watched the tears roll down Blankenship's chapped, pitted cheeks. He cleared his throat. 'Look, fella . . .' he began. He felt at a loss. He felt like telling Blankenship that things were tough all over.

Blankenship sniffed and telescoped his neck and after a moment looked at Elliot. His look was disconcertingly trustful; he was used to being counseled.

'Really, you know, it's ridiculous for you to tell me your problems have to do with Nam. You were never over there. It was me over there, Blankenship. Not you.'

Blankenship leaned forward and put his forehead on his knees.

'Your troubles have to do with here and now,' Elliot told his client. 'Fantasies aren't helpful.'

His voice sounded overripe and hypocritical in his own ears. What a dreadful business, he thought. What an awful job this is. Anger was driving him crazy.

Blankenship straightened up and spoke through his tears. 'This dream . . .' he said. 'I'm scared.'

Elliot felt ready to endure a great deal in order not to hear Blankenship' s dream.

'I'm not the one you see about that,' he said. In the end he knew his duty. He sighed. 'OK. All right. Tell me about it.'

'Yeah?' Blankenship asked with leaden sarcasm. 'Yeah? You think dreams are friggin' boring!'

'No, no,' Elliot said. He offered Blankenship a tissue and Blankenship took one. 'That was sort of off the top of my head. I didn't really mean it.'

Blankenship fixed his eyes on dreaming distance. 'There's a feeling that goes with it. With the dream.' Then he shook his head in revulsion and looked at Elliot as though he had only just awakened. 'So what do you think? You think it's boring?'

'Of course not,' Elliot said. 'A physical feeling?'

'Ya. It's like I'm floating in rubber.'

He watched Elliot stealthily, aware of quickened attention. Elliot had caught dengue in Vietnam and during his weeks of delirium had felt vaguely as though he were floating in rubber.

'What are you seeing in this dream?'

Blankenship only shook his head. Elliot suffered a brief but intense attack of rage.

'Hey, Blankenship,' he said equably, 'here I am, man. You can see I'm listening.'

'What I saw was black,' Blankenship said. He spoke in an odd tremolo. His behavior was quite different from anything Elliot had come to expect from him.

'Black? What was it?'

'Smoke. The sky maybe.'

'The sky?' Elliot asked.

'It was all black. I was scared.'

In a waking dream of his own, Elliot felt the muscles on his neck distend. He was looking up at a sky that was black, filled with smoke-swollen clouds, lit with fires, damped with blood and rain.

'What were you scared of?' he asked Blankenship.

'I don't know,' Blankenship said.

Elliot could not drive the black sky from his inward eye. It was as though Blankenship's dream had infected his own mind.

'You don't know? You don't know what you were scared of?'

Blankenship's posture was rigid. Elliot, who knew the aspect of true fear, recognized it there in front of him.

'The Nam,' Blankenship said.

'You're not even old enough,' Elliot told him.

Blankenship sat trembling with joined palms between his thighs. His face was flushed and not in the least ennobled by pain. He had trouble with alcohol and drugs. He had trouble with everything.

'So wherever your black sky is, it isn't Vietnam.'

Things were so unfair, Elliot thought. It was unfair of Blankenship to appropriate the condition of a Vietnam veteran. The trauma inducing his post-traumatic stress had been nothing more serious than his own birth, a routine procedure. Now, in addition to the poverty, anxiety and confusion that would always be his life's lot, he had been visited with irony. It was all arbitrary and some people simply got elected. Everyone knew that who had been where Blankenship had not.

'Because, I assure you, Mr. Blankenship, you were never there.'

'Whaddaya mean?' Blankenship asked.

*

When Blankenship was gone, Elliot leafed through his file and saw that the psychiatrists had passed him upstairs without recording a diagnosis. Disproportionately angry, he went out to the secretary's desk.

'Nobody wrote up that last patient,' he said. 'I'm not supposed to see people without a diagnosis. The shrinks are just passing the buck.'

The secretary was a tall, solemn redhead with prominent front teeth and a slight speech disorder. 'Dr. Sayyid will have kittens if he hears you call him a shrink, Chas. He's already complained. He hates being called a shrink.'

'Then he came to the wrong country,' Elliot said. 'He can go back to his own.'

The woman giggled. 'He *is* the doctor, Chas.'

'Hates being called a shrink!' He threw the file on the secretary's table and stormed back toward his office. 'That fucking little zip couldn't give you a decent haircut. He's a prescription clerk.'

The secretary looked about her guiltily and shook her head. She was used to him.

Elliot succeeded in calming himself down after a while, but the image of black sky remained with him. At first he thought he would be able to shrug the whole thing off. After a few minutes, he picked up his phone and dialed Blankenship's probation officer.

'The Vietnam thing is all he has,' the probation officer explained. 'I guess he picked it up around.'

'His descriptions are vivid,' Elliot said.

'You mean they sound authentic?'

'I mean he had me going today. He was ringing my bells.'

'Good for Blanky. Think he believes it himself?'

'Yes,' Elliot said. 'He believes it himself now.'

Elliot told the probation officer about Blankenship's current arrest, which was for showering illegally at midnight in the Wyndham Regional High School. He asked what Probation knew about Blankenship's present relationship with his family.

'You kiddin'?' the P.O. asked. 'They're all locked down. The whole family's inside. The old man's in Bridgewater. Little Donny's in San Quentin or somewhere. Their dog's in the pound.'

Elliot had lunch alone in the hospital staff cafeteria. On the far side of the double-glazed windows, the day was darkening as an expected snowstorm gathered. Along Route 7, ancient elms stood frozen against the gray sky. When he had finished his sandwich and coffee, he sat staring out at the winter afternoon. His anger had given way to an insistent anxiety.

On the way back to his office, he stopped at the hospital gift shop for a copy of *Sports Illustrated* and a candy bar. When he was inside again, he closed the door and put his feet up. It was Friday and he had no appointments for the remainder of the day, nothing to do but write a few letters and read the office mail.

Elliot's cubicle in the social services department was windowless and lined with bookshelves. When he found himself unable to concentrate on the magazine and without any heart for his paperwork, he ran his eye over the row of books beside his chair. There were volumes by Heinrich Muller and Carlos Castaneda, Jones's life of Freud and *The Golden Bough*. The books aroused a revulsion in Elliot. Their present uselessness repelled him.

Over and over again, detail by detail, he tried to recall his conversation with Blankenship.

'You were never there,' he heard himself explaining. He was trying to get the whole incident straightened out after the fact. Something was wrong. Dread crept over him like a paralysis. He ate his candy bar without tasting it. He knew that the craving for sweets was itself a bad sign.

Blankenship had misappropriated someone else's dream and made it his own. It made no difference whether you had been there, after all. The dreams had crossed the ocean. They were in the air.

He took his glasses off and put them on his desk and sat with his arms folded, looking into the well of light from his desk lamp. There seemed to be nothing but whirl inside him. Unwelcome things came and went in his mind's eye. His heart beat faster. He could not control the headlong promiscuity of his thoughts.

It was possible to imagine larval dreams traveling in suspended animation undetectable in a host brain. They could be divided and regenerate like flatworms, hide in seams and bedding, in war stories, laughter, snapshots. They could rot your socks and turn your memory into a black and green blister. Green for the hills, black for the sky above. At daybreak they hung themselves up in rows like bats. At dusk they went out to look for dreamers.

Elliot put his jacket on and went into the outer office, where the secretary sat frowning into the measured sound and light of her machine. She must enjoy its sleekness and order, he thought. She was divorced. Four red-headed kids between ten and seventeen lived with her in an unpainted house across from Stop & Shop. Elliot liked her and had come to find her attractive. He managed a smile for her.

'Ethel, I think I'm going to pack it in,' he declared. It seemed awkward to be leaving early without a reason.

'Jack wants to talk to you before you go, Chas.'

Elliot looked at her blankly.

Then his colleague, Jack Sprague, having heard his voice, called from the adjoining cubicle. 'Chas, what about Sunday's games? Shall I call you with the spread?'

'I don't know,' Elliot said. 'I'll phone you tomorrow.'

'This is a big decision for him,' Jack Sprague told the secretary. 'He might lose twenty-five bucks.'

At present, Elliot drew a slightly higher salary than Jack Sprague, although Jack had a Ph.D. and Elliot was only an M.S.W. Different branches of the state government employed them.

'Twenty-five bucks,' said the woman. 'If you guys have no better use for twenty-five bucks, give it to me.'

'Where are you off to, by the way?' Sprague asked.

Elliot began to answer, but for a moment no reply occurred to him. He shrugged. 'I have to get back,' he finally stammered. 'I promised Grace.'

'Was that Blankenship I saw leaving?'

Elliot nodded.

'It's February,' Jack said. 'How come he's not in Florida?'

'I don't know,' Elliot said. He put on his coat and walked to the door. 'I'll see you.'

'Have a nice weekend,' the secretary said. She and Sprague looked after him indulgently as he walked toward the main corridor.

'Are Chas and Grace going out on the town?' she said to Sprague. 'What do you think?'

'That would be the day,' Sprague said. 'Tomorrow he'll come back over here and read all day. He spends every weekend holed up in this goddamn office while she does something or other at the church.' He shook his head. 'Every night he's at A.A. and she's home alone.'

Ethel savored her overbite. 'Jack,' she said teasingly, 'are you thinking what I think you're thinking? Shame on you.'

'I'm thinking I'm glad I'm not him, that's what I'm thinking. That's as much as I'll say.'

'Yeah, well, I don't care,' Ethel said. 'Two salaries and no kids, that's the way to go, boy.'

Elliot went out through the automatic doors of the emergency bay and the cold closed over him. He walked across the hospital parking lot with his eyes on the pavement, his hands thrust deep in his overcoat pockets, skirting patches of shattered ice. There was no wind, but the motionles air stung; the metal frames of his glasses burned his skin. Curlicues of mud-brown ice coated the soiled snowbanks along the street. Although it was still afternoon, the street lights had come on.

The lock on his car door had frozen and he had to breathe on the keyhole to fit the key. When the engine turned over, Jussi Björling's recording of the Handel Largo filled the car interior. He snapped it off at once.

Halted at the first stoplight, he began to feel the want of a destination. The fear and impulse to flight that had got him out of the office faded, and he had no desire to go home. He was troubled by a peculiar impatience that might have been with time itself. It was as though he were waiting for something. The sensation made him feel anxious; it was unfamiliar but not altogether unpleasant. When the light changed he drove on, past the Gulf station and the firehouse and between the greens of Ilford Common. At the far end of the common he swung into the parking lot of the Packard Conway Library and stopped with the engine running. What he was experiencing, he thought, was the principle of possibility.

He turned off the engine and went out again into the cold. Behind the leaded library windows he could see the librarian pouring coffee in her tiny private office. The librarian was a Quaker of socialist convictions named Candace Music, who was Elliot's cousin.

The Conway Library was all dark wood and etched mirrors, a Gothic saloon. Years before, out of work and booze-whipped, Elliot had gone to hide there. Because Candace was a classicist's widow and knew some Greek, she was one of the few people in the valley with whom Elliot had cared to speak in those days. Eventually, it had seemed to him that all their conversations tended toward Vietnam, so he had gone less and less often. Elliot was the only Vietnam veteran Candace knew well enough to chat with, and he had come to suspect that he was being probed for the edification of the East Ilford Friends Meeting. At that time he had still pretended to talk easily about his war and had prepared little discourses and picaresque anecdotes to recite on demand. Earnest seekers like Candace had caused him great secret distress.

Candace came out of her office to find him at the checkout desk. He watched her brow furrow with concern as she composed a smile. 'Chas, what a surprise. You haven't been in for an age.'

'Sure I have, Candace. I went to all the Wednesday films last fall. I work just across the road.'

'I know, dear,' Candace said. 'I always seem to miss you.'

A cozy fire burned in the hearth, an antique brass clock ticked along on the marble mantel above it. On a couch near the fireplace an old man sat upright, his mouth open, asleep among half a dozen soiled plastic bags. Two teenage girls whispered over their homework at a table under the largest window.

'Now that I'm here,' he said, laughing, 'I can't remember what I came to get.'

'Stay and get warm,' Candace told him. 'Got a minute? Have a cup of coffee.'

Elliot had nothing but time, but he quickly realized that he did not want to stay and pass it with Candace. He had no clear idea of why he had come to the library. Standing at the checkout desk, he accepted coffee. She attended him with an air of benign supervision, as though he were a Chinese peasant and she a medical missionary, like her father. Candace was tall and plain, more handsome in her middle sixties than she had ever been.

'Why don't we sit down?'

He allowed her to gentle him into a chair by the fire. They made a threesome with the sleeping old man.

'Have you given up translating, Chas? I hope not.'

'Not at all,' he said. Together they had once rendered a few fragments of Sophocles into verse. She was good at clever rhymes.

'You come in so rarely, Chas. Ted's books go to waste.'

After her husband's death, Candace had donated his books to the

Conway, where they reposed in a reading room inscribed to his memory, untouched among foreign-language volumes, local gene-alogies and books in large type for the elderly.

'I have a study in the barn,' he told Candace. 'I work there. When I have time.' The lie was absurd, but he felt the need of it.

'And you're working with Vietnam veterans,' Candace declared.

'Supposedly,' Elliot said. He was growing impatient with her nodding solicitude.

'Actually,' he said, 'I came in for the new Oxford *Classical World*. I thought you'd get it for the library and I could have a look before I spent my hard-earned cash.'

Candace beamed. 'You've come to the right place, Chas, I'm happy to say.' He thought she looked disproportionately happy. 'I have it.'

'Good,' Elliot said, standing. 'I'll just take it, then. I can't really stay.'

Candace took his cup and saucer and stood as he did. When the library telephone rang, she ignored it, reluctant to let him go. 'How's Grace?' she asked.

'Fine,' Elliot said. 'Grace is well.'

At the third ring she went to the desk. When her back was turned, he hesitated for a moment and then went outside.

The gray afternoon had softened into night, and it was snowing. The falling snow whirled like a furious mist in the headlight beams on Route 7 and settled implacably on Elliot's cheeks and eyelids. His heart, for no good reason, leaped up in childlike expectation. He had run away from a dream and encountered possibility. He felt in possession of a promise. He began to walk toward the roadside lights.

Only gradually did he begin to understand what had brought him there and what the happy anticipation was that fluttered in his breast. Drinking, he had started his evenings from the Conway Library. He would arrive hung over in the early afternoon to browse and read. When the old pain rolled in with dusk, he would walk down to the Midway Tavern for a remedy. Standing in the snow outside the library, he realized that he had contrived to promise himself a drink.

Ahead, through the storm, he could see the beer signs in the Midway's window warm and welcoming. Snowflakes spun around his head like an excitement.

Outside the Midway's package store, he paused with his hand on the doorknob. There was an old man behind the counter whom Elliot remembered from his drinking days. When he was inside, he realized that the old man neither knew nor cared who he was. The package store was thick with dust; it was on the counter, the shelves, the bottles themselves. The old counterman looked dusty. Elliot bought a bottle of King William Scotch and put it in the inside pocket of his overcoat.

Passing the windows of the Midway Tavern, Elliot could see the ranks of bottles aglow behind the bar. The place was crowded with men leaving the afternoon shifts at the shoe and felt factories. No one turned to note him when he passed inside. There was a single stool vacant at the bar and he took it. His heart beat faster. Bruce Springsteen was on the jukebox.

The bartender was a club fighter from Pittsfield called Jackie G., with whom Elliot had often gossiped. Jackie G. greeted him as though he had been in the previous evening. 'Say, babe?'

'How do,' Elliot said.

A couple of the men at the bar eyed his shirt and tie. Confronted with the bartender, he felt impelled to explain his presence. 'Just thought I'd stop by,' he told Jackie G. 'Just thought I'd have one. Saw the light. The snow . . .' He chuckled expansively.

'Good move,' the bartender said. 'Scotch?'

'Double,' Elliot said.

When he shoved two dollars forward along the bar, Jackie G. pushed one of the bills back to him. 'Happy hour, babe.'

'Ah,' Elliot said. He watched Jackie pour the double. 'Not a moment too soon.'

For five minutes or so, Elliot sat in his car in the barn with the engine running and his Handel tape on full volume. He had driven over from East Ilford in a Baroque ecstasy, swinging and swaying and singing along. When the tape ended, he turned off the engine and poured some Scotch into an apple juice container to store providentially beneath the car seat. Then he took the tape and the Scotch into the house with him. He was lying on the sofa in the dark living room, listening to the Largo, when he heard his wife's car in the driveway. By the time Grace had made her way up the icy back-porch steps, he was able to hide the Scotch and rinse his glass clean in the kitchen sink. The drinking life, he thought, was lived moment by moment.

Soon she was in the tiny cloakroom struggling off with her overcoat.

In the process she knocked over a cross-country ski, which stood propped against the cloakroom wall. It had been more than a year since Elliot had used the skis.

She came into the kitchen and sat down at the table to take off her boots. Her lean, freckled face was flushed with the cold, but her eyes looked weary. 'I wish you'd put those skis down in the barn,' she told him. 'You never use them.'

'I always like to think,' Elliot said, 'that I'll start the morning off skiing.'

'Well, you never do,' she said. 'How long have you been home?'

'Practically just walked in,' he said. Her pointing out that he no longer skied in the morning enraged him. 'I stopped at the Conway Library to get the new Oxford *Classical World*. Candace ordered it.'

Her look grew troubled. She had caught something in his voice. With dread and bitter satisfaction, Elliot watched his wife detect the smell of whiskey.

'Oh God,' she said. 'I don't believe it.'

Let's get it over with, he thought. Let's have the song and dance.

She sat up straight in her chair and looked at him in fear.

'Oh, Chas,' she said, 'how could you?'

For a moment he was tempted to try to explain it all.

'The fact is,' Elliot told his wife, 'I hate people who start the day cross-country skiing.'

She shook her head in denial and leaned her forehead on her palm and cried.

He looked into the kitchen window and saw his own distorted image. 'The fact is I think I'll start tomorrow morning by stringing head-high razor wire across Anderson's trail.'

The Andersons were the Elliots' nearest neighbors. Loyall Anderson was a full professor of government at the state university, thirty miles away. Anderson and his wife were blond and both of them were over six feet tall. They had two blond children, who qualified for the gifted class in the local school but attended regular classes in token of the Andersons' opposition to elitism.

'Sure,' Elliot said. 'Stringing wire's good exercise. It's life-affirming in its own way.'

The Andersons started each and every day with a brisk morning glide along a trail that they partly maintained. They skied well and presented a pleasing, wholesome sight. If, in the course of their adventure, they encountered a snowmobile, Darlene Anderson would affect to choke and cough, indicating her displeasure. If the snowmobile approached them from behind and the trail was narrow, the Andersons would decline to let it pass, asserting their statutory right-of-way.

'I don't want to hear your violent fantasies,' Grace said.

Elliot was picturing razor wire, the army kind. He was picturing the decapitated Andersons, their blood and jaunty ski caps bright on the white trail. He was picturing their severed heads, their earnest blue eyes and large white teeth reflecting the virginal morning snow. Although Elliot hated snowmobiles, he hated the Andersons far more.

He looked at his wife and saw that she had stopped crying. Her long, elegant face was rigid and lipless.

'Know what I mean? One string at mommy-and-daddy level for Loyall and Darlene. And a bitty wee string at kiddie level for Skippy and Samantha, those cunning little whizzes.'

'Stop it,' she said to him.

'Sorry,' Elliot told her.

Stiff with shame, he went and took his bottle out of the cabinet into which he had thrust it and poured a drink. He was aware of her eyes on him. As he drank, a fragment from old Music's translation of *Medea* came into his mind. 'Old friend, I have to weep. The gods and I went mad together and made things as they are.' It was such a waste; eighteen months of struggle thrown away. But there was no way to get the stuff back in the bottle.

'I'm very sorry,' he said. 'You know I'm very sorry, don't you, Grace?'

The delectable Handel arias spun on in the next room.

'You must stop,' she said. 'You must make yourself stop before it takes over.'

'It's out of my hands,' Elliot said. He showed her his empty hands. 'It's beyond me.'

'You'll lose your job, Chas.' She stood up at the table and leaned on it, staring wide-eyed at him. Drunk as he was, the panic in her voice frightened him. 'You'll end up in jail again.'

'One engages,' Elliot said, 'and then one sees.'

'How can you have done it?' she demanded. 'You promised me.'

'First the promises,' Elliot said, 'and then the rest.'

'Last time was supposed to be the last time,' she said.

'Yes,' he said, 'I remember.'

'I can't stand it,' she said. 'You reduce me to hysterics.' She wrung her hands for him to see. 'See? Here I am, I'm in hysterics.'

'What can I say?' Elliot asked. He went to the bottle and refilled his glass. 'Maybe you shouldn't watch.'

'You want me to be forbearing, Chas? I'm not going to be.'

'The last thing I want,' Elliot said, 'is an argument.'

'I'll give you a fucking argument. You didn't have to drink. All you had to do was come home.'

'That must have been the problem,' he said.

Then he ducked, alert at the last possible second to the missile that came for him at hairline level. Covering up, he heard the shattering of glass, and a fine rain of crystals enveloped him. She had sailed the sugar bowl at him; it had smashed against the wall above his head and there was sugar and glass in his hair.

'You bastard!' she screamed. 'You are undermining me!'

'You ought not to throw things at me,' Elliot said. 'I don't throw things at you.'

He left her frozen into her follow-through and went into the living room to turn the music off. When he returned she was leaning back against the wall, rubbing her right elbow with her left hand. Her eyes were bright. She had picked up one of her boots from the middle of the kitchen floor and stood holding it.

'What the hell do you mean, that must have been the problem?'

He set his glass on the edge of the sink with an unsteady hand and turned to her. 'What do I mean? I mean that most of the time I'm putting one foot in front of the other like a good soldier and I'm out of it from the neck up. But there are times when I don't think I will ever be dead enough—or dead long enough—to get the taste of this life off my teeth. That's what I mean!'

She looked at him dry-eyed. 'Poor fella,' she said.

'What you have to understand, Grace, is that this drink I'm having'—he raised the glass toward her in a gesture of salute—'is the only worthwhile thing I've done in the last year and a half. It's the only thing in my life that means jack shit, the closest thing to satisfaction I've had. Now how can you begrudge me that? It's the best I'm capable of.'

'You'll go too far,' she said to him. 'You'll see.'

'What's that, Grace? A threat to walk?' He was grinding his teeth. 'Don't make me laugh. You, walk? You, the friend of the unfortunate?'

'Don't you hit me,' she said when she looked at his face. 'Don't you dare.'

'You, the Christian Queen of Calvary, walk? Why, I don't believe that for minute.'

She ran a hand through her hair and bit her lip. 'No, we stay,' she said. Anger and distraction made her look young. Her cheeks blazed rosy against the general pallor of her skin. 'In my family we stay until the fella dies. That's the tradition. We stay and pour it for them and they die.'

He put his drink down and shook his head.

'I thought we'd come through,' Grace said. 'I was sure.'

'No,' Elliot said. 'Not altogether.'

They stood in silence for a minute. Elliot sat down at the oilcloth-covered table. Grace walked around it and poured herself a whiskey.

'You are undermining me, Chas. You are making things impossible for me and I just don't know.' She drank and winced. 'I'm not going to stay through another drunk. I'm telling you right now. I haven't got it in me. I'll die.'

He did not want to look at her. He watched the flakes settle against the glass of the kitchen door. 'Do what you feel the need of,' he said.

'I just can't take it,' she said. Her voice was not scolding but measured and reasonable. 'It's February. And I went to court this morning and lost Vopotik.'

Once again, he thought, my troubles are going to be obviated by those of the deserving poor. He said, 'Which one was that?'

'Don't you remember them? The three-year-old with the broken fingers?'

He shrugged. Grace sipped her whiskey.

'I told you. I said I had a three-year-old with broken fingers, and you said, "Maybe he owed somebody money."'

'Yes,' he said, 'I remember now.'

'You ought to see the Vopotiks, Chas. The woman is young and obese. She's so young that for a while I thought I could get to her as a juvenile. The guy is a biker. They believe the kid came from another planet to control their lives. They believe this literally, both of them.'

'You shouldn't get involved that way,' Elliot said. 'You should leave it to the caseworkers.'

'They scared their first caseworker all the way to California. They were following me to work.'

'You didn't tell me.'

'Are you kidding?' she asked. 'Of course I didn't.' To Elliot's surprise, his wife poured herself a second whiskey. 'You know how they address the child? As "dude." She says to it, "Hey, dude."' Grace shuddered with loathing. 'You can't imagine! The woman munching Twinkies. The kid smelling of shit. They're high morning, noon and night, but you can't get anybody for that these days.'

'People must really hate it,' Elliot said, 'when somebody tells them they're not treating their kids right.'

'They definitely don't want to hear it,' Grace said. 'You're right.' She sat stirring her drink, frowning into the glass. 'The Vopotik child will die, I think.'

'Surely not,' Elliot said.

'This one I think will die,' Grace said. She took a deep breath and puffed out her cheeks and looked at him forlornly. 'The situation's extreme. Of course, sometimes you wonder whether it makes any difference. That's the big question, isn't it?'

'I would think,' Elliot said, 'that would be the one question you didn't ask.'

'But you do,' she said. 'You wonder: Ought they to live at all? To continue the cycle?' She put a hand to her hair and shook her head as if in confusion. 'Some of these folks, my God, the poor things cannot put Wednesday on top of Tuesday to save their lives.'

'It's a trick,' Elliot agreed, 'a lot of them can't manage.'

'And kids are small, they're handy and underfoot. They make noise. They can't hurt you back.'

'I suppose child abuse is something people can do together,' Elliot said.

'Some kids are obnoxious. No question about it.'

'I wouldn't know,' Elliot said.

'Maybe you should stop complaining. Maybe you're better off. Maybe your kids are better off unborn.'

'Better off or not,' Elliot said, 'it looks like they'll stay that way.'

'I mean our kids, of course,' Grace said. 'I'm not blaming you, understand? It's just that here we are with you drunk again and me losing Vopotik, so I thought why not get into the big unaskable questions.' She got up and folded her arms and began to pace up and down the kitchen. 'Oh,' she said when her eye fell upon the bottle, 'that's good stuff, Chas. You won't mind if I have another? I'll leave you enough to get loaded on.'

Elliot watched her pour. So much pain, he thought; such anger and confusion. He was tired of pain, anger and confusion; they were what had got him in trouble that very morning.

The liquor seemed to be giving him a perverse lucidity when all he now required was oblivion. His rage, especially, was intact in its salting of alcohol. Its contours were palpable and bleeding at the borders. Booze was good for rage. Booze could keep it burning through the darkest night.

'What happened in court?' he asked his wife.

She was leaning on one arm against the wall, her long, strong body flexed at the hip. Holding her glass, she stared angrily toward the invisible fields outside. 'I lost the child,' she said.

Elliot thought that a peculiar way of putting it. He said nothing.

'The court convened in an atmosphere of high hilarity. It may be Hate Month around here but it was buddy-buddy over at Ilford Courthouse. The room was full of bikers and bikers' lawyers. A colorful crowd. There was a lot of bonding.' She drank and shivered. 'They didn't think too well of me. They don't think too well of broads as lawyers. Neither does the judge. The judge has the common touch. He's one of the boys.'

'Which judge?' Elliot asked.

'Buckley. A man of about sixty. Know him? Lots of veins on his nose?'

Elliot shrugged.

'I thought I had done my homework,' Grace told him. 'But suddenly I had nothing but paper. No witnesses. It was Margolis at Valley Hospital who spotted the radiator burns. He called us in the first place. Suddenly he's got to keep his reservation for a campsite in St. John. So Buckley threw his deposition out.' She began to chew on a fingernail. 'The caseworkers have vanished—one's in L.A., the other's in Nepal. I went in there and got run over. I lost the child.'

'It happens all the time,' Elliot said. 'Doesn't it?'

'This one shouldn't have been lost, Chas. These people aren't simply confused. They're weird. They stink.'

'You go messing into anybody's life,' Elliot said, 'that's what you'll find.'

'If the child stays in that house,' she said, 'he's going to die.'

'You did your best,' he told his wife. 'Forget it.'

She pushed the bottle away. She was holding a water glass that was almost a third full of whiskey.

'That's what the commissioner said.'

Elliot was thinking of how she must have looked in court to the cherry-faced judge and the bikers and their lawyers. Like the schoolteachers who had tormented their childhoods, earnest and tight-assed, humorless and self-righteous. It was not surprising that things had gone against her.

He walked over to the window and faced his reflection again. 'Your optimism always surprises me.'

'My optimism? Where I grew up our principal cultural expression was the funeral. Whatever keeps me going, it isn't optimism.'

'No?' he asked. 'What is it?'

'I forget,' she said.

'Maybe it's your religious perspective. Your sense of the divine plan.'

She sighed in exasperation. 'Look, I don't think I want to fight anymore. I'm sorry I threw the sugar at you. I'm not your keeper. Pick on someone your own size.'

'Sometimes,' Elliot said, 'I try to imagine what it's like to believe that the sky is full of care and concern.'

'You want to take everything from me, do you?' She stood leaning against the back of her chair. 'That you can't take. It's the only part of my life you can't mess up.'

He was thinking that if it had not been for her he might not have survived. There could be no forgiveness for that. 'Your life? You've got all this piety strung out between Monadnock and Central America. And look at yourself. Look at your life.'

'Yes,' she said, 'look at it.'

'You should have been a nun. You don't know how to live.'

'I know that,' she said. 'That's why I stopped doing counseling. Because I'd rather talk the law than life.' She turned to him. 'You got everything I had, Chas. What's left I absolutely require.'

'I swear I would rather be a drunk,' Elliot said, 'than force myself to believe such trivial horseshit.'

'Well, you're going to have to do it without a straight man,' she said, 'because this time I'm not going to be here for you. Believe it or not.'

'I don't believe it,' Elliot said. 'Not my Grace.'

'You're really good at this,' she told him. 'You make me feel ashamed of my own name.'

'I love your name,' he said.

The telephone rang. They let it ring three times, and then Elliot went over and answered it.

'Hey, who's that?' a good-humored voice on the phone demanded. Elliot recited their phone number.

'Hey, I want to talk to your woman, man. Put her on.'

'I'll give her a message,' Elliot said.

'You put your woman on, man. Run and get her.'

Elliot looked at the receiver. He shook his head. 'Mr. Vopotik?'

'Never you fuckin' mind, man. I don't want to talk to you. I want to talk to the skinny bitch.'

Elliot hung up.

'Is it him?' she asked.

'I guess so.'

They waited for the phone to ring again and it shortly did.

'I'll talk to him,' Grace said. But Elliot already had the phone.

'Who are you, asshole?' the voice inquired. 'What's your fuckin' name, man?'

'Elliot,' Elliot said.

'Hey, don't hang up on me, Elliot. I won't put up with that. I told you go get that skinny bitch, man. You go do it.'

There were sounds of festivity in the background on the other end of the line—a stereo and drunken voices.

'Hey,' the voice declared. 'Hey, don't keep me waiting, man.'

'What do you want to say to her?' Elliot asked.

'That's none of your fucking business, fool. Do what I told you.'

'My wife is resting,' Elliot said. 'I'm taking her calls.'

He was answered by a shout of rage. He put the phone aside for a moment and finished his glass of whiskey. When he picked it up again the man on the line was screaming at him. 'That bitch tried to break up my family, man! She almost got away with it. You know what kind of pain my wife went through?'

'What kind?' Elliot asked.

For a few seconds he heard only the noise of the party. 'Hey, you're not drunk, are you, fella?'

'Certainly not,' Elliot insisted.

'You tell that skinny bitch she's gonna pay for what she did to my family, man. You tell her she can run but she can't hide. I don't care where you go—California, anywhere—I'll get to you.'

'Now that I have you on the phone,' Elliot said, 'I'd like to ask you a couple of questions. Promise you won't get mad?'

'Stop it!' Grace said to him. She tried to wrench the phone from his grasp, but he clutched it to his chest.

'Do you keep a journal?' Elliot asked the man on the phone. 'What's your hat size?'

'Maybe you think I can't get to you,' the man said. 'But I can get to you, man. I don't care who you are, I'll get to you. The brothers will get to you.'

'Well, there's no need to go to California. You know where we live.'

'For God's sake,' Grace said.

'Fuckin' right,' the man on the telephone said. 'Fuckin' right I know.'

'Come on over,' Elliot said.

'How's that?' the man on the phone asked.

'I said come on over. We'll talk about space travel. Comets and stuff. We'll talk astral projection. The moons of Jupiter.'

'You're making a mistake, fucker.'

'Come on over,' Elliot insisted. 'Bring your fat wife and your beat-up kid. Don't be embarrassed if your head's a little small.'

The telephone was full of music and shouting. Elliot held it away from his ear.

'Good work,' Grace said to him when he had replaced the receiver.

'I hope he comes,' Elliot said. 'I'll pop him.'

He went carefully down the cellar stairs, switched on the overhead light and began searching among the spiderwebbed shadows and fouled fishing line for his shotgun. It took him fifteen minutes to find it and his cleaning case. While he was still downstairs, he heard the telephone ring again and his wife answer it. He came upstairs and spread his shooting gear across the kitchen table. 'Was that him?'

She nodded wearily. 'He called back to play us the chain saw.'

'I've heard that melody before,' Elliot said.

He assembled his cleaning rod and swabbed out the shotgun barrel. Grace watched him, a hand to her forehead. 'God,' she said. 'What have I done? I'm so drunk.'

'Most of the time,' Elliot said, sighting down the barrel, 'I'm helpless in the face of human misery. Tonight I'm ready to reach out.'

'I'm finished,' Grace said. 'I'm through, Chas. I mean it.'

Elliot rammed three red shells into the shotgun and pumped one forward into the breech with a satisfying report. 'Me, I'm ready for some radical problem-solving. I'm going to spray that no-neck Slovak all over the yard.'

'He isn't a Slovak,' Grace said. She stood in the middle of the kitchen with her eyes closed. Her face was chalk white.

'What do you mean?' Elliot demanded. 'Certainly he's a Slovak.'

'No he's not,' Grace said.

'Fuck him anyway. I don't care what he is. I'll grease his ass.'

He took a handful of deer shells from the box and stuffed them in his jacket pockets.

'I'm not going to stay with you, Chas. Do you understand me?'

Elliot walked to the window and peered out at his driveway. 'He won't be alone. They travel in packs.'

'For God's sake!' Grace cried, and in the next instant bolted for the downstairs bathroom. Elliot went out, turned off the porch light and switched on a spotlight over the barn door. Back inside, he could hear Grace in the toilet being sick. He turned off the light in the kitchen.

He was still standing by the window when she came up behind him. It seemed strange and fateful to be standing in the dark near her, holding the shotgun. He felt ready for anything.

'I can't leave you alone down here drunk with a loaded shotgun,' she said. 'How can I?'

'Go upstairs,' he said.

'If I went upstairs it would mean I didn't care what happened. Do you understand? If I go it means I don't care anymore. Understand?'

'Stop asking me if I understand,' Elliot said. 'I understand fine.'

'I can't think,' she said in a sick voice. 'Maybe I don't care. I don't know. I'm going upstairs.'

'Good,' Elliot said.

*

When she was upstairs, Elliot took his shotgun and the whiskey into the dark living room and sat down in an armchair beside one of the lace-curtained windows. The powerful barn light illuminated the length of his driveway and the whole of the back yard. From the window at which he sat, he commanded a view of several miles in the direction of East Ilford. The two-lane blacktop road that ran there was the only one along which an enemy could pass.

He drank and watched the snow, toying with the safety of his 12-gauge Remington. He felt neither anxious nor angry now but only impatient to be done with whatever the night would bring. Drunkenness and the silent rhythm of the falling snow combined to make him feel outside of time and syntax.

Sitting in the dark room, he found himself confronting Blankenship's dream. He saw the bunkers and wire of some long-lost perimeter. The rank smell of night came back to him, the dread evening and quick dusk, the mysteries of outer darkness: fear, combat and death. Enervated by liquor, he began to cry. Elliot was sympathetic with other people's tears but ashamed of his own. He thought of his own tears as childish and excremental. He stifled whatever it was that had started them.

Now his whiskey tasted thin as water. Beyond the lightly frosted glass, illuminated snowflakes spun and settled sleepily on weighted pine boughs. He had found a life beyond the war after all, but in it he was still sitting in darkness, armed, enraged, waiting.

His eyes grew heavy as the snow came down. He felt as though he could be drawn up into the storm and he began to imagine that. He imagined his life with all its artifacts and appetites easing up the spout into white oblivion, everything obviated and foreclosed. He thought maybe he could go for that.

When he awakened, his left hand had gone numb against the trigger guard of his shotgun. The living room was full of pale, delicate light. He looked outside and saw that the storm was done with and the sky radiant and cloudless. The sun was still below the horizon.

Slowly Elliot got to his feet. The throbbing poison in his limbs served to remind him of the state of things. He finished the glass of whiskey on the windowsill beside his easy chair. Then he went to the hall closet to get a ski jacket, shouldered his shotgun and went outside.

There were two cleared acres behind his house; beyond them a trail descended into a hollow of pine forest and frozen swamp. Across the hollow, white pastures stretched to the ridge line, lambent under the lightening sky. A line of skeletal elms weighted with snow marked the course of frozen Shawmut Brook.

He found a pair of ski goggles in a jacket pocket and put them on and set out toward the tree line, gripping the shotgun, step by careful step in the knee-deep snow. Two raucous crows wheeled high overhead, their cries exploding the morning's silence. When the sun came over the ridge, he stood where he was and took in a deep breath. The risen sun warmed his face and he closed his eyes. It was windless and very cold.

Only after he had stood there for a while did he realize how tired he had become. The weight of the gun taxed him. It seemed infinitely wearying to contemplate another single step in the snow. He opened his eyes and closed them again. With sunup the world had gone blazing blue and white, and even with his tinted goggles its whiteness dazzled him and made his head ache. Behind his eyes, the hypnagogic patterns formed a monsoon-heavy tropical sky. He yawned. More than anything, he wanted to lie down in the soft, pure snow. If he could do that, he was certain he could go to sleep at once.

He stood in the middle of the field and listened to the crows. Fear, anger and sleep were the three primary conditions of life. He had learned that over there. Once he had thought fear the worst, but he had learned that the worst was anger. Nothing could fix it, neither alcohol nor medicine. It was a worm. It left him no peace. Sleep was the best.

He opened his eyes and pushed on until he came to the brow that overlooked the swamp. Just below, gliding along among the frozen cattails and bare scrub maple, was a man on skis. Elliot stopped to watch the man approach.

The skier's face was concealed by a red and blue ski mask. He wore snow goggles, a blue jumpsuit and a red woollen Norwegian hat. As he came, he leaned into the turns of the trail, moving silently and gracefully along. At the foot of the slope on which Elliot stood, the man looked up, saw him and slid to a halt. The man stood staring at him for a moment and then began to herringbone up the slope. In no time at all the skier stood no more than ten feet away, removing his goggles, and inside the woollen mask Elliot recognized the clear blue eyes of his neighbor, Professor Loyall Anderson. The shotgun Elliot was carrying seemed to grow heavier. He yawned and shook his head, trying unsuccessfully to clear it. The sight of Anderson's eyes gave him a little thrill of revulsion.

'What are you after?' the young professor asked him, nodding toward the shotgun Elliot was cradling.

'Whatever there is,' Elliot said.

Anderson took a quick look at the distant pasture behind him and then turned back to Elliot. The mouth hole of the professor's mask filled with teeth. Elliot thought that Anderson's teeth were quite as he had imagined them earlier. 'Well, Polonski's cows are locked up,' the professor said. 'So they at least are safe.'

Elliot realized that the professor had made a joke and was smiling. 'Yes,' he agreed.

Professor Anderson and his wife had been the moving force behind an initiative to outlaw the discharge of firearms within the boundaries of East Ilford Township. The initiative had been defeated, because East Ilford was not that kind of town.

'I think I'll go over by the river,' Elliot said. He said it only to have something to say, to fill the silence before Anderson spoke again. He was afraid of what Anderson might say to him and of what might happen.

'You know,' Anderson said, 'that's all bird sanctuary over there now.'

'Sure,' Elliot agreed.

Outfitted as he was, the professor attracted Elliot's anger in an elemental manner. The mask made him appear a kind of doll, a kachina figure or a marionette. His eyes and mouth, all on their own, were disagreeable.

Elliot began to wonder if Anderson could smell the whiskey on his breath. He pushed the little red bull's-eye safety button on his gun to Off.

'Seriously,' Anderson said, 'I'm always having to run hunters out of there. Some people don't understand the word "posted."'

'I would never do that,' Elliot said. 'I would be afraid.'

Anderson nodded his head. He seemed to be laughing. 'Would you?' he asked Elliot merrily.

In imagination, Elliot rested the tip of his shotgun barrel against Anderson's smiling teeth. If he fired a load of deer shot into them, he thought, they might make a noise like broken china. 'Yes,' Elliot said. 'I wouldn't know who they were or where they'd been. They might resent my being alive. Telling them where they could shoot and where not.'

Anderson's teeth remained in place. 'That's pretty strange,' he said. 'I mean, to talk about resenting someone for being alive.'

'It's all relative,' Elliot said. 'They might think, "Why should he be alive when some brother of mine isn't?" Or they might think, "Why should he be alive when I'm not?"'

'Oh,' Anderson said.

'You see?' Elliot said. Facing Anderson, he took a long step backward. 'All relative.'

'Yes,' Anderson said.

'That's so often true, isn't it?' Elliot asked. 'Values are often relative.'

'Yes,' Anderson said. Elliot was relieved to see that he had stopped smiling.

'I've hardly slept, you know,' Elliot told Professor Anderson. 'Hardly at all. All night. I've been drinking.'

'Oh,' Anderson said. He licked his lips in the mouth of the mask. 'You should get some rest.'

'You're right,' Elliot said.

'Well,' Anderson said, 'got to go now.'

Elliot thought he sounded a little thick in the tongue. A little slow in the jaw.

'It's a nice day,' Elliot said, wanting now to be agreeable.

'It's great,' Anderson said, shuffling on his skis.

'Have a nice day,' Elliot said.

'Yes,' Anderson said, and pushed off.

Elliot rested the shotgun across his shoulders and watched Anderson withdraw through the frozen swamp. It was in fact a nice day, but Elliot took no comfort in the weather. He missed night and the falling snow.

As he walked back toward his house, he realized that now there would be whole days to get through, running before the antic energy of whiskey. The whiskey would drive him until he dropped. He shook his head in regret. 'It's a revolution,' he said aloud. He imagined himself talking to his wife.

Getting drunk was an insurrection, a revolution—a bad one. There would be outsize bogus emotions. There would be petty moral blackmail and cheap remorse. He had said dreadful things to his wife. He had bullied Anderson with his violence and unhappiness, and Anderson would not forgive him. There would be damn little justice and no mercy.

Nearly to the house, he was startled by the desperate feathered drumming of a pheasant's rush. He froze, and out of instinct brought the gun up in the direction of the sound. When he saw the bird break from its cover and take wing, he tracked it, took a breath and fired once. The bird was a little flash of opulent color against the bright blue sky. Elliot felt himself flying for a moment. The shot missed.

Lowering the gun, he remembered the deer shells he had loaded. A hit with the concentrated shot would have pulverized the bird, and he was glad he had missed. He wished no harm to any creature. Then he thought of himself wishing no harm to any creature and began to feel fond and sorry for himself. As soon as he grew aware of the emotion he was indulging, he suppressed it. Pissing and moaning, mourning and weeping, that was the nature of the drug.

The shot echoed from the distant hills. Smoke hung in the air. He turned and looked behind him and saw, far away across the pasture, the tiny blue and red figure of Professor Anderson motionless against the snow. Then Elliot turned again toward his house and took a few labored steps and looked up to see his wife at the bedroom window. She stood perfectly still, and the morning sun lit her nakedness. He stopped where he was. She had heard the shot and run to the window. What had she thought to see? Burnt rags and blood on the snow. How relieved was she now? How disappointed?

Elliot thought he could feel his wife trembling at the window. She was hugging herself. Her hands clasped her shoulders. Elliot took his snow goggles off and shaded his eyes with his hand. He stood in the field staring.

The length of the gun was between them, he thought. Somehow she had got out in front of it, to the wrong side of the wire. If he looked long enough he would find everything out there. He would find himself down the sight.

How beautiful she is, he thought. The effect was striking. The window was so clear because he had washed it himself, with vinegar. At the best of times he was a difficult, fussy man.

Elliot began to hope for forgiveness. He leaned the shotgun on his forearm and raised his left hand and waved to her. Show a hand, he thought. Please just show a hand.

He was cold, but it had got light. He wanted no more than the gesture. It seemed to him that he could build another day on it. Another day was all you needed. He raised his hand higher and waited.

ERRAND

Raymond Carver

Chekhov. On the evening of 22 March 1897, he went to dinner in Moscow with his friend and confidant Alexei Suvorin. This Suvorin was a very rich newspaper and book publisher, a reactionary, a self-made man whose father was a private at the battle of Borodino. Like Chekhov, he was the grandson of a serf. They had that in common: each had peasant's blood in his veins. Otherwise, politically and temperamentally, they were miles apart. Nevertheless, Suvorin was one of Chekhov's few intimates, and Chekhov enjoyed his company.

Naturally, they went to the best restaurant in the city, a former town house called the Hermitage—a place where it could take hours, half the night even, to get through a ten-course meal that would, of course, include several wines, liqueurs, and coffee. Chekhov was impeccably dressed, as always—a dark suit and waistcoat, his usual pince-nez. He looked that night very much as he looks in the photographs taken of him during this period. He was relaxed, jovial. He shook hands with the maitre d', and with a glance took in the large dining room. It was brilliantly illuminated by ornate chandeliers, the tables occupied by elegantly dressed men and women. Waiters came and went ceaselessly. He had just been seated across the table from Suvorin when suddenly, without warning, blood began gushing from his mouth. Suvorin and two waiters helped him to the gentlemen's room and tried to stanch the flow of blood with ice packs. Suvorin saw him back to his own hotel and had a bed prepared for Chekhov in one of the rooms of the suite. Later, after another hemorrhage, Chekhov allowed himself to be moved to a clinic that specialized in the treatment of tuberculosis and related respiratory infections. When Suvorin visited him there, Chekhov apologized for the 'scandal' at the restaurant three nights earlier but continued to insist there was nothing seriously wrong. 'He laughed and jested as usual,' Suvorin noted in his diary, 'while spitting blood into a large vessel.'

Maria Chekhov, his younger sister, visited Chekhov in the clinic during the last days of March. The weather was miserable; a sleet storm was in progress, and frozen heaps of snow lay everywhere. It was hard for her to wave down a carriage to take her to the hospital. By the time she arrived she was filled with dread and anxiety.

'Anton Pavlovich lay on his back,' Maria wrote in her *Memoirs*. 'He was not allowed to speak. After greeting him, I went over to the table to hide my emotions.' There, among bottles of champagne, jars of caviar, bouquets of flowers from well-wishers, she saw something that terrified her: a freehand drawing, obviously done by a specialist in these matters, of Chekhov's lungs. It was the kind of sketch a doctor often makes in order to show his patient what he thinks is taking place. The lungs were outlined in blue, but the upper parts were filled in with red. 'I realized they were diseased,' Maria wrote.

Leo Tolstoy was another visitor. The hospital staff were awed to find themselves in the presence of the country's greatest writer. The most famous man in Russia? Of course they had to let him in to see Chekhov, even though 'nonessential' visitors were forbidden. With much obsequiousness on the part of the nurses and resident doctors, the bearded, fierce-looking old man was shown into Chekhov's room. Despite his low opinion of Chekhov's abilities as a playwright (Tolstoy felt the plays were static and lacking in any moral vision. 'Where do your characters take you?' he once demanded of Chekhov. 'From the sofa to the junk room and back'), Tolstoy liked Chekhov's short stories. Furthermore, and quite simply, he loved the man. He told Gorky, 'What a beautiful, magnificent man: modest and quiet, like a girl. He even walks like a girl. He's simply wonderful.' And Tolstoy wrote in his journal (everyone kept a journal or a diary in those days), 'I am glad I love . . . Chekhov.'

Tolstoy removed his woollen scarf and bearskin coat, then lowered himself into a chair next to Chekhov's bed. Never mind that Chekhov was taking medication and not permitted to talk much less carry on a conversation. He had to listen, amazedly, as the Count began to discourse on his theories of the immortality of the soul. Concerning that visit, Chekhov later wrote, 'Tolstoy assumes that all of us (humans and animals alike) will live on in a principle (such as reason or love) the essence and goals of which are a mystery to us . . . I have no use for that kind of immortality. I don't understand it, and Lev Nikolayevich was astonished I didn't.'

Nevertheless, Chekhov was impressed with the solicitude shown by

Tolstoy's visit. But, unlike Tolstoy, Chekhov didn't believe in an afterlife and never had. He didn't believe in anything that couldn't be apprehended by one or more of his five senses. And as far as his outlook on life and writing went, he once told someone that he lacked 'a political, religious, and philosophical world view. I change it every month, so I'll have to limit myself to the description of how my heroes love, marry, give birth, die, and how they speak.'

Earlier, before his TB was diagnosed, Chekhov had remarked, 'When a peasant has consumption, he says, "There's nothing I can do. I'll go off in the spring with the melting of the snows."' (Chekhov himself died in the summer, during a heat wave.) But once Chekhov's own tuberculosis was discovered he continually tried to minimize the seriousness of his condition. To all appearances, it was as if he felt, right up to the end, that he might be able to throw off the disease as he would a lingering catarrh. Well into his final days, he spoke with seeming conviction of the possibility of an improvement. In fact, in a letter written shortly before his end he went so far as to tell his sister that he was 'getting fat' and felt much better now that he was in Badenweiler.

Badenweiler is a spa and resort city in the western area of the Black Forest, not far from Basel. The Vosges are visible from nearly anywhere in the city, and in those days the air was pure and invigorating. Russians had been going there for years to soak in the hot mineral baths and promenade on the boulevards. In June, 1904, Chekhov went there to die.

Earlier that month, he'd made a difficult journey by train from Moscow to Berlin. He traveled with his wife, the actress Olga Knipper, a woman he'd met in 1898 during rehearsals for *The Seagull*. Her contemporaries describe her as an excellent actress. She was talented, pretty, and almost ten years younger than the playwright. Chekhov had been immediately attracted to her, but was slow to act on his feelings. As always, he preferred a flirtation to marriage. Finally, after a three-year courtship involving many separations, letters, and the inevitable misunderstandings, they were at last married, in a private ceremony in Moscow, on 25 May 1901. Chekhov was enormously happy. He called Olga his 'pony', and sometimes 'dog' or 'puppy'. He was also fond of addressing her as 'little turkey' or simply as 'my joy'.

In Berlin, Chekhov consulted with a renowned specialist in pulmonary disorders, a Dr Karl Ewald. But, according to an eyewitness, after the doctor examined Chekhov he threw up his hands and left the room without a word. Chekhov was too far gone for help: this Dr Ewald was furious with himself for not being able to work miracles, and with Chekhov for being so ill.

A Russian journalist happened to visit the Chekhovs at their hotel and sent back this dispatch to his editor: 'Chekhov's days are numbered. He seems mortally ill, is terribly thin, coughs all the time, gasps for breath at the slightest movement, and is running a high temperature.' This same journalist saw the Chekhovs off at Potsdam Station when they boarded their train for Badenweiler. According to his account, 'Chekhov had trouble making his way up the small staircase at the station. He had to sit down for several minutes to catch his breath.' In fact, it was painful for Chekhov to move: his legs ached continually and his insides hurt. The disease had attacked his intestines and spinal cord. At this point he had less than a month to live. When Chekhov spoke of his condition now, it was, according to Olga, 'with an almost reckless indifference'.

Dr Schwöhrer was one of the many Badenweiler physicians who earned a good living by treating the well-to-do who came to the spa seeking relief from various maladies. Some of his patients were ill and infirm, others simply old and hypochondriacal. But Chekhov's was a special case: he was clearly beyond help and in his last days. He was also very famous. Even Dr Schwöhrer knew his name: he'd read some of Chekhov's stories in a German magazine. When he examined the writer early in June, he voiced his appreciation of Chekhov's art but kept his medical opinions to himself. Instead, he prescribed a diet of cocoa, oatmeal drenched in butter, and strawberry tea. This last was supposed to help Chekhov sleep at night.

On 13 June, less than three weeks before he died, Chekhov wrote a letter to his mother in which he told her his health was on the mend. In it he said, 'It's likely that I'll be completely cured in a week.' Who knows why he said this? What could he have been thinking? He was a doctor himself, and he knew better. He was dying, it was as simple and as unavoidable as that. Nevertheless, he sat out on the balcony of his hotel room and read railway timetables. He asked for information on sailings of boats bound for Odessa from Marseilles. But he *knew*. At this stage he had to have known. Yet in one of the last letters he ever wrote he told his sister he was growing stronger by the day.

He no longer had any appetite for literary work, and hadn't for a long time. In fact, he had very nearly failed to complete *The Cherry Orchard* the year before. Writing that play was the hardest thing he'd ever done in his life. Toward the end, he was able to manage only six or seven lines a day. 'I've started losing heart,' he wrote Olga. 'I feel I'm finished as a writer, and every sentence strikes me as worthless and of no use whatever.' But he didn't stop. He finished his play in October 1903. It was the last thing he ever wrote, except for letters and a few entries in his notebook.

A little after midnight on 2 July 1904, Olga sent someone to fetch Dr Schwöhrer. It was an emergency: Chekhov was delirious. Two young Russians on holiday happened to have the adjacent room, and Olga hurried next door to explain what was happening. One of the youths was in his bed asleep, but the other was still awake, smoking and reading. He left the hotel at a run to find Dr Schwöhrer. 'I can still hear the sound of the gravel under his shoes in the silence of that stifling July night,' Olga wrote later on in her memoirs. Chekhov was hallucinating, talking about sailors, and there were snatches of something about the Japanese. 'You don't put ice on an empty stomach,' he said when she tried to place an ice pack on his chest.

Dr Schwöhrer arrived and unpacked his bag, all the while keeping his gaze fastened on Chekhov, who lay gasping in the bed. The sick man's pupils were dilated and his temples glistened with sweat. Dr Schwöhrer's face didn't register anything. He was not an emotional man, but he knew Chekhov's end was near. Still, he was a doctor, sworn to do his utmost, and Chekhov held on to life, however tenuously. Dr Schwöhrer prepared a hypodermic and administered an injection of camphor, something that was supposed to speed up the heart. But the injection didn't help—nothing, of course, could have helped. Nevertheless, the doctor made known to Olga his intention of sending for oxygen. Suddenly, Chekhov roused himself, became lucid, and said quietly, 'What's the use? Before it arrives I'll be a corpse.'

Dr Schwöhrer pulled on his big moustache and stared at Chekhov. The writer's cheeks were sunken and gray, his complexion waxen; his breath was raspy. Dr Schwöhrer knew the time could be reckoned in minutes. Without a word, without conferring with Olga, he went over to an alcove where there was a telephone on the wall. He read the instructions for using the device. If he activated it by holding his finger on a button and turning a handle on the side of the phone, he could reach the lower regions of the hotel—the kitchen. He picked up the receiver, held it to his ear, and did as the instructions told him. When someone finally answered, Dr Schwöhrer ordered a bottle of the hotel's best champagne. 'How many glasses?' he was asked. 'Three glasses!' the doctor shouted into the mouthpiece. 'And hurry, do you hear?' It was one of those rare moments of inspiration that can easily enough be overlooked later on, because the action is so entirely appropriate it seems inevitable.

The champagne was brought to the door by a tired-looking young man whose blond hair was standing up. The trousers of his uniform were wrinkled, the creases gone, and in his haste he'd missed a loop while buttoning his jacket. His appearance was that of someone who'd been resting (slumped in a chair, say, dozing a little), when off in the distance the phone had clamored in the early-morning hours—great God in Heaven!—and the next thing he knew he was being shaken awake by a superior and told to deliver a bottle of Moët to Room 211. 'And hurry, do you hear?'

The young man entered the room carrying a silver ice bucket with the champagne in it and a silver tray with three cut-crystal glasses. He found a place on the table for the bucket and glasses, all the while craning his neck, trying to see into the other room, where someone panted ferociously for breath. It was a dreadful, harrowing sound, and the young man lowered his chin into his collar and turned away as the ratchety breathing worsened. Forgetting himself, he stared out the open window toward the darkened city. Then this big imposing man with a thick moustache pressed some coins into his hand—a large tip, by the feel of it—and suddenly the young man saw the door open. He took some steps and found himself on the landing, where he opened his hand and looked at the coins in amazement.

Methodically, the way he did everything, the doctor went about the business of working the cork out of the bottle. He did it in such a way as to minimize, as much as possible, the festive explosion. He poured three glasses and, out of habit, pushed the cork back into the neck of the bottle. He then took the glasses of champagne over to the bed.

Olga momentarily released her grip on Chekhov's hand—a hand, she said later, that burned her fingers. She arranged another pillow behind his head. Then she put the cool glass of champagne against Chekhov's palm and made sure his fingers closed around the stem. They exchanged looks—Chekhov, Olga, Dr Schwöhrer. They didn't touch glasses. There was no toast. What on earth was there to drink to? To death? Chekhov summoned his remaining strength and said, 'It's been so long since I've had champagne.' He brought the glass to his lips and drank. In a minute or two Olga took the empty glass from his hand and set it on the nightstand. Then Chekhov turned onto his side. He closed his eyes and sighed. A minute later, his breathing stopped.

Dr Schwöhrer picked up Chekhov's hand from the bedsheet. He held his fingers to Chekhov's wrist and drew a gold watch from his vest pocket, opening the lid of the watch as he did so. The second hand on the watch moved slowly, very slowly. He let it move around the face of the watch three times while he waited for signs of a pulse. It was three o'clock in the morning and still sultry in the room. Badenweiler was in the grip of its worst heat wave in years. All the windows in both rooms stood open, but there was no sign of a breeze. A large, black-winged moth flew through a window and banged wildly against the electric lamp. Dr Schwöhrer let go of Chekhov's wrist. 'It's over,' he said. He closed the lid of his watch and returned it to his vest pocket.

At once Olga dried her eyes and set about composing herself. She thanked the doctor for coming. He asked if she wanted some medication—laudanum, perhaps, or a few drops of valerian. She shook her head. She did have one request, though: before the authorities were notified and the newspapers found out, before the time came when Chekhov was no longer in her keeping, she wanted to be alone with him for a while. Could the doctor help with this? Could he withhold, for a while anyway, news of what had just occurred?

Dr Schwöhrer stroked his moustache with the back of a finger. Why not? After all, what difference would it make to anyone whether this matter became known now or a few hours from now? The only detail that remained was to fill out a death certificate, and this could be done at his office later on in the morning, after he'd slept a few hours. Dr Schwöhrer nodded his agreement and prepared to leave. He murmured a few words of condolence. Olga inclined her head. 'An honor,' Dr Schwöhrer said. He picked up his bag and left the room and, for that matter, history.

It was at this moment that the cork popped out of the champagne bottle; foam spilled down onto the table. Olga went back to Chekhov's bedside. She sat on a footstool, holding his hand, from time to time stroking his face. 'There were no human voices, no everyday sounds,' she wrote. 'There was only beauty, peace, and the grandeur of death.'

She stayed with Chekhov until daybreak, when thrushes began to call from the garden below. Then came the sound of tables and chairs being moved about down there. Before long, voices carried up to her. It was then a knock sounded at the door. Of course she thought it must be an official of some sort—the medical examiner, say, or someone from the police who had questions to ask and forms for her to fill out, or maybe, just maybe, it could be Dr Schwöhrer returning with a mortician to render assistance in embalming and transporting Chekhov's remains back to Russia.

But, instead, it was the same blond young man who'd brought the champagne a few hours earlier. This time, however, his uniform trousers were neatly pressed, with stiff creases in front, and every button on his snug green jacket was fastened. He seemed quite another person. Not only was he wide awake but his plump cheeks were smooth-shaven, his hair was in place, and he appeared anxious to please. He was holding a porcelain vase with three long-stemmed yellow roses. He presented these to Olga with a smart click of his heels. She stepped back and let him into the room. He was there, he said, to collect the glasses, ice bucket, and tray, yes. But he also wanted to say that, because of the extreme heat, breakfast would be served in the garden this morning. He hoped this weather wasn't too bothersome; he apologized for it.

The woman seemed distracted. While he talked, she turned her eyes away and looked down at something in the carpet. She crossed her arms and held her elbows. Meanwhile, still holding his vase, waiting for a sign, the young man took in the details of the room. Bright sunlight flooded through the open windows. The room was tidy and seemed undisturbed, almost untouched. No garments were flung over chairs, no shoes, stockings, braces, or stays were in evidence, no open suitcases. In short, there was no clutter, nothing but the usual heavy pieces of hotel-room furniture. Then, because the woman was still looking down, he looked down, too, and at once spied a cork near the toe of his shoe. The woman did not see it—she was looking somewhere else. The young man wanted to bend over and pick up the cork, but he was still holding the roses and was afraid of seeming to intrude even more by drawing any further attention to himself. Reluctantly, he left the cork where it was and raised his eyes. Everything was in order except for the uncorked, half-empty bottle of champagne that stood alongside two crystal glasses over on the little table. He cast his gaze about once more. Through an open door he saw that the third glass was in the bedroom, on the nightstand. But someone still occupied the bed! He couldn't see a face, but the figure under the covers lay perfectly motionless and quiet. He noted the figure and looked elsewhere. Then for a reason he couldn't understand, a feeling of uneasiness took hold of him. He cleared his throat and moved his weight to the other leg. The woman still didn't look up or break her silence. The young man felt his cheeks grow warm. It occurred to him, quite without his having thought it through, that he should perhaps suggest an alternative to breakfast in the garden. He coughed, hoping to focus the woman's attention, but she didn't look at him. The distinguished foreign guests could, he said, take breakfast in their rooms this morning if they wished. The young man (his name hasn't survived, and it's likely he perished in the Great War) said he would be happy to bring up a tray. Two trays, he added, glancing uncertainly once again in the direction of the bedroom.

He fell silent and ran a finger around the inside of his collar. He didn't understand. He wasn't even sure the woman had been listening. He didn't know what else to do now; he was still holding the vase. The sweet odor of the roses filled his nostrils and inexplicably caused a pang of regret. The entire time he'd been waiting, the woman had apparently been lost in thought. It was as if all the while he'd been standing there, talking, shifting his weight, holding his flowers, she had been someplace else, somewhere far from Badenweiler. But now she came back to herself, and her face assumed another expression. She raised her eyes, looked at him, and then shook her head. She seemed to be struggling to understand what on earth this young man could be doing there in the room holding a vase with three yellow roses. Flowers? She hadn't ordered flowers.

The moment passed. She went over to her handbag and scooped up some coins. She drew out a number of banknotes as well. The young man touched his lips with his tongue; another large tip was forthcoming, but for what? What did she want him to do? He'd never before waited on such guests. He cleared his throat once more.

No breakfast, the woman said. Not yet, at any rate. Breakfast wasn't the important thing this morning. She required something else. She needed him to go out and bring back a mortician. Did he understand her? Herr Chekhov was dead, you see. *Comprenez-vous?* Young man? Anton Chekhov was dead. Now listen carefully to me, she said. She wanted him to go downstairs and ask someone at the front desk where he could go to find the most respected mortician in the city. Someone reliable, who took great pains in his work and whose manner was appropriately reserved. A mortician, in short, worthy of a great artist. Here, she said, and pressed the money on him. Tell them downstairs that I have specifically requested you to perform this duty for me. Are you listening? Do you understand what I'm saying to you?

The young man grappled to take in what she was saying. He chose not to look again in the direction of the other room. He had sensed that something was not right. He became aware of his heart beating rapidly under his jacket, and he felt perspiration break out on his forehead. He didn't know where he should turn his eyes. He wanted to put the vase down.

Please do this for me, the woman said. I'll remember you with gratitude. Tell them downstairs that I insist. Say that. But don't call any unnecessary attention to yourself or to the situation. Just say that this is necessary, that I request it—and that's all. Do you hear me? Nod if you understand. Above all, don't raise an alarm. Everything else, all the rest, the commotion—that'll come soon enough. The worst is over. Do we understand each other?

The young man's face had grown pale. He stood rigid, clasping the vase. He managed to nod his head.

After securing permission to leave the hotel he was to proceed quietly and resolutely, though without any unbecoming haste, to the mortician's. He was to behave exactly as if he were engaged on a very important errand, nothing more. He *was* engaged on an important errand, she said. And if it would help keep his movements purposeful he should imagine himself as someone moving down the busy sidewalk carrying in his arms a porcelain vase of roses that he had to deliver to an important man. (She spoke quietly, almost confidentially, as if to a relative or a friend.) He could even tell himself that the man he was going to see was expecting him, was perhaps impatient for him to arrive with his flowers. Nevertheless, the young man was not to become excited and run, or otherwise break his stride. Remember the vase he was carrying! He was to walk briskly, comporting himself at all times in as dignified a manner as possible. He should keep walking until he came to the mortician's house and stood before the door. He would then raise the brass knocker and let it fall, once, twice, three times. In a minute the mortician himself would answer.

This mortician would be in his forties, no doubt, or maybe early fifties—bald, solidly built, wearing steel-frame spectacles set very low on his nose. He would be modest, unassuming, a man who would ask only the most direct and necessary questions. An apron. Probably he would be wearing an apron. He might even be wiping his hands on a dark towel while he listened to what was being said. There'd be a faint whiff of formaldehyde on his clothes. But it was all right, and the young man shouldn't worry. He was nearly a grown-up now and shouldn't be frightened or repelled by any of this. The mortician would hear him out. He was a man of restraint and bearing, this mortician, someone who could help allay people's fears in this situation, not increase them. Long ago he'd acquainted himself with death in all its various guises and forms; death held no surprises for him any longer, no hidden secrets. It was this man whose services were required this morning.

The mortician takes the vase of roses. Only once while the young man is speaking does the mortician betray the least flicker of interest, or indicate that he's heard anything out of the ordinary. But the one time the young man mentions the name of the deceased, the mortician's eyebrows rise just a little. Chekhov, you say? Just a minute, and I'll be with you.

Do you understand what I'm saying, Olga said to the young man. Leave the glasses. Don't worry about them. Forget about crystal wineglasses and such. Leave the room as it is. Everything is ready now. We're ready. Will you go?

But at that moment the young man was thinking of the cork still resting near the toe of his shoe. To retrieve it he would have to bend over, still gripping the vase. He would do this. He leaned over. Without looking down, he reached out and closed it into his hand.

WHERE *IS* HERE?

Joyce Carol Oates

For years they had lived without incident in their house in a quiet residential neighborhood when, one November evening at dusk, the doorbell rang, and the father went to answer it, and there on his doorstep stood a man he had never seen before. The stranger apologized for disturbing him at what was probably the dinner hour and explained that he'd once lived in the house—'I mean, I was a child in this house'—and since he was in the city on business he thought he would drop by. He had not seen the house since January 1949 when he'd been eleven years old and his widowed mother had sold it and moved away but, he said, he thought of it often, dreamt of it often, and never more powerfully than in recent months. The father said, 'Would you like to come inside for a few minutes and look around?' The stranger hesitated, then said firmly, 'I think I'll just poke around outside for a while, if you don't mind. That might be sufficient.' He was in his late forties, the father's approximate age. He wore a dark suit, conservatively cut; he was hatless, with thin silver-tipped neatly combed hair; a plain, sober, intelligent face and frowning eyes. The father, reserved by nature, but genial and even gregarious when taken unaware, said amiably, 'Of course we don't mind. But I'm afraid many things have changed since 1949.'

So, in the chill, damp, deepening dusk, the stranger wandered around the property while the mother set the dining room table and the father peered covertly out the window. The children were upstairs in their rooms. 'Where is he now?' the mother asked. 'He just went into the garage,' the father said. 'The garage! What does he want in there!' the mother said uneasily. 'Maybe you'd better go out there with him . . .' 'He wouldn't want anyone with him,' the father said. He moved stealthily to another window, peering through the curtains. A moment passed in silence. The mother, paused in the act of setting down plates, neatly folded paper napkins, and stainless-steel cutlery, said impatiently, 'And where is he now? I don't like this.' The father said, 'Now he's coming out of the garage,' and stepped back hastily from the window. 'Is he going now?' the mother asked. 'I wish I'd answered the door.' The father watched for a moment in silence then said, 'He's headed into the backyard.' 'Doing what?' the mother asked. 'Not doing anything, just walking,' the father said. 'He seems to have a slight limp.' 'Is he an older man?' the mother asked. 'I didn't notice,' the father confessed. 'Isn't that just like you!' the mother said.

She went on worriedly, 'He could be anyone, after all. Any kind of thief, or mentally disturbed person, or even murderer. Ringing our doorbell like that with no warning and you don't even know what he looks like!'

The father had moved to another window and stood quietly watching, his cheek pressed against the glass. 'He's gone down to the old swings. I hope he won't sit in one of them, for memory's sake, and try to swing—the posts are rotted almost through.' The mother drew breath to speak but sighed instead, as if a powerful current of feeling had surged through her. The father was saying, 'Is it possible he remembers those swings from his childhood? I can't believe they're actually that old.' The mother said vaguely, 'They were old when we bought the house.' The father said, 'But we're talking about forty years or more, and that's a long time.' The mother sighed again, involuntarily. 'Poor man!' she murmured. She was standing before her table but no longer seeing it. In her hand were objects—forks, knives, spoons—she could not have named. She said, 'We can't bar the door against him. That would be cruel.' The father said, 'What? No one has barred any door against anyone.' 'Put yourself in his place,' the mother said. 'He told me he didn't want to come inside,' the father said. 'Oh— isn't that just like you!' the mother said in exasperation.

Without a further word she went to the back door and called out for the stranger to come inside, if he wanted, when he had finished looking around outside.

They introduced themselves rather shyly, giving names, and forgetting names, in the confusion of the moment. The stranger's handshake was cool and damp and tentative. He was smiling hard, blinking moisture from his eyes; it was clear that entering his childhood home was enormously exciting yet intimidating to him. Repeatedly he said, 'It's so nice of you to invite me in—I truly hate to disturb you—I'm really so grateful, and so—' But the perfect word eluded him. As he spoke his eyes darted about the kitchen almost like eyes out of control. He stood in an odd stiff posture, hands gripping the lapels of his suit as if he meant to crush them. The mother, meaning to break the awkward silence, spoke warmly of their satisfaction with the house and with the neighborhood, and the father concurred, but the stranger listened only politely, and continued to stare, and stare hard. Finally he said that the kitchen had been so changed—'so modernized'—he almost didn't recognize it. The floor tile, the size of the windows, something about the position of the cupboards—all were different. But the sink was in the same place, of course; and the refrigerator and stove; and the door leading down to the basement— 'That *is* the door leading down to the basement, isn't it?' He spoke strangely, staring at the door. For a moment it appeared he might ask to be shown the basement but the moment passed, fortunately—this was not a part of their house the father and mother would have been comfortable showing to a stranger.

Finally, making an effort to smile, the stranger said, 'Your kitchen is so—pleasant.' He paused. For a moment it seemed he had nothing further to say. Then, 'A—controlled sort of place. My mother—When we lived here—' His words trailed off into a dreamy silence and the mother and father glanced at each other with carefully neutral expressions.

On the windowsill above the sink were several lushly blooming African violet plants in ceramic pots and these the stranger made a show of admiring. Impulsively he leaned over to sniff the flowers— 'Lovely!'—though African violets have no smell. As if embarrassed he said, 'Mother too had plants on this windowsill but I don't recall them ever blooming.'

The mother said tactfully, 'Oh they were probably the kind that don't bloom—like ivy.'

In the next room, the dining room, the stranger appeared to be even more deeply moved. For some time he stood staring, wordless. With fastidious slowness he turned on his heel, blinking, and frowning, and tugging at his lower lip in a rough gesture that must have hurt. Finally, as if remembering the presence of his hosts, and the necessity for some display of civility, the stranger expressed his admiration for the attractiveness of the room, and its coziness. He'd remembered it as cavernous, with a ceiling twice as high. 'And dark most of the time,' he said wonderingly. 'Dark by day, dark by night.' The mother turned the lights of the little brass chandelier to their fullest: shadows were dispersed like ragged ghosts and the cut-glass fruit bowl at the center of the table glowed like an exquisite multifaceted jewel. The stranger exclaimed in surprise. He'd extracted a handkerchief from his pocket and was dabbing carefully at his face, where beads of perspiration shone. He said, as if thinking aloud, still wonderingly, 'My father was a unique man. Everyone who knew him admired him. He sat *here*,' he said, gingerly touching the chair that was in fact the father's chair, at one end of the table. 'And Mother sat *there*,' he said, merely pointing. 'I don't recall my own place or my sister's but I suppose it doesn't matter . . . I see you have four place settings, Mrs . . .? Two children, I suppose?' 'A boy eleven, and a girl thirteen,' the mother said. The stranger stared not at her but at the table, smiling. 'And so too *we* were—I mean, there were two of us: my sister and me.'

The mother said, as if not knowing what else to say, 'Are you—close?'

The stranger shrugged, distractedly rather than rudely, and moved on to the living room.

This room, cozily lit as well, was the most carefully furnished room in the house. Deep-piled wall-to-wall carpeting in hunter green, cheerful chintz drapes, a sofa and matching chairs in nubby heather green, framed reproductions of classic works of art, a gleaming gilt-framed mirror over the fireplace: wasn't the living room impressive as a display in a furniture store? But the stranger said nothing at first. Indeed, his eyes narrowed sharply as if he were confronted with a disagreeable spectacle. He whispered, 'Here too! Here too!'

He went to the fireplace, walking, now, with a decided limp; he drew his fingers with excruciating slowness along the mantel as if testing its materiality. For some time he merely stood, and stared, and listened. He tapped a section of wall with his knuckles—'There used to be a large water stain here, like a shadow.'

'Was there?' murmured the father out of politeness, and 'Was there!' murmured the mother. Of course, neither had ever seen a water stain there.

Then, noticing the window seat, the stranger uttered a soft surprised cry, and went to sit in it. He appeared delighted: hugging his knees like a child trying to make himself smaller. 'This was one of my happy places! At least when Father wasn't home. I'd hide away here for hours, reading, daydreaming, staring out the window! Sometimes Mother would join me, if she was in the mood, and we'd plot together—oh, all sorts of fantastical things!' The stranger remained sitting in the window seat for so long, tears shining in his eyes, that the father and mother almost feared he'd forgotten them. He was stroking the velvet fabric of the cushioned seat, gropingly touching the leaded windowpanes. Wordlessly, the father and mother exchanged a glance: who was this man, and how could they tactfully get rid of him? The father made a face signaling impatience and the mother shook her head without seeming to move it. For they couldn't be rude to a guest in their house.

The stranger was saying in a slow, dazed voice, 'It all comes back to me now. How could I have forgotten! Mother used to read to me, and tell me stories, and ask me riddles I couldn't answer. "What creature walks on four legs in the morning, two legs at midday, three legs in the evening?" "What is round, and flat, measuring mere inches in one direction, and infinity in the other?" "Out of what does our life arise? Out of what does our consciousness arise? Why are we here? Where *is* here?"'

The father and mother were perplexed by these strange words and hardly knew how to respond. The mother said uncertainly, 'Our daughter used to like to sit there too, when she was younger. It *is* a lovely place.' The father said with surprising passion, 'I hate riddles— they're moronic some of the time and obscure the rest of the time.' He spoke with such uncharacteristic rudeness, the mother looked at him in surprise.

Hurriedly she said, 'Is your mother still living, Mr . . .?' 'Oh no. Not at all,' the stranger said, rising abruptly from the window seat, and looking at the mother as if she had said something mildly preposterous. 'I'm sorry,' the mother said. 'Please don't be,' the stranger said. 'We've all been dead—*they've* all been dead—a long time.'

The stranger's cheeks were deeply flushed as if with anger and his breath was quickened and audible.

The visit might have ended at this point but so clearly did the stranger expect to continue on upstairs, so purposefully, indeed almost defiantly, did he limp his way to the stairs, neither the father nor the mother knew how to dissuade him. It was as if a force of nature, benign at the outset, now uncontrollable, had swept its way into their house!

The mother followed after him saying nervously, 'I'm not sure what condition the rooms are in, upstairs. The children's rooms especially—' The stranger muttered that he did not care in the slightest about the condition of the household and continued on up without a backward glance.

The father, his face burning with resentment and his heart accelerating as if in preparation for combat, had no choice but to follow the stranger and the mother up the stairs. He was flexing and unflexing his fingers as if to rid them of stiffness.

On the landing, the stranger halted abruptly to examine a stained-glass fanlight—'My God, I haven't thought of this in years!' He spoke excitedly of how, on tiptoe, he used to stand and peek out through the diamonds of colored glass, red, blue, green, golden yellow: seeing with amazement the world outside so *altered*. 'After such a lesson it's hard to take the world on its own terms, isn' t it?' he asked. The father asked, annoyed, 'On what terms should it be taken, then?' The stranger replied, regarding him levelly, with a just perceptible degree of disdain, 'Why, none at all.'

It was the son's room—by coincidence, the stranger's old room—the stranger most wanted to see. Other rooms on the second floor, the 'master' bedroom in particular, he decidedly did not want to see. As he spoke of it, his mouth twitched as if he had been offered something repulsive to eat.

The mother hurried on ahead to warn the boy and to straighten up his room a bit. No one had expected a visitor this evening! 'So you have two children,' the stranger murmured, looking at the father with a small quizzical smile. 'Why?' The father stared at him as if he hadn't heard correctly. '"Why"?' he asked. 'Yes. *Why*?' the stranger repeated. They looked at each other for a long strained moment, then the stranger said quickly, 'But you love them—of course.' The father controlled his temper and said, biting off his words, 'Of course.'

'Of course, of course,' the stranger murmured, tugging at his necktie and loosening his collar, 'otherwise it would all come to an end.' The two men were of approximately the same height but the father was heavier in the shoulders and torso; his hair had thinned more severely so that the scalp of the crown was exposed, flushed, damp with perspiration, sullenly alight.

*

With a stiff avuncular formality the stranger shook the son's hand. 'So this is your room, now! So you live here, now!' he murmured, as if the fact were an astonishment. Not used to shaking hands, the boy was stricken with shyness and cast his eyes down. The stranger limped past him, staring. 'The same!—the same!—walls, ceiling, floor— window—' He drew his fingers slowly along the windowsill; around the frame; rapped the glass, as if, again, testing materiality; stooped to look outside—but it was night, and nothing but his reflection bobbed in the glass, ghostly and insubstantial. He groped against the walls, he opened the closet door before the mother could protest, he sat heavily on the boy's bed, the springs creaking beneath him. He was panting, red-faced, dazed. 'And the ceiling overhead,' he whispered. He nodded slowly and repeatedly, smiling. 'And the floor beneath. That is what *is*.'

He took out his handkerchief again and fastidiously wiped his face. He made a visible effort to compose himself.

The father, in the doorway, cleared his throat and said, 'I'm afraid it's getting late—it's almost six.'

The mother said, 'Oh yes I'm afraid—I'm afraid it *is* getting late. There's dinner, and the children have their homework—'

The stranger got to his feet. At his full height he stood for a precarious moment swaying, as if the blood had drained from his head and he was in danger of fainting. But he steadied himself with a hand against the slanted dormer ceiling. He said, 'Oh yes!—I know!—I've disturbed you terribly!—you've been so *kind*.' It seemed, surely, as if the stranger *must* leave now, but, as chance had it, he happened to spy, on the boy's desk, an opened mathematics textbook and several smudged sheets of paper, and impulsively offered to show the boy a mathematical riddle—'You can take it to school tomorrow and surprise your teacher!'

So, out of dutiful politeness, the son sat down at his desk and the stranger leaned familiarly over him, demonstrating adroitly with a ruler and a pencil how 'what we call "infinity"' can be contained within a small geometrical figure on a sheet of paper. 'First you draw a square; then you draw a triangle to fit inside the square; then you draw a second triangle, and a third, and a fourth, each to fit inside the square, but without their points coinciding, and as you continue—here, son, I'll show you—give me your hand, and I'll show you—the border of the triangles' common outline gets more complex and measures larger, and larger, and larger—and soon you'll need a magnifying glass to see the details, and then you'll need a microscope, and so on and so forth, forever, laying triangles neatly down to fit inside the original square *without their points coinciding*—!' The stranger spoke with increasing fervor; spittle gleamed in the corners of his mouth. The son stared at the geometrical shapes rapidly materializing on the sheet of paper before him with no seeming comprehension but with a rapt staring fascination as if he dared not look away.

After several minutes of this the father came abruptly forward and dropped his hand on the stranger's shoulder. 'The visit is over,' he said calmly. It was the first time since they'd shaken hands that the two men had touched, and the touch had a galvanic effect upon the stranger: he dropped ruler and pencil at once, froze in his stooped posture, burst into frightened tears.

Now the visit truly was over; the stranger, at last, *was* leaving, having wiped away his tears and made a stoical effort to compose himself; but on the doorstep, to the father's astonishment, he made a final, preposterous appeal—he wanted to see the basement. 'Just to sit on the stairs? In the dark? For a few quiet minutes? And you could close the door and forget me, you and your family could have your dinner and—'

The stranger was begging but the father was resolute. Without raising his voice he said, 'No. *The visit is over.*'

He shut the door, and locked it.

Locked it! His hands were shaking and his heart beat angrily.

He watched the stranger walk away—out to the sidewalk, out to the street, disappearing in the darkness. Had the streetlights gone out?

Behind the father the mother stood apologetic and defensive, wringing her hands in a classic stance. 'Wasn't that sad! Wasn't that— *sad!* But we had no choice but to let him in, it was the only decent thing to do.' The father pushed past her without comment. In the living room he saw that the lights were flickering as if on the brink of going out; the patterned wallpaper seemed drained of color; a shadow lay upon it shaped like a bulbous cloud or growth. Even the robust green of the carpeting looked faded. Or was it an optical illusion? Everywhere the father looked, a pulse beat mute with rage. '*I* wasn't the one who opened the door to that man in the first place,' the mother said, coming up behind the father and touching his arm. Without seeming to know what he did the father violently jerked his arm and thrust her away.

'Shut up. We'll forget it,' he said.

'But—'

'We'll forget it.'

The mother entered the kitchen walking slowly as if she'd been struck a blow. In fact, a bruise the size of a pear would materialize on her forearm by morning. When she reached out to steady herself she misjudged the distance of the door frame—or did the doorframe recede an inch or two—and nearly lost her balance.

In the kitchen the lights were dim and an odor of sourish smoke, subtle but unmistakable, made her nostrils pinch.

She slammed open the oven door. Grabbed a pair of pot holders with insulated linings. '*I* wasn't the one, God damn you,' she cried, panting, 'and you know it.'

THE MANAGEMENT OF GRIEF

Bharati Mukherjee

A woman I don't know is boiling tea the Indian way in my kitchen. There are a lot of women I don't know in my kitchen, whispering, and moving tactfully. They open doors, rummage through the pantry, and try not to ask me where things are kept. They remind me of when my sons were small, on Mother's Day or when Vikram and I were tired, and they would make big, sloppy omelets. I would lie in bed pretending I didn't hear them.

Dr. Sharma, the treasurer of the Indo-Canada Society, pulls me into the hallway. He wants to know if I am worried about money. His wife, who has just come up from the basement with a tray of empty cups and glasses, scolds him. 'Don't bother Mrs. Bhave with mundane details.' She looks so monstrously pregnant her baby must be days overdue. I tell her she shouldn't be carrying heavy things. 'Shaila,' she says, smiling, 'this is the fifth.' Then she grabs a teenager by his shirttails. He slips his Walkman off his head. He has to be one of her four children, they have the same domed and dented foreheads. 'What's the official word now?' she demands. The boy slips the headphones back on. 'They're acting evasive, Ma. They're saying it could be an accident or a terrorist bomb.'

All morning, the boys have been muttering, Sikh Bomb, Sikh Bomb. The men, not using the word, bow their heads in agreement. Mrs. Sharma touches her forehead at such a word. At least they've stopped talking about space debris and Russian lasers.

Two radios are going in the dining room. They are tuned to different stations. Someone must have brought the radios down from my boys' bedrooms. I haven't gone into their rooms since Kusum came running across the front lawn in her bathrobe. She looked so funny, I was laughing when I opened the door.

The big TV in the den is being whizzed through American networks and cable channels.

'Damn!' some man swears bitterly. 'How can these preachers carry on like nothing's happened?' I want to tell him we're not that important. You look at the audience, and at the preacher in his blue robe with his beautiful white hair, the potted palm trees under a blue sky, and you know they care about nothing.

The phone rings and rings. Dr. Sharma's taken charge. 'We're with her,' he keeps saying. 'Yes, yes, the doctor has given calming pills. Yes, yes, pills are having necessary effect.' I wonder if pills alone explain this calm. Not peace, just a deadening quiet. I was always controlled, but never repressed. Sound can reach me, but my body is tensed, ready to scream. I hear their voices all around me. I hear my boys and Vikram cry, 'Mommy, Shaila!' and their screams insulate me, like headphones.

The woman boiling water tells her story again and again. 'I got the news first. My cousin called from Halifax before six A.M., can you imagine? He'd gotten up for prayers and his son was studying for medical exams and he heard on a rock channel that something had happened to a plane. They said first it had disappeared from the radar, like a giant eraser just reached out. His father called me, so I said to him, what do you mean, "something bad"? You mean a hijacking? And he said, *behn*, there is no confirmation of anything yet, but check with your neighbors because a lot of them must be on that plane. So I called poor Kusum straightaway. I knew Kusum's husband and daughter were booked to go yesterday.'

Kusum lives across the street from me. She and Satish had moved in less than a month ago. They said they needed a bigger place. All these people, the Sharmas and friends from the Indo-Canada Society, had been there for the housewarming. Satish and Kusum made homemade tandoori on their big gas grill and even the white neighbors piled their plates high with that luridly red, charred, juicy chicken. Their younger daughter had danced, and even our boys had broken away from the Stanley Cup telecast to put in a reluctant appearance. Everyone took pictures for their albums and for the community newspapers—another of our families had made it big in Toronto—and now I wonder how many of those happy faces are gone. 'Why does God give us so much if all along He intends to take it away?' Kusum asks me.

I nod. We sit on carpeted stairs, holding hands like children. 'I never once told him that I loved him,' I say. I was too much the well brought up woman. I was so well brought up I never felt comfortable calling my husband by his first name.

'It's all right,' Kusum says. 'He knew. My husband knew. They felt it. Modern young girls have to say it because what they feel is fake.'

Kusum's daughter, Pam, runs in with an overnight case. Pam's in her McDonald's uniform. 'Mummy! You have to get dressed!' Panic makes her cranky. 'A reporter's on his way here.'

'Why?'

'You want to talk to him in your bathrobe?' She starts to brush her mother's long hair. She's the daughter who's always in trouble. She dates Canadian boys and hangs out in the mall, shopping for tight sweaters. The younger one, the goody-goody one according to Pam, the one with a voice so sweet that when she sang *bhajans* for Ethiopian relief even a frugal man like my husband wrote out a hundred dollar check, *she* was on that plane. *She* was going to spend July and August with grandparents because Pam wouldn't go. Pam said she'd rather waitress at McDonald's. 'If it's a choice between Bombay and Wonderland, I'm picking Wonderland,' she'd said.

'Leave me alone,' Kusum yells. 'You know what I want to do? If I didn't have to look after you now, I'd hang myself.'

Pam's young face goes blotchy with pain. 'Thanks,' she says, 'don't let me stop you.'

'Hush,' pregnant Mrs. Sharma scolds Pam. 'Leave your mother alone. Mr. Sharma will tackle the reporters and fill out the forms. He'll say what has to be said.'

Pam stands her ground. 'You think I don't know what Mummy's thinking? *Why her?* that's what. That's sick! Mummy wishes my little sister were alive and I were dead.'

Kusum's hand in mine is trembly hot. We continue to sit on the stairs.

She calls before she arrives, wondering if there's anything I need. Her name is Judith Templeton and she's an appointee of the provincial government. 'Multiculturalism?' I ask, and she says, 'partially,' but that her mandate is bigger. 'I've been told you knew many of the people on the flight,' she says. 'Perhaps if you'd agree to help us reach the others . . .?'

She gives me time at least to put on tea water and pick up the mess in the front room. I have a few *samosas* from Kusum's housewarming that I could fry up, but then I think, Why prolong this visit?

Judith Templeton is much younger than she sounded. She wears a blue suit with a white blouse and a polka dot tie. Her blond hair is cut short, her only jewelry is pearl drop earrings. Her briefcase is new and expensive looking, a gleaming cordovan leather. She sits with it across her lap. When she looks out the front windows onto the street, her contact lenses seem to float in front of her light blue eyes.

'What sort of help do you want from me?' I ask. She has refused the tea, out of politeness, but I insist, along with some slightly stale biscuits.

'I have no experience,' she admits. 'That is, I have an MSW and I've worked in liaison with accident victims, but I mean I have no experience with a tragedy of this scale—'

'Who could?' I ask.

'—and with the complications of culture, language, and customs. Someone mentioned that Mrs. Bhave is a pillar—because you've taken it more calmly.'

At this, perhaps, I frown, for she reaches forward, almost to take my hand. 'I hope you understand my meaning, Mrs. Bhave. There are hundreds of people in Metro directly affected, like you, and some of them speak no English. There are some widows who've never handled money or gone on a bus, and there are old parents who still haven't eaten or gone outside their bedrooms. Some houses and apartments have been looted. Some wives are still hysterical. Some husbands are in shock and profound depression. We want to help, but our hands are tied in so many ways. We have to distribute money to some people, and there are legal documents—these things can be done. We have interpreters, but we don't always have the human touch, or maybe the right human touch. We don't want to make mistakes, Mrs. Bhave, and that's why we'd like to ask you to help us.'

'More mistakes, you mean,' I say.

'Police matters are not in my hands,' she answers.

'Nothing I can do will make any difference,' I say. 'We must all grieve in our own way.'

'But you are coping very well. All the people said, Mrs. Bhave is the strongest person of all. Perhaps if the others could see you, talk with you, it would help them.'

'By the standards of the people you call hysterical, I am behaving very oddly and very badly, Miss Templeton.' I want to say to her, *I wish*

I could scream, starve, walk into Lake Ontario, jump from a bridge. 'They would not see me as a model. I do not see myself as a model.'

I am a freak. No one who has ever known me would think of me reacting this way. This terrible calm will not go away.

She asks me if she may call again, after I get back from a long trip that we all must make. 'Of course,' I say. 'Feel free to call, anytime. '

Four days later, I find Kusum squatting on a rock overlooking a bay in Ireland. It isn't a big rock, but it juts sharply out over water. This is as close as we'll ever get to them. June breezes balloon out her sari and unpin her knee-length hair. She has the bewildered look of a sea creature whom the tides have stranded.

It's been one hundred hours since Kusum came stumbling and screaming across my lawn. Waiting around the hospital, we've heard many stories. The police, the diplomats, they tell us things thinking that we're strong, that knowledge is helpful to the grieving, and maybe it is. Some, I know, prefer ignorance, or their own versions. The plane broke into two, they say. Unconsciousness was instantaneous. No one suffered. My boys must have just finished their breakfasts. They loved eating on planes, they loved the smallness of plates, knives, and forks. Last year they saved the airline salt and pepper shakers. Half an hour more and they would have made it to Heathrow.

Kusum says that we can't escape our fate. She says that all those people—our husbands, my boys, her girl with the nightingale voice, all those Hindus, Christians, Sikhs, Muslims, Parsis, and atheists on that plane—were fated to die together off this beautiful bay. She learned this from a swami in Toronto.

I have my Valium.

Six of us 'relatives'—two widows and four widowers—choose to spend the day today by the waters instead of sitting in a hospital room and scanning photographs of the dead. That's what they call us now: relatives. I've looked through twenty-seven photos in two days. They're very kind to us, the Irish are very understanding. Sometimes understanding means freeing a tourist bus for this trip to the bay, so we can pretend to spy our loved ones through the glassiness of waves or in sun-speckled cloud shapes.

I could die here, too, and be content.

'What is that, out there?' She's standing and flapping her hands and for a moment I see a head shape bobbing in the waves. She's standing in the water, I, on the boulder. The tide is low, and a round, black, head-sized rock has just risen from the waves. She returns, her sari end dripping and ruined and her face is a twisted remnant of hope, the way mine was a hundred hours ago, still laughing but inwardly knowing that nothing but the ultimate tragedy could bring two women together at six o'clock on a Sunday morning. I watch her face sag into blankness.

'That water felt warm, Shaila,' she says at length.

'You can't,' I say. 'We have to wait for our turn to come.'

I haven't eaten in four days, haven't brushed my teeth.

'I know,' she says. 'I tell myself I have no right to grieve. They are in a better place than we are. My swami says I should be thrilled for them. My swami says depression is a sign of our selfishness.'

Maybe I'm selfish. Selfishly I break away from Kusum and run, sandals slapping against stones, to the water's edge. What if my boys aren't lying pinned under the debris? What if they aren't stuck a mile below that innocent blue chop? What if, given the strong currents . . .

Now I've ruined my sari, one of my best. Kusum has joined me, knee-deep in water that feels to me like a swimming pool. I could settle in the water, and my husband would take my hand and the boys would slap water in my face just to see me scream.

'Do you remember what good swimmers my boys were, Kusum?'

'I saw the medals,' she says.

One of the widowers, Dr. Ranganathan from Montreal, walks out to us, carrying his shoes in one hand. He's an electrical engineer. Someone at the hotel mentioned his work is famous around the world, something about the place where physics and electricity come together. He has lost a huge family, something indescribable. 'With some luck,' Dr. Ranganathan suggests to me, 'a good swimmer could make it safely to some island. It is quite possible that there may be many, many microscopic islets scattered around.'

'You're not just saying that?' I tell Dr. Ranganathan about Vinod, my elder son. Last year he took diving as well.

'It's a parent's duty to hope,' he says. 'It is foolish to rule out possibilities that have not been tested. I myself have not surrendered hope.'

Kusum is sobbing once again. 'Dear lady,' he says, laying his free hand on her arm, and she calms down.

'Vinod is how old?' he asks me. He's very careful, as we all are. *Is*, not was.

'Fourteen. Yesterday he was fourteen. His father and uncle were going to take him down to the Taj and give him a big birthday party. I couldn't go with them because I couldn't get two weeks off from my stupid job in June.' I process bills for a travel agent. June is a big travel month.

Dr. Ranganathan whips the pockets of his suit jacket inside out. Squashed roses, in darkening shades of pink, float on the water. He tore the roses off creepers in somebody's garden. He didn't ask anyone if he could pluck the roses, but now there's been an article about it in the local papers. When you see an Indian person, it says, please give him or her flowers.

'A strong youth of fourteen,' he says, 'can very likely pull to safety a younger one.'

My sons, though four years apart, were very close. Vinod wouldn't let Mithun drown. *Electrical engineering,* I think, foolishly perhaps: this man knows important secrets of the universe, things closed to me. Relief spins me lightheaded. No wonder my boys' photographs haven't turned up in the gallery of photos of the recovered dead. 'Such pretty roses,' I say.

'My wife loved pink roses. Every Friday I had to bring a bunch home. I used to say, Why? After twenty odd years of marriage you're still needing proof positive of my love?' He has identified his wife and three of his children. Then others from Montreal, the lucky ones, intact families with no survivors. He chuckles as he wades back to shore. Then he swings around to ask me a question. 'Mrs. Bhave, you are wanting to throw in some roses for your loved ones? I have two big ones left.'

But I have other things to float: Vinod's pocket calculator; a half-painted model B-52 for my Mithun. They'd want them on their island. And for my husband? For him I let fall into the calm, glassy waters a poem I wrote in the hospital yesterday. Finally he'll know my feelings for him.

'Don't tumble, the rocks are slippery,' Dr. Ranganathan cautions. He holds out a hand for me to grab.

Then it's time to get back on the bus, time to rush back to our waiting posts on hospital benches.

*

Kusum is one of the lucky ones. The lucky ones flew here, identified in multiplicate their loved ones, then will fly to India with the bodies for proper ceremonies. Satish is one of the few males who surfaced. The photos of faces we saw on the walls in an office at Heathrow and here in the hospital are mostly of women. Women have more body fat, a nun said to me matter-of-factly. They float better.

Today I was stopped by a young sailor on the street. He had loaded bodies, he'd gone into the water when—he checks my face for signs of strength—when the sharks were first spotted. I don't blush, and he breaks down. 'It's all right,' I say. 'Thank you.' I had heard about the sharks from Dr. Ranganathan. In his orderly mind, science brings understanding, it holds no terror. It is the shark's duty. For every deer there is a hunter, for every fish a fisherman.

The Irish are not shy; they rush to me and give me hugs and some are crying. I cannot imagine reactions like that on the streets of Toronto. Just strangers, and I am touched. Some carry flowers with them and give them to any Indian they see.

After lunch, a policeman I have gotten to know quite well catches hold of me. He says he thinks he has a match for Vinod. I explain what a good swimmer Vinod is.

'You want me with you when you look at photos?' Dr. Ranganathan walks ahead of me into the picture gallery. In these matters, he is a scientist, and I am grateful. It is a new perspective. 'They have performed miracles,' he says. 'We are indebted to them.'

The first day or two the policemen showed us relatives only one picture at a time; now they're in a hurry, they're eager to lay out the possibles, and even the probables.

The face on the photo is of a boy much like Vinod; the same intelligent eyes, the same thick brows dipping into a V. But this boy's features, even his cheeks, are puffier, wider, mushier.

'No.' My gaze is pulled by other pictures. There are five other boys who look like Vinod.

The nun assigned to console me rubs the first picture with a fingertip. 'When they've been in the water for a while, love, they look a little heavier.' The bones under the skin are broken, they said on the first day—try to adjust your memories. It's important.

'It's not him. I'm his mother. I'd know.'

'I know this one!' Dr. Ranganathan cries out suddenly from the back of the gallery. 'And this one!' I think he senses that I don't want to find my boys. 'They are the Kutty brothers. They were also from Montreal.' I don't mean to be crying. On the contrary, I am ecstatic. My suitcase in the hotel is packed heavy with dry clothes for my boys.

The policeman starts to cry. 'I am so sorry, I am so sorry, ma'am. I really thought we had a match.'

With the nun ahead of us and the policeman behind, we, the unlucky ones without our children's bodies, file out of the makeshift gallery.

From Ireland most of us go on to India. Kusum and I take the same direct flight to Bombay, so I can help her clear customs quickly. But we have to argue with a man in uniform. He has large boils on his face. The boils swell and glow with sweat as we argue with him. He wants Kusum to wait in line and he refuses to take authority because his boss is on a tea break. But Kusum won't let her coffins out of sight, and I shan't desert her though I know that my parents, elderly and diabetic, must be waiting in a stuffy car in a scorching lot.

'You bastard!' I scream at the man with the popping boils. Other passengers press closer. 'You think we're smuggling contraband in those coffins!'

Once upon a time we were well brought up women; we were dutiful wives who kept our heads veiled, our voices shy and sweet.

In India, I become, once again, an only child of rich, ailing parents. Old friends of the family come to pay their respects. Some are Sikh, and inwardly, involuntarily, I cringe. My parents are progressive people; they do not blame communities for a few individuals.

In Canada it is a different story now.

'Stay longer,' my mother pleads. 'Canada is a cold place. Why would you want to be all by yourself?' I stay.

Three months pass. Then another.

'Vikram wouldn't have wanted you to give up things!' they protest. They call my husband by the name he was born with. In Toronto he'd changed to Vik so the men he worked with at his office would find his name as easy as Rod or Chris. 'You know, the dead aren't cut off from us!'

My grandmother, the spoiled daughter of a rich *zamindar*, shaved her head with rusty razor blades when she was widowed at sixteen. My grandfather died of childhood diabetes when he was nineteen, and she saw herself as the harbinger of bad luck. My mother grew up without parents, raised indifferently by an uncle, while her true mother slept in a hut behind the main estate house and took her food with the servants. She grew up a rationalist. My parents abhor mindless mortification.

The zamindar's daughter kept stubborn faith in Vedic rituals; my parents rebelled. I am trapped between two modes of knowledge. At thirty-six, I am too old to start over and too young to give up. Like my husband's spirit, I flutter between worlds.

Courting aphasia, we travel. We travel with our phalanx of servants and poor relatives. To hill stations and to beach resorts. We play contract bridge in dusty gymkhana clubs. We ride stubby ponies up crumbly mountain trails. At tea dances, we let ourselves be twirled twice round the ballroom. We hit the holy spots we hadn't made time for before. In Varanasi, Kalighat, Rishikesh, Hardwar, astrologers and palmists seek me out and for a fee offer me cosmic consolations.

Already the widowers among us are being shown new bride candidates. They cannot resist the call of custom, the authority of their parents and older brothers. They must marry; it is the duty of a man to look after a wife. The new wives will be young widows with children, destitute but of good family. They will make loving wives, but the men will shun them. I've had calls from the men over crackling Indian telephone lines. 'Save me,' they say, these substantial, educated, successful men of forty. 'My parents are arranging a marriage for me.' In a month they will have buried one family and returned to Canada with a new bride and partial family.

I am comparatively lucky. No one here thinks of arranging a husband for an unlucky widow.

Then, on the third day of the sixth month into this odyssey, in an abandoned temple in a tiny Himalayan village, as I make my offering of flowers and sweetmeats to the god of a tribe of animists, my husband descends to me. He is squatting next to a scrawny *sadhu* in moth-eaten robes. Vikram wears the vanilla suit he wore the last time I hugged him. The *sadhu* tosses petals on a butter-fed flame, reciting Sanskrit mantras and sweeps his face of flies. My husband takes my hands in his.

You're beautiful, he starts. Then, *What are you doing here?*

Shall I stay? I ask. He only smiles, but already the image is fading. *You must finish alone what we started together.* No seaweed wreathes his mouth. He speaks too fast just as he used to when we were an envied family in our pink split-level. He is gone.

In the windowless altar room, smoky with joss sticks and clarified butter lamps, a sweaty hand gropes for my blouse. I do not shriek. The *sadhu* arranges his robe. The lamps hiss and sputter out.

When we come out of the temple, my mother says, 'Did you feel something weird in there?'

My mother has no patience with ghosts, prophetic dreams, holy men, and cults.

'No,' I lie. 'Nothing.'

But she knows that she's lost me. She knows that in days I shall be leaving.

Kusum's put her house up for sale. She wants to live in an ashram in Hardwar. Moving to Hardwar was her swami's idea. Her swami runs two ashrams, the one in Hardwar and another here in Toronto.

'Don't run away,' I tell her.

'I'm not running away,' she says. 'I'm pursuing inner peace. You think you or that Ranganathan fellow are better off?'

Pam's left for California. She wants to do some modelling, she says. She says when she comes into her share of the insurance money she'll open a yoga-cum-aerobics studio in Hollywood. She sends me postcards so naughty I daren't leave them on the coffee table. Her mother has withdrawn from her and the world.

The rest of us don't lose touch, that's the point. Talk is all we have, says Dr. Ranganathan, who has also resisted his relatives and returned to Montreal and to his job, alone. He says, whom better to talk with than other relatives? We've been melted down and recast as a new tribe.

He calls me twice a week from Montreal. Every Wednesday night and every Saturday afternoon. He is changing jobs, going to Ottawa. But Ottawa is over a hundred miles away, and he is forced to drive two hundred and twenty miles a day. He can't bring himself to sell his house. The house is a temple, he says; the king-sized bed in the master bedroom is a shrine. He sleeps on a folding cot. A devotee.

*

There are still some hysterical relatives. Judith Templeton's list of those needing help and those who've 'accepted' is in nearly perfect balance. Acceptance means you speak of your family in the past tense and you make active plans for moving ahead with your life. There are courses at Seneca and Ryerson we could be taking. Her gleaming leather briefcase is full of college catalogues and lists of cultural societies that need our help. She has done impressive work, I tell her.

'In the textbooks on grief management,' she replies—I am her confidante, I realize, one of the few whose grief has not sprung bizarre obsessions—'there are stages to pass through: rejection, depression, acceptance, reconstruction.' She has compiled a chart and finds that six months after the tragedy, none of us still reject reality, but only a handful are reconstructing. 'Depressed Acceptance' is the plateau we've reached. Remarriage is a major step in reconstruction (though she's a little surprised, even shocked, over *how* quickly some of the men have taken on new families). Selling one's house and changing jobs and cities is healthy.

How do I tell Judith Templeton that my family surrounds me, and that like creatures in epics, they've changed shapes? She sees me as calm and accepting but worries that I have no job, no career. My closest friends are worse off than I. I cannot tell her my days, even my nights, are thrilling.

She asks me to help with families she can't reach at all. An elderly couple in Agincourt whose sons were killed just weeks after they had brought their parents over from a village in Punjab. From their names, I know they are Sikh. Judith Templeton and a translator have visited them twice with offers of money for air fare to Ireland, with bank forms, power-of-attorney forms, but they have refused to sign, or to leave their tiny apartment. Their sons' money is frozen in the bank. Their sons' investment apartments have been trashed by tenants, the furnishings sold off. The parents fear that anything they sign or any money they receive will end the company's or the country's obligations to them. They fear they are selling their sons for two airline tickets to a place they've never seen.

The high-rise apartment is a tower of Indians and West Indians, with a sprinkling of Orientals. The nearest bus stop kiosk is lined with women in saris. Boys practice cricket in the parking lot. Inside the building, even I wince a bit from the ferocity of onion fumes, the distinctive and immediate Indianness of frying *ghee*, but Judith Templeton maintains a steady flow of information. These poor old people are in imminent danger of losing their place and all their services.

I say to her, 'They are Sikh. They will not open up to a Hindu woman.' And what I want to add is, as much as I try not to, I stiffen now at the sight of beards and turbans. I remember a time when we all trusted each other in this new country, it was only the new country we worried about.

The two rooms are dark and stuffy. The lights are off, and an oil lamp sputters on the coffee table. The bent old lady has let us in, and her husband is wrapping a white turban over his oiled, hip-length hair. She immediately goes to the kitchen, and I hear the most familiar sound of an Indian home, tap water hitting and filling a teapot.

They have not paid their utility bills, out of fear and the inability to write a check. The telephone is gone; electricity and gas and water are soon to follow. They have told Judith their sons will provide. They are good boys, and they have always earned and looked after their parents.

We converse a bit in Hindi. They do not ask about the crash and I wonder if I should bring it up. If they think I am here merely as a translator, then they may feel insulted. There are thousands of Punjabi-speakers, Sikhs, in Toronto to do a better job. And so I say to the old lady, 'I too have lost my sons, and my husband, in the crash.'

Her eyes immediately fill with tears. The man mutters a few words which sound like a blessing. 'God provides and God takes away,' he says.

I want to say, But only men destroy and give back nothing. 'My boys and my husband are not coming back,' I say. 'We have to understand that.'

Now the old woman responds. 'But who is to say? Man alone does not decide these things.' To this her husband adds his agreement.

Judith asks about the bank papers, the release forms. With a stroke of the pen, they will have a provincial trustee to pay their bills, invest their money, send them a monthly pension.

'Do you know this woman?' I ask them.

The man raises his hand from the table, turns it over and seems to regard each finger separately before he answers. 'This young lady is always coming here, we make tea for her and she leaves papers for us to sign.' His eyes scan a pile of papers in the corner of the room. 'Soon we will be out of tea, then will she go away?'

The old lady adds, 'I have asked my neighbors and no one else gets *angrezi* visitors. What have we done?'

'It's her job,' I try to explain. 'The government is worried. Soon you will have no place to stay, no lights, no gas, no water.'

'Government will get its money. Tell her not to worry, we are honorable people.'

I try to explain the government wishes to give money, not take. He raises his hand. 'Let them take,' he says. 'We are accustomed to that. That is no problem.'

'We are strong people,' says the wife. 'Tell her that.'

'Who needs all this machinery?' demands the husband. 'It is unhealthy, the bright lights, the cold air on a hot day, the cold food, the four gas rings. God will provide, not government.'

'When our boys return,' the mother says. Her husband sucks his teeth. 'Enough talk,' he says.

Judith breaks in. 'Have you convinced them?' The snaps on her cordovan briefcase go off like firecrackers in that quiet apartment. She lays the sheaf of legal papers on the coffee table. 'If they can't write their names, an X will do—I've told them that.'

Now the old lady has shuffled to the kitchen and soon emerges with a pot of tea and two cups. 'I think my bladder will go first on a job like this,' Judith says to me, smiling. 'If only there was some way of reaching them. Please thank her for the tea. Tell her she's very kind.'

I nod in Judith's direction and tell them in Hindi, 'She thanks you for the tea. She thinks you are being very hospitable but she doesn't have the slightest idea what it means.'

I want to say, Humor her. I want to say, My boys and my husband are with me too, more than ever. I look in the old man's eyes and I can read his stubborn, peasant's message: *I have protected this woman as best I can. She is the only person I have left. Give to me or take from me what you will, but I will not sign for it. I will not pretend that I accept.*

In the car, Judith says, 'You see what I'm up against? I'm sure they're lovely people, but their stubbornness and ignorance are driving me crazy. They think signing a paper is signing their sons' death warrants, don't they?'

I am looking out the window. I want to say, *In our culture, it is a parent's duty to hope.*

'Now Shaila, this next woman is a real mess. She cries day and night, and she refuses all medical help. We may have to—'

'—Let me out at the subway,' I say.

'I beg your pardon?' I can feel those blue eyes staring at me.

It would not be like her to disobey. She merely disapproves, and slows at a corner to let me out. Her voice is plaintive. 'Is there anything I said? Anything I did?'

I could answer her suddenly in a dozen ways, but I choose not to. 'Shaila? Let's talk about it,' I hear, then slam the door.

A wife and mother begins her new life in a new country, and that life is cut short. Yet her husband tells her: Complete what we have started. We who stayed out of politics and came halfway around the world to avoid religious and political feuding have been the first in the New World to die from it. I no longer know what we started, nor how to complete it. I write letters to the editors of local papers and to members of Parliament. Now at least they admit it was a bomb. One MP answers back, with sympathy, but with a challenge. You want to make a difference? Work on a campaign. Work on mine. Politicize the Indian voter.

My husband's old lawyer helps me set up a trust. Vikram was a saver and a careful investor. He had saved the boys' boarding school and college fees. I sell the pink house at four times what we paid for it and take a small apartment downtown. I am looking for a charity to support.

We are deep in the Toronto winter, gray skies, icy pavements. I stay indoors, watching television. I have tried to assess my situation, how best to live my life, to complete what we began so many years ago. Kusum has written me from Hardwar that her life is now serene. She has seen Satish and has heard her daughter sing again. Kusum was on a pilgrimage, passing through a village when she heard a young girl's voice, singing one of her daughter's favorite *bhajans*. She followed the music through the squalor of a Himalayan village, to a hut where a young girl, an exact replica of her daughter, was fanning coals under the kitchen fire. When she appeared, the girl cried out, 'Ma!' and ran away. What did I think of that?

I think I can only envy her.

Pam didn't make it to California, but writes me from Vancouver. She works in a department store, giving make-up hints to Indian and Oriental girls. Dr. Ranganathan has given up his commute, given up his house and job, and accepted an academic position in Texas where no one knows his story and he has vowed not to tell it. He calls me now once a week.

I wait, I listen, and I pray, but Vikram has not returned to me. The voices and the shapes and the nights filled with visions ended abruptly several weeks ago.

I take it as a sign.

One rare, beautiful, sunny day last week, returning from a small errand on Yonge Street, I was walking through the park from the subway to my apartment. I live equidistant from the Ontario Houses of Parliament and the University of Toronto. The day was not cold, but something in the bare trees caught my attention. I looked up from the gravel, into the branches and the clear blue sky beyond. I thought I heard the rustling of larger forms, and I waited a moment for voices. Nothing.

'What?' I asked.

Then as I stood in the path looking north to Queen's Park and west to the university, I heard the voices of my family one last time. *Your time has come*, they said. *Go, be brave.*

I do not know where this voyage I have begun will end. I do not know which direction I will take. I dropped the package on a park bench and started walking.

THE PALATSKI MAN

Stuart Dybek

He reappeared in spring, some Sunday morning, perhaps Easter, when
the twigs of the catalpa trees budded and lawns smelled of mud and
breaking seeds. Or Palm Sunday, returning from mass with handfuls
of blessed, bending palms to be cut into crosses and pinned on your
Sunday dress and the year-old palms removed by her brother, John,
from behind the pictures of Jesus with his burning heart and the Virgin
with her sad eyes, to be placed dusty and crumbling in an old coffee
can and burned in the backyard. And once, walking back from church,
Leon Sisca said these are what they lashed Jesus with. And she said no
they aren't, they used whips. They used these, he insisted. What do
you know, she said. And he told her she was a dumb girl and lashed
her across her bare legs with his blessed palms. They stung her; she
started to cry, that anyone could do such a thing, and he caught her
running down Twenty-fifth Street with her skirt flying and got her
against a fence, and grabbing her by the hair, he stuck his scratchy
palms in her face, and suddenly he was lifted off the ground and flung
to the sidewalk, and she saw John standing over him very red in the
face; and when Leon Sisca tried to run away, John blocked him, and
Leon tried to dodge around him as if they were playing football; and
as he cut past, John slapped him across the face; Leon's head snapped
back and his nose started to bleed. John didn't chase him and he ran
halfway down the block, turned around and yelled through his tears
with blood dripping on his white shirt: I hate you goddamn you I hate
you! All the dressed-up people coming back from church saw it
happen and shook their heads. John said c'mon Mary let's go home.

No, it wasn't that day, but it was in that season on a Sunday that he
reappeared, and then every Sunday after that through the summer and
into the fall, when school would resume and the green catalpa leaves
fall like withered fans into the birdbaths, turning the water brown, the
Palatski Man would come.

He was an old man who pushed a white cart through the
neighborhood streets ringing a little golden bell. He would stop at each

corner, and the children would come with their money to inspect the taffy apples sprinkled with chopped nuts, or the red candy apples on pointed sticks, or the *palatski* displayed under the glass of the white cart. She had seen taffy apples in the candy stores and even the red apples sold by clowns at circuses, but she had never seen *palatski* sold anywhere else. It was two crisp wafers stuck together with honey. The taste might have reminded you of an ice-cream cone spread with honey, but it reminded Mary of Holy Communion. It felt like the Eucharist in her mouth, the way it tasted walking back from the communion rail after waiting for Father Mike to stand before her wearing his rustling silk vestments with the organ playing and him saying the Latin prayer over and over faster than she could ever hope to pray and making a sign of the cross with the host just before placing it on someone's tongue. She knelt at the communion rail close enough to the altar to see the silk curtains drawn inside the open tabernacle and the beeswax candles flickering and to smell the flowers. Father Mike was moving down the line of communicants, holding the chalice, with the altar boy, an eighth-grader, sometimes even John, standing beside him in a lace surplice, holding the paten under each chin; and she would close her eyes and open her mouth, sticking her tongue out, and hear the prayer and feel the host placed gently on her tongue. Sometimes Father's hand brushed her bottom lip, and she would feel a spark from his finger, which Sister said was static electricity, not the Holy Spirit.

Then she would walk down the aisle between the lines of communicants, searching through half-shut eyes for her pew, her mind praying Jesus help me find it. And when she found her pew, she would kneel down and shut her eyes and bury her face in her hands praying over and over thank you Jesus for coming to me, feeling the host stuck to the roof of her mouth, melting against her tongue like a warm, wheaty snowflake; and she would turn the tip of her tongue inward and lick the host off the ridges of her mouth till it was loosened by saliva and swallowed into her soul.

Who was the Palatski Man? No one knew or even seemed to care. He was an old man with an unremembered face, perhaps a never-seen face, a head hidden by a cloth-visored cap, and eyes concealed behind dark glasses with green, smoked lenses. His smile revealed only a gold crown and a missing tooth. His only voice was the ringing bell, and his hands were rough and red as if scrubbed with sandpaper and their skin very hard when you opened your hand for your change and his fingers brushed yours. His clothes were always the same—white—not starched and dazzling, but the soft white of many washings and wringings.

No one cared and he was left alone. The boys didn't torment him as they did the peddlers during the week. There was constant war between the boys and the peddlers, the umbrella menders, the knife sharpeners, anyone whose business carried him down the side streets or through the alleys. The peddlers came every day, spring, summer, and autumn, through the alleys behind the backyard fences crying, 'Rags ol irn, rags ol irn!' Riding their ancient, rickety wagons with huge wooden-spoked wheels, heaped high with scraps of metal, frames of furniture, coal-black cobwebbed lumber, bundles of rags and filthy newspapers. The boys called them the Ragmen. They were all old, hunched men, bearded and bald, who bargained in a stammered foreign English and dressed in clothes extracted from the bundles of rags in their weather-beaten wagons.

Their horses seemed even more ancient than their masters, and Mary was always sorry for them as she watched their slow, arthritic gait up and down the alleys. Most of them were white horses, a dirty white as if their original colors had turned white with age, like the hair on an old man's head. They had enormous hooves with iron shoes that clacked down the alleys over the broken glass, which squealed against the concrete when the rusty, metal-rimmed wheels of the wagon ground over it. Their muzzles were pink without hair, and their tongues lolled out gray; their teeth were huge and yellow. Over their eyes were black blinders, around their shoulders a heavy black harness that looked always ready to slip off, leather straps hung all about their bodies. They ate from black, worn leather sacks tied over their faces, and as they ate, the flies flew up from their droppings and climbed all over their thick bodies and the horses swished at them with stringy tails.

The Ragmen drove down the crooked, interconnecting alleys crying, 'Rags ol irn, rags ol irn,' and the boys waited for a wagon to pass, hiding behind fences or garbage cans; and as soon as it passed they would follow, running half bent over so that they couldn't be seen if the Ragman turned around over the piles heaped on his wagon. They would run to the tailgate and grab on to it, swinging up, the taller ones, like John, stretching their legs onto the rear axle, the shorter ones just hanging as the wagon rolled along. Sometimes one of the bolder boys would try to climb up on the wagon itself and throw off some of the junk. The Ragman would see him and pull the reins, stopping the wagon. He would begin gesturing and yelling at the boys, who jumped from the wagon and stood back laughing and hollering, 'Rags ol irn, rags ol irn!' Sometimes he'd grab a makeshift whip, a piece of clothesline tied to a stick, and stagger after them as they scattered laughing before him, disappearing over fences and down gangways only to reappear again around the corner of some other alley; or, lying flattened on a garage roof, they'd suddenly jump up and shower the wagon with garbage as it passed beneath.

Mary could never fully understand why her brother participated. He wasn't a bully like Leon Sisca and certainly not cruel like Denny Zmiga, who tortured cats. She sensed the boys vaguely condemned the Ragmen for the sad condition of their horses. But that was only a small part of it, for often the horses as well as their masters were harassed. She thought it was a venial sin and wondered if John confessed it the Thursday before each First Friday, when they would go together to confession in the afternoon: Bless me Father for I have sinned, I threw garbage on a Ragman five times this month. For your penance say five Our Fathers and five Hail Marys, go in peace. She never mentioned this to him, feeling that whatever made him do it was a part of what made him generally unafraid, a part of what the boys felt when they elected him captain of the St. Roman Grammar School baseball team. She couldn't bear it if he thought she was a dumb girl. She never snitched on him. If she approached him when he was surrounded by his friends, he would loudly announce, 'All right, nobody swear while Mary's here.'

At home he often took her into his confidence. This was what she liked the most, when, after supper, while her parents watched TV in the parlor, he would come into her room, where she was doing her homework, and lie down on her bed and start talking, telling her who among his friends was a good first sacker, or which one of the girls in his class tried to get him to dance with her at the school party, just talking and sometimes even asking her opinion on something like if she thought he should let his hair grow long like that idiot Peter

Noskin, who couldn't even make the team as a right fielder. What did she think of guys like that? She tried to tell him things back. How Sister Mary Valentine had caught Leon Sisca in the girls' washroom yesterday. And then one night he told her about Raymond Cruz, which she knew was a secret because their father had warned John not to hang around with him even if he was the best pitcher on the team. He told her how after school he and Raymond Cruz had followed a Ragman to Hobotown, which was far away, past Western Avenue, on the other side of the river, down by the river and the railroad tracks, and that they had a regular town there without any streets. They lived among huge heaps of junk, rubbled lots tangled with smashed, rusting cars and bathtubs, rotting mounds of rags and paper, woodpiles infested with river rats. Their wagons were all lined up and the horses kept in a deserted factory with broken windows. They lived in shacks that were falling apart, some of them made out of old boxcars, and there was a blacksmith with a burning forge working in a ruined shed made of bricks and timbers with a roof of canvas.

He told her how they had snuck around down the riverbank in the high weeds and watched the Ragmen come in from all parts of the city, pulled by their tired horses, hundreds of Ragmen arriving in silence, and how they assembled in front of a great fire burning in the middle of all the shacks, where something was cooking in a huge, charred pot.

Their scroungy dogs scratched and circled around the fire while the Ragmen stood about and seemed to be trading among one another: bales of worn clothing for baskets of tomatoes, bushels of fruit for twisted metals, cases of dust-filled bottles for scorched couches and lamps with frazzled wires. They knelt, peering out of the weeds and watching them, and then Ray whispered let's sneak around to the building where the horses are kept and look at them.

So they crouched through the weeds and ran from shack to shack until they came to the back of the old factory. They could smell the horses and hay inside and hear the horses sneezing. They snuck in through a busted window. The factory was dark and full of spiderwebs, and they felt their way through a passage that entered into a high-ceilinged hall where the horses were stabled. It was dim; rays of sun sifted down through the dust from the broken roof. The horses didn't look the same in the dimness without their harnesses. They looked huge and beautiful, and when you reached to pat them, their muscles quivered so that you flinched with fright.

'Wait'll the guys hear about this,' John said.

And Ray whispered, 'Let's steal one! We can take him to the river and ride him.'

John didn't know what to say. Ray was fourteen. His parents were divorced. He had failed a year in school and often hung around with high-school guys. Everybody knew that he had been caught in a stolen car but that the police let him go because he was so much younger than the other guys. He was part Mexican and knew a lot about horses. John didn't like the idea of stealing.

'We couldn't get one out of here,' he said.

'Sure we could,' Ray said. 'We could get on one and gallop out with him before they knew what was going on.'

'Suppose we get caught,' John said.

'Who'd believe the Ragmen anyway?' Ray asked him. 'They can't even speak English. You chicken?'

So they picked out a huge white horse to ride, who stood still and uninterested when John boosted Ray up on his back and then Ray reached down and pulled him up. Ray held his mane and John held on to Ray's waist. Ray nudged his heels into the horse's flanks and he began to move, slowly swaying toward the light of the doorway.

'As soon as we get outside,' Ray whispered, 'hold on. I'm gonna goose him.'

John's palms were sweating by this time because being on this horse felt like straddling a blimp as it rose over the roofs. When they got to the door, Ray hollered, 'Heya!' and kicked his heels hard, and the horse bolted out, and before he knew what had happened, John felt himself sliding, dropping a long way, and then felt the sudden hard smack of the hay-strewn floor. He looked up and realized he had never made it out of the barn, and then he heard the shouting and barking of the dogs and, looking out, saw Ray half riding, half hanging from the horse, which reared again and again, surrounded by the shouting Ragmen, and he saw the look on Ray's face as he was bucked from the horse into their arms. There was a paralyzed second when they all glanced toward him standing in the doorway of the barn, and then he whirled around and stumbled past the now-pitching bulks of horses whinnying all about him and found the passage, struggling through it, bumping into walls, spiderwebs sticking to his face, with the shouts and barks gaining on him, and then he was out the window and running up a hill of weeds, crushed coal slipping under his feet, skidding up and down two more hills, down railroad tracks, not turning around, just running until he could no longer breathe, and above him he saw a bridge and clawed up the grassy embankment till he reached it.

It was rush hour and the bridge was crowded with people going home, factory workers carrying lunch pails and businessmen with attaché cases. The street was packed with traffic, and he didn't know where he was or what he should do about Ray. He decided to go home and see what would happen. He'd call Ray that night, and if he wasn't home, then he'd tell them about the Ragmen. But he couldn't find his way back. Finally he had to ask a cop where he was, and the cop put him on a trolley car that got him home.

He called Ray about eight o'clock, and his mother answered the phone and told him Ray had just got in and went right to bed, and John asked her if he could speak to him, and she said she'd go see, and he heard her set down the receiver and her footsteps walk away. He realized his own heartbeat was no longer deafening and felt the knots in his stomach loosen. Then he heard Ray's mother say that she was sorry but that Ray didn't want to talk to him.

The next day, at school, he saw Ray and asked him what happened, if he was angry that he had run out on him, and Ray said, no, nothing happened, to forget it. He kept asking Ray how he got away, but Ray wouldn't say anything until John mentioned telling the other guys about it. Ray said if he told anybody he'd deny it ever happened, that there was such a place. John thought he was just kidding, but when he told the guys, Ray told them John made the whole thing up, and they almost got into a fight, pushing each other back and forth, nobody taking the first swing, until the guys stepped between them and broke it up. John lost his temper and said he'd take any of the guys who wanted to go next Saturday to see for themselves. They could go on their bikes and hide them in the weeds by the river and sneak up on the Ragmen. Ray said go on.

So on Saturday John and six guys met at his place and peddled toward the river and railroad tracks, down the busy trucking streets, where the semis passed you so fast your bike seemed about to be sucked away by the draft. They got to Western Avenue and the river, and it looked the same and didn't look the same. They left the street and pumped their bikes down a dirt road left through the weeds by bulldozers, passing rusty barges moored to the banks, seemingly abandoned in the oily river. They passed a shack or two, but they were empty. John kept looking for the three mounds of black cinders as a landmark but couldn't find them. They rode their bikes down the railroad tracks, and it wasn't like being in the center of the city at all, with the smell of milkweeds and the noise of birds and crickets all about them and the spring sun glinting down the railroad tracks. No one was around. It was like being far out in the country. They rode until they could see the skyline of downtown, skyscrapers rising up through the smoke of chimneys like a horizon of jagged mountains in the mist. By now everyone was kidding him about the Ragmen, and finally he had to admit he couldn't find them, and they gave up. They all peddled back, kidding him, and he bought everybody Cokes, and they admitted they had had a pretty good time anyway, even though he sure as hell was some storyteller.

And he figured something must have happened to Ray. It hit him Sunday night, lying in bed trying to sleep, and he knew he'd have to talk to him about it Monday when he saw him at school, but on Monday Ray was absent and was absent on Tuesday, and on Wednesday they found out that Ray had run away from home and no one could find him.

No one ever found him, and he wasn't there in June when John and his classmates filed down the aisle, their maroon robes flowing and white tassels swinging almost in time to the organ, to receive their diplomas and shake hands with Father Mike. And the next week it was summer, and she was permitted to go to the beach with her girlfriends. Her girlfriends came over and giggled whenever John came into the room.

On Sundays they went to late mass. She wore her flowered-print dress and a white mantilla in church when she sat beside John among the adults. After mass they'd stop at the corner of Twenty-fifth Street on their way home and buy *palatski* and walk home eating it with its crispness melting and the sweet honey crust becoming chewy. She remembered how she used to pretend it was manna they'd been rewarded with for keeping the Sabbath. It tasted extra good because she had skipped breakfast. She fasted before receiving Communion.

Then it began to darken earlier, and the kids played tag and rolivio in the dusk and hid from each other behind trees and in doorways, and the girls laughed and blushed when the boys chased and tagged them. She had her own secret hiding place down the block, in a garden under a lilac bush, where no one could find her; and she would lie there listening to her name called in the darkness, Mary Mary free free free, by so many voices.

She shopped downtown with her mother at night for new school clothes, skirts, not dresses, green ribbons for her dark hair, and shoes without buckles, like slippers a ballerina wears. And that night she tried them on for John, dancing in her nightgown, and he said you're growing up. And later her mother came into her room—only the little bed lamp was burning—and explained to her what growing up was like. And after her mother left, she picked up a little rag doll that was kept as an ornament on her dresser and tried to imagine having a child, really having a child, it coming out of her body, and she looked at herself in the mirror and stood close to it and looked at the colors of her eyes: brown around the edges and then turning a milky gray that seemed to be smoking behind crystal and toward the center the gray turning green, getting greener till it was almost violet near her pupils And in the black mirror of her pupils she saw herself looking at herself.

The next day, school started again and she was a sixth-grader. John was in high school, and Leon Sisca, who had grown much bigger over the summer and smoked, sneered at her and said, 'Who'll protect you now?' She made a visit to the church at lunchtime and dropped a dime in the metal box by the ruby vigil lights and lit a candle high up on the rack with a long wax wick and said a prayer to the Blessed Virgin.

And it was late in October, and leaves wafted from the catalpa trees on their way to church on Sunday and fell like withered fans into the birdbaths, turning the water brown. They were walking back from mass, and she was thinking how little she saw John anymore, how he no longer came to her room to talk, and she said, 'Let's do something together.'

'What?' he asked.

'Let's follow the Palatski Man.'

'Why would you want to do that?'

'I don't know,' she said. 'We could find out where he lives, where he makes his stuff. He won't come around pretty soon. Maybe we could go to his house in the winter and buy things from him.'

John looked at her. Her hair, like his, was blowing about in the wind. 'All right,' he said.

So they waited at a corner where a man was raking leaves into a pile to burn, but each time he built the pile and turned to scrape a few more leaves from his small lawn, the wind blew and the leaves whirled off from the pile and sprayed out as if alive over their heads, and then the wind suddenly died, and they floated back about the raking man into the grass softly, looking like wrinkled snow. And in a rush of leaves they closed their eyes against, the Palatski Man pushed by.

They let him go down the block. He wasn't hard to follow, he went so slow, stopping at corners for customers. They didn't have to sneak behind him because he never turned around. They followed him down the streets, and one street became another until they were out of their neighborhood, and the clothes the people wore became poorer and brighter. They went through the next parish, and there was less stopping because it was a poorer parish where more Mexicans lived, and the children yelled in Spanish, and they felt odd in their new Sunday clothes.

'Let's go back,' John said.

But Mary thought there was something in his voice that wasn't sure, and she took his arm and mock-pleaded, 'No-o-o-o, this is fun, let's see where he goes.'

The Palatski Man went up the streets, past the trucking lots full of semis without cabs, where the wind blew more grit and dirty papers than leaves, where he stopped hardly at all. Then past blocks of mesh-windowed factories shut down for Sunday and the streets empty and the pavements powdered with brown glass from broken beer bottles. They walked hand in hand a block behind the white, bent figure of the Palatski Man pushing his cart over the fissured sidewalk. When he crossed streets and looked from side to side for traffic, they jumped into doorways, afraid he might turn around.

He crossed Western Avenue, which was a big street and so looked emptier than any of the others without traffic on it. They followed him down Western Avenue and over the rivet-studded, aluminum-girdered bridge that spanned the river, watching the pigeons flitting through the cables. Just past the bridge he turned into a pitted asphalt road that trucks used for hauling their cargoes to freight trains. It wound into the acres of endless lots and railroad yards behind the factories along the river.

John stopped. 'We can't go any further,' he said.

'Why?' she asked. 'It's getting interesting.'

'I've been here before,' he said.

'When?'

'I don't remember, but I feel like I've been here before.'

'C'mon, silly,' she said, and tugged his arm with all her might and opened her eyes very wide, and John let himself be tugged along, and they both started laughing. But by now the Palatski Man had disappeared around a curve in the road, and they had to run to catch up. When they turned the bend, they just caught sight of him going over a hill, and the asphalt road they had to run up had turned to cinder. At the top of the hill Mary cried, 'Look!' and pointed off to the left, along the river. They saw a wheat field in the center of the city, with the wheat blowing and waving, and the Palatski Man, half man and half willowy grain, was pushing his cart through the field past a scarecrow with straw arms outstretched and huge black crows perched on them.

'It looks like he's hanging on a cross,' Mary said.

'Let's go,' John said, and she thought he meant turn back home and was ready to agree because his voice sounded so determined, but he moved forward instead to follow the Palatski Man.

'Where can he be going?' Mary said.

But John just looked at her and put his finger to his lips. They followed single file down a trail trod smooth and twisting through the wheat field. When they passed the scarecrow, the crows flapped off in great iridescent flutters, cawing at them while the scarecrow hung as if guarding a field of wings. Then, at the edge of the field, the cinder path resumed sloping downhill toward the river.

John pointed and said, 'The mounds of coal.'

And she saw three black mounds rising up in the distance and sparkling in the sun.

'C'mon,' John said, 'we have to get off the path.'

He led her down the slope and into the weeds that blended with the river grasses, rushes, and cattails. They sneaked through the weeds, which pulled at her dress and scratched her legs. John led the way; he seemed to know where he was going. He got down on his hands and knees and motioned for her to do the same, and they crawled forward without making a sound. Then John lay flat on his stomach, and she crawled beside him and flattened out. He parted the weeds, and she looked out and saw a group of men standing around a kettle on a fire and dressed in a strange assortment of ill-fitting suits, either too small or too large and baggy. None of the suit pieces matched, trousers blue and the suitcoat brown, striped pants and checked coats, countless combinations of colors. They wore crushed hats of all varieties: bowlers, straws, stetsons, derbies, homburgs. Their ties were the strangest of all, misshapen and dangling to their knees in wild designs of flowers, swirls, and polka dots.

'Who are they?' she whispered.

'The Ragmen. They must be dressed for Sunday,' John hissed.

And then she noticed the shacks behind the men, with the empty wagons parked in front and the stacks of junk from uprooted basements and strewn attics, even the gutted factory just the way John had described it. She saw the dogs suddenly jump up barking and whining, and all the men by the fire turn around as the Palatski Man wheeled his cart into their midst.

He gestured to them, and they all parted as he walked to the fire, where he stood staring into the huge black pot. He turned and said something to one of them, and the man began to stir whatever was in the pot, and then the Palatski Man dipped a small ladle into it and raised it up, letting its contents pour back into the pot, and Mary felt herself get dizzy and gasp as she saw the bright red fluid in the sun and heard John exclaim, 'Blood!' And she didn't want to see any more, how the men came to the pot and dipped their fingers in it and licked them off, nodding and smiling. She saw the horses filing out of their barn, looking ponderous and naked without their harnesses. She hid her face in her arms and wouldn't look, and then she heard the slow, sorrowful chanting and off-key wheezing behind it. And she looked up and realized all the Ragmen, like a choir of bums, had removed their crushed hats and stood bareheaded in the wind, singing. Among them someone worked a dilapidated accordion, squeezing out a mournful, foreign melody. In the center stood the Palatski Man, leading them with his arms like a conductor and sometimes intoning a word that all would echo in a chant. Their songs rose and fell but always rose again, sometimes nasal, then shifting into a rich baritone, building always louder and louder, more sorrowful, until the Palatski Man rang his bell and suddenly everything was silent. Not men or dogs or accordion or birds or crickets or wind made a sound. Only her breathing and a far-off throb that she seemed to feel more than hear, as if all the church bells in the city were tolling an hour. The sun was in the center of the sky. Directly below it stood the Palatski Man raising a *palatski*.

The Ragmen had all knelt. They rose and started a procession leading to where she and John hid in the grass. Then John was up and yelling, 'Run!' and she scrambled to her feet, John dragging her by the arm. She tried to run but her legs wouldn't obey her. They felt so rubbery pumping through the weeds and John pulling her faster than she could go with the weeds tripping her and the vines clutching like fingers around her ankles.

Ragmen rose up in front of them and they stopped and ran the other way but Ragmen were there too. Ragmen were everywhere in an embracing circle, so they stopped and stood still, holding hands.

'Don't be afraid,' John told her.

And she wasn't. Her legs wouldn't move and she didn't care. She just didn't want to run anymore, choking at the acrid smell of the polluted river. Through her numbness she heard John's small voice lost over and over in the open daylight repeating, 'We weren't doin' anything.'

The Ragmen took them back to where the Palatski Man stood before the fire and the bubbling pot. John started to say something but stopped when the Palatski Man raised his finger to his lips. One of the Ragmen brought a bushel of shiny apples and another a handful of pointed little sticks. The Palatski Man took an apple and inserted the stick and dipped it into the pot and took it out coated with red. The red crystallized and turned hard, and suddenly she realized it was a red candy apple that he was handing her. She took it from his hand and held it dumbly while he made another for John and a third for himself. He bit into his and motioned for them to do the same. She looked up at John standing beside her, flushed and sweaty, and she bit into her apple. It was sweeter than anything she'd ever tasted, with the red candy crunching in her mouth, melting, mingling with apple juice.

And then from his cart he took a giant *palatski*, ten times bigger than any she had ever seen, and broke it again and again, handing the tiny bits to the circle of Ragmen, where they were passed from mouth to mouth. When there was only a small piece left, he broke it three ways and offered one to John. She saw it disappear in John's hand and watched him raise his hand to his mouth and at the same time felt him squeeze her hand very hard. The Palatski Man handed her a part. Honey stretched into threads from its torn edges. She put it in her mouth, expecting the crisp wafer and honey taste, but it was so bitter it brought tears to her eyes. She fought them back and swallowed, trying not to screw up her face, not knowing whether he had tricked her or given her a gift she didn't understand. He spoke quietly to one of the Ragmen in a language she couldn't follow and pointed to an enormous pile of rags beside a nearby shack. The man trudged to the pile and began sorting through it and returned with a white ribbon of immaculate, shining silk. The Palatski Man gave it to her, then turned and walked away, disappearing into the shack. As soon as he was gone, the circle of Ragmen broke and they trudged away, leaving the children standing dazed before the fire.

'Let's get out of here,' John said. They turned and began walking slowly, afraid the Ragmen would regroup at any second, but no one paid any attention to them. They walked away. Back through the wheat field, past silently perched crows, over the hill, down the cinder path that curved and became the pitted asphalt road. They walked over the Western Avenue bridge, which shook as a green trolley, empty with Sunday, clattered across it. They stopped in the middle of the bridge, and John opened his hand, and she saw the piece of *palatski* crushed into a little sour ball, dirty and pasty with sweat.

'Did you eat yours?' he asked.

'Yes,' she said.

'I tried to stop you,' he said. 'Didn't you feel me squeezing your hand? It might have been poisoned.'

'No,' she lied, so he wouldn't worry, 'it tasted fine.'

'Nobody believed me,' John said.

'I believed you.'

'They'll see now.'

And then he gently took the ribbon that she still unconsciously held in her hand—she had an impulse to clench her fist but didn't—and before she could say anything, he threw it over the railing into the river. They watched it, caught in the drafts of wind under the bridge, dipping and gliding among the wheeling pigeons, finally touching the green water and floating away.

'You don't want the folks to see that,' John said. 'They'd get all excited and nothing happened. I mean nothing really happened, we're both all right.'

'Yes,' she said. They looked at each other. Sunlight flashing through latticed girders made them squint; it reflected from the slits of eyes and off the river when their gaze dropped. Wind swooped over the railing and tangled their hair.

'You're the best girl I ever knew,' John told her.

They both began to laugh, so hard they almost cried, and John stammered out, 'We're late for dinner—I bet we're gonna really get it,' and they hurried home.

They were sent to bed early that night without being permitted to watch TV. She undressed and put on her nightgown and climbed under her covers, feeling the sad, hollow Sunday-night feeling when the next morning will be Monday and the weekend is dying. The feeling always reminded her of all the past Sunday nights she'd had it, and she thought of all the future Sunday nights when it would come again. She wished John could come into her room so they could talk. She lay in bed tossing and seeking the cool places under her pillow with her arms and in the nooks of her blanket with her toes. She listened to the whole house go to sleep: the TV shut off after the late news, the voices of her parents discussing whether the doors had been locked for the night. She felt herself drifting to sleep and tried to think her nightly prayer, the Hail Mary before she slept, but it turned into a half dream that she woke out of with a faint recollection of Gabriel's wings, and she lay staring at the familiar shapes of furniture in her dark room. She heard the wind outside like a low whinny answered by cats. At last she climbed out of her bed and looked out the lace-curtained window. Across her backyard, over the catalpa tree, the moon hung low in the cold sky. It looked like a giant *palatski* snagged in the twigs. And then she heard the faint tinkle of the bell.

He stood below, staring up, the moon, like silver eyeballs, shining in the centers of his dark glasses. His horse, a windy white stallion, stamped and snorted behind him, and a gust of leaves funneled along the ground and swirled through the streetlight, and some of them stuck in the horse's tangled mane while its hooves kicked sparks in the dark alley. He offered her a *palatski*.

She ran from the window to the mirror and looked at herself in the dark, feeling her teeth growing and hair pushing through her skin in the tender parts of her body that had been bare and her breasts swelling like apples from her flat chest and her blood burning, and then in a lapse of wind, when the leaves fell back to earth, she heard his gold bell jangle again as if silver and knew that it was time to go.

GET SOME YOUNG

Barry Hannah

Since he had returned from Korea he and his wife lived in mutual disregard, which turned three times a month into animal passion then diminished on the sharp incline to hatred, at last collecting in time into silent equal fatigue. His face was ordinarily rimmed with a short white beard and his lips frozen like those of a perch, such a face as you see in shut-ins and winos. But he did not drink much anymore, he simply often forgot his face as he did that of his wife in the blue house behind his store. He felt clever in his beard and believed that his true expressions were hidden.

Years ago when he was a leader of the Scouts he had cut way down on his drink. It seemed he could not lead the Scouts without going through their outings almost full drunk. He would get too angry at particular boys. Then in a hollow while they ran ahead planting pine trees one afternoon he was thrust by his upper bosom into heavy painful sobs. He could not stand them anymore and he quit the Scouts and the bonded whiskey at the same time. Now and then he would snatch a dram and return to such ecstasy as was painful and barbed with sorrow when it left.

This man Tuck last year stood behind the counter heedless of his forty-first birthday when two lazy white girls came in and raised their T-shirts then ran away. He worried they had mocked him in his own store and only in a smaller way was he certain he was still desirable and they could not help it, minxes. But at last he was more aggrieved over this than usual and he felt stuffed as with hot meat breaking forth unsewed at the seams. Yes girls, but through his life he had been stricken by young men too and became ruinously angry at them for teasing him with their existence. It was not clear whether he wished to ingest them or exterminate them or yet again, wear their bodies as a younger self, all former prospects delivered to him again. They would come in his life and then suddenly leave, would they, would they now? Particular Scouts, three of them, had seemed to know their own charms very well and worked him like a gasping servant in their behalf. Or so it had felt, mad wrath at the last, the whiskey put behind him.

The five boys played in the Mendenhall pool room for a few hours, very seriously, like international sportsmen in a castle over a bog, then they went out on the sidewalks mimicking the denizens of this gritty burg who stood and ambled about like escaped cattle terrified of sudden movements from any quarter. The boys were from the large city some miles north. When they failed at buying beer even with the big hairy Walthall acting like Peter Gunn they didn't much care anyway because they had the peach wine set by growing more alcoholic per second. Still, they smoked and a couple of them swore long histrionic oaths in order to shake up a meek druggist. Then they got in the blue Chevrolet Bel Air and drove toward their camp on the beach of the Strong River. They had big hearts and somehow even more confidence because there were guns in the car. They hoped some big-nosed crimp-eyed seed would follow them but none did. Before the bridge road took them to the water they stopped at the store for their legitimate country food. They had been here many times but they were all some bigger now. They did not know the name of the man in there and did not want to know it.

Bean, Arden Pal, Lester Silk, Walthall, and Swanly were famous to one another. None of them had any particular money or any special girl. Swanly, the last in the store, was almost too good-looking, like a Dutch angel, and the others felt they were handsome too in his company as the owner of a pet of great beauty might feel, smug in his association. But Swanly was not vain and moved easily about, graceful as a tennis player from the era of Woodrow Wilson, though he had never played the game.

From behind the cash register on his barstool Tuck from his hidden whitened fuzzy face watched Swanly without pause. On his fourth turn up the aisle Swanly noticed this again and knew certainly there was something wrong.

Mister, you think I'd steal from you?

What are you talking about?

You taking a picture of me?

I was noticing you've grown some from last summer.

You'd better give me some cigarettes now so we can stamp that out.

The other boys giggled.

I'm just a friendly man in a friendly store, said Tuck.

The smothered joy of hearing this kept the rest of them shaking the whole remaining twenty minutes they roamed the aisles. They got Viennas, sardines, Pall Malls, Winstons, Roi-Tans, raisins; tamales in the can, chili and beans, peanut butter, hoop and rat cheese, bologna, salami, white bread, mustard, mayonnaise, Nehi, root beer, Orange Crush; carrots, potatoes, celery, sirloin, Beech-Nut, a trotline, chicken livers, chocolate and vanilla Moon Pies, four pairs of hunting socks, batteries, kitchen matches. On the porch Swanly gave Walthall the cigarettes because he did not smoke.

Swanly was a prescient boy. He hated that their youth might end. He saw the foul gloom of job and woman ahead, all the toting and fetching, all the counting of diminished joys like sheep with plague; the arrival of beard hair, headaches, the numerous hospital trips, the taxes owed and the further debts, the mean and ungrateful children, the washed and waxen dead grown thin and like bad fish heaved into the outer dark. He had felt his own beauty drawn from him in the first eruption of sperm, an accident in the bed of an aunt by marriage whose smell of gardenia remained wild and deep in the pillow. Swanly went about angry and frightened and much saddened him.

Walthall lived on some acreage out from the city on a farm going quarter speed with peach and pecan trees and a few head of cattle. Already he had made his own peach brandy. Already he had played viola with high seriousness. Already he had been deep with a 'woman' in Nashville and he wrote poems about her in the manner of E. A. Poe at his least in bonging rhymes. In every poem he expired in some way and he wanted the 'woman' to watch this. Already he could have a small beard if he wanted, and he did, and he wanted a beret too. He had found while visiting relatives around the community of Rodney a bound flock of letters in an abandoned house, highly erotic missiles cast forth by a swooning inmate of Whitfield, the state asylum, to whatever zestfully obliging woman once lived there. These he would read to the others once they were outside town limits and then put solemnly away in a satchel where he also kept his poetry. A year ago Walthall was in a college play, a small atmospheric part but requiring much dramatic amplitude even on the streets thereafter. Walthall bought an ancient Jaguar sedan for nothing, and when it ran, smelling like Britain on the skids or the glove of a soiled duke, Walthall sat in it aggressive in his leisure as he drove about subdivisions at night looking in windows for naked people. Walthall was large but not athletic and his best piece of acting was collapsing altogether as if struck by a deer rifle from somewhere. For Walthall reckoned he had many enemies, many more than even knew of his existence.

Swanly was at some odds with Walthall's style. He would not be instructed in ways of the adult world, he did not like talking sex. Swanly was cowlicked and blithe in his boy ways and he meant to stay that way. He was hesitant even to learn new words. Of all the boys, Swanly most feared and loathed Negroes. He had watched the Negro young precocious in their cursing and dancing and he abhorred this. The only role he saw fit in maturity was that of a blond German cavalry captain. Among Walthall's recondite possessions, he coveted only the German gear from both world wars. Swanly would practice with a monocle and cigarette and swagger stick. It was not that he opposed those of alien races so much but that he aspired to the ideal of the Nordic horseman with silver spurs whom he had never seen. The voices of Nat King Cole and Johnny Mathis pleased him greatly. On the other hand he was careful never to eat certain foods he viewed as negroid, such as Raisinets at the movies. There was a special earnest purity about him.

The boys had been to Florida two years ago in the 1954 Bel Air owned by the brother of Arden Pal. They were stopped in Perry by a kind patrolman who thought they looked like runaway youth. But his phone call to Pal's home put it right. They went rightly on their way to the sea but for a while everybody but Swanly was depressed they were taken for children. It took them many cigarettes and filthy songs to get their confidence back. Uh found your high school ring in muh baby's twat, sang Walthall with the radio. You are muh cuntshine, muh only cuntshine, they sang to another tune. From shore to shore AM teenage castrati sang about this angel or that, chapels and heaven. It was a most spiritual time. But Swanly stared fixedly out the window at the encroaching palms, disputing the sunset with his beauty, his blond hair a crown over his forehead. He felt bred out of a golden mare with a saber in his hand, hair shocked back in stride with the wind. Other days he felt ugly, out of an ass, and the loud and vulgar world too soon pinched his face.

The little river rushed between the milky bluffs like cola. Pal dug into a clay bank for a sleeping grotto, his tarp over it. He placed three pictures of draped bohemian women from the magazine *Esquire* on the hard clay walls and under them he placed his flute case, pistol, and Mossberg carbine with telescope mounted there beside two candles in holes, depicting high adventure and desire, the grave necessities of men.

The short one called Lester Silk was newly arrived to the group. He was the veteran army brat of several far-flung bases. Now his retired father was going to seed through smoke and ceaseless hoisting on his own petard of Falstaff beers. Silk knew much of weapons and spoke often of those of the strange sex, men and women, who had preyed the perimeters of his youth. These stories were vile and wonderful to the others yet all the while they felt that Silk carried death in him in some old way. He was not nice. Others recalled him as only the short boy, big nose and fixed leer—nothing else. His beard was well on and he seemed ten years beyond the rest.

Bean's father, a salesman, had fallen asleep on a highway cut through a bayou and driven off into the water. The police called from Louisiana that night. All of the boys were at the funeral. Right after it Bean took his shotgun out hunting meadowlarks. The daughter of his maid was at the house with her mother helping with the funeral buffet. She was Bean's age. She told Bean it didn't seem nice him going hunting directly after his father's funeral. He told her she was only a darkie and to shut up, he made all the rules now. Her feelings were hurt and her mother hugged her, crying, as they watched young Bean go off over the hill to the pine meadows with his chubby black mutt Spike. Bean was very thin now. He had a bad complexion. He ran not on any team but only around town and the gravel roads through the woods. Almost every hour out of school he ran, looking ahead in forlorn agony and saying nothing to anybody. He was The Runner, the boy with a grim frown. When he ran he had wicked ideas on girls. They were always slaves and hostages. His word could free them or cause them to go against all things sacred. Or he would leave them. Don't leave, don't leave. I'll do anything. But I must go. After the death of his father he began going to the police station when he was through with his run. He begged to go along on a call. He hoped somebody would be shot. He wished he lived in a larger city where there was more crime. When he got a wife he would protect her and then she

would owe him a great deal. Against all that was sacred he would
prevail on her, he might be forced to tie her up in red underwear and
attach a yoke to her. Bean was vigilant about his home and his guns
were loaded. He regarded trespass as a dire offense and studied the tire
marks and footprints neighbor and stranger made on the verge of his
lawn. Bean's dog was as hair-triggered as he was, ruffing and flinching
around the house like a creature beset by trespass at all stations. Both
of them protected Bean's mother to distraction. She hauled him to and
fro to doctors for his skin and in the waiting room thin Bean would rise
to oppose whoever might cross his mother. Of all the boys, Bean most
loved Swanly.

Three boys, Bean among them, waded out into a gravel pool now,
a pool that moved heavy in its circumference but was still and deep in
its center like a woman in the very act of conception. The water moved
past them into a deep pit of sand under the bridge and then under the
bluffs on either side, terra-cotta besieged by black roots. An ageless
hermit bothersome to no one lived in some kind of tin house in the
bank down the way a half mile and they intended to worry him. It was
their fourth trip to the Strong and something was urgent now as they
had to make plans. They were not at peace and were hungry for an act
before the age of school job money and wife. The bittersweet Swanly
named it school job money whore, and felt ahead of him the awful
tenure in which a man shuffles up and down the lanes of a great
morgue. Swanly's father was a failure except for Swanly himself who
was beautiful past the genes of either parent. He worshiped Swanly,
idolized him, and heeded him, all he said. He watched the smooth lad
live life in his walk, talk, and long silent tours in the bathtub. He
believed in Swanly as he did not himself or in his wife. It was Swanly's
impression there was no real such thing as maturity, no, people simply
began acting like grown-ups, the world a farce of playing house.
Swanly of all the others most wanted an act, standing there to his waist
in the black water.

The storekeeper Tuck knew for twenty years about the clothesline
strung from the shed at the rear of the yard of the house behind the
store. The T-bar stood at the near end with high clover at its base. Yet
that night two weeks ago. His throat still hurt and had a red welt across
it. He ran through his lawn and necked himself on the wire. Blind in
the dark in a fury. What was it? All right. He had given himself up to

age but although he did not like her he thought his wife would hold out against it. After all she was ten years younger. But he saw she was growing old in the shoulders and under the eyes, all of a sudden. That might cause pity, but like the awful old she had begun clutching things, having her things, this time a box of Red Hots she wouldn't share, clutching it to her titties, this owning things more and more, small things and big, when he saw that he took a run across the yard, hard on baked mud, apoplectic, and the wire brought him down, a cutlass out of the dark. Now he was both angry and puny, riven and welted and all kind of ointment sticky at his shirt collar. It was intolerable especially now he'd seen the youth, oh wrath of loss, fair gone sprite. His very voice was bruised, the wound deep to the thorax.

Swanly, out in the river in old red shorts, was not a spoiled child. His father intended to spoil him but Swanly would not accept special privileges. He did not prevail by his looks or by his pocket money, a lot at hand always compared with the money of his partners, and he was not soft in any way so far that they knew. He could work, had worked, and he gave himself chores. He went to church occasionally, sitting down and eyed blissfully by many girls, many much older than Swanly. Even to his sluttish pill-addicted mother he was kind, even when she had some pharmaceutical cousin over on the occasion of his father being on the road. He even let himself be used as an adornment of her with his mild temper and sad charm. She would say he would at any moment be kidnapped by Hollywood. And always he would disappear conveniently to her and the cousin as if he had never been there at all except as the ghost in the picture she kept.

Walthall with his German Mauser was naked in the pool. He had more hair than the others and on his chin the outline of a goatee. On his head was a dusty black beret and his eyes were set downriver at a broad and friendly horizon. But he would go in the navy. There was no money for college right away. His impressions were quicker and deeper than those of the others. By the time he knew something, it was in his roots as a passion. He led all aspirants in passion for music, weapons, girls, books, drinking, and wrestling, where operatic goons in mode just short of drag queens grappled in the city auditorium. Walthall, an actor, felt the act near too. He was a connoisseur and this act would be most delicious. He called the hermit's name.

Sunballs! Sunballs! hefting the Mauser, Lester Silk just behind him a foot shorter and like a wet rat with his big nose. Swanly stood in patient beatitude but with an itch on, Arden Pal and Bean away at the bluff. You been wantin' it, Sunballs! Been beggin' for it, called Silk.

Come get some! cried Bean, at that distance to Walthall a threatening hood ornament.

None could be heard very far in the noise of the river.

Tuck, who had followed in his car, did hear them from the bridge.

What could they want with that wretch Sunballs? he imagined.

He was not without envy of the hermit. What a mighty wound to the balls it must take to be like that, that hiding shuffling thing, harmless and beholden to no man. Without woman, without friend, without the asking of lucre, without all but butt-bare necessity. Haunt of the possum, coon, and crane, down there. Old Testament specters with birds all over them eating honey out of roadkill. Too good for men. Sunballs was not that old, either. But he was suddenly angry at the man. Above the fray, absent, out, was he? Well.

Tuck knelt beneath a cluster of poison sumac on the rim of the bluff. He saw the three naked in the water. There was Swanly in the pool, the blond hair, the tanned skin. Who dared give a south Mississippi pissant youth such powerful flow and comeliness? Already Tuck in his long depressed thinking knew the boy had no good father, his home would stink of distress. He had known his type in the Scouts, always something deep-warped at home with them, beauty thrown up out of manure like. The mother might be beautiful but this lad had gone early and now she was a tramp needed worship by any old bunch of rags around a pecker. A boy like that you had to take it slow but not that much was needed to replace the pa, in his dim criminal weakness. You had to show them strength then wait until possibly that day, that hour, that hazy fog of moment when thought required act, the kind hand of Tuck in an instant of transfer to all nexus below the navel, no more to be denied than those rapids they're hollering down, nice lips on the boy too.

You had to show them something, then be patient.

They hated Sunballs? I could thrash Sunballs. I can bury him, he thought. I am their man.

Tuck was angered against the hermit now but sickened too. The line of pain over his thorax he attributed now directly to the hermit. The hermit was confusion.

I am a vampire I am a vampire, Tuck said aloud. They shook me out of my nest and I can't be responsible for what might happen.

He knew the boy would be back at his store.

The storekeeper's sons were grown and fattish and ugly. They married and didn't even leave the community, were just up the road there nearly together. They both of them loved life and the parts hereabouts and he could not forgive them for it.

The boy would know something was waiting for him. It would take time but the something was nearly here. There had been warmth in their exchange, not all yet unpromising.

That night in another heat his wife spoke back to him. You ain't wanted it like this in a long time. What's come over you. Now you be kindly be gentle you care for what you want, silly fool.

As he spent himself he thought, Once after Korea there was a chance for me. I had some fine stories about Pusan, Inchon, and Seoul, not all of them lies. That I once vomited on a gook in person. Fear of my own prisoner in the frozen open field there, not contempt as I did explain. But still. There was some money, higher education maybe, big house in downtown Hawaii. But I had to put it all down that hole, he said pulling back from the heat of his spouse. The fever comes on you, you gasp like a man run out of the sea by stingrays. Fore you know it you got her spread around you like a tree and fat kids. You married a tree with a nest in it blown and rained on every which way. You a part of the tree too with your arms out legs out roots down ain't going nowhere really even in an automobile on some rare break to Florida, no you just a rolling tree.

But you get some scot-free thief of time like Sunballs, he thinks he don't have to pay the toll. You know somebody else somewhere is paying it for him, though. This person rooted in his tree sweats the toll for Sunballs never you doubt it. That wretch with that joker's name eases in the store wanting to know whether he's paying sales tax, why is this bit of bait up two cents from last time? Like maybe I ought to take care of it for him. Like he's a double agent don't belong to no country. Times twenty million you got the welfare army, biggest thing ever invaded this USA, say gimme the money, the ham, the cheese, the car, the moon, worse than Sherman's march. The babysitting, the hospital, throw in a smoking Buick, and bad on gas mileage if you please. Thanks very much kiss my ass. Army leech out this country white and clay-dry like those bluffs over that river down there. Pass a man with an honest store and friendly like me, what you see is a man sucked dry, the suckee toting dat barge. The suckers drive by thirteen to the Buick like a sponge laughing at you with all its mouths, got that music too, mouths big from sucking the national tit sing it out like some banshee rat speared in the jungle.

Tuck had got himself in a sleepy wrath but was too tired to carry it out and would require a good short sleep, never any long ones anymore, like your old self don't want to miss any daylight, to lift himself and resume. That Swanly they called him, so fresh he couldn't even handle a Pall Mall.

There he was, the boy back alone like Tuck knew he would be. Something had happened between them. No wonder you kept climbing out of bed with this thing in the world this happy thing all might have come to.

It ain't pondering or chatting or wishing it's only the act, from dog to man to star all nature either exploding or getting ready to.

Tuck had seen a lot of him in the pool, the move of him. This one would not play sports. There was a lean sun-browned languor to him more apt for man than boy games. It went on beyond what some thick coach could put to use.

A sacred trust prevailing from their luck together would drive them beyond all judgment, man and adolescent boy against every ugly thing in that world, which would mean nothing anymore. He would look at fresh prospects again the same as when he the young warrior returned to these shores in '53. It would not matter how leeched and discommoded he had been for three decades. Put aside, step to joy.

You boys getting on all right sleeping over there? Tuck asked Swanly.

Where'd you hear we slept anywhere? The boy seemed in a trance between the aisles, the cans around him assorted junk of lowly needs. His hair was out of place from river, wind, and sand. Smears of bracken were on his pants knees, endearing him almost too much to Tuck. My dead little boyhood, Tuck almost sobbed.

I mean is nature being kind to you.

The boy half looked at him, panting a bit, solemn and bothered.

Are you in the drama club, young man?

Swanly sighed.

You sell acting lessons here at the store?

Good. Very quick. Somebody like you would be.

You don't know me at all.

Fourth year you've been at the river. I've sort of watched you grow at the store here, in a way. This time just a little sad, or mad. We got troubles?

We. Swanly peeked straight at him then quickly away.

When I was a little guy, Tuck spoke in his mind, I held two marbles in my hand just the blue-green like his eyes. It was across the road under those chinaberries and us tykes had packed the clay down in a near perfect circle. Shot all day looking at those pretty agates. Too good to play with. My fist was all sweaty around them. I'd almost driven them through my palm. The beauty of the balls. There inside my flesh. Such things drive you to a church you never heard of before, worship them.

I have no troubles, the boy said. No we either. No troubles.

You came back to the real world.

I thought I was in it.

You've come back all alone.

Outside there's a sign that says store, mister.

Down at the river pirates playhouse, you all.

Where you get your reality anyway? said the boy. Gas oil tobacco bacon hooks?

You know, wives can really be the gate of hell. They got that stare. They want to lock you down, get some partner to stoop down to that tiny peephole look at all the little shit with them. If you can forgive my language, ladies.

So you would be standing there 'mongst the Chesterfields seeing all the big?

Tuck did not take this badly. He liked the wit.

I might be. Some of us see the big things behind all the puny.

The hermit Sunballs appeared within the moment, the screen door slamming behind him like a shot. He walked on filthy gym shoes of one aspect with the soil of his wanderings, ripped up like the roots of it. You would not see such annealed textures at the ankles of a farmer, not this color of city gutters back long past. All of him the color of putty almost, as your eyes rose. The clothes vaporish like bus exhaust. The fingers whiter in the air like a potter's but he had no work and you knew this instantly. He held a red net sack for oranges, empty. It was not known why he had an interesting name like Sunballs. You would guess the one who had named him was the cleverer. Nothing in him vouched for parts solar. More perhaps of a star gray and dead or old bait or of a sex organ on the drowned. Hair thicket of red rust on gray atop him.

He pored over the tin tops in the manner of a devout scholar. The boy watched him in fury. It was the final waste product of all maturity he saw, a creature fired-out full molded by the world, the completed grown-up.

Whereas with an equal fury the storekeeper saw the man as the final insult to duty, friendless, wifeless, jobless, motherless, stateless, and not even black. He could not bear the nervous hands of the creature over his goods, arrogant discriminating moocher. He loathed the man so much a pain came in his head and his heartbeat had thrown a sweat on him. The presence of the boy broke open all gates and he loathed in particular with a hatred he had seldom known, certainly never in Korea, where people wearing gym shoes and smelling of garlic shot at him. Another mouth, Tuck thought, seeking picking choosing. He don't benefit nobody's day. Squandered every chance of his white skin, down in his river hole. Mocks even a healthy muskrat in personal hygiene. Not native to nothing. Hordes of them, Tuck imagined, pouring across the borders of the realm from bumland. His progeny lice with high attitudes.

Tuck saw the revulsion of the boy.

You ten cents higher than the store in Pinola, spoke Sunballs. His voice was shallow and thin as if he had worn it down screaming. A wreckage of teeth added a whistle at the end.

Tuck was invested by red blindness.

But Swanly spoke first. I warn you. Don't come near me. I can't be responsible, you.

The hermit whispered a breeze off rags where feral beings had swarmed. Ere be a kind of storeman take his neighbor by the short hairs like they got you dead in an airport and charges for water next thing you know.

What did you say? demanded the storekeeper coming around the register. You say neighbor and airport? You never even crossed through an airport I bet, you filthy mouthbroom.

Sunballs stood back from the beauty of Swanly but was not afraid of the anger of Tuck. He was too taken with this startling pretty boy.

Oh yes, my man, airport I have been in and the airplane crash is why I am here.

He pointed at the oiled floor swept clean by the wife who was now coming in from the rear in attendance to the loud voices, so rare in this shop, where the savage quiet reigned almost perpetual both sides of the mutual gloom, the weary armistice, then the hate and lust and panting. Only lately had her own beauty ebbed and not truly very much. She was younger with long muscular legs and dressed like a well-kept city woman in beach shorts. Her hair was brunette and chopped shortish and she had the skin of a Mexican. Her lips were pulled together in a purse someone might mistake for delight by their expression, not petulance. Her name was Bernadette and when Tuck saw her he flamed with nostalgia, not love. Brought back to his own hard tanned youth returned from the Orient on a ship in San Diego. Swanly looked over to her, and the two of them, boy and married woman, in the presence of the gasping hermit, fell in love.

What's wrong out here? she asked gently, her eyes never off the boy.

Said they can have it if that's what's there in the modern world, continued Sunballs. It was a good job I had too, I'm no liar. They was treating me special flying me to Kalamazoo, Michigan, on a Constellation. We was set upon by them flight stewards, grown men in matching suits, but they was these beatniks underneath, worse, these flight stewards, called, they attended themselves, it didn't matter men women or children, they was all homos all the time looking in a mirror at each other, didn't stir none atall for nobody else in their abomination once the airplane began crashing. It took forever rolling back and forth downward near like a corkscrew but we known it was plowing into ground directly. These two funny fellows you know, why when we wrecked all up with several dead up front and screaming, why they was in the back in the rear hull a'humpin' each other their eyes closed 'blivious to the crash they trying to get one last 'bomination in and we unlatched ourselves, stood up in the hulk and they still goin' at it, there's your modern world I say, two smoky old queers availing theyselve and the captain come back with half a burnt face say what the hell we got. Ever damn thing about it a crime against nature. No money no Kalamazoo never bring me back in, damn them, yes I seen it what it come down to in your modern world.

Tuck watched Swanly and his wife in long locked estimation of each other, the words of the hermit flying over like faraway geese.

People is going over to the other side of everything, I say, and it all roots out from the evil of price, the cost of everything being so goddamned high. Nothing ain't a tenth its value and a man's soul knows it's true.

What? Tuck said, down from his rage and confused by everybody. You ain't flapped on like this in the seven years you been prowling round.

Sunballs would not stop. Old man Bunch Lewis up north in the state, he run a store and has a hunchback. The hermit spoke with relish, struck loquacious by the act of love proceeding almost visibly between the boy and the wife, each to each, the female lips moving without words. It behooved him, he thought, to announce himself a wry soldier of the world.

Fellow come in seen Lewis behind the counter with a ten-dollar shirt in his hands. Said Lewis, What's that on your back? Lewis got all fierce, he say, You know it's a hump I'm a humpback you son of a bitch. Fellow say, Well I thought it might be your ass, everything else in this store so high. What he say.

Neither the storekeeper nor his wife had ever heard the first word of wit from this man.

The hermit put a hand to his rushy wad of hair as if to groom it. The plain common man even in this humble state can't afford no clothes where you got the Bunch Lewises a'preying on them, see. After this appeal he paused, shot out for a time, years perhaps.

This isn't a plain common boy here, though, is he, son? Bernadette said, as if her voice had fled out and she powerless. The question called out of her in a faint tone between mother love and bald lechery. Is it real? Has this boy escaped out of a theater somewheres? demanded the hermit. His eyes were on the legs of the wife, her feet set in fashion huaraches like a jazz siren between the great wars.

You never even looked at my wife before, said Tuck. Pissmouth.

Hush everybody. You getting the air dirty, said Bernadette.

Her own boys were hammy and homely and she wandered in a moment of conception, giving birth to Swanly all over again as he stood there, a pained ecstasy in the walls of her womb. He was what she had intended by everything female about her and she knew hardly any woman ever chanced to see such a glorious boy.

Tuck was looking at her afresh and he was shocked. Why my wife, she's a right holy wonder, she is, he thought. Or is she just somebody I've not ever seen now?

Out of the south Mississippi fifth-grown pines, the rabbitweed, the smaller oaks and hickories, the white clay and the coon-toed bracken, she felt away on palisades over a sea of sweetening terror.

She said something nobody caught. Swanly in shyness and because he could not hold his feelings edged away with a can of sardines and bottle of milk unpaid for, but he was not conscious of this.

I am redeemed, she said again, even more softly.

Sunballs left with a few goods unpaid for and he was very conscious of this. Tuck stared at him directly as he went out the door but saw little. It must have been the hermit felt something was owed for his narration.

The wife walked to the screen and looked out carefully.

You stay away from that boy, she called, and they heard her.

When Tuck was alone behind the register again he sensed himself alien to all around him and his aisles seemed a fantastic dump of road offal brought in by a stranger.

He was in the cold retreat from Chosin marching backwards, gooks in the hills who'd packed in artillery by donkey. You could smell the garlic coming off them at a half mile but My sweet cock that was my living room compared to this now, he thought.

All the fat on him, the small bags under his eyes, the hint of rung at his belt he summoned out of himself. He must renew his person. Some moments would come and he could do this simply by want. Tuck felt himself grow leaner and handsomer.

Walthall had wanted the peach wine to become brandy but alas. He brought his viola to the river camp and Pal his bass flute, two instruments unrecognized by anybody in his school, his city, and they played them passing strange with less artistry than vengeance sitting opposed on a sunken petrified log like an immense crocodile forced up by saurian times, in the first rush of small rapids out of the pool. This river in this place transported them to Germany or the Rockies or New England, anywhere but here, and the other boys, especially the hearkening beatific Swanly, listened, confident paralyzed hipsters, to the alien strains of these two mates, set there in great parlor anguish swooning like people in berets near death.

Bean, the sternest and most religious of them all, set his gun on his knees, feeling a lyric militancy and praying for an enemy. Like the others, this boy was no drinking man but unlike them he did not drink the wine from the fruit jars. For the others, the wine went down like a ruined orchard, acid to the heart, where a ball of furred heat made them reminiscent of serious acts never acted, women never had.

The wine began dominating and the boys were willing slaves. When the music paused Lester Silk, son of the decaying army man who never made anything but fun of poetry and grabbed his scrotum and acted the fairy whenever it occurred at school, said, I believe in years to come I will meet a pale woman from Texas who plays clarinet in the symphony. Then we shall dally, there will be a rupture over my drinking, she'll tear up my pictures and for penance over the freedoms she allowed me she will go off to the nun mountains in a faraway state and be killed accidentally by masked gunmen. Forever afterward I will whup my lap mournfully in her memory.

Somebody must die when you hear that music out here, I feel it, said Swanly, cool-butted and naked in the little rapids but full hot with the peach wine after five swallows.

Walthall, stopping the viola, wore a necklace of twine and long mail-order Mauser shells. He exclaimed, Send not to ask for when the bell tolls. I refuse to mourn the death by fire of a child's Christmas on Fern Hill. Do not go gently in my sullen craft, up yours. He raised the fruit jar from his rock.

All that separates me from Leslie Caron must die, said Arden Pal. He held his flute up like a saber, baroque over the flat rocks and frothing tea of the rapids. Pal was a gangling youth of superfluous IQ already experiencing vile depressions. His brain made him feel constantly wicked but he relieved himself through botany and manic dilettantism.

Like a piece of languid Attic statuary Swanly lay out with a sudden whole nudeness under the shallow water. He might have been something caught in the forest and detained for study, like a white deer missing its ilk, because he was sad and in love and greatly confused.

Bernadette cooked two chickens, made a salad, then Irish Creme cookies, for the boys' health, she said, for their wretched motherless pirates' diets, and Tuck drove her down to the bridge with it all in a basket. Catastrophic on both sides of the washboard gravel was the erosion where ditches of white limesoil had been clawed into deep small canyons by heavy rains, then swerved into the bogs in wild fingers. Tuck pretended he was confused as to where the boys might be in camp and guessed loudly while pulling off before the bridge into the same place he had been earlier. Ah, he said, the back of their car, Hinds County, I recognize it.

But he said he would wait and that was perfect by Bernadette. Then he followed her, tree to tree, at a distance. Bernadette came to the head of the bluff and he saw her pause, then freeze, cradling the food basket covered in blue cloth with white flowers printed on. Through a nearer gully he saw what she saw.

Hairy Walthall, at the viola with his root floating in the rills, might have seemed father to Swanly, who was hung out like a beige flag in the shallows. She could not see Arden Pal but she heard the deep weird flute. Swanly moved as a liquid one with the river, the bed around him slick tobacco shale, and Bernadette saw all this through a haze of inept but solemn chamber music. She did not know it was inept and a wave of terrible exhilaration overcame her.

Tuck looked on at the boys from his own vantage, stroking the wound to his throat.

The hermit Sunballs was across the river before them in a bower of wild muscadine, prostrate and gripping the lip of the bluff. He owned a telescope, which he was now using. He viewed all of Swanly he could. The others were of no concern. For a while Tuck and his wife could not see him, flat to the earth and the color of organic decay. None of them for that matter would have recognized their own forms rapt and helpless to the quick, each with their soul drawn out through their eyes, beside themselves, stricken into painful silence.

It was habitual with Pal as he played the flute, however, that his eyes went everywhere. He was unsure at first then he thought he had invoked ghosts by his music, the ancient river dead roused from their Civil War ghoulments by the first flute since in these parts. He was startled by this for the seconds the thought lasted then he was frightened because they were on both bluffs and he mistook the telescope pushed out of the vines for a weapon. Perhaps they were the law, but next he knew they were not, seeing one was a woman.

They're watching you, Swanly!

The boys, except Swanly, came out of the water and thrashed back to the camp incensed and indignant. Pal pointed his flute at the telescope, which receded. Then the hermit's face came briefly into the frame of vine leaves. He could not tear himself away.

Swanly stood wobbling in the shallows, his hand to the slick shale rock, then at last stood up revealed and fierce in his nakedness. He swayed on the slick rocks, outraged, screaming. Then he vomited.

Keep your eyes off me! Keep away! he bawled upwards at the hermit, who then disappeared.

Pal pointed upwards to the right. They watched too, Swanly! But Swanly didn't seem to understand this.

Walthall fired his Mauser twice in the air and the blasts made rocking echoes down the river beach to beach.

Bernadette and Tuck melted back onto the rooted path in the high cane and the woman came cautiously with her basket, trailed fifty yards behind by her husband who was trembling and homicidal toward the hermit. Also he knew the boy loved his wife more than him. The boy's nakedness to him had had no definition but was a long beige flag of taunting and every fine feeling of his seemed mocked and whored by the presence of the hermit. Tuck felt himself only a raving appendage to the event, a thing tacked on to the crisis of his wife.

Yoo hoo! Oh bad bad boys. I've got a treat for you, called Bernadette. All wet in their pants they stared up to the woman clearing the cane above them, their beds spread below her. Their sanctuary ruined. Only Swanly knew who she was.

Oh no, is it a woman of the church? said Walthall.

There will always be a woman around to wreck things, said Pal.

No, she's all right, Swanly intervened, though he was still sick. He came up from the shore roots and struggled into his shorts slowly. He seemed paralyzed and somewhere not with them, an odd sleepiness on him. Be nice, all of you, he added.

Big Mama Busybod, said Walthall. Courtesy of the Southern regions.

Out in the sun they saw she was not a bad-looking case though she seemed arrested by a spiritual idea and did not care her hair was blowing everywhere like a proper woman of the '50s would.

Her husband came behind, mincing over the stone beach. She turned.

I heard the shots, he said.

Fools. Eat, said Bernadette. But she remained startled by Swanly and could not turn her face long from him.

Tuck didn't understand it, but his jaw began flapping. You boys ever bait a trotline with soap? Yes Ivory soap. Tuck pointed under the bridge where their line was set on the near willow. Tuck was not convinced he even existed now outside the river of want he poured toward Swanly. He was not interested in what he continued to say, like something in a storekeeper's costume activated by a pullstring and thrust into a playhouse by a child. Fish began biting on the substances of modern industry in the '40s, boys. Why they're like contemporary men they ain't even that hungry just more curious. Or a woman. They get curious and then the bait eats them, huh.

Yes sir, said Walthall, annoyed.

Tuck kept on in despondent sagery then trailed off as the boys ate and he next simply sat down on a beach boulder and stared away from them into the late bower of Sunballs across the river.

When he twisted to look he was astounded by the extent of bosom his wife was visiting on Swanly. She was bared like some tropical hula but not. Swanly ate his chicken kneeling in front of her with his bare smooth chest slightly burned red and of such an agreeable shape he seemed made to fly through night winds like the avatar on the bow of a ship. That hussy had dropped her shawl down and Tuck noticed more of her in truth, her mothersome cleavage, than he had in years, faintly freckled and still not a bad revelation. Not in years atop her.

It was eleven years ago when he had pursued illicit love with another woman. This was when his boys were small and cute. He could not get over how happy he was and blameless and blessed-feeling, as if in the garden before the fall. She was a young woman with practical headquarters in the Jackson Country Club, a thing he felt giant pride about, her sitting there in a swimsuit nursing a Tom Collins, high-heeled beach shoes on her feet, talking about storms how she loved them. Now she was a fat woman and his children were fat men and it was not their fatness that depressed him so much as it was watching visible time on them, the horrible millions of minutes collected and evident, the murdered idle thousands of hours, his time more than theirs in their change. They had an unfortunate disease where you saw everything the minute you saw them, the awful feckless waiting, the lack of promise, the bulk of despair. The woman had been attracted to him through his handsome little boys and she would excite him by exclaiming, Oh what wonderful seed you have. He stayed up like a happy lighthouse with rotating beam. She had no children, never would, but she whispered to him he might break her will if he didn't stop being so good. All the while he had loved Bernadette too, even more, was that possible? The woman didn't mind. What kind of man am I? Tuck thought. Was time working every perversion it had on him, were there many like him? He felt multiplied in arms and legs, a spider feeling eight ways, he was going into the insect kingdom. Oh yes, lost to the rest.

He loved his boys but my God they were like old uncles, older than him, mellow and knee-slapping around a campfire. He loved his wife, but no he didn't, it was an embattled apathy each morning goaded into mere courtesy, that was what, and he felt wild as a prophet mocking an army of the righteous below him at the gate.

Now isn't that better? his wife said to the boys, who had fed themselves with hesitation before they fell to trough like swine.

You're too thoughtful of us, ma'am, said Swanly.

I'm Bernadette, she said.

You are desperate, thought Tuck. I sort of like it. Hanging all out there, little Mama.

Was it how you like it? she said only to the boy.

My mother never cooked for me like that.

Ah.

Nobody ever has.

Oh. What's wrong?

That hermit, you know. He saw me without anything on.

She could see he was still trembling, warm as it was. I know how it is. She looked more deeply into his eyes. Believe me.

What is it? said Tuck, coming up.

This boy's been spied on by that creature Sunballs.

Tuck leaned in to Swanly. The boy was evilly shaken like a maiden thing out of the last century. He was all boy but between genders, hurt deep to his modesty. Tuck was greatly curious and fluttered-up. All execrable minutes, all time regained. I would live backwards in time until I took the shape of the boy myself. My own boyself was eat up by the gooks and then this strolling wench, my boyself was hostaged by her, sucking him out to her right in front of me, all over again as with me. Woman's thing stays hungry, it don't diminish, it's always something. A need machine, old beard lost its teeth harping on like a holy fool in the desert. They're always with themselves having sex with themselves, two lips forever kissing each other down there and they got no other subject. Even so, I feel love for her all over again.

Lester Silk, Bean, and Pal studied this trio isolated there where the water on rills avid over pebbles made a laughing noise. Walthall raised his viola and spread his arms out like a crucified musician and he stood there in silence evoking God knows what but Arden Pal asked the others what was going on.

Wake up and smell the clue, whispered Silk. Walthall wants the woman and our strange boy Swanly's already got her.

Swanly's okay, Silk. He's not strange.

Maybe not till now.

Leave him alone, said Bean. Swanly's a right guy. He has been through some things that's all. Ask me.

You mean a dead daddy like you?

I'd say you look hard enough, a dead both, but he wouldn't admit it. Bean intended to loom there in his acuity for a moment, looking into the breech of his gun which he had opened with the lever. It was a rare lever action shotgun, 20-gauge. Bean worshiped shells and bullets. Ask me, he's a full orphan.

They blending with him, said Arden Pal. They watched us naked too. She didn't jump back in the bushes like a standard woman when I caught her.

Swanly came over getting his shirt.

She's giving me something. I'm feeling poorly, he said.

The rest did not speak and the three, Tuck, Bernadette, and Swanly, walked up the shallow bluff and into the woods.

Silk sighed. I don't quite believe I ever seen nothing like that. Old store boy there looks like somebody up to the eight count.

Walthall, who had actually had a sort of girl, since with stubborn farm boy will he would penetrate nearly anything sentient, was defeated viola and all. Lord my right one for mature love like that. No more did he heed the calling of his music and he was sore in gloom.

Bean could not sit still and he walked here and there rolling two double-aught buckshot shells in his palm, looking upward to the spying bower of the hermit, but no offending eye there now, as he would love.

They closed the store as Swanly began talking. She went to the house and got something for his belly and some nerve pills too and diet pills as well. Bernadette was fond of both diet and nerve pills, and sometimes her husband was too, quite positively. Some mornings they were the only promise he could fetch in and he protected his thefts of single pills from his wife's cabinet with grim slyness. In narcosis she was fond of him and in amphetamine zeal he returned affection to her which she mistook for actual interest. The doctor in Magee was a firm believer in Dexamil as panacea and gave her anything she wanted. The pain of wanting in her foreign eyes got next to him. In a fog of charity he saw her as a lovely spy in the alien pines. He saw a lot of women and few men who weren't in the act of bleeding as they spoke, where they stood. The pharmacist was more a partisan of Demerol and John Birch and his prices were high since arsenals were expensive. His constant letters to Senator McCarthy, in his decline, almost consumed his other passions for living, such as they were. But the pharmacist liked Bernadette too, and when she left, detained as long as he could prolong the difficulty of her prescription, he went in the back room where a mechanic's calendar with a picture of a woman lying cross-legged in a dropped halter on the hood of a Buick was nailed to the wall and laid hand to himself. One night the doctor and the pharmacist met in this room and began howling like wolves in lonely ardor. Bernadette's name was mentioned many times, then they would howl again. They wore female underwear but were not sodomites. Both enjoyed urban connections and their pity for Bernadette in her aging beauty out in the river boonies was painful without limit; and thus in the proper lingerie they acted it out.

Swanly, after the pills, began admitting to the peach wine as if it were a mortal offense. Bernadette caught his spirit. They adjourned to the house where he could lie comfortably with her Oriental shawl over him.

We don't have strong drink here. Not much. She looked to Tuck. You don't have to drink to have a full experience.

Tuck said, No, not drink. Hardly.

No. I'm having fun just talking. Talking to you is fine. Because I haven't been much of a talker. That's good medicine. My tongue feels all light.

Talk on, child. She gave Swanly another pill.

Tuck went to relieve himself and through the window he saw the clothesline over the green clover and he speculated that through time simple household things might turn on you in a riot of overwhelming redundancy. He had heard of a man whose long dear companion, a buckskin cat, had walked between his legs one night and tripped and killed him as he went down headfirst onto a commode. Cheered that this was not him he went back to listen to the boy.

But after all you wouldn't have just anybody look at you all bared. Surely not that awful person, Bernadette was saying. I'd not let him see me for heaven's sake.

It seems he ought to pay. I feel tortured and all muddy. I can't forget it.

Just talk it out, that's best. It seems there's always a monster about, doesn't it?

I feel I could talk all afternoon into the night.

We aren't going anywhere.

We aren't going anywhere, added Tuck.

I'm feeling all close to you if that's all right.

Some people are sent to us. We have been waiting all our lives for somebody and don't even know it.

Older ones are here to teach and guide the young, Tuck said.

Bernadette glanced at Tuck then looked again. He had come back with his hair combed and he had shaved. He was so soft in the face she felt something new for him. In this trinity already a pact was sealed and they could no more be like others. There was a tingling and a higher light around them. A flood of goodwill took her as if they had been hurled upon a foreign shore, all fresh. The boy savior, child, and paramour at once. Swanly spoke on, it hardly mattered what he said. Each word a pleasant weight on her bosom.

Walthall and the rest stared into the fire sighing, three of them having their separate weather, their separate fundament, in peach wine. Pal could swallow no more and heaved out an arc of puke luminous over the fire, crying, Thar she blows, my dear youth. This act was witnessed like a miracle by the others.

God in heaven, this stuff was so good for a while, said Silk.

Fools, said Bean.

Bean don't drink because he daddy daid, said Walthall. So sad, so sad, so gone, so Beat.

Yeh. It might make him cry, said Pal.

Or act human, said Silk.

Let it alone. Bean had stood unmoved by their inebriation for two hours, caressing his 20-gauge horse gun.

Teenage love, teenage heart. My face broke out the other night but I'm in love wit yewwww! sang Walthall.

What you think Swanly's doing, asked Pal.

Teenage suckface. Dark night of the suck.

They are carrying him away, far far away, Silk declared.

Or him them.

Having a bit of transversion, them old boy and girl.

You mean travesty. Something stinketh, I tell you.

We know.

The hermit made Swanly all sick. We should put a stop to his mischief, said Bean all sober.

That person saw the peepee full out of ourn good friend ourn little buddy.

This isn't to laugh about. Swanly's deep and he's a hurting man.

Boy, said Pal. He once told me every adult had a helpless urge to smother the young so they could keep company with the dead, which were themselves.

You'd have to love seeing small animals suffer to hurt Swanly. The boy's damn near an angel. I swear he ain't even rightly one of us, said Silk. Bean did not care for Silk, who had only joined them lately. But Silk redeemed himself, saying, Christ I'm just murky. Swanly's deep.

You know what, Walthall spoke, I felt sorry for all three of them when they left here. Yes the woman is aged but fine, but it was like a six-legged crippled thing.

So it was, said Pal. I declare nothing happy is going on wherever they are.

Whosoever you are, be that person with all your might. Time goes by faster than we thought. It is a thief so quiet. You must let yourself be loved and you must love, parts of you that never loved must open and love. You must announce yourself in all particulars so you can have yourself.

Tuck going on at dawn. Bernadette was surprised again by him. Another man, fluent, had risen in his place. She was in her pink sleeping gown but the others wore their day clothes and were not sleepy.

Listen, the birds are singing for us out there and it's a morning, a real morning, Bernadette said. A true morning out of all the rest of the mornings.

By noon they were hoarse and languid and commended themselves into a trance wherein all wore bedsheets and naked underneath they moved about the enormous bed like adepts in a rite. The question was asked of Swanly by Tuck whether he would care to examine their lovely Bernadette since he had never seen a woman and Swanly said yes and Bernadette lay back opening the sheet and then spreading herself so Swanly saw a woman as he had never seen her for a long while and she only a little shy and the boy smiled wearily assenting to her glory and was pulled inward through love and death and constant birth gleefully repeated by the universe. Then husband and wife embraced with the boy between them on the edge of the bed, none of them recalling how they were there but all talk ceased and they were as those ignorant animals amongst the fruit of Eden just hours before the thunder.

Long into the afternoon they awoke with no shame and only the shyness of new dogs in a palace and then an abashed hunger for the whole ritual again set like a graven image in all their dreams. The boy had been told things and he felt very elegant, a crowned orphan now orphan no more. Bernadette, touched in all places, felt dear and coveted. All meanness had been driven from Tuck and he was blank in an ecstasy of separate parts like a creature torn to bits at the edge of a sea. Around them were their scattered clothes, the confetti of delirium. They embraced and were suspended in a bulb of void delicate as a drop of water.

Sunballs came around the store since it was closed and he wore a large knife on his belt in a scabbard with fringe on it and boots in white leather and high to the knee, which he had without quite knowing their use rescued out of a country lane near the bridge, the jetsam of a large majorette seduced in a car he had been watching all night. At the feet he looked blindingly clean as in a lodge ceremony. He walked quickly as if appointed and late. He looked in one window of the blue house, holding the sill, before he came to the second and beheld them all naked gathering and ungathering in languor, unconscious in their innocence. He watched a goodly while, his hands formally at his side, bewitched like a pole-axed angel. Then he commenced rutting on the scabbard of his knife grabbed desperately to his loins but immediately also to call out scolding as somebody who had walked up on murder.

Cursed and stunned Tuck and Bernadette snatched the covering but Swanly sat peering at the fiend outside until overcome by grief and then nausea. His nudity was then like one dead, cut down from joy. Still, he was too handsome, and Sunballs could not quit his watching while Swanly retched himself sore.

He might well be dying, thought Sunballs, and this fascinated him, these last heavings of beauty. He began to shake and squalled even louder. There was such a clamor from the two adults he awoke to himself and hastened back to the road and into the eroded ditch unbraked until he reached his burrow. Under his bluff the river fled deep and black with a sheen of new tar, and the hermit emerged once on his filthy terrace to stand over it in conversation with his erection, his puny calves in the white boots.

The boys labored with oaths down the bedrocks of the river. All was wretched and foul since waking under the peach wine, which they now condemned, angry at daylight itself. Only Bean was ready to the task. They went through a bend in silence and approached water with no beach. They paused for a while then flung in and waded cold to their chests. Bean, the only one armed, carried the cavalry shotgun above his head.

I claim this land for the Queen of Spain, Bean said. God for a hermit to shoot. My kingdom for a hermit. Then he went underwater but the shotgun stayed up and dry, waggled about.

When he came up he saw the hermit leering down from his porch on the bluff. Bean, choked and bellicose, thought he heard Sunballs laughing at him. He levered in a round and without hesitation would have shot the man out of his white boots had this person not been snatched backwards by Tuck. All of them saw the arm come around his neck and the female boots striding backwards in air, then dust in vacant air, the top of a rust hut behind it. A stuffed holler went off the bluff and scattered down the pebble easements westerly and into the cypresses on either side. Then there was silence.

He was grabbed by something, said Walthall, something just took Sunballs away.

By hell, I thought he was shot before I pulled the trigger, swore Bean. Bean had horrified himself. The horse gun in his hand was loathsome.

Don't hit me no more in the eye! a voice cried from above.

Then there were shouts from both men and much stomping on the terrace.

Tuck shrieked out, his voice like a great bird driving past. They heard then the hysterical voice of Swanly baying like a woman. The boys were spooked but drawn. They went to finding a path upwards even through the wine sickness.

Swanly, he ain't right and that's him, said Pal.

Well somebody's either humping or killing somebody.

We charging up there like we know what to do about it.

I could've killed him, said Bean, dazed still. Damn you Swanly. For you, damn you.

Then they were up the fifty feet or more and lost in cane through which they heard groans and sobs. They turned to this and crashed through and to the man they were afraid. At the edge of the brake, they drew directly upon a bin buried three-quarters in the top of the bluff, this house once a duckblind. In front of it from the beaten clay porch they heard sounds and they pressed around to them like harried pilgrims anxious for bad tidings. They saw the river below open up in a wide bend deep and strong through a passage of reigning boulders on either side and then just beside them where they had almost overwalked them, Bernadette and Swanly together on the ground, Swanly across her lap and the woman with her breasts again nearly out of their yoke in a condition of the Pietà, but Swanly red and mad in the face, both of them covered with dust as if they had rolled through a desert together. This put more fear in them than would have a ghoul, and they looked quickly away where Tuck sat holding his slashed stomach, beside him the hermit spread with outstretched boots, swatted down as from some pagan cavalry. Sunballs covered his eyes with his hands.

They thought in those seconds that Tuck had done himself in. The

big hunting knife was still in his hand and he gazed over the river as
if dying serenely. But this was only exhaustion and he looked up at
them unsurprised and baleful as if nothing more could shock him.

I can't see, moaned Sunballs. He never stopped hitting my eyes.

Good, good, spoke Tuck. I'm not sorry. Cut your tongue out next, tie
you up in a boat down that river. See how you spy on those sharks in
the Gulf of Mexico.

I ain't the trouble, moaned the hermit. You got big sons wouldn't
think so either.

Nothing stands between me and that tongue, keep wagging it.

Them ole boys of yours could sorely be enlightened.

Sunballs moved his hands and the boys viewed the eyes bruised like
a swollen burglar's mask, the red grief of pounded meat in the sockets.
The fingers of both Tuck's hands were mud red and fresher around the
knife handle. But Tuck was spent, a mere chattering head, and the
hermit in his agony rolled over and stared blind into his own vomit.
His wadded hair was white-flecked by it and the boys didn't look any
more at him.

It was Swanly they loved and could not bear to see. He was not the
bright shadow of their childhoods anymore, he was not the boy of
almost candescent complexion, he was not the pal haunting in the
remove of his beauty, slim and clean in his limbs. This beauty had been
a strange thing. It had always brought on some distress and then
infinite kindness in others and then sadness too. But none of them were
cherubs any longer and they knew all this and hated it, seeing him now
across the woman's lap, her breasts over his twisted face. Eden in the
bed of Eros, all Edenwide all lost. He was neither child, boy, nor man,
and he was dreadful. Bean could barely carry on and knelt before him
in idiocy. Walthall was enraged, big hairy Walthall, viola torn to bits
inside him. He could not forgive he was ever obliged to see this.

We're taking our friend with us.

You old can have each other, said Bean. He had forgot the shotgun
in his hand.

Bury each other. Take your time.

The woman looked up, her face flocked with dust.

We're not nasty. We were good people.

Sure. Hag.

Come on away, Bean, Pal directed him.

Bring Swanly up. Hold him, somebody, help me. Walthall was large and clumsy. He could not see the way to handle Swanly.

Bernadette began to lick the dust from Swanly's cheek

There ain't nothing only a tiny light, and a round dark, sighed Sunballs. It ain't none improved.

We are bad. Tuck spoke. Damn us, damn it all.

Silk and Pal raised Swanly up and although he was very sick he could walk. There was an expression simian wasted on his face, blind to those who took him now, blind to the shred of clothes remaining to him, his shorts low on his hips.

They kept along the gravel shoulder the mile back to their camp. Bean with the handsome gun, relic of swaggering days in someone else's life. He seemed deputized and angry, walking Swanly among the others. Sometimes Swanly fell from under him completely, his legs surrendered, while they pulled him on, no person speaking.

In the halls of his school thenceforward Swanly was wolfish in his glare and often dirty. In a year no one was talking to him at all. The exile seemed to make him smile but as if at others inside himself he knew better than them.

His mother, refractory until this change in her son, withdrew into silent lesbian despair with another of her spirit then next into a church and out of this world, where her husband continued to make his inardent struggles.

Some fourteen years later, big Walthall, rich but sad, took a sudden turn off the regular highway on the way to a Florida vacation. He was struck by a nostalgia he could not account for, like a bole of overweening sad energy between his eyes. He drove right up to the store and later he swore to Bean and Pal that although Tuck had died, an almost unrecognizable and clearly mad old woman hummed, nearly toothless, behind the cash register. She was wearing Swanly's old jersey, what was left of it, and the vision was so awful he fled almost immediately and was not right in Boca Raton nor much better when he came back home.

When Walthall inquired about the whereabouts of Swanly the woman began to scream without pause.

THE FARM

Joy Williams

It was a dark night in August. Sarah and Tommy were going to their
third party that night, the party where they would actually sit down to
dinner. They were driving down Mixtuxet Avenue, a long black avenue
of trees that led out of the village, away from the shore and the coastal
homes into the country. Tommy had been drinking only soda that
night. Every other weekend, Tommy wouldn't drink. He did it, he said,
to keep trim. He did it because he could.

Sarah was telling a long story as she drove. She kept asking Tommy
if she had told it to him before, but he was noncommittal. When
Tommy didn't drink, Sarah talked and talked. She was telling him a
terrible story that she had read in the newspaper about an alligator at
a jungle farm attraction in Florida. The alligator had eaten a child who
had crawled into its pen. The alligator's name was Cookie. Its owner
had shot it immediately. The owner was sad about everything, the
child, the parents' grief, Cookie. He was quoted in the paper as saying
that shooting Cookie was not an act of revenge.

When Tommy didn't drink, Sarah felt cold. She was shivering in the
car. There were goosepimples on her tanned, thin arms. Tommy sat
beside her smoking, saying nothing.

There had been words between them earlier. The parties here had an
undercurrent of sexuality. Sarah could almost hear it, flowing around
them all, carrying them all along. In the car, on the night of the
accident, Sarah was at that point in the evening when she felt guilty.
She wanted to make things better, make things nice. She had gone
through her elated stage, her jealous stage, her stubbornly resigned
stage and now she felt guilty. Had they talked about divorce that night,
or had that been before, on other evenings? There was a flavor she
remembered in their talks about divorce, a scent. It was hot, as Italy
had been hot when they had been there. Dust, bread, sun, a burning at
the back of the throat from too much drinking.

But no, they hadn't been talking about divorce that night. The
parties had been crowded. Sarah had hardly seen Tommy. Then, on her

way to the bathroom, she had seen him sitting with a girl on a bed in one of the back rooms. He was telling the girl about condors, about hunting for condors in small, light planes.

'Oh, but you didn't hurt them, did you?' the girl asked. She was someone's daughter, a little overweight but with beautiful skin and large green eyes.

'Oh no,' Tommy assured her, 'we weren't hunting to hurt.'

Condors. Sarah looked at them sitting on the bed. When they noticed her, the girl blushed. Tommy smiled. Sarah imagined what she looked like, standing in the doorway. She wished that they had shut the door.

That had been at the Steadmans'. The first party had been at the Perrys'. The Perrys never served food. Sarah had had two or three drinks there. The bar had been set up beneath the grape arbor and everyone stood outside. It had still been light at the Perrys' but at the Steadmans' it was dark and people drank inside. Everyone spoke about the end of summer as though it were a bewildering and unnatural event.

They had stayed at the Steadmans' longer than they should have and they were going to be late for dinner. Nevertheless, they were driving at a moderate speed, through a familiar landscape, passing houses that they had been entertained in many times. There were the Salts and the Hollands and the Greys and the Dodsons. The Dodsons kept their gin in the freezer and owned two large and dappled crotch-sniffing dogs. The Greys imported Southerners for their parties. The women all had lovely voices and knew how to make spoon bread and pickled tomatoes and artillery punch. The men had smiles when they'd say to Sarah, 'Why, let me get you another. You don't have a thing in that glass, ah swear.' The Hollands gave the kind of dinner party where the shot was still in the duck and the silver should have been in a vault. Little whiskey was served but there was always excellent wine. The Salts were a high-strung couple who often quarreled. Jenny Salt was on some type of medication for tension and often dropped the canapés she attempted to serve. Jenny and her husband, Pete, had a room in which there was nothing but a large doll house where witty mâché figures carried on assignations beneath tiny clocks and crystal chandeliers. Once, when Sarah was examining the doll house's library where two figures were hunched over a chess game which was just about to be

won, Pete had always said, on the twenty-second move, Pete told
Sarah that she had pretty eyes. She had moved away from him
immediately. She had closed her eyes. In another room, with the other
guests, she had talked about the end of summer.

On that night, at the end of summer, the night of the accident, Sarah
was still talking as they passed the Salts' house. She was talking about
Venice. She and Tommy had been there once. They had drunk in the
Plaza and listened to the orchestras. Sarah quoted D. H. Lawrence on
Venice . . . 'Abhorrent green and slippery city . . .' But she and Tommy
had liked Venice. They drank standing up at little bars. Sarah had had
a cold and she drank grappa and the cold had disappeared for the rest
of her life.

After the Salts' house, the road swerved north and became very
dark. There were no lights, no houses for several miles. There were
stone walls, an orchard of sickly peach trees, a cider mill. There was St.
James Episcopal Church where Tommy took their daughter, Martha, to
Sunday school. The Sunday school was highly fundamental. There
were many arguments among the children and their teachers as to the
correct interpretation of Bible story favorites. For example, when
Lazarus rose from the dead, was he stlll sick? Martha liked the fervor
at St. James. Each week, her dinner graces were becoming more
impassioned and fantastic. Martha was seven.

Each Sunday, Tommy takes Martha to her little classes at St. James.
Sarah can imagine the child sitting there at a low table with her jars of
colors. Tommy doesn't go to church himself and Martha's classes are
two hours long. Sarah doesn't know where Tommy goes. She suspects
he is seeing someone. When they come home on Sundays, Tommy is
sleek, exhilarated. The three of them sit down to the dinner Sarah has
prepared.

Over the years, Sarah suspects, Tommy has floated to the surface of
her. They are swimmers now, far apart, on the top of the sea.

Sarah at last fell silent. The road seemed endless as in a dream. They
seemed to be slowing down. She could not feel her foot on the
accelerator. She could not feel her hands on the wheel. Her mind was
an untidy cupboard filled with shining bottles. The road was dark and
silvery and straight. In the space ahead of her, there seemed to be
something. It beckoned, glittering. Sarah's mind cleared a little. She
saw Martha with her hair cut oddly short. Sarah gently nibbled on the

inside of her mouth to keep alert. She saw Tommy choosing a succession of houses, examining the plaster, the floorboards, the fireplaces, deciding where windows should be placed, walls knocked down. She saw herself taking curtains down from a window so that there would be a better view of the sea. The curtains knocked her glass from the sill and it shattered. The sea was white and flat. It did not command her to change her life. It demanded of her, nothing. She saw Martha sleeping, her paint-smudged fingers curled. She saw Tommy in the city with a woman, riding in a cab. The woman wore a short fur jacket and Tommy stroked it as he spoke. She saw a figure in the road ahead, its arms raised before its face as though to block out the sight of her. The figure was a boy who wore dark clothing, but his hair was bright, his face was shining. She saw her car leap forward and run him down where he stood.

Tommy had taken responsibility for the accident. He had told the police he was driving. The boy apparently had been hitchhiking and had stepped out into the road. At the autopsy, traces of a hallucinogen were found in the boy's system. The boy was fifteen years old and his name was Stevie Bettencourt. No charges were filed.

'My wife,' Tommy told the police, 'was not feeling well. My wife,' Tommy said, 'was in the passenger seat.'

Sarah stopped drinking immediately after the accident. She felt nauseated much of the time. She slept poorly. Her hands hurt her. The bones in her hands ached. She remembered that this was the way she felt the last time she had stopped drinking. It had been two years before. She remembered why she had stopped and she remembered why she had started again. She had stopped because she had done a cruel thing to her little Martha. It was spring and she and Tommy were giving a dinner party. Sarah had two martinis in the late afternoon when she was preparing dinner and then she had two more martinis with her guests. Martha had come downstairs to say a polite goodnight to everyone as she had been taught. She had put on her nightie and brushed her teeth. Sarah poured a little more gin in her glass and went upstairs with her to brush out her hair and put her to bed. Martha had long, thick blond hair of which she was very proud. On that night she wore it in a pony tail secured by an elasticized holder with two small colored balls on the end. Sarah's fingers were clumsy and she could not

get it off without pulling Martha's hair and making her cry. She got a
pair of scissors and carefully began snipping at the stubborn elastic.
The scissors were large, like shears, and they had been difficult to
handle. A foot of Martha's gathered hair had abruptly fallen to the
floor. Sarah remembered trying to pat it back into place on the child's
head.

So Sarah had stopped drinking the first time. She did not feel
renewed. She felt exhausted and wary. She read and cooked. She
realized how little she and Tommy had to talk about. Tommy drank
Scotch when he talked to her at night. Sometimes Sarah would silently
count as he spoke to see how long the words took. When he was away
and he telephoned her, she could hear the ice tinkling in the glass.

Tommy was in the city four days a week. He often changed hotels.
He would bring Martha little bars of soap wrapped in the different
colored papers of the hotels. Martha's drawers were full of the soaps
scenting her clothes. When Tommy came home on the weekends he
would work on the house and they would give parties at which
Tommy was charming. Tommy had a talent for holding his liquor and
for buying old houses, restoring them and selling them for three times
what he had paid for them. Tommy and Sarah had moved six times in
eleven years. All their homes had been fine old houses in excellent
locations two or three hours from New York. Sarah would stay in the
country while Tommy worked in the city. Sarah did not know her way
around New York.

For three weeks, Sarah did not drink. Then it was her birthday.
Tommy gave her a slim gold necklace and fastened it around her neck.
He wanted her to come to New York with him, to have dinner, see a
play, spend the night with him in the fine suite the company had given
him at the hotel. They had got a babysitter for Martha, a marvelous
woman who polished the silver in the afternoon when Martha napped.
Sarah drove. Tommy had never cared for driving. His hand rested on
her thigh. Occasionally, he would slip his hand beneath her skirt. Sarah
was sick with the thought that this was the way he touched other
women.

By the time they were in Manhattan, they were arguing. They had
been married for eleven years. Both had had brief marriages before.
They could argue about anything. In midtown, Tommy stormed out of
the car as Sarah braked for a light. He took his suitcase and disappeared.

Sarah drove carefully for many blocks. When she had the opportunity, she would pull to the curb and ask someone how to get to Connecticut. No one seemed to know. Sarah thought she was probably phrasing the question poorly but she didn't know how else to present it. After half an hour, she made her way back to the hotel where Tommy was staying. The doorman parked the car and she went into the lobby. She looked into the hotel bar and saw Tommy in the dimness, sitting at a small table. He jumped up and kissed her passionately. He rubbed his hands up and down her sides. 'Darling, darling,' he said, 'I want you to have a happy birthday.'

Tommy ordered drinks for both of them. Sarah sipped hers slowly at first but then she drank it and he ordered others. The bar was subdued. There was a piano player who sang about the lord of the dance. The words seemed like those of a hymn. The hymn made her sad but she laughed. Tommy spoke to her urgently and gaily about little things. They laughed together like they had when they were first married. They had always drunk a lot together then and fallen asleep, comfortably and lovingly entwined on white sheets.

They went to their room to change for the theater. The maid had turned back the beds. There was a fresh rose in a bud vase on the writing desk. They had another drink in the room and got undressed. Sarah awoke the next morning curled up on the floor with the bedspread tangled around her. Her mouth was sore. There was a bruise on her leg. The television set was on with no sound. The room was a mess although Sarah could see that nothing had been really damaged. She stared at the television where black-backed gulls were dive-bombing on terrified and doomed cygnets in a documentary about swans. Sarah crept into the bathroom and turned on the shower. She sat in the tub while the water beat upon her. Pinned to the outside of the shower curtain was a note from Tommy, who had gone to work. 'Darling,' the note said, 'we had a *good* time on your birthday. I can't say I'm sorry we never got out. I'll call you for lunch. Love.'

Sarah turned the note inward until the water made the writing illegible. When the phone rang just before noon, she did not answer it.

There is a certain type of conversation one hears only when one is drunk and it is like a dream, full of humor and threat and significance, deep significance. And the way one witnesses things when one is drunk is different as well. It is like putting a face mask against the surface of the sea and looking into things, into their baffled and guileless hearts.

When Sarah had been a drinker, she felt that she had a fundamental and inventive grasp of situations, but now that she drank no longer, she found herself in the midst of a great and impenetrable silence which she could in no way interpret.

It was a small village. Many of the people who lived there did not even own cars. The demands of life were easily met in the village and it was pretty there besides. It was divided between those who always lived there and who owned fishing boats and restaurants and the city people who had more recently discovered the area as a summer place and winter weekend investment. On the weekends, the New Yorkers would come up with their houseguests and their pâté and cheeses and build fires and go cross-country skiing. Tommy came home to Sarah on weekends. They did things together. They agreed on where to go. During the week she was on her own.

Once, alone, she saw a helicopter carrying a tree in a sling across the Sound. The wealthy could afford to leave nothing behind.

Once, with the rest of the town, she saw five boats burning in their storage shrouds. Each summer resort has its winter pyromaniac.

Sarah did not read any more. Her eyes hurt when she read and her hands ached all the time. During the week, she marketed and walked and cared for Martha.

It was three months after Stevie Bettencourt was killed when his mother visited Sarah. She came to the door and knocked on it and Sarah let her in.

Genevieve Bettencourt was a woman Sarah's age although she looked rather younger. She had been divorced almost from the day that Stevie was born. She had another son named Bruce who lived with his father in Nova Scotia. She had an old powder-blue Buick parked on the street before Sarah's house. The Buick had one white door.

The two women sat in Sarah's handsome, sunny living room. It was very calm, very peculiar, almost thrilling. Genevieve looked all around the room. Off the living room were the bedrooms. The door to Sarah's and Tommy's was closed but Martha's door was open. She had a little hanging garden against the window. She had a hamster in a cage. She had an enormous bookcase filled with dolls and books.

Genevieve said to Sarah, 'That room wasn't there before. This used to be a lobster pound. I know a great deal about this town. People like you have nothing to do with what I know about this town. Do you remember the way things were, ever?'

'No,' Sarah said.

Genevieve sighed. 'Does your daughter look like you or your husband?'

'No one's ever told me she looked like me,' Sarah said quietly.

On the glass-topped table before them there was a little wooden sculpture cutout that Tommy had bought. A man and woman sat on a park bench. Each wore a startled and ambiguous expression. Each had a terrier on the end of a string. The dogs were a puzzle. One fit on top of the other. Sarah was embarrassed about it being there. Tommy had put it on the table during the weekend and Sarah hadn't moved it. Genevieve didn't touch it.

'I did not want my life to know you,' Genevieve said. She removed a hair from the front of her white blouse and dropped it to the floor. She looked out the window at the sun. The floor was of a very light and varnished pine. Sarah could see the hair upon it.

'I'm so sorry,' Sarah said. 'I'm so very, very sorry.' She stretched her neck and put her head back.

'Stevie was a mixed-up boy,' Genevieve said. 'They threw him off the basketball team. He took pills. He had bad friends. He didn't study and he got a D in geometry and they wouldn't let him play basketball.'

She got up and wandered around the room. She wore green rubber boots, dirty jeans and a beautiful, hand-knit sweater. 'I once bought all my fish here,' she said. 'The O'Malleys owned it. There were practically no windows. Just narrow high ones over the tanks. Now it's all windows, isn't it? Don't you feel exposed?'

'No, I . . .' Sarah began. 'There are drapes,' she said.

'Off to the side, where you have your garden, there are whale bones if you dig deep enough. I can tell you a lot about this town.'

'My husband wants to move,' Sarah said.

'I can understand that, but you're the real drinker, after all, aren't you, not him.'

'I don't drink any more,' Sarah said. She looked at the woman dizzily.

Genevieve was not pretty but she had a clear, strong face. She sat down on the opposite side of the room. 'I guess I would like something,' she said. 'A glass of water.' Sarah went to the kitchen and poured a glass of Vichy for them both. Her hands shook.

'We are not strangers to one another,' Genevieve said. 'We could be friends.'

'My first husband always wanted to be friends with my second husband,' Sarah said after a moment. 'I could never understand it.' This had somehow seemed analogous when she was saying it but now it did not. 'It is not appropriate that we be friends,' she said.

Genevieve continued to sit and talk. Sarah found herself concentrating desperately on her articulate, one-sided conversation. She suspected that the words Genevieve was using were codes for other words, terrible words. Genevieve spoke thoughtlessly, dispassionately, with erratic flourishes of language. Sarah couldn't believe that they were chatting about food, men, the red clouds massed above the sea.

'I have a friend who is a designer,' Genevieve said. 'She hopes to make a great deal of money someday. Her work has completely altered her perceptions. Every time she looks at a view, she thinks of sheets. "Take out those mountains," she will say, "lighten that cloud a bit and it would make a great sheet." When she looks at the sky, she thinks of lingerie. Now when I look at the sky, I think of earlier times, happier times when I looked at the sky. I have never been in love, have you?'

'Yes,' Sarah said, 'I'm in love.'

'It's not a lucky thing, you know, to be in love.'

There was a soft scuffling at the door and Martha came in. 'Hello,' she said. 'School was good today. I'm hungry.'

'Hello, dear,' Genevieve said. To Sarah, she said, 'Perhaps we can have lunch sometime.'

'Who is that?' Martha asked Sarah after Genevieve had left.

'A neighbor,' Sarah said, 'one of Mommy's friends.'

When Sarah told Tommy about Genevieve coming to visit her, he said, 'It's harassment. It can be stopped.'

It was Sunday morning. They had just finished breakfast and Tommy and Martha were drying the dishes and putting them away. Martha was wearing her church-school clothes and she was singing a song she had learned the Sunday before.

'. . . I'm going to the Mansion on the Happy Days' Express . . .' she sang.

Tommy squeezed Martha's shoulders. 'Go get your coat, sweetie,' he said. When the child had gone, he said to Sarah, 'Don't speak to this woman. Don't allow it to happen again.'

'We didn't talk about that.'

'What else could you talk about? It's weird.'

'No one talks about that. No one, ever.'

Tommy was wearing a corduroy suit and a tie Sarah had never seen before. Sarah looked at the pattern in the tie. It was random and bright.

'Are you having an affair?' Sarah asked.

'No,' he said easily. 'I don't understand you, Sarah. I've done everything I could to protect you, to help you straighten yourself out. It was a terrible thing but it's over. You have to get over it. Now, just don't see her again. There's no way that she can cause trouble if you don't speak to her.'

Sarah stopped looking at Tommy's tie. She moved her eyes to the potatoes she had peeled and put in a bowl of water.

Martha came into the kitchen and held on to her father's arm. Her hair was long and thick, but it was getting darker. It was as though it had never been cut.

After they left, Sarah put the roast in the oven and went into the living room. The large window was full of the day, a colorless windy day without birds. Sarah sat on the floor and ran her fingers across the smooth, varnished wood. Beneath the expensive flooring was cold cement. Tanks had once lined the walls. Lobsters had crept back and forth across the mossy glass. The phone rang. Sarah didn't look at it, suspecting it was Genevieve. Then she picked it up.

'Hello,' said Genevieve, 'I thought I might drop by. It's a bleak day, isn't it. Cold. Is your family at home?'

'They go out on Sunday,' Sarah said. 'It gives me time to think. They go to church.'

'What do you think about?' The woman's voice seemed far away. Sarah strained to hear her.

'I'm supposed to cook dinner. When they come back we eat dinner.'

'I can prepare clams in forty-three different ways,' Genevieve said.

'This is a roast. A roast pork.'

'Well, may I come over?'

'All right,' Sarah said.

She continued to sit on the floor, waiting for Genevieve, looking at the water beneath the sky. The water on the horizon was a wide, satin ribbon. She wished that she had the courage to swim on such a bitter, winter day. To swim far out and rest, to hesitate and then to return. Her life was dark, unexplored. Her abstinence had drained her. She felt sluggish, robbed. Her body had no freedom.

She sat, seeing nothing, the terrible calm light of the day around her. The things she remembered were so far away, bathed in a different light. Her life seemed so remote to her. She had sought happiness in someone, knowing she could not find it in herself and now her heart was strangely hard. She rubbed her head with her hands.

Her life with Tommy was broken, irreparable. Her life with him was over. His infidelities kept getting mixed up in her mind with the death of the boy, with Tommy's false admission that he had been driving when the boy died. Sarah couldn't understand anything. Her life seemed so random, so needlessly constructed and now threatened in a way which did not interest her.

'Hello,' Genevieve called. She had opened the front door and was standing in the hall. 'You didn't hear my knock.'

Sarah got up. She was to entertain this woman. She felt anxious, adulterous. The cold rose from Genevieve's skin and hair. Sarah took her coat and hung it in the closet. The fresh cold smell lingered on her hands.

Sarah moved into the kitchen. She took a package of rolls out of the freezer.

'Does your little girl like church?' Genevieve asked.

'Yes, very much.'

'It's a stage,' said Genevieve. 'I'm Catholic myself. As a child, I used to be fascinated by the martyrs. I remember a picture of St. Lucy, carrying her eyes like a plate of eggs, and St. Agatha. She carried her breasts on a plate.'

Sarah said, 'I don't understand what we're talking about. I know you're just using these words, that they mean other words, I . . .'

'Perhaps we could take your little girl to a movie sometime, a matinee, after she gets out of school.'

'Her name is Martha,' Sarah said. She saw Martha grown up, her hair cut short once more, taking rolls out of the freezer, waiting.

'Martha, yes,' Genevieve said. 'Have you wanted more children?'

'No,' Sarah said. Their conversation was illegal, unspeakable. Sarah couldn't imagine it ever ending. Her fingers tapped against the ice-cube trays. 'Would you care for a drink?'

'A very tall glass of vermouth,' Genevieve said. She was looking at a little picture Martha had made, that Sarah had tacked to the wall. It was a very badly drawn horse. 'I wanted children. I wanted to fulfill myself. One can never fulfill oneself. I think it is an impossibility.'

Sarah made Genevieve's drink very slowly. She did not make one for herself.

'When Stevie was Martha's age, he knew everything about whales. He kept notebooks. Once, on his birthday, I took him to the whaling museum in New Bedford.' She sipped her drink. 'It all goes wrong somewhere,' she said. She turned her back on Sarah and went into the other room. Sarah followed her.

'There are so many phrases for "dead," you know,' Genevieve was saying. 'The kids think them up, or they come out of music or wars. Stevie had one that he'd use for dead animals and rock stars. He'd say they'd "bought the farm."'

Sarah nodded. She was pulling and peeling at the nails of her hands.

'I think it's pretty creepy. A dark farm, you know. Weedy. Run-down. Broken machinery everywhere. A real job.'

Sarah raised her head. 'You want us to share Martha, don't you,' she said. 'It's only right, isn't it?'

'. . . the paint blown away, acres and acres of tangled, black land, a broken shutter over the well.'

Sarah lowered her head again. Her heart was cold, horrified. The reality of the two women, placed by hazard in this room, this bright functional tasteful room that Tommy had created, was being tested. Reality would resist, for days, perhaps weeks, but then it would yield. It would yield to this guest, this visitor, for whom Sarah had made room.

'Would you join me in another drink?' Genevieve asked. 'Then I'll go.'

'I mustn't drink,' Sarah said.

'You don't forget,' Genevieve said, 'that's just an old saw.' She went into the kitchen and poured more vermouth for herself. Sarah could smell the meat cooking. From another room, the clock chimed.

'You must come to my home soon,' Genevieve said. She did not sit down. Sarah looked at the pale green liquid in the glass.

'Yes,' Sarah said, 'soon.'

'We must not greet one another on the street, however. People are quick to gossip.'

'Yes,' Sarah said. 'They would condemn us.' She looked heavily at Genevieve, full of misery and submission.

There was knocking on the door. 'Sarah,' Tommy's voice called, 'why is the door locked?' She could see his dark head at the window.

'I must have thrown the bolt,' Genevieve said. 'It's best to lock your house in the winter, you know. It's the kids mostly. They get bored. Stevie was a robber once or twice, I'm sure.' She put down her glass, took her coat from the closet and went out. Sarah heard Martha say, 'That's Mommy's friend.'

Tommy stood in the doorway and stared at Sarah. 'Why did you lock the door?' he asked again.

Sarah imagined seeing herself, naked. She said, 'There are robbers.'

Tommy said, 'If you don't feel safe here, we'll move. I've been looking at a wonderful place about twenty miles from here, on a cove. It only needs a little work. It will give us more room. There's a barn, some fence. Martha could have a horse.'

Sarah looked at him with an intent, halted expression, as though she were listening to a dialogue no one present was engaged in. Finally, she said, 'There are robbers. Everything has changed.'

MR. GREEN

Robert Olen Butler

I am a Catholic, the daughter of a Catholic mother and father, and I do not believe in the worship of my ancestors, especially in the form of a parrot. My father's parents died when he was very young and he became a Catholic in an orphanage run by nuns in Hanoi. My mother's mother was a Catholic but her father was not and, like many Vietnamese, he was a believer in what Confucius taught about ancestors. I remember him taking me by the hand while my parents and my grandmother were sitting under a banana tree in the yard and he said, 'Let's go talk with Mr. Green.' He led me into the house and he touched his lips with his forefinger to tell me that this was a secret. Mr. Green was my grandfather's parrot and I loved talking to him, but we passed Mr. Green's roost in the front room. Mr. Green said, 'Hello, kind sir,' but we didn't even answer him.

My grandfather took me to the back of his house, to a room that my mother had said was private, that she had yanked me away from when I once had tried to look. It had a bead curtain at the door and we passed through it and the beads rustled like tall grass. The room was dim, lit by candles, and it smelled of incense, and my grandfather stood me before a little shrine with flowers and a smoking incense bowl and two brass candlesticks and between them a photo of a man in a Chinese mandarin hat. 'That's my father,' he said, nodding toward the photo. 'He lives here.' Then he let go of my hand and touched my shoulder. 'Say a prayer for my father.' The face in the photo was tilted a little to the side and was smiling faintly, like he'd asked me a question and he was waiting for an answer that he expected to like. I knelt before the shrine as I did at Mass and I said the only prayer I knew by heart, The Lord's Prayer.

But as I prayed, I was conscious of my grandfather. I even peeked at him as he stepped to the door and parted the beads and looked toward the front of the house. Then he returned.and stood beside me and I finished my prayer as I listened to the beads rustling into silence behind us. When I said 'Amen' aloud, my grandfather knelt beside me and leaned near and whispered, 'Your father is doing a terrible thing. If he must be a Catholic, that's one thing. But he has left the spirits of his ancestors to wander for eternity in loneliness.' It was hard for me to believe that my father was doing something as terrible as this, but it was harder for me to believe that my grandfather, who was even older than my father, could be wrong.

My grandfather explained about the spirit world, how the souls of our ancestors continue to need love and attention and devotion. Given these things, they will share in our lives and they will bless us and even warn us about disasters in our dreams. But if we neglect the souls of our ancestors, they will become lost and lonely and will wander around in the kingdom of the dead no better off than a warrior killed by his enemy and left unburied in a rice paddy to be eaten by black birds of prey.

When my grandfather told me about the birds plucking out the eyes of the dead and about the possibility of our own ancestors, our own family, suffering just like that if we ignore them, I said, 'Don't worry, Grandfather, I will always say prayers for you and make offerings for you, even if I'm a Catholic.'

I thought this would please my grandfather, but he just shook his head sharply, like he was mad at me, and he said, 'Not possible.'

'I can,' I said.

Then he looked at me and I guess he realized that he'd spoken harshly. He tilted his head slightly and smiled a little smile—just like his father in the picture—but what he said wasn't something to smile about. 'You are a girl,' he said. 'So it's not possible for you to do it alone. Only a son can oversee the worship of his ancestors.'

I felt a strange thing inside me, a recoiling, like I'd stepped barefoot on a slug, but how can you recoil from your own body? And so I began to cry. My grandfather patted me and kissed me and said it was all right, but it wasn't all right for me. I wanted to protect my grandfather's soul, but it wasn't in my power. I was a girl. We waited together before the shrine and when I'd stopped crying, we went back to the front room and my grandfather bowed to his parrot and said, 'Hello, kind sir,' and Mr. Green said, 'Hello, kind sir,' and even though I loved the parrot, I would not speak to him that day because he was a boy and I wasn't.

This was in our town, which was on the bank of the Red River just south of Hanoi. We left that town not long after. I was seven years old and I remember hearing my grandfather arguing with my parents. I was sleeping on a mat at the back of our house and I woke up and I heard voices and my grandfather said, 'Not possible.' The words chilled me, but then I listened more closely and I knew they were discussing the trip we were about to go on. Everyone was very frightened and excited. There were many families in our little town who were planning to leave. They had even taken the bell out of the church tower to carry with them. We were all Catholics. But Grandfather did not have the concerns of the Catholics. He was concerned about the spirits of his ancestors. This was the place where they were born and died and were buried. He was afraid that they would not make the trip. 'What then?' he cried. And later he spoke of the people of the South and how they would hate us, being from the North. 'What then?' he said.

Mr. Green says that, too. 'What then?' he has cried to me a thousand times, ten thousand times, in the past sixteen years. Parrots can live for a hundred years. And though I could not protect my dead grandfather's soul, I could take care of his parrot. When my grandfather died in Saigon in 1972, he made sure that Mr. Green came to me. I was twenty-four then and newly married and I still loved Mr. Green. He would sit on my shoulder and take the top of my ear in his beak, a beak that could crush the hardest shell, and he would hold my ear with the greatest gentleness and touch me with his tongue.

I have brought Mr. Green with me to the United States of America, and in the long summers here in New Orleans and in the warm springs and falls and even in many days of our mild winters, he sits on my screened-in back porch, near the door, and he speaks in the voice of my grandfather. When he wants to get onto my shoulder and go with me into the community garden, he says, 'What then?' And when I first come to him in the morning, he says, 'Hello, kind sir.'

He loves me. That is, I am the only person who can go near him without his attempting to draw blood. But he loved my grandfather before me, and there are times when he seems to hold the spirit of my grandfather and all his knowledge. Mr. Green sits on my shoulder and presses close to my head and he repeats the words that he has heard from my husband and my children. My children even teach him English words. He says all these things, but without any feeling. The

Vietnamese words of my grandfather, however, come out powerfully, like someone very strong is inside him. And whenever he speaks with my grandfather's voice, Mr. Green's eyes dilate and contract over and over, which is a parrot's display of happiness. Yesterday I tried to give him some drops that the veterinarian prescribed for him and Mr. Green said, 'Not possible,' and even though he is sick, his eyes showed how pleased he was to defy me.

When we all lived in Saigon at last, my grandfather discovered the bird market on Hàm Nghi Street and he would take me there. Actually, in the street market of Hàm Nghi there were animals of all kinds— dogs and monkeys and rabbits and turtles and even wildcats. But when my grandfather took my hand and said to me, 'Come, little one,' and we walked down Trần Hu'ng Đạo, where our house was, and we came to Hàm Nghi, he always took me to the place with the birds.

The canaries were the most loved by everyone who came to the market, and my grandfather sang with them. They all hopped to the side of their cages that was closest to my grandfather and he whistled and hummed and even sang words, songs from the North that he sang quite low, so that only the birds could hear. He did not want the people of Saigon to realize he was from the North. And the canaries all opened their mouths and the air filled with their sounds, their throats ruffling and puffing, and I looked at my grandfather's throat to see if it moved the way the throats of these birds moved. It did not move at all. His skin was slack there, and in all the times I saw him charm the birds, I never saw his throat move, like he didn't really mean the sounds he made. The people all laughed when they saw what he could do and they said that my grandfather was a wizard, but he would just ignore them.

The canaries seemed to be his favorite birds on Hàm Nghi, though he spent time with them all. The dark-plumed ones—the magpies and the blackbirds—were always singing on their own, especially the blackbuds with their orange beaks. My grandfather came near the blackbirds and they were gabbling among themselves and he frowned at them, like they were fools to be content only with their own company. They did not need him to prompt their songs. He growled at them, 'You're just a bunch of old women,' and we moved on to the doves that were big-eyed and quiet and he cooed at them and he told them how pretty they were and we looked at the moorhens, pecking at the bottoms of their cages like chickens, and the cranes with their wonderful necks curling and stretching.

We visited all the birds and my grandfather loved them, and the first time we went to Hàm Nghi, we ended up at the cages crowded with sparrows. He bent near their chattering and I liked these birds very much. They were small and their eyes were bright, and even though the birds were crowded, they were always in motion, hopping and fluffing up and shaking themselves like my vain friends. I was a quiet little girl, but I, too, would sometimes look at myself in a mirror and primp and puff myself up, even as in public I tried to hold myself apart a little bit from the other girls.

I was surprised and delighted that first day when my grandfather motioned to the birdseller and began to point at sparrows and the merchant reached into the cage and caught one bird after another and he put them all into a cardboard box. My grandfather bought twelve birds and they did not fly as they sat in the box. 'Why aren't they flying?' I asked.

'Their wings are clipped,' my grandfather said.

This was all right with me. They clearly weren't in any pain and they could still hop and they would never fly away from me. I wouldn't even need a cage for my vain little friends.

I'm sure that my grandfather knew what I was thinking. But he said nothing. When we got home, he gave me the box and told me to take the birds to show my mother. I found her on the back stoop slicing vegetables. I showed her the box and she said that Grandfather was wonderful. She set the box down and told me to stay with her, I could help her. I crouched beside her and waited and I could hear the chattering of the sparrows from the box.

We had always kept chickens and ducks and geese. Some of them were pecking around near us even as I crouched there with my mother. I knew that we ate those animals, but for some reason Hàm Nghi seemed like a different place altogether and the sparrows could only be for song and friendship. But finally my mother finished cutting the vegetables and she reached into the box and drew out a sparrow, its feet dangling from the bottom of her fist and its head poking out of the top. I looked at its face and I knew it was a girl and my mother said, 'This is the way it's done,' and she fisted her other hand around the sparrow's head and she twisted.

I don't remember how long it took me to get used to this. But I would always drift away when my grandfather went to the sparrow cages on Hàm Nghi. I did not like his face when he bought them. It seemed the same as when he cooed at the doves or sang with the canaries. But I must have decided that it was all part of growing up, of becoming a woman like my mother, for it was she who killed them, after all. And she taught me to do this thing and I wanted to be just like her and I twisted the necks of the sparrows and I plucked their feathers and we roasted them and ate them and my grandfather would take a deep breath after the meal and his eyes would close in pleasure.

There were parrots, too, on Hàm Nghi. They all looked very much like Mr. Green. They were the color of breadfruit leaves with a little yellow on the throat. My grandfather chose one bird each time and cocked his head at it, copying the angle of the bird's head, and my grandfather said, 'Hello,' or 'What's your name?'—things he never said to Mr. Green. The parrots on Hàm Nghi did not talk to my grandfather, though once one of them made a sound like the horns of the little cream and blue taxis that rushed past in the streets. But they never spoke any words, and my grandfather took care to explain to me that these parrots were too recently captured to have learned anything. He said that they were probably not as smart as Mr. Green either, but one day they would speak. Once after explaining this, he leaned near me and motioned to a parrot that was digging for mites under his wing and said, 'That bird will still be alive and speaking to someone when you have grown to be an old woman and have died and are buried in the ground.'

I am forty-one years old now. I go each day to the garden on the bank of the bayou that runs through this place they call Versailles. It is part of New Orleans, but it is far from the center of the town and it is full of Vietnamese who once came from the North. My grandfather never saw the United States. I don't know what he would think. But I come to this garden each day and I crouch in the rich earth and I wear my straw hat and my black pantaloons and I grow lettuce and collards and turnip greens and mint, and my feet, which were once quite beautiful, grow coarse. My family likes the things I bring to the table.

Sometimes Mr. Green comes with me to this garden. He rides on my shoulder and he stays there for a long time, often imitating the cardinals, the sharp ricochet sound they make. Then finally Mr. Green climbs down my arm and drops to the ground and he waddles about in the garden, and when he starts to bite off the stalk of a plant, I cry, 'Not possible' to him and he looks at me like he is angry, like I've dared to use his own words, his and his first master's, against him. I always bring twigs with me and I throw him one to chew on so that neither of us has to back down. I have always tried to preserve his dignity. He is at least fifty years older than me. My grandfather was eighteen when he himself caught Mr. Green on a trip to the highlands with his father.

So Mr. Green is quite old and old people sometimes lose their understanding of the things around them. It is not strange, then, that a few weeks ago Mr. Green began to pluck his feathers out. I went to the veterinarian when it became clear what was happening. A great bare spot had appeared on Mr. Green's chest and I had been finding his feathers at the foot of his perch, so I watched him one afternoon through the kitchen window. He sat there on his perch beside the door of the back porch and he pulled twelve feathers from his chest, one at a time, and felt each with his tongue and then dropped it to the floor. I came out onto the porch and he squawked at me, as if he was doing something private and I should have known better than to intrude. I sat down on the porch and he stopped.

I took Mr. Green to the veterinarian and he said that when parrots do this, it may be because they lack a certain vitamin or mineral. But more often the reason is that the bird is bored. I tried to convince myself that this is what it meant when Mr. Green stopped plucking his feathers as soon as I appeared on the porch. Keep him busy, the doctor said. So I got Mr. Green a new climbing tree with lots of fresh bark to peel and I spent more time with him. I took him to the garden even when he didn't ask to go and I brought my sewing and even some of my cooking—the preparation of the foods—out onto the porch, and while I did these household things, I talked to him. It was just idle chatter but there were plenty of words, and often Mr. Green looked at me sharply as I spoke and I could hear how I sounded, chattering away like a blackbird.

But I felt driven to do something for him. He was old and he was sick and I felt I had to do something. My grandfather took six months to die and he lay in a bed on the top floor of our house and Mr. Green was always on a perch beside him. I remember a wind chime at the window. It was made of brass and I've never had a wind chime in my home because when I hear one, another sound always comes with it, the deep rattling cough of my grandfather. I would visit him in his room with my mother and once he called me back as we were about to leave. I came to him and my mother had gone on out the door and I could hear her talking rapidly with my grandmother. My grandfather motioned me to come very near and he twisted his body in the bed. His face crumpled in pain as he did it, but he forced himself because he wanted to tell me a secret. I leaned cbse to him. 'Do you hear them talking?' he said. He nodded toward the door and he obviously meant my mother and grandmother.

'Yes,' I said.

He frowned. 'How foolish they sound. Chattering and yammering. All the women sound like that. You don't want to grow up sounding like all these foolish women, do you?'

I did not know how to answer his question. I wanted very much to be like my mother, and when my grandfather said this, I felt the recoiling begin inside me and the tears begin to rise. But my mother called my name at that moment and I did not have to find an answer to my grandfather's question. I turned my back on him and ran across the room without saying a word. As I got to the door, however, Mr. Green cried, 'What then?' and it sounded as if he had actually finished my grandfather's thought. You will grow up to be a woman—what then?

And maybe he did finish the thought. Parrots are very smart. Mr. Green in particular. And he knows more than just my grandfather's words. The Buddhists believe in the transmigration of souls, though I suppose it's impossible to transmigrate into some creature that's already alive. But after a few days of angry looks from Mr. Green when I filled the porch with talk that was intended to save his life, he began to cry, 'Not possible' over and over until I stopped speaking. Perhaps a male voice would have been acceptable to him, but mine was not, and then Mr. Green began to pluck himself once more, even with me sitting there in the room. I went to him when he began to do this and I said, 'Not possible,' but he ignored me. He did not even raise his head to look at me but tore away at his feathers, each one making a faint popping sound as it came out. Then the next day he began to cough.

I knew the cough well. But I took Mr. Green to the veterinarian and he told me what I expected, that the cough was not the bird's. This was a sound he was imitating. 'Did someone in your household recently have a cold or the flu?' the doctor said.

'It is my grandfather,' I said.

On the last visit to my grandfather's room he began to cough. My mother went to him and he waved her away. She backed off and I came forward, wanting to help him. He was sitting up now and hunched over and the cough rattled deep inside his chest and then there was a sudden silence and I drew nearer, thinking that my step forward had actually helped, but my grandfather lifted his face and his eyes were very sad, and I knew he was disappointed. My brothers were not yet born and I held my breath so that this silence would go on, but the sound raked up from his chest and filled the room again.

This morning I went to the back porch and Mr. Green was pulling out a feather and he did not acknowledge me, even to taunt me by calling me 'sir.' He dropped the feather and began to pluck another from beneath his left wing. His chest was naked now and the skin looked as slack as my grandfather's throat. I stood before him and I offered my arm for him to come and sit on my shoulder. Yesterday he had said, 'Not possible,' but today he said nothing. He dropped a feather and leaned over and bit me hard on my arm. I bled. But I did not move my arm and he looked at me. His eyes were steady in their sadness, fully dilated, as if he was considering all of this. I pushed my arm to him again and he knew that he had no choice, so he climbed on, but he did not go to my shoulder.

I held my arm aloft and carried Mr. Green outside. The sun had still not burned the fog off the bayou and I went straight into the garden. My feet were bare, like a child's, and the earth was soft and wet and I crouched there and I quickly reached to Mr. Green and grasped him at his chest, lifted him and caught him with my other hand before he could struggle. His wings were pinned and he was bigger in my hands than I had ever imagined. But a Vietnamese woman is experienced in these things and Mr. Green did not have a chance even to make a sound as I laid him on his side, pinned him with my knee, slid my hands up and wrung his neck.

I pray for the soul of my grandfather. I do not bear him any anger. Sometimes I go to Mass during the week. Versailles has a Catholic church just for the Vietnamese and the Mass is celebrated in our language. I sit near the back and I look at the section where all the old women go. They take the Eucharist every day of their lives and they sit together wearing their traditional dresses and with their hair in scarves rolled up on their heads and I wonder if that is where I will finally end up, in the old women's section at Mass each day. No one in my church will likely live as long as a parrot. But our savior lived only thirty-three years, so maybe it's not important. There were women around Jesus when He died, the two Marys. They couldn't do anything for Him. But neither could the men, who had all run away.

THE PUGILIST AT REST

Thom Jones

Hey Baby got caught writing a letter to his girl when he was supposed to be taking notes on the specs of the M-14 rifle. We were sitting in a stifling hot Quonset hut during the first weeks of boot camp, August 1966, at the Marine Corps Recruit Depot in San Diego. Sergeant Wright snatched the letter out of Hey Baby's hand, and later that night in the squad bay he read the letter to the Marine recruits of Platoon 263, his voice laden with sarcasm. *'Hey, Baby!'* he began, and then as he went into the body of the letter he worked himself into a state of outrage and disgust. It was a letter to *Rosie Rottencrotch*, he said at the end, and what really mattered, what was really at issue and what was of utter importance was not *Rosie Rottencrotch* and her steaming-hot panties but rather the muzzle velocity of the M-14 rifle.

Hey Baby paid for the letter by doing a hundred squat thrusts on the concrete floor of the squad bay, but the main prize he won that night was that he became forever known as Hey Baby to the recruits of Platoon 263—in addition to being a shitbird, a faggot, a turd, a maggot, and other such standard appellations. To top it all off, shortly after the incident, Hey Baby got a Dear John from his girl back in Chicago, of whom Sergeant Wright, myself, and seventy-eight other Marine recruits had come to know just a little.

Hey Baby was not in the Marine Corps for very long. The reason for this was that he started in on my buddy, Jorgeson. Jorgeson was my main man, and Hey Baby started calling him Jorgepussy and began harassing him and pushing him around. He was down on Jorgeson because whenever we were taught some sort of combat maneuver or tactic, Jorgeson would say, under his breath, 'You could get *killed* if you try that.' Or, 'Your ass is *had*, if you do that.' You got the feeling that Jorgeson didn't think loving the American flag and defending democratic ideals in Southeast Asia were all that important. He told me that what he really wanted to do was have an artist's loft in the SoHo district of New York City, wear a beret, eat liver-sausage sandwiches made with stale baguettes, drink Tokay wine, smoke dope, paint pictures, and listen to the wailing, sorrowful songs of that French singer Edith Piaf, otherwise known as 'The Little Sparrow.'

After the first half hour of boot camp most of the other recruits wanted to get out, too, but they nourished dreams of surfboards, Corvettes, and blond babes. Jorgeson wanted to be a beatnik and hang out with Jack Kerouac and Neal Cassady, slam down burning shots of amber whiskey, and hear Charles Mingus play real cool jazz on the bass fiddle. He wanted to practice Zen Buddhism, throw the I Ching, eat couscous, and study astrology charts. All of this was foreign territory to me. I had grown up in Aurora, Illinois, and had never heard of such things. Jorgeson had a sharp tongue and was so supercilious in his remarks that I didn't know quite how seriously I should take this talk, but I enjoyed his humor and I did believe he had the sensibilities of an artist. It was not some vague yearning. I believed very much that he could become a painter of pictures. At that point he wasn't putting his heart and soul into becoming a Marine. He wasn't a true believer like me.

Some weeks after Hey Baby began hassling Jorgeson, Sergeant Wright gave us his best speech: 'You men are going off to war, and it's not a pretty thing,' etc. & etc., 'and if Luke the Gook knocks down one of your buddies, a fellow-Marine, you are going to risk your life and go in and get that Marine and you are going to bring him out. Not because I said so. No! You are going after that Marine because *you* are a Marine, a member of the most elite fighting force in the world, and that man out there who's gone down is a Marine, and he's your *buddy*. He is your brother! Once you are a Marine, you are *always* a Marine and you will never let another Marine down.' Etc. & etc. 'You can take a Marine out of the Corps but you can't take the Corps out of a Marine.' Etc. & etc. At the time it seemed to me a very good speech, and it stirred me deeply. Sergeant Wright was no candy ass. He was one squared-away dude, and he could call cadence. Man, it puts a lump in my throat when I remember how that man could sing cadence. Apart from Jorgeson, I think all of the recruits in Platoon 263 were proud of Sergeant Wright. He was the real thing, the genuine article. He was a crackerjack Marine.

In the course of training, lots of the recruits dropped out of the original platoon. Some couldn't pass the physical-fitness tests and had to go to a special camp for pussies. This was a particularly shameful shortcoming, the most humiliating apart from bed-wetting. Other recruits would get pneumonia, strep throat, infected foot blisters, or whatever, and lose time that way. Some didn't qualify at the rifle range. One would break a leg. Another would have a nervous breakdown (and this was also deplorable). People dropped out right and left. When the recruit corrected whatever deficiency he had, or when he got better, he would be picked up by another platoon that was in the stage of basic training that he had been in when his training was interrupted. Platoon 263 picked up dozens of recruits in this fashion. If everything went well, however, you got through with the whole business in twelve weeks. That's not a long time, but it seemed like a long time. You did not see a female in all that time. You did not see a newspaper or a television set. You did not eat a candy bar. Another thing was the fact that you had someone on top of you, watching every move you made. When it was time to 'shit, shower, and shave,' you were given just ten minutes, and had to confront lines and so on to complete the entire affair. Head calls were so infrequent that I spent a lot of time that might otherwise have been neutral or painless in the eye-watering anxiety that I was going to piss my pants. We *ran* to chow, where we were faced with enormous steam vents that spewed out a sickening smell of rancid, super-heated grease. Still, we entered the mess hall with ravenous appetites, ate a huge tray of food in just a few minutes, and then *ran* back to our company area in formation, choking back the burning bile of a meal too big to be eaten so fast. God forbid that you would lose control and vomit.

If all had gone well in the preceding hours, Sergeant Wright would permit us to smoke one cigarette after each meal. Jorgeson had shown me the wisdom of switching from Camels to Pall Malls—they were much longer, packed a pretty good jolt, and when we snapped open our brushed-chrome Zippos, torched up, and inhaled the first few drags, we shared the overmastering pleasure that tobacco can bring if you use it seldom and judiciously. These were always the best moments of the day—brief respites from the tyrannical repression of recruit training. As we got close to the end of it all Jorgeson liked to play a little game. He used to say to me (with fragrant blue smoke curling out of his nostrils), 'If someone said, "I'll give you ten thousand dollars to do all of this again," what would you say?' 'No way, Jack!' He would keep on upping it until he had John Beresford Tipton, the guy from 'The Millionaire,' offering me a check for a million bucks. 'Not for any money,' I'd say.

While they were all smoldering under various pressures, the recruits were also getting pretty 'salty'—they were beginning to believe. They were beginning to think of themselves as Marines. If you could make it through this, the reasoning went, you wouldn't crack in combat. So I remember that I had tears in my eyes when Sergeant Wright gave us the spiel about how a Marine would charge a machine-gun nest to save his buddies, dive on a hand grenade, do whatever it takes—and yet I was ashamed when Jorgeson caught me wiping them away. All of the recruits were teary except Jorgeson. He had these very clear cobalt-blue eyes. They were so remarkable that they caused you to notice Jorgeson in a crowd. There was unusual beauty in these eyes, and there was an extraordinary power in them. Apart from having a pleasant enough face, Jorgeson was small and unassuming except for these eyes. Anyhow, when he caught me getting sentimental he gave me this look that penetrated to the core of my being. It was the icy look of absolute contempt, and it caused me to doubt myself. I said, 'Man! Can't you get into it? For Christ's sake!'

'I'm not like you,' he said. 'But I am into it, more than you could ever know. I never told you this before, but I am Kal-El, born on the planet Krypton and rocketed to Earth as an infant, moments before my world exploded. Disguised as a mild-mannered Marine, I have resolved to use my powers for the good of mankind. Whenever danger appears on the scene, truth and justice will be served as I slip into the green U.S.M.C. utility uniform and become Earth's greatest hero.'

I got highly pissed and didn't talk to him for a couple of days after this. Then, about two weeks before boot camp was over, when we were running out to the parade field for drill with our rifles at port arms, all assholes and elbows, I saw Hey Baby give Jorgeson a nasty shove with his M-14. Hey Baby was a large and fairly tough young man who liked to displace his aggressive impulses on Jorgeson, but he wasn't as big or as tough as I.

Jorgeson nearly fell down as the other recruits scrambled out to the parade field, and Hey Baby gave a short, malicious laugh. I ran past Jorgeson and caught up to Hey Baby; he picked me up in his peripheral vision, but by then it was too late. I set my body so that I could put everything into it, and with one deft stroke I hammered him in the temple with the sharp edge of the steel butt plate of my M-14. It was not exactly a premeditated crime, although I had been laying to get him. My idea before this had simply been to lay my hands on him, but now I had blood in my eye. I was a skilled boxer, and I knew the temple was a vulnerable spot; the human skull is otherwise hard and durable, except at its base. There was a sickening crunch, and Hey Baby dropped into the ice plants along the side of the company street.

The entire platoon was out on the parade field when the house mouse screamed at the assistant D.I., who rushed back to the scene of the crime to find Hey Baby crumpled in a fetal position in the ice plants with blood all over the place. There was blood from the scalp wound as well as a froth of blood emitting from his nostrils and his mouth. Blood was leaking from his right ear. Did I see skull fragments and brain tissue? It seemed that I did. To tell you the truth, I wouldn't have cared in the least if I had killed him, but like most criminals I was very much afraid of getting caught. It suddenly occurred to me that I could be headed for the brig for a long time. My heart was pounding out of my chest. Yet the larger part of me didn't care. Jorgeson was my buddy, and I wasn't going to stand still and let someone fuck him over.

The platoon waited at parade rest while Sergeant Wright came out of the duty hut and took command of the situation. An ambulance was called, and it came almost immediately. A number of corpsmen squatted down alongside the fallen man for what seemed an eternity. Eventually they took Hey Baby off with a fractured skull. It would be the last we ever saw of him. Three evenings later, in the squad bay, the assistant D.I. told us rather ominously that Hey Baby had recovered consciousness. That's all he said. What did *that* mean? I was worried, because Hey Baby had seen me make my move, but, as it turned out, when he came to he had forgotten the incident and all events of the preceding two weeks. Retrograde amnesia. Lucky for me. I also knew that at least three other recruits had seen what I did, but none of them reported me. Every member of the platoon was called in and grilled by a team of hard-ass captains and a light colonel from the Criminal Investigation Detachment. It took a certain amount of balls to lie to them, yet none of my fellow-jarheads reported me. I was well liked and Hey Baby was not. Indeed, many felt that he got exactly what was coming to him.

*

The other day—Memorial Day, as it happened—I was cleaning some stuff out of the attic when I came upon my old dress-blue uniform. It's a beautiful uniform, easily the most handsome worn by any of the U.S. armed forces. The rich color recalled Jorgeson's eyes for me—not that the color matched, but in the sense that the color of each was so startling. The tunic does not have lapels, of course, but a high collar with red piping and the traditional golden eagle, globe, and anchor insignia on either side of the neck clasp. The tunic buttons are not brassy—although they are in fact made of brass—but are a delicate gold in color, like Florentine gold. On the sleeves of the tunic my staff sergeant's chevrons are gold on red. High on the left breast is a rainbow display of fruit salad representing my various combat citations. Just below these are my marksmanship badges; I shot Expert in rifle as well as pistol.

I opened a sandalwood box and took my various medals out of the large plastic bag I had packed them in to prevent them from tarnishing. The Navy Cross and the two Silver Stars are the best; they are such pretty things they dazzle you. I found a couple of Thai sticks in the sandalwood box as well. I took a whiff of the box and smelled the smells of Saigon—the whores, the dope, the saffron, cloves, jasmine, and patchouli oil. I put the Thai sticks back, recalling the three-day hangover that particular batch of dope had given me more than twenty-three years before. Again I looked at my dress-blue tunic. My most distinctive badge, the crowning glory, and the one of which I am most proud, is the set of Airborne wings. I remember how it was, walking around Oceanside, California—the Airborne wings and the high-and-tight haircut were recognized by all the Marines; they meant you were the crème de la crème, you were a recon Marine.

Recon was all Jorgeson's idea. We had lost touch with each other after boot camp. I was sent to com school in San Diego, where I had to sit in a hot Class A wool uniform all day and learn the Morse code. I deliberately flunked out, and when I was given the perfunctory option for a second shot, I told the colonel, 'Hell no, sir. I want to go 003— infantry. I want to be a ground-pounder. I didn't join the service to sit at a desk all day.'

I was on a bus to Camp Pendleton three days later, and when I got there I ran into Jorgeson. I had been thinking of him a lot. He was a clerk in headquarters company. Much to my astonishment, he was fifteen pounds heavier, and had grown two inches, and he told me he was hitting the weight pile every night after running seven miles up and down the foothills of Pendleton in combat boots, carrying a rifle and a full field pack. After the usual what's-been-happening? b.s., he got down to business and said, 'They need people in Force Recon, what do you think? Headquarters is one boring motherfucker.'

I said, 'Recon? Paratrooper? You got to be shittin' me! When did you get so gung-ho, man?'

He said, 'Hey, you were the one who *bought* the program. Don't fade on me now, goddamm it! Look, we pass the physical fitness test and then they send us to jump school at Benning. If we pass that, we're in. And we'll pass. Those doggies ain't got jack. Semper fi, motherfucker! Let's do it.'

There was no more talk of Neal Cassady, Edith Piaf, or the artist's loft in SoHo. I said, 'If Sergeant Wright could only see you now!'

We were just three days in country when we got dropped in somewhere up north near the DMZ. It was a routine reconnaissance patrol. It was not supposed to be any kind of big deal at all—just acclimation. The morning after our drop we approached a clear field. I recall that it gave me a funny feeling, but I was too new to fully trust my instincts. *Everything* was spooky; I was fresh meat, F.N.G.—a Fucking New Guy.

Before moving into the field, our team leader sent Hanes—a lance corporal, a short-timer, with only tvelve days left before his rotation was over—across the field as a point man. This was a bad omen and everyone knew it. Hanes had two Purple Hearts. He followed the order with no hesitation and crossed the field without drawing fire. The team leader signaled for us to fan out and told me to circumvent the field and hump through the jungle to investigate a small mound of loose red dirt that I had missed completely but that he had picked up with his trained eye. I remember I kept saying, 'Where?' He pointed to a heap of earth about thirty yards along the tree line and about ten feet back in the bushes. Most likely it was an anthill, but you never knew—it could have been an NVA tunnel. 'Over there,' he hissed. 'Goddamn it, do I have to draw pictures for you?'

I moved smartly in the direction of the mound while the rest of the team reconverged to discuss something. As I approached the mound

I saw that it was in fact an anthill, and I looked back at the team and saw they were already halfway across the field, moving very fast.

Suddenly there were several loud hollow pops and the cry 'Incoming!' Seconds later the first of a half-dozen mortar rounds landed in the loose earth surrounding the anthill. For a millisecond, everything went black. I was blown back and lifted up on a cushion of warm air. At first it was like the thrill of a carnival ride, but it was quickly followed by that stunned, jangly, electric feeling you get when you hit your crazy bone. Like that, but not confined to a small area like the elbow. I felt it shoot through my spine and into all four limbs. A thick plaster of sand and red clay plugged up my nostrils and ears. Grit was blown in between my teeth. If I hadn't been wearing a pair of Ray-Ban aviator shades, I would certainly have been blinded permanently—as it was, my eyes were loaded with grit. (I later discovered that fine red earth was somehow blown in behind the crystal of my pressure-tested Rolex Submariner, underneath my fingernails and toenails, and deep into the pores of my skin.) When I was able to, I pulled out a canteen filled with lemon-lime Kool-Aid and tried to flood my eyes clean. This helped a little, but my eyes still felt like they were on fire. I rinsed them again and blinked furiously.

I rolled over on my stomach in the prone position and leveled my field-issue M-16. A company of screaming NVA soldiers ran into the field, firing as they came—I saw their green tracer rounds blanket the position where the team had quickly congregated to lay out a perimeter, but none of our own red tracers were going out. Several of the Marines had been killed outright by the mortar rounds. Jorgeson was all right, and I saw him cast a nervous glance in my direction. Then he turned to the enemy and began to fire his M-16. I clicked my rifle on to automatic and pulled the trigger, but the gun was loaded with dirt and it wouldn't fire.

Apart from Jorgeson, the only other American putting out any fire was Second Lieutenant Milton, also a fairly new guy, a 'cherry,' who was down on one knee firing his .45, an exercise in almost complete futility. I assumed that Milton's 16 had jammed, like mine, and watched as AK-47 rounds, having penetrated his flak jacket and then his chest, ripped through the back of his field pack and buzzed into the jungle beyond }ike a deadly swarm of bees. A few seconds later, I heard the swoosh of an RPG rocket, a dud round that dinged the lieutenant's left shoulder before it flew off in the bush behind him. It took off his whole arm, and for an instant I could see the white bone and ligaments of his shoulder, and then red flesh of muscle tissue, looking very much like fresh prime beef, well marbled and encased in a thin layer of yellowish-white adipose tissue that quickly became saturated with dark-red blood. What a lot of blood there was. Still, Milton continued to fire his .45. When he emptied his clip, I watched him remove a fresh one from his web gear and attempt to load the pistol with one hand. He seemed to fumble with the fresh clip for a long time, until at last he dropped it, along with his .45. The lieutenant's head slowly sagged forward, but he stayed up on one knee with his remaining arm extended out to the enemy, palm upward in the soulful, heartrending gesture of Al Jolson doing a rendition of 'Mammy.'

A hail of green tracer rounds buzzed past Jorgeson, but he coolly returned fire in short, controlled bursts. The light, tinny pops from his M-16 did not sound very reassuring, but I saw several NVA go down. AK-47 fire kicked up red dust all around Jorgeson's feet. He was basically out in the open, and if ever a man was totally alone it was Jorgeson. He was dead meat and he had to know it. It was very strange that he wasn't hit immediately.

Jorgeson zigged his way over to the body of a large black Marine who carried an M-60 machine gun. Most of the recon Marines carried grease guns or Swedish Ks; an M-60 was too heavy for traveling light and fast, but this Marine had been big and he had been paranoid. I had known him least of anyone in the squad. In three days he had said nothing to me, I suppose because I was F.N.G., and had spooked him. Indeed, now he was dead. That august seeker of truth, Schopenhauer, was correct: *We are like lambs in a field, disporting themselves under the eye of the butcher, who chooses out first one and then another for his prey. So it is that in our good days we are all unconscious of the evil Fate may have presently in store for us—sickness, poverty, mutilation, loss of sight or reason.*

It was difficult to judge how quickly time was moving. Although my senses had been stunned by the concussion of the mortar rounds, they were, however paradoxical this may seem, more acute than ever before. I watched Jorgeson pick up the machine gun and begin to spread an impressive field of fire back at the enemy. *Thuk thuk thuk, thuk thuk thuk, thuk thuk tkuk!* I saw several more bodies fall, and began to think that things might turn out all right after all. The NVA dropped for cover, and many of them turned back and headed for the tree line. Jorgeson fired off a couple of bandoliers, and after he stopped to load another, he turned back and looked at me with those blue eyes and a smile like 'How am I doing?' Then I heard the steel-cork pop of an M-79 launcher and saw a rocket grenade explode through Jorgeson's upper abdomen, causing him to do something like a back flip. His M-60 machine gun flew straight up into the air. The barrel was glowing red like a hot poker, and continued to fire in a 'cook off' until the entire bandolier had run through.

In the meantime I had pulled a cleaning rod out of my pack and worked it through the barrel of my M-16. When I next tried to shoot, the Tonka-toy son of a bitch remained jammed, and at last I frantically broke it down to find the source of the problem. I had a dirty bolt. Fucking dirt everywhere. With numbed fingers I removed the firing pin and worked it over with a toothbrush, dropping it in the red dirt, picking it up, cleaning it, and dropping it again. My fingers felt like Novocain, and while I could see far away, I was unable to see up close. I poured some more Kool-Aid over my eyes. It was impossible for me to get my weapon clean. Lucky for me, ultimately.

Suddenly NVA soldiers were running through the field shoving bayonets into the bodies of the downed Marines. It was not until an NVA trooper kicked Lieutenant Milton out of his tripod position that he finally fell to the ground. Then the soldiers started going through the dead Marines' gear. I was still frantically struggling with my weapon when it began to dawn on me that the enemy had forgotten me in the excitement of the firefight. I wondered what had happened to Hanes and if he had gotten clear. I doubted it, and hopped on my survival radio to call in an air strike when finally a canny NVA trooper did remember me and headed in my direction most ricky-tick.

With a tight grip on the spoon, I pulled the pin on a fragmentation grenade and then unsheathed my K-bar. About this time Jorgeson let off a horrendous shriek—a gut shot is worse than anything. Or did Jorgeson scream to save my life? The NVA moving in my direction turned back to him, studied him for a moment, and then thrust a bayonet into his heart. As badly as my own eyes hurt, I was able to see Jorgeson's eyes—a final flash of glorious azure before they faded into the unfocused and glazed gray of death. I repinned the grenade, got up on my knees, and scrambled away until finally I was on my feet with a useless and incomplete handful of M-16 parts, and I was running as fast and as hard as I have ever run in my life. A pair of Phantom F-4s came in very low with delayed-action high-explosive rounds and napalm. I could feel the almost unbearable heat waves of the latter, volley after volley. I can still feel it and smell it to this day.

Concerning Lance Corporal Hanes: they found him later, fried to a crisp by the napalm, but it was nonetheless ascertained that he had been mutilated while alive. He was like the rest of us—eighteen, nineteen, twenty years old. What did we know of life? Before Vietnam, Hanes didn't think he would ever die. I mean, yes, he knew that in theory he would die, but he *felt* like he was going to live forever. I know that I felt that way. Hanes was down to twelve days and a wake-up. When other Marines saw a short-timer get greased, it devastated their morale. However, when I saw them zip up the body bag on Hanes I became incensed. Why hadn't Milton sent him back to the rear to burn shit or something when he got so short? Twelve days to go and then mutilated. Fucking Milton! Fucking second lieutenant!

Theogenes was the greatest of gladiators. He was a boxer who served under the patronage of a cruel nobleman, a prince who took great delight in bloody spectacles. Although this was several hundred years before the times of those most enlightened of men Socrates, Plato, and Aristotle, and well after the Minoans of Crete, it still remains a high point in the history of Western civilization and culture. It was the approximate time of Homer, the greatest poet who ever lived. Then, as now, violence, suffering, and the cheapness of life were the rule.

The sort of boxing Theogenes practiced was not like modern-day boxing with those kindergarten Queensberry Rules. The two contestants were not permitted the freedom of a ring. Instead, they were strapped to flat stones, facing each other nose-to-nose. When the signal was given, they would begin hammering each other with fists encased in heavy leather thongs. It was a fight to the death. Fourteen hundred and twenty-five times Theogenes was strapped to the stone and fourteen hundred and twenty-five times he emerged a victor.

Perhaps it is Theogenes who is depicted in the famous Roman statue (based on the earlier Greek original) of 'The Pugilist at Rest.' I keep a grainy black-and-white photograph of it in my room. The statue

depicts a muscular athlete approaching his middle age. He has a thick
beard and a full head of curly hair. In addition to the telltale broken
nose and cauliflower ears of a boxer, the pugilist has the slanted,
drooping brows that bespeak torn nerves. Also, the forehead is piled
with scar tissue. As may be expected, the pugilist has the musculature
of a fighter. His neck and trapezius muscles are well developed. His
shoulders are enormous; his chest is thick and flat, without the bulging
pectorals of the bodybuilder. His back, oblique, and abdominal
muscles are highly pronounced, and he has that greatest asset of the
modern boxer—sturdy legs. The arms are large, particularly the
forearms, which are reinforced with the leather wrappings of the
cestus. It is the body of a small heavyweight—lithe rather than bulky,
but by no means lacking in power: a Jack Johnson or a Dempsey, say.
If you see the authentic statue at the Terme Museum, in Rome, you will
see that the seated boxer is really not much more than a light-
heavyweight. People were small in those days. The important thing
was that he was perfectly proportioned.

The pugilist is sitting on a rock with his forearms balanced on his
thighs. That he is seated and not pacing implies that he has been
through all this many times before. It appears that he is conserving his
strength. His head is turned as if he were looking over his shoulder—
as if someone had just whispered something to him. It is in this that the
'art' of the sculpture is conveyed to the viewer. Could it be that
someone has just summoned him to the arena? There is a slight look of
befuddlement on his face, but there is no trace of fear. There is an air
about him that suggests that he is eager to proceed and does not wish
to cause anyone any trouble or to create a delay, even though his life
will soon be on the line. Besides the deformities on his noble face, there
is also the suggestion of weariness and philosophical resignation. *All
the world's a stage, and all the men and women merely players*. Exactly! He
knew this more than two thousand years before Shakespeare penned
the line. How did he come to be at this place in space and time? Would
he rather be safely removed to the countryside—an obscure, stinking
peasant shoving a plow behind a mule? Would that be better? Or does
he revel in his role? Perhaps he once did, but surely not now. Is this the
great Theogenes or merely a journeyman fighter, a former slave or
criminal bought by one of the many contractors who for months
trained the condemned for their brief moment in the arena? I wonder

if Marcus Aurelius loved the 'Pugilist' as I do, and came to study it and to meditate before it.

I cut and ran from that field in Southeast Asia. I've read that Davy Crockett, hero of the American frontier, was cowering under a bed when Santa Anna and his soldiers stormed into the Alamo. What is the truth? Jack Dempsey used to get so scared before his fights that he sometimes wet his pants. But look what he did to Willard and to Luis Firpo, the Wild Bull of the Pampas! It was something close to homicide. What is courage? What is cowardice? The magnificent Roberto Duran gave us 'No más,' but who had a greater fighting heart than Duran?

I got over that first scare and saw that I was something quite other than that which I had known myself to be. Hey Baby proved only my warm-up act. There was a reservoir of malice, poison, and vicious sadism in my soul, and it poured forth freely in the jungles and rice paddies of Vietnam. I pulled three tours. I wanted some payback for Jorgeson. I grieved for Lance Corporal Hanes. I grieved for myself and what I had lost. I committed unspeakable crimes and got medals for it.

It was only fair that I got a head injury myself. I never got a scratch in Vietnam, but I got tagged in a boxing smoker at Pendleton. Fought a bad-ass light-heavyweight from artillery. Nobody would fight this guy. He could box. He had all the moves. But mainly he was a puncher—it was said that he could punch with either hand. It was said that his hand speed was superb. I had finished off at least a half rack of Hamm's before I went in with him and started getting hit with head shots I didn't even see coming. They were right. His hand speed was superb.

I was twenty-seven years old, smoked two packs a day, was a borderline alcoholic. I shouldn't have fought him—I knew that—but he had been making noise. A very long time before, I had been the middleweight champion of the 1st Marine Division. I had been a so-called war hero. I had been a recon Marine. But now I was a garrison Marine and in no kind of shape.

He put me down almost immediately, and when I got up I was terribly afraid. I was tight and I could not breathe. It felt like he was hitting me in the face with a ball-peen hammer. It felt like he was busting light bulbs in my face. Rather than one opponent, I saw three.

I was convinced his gloves were loaded, and a wave of self-pity ran through me.

I began to move. He made a mistake by expending a lot of energy trying to put me away quickly. I had no intention of going down again, and I knew I wouldn't. My buddies were watching, and I had to give them a good show. While I was afraid, I was also exhilarated; I had not felt this alive since Vietnam. I began to score with my left jab, and because of this I was able to withstand his bull charges and divert them. I thought he would throw his bolt, but in the beginning he was tireless. I must have hit him with four hundred left jabs. It got so that I could score at will, with either hand, but he would counter, trap me on the ropes, and pound. He was the better puncher and was truly hurting me, but I was scoring, and as the fight went on the momentum shifted and I took over. I staggered him again and again. The Marines at ringside were screaming for me to put him away, but however much I tried, I could not. Although I could barely stand by the end, I was sorry that the fight was over. Who had won? The referee raised my arm in victory, but I think it was pretty much a draw. Judging a prizefight is a very subjective thing.

About an hour after the bout, when the adrenaline had subsided, I realized I had a terrible headache. It kept getting worse, and I rushed out of the NCO Club, where I had gone with my buddies to get loaded.

I stumbled outside, struggling to breathe, and I headed away from the company area toward Sheepshit Hill, one of the many low brown foothills in the vicinity. Like a dog who wants to die alone, so it was with me. Everything got swirly, and I dropped in the bushes.

I was unconscious for nearly an hour, and for the next two weeks I walked around like I was drunk, with double vision. I had constant headaches and seemed to have grown old overnight. My health was gone.

I became a very timid individual. I became introspective. I wondered what had made me act the way I had acted. Why had I killed my fellowmen in war, without any feeling, remorse, or regret? And when the war was over, why did I continue to drink and swagger around and get into fistfights? Why did I like to dish out pain, and why did I take positive delight in the suffering of others? Was I insane? Was it too much testosterone? Women don't do things like that. The rapacious Will to Power lost its hold on me. Suddenly I began to feel sympathetic to the cares and sufferings of all living creatures. You lose your health and you start thinking this way.

Has man become any better since the times of Theogenes? The world is replete with badness. I'm not talking about that old routine where you drag out the Spanish Inquisition, the Holocaust, Joseph Stalin, the Khmer Rouge, etc. It happens in our own backyard. Twentieth-century America is one of the most materially prosperous nations in history. But take a walk through an American prison, a nursing home, the slums where the homeless live in cardboard boxes, a cancer ward. Go to a Vietnam vets' meeting, or an A.A. meeting, or an Overeaters Anonymous meeting. *How hollow and unreal a thing is life, how deceitful are its pleasures, what horrible aspects it possesses.* Is the world not rather like a hell, as Schopenhauer, that clearheaded seer—who has helped me transform my suffering into an object of understanding—was so quick to point out? They called him a pessimist and dismissed him with a word, but it is peace and self-renewal that I have found in his pages.

About a year after my fight with the guy from artillery I started having seizures. I suffered from a form of left-temporal-lobe seizure which is sometimes called Dostoyevski's epilepsy. It's so rare as to be almost unknown. Freud, himself a neurologist, speculated that Dostoyevski was a hysterical epileptic, and that his fits were unrelated to brain damage—psychogenic in origin. Dostoyevski did not have his first attack until the age of twenty-five, when he was imprisoned in Siberia and received fifty lashes after complaining about the food. Freud figured that after Dostoyevski's mock execution, the four years' imprisonment in Siberia, the tormented childhood, the murder of his tyrannical father, etc. & etc.—he had all the earmarks of hysteria, of grave psychological trauma. And Dostoyevski had displayed the trademark features of the psychomotor epileptic long before his first attack. These days physicians insist there is no such thing as the 'epileptic personality. ' I think they say this because they do not want to add to the burden of the epileptic's suffering with an extra stigma. Privately they do believe in these traits. Dostoyevski was nervous and depressed, a tormented hypochondriac, a compulsive writer obsessed with religious and philosophic themes. He was hyperloquacious, raving, etc. & etc. His gambling addiction is well known. By most accounts he was a sick soul.

The peculiar and most distinctive thing about his epilepsy was that in the split second before his fit—in the aura, which is in fact officially a part of the attack—Dostoyevski experienced a sense of felicity, of ecstatic well-being unlike anything an ordinary mortal could hope to imagine. It was the experience of satori. Not the nickel-and-dime satori of Abraham Maslow, but the Supreme. He said that he wouldn't trade ten years of life for this feeling, and I, who have had it, too, would have to agree. I can't explain it, I don't understand it—it becomes slippery and elusive when it gets any distance on you—but I have felt this down to the core of my being. Yes, God exists! But then it slides away and I lose it. I become a doubter. Even Dostoyevski, the fervent Christian, makes an almost airtight case against the possibility of the existence of God in the Grand Inquisitor digression in *The Brothers Karamazov*. It is probably the greatest passage in all of world literature, and it tilts you to the court of the atheist. This is what happens when you approach Him with the intellect.

It is thought that St. Paul had a temporal-lobe fit on the road to Damascus. Paul warns us in First Corinthians that God will confound the intellectuals. It is known that Muhammad composed the Koran after attacks of epilepsy. Black Elk experienced fits before his grand 'buffalo' vision. Joan of Arc is thought to have been a left-temporal-lobe epileptic. Each of these in a terrible flash of brain lightning was able to pierce the murky veil of illusion which is spread over all things. Just so did the scales fall from my eyes. It is called the 'sacred disease.'

But what a price. I rarely leave the house anymore. To avoid falling injuries, I always wear my old boxer's headgear, and I always carry my mouthpiece. Rather more often than the aura where 'every common bush is afire with God,' I have the typical epileptic aura, which is that of terror and impending doom. If I can keep my head and think of it, and if there is time, I slip the mouthpiece in and thus avoid biting my tongue. I bit it in half once, and when they sewed it back together it swelled enormously, like a huge red-and-black sausage. I was unable to close my mouth for more than two weeks.

The fits are coming more and more. I'm loaded on Depakene, phenobarbital, Tegretol, Dilantin—the whole shit load. A nurse from the V.A. bought a pair of Staffordshire terriers for me and trained them to watch me as I sleep, in case I have a fit and smother facedown in my bedding. What delightful companions these dogs are! One of them,

Gloria, is especially intrepid and clever. Inevitably, when I come to I find that the dogs have dragged me into the kitchen, away from blankets and pillows, rugs, and objects that might suffocate me; and that they have turned me on my back. There's Gloria, barking in my face. Isn't this incredible?

My sister brought a neurosurgeon over to my place around Christmas—not some V.A. butcher but a guy from the university hospital. He was a slick dude in a nine-hundred-dollar suit. He came down on me hard, like a used-car salesman. He wants to cauterize a small spot in a nerve bundle in my brain. 'It's not a lobotomy, it's a *cingulotomy*,' he said.

Reckless, desperate, last-ditch psychosurgery is still pretty much unthinkable in the conservative medical establishment. That's why he made a personal visit to my place. A house call. Drumming up some action to make himself a name. 'See that bottle of Thorazine?' he said. 'You can throw that poison away,' he said. 'All that amitriptyline. That's garbage, you can toss that, too.' He said, 'Tell me something. How can you take all of that shit and still walk?' He said, 'You take enough drugs to drop an elephant.'

He wants to cut me. He said that the feelings of guilt and worthlessness, and the heaviness of a heart blackened by sin, will go away. 'It is *not* a lobotomy,' he said.

I don't like the guy. I don't trust him. I'm not convinced, but I can't go on like this. If I am not having a panic attack I am engulfed in tedious, unrelenting depression. I am overcome with a deadening sense of languor; I can't *do* anything. I wanted to give my buddies a good show! What a goddamn fool. I am a goddamn fool!

It has taken me six months to put my thoughts in order, but I wanted to do it in case I am a vegetable after the operation. I know that my buddy Jorgeson was a real American hero. I wish that he had lived to be something else, if not a painter of pictures then even some kind of fuckup with a factory job and four divorces, bankruptcy petitions, in and out of jail. I wish he had been that. I wish he had been *anything* rather than a real American hero. So, then, if I am to feel somewhat *indifferent* to life after the operation, all the better. If not, not.

If I had a more conventional sense of morality I would shitcan those dress blues, and I'd send that Navy Cross to Jorgeson's brother. Jorgeson was the one who won it, who pulled the John Wayne number up there near Khe Sanh and saved my life, although I lied and took the credit for all of those dead NVA. He had created a stunning body count—nothing like Theogenes, but Jorgeson only had something like twelve minutes total in the theater of war.

The high command almost awarded me the Medal of Honor, but of course there were no witnesses to what I claimed I had done, and I had saved no one's life. When I think back on it, my tale probably did not sound as credible as I thought it had at the time. I was only nineteen years old and not all that practiced a liar. I figure if they *had* given me the Medal of Honor, I would have stood in the ring up at Camp Las Pulgas in Pendleton and let that light-heavyweight from artillery fucking kill me.

Now I'm thinking I might call Hey Baby and ask how he's doing. No shit, a couple of neuropsychs—we probably have a lot in common. I could apologize to him. But I learned from my fits that you don't have to do that. Good and evil are only illusions. Still, I cannot help but wonder sometimes if my vision of the Supreme Reality was any more real than the demons visited upon schizophrenics and madmen. Has it all been just a stupid neurochemical event? Is there no God at all? The human heart rebels against this.

If they fuck up the operation, I hope I get to keep my dogs somehow—maybe stay at my sister's place. If they send me to the nuthouse I lose the dogs for sure.

ANCIENT HISTORY

Richard Bausch

In the car on the way south, after hours of quiet between them, of only the rattle and static of the radio, she began to talk about growing up so close to Washington: how it was to have all the shrines of Democracy as a part of one's daily idea of home; she had taken it all for granted, of course. 'But your father was always a tourist in his own city,' she said. 'It really excited him. That's why we spent our honeymoon there. Everybody thought we'd got tickets to travel, and we weren't fifteen minutes from home. We checked into the Lafayette Hotel, right across from the White House. The nicest old hotel. I was eighteen years old, and all my heroes were folksingers. Jack Kennedy was president. Lord, it seems so much closer than it is.' She was watching the country glide past the window, and so Charles couldn't see her face. He was driving. The road was wet, probably icy in places. On either side were brown, snowpatched hills, and the sky seemed to move like a smoke along the crests. 'My God. Charles, I was exactly your age now. Isn't that amazing. Well, I don't suppose you find it so amazing.'

'It's amazing, Mom.' He smiled at her.

'Yes, well, you wait. Wait till you're my age. You'll see.'

A little later, she said, 'All the times you and your father and I have been down here, and I still feel like it's been a thousand years.'

'It's strange to be coming through when the trees are all bare,' said Charles. Aunt Lois had asked them to come. She didn't want to be alone on Christmas, and she didn't want to travel anymore; she had come north to visit every Christmas for fifteen years, and now that Lawrence was gone she didn't feel there was any reason to put herself through the journey again, certainly not to sit in that house with Charles's mother and pine for some other Christmas. She was going to stay put, and if people wanted to see her, they could come south. 'Meaning us,' Charles's mother said. And Aunt Lois said, 'That's exactly what I meant, Marie. I'm glad you're still quick on the uptake.' They were talking on the telephone, but Aunt Lois's voice was so clear and resonant that Charles, sitting across the room from his mother, could hear every word. His mother held the receiver an inch from her ear and looked at him and smiled. They'd go. Aunt Lois was not about to budge. 'We do want to see her,' Charles's mother said, 'and I guess we don't really want to be here for Christmas, do we?'

Charles shook his head no.

'I guess we don't want Christmas to come at all,' she said into the phone. Charles heard Aunt Lois say that it was coming anyway, and nothing would stop it. When his mother had hung up, he said, 'I don't think I want to go through it anywhere,' meaning Christmas.

She said, 'We could just stay here and not celebrate it or something. Or we could have a bunch of people over, like we did on Thanksgiving.'

'No,' Charles said, 'let's go.'

'I know one thing,' she said. 'Your father wouldn't want us moping around on his favorite holiday.'

'I'm not moping.' Charles said.

'Good. Dad wouldn't like it.'

It had been four months, and she had weathered her grief, had shown him how strong she was, yet sometimes such a bewildered look came into her eyes. He saw in it something of his own bewilderment: his father had been young and vigorous, his heart had been judged to be strong—and now life seemed so frail and precarious.

Driving south, Charles looked over at his mother and wondered how he would ever be able to let her out of his sight. 'Mom,' he said, 'let's travel somewhere.'

'I thought we were doing just that,' she said.

'Let's close the house up and go to Europe or someplace.'

'We don't have that kind of money; are you kidding? There's money for you to go to school, and that's about it. And you know it, Charles.'

'It wouldn't cost that much to go somewhere for a while. There's all kinds of package deals—discounts and special fares—it wouldn't cost that much.'

'Why don't *you* go?'

'By myself?'

'Isn't there a friend you'd like to go with—somebody with the money to go?'

'I thought *we'd* go.'

'Don't you think I'd get in your way a little? A young man like you, in one of those touring groups with his mother?'

'I thought it might be a good thing,' he muttered.

She turned a little on the seat, to face him. 'Don't mope, Charles.'

'I'm not. I just thought it might be fun to travel together.'

'We travel everywhere together these days,' she said.

He stared ahead at the road.

'You know,' she said after a moment, 'I think Aunt Lois was a little surprised that we took her up on her invitation.'

'Wouldn't you like traveling together?' Charles said.

'I think you should go with somebody else if you go. I'm glad we're taking *this* trip together. I really am. But for me to go on a long trip like that with you—well, it just seems, I don't know, uncalled-for.'

'Why uncalled-for?' he asked.

'Let's take one trip at a time,' she said.

'Yes, but why uncalled-for?'

'We'll talk about it later.' This was her way of curtailing a discussion; she would say, very calmly, as if there were all the time in the world, 'We'll talk about it later,' and of course her intention was that the issue, whatever its present importance, would be forgotten, the subject would be closed. If it was broached again, she was likely to show impatience and, often, a kind of dismay, as if one had shown very bad manners calling up so much old-hat, so much ancient history.

'I'm not doing anything out of duty,' Charles said.

'Who said anything about duty?'

'I just wanted you to know.'

'What an odd thing to say.'

'Well, you said that about it being uncalled-for.'

'I just meant it's not necessary, Charles. Besides, don't you think it's time for you to get on with the business of your own life?'

'I don't see how traveling together is stopping me,' he said.

'All right, but I don't want to talk about it now.'

'Okay, then.'

'Aren't you going a little fast?'

He slowed down.

A few moments later, she said, 'You're driving. I guess I shouldn't have said anything.'

'I *was* going too fast,' he said.

'I'm kind of jumpy, too.'

They lapsed into silence. It had begun to rain a little, and Charles turned the windshield wipers on. Other cars, coming by them, threw a muddy spray up from the road.

'Of all things,' his mother said, 'I really am nervous all of a sudden.'

Aunt Lois's house was a little three-bedroom rambler in a row of three-bedroom ramblers just off the interstate. At the end of her block was an overpass sixty feet high, which at the same time each clear winter afternoon blotted out the sun; a wide band of shade stretched across the lawn and the house, and the sidewalk often stayed frozen longer than the rest of the street. Aunt Lois kept a five-pound bag of rock salt in a child's wagon on her small front porch, and in the evenings she would stand there and throw handfuls of it on the walk. Charles's father would tease her about it, as he teased her about everything: her chain-smoking, her love of country music—which she denied vehemently—her fear of growing fat, and her various disasters with men, about which she was apt to hold forth at great length and with very sharp humor, with herself as the butt of the jokes, the bumbling central character.

She stood in the light of her doorway, arms folded tight, and called to them to be careful of ice patches on the walk. There was so much rock salt it crackled under their feet, and Charles thought of the gravel walk they had all traversed following his father's body in the funeral procession, the last time he had seen Aunt Lois. He shivered as he looked at her there now, outlined in the light.

'I swear,' she was saying, 'I can't believe you actually decided to come.'

'Whoops,' Charles's mother said, losing her balance slightly. She leaned on his arm as they came up onto the porch. Aunt Lois stood back from the door. Charles couldn't shake the feeling of the long funeral walk, that procession in his mind. He held tight to his mother's elbow as they stepped up through Aunt Lois's door. Her living room was warm, and smelled of cake. There was a fire in the fireplace. The lounge chair his father always sat in was on the other side of the room. Aunt Lois had moved it. Charles saw that the imprint of its legs was still in the nap of the carpet. Aunt Lois was looking at him.

'Well,' she said, smiling and looking away. She had put pinecones and sprigs of pine along the mantel. On the sofa the Sunday papers lay scattered. 'I was beginning to worry,' she said, closing the door. 'It's been such a nasty day for driving.' She took their coats and hung them in the closet by the front door. She was busying herself, bustling around the room. 'Sometimes I think I'd rather drive in snow than rain like this.' Finally she looked at Charles. 'Don't I get a hug?'

He put his arms around her, felt the thinness of her shoulders. One of the things his father used to say to her was that she couldn't get fat if it was required, and the word *required* had had some other significance for them both, for all the adults. Charles had never fully understood it; it had something to do with when they were all in school. He said 'Aunt Lois, you couldn't get fat if it was required.'

'Don't,' she said, waving a hand in front of her face and blinking. 'Lord, boy, you even sound like him.'

He said, 'We had a smooth trip.' There wasn't anything else he could think of. She had moved out of his arms and was embracing his mother. The two women stood there holding tight, and his mother sniffled.

'I'm so glad you're here,' Aunt Lois said. 'I feel like you've come home.'

Charles's mother said, 'What smells so good?' and wiped her eyes with the gloved backs of her hands.

'I made spice cake. Or I *tried* spice cake. I burned it, of course.'

'It smells good,' Charles said.

'It does,' said his mother.

Aunt Lois said, 'I hope you like it *very* brown.' And then they were at a loss for something else to say. Charles looked at the empty lounge chair, and Aunt Lois turned and busied herself with the clutter of newspapers on the sofa. 'I'll just get this out of the way,' she said.

'I've got to get the suitcases out of the trunk,' Charles said.

They hadn't heard him. Aunt Lois was stacking the newspapers, and his mother strolled about the room like a daydreaming tourist in a museum. He let himself out and walked to the car, feeling the cold, and the aches and stiffnesses of having driven all day. It was misting now, and a wind was blowing. Cars and trucks rumbled by on the overpass, their headlights fanning out into the fog. He stood and watched them go by, and quite suddenly he did not want to be here. In the house, in the warm light of the window, his mother and Aunt Lois moved, already arranging things, already settling themselves for what would be the pattern of the next few days; and Charles, fumbling with the car keys in the dark, feeling the mist on the back of his neck, had the disquieting sense that he had come to the wrong place. The other houses, shrouded in darkness, with only one winking blue light in the window of the farthest one, seemed alien and unfriendly somehow. 'Aw, Dad,' he said under his breath.

As he got the trunk open, Aunt Lois came out and made her way to him, moving very slowly, her arms out for balance. She had put on an outlandish pair of floppy yellow boots, and her flannel bathrobe collar jutted above the collar of her raincoat. 'Marie seems none the worse for wear,' she said to him. 'How are you two getting along?'

'We had a smooth trip,' Charles said.

'I didn't mean the trip.'

'We're okay, Aunt Lois.'

'She says you want to go to Europe with her.'

'It didn't take her long,' Charles said, 'did it. I just suggested it in the car on the way here. It was just an idea.'

'Let me take one of those bags, honey. I don't want her to think I came out here just to jabber with you, although that's exactly why I did come out.'

Charles handed her his own small suitcase.

'You like my boots?' she said. 'I figured I could attract a handsome fireman with them.' She modeled them for him, turning.

'They're a little big for you, Aunt Lois.'

'You're no fun.'

He was struggling with his mother's suitcases.

'I guess you noticed that I moved the chair. You looked a little surprised. But when I got back here after the funeral I walked in there and—well, there it was, right where he always was whenever you all visited. I used to tease him about sleeping in it all day—you remember. We all used to tease him about it. Well, I didn't want you to walk in and see it that way—'

Charles closed the trunk of the car and hefted the suitcases, facing her.

'You want to go home, don't you,' she said.

It seemed to him that she had always had a way of reading him. 'I want everything to be back the way it was,' he said.

'I know,' Aunt Lois said.

He followed her back to the house. On the porch she turned and gave him a sad look and then forced a smile. 'You're an intelligent young man, and a very good one, too. So serious and sweet—a very dear, sweet boy.'

He might have mumbled a thank-you, he didn't really know. He was embarrassed and confused and sick at heart; he had thought he wanted this visit. Aunt Lois kissed him on the cheek, then stood back and sighed. 'I'm going to need your help about something. Boy, am I ever.'

'What's the matter?' he said.

'It's nothing. It's just a situation.' She sighed again. She wasn't looking at him now. 'I don't know why, but I find it—well, reassuring, somehow, that we—we—leave such a gaping hole in everything when we go.'

He just stood there, weighted down with the bags.

'Well,' she said, and opened the door for him.

Charles's mother said she wanted to sit up and talk, but she kept nodding off. Finally she was asleep. When Aunt Lois began gently to wake her, to walk her in to her bed, Charles excused himself and made his way to his own bed. A few moments later he heard Aunt Lois in the kitchen. As had always been her custom, she would drink one last cup of coffee before retiring. He lay awake, hearing the soft tink of her cup against the saucer, and at last he began to drift. But in a little while he was fully awake again. Aunt Lois was moving through the house turning the lights off, and soon she too was down for the night. Charles stared through the shadows of the doorway to what he knew was the entrance to the living room, and listened to the house settle into itself. Outside, there were the hum and whoosh of traffic on the overpass, and the occasional sighing rush of rain at the window, like surf. Yet he knew he wouldn't sleep. He was thinking of summer nights in a cottage on Cape Cod, when his family was happy, and he lay with the sun burning in his skin and listened to the adults talking and laughing out on the screened porch, the sound of the bay rushing like this rain at this window. He couldn't sleep. Turning in the bed, he cupped his hands over his face.

A year ago, two years—at some time and in some way that was beyond him—his parents had grown quiet with each other, a change had started, and he could remember waking up one morning near the end of his last school year with a deep sense that something somewhere would go so wrong, was already so wrong that there would be no coming back from it. There was a change in the chemistry of the household that sapped his will, that took the breath out of him and left him in an exhaustion so profound that even the small energy necessary for speech seemed unavailable to him. This past summer, the first summer out of high school, he had done nothing with himself; he had found nothing he wanted to do, nothing he could feel anything at all about. He looked for a job because his parents insisted that he do so; it was an ordeal of walking, of managing to talk, to fill out applications, and in the end he found nothing. The summer wore on and his father grew angry and sullen with him. Charles was a disappointment and knew it; he was overweight, and seemed lazy, and he couldn't find a way to explain himself. His mother thought there might be something physically wrong, and so then there were doctors, and medical examinations to endure. What he wanted was to stay in the house and have his parents be the people that they once were—happy, fortunate people with interest in each other and warmth and humor between them. And then one day in September his father keeled over on the sidewalk outside a restaurant in New York, and Charles had begun to be this person he now was, someone hurting in this irremediable way, lying awake in his aunt's house in the middle of a cold December night, wishing with all his heart it were some other time, some other place.

In the morning, after breakfast, Aunt Lois began to talk about how good it would be to have people at her table for dinner on Christmas Eve. She had opened the draperies wide, to watch the snow fall outside. The snow had started before sunrise, but nothing had accumulated yet; it was melting as it hit the ground. Aunt Lois talked about how Christmasy it felt, and about getting a tree to put up, about making a big turkey dinner. 'I don't think anybody should be alone on Christmas,' she said. 'Do you, Marie?'

'Not unless they want to,' Marie said.

'Right, and who wants to be alone on Christmas?'

'Lois, I suppose you're going to come to the point soon.'

'Well,' Aunt Lois said, 'I guess I am driving at something. I've invited someone over to dinner on Christmas Eve.'

'Who.'

'It's someone you know.'

'Lois, please.'

'I ran into him on jury duty last June,' Aunt Lois said. 'Can you imagine? After all these years—and we've become very good friends again. I mean I'd court him if I thought I had a chance.'

'Lois, who are we talking about?'

'Well,' Aunt Lois said, 'It's Bill Downs.'

Marie stood. 'You're not serious.'

'It has nothing to do with anything,' Lois said. 'To tell you the truth, I invited them before I knew you were coming.'

'Them?'

'He has a cousin visiting. I told him they could both come.'

'Who's Bill Downs?' Charles asked.

'He's nobody,' said his mother.

'He's somebody from a long time ago,' Aunt Lois said. They had spoken almost in unison. Aunt Lois went on: 'His cousin just lost his wife. Well—last year. Bill didn't want him to be alone. He says he's a very interesting man—'

'Lois, I don't care if he's the King of England.'

'I didn't mean anything by it,' Aunt Lois said. 'Don't make it into something it isn't. Look at us, anyway—look how depleted we are. I want people here. I don't want it just the three of us on Christmas. You have Charles; I'm the last one in this family, Marie. And this—this isn't just your grief. Lawrence was my brother. I didn't want to be alone—do you want me to spell it out for you?'

Marie now seemed too confused to speak. She only glanced at Charles, then turned and left the room. Her door closed quietly. Aunt Lois sat back against the cushions of the sofa and shut her eyes for a moment.

'Who's Bill Downs?' Charles said.

When she opened her eyes it was as if she had just noticed him there. 'The whole thing is just silly. We were all kids together. It was a million years ago.'

Charles said nothing. In the fireplace a single charred log hissed. Aunt Lois sat forward and took a cigarette from her pack and lighted it. 'I wonder what you're thinking.'

'I don't know.'

'Do you have a steady girl, Charles?'

He nodded. The truth was that he was too shy, too aware of his girth and the floridness of his complexion, too nervous and clumsy to be more than the clownish, kindly friend he was to the girls he knew.

'Do you think you'll go on and marry her?'

'Who?' he said.

'Your girl.'

'Oh,' he said, 'probably not.'

'Some people do, of course. And some don't. Some people go on and meet other people. Do you see? When I met your mother, your father was away at college.'

'I think I had this figured out already, Aunt Lois.'

'Well—then that's who Bill Downs is.' She got to her feet, with some effort, then stood gazing down at him. 'This just isn't the way it looks, though. And everybody will just have to believe me about it.'

'I believe you, ' Charles said.

'She doesn't,' said Aunt Lois, 'and now she's probably going to start lobbying to go home.'

Charles shook his head.

'I hope you won't let her talk you into it.'

'Nobody's going anywhere,' Marie said, coming into the room. She sat down on the sofa and opened the morning paper, and when she spoke now it was as if she were not even attentive to her own words. 'Though it would serve you right if everybody deserted you out of embarrassment.'

'You might think about me a little, Marie. You might think how *I* feel in all this.'

Marie put the newspaper down on her lap and looked at her. 'I am thinking of you. If I wasn't thinking of you I'd be in the car this minute, heading north, whether Charles would come or not.'

'Well, fine,' Aunt Lois said, and stormed out of the room.

A little later, Charles and Marie went into the city. They parked the car in a garage on H Street and walked over to Lafayette Square. It was still snowing, but the ground was too warm; it wouldn't stick. Charles said, 'Might as well be raining,' and realized that neither of them had spoken since they had pulled away from Aunt Lois's house.

'Charles,' his mother said, and then seemed to stop herself. 'Never mind.'

'What?' he said.

'Nothing. It's easy to forget that you're only eighteen. I forget sometimes, that's all.'

Charles sensed that this wasn't what she had started to say, but kept silent. They crossed the square and entered a sandwich shop on Seventeenth Street, to warm themselves with a cup of coffee. They sat at a table by the window and looked out at the street, the people walking by— shoppers mostly, burdened with packages.

'Where's the Lafayette Hotel from here?' Charles asked.

'Oh, honey, they tore that down a long time ago.'

'Where was it?'

'You can't see it from here.' She took a handkerchief out of her purse and touched the corners of her eyes with it. 'The cold makes my eyes sting. How about you?'

'It's the wind,' Charles said.

She looked at him. 'My ministering angel.'

'Mom,' he said.

Now she looked out the window. 'Your father would be proud of you now.' She bowed her head slightly, fumbling with her purse, and then she was crying. She held the handkerchief to her nose, and the tears dropped down over her hand.

'Mom,' he said, reaching for her wrist.

She withdrew from him a little. 'No, you don't understand.'

'Let's go,' Charles said.

'I don't think I could stand to be home now, Charles. Not on Christmas. Not this Christmas.'

Charles paid the check and then went back to the table to help her into her coat. 'Goddamn Lois,' she said, pulling the furry collar up to cover her ears.

'Tell me about your girlfriend,' Aunt Lois said.

He shrugged this off.

They were sitting in the kitchen, breaking up bread for the dressing, while Marie napped on the sofa in the living room. Aunt Lois had brought the turkey out and set it on the counter. The meat deep in its breast still had to thaw, she told Charles. She was talking just to talk. Things had been very cool since the morning, and Charles was someone to talk to.

'Won't even tell me her name?'

'I'm not really going with anybody,' he said.

'A handsome boy like you.'

'Aunt Lois, could we talk about something else?'

She said, 'All right. Tell me what you did all fall.'

'I took care of the house.'

'Did you read any good books or see any movies or take anybody out besides your mother?'

'Sure,' he said.

'Okay, tell me about it.'

'What do you want to know?'

'I want to know what you did all fall.'

'What is this?' Charles said.

She spoke quickly. 'I apologize for prying. I won't say another word.'

'Look,' he said, 'Aunt Lois, I'm not keeping myself from anything right now. I couldn't have concentrated in school in September.'

'I know,' she said, 'I know.'

There was a long silence.

'I wonder if it's too late for me to get married and have a bunch of babies,' she said suddenly. 'I think I'd like the noise they'd make.'

That night, they watched Christmas specials. Charles dozed in the lounge chair by the fireplace, a magazine on his lap, and the women sat on the sofa. No one spoke. On television, celebrities sang old Christmas songs, and during the commercials other celebrities appealed to the various yearnings for cheer and happiness and possessions, and the thrill of giving. In a two-hour cartoon with music and production numbers, Scrooge made his night-long journey to wisdom and love; the Cratchits were portrayed as church mice. Aunt Lois remarked that this was cute, and no one answered her. Charles feigned sleep. When the news came on, Aunt Lois turned the television off, and they said good night. Charles kissed them both on the cheek, and went to his room. For a long while after he lay down, he heard them talking low. They had gone to Aunt Lois's room. He couldn't distinguish words, but the tones were chilly and serious. He rolled over on his side and punched the pillow into shape and stared at the faint outline of trees outside the window, trying not to hear. The voices continued, and he heard his mother's voice rising, so that he could almost make out words now. His mother said something about last summer, and then both women were silent. A few moments later, Aunt Lois came marching down the hall past his door, on into the kitchen, where she opened cabinets and slammed them, and ran water. She was going to make coffee, she said, when Marie called to her. If she wanted a cup of coffee in her own house at any hour of the night she'd have coffee.

Charles waited a minute or so, then got up, put his robe on, and went in to her. She sat at the table, arms folded, waiting for the water to boil.

'It's sixty dollars for a good Christmas tree,' she said. 'A ridiculous amount of money.'

Charles sat down across from her.

'You're just like your father,' she said, 'you placate. And I think he placated your mother too much—that's what I think.'

He said, 'Come on, Aunt Lois.'

'Well, she makes me so mad. I can't help it. She doesn't want to go home and she doesn't want to stay here and she won't listen to the slightest suggestion about you or the way you've been nursemaiding her for four months. And she's just going to stay mad at me all week. Now, you tell me.'

'I just wish everybody would calm down,' Charles said.

She stood and turned her back to him and set about making her coffee.

According to the medical report, Charles's father had suffered a massive coronary occlusion, and death was almost instantaneous; it could not have been attended with much pain. Perhaps there had been a second's recognition, but little more than that. The doctor wanted Charles and his mother to know that the speed with which an attack like that kills is a blessing. In his sleep, Charles heard the doctor's voice saying this, and then he was watching his father fall down on the sidewalk outside the restaurant; people walked by and stared, and Charles looked at their faces, the faces of strangers.

He woke trembling in the dark, the only one awake on Christmas Eve morning. He lay on his side, facing the window, and watched the dawn arrive, and at last someone was up, moving around in the kitchen.

It was his mother. She was making coffee. 'You're up early,' she said. 'I dreamed about Dad.'

'I dream about him too,' she said. She opened the refrigerator. 'Good God, there's a leg of lamb in here. Where did this come from? What in the world is that woman thinking of? The turkey's big enough for eight people.'

'Maybe it's for tomorrow.'

'And don't always defend her, either, Charles. She's not infallible, you know.'

'I never said she was.'

'None of them—your father wasn't. I mean—' she closed the refrigerator and took a breath. 'He wouldn't want you to put him on a pedestal.'

'I didn't,' Charles said.

'People are people,' she said. 'They don't always add up.'

This didn't seem to require a response.

'And I've known Lois since she was seventeen years old. I know how she thinks.'

'I'm not defending anybody,' he said, 'I'm just the one in between everything here. I wish you'd both just leave me out of it.'

'Go get dressed,' she said. 'Nobody's putting you in between anybody.'

'Mom.'

'No—you're right. I won't involve you. Now really, go get dressed.' She looked as though she might begin to cry again. She patted him on the wrist and then went back to the refrigerator. 'I wanted something in here,' she said, opening it. There were dark blue veins forking over her ankles. She looked old and thin and afraid and lonely, and he turned his eyes away.

The three of them went to shop for a tree. Charles drove. They looked in three places and couldn't agree on anything, and when it began to rain Aunt Lois took matters into her own hands. She made them wait in the car while she picked out the tree she wanted for what was, after all, her living room. They got the tree home, and had to saw off part of the trunk to get it up, but when it was finished, ornamented and wound with popcorn and tinsel, they all agreed that it was a handsome tree—a round, long-needled pine that looked like a jolly rotund elf, with its sawed-off trunk and its top listing slightly to the left under the weight of a tinfoil star. They turned its lights on and stood admiring it, and for a while there was something of the warmth of other Christmases in the air. Work on the decorations, and all the cooperation required to get everything accomplished seemed to have created a kind of peace between the two women. They spent the early part of the evening wrapping presents for the morning, each in his own room with his gifts for the others, and then Aunt Lois put the television on, and went about her business, getting the dinner ready. She wanted no help from anyone, she said, but Marie began to help anyway, and Aunt Lois did nothing to stop her. Charles sat in the lounge chair and watched a parade. It was the halftime of a football game, but he was not interested in it, and soon he had begun to doze again. He sank deep, and there were no dreams, and then Aunt Lois was telling him to wake up. 'Charles,' she said, 'they're here.' He sat forward in the chair, a little startled, and Aunt Lois laughed. 'Wake up, son,' she said. Charles saw a man standing by the Christmas tree, smiling at him. Another man sat on the sofa, his legs spread a little to make room for his stomach; he looked blown up, his neck bulging over the collar of his shirt.

'Charles,' Aunt Lois said, indicating the man on the sofa, 'this is Mr. Rainy.'

Mr. Rainy was smiling in an almost imbecilic way, not really looking at anyone.

'This is Charles,' Aunt Lois said to him.

They shook hands. 'Nice to meet you,' Mr. Rainy said. He had a soft, high-pitched voice.

'And this is Mr. Downs.'

Charles looked at him, took the handshake he offered. Bill Downs was tall and a little stooped, and he seemed very uneasy. He looked around the room, and his hands went into his pockets and then flew up to his hair, which was wild-looking and very sparse.

'Marie will be out any time, I'm sure,' Aunt Lois said in a voice that, to Charles at least, sounded anything but sure. 'In the meantime, can I get anybody a drink?'

No one wanted anything right away. Mr. Rainy had brought two bottles of champagne, which Aunt Lois took from him and put on ice in the kitchen. The two men sat on the sofa across from Charles, and the football game provided them with something to look at. Charles caught himself watching Bill Downs, and thinking about how his mother had once felt something for him. It was hard to picture them together, as it was hard not to stare at the man, at his skinny hands, never still in the long-legged lap, and the nervous way he looked around the room. He did not look past forty years old, except for the thinning hair.

'You boys get your football watching before dinner,' Aunt Lois said, coming back into the room. 'I won't have it after we begin to eat.'

'I'm not much of a football fan,' Bill Downs said.

Charles almost blurted out that his father had loved football. He kept silent. In the next moment, Marie made her entrance. It struck Charles exactly that way: that it was an entrance, thoroughly dramatic and calculated to have an effect. It was vivacious in a nervous, almost automatic way. She crossed the room to kiss him on the forehead and then she turned to face the two men on the sofa. 'Bill, you haven't changed a bit.'

Downs was clambering over himself to get to his feet. 'You either, Marie.'

'Merry Christmas,' Mr. Rainy said, also trying to rise.

'Oh, don't get up,' Marie was saying.

Charles sat in his chair and watched them make their way through the introductions and the polite talk before dinner. He watched his mother, mostly. He knew exactly what she was feeling, understood the embarrassment and the nervousness out of which every gesture and word came, and yet something in him hated her for it, felt betrayed by it. When she went with the two men into the kitchen to open one of the bottles of champagne, he got out of the chair and faced Aunt Lois, whose expression seemed to be saying 'Well?' as if this were only what one should have expected. He shook his head, and she said, 'Come on.'

They went into the kitchen. Marie was leaning against the counter with a glass of champagne in her hand. Charles decided that he couldn't look at her. She and Bill Downs were talking about the delicious smell of the turkey.

'I didn't have Thanksgiving dinner this year,' Mr. Rainy was saying. 'You know, I lost my wife. I just didn't feel like anything, you know.'

'This is a hard time of year,' Aunt Lois said.

'I simply don't know how to act anymore,' Mr. Rainy said.

Charles backed quietly away from them. He took himself to the living room and the television, where everyone seemed to know everyone else. They were all celebrating Christmas on television, and then the football game was on again. Charles got into his coat and stepped out onto the porch, intending at first just to take a few deep breaths, to shake if he could this feeling of betrayal and anger that had risen in him. It was already dark. The rain had turned to mist again. When the wind blew, cold drops splattered on the eaves of the porch. The cars and trucks racing by on the overpass at the end of the block seemed to traverse a part of the sky. Charles moved to the steps of the porch, and behind him the door opened. He turned to see his mother, who came out after glancing into the house, apparently wanting to be sure they would be alone. She wasn't wearing her coat, and he started to say something about the chill she would get when the expression on her face stopped him.

'What do you expect from me, Charles?'

He couldn't speak for a moment.

She advanced across the porch, already shivering. 'What am I supposed to do?'

'I don't know what you're talking about.'

'Oh, God.' She paced back and forth in front of him, her arms wrapped around herself. Somewhere off in the misty dark, a group of people were singing carols. The voices came in on a gust of wind, and when the wind died they were gone. 'God,' she said again. Then she muttered, 'Christmas.'

'I wish it was two years ago,' Charles said suddenly.

She had stopped pacing. 'It won't ever be two years ago, and you'd better get used to that right now.'

Charles was silent.

'You're turning what you remember into a paradise,' she said, 'and I've helped you get a good start on it.'

'I'm not,' Charles said, 'I'm not doing that at all. I remember the way it was last summer when I wasn't—when I couldn't do anything and he couldn't make me do anything, and you and he were so different with each other—' He halted. He wasn't looking at her.

'Go on,' she said.

He said, 'Nothing.'

'What went on between your father and me is nobody's business.'

'I didn't say it was.'

'It had nothing to do with you, Charles.'

'All right,' he said.

She was shivering so hard now that her voice quavered when she spoke. 'I wish I could *make* it all right, but I can't.'

Charles reached for her, put his arms around her, and she cried into the hollow of his shoulder. They stood that way for a while, and the wind blew and again there was the sound of the carolers.

'Mom,' Charles said, 'he was going to leave us, wasn't he.'

She removed herself, produced a handkerchief from somewhere in her skirt, and touched it to her nose, still trembling, staring down. Then she breathed out as if something had given way inside her, and Charles could see that she was gathering herself, trying not to show whatever it was that had just gone through her. When she raised her eyes she gave him the softest, the kindest look. 'Not you,' she said. Then: 'Don't think such things.' She turned from him, stepped up into the doorway, and the light there made a willowy shadow of her. 'Don't stay out here too long, son. Don't be rude.'

When she had closed the door, he walked down the street to the overpass and stood below it, his hands deep in his coat pockets. It wasn't extremely cold out yet, but he was cold. He was cold, and he shook, and above him the traffic whooshed by. He turned and faced the house, beginning to cry now, and a sound came out of him that he put his hands to his mouth to stop. When a car came along the road he ducked back into the deeper shadow of the overpass, but he had been seen. The car pulled toward him, and a policeman shined a light on him.

'What're you doing there, fella?'

'Nothing,' Charles said. 'My father died.'

The policeman kept the light on him for a few seconds, then turned it off. He said, 'Go on home, son,' and drove away.

Charles watched until the taillights disappeared in the mist. It was quiet; even the traffic on the overpass had ceased for a moment. The police car came back, slowing as it passed him, then going on, and once more it was quiet. He turned and looked at the house with its Christmas tree shimmering in the window, and in that instant it seemed to contain only the light and tangle of adulthood; it was their world, so far from him. He wiped his eyes with the backs of his hands, beginning to cry again. No, it wasn't so far. It wasn't so far at all. Up the street, Aunt Lois opened her door and called his name. But she couldn't see him, and he didn't answer her.

FIRELIGHT

Tobias Wolff

My mother swore we'd never live in a boardinghouse again, but circumstances did not allow her to keep this promise. She decided to change cities; we had to sleep somewhere. This boardinghouse was worse than the last, unfriendly, funereal, heavy with the smells that disheartened people allow themselves to cultivate. On the floor below ours a retired merchant seaman was coughing his lungs out. He was a friendly old guy, always ready with a compliment for my mother as we climbed past the dim room where he sat smoking on the edge of his bed. During the day we felt sorry for him, but at night, as we lay in wait for the next racking seizure, feeling the silence swell with it, we hated him. I did, anyway.

My mother said this was only temporary. We were definitely getting out of there. To show me and maybe herself that she meant business, she went through the paper during breakfast every Saturday morning and circled the advertisements for furnished apartments that sounded, as she put it, 'right for our needs.' I liked that expression. It made me feel as if our needs had some weight in the world, and would have to be reckoned with. Then, putting on her shrewd face, my mother compared the rents and culled out the most expensive apartments and also the very cheap ones. We knew the story on those, the dinky fridge and weeping walls, the tub sinking through the bathroom floor, the wife-beater upstairs. We'd been that route. When my mother had five or six possibilities, she called to make sure they were still open and we spent the day going from one to another.

We couldn't actually take a place yet. The landlords wanted first and last months' rent, plus cleaning deposit, and it was going to be a while before my mother could put all that together. I understood this, but every Saturday my mother repeated it again so I wouldn't get carried away. We were just looking. Getting a feel for the market.

There is pleasure to be found in the purchase of goods and services. I enjoy it myself now, playing the part of a man who knows what he wants and can take it home with him. But in those days I was mostly happy just to look at things. And that was lucky for me, because we did a power of looking, and no buying.

My mother wasn't one of those comparison shoppers who head straight for the price tag, shaking their faces and beefing about the markup to everyone in sight. She had no great interest in price. She had no money, either, but it went deeper than that. She liked to shop because she felt at home in stores and was interested in the merchandise. Sales clerks waited on her without impatience, seeing there was nothing mean or trivial in her curiosity, this curiosity that kept her so young and drove her so hard. She just had to see what was out there.

We'd always shopped, but that first fall in Seattle, when we were more broke than we'd ever been, we really hit our stride. We looked at leather luggage. We looked at televisions in large Mediterranean consoles. We looked at antiques and Oriental rugs. Looking at Oriental rugs isn't something you do lightly, because the men who sell them have to work like dogs, dragging them down from these tall teetering piles and then humping them over to you, sweating and gasping, staggering under the weight, their faces woolly with lint. They tend to be small men. You can't be squeamish. You have to be free of shame, absolutely sure of your right to look at what you cannot buy. And so we were.

When the new fashions came in, my mother tried them on while I watched. She had once been a model and knew how to strike attitudes before the mirror, how to walk casually away and then stop, canting one hip and glancing over her shoulder as if someone had just called her name. When she turned to me I expressed my judgments with a smile, a shrug, a sour little shake of the head. I thought she was beautiful in everything but I felt obliged to discriminate. She didn't like too much admiration. It suffocated her.

We looked at copper cookware. We looked at lawn furniture and pecan dining room sets. We spent one whole day at a marina, studying the inventory of a bankrupt Chris-Craft dealership. *The Big Giveaway*, they called it. It was the only sale we ever made a point of going to.

My mother wore a smart gray suit when we went house hunting. I wore my little gentleman's outfit, a V-neck sweater with a bow tie. The sweater had the words *Fraternity Row* woven across the front. We looked respectable, as, on the whole, we were. We also looked solvent.

On this particular day we were touring apartments in the university district. The first three we looked at were decent enough, but the fourth was a wreck—the last tenant, a woman, must have lived there like an animal in a cave. Someone had tried to clean it up but the job was hopeless. The place smelled like rotten meat, even with the windows open and the cold air blowing through. Everything felt sticky. The landlord said that the woman had been depressed over the breakup of her marriage. Though he talked about a paint job and new carpets, he seemed discouraged and soon fell silent. The three of us walked through the rooms, then back outside. The landlord could tell we weren't biting. He didn't even offer us a card.

We had one more apartment to look at, but my mother said she'd seen enough. She asked me if I wanted to go down to the wharf, or home, or what. Her mouth was set, her face drawn. She tried to sound agreeable but she was in a black mood. I didn't like the idea of going back to the house, back to the room, so I said why didn't we walk up to the university and take a look around.

She squinted up the street. I thought she was going to say no. 'Sure,' she said. 'Why not? As long as we're here.'

We started walking. There were big maples along the sidewalk. Fallen leaves scraped and eddied around our legs as the breeze gusted.

'You don't *ever* let yourself go like that,' my mother said, hugging herself and looking down. 'There's no excuse for it.'

She sounded mortally offended. I knew I hadn't done anything, so I kept quiet. She said, 'I don't care what happens, there is no excuse to give up like that. Do you hear what I'm saying?'

'Yes, ma'am.'

A group of Chinese came up behind us, ten or twelve of them, all young men, talking excitedly. They parted around us, still talking, and rejoined like water flowing around a stone. We followed them up the street and across the road to the university, where we wandered among the buildings as the light began to fail and the wind turned raw. This was the first really cold day since we'd moved here and I wasn't dressed for it. But I said nothing, because I still didn't want to go home. I had never set foot on a campus before and was greedily measuring it against my idea of what it should look like. It had everything. Old-looking buildings with stone archways and high, arched windows. Rich greenswards. Ivy. The leaves of the ivy had turned red. High on the west-facing walls, in what was left of the sunshine, the red leaves glittered as the wind stirred them. Every so often a great roar went up from Husky Stadium, where a game was in progress. Each time I heard it I felt a thrill of complicity and belonging. I believed that I was in place here, and that the students we passed on the brick walkways would look at me and see one of themselves—*Fraternity Row*—if it weren't for the woman beside me, her hand on my shoulder. I began to feel the weight of that hand.

My mother didn't notice. She was in good spirits again, flushed with the cold and with memories of days like this at Yale and Trinity, when she used to get free tickets to football games from a girlfriend who dated a player. She had dated one of the players herself, an All-American quarterback from Yale named Dutch Diefenbacker. He'd wanted to marry her, she added carelessly.

'You mean he actually asked you?'

'He gave me a ring. My father sold it to him. He'd bought it for this woman he had a crush on, but she wouldn't accept it. What she actually said was "Why, I wouldn't marry an old man like you!"' My mother laughed.

'Wait a minute,' I said. 'You had a chance to marry an All-American from Yale?'

'Sure.'

'So why didn't you?'

We stopped beside a fountain clotted with leaves. My mother stared into the water. 'I don't know. I was pretty young then, and Dutch wasn't what you'd call a scintillating guy. He was nice . . . just dull. Very dull.' She drew a deep breath and said, with some violence, 'God, he was boring!'

'I would've married him,' I said. I'd never heard about this before. That my mother, out of schoolgirl snobbery, had deprived me of an All-American father from Yale was outrageous. I would be rich now, and have a collie. Everything would be different.

We circled the fountain and headed back the way we'd come. When we reached the road my mother asked me if I wanted to look at the apartment we'd skipped. 'Oh, what the heck,' she said, seeing me hesitate. 'It's around here somewhere. We might as well make a clean sweep.'

I was cold, but because I hadn't said anything so far I thought it would sound false if I complained now, false and babyish. She stopped two girls wearing letter sweaters—*co-eds*, I thought, finding a cheap, keen excitement in the word—and while they gave her directions I studied the display in a bookstore window, as if I just happened to be standing beside this person who didn't know her way around.

The evening was clear and brief. At a certain moment the light flared weakly, and then it was gone. We walked several blocks, into a neighborhood of Victorian houses whose windows, seen from the empty street, glowed with rich, exclusive light. The wind blew at our backs. I was starting to shake. I still didn't tell my mother. I knew I should have said something earlier, that I'd been stupid not to, and now I fastened all my will on the effort to conceal this stupidity by maintaining it.

We stopped in front of a house with a turret. The upper story was dark. 'We're late,' I said.

'Not that late,' my mother said. 'Besides, the apartment's on the ground floor.'

She walked up to the porch while I waited on the sidewalk. I heard the muted chime of bells, and watched the windows for movement.

'Nuts . . . I should've called,' my mother said. She'd just turned away when one of the two doors swung open and a man leaned out, a big man silhouetted in the bright doorway. 'Yes?' he said. He sounded impatient, but when my mother turned to face him he added, more gently, 'What can I do for you?' His voice was so deep I could almost feel it, like coal rumbling down a chute.

She told him we were here about the apartment. 'I guess we're a little late,' she said.

'An hour late,' he said.

My mother exclaimed surprise, said we'd been walking around the university and completely lost track of time. She was very apologetic but made no move to go, and it must have been clear to him that she had no intention of going until she'd seen the apartment. It was clear enough to me. I went down the walkway and up the porch steps.

He was big in every direction—tall and rotund with a massive head, a trophy head. He had the kind of size that provokes, almost inevitably, the nickname 'Tiny,' though I'm sure nobody ever called him that. He was too solemn, preoccupied, like a buffalo in the broadness and gravity of his face. He looked down at us through black-framed glasses. 'Well, you're here,' he said, not unkindly, and we followed him inside.

The first thing I saw was the fire. I was aware of other things, furniture, the church-like expanse of the room, but my eyes went straight to the flames. They burned with a hissing sound in a fireplace I could have walked into without stooping, or just about. A girl lay on her stomach in front of the fire, one bare foot raised and slowly twisting, her chin propped in her hand. She was reading a book. She went on reading it for a few moments after we came in, then sat up and said, very precisely, 'Good evening.' She had boobs. I could see them pushing at the front of her blouse. But she wasn't pretty. She was owlish and large and wore the same kind of glasses as the man, whom she closely and unfortunately resembled. She blinked constantly. I felt immediately at ease with her. I smiled and said 'Hi,' instead of assuming the indifference, even hostility, with which I treated pretty girls.

Something was in the oven, something chocolate. I went over to the fire and stood with my back to it, flexing my hands behind me.

'Oh yes, it's quite comfortable,' the man said in answer to a comment of my mother's. He peered around curiously as if surprised to find himself here. The room was big, the biggest I'd ever seen in an apartment. We could never afford to live here, but I was already losing my grip on that fact.

'I'll go get my wife,' the man said, then stayed where he was, watching my mother.

She was turning slowly, nodding to herself in a pensive way. 'All this room,' she said. 'It makes you feel so free. How can you bear to give it up?'

At first he didn't answer. The girl started picking at something on the rug. Then he said, 'We're ready for a bit of a change. Aren't we, Sister?'

She nodded without looking up.

A woman came in from the next room, carrying a plate of brownies. She was tall and thin. Deep furrows ran down her cheeks, framing her mouth like parentheses. Her gray hair was pulled into a ponytail. She moved toward us with slow, measured steps, as if carrying gifts to the altar, and set the plate on the coffee table. 'You're just in time to have some of Dr. Avery's brownies,' she said.

I thought she was referring to a recipe. Then the man hurried over and scooped up a handful, and I understood. I understood not only that he was Dr. Avery, but also that the brownies belonged to him; his descent on the plate bore all the signs of jealous ownership. I was nervous about taking one, but Sister did it and survived, and even went back for another. I had a couple myself. As we ate, the woman slipped her arm behind Dr. Avery's back and leaned against him. The little I'd seen of marriage had disposed me to view public affection between husbands and wives as pure stagecraft—*Look, this is a home where people hug each other*—but she was so plainly happy to be where she was that I couldn't help feeling happy with her.

My mother prowled the room restlessly. 'Do you mind if I look around?' she said.

Mrs. Avery asked Sister to show us the rest of the apartment.

More big rooms. Two of them had fireplaces. Above the mantel in the master bedroom hung a large photograph of a man with dark, thoughtful eyes. When I asked Sister who it was, she said, a shade importantly, 'Gurdjieff.'

I didn't mind her condescension. She was older, and bigger, and I suspected smarter than me. Condescension seemed perfectly in order.

'Gurdjieff,' my mother said. 'I've heard of him.'

'*Gurdjieff*,' Sister repeated, as though she'd said it wrong.

We went back to the living room and sat around the fire, Dr. and Mrs. Avery on the couch, my mother in a rocking chair across from them. Sister and I stretched out on the floor. She opened her book, and a moment later her foot rose into the air again and began its slow twisting motion. My mother and Mrs. Avery were talking about the apartment. I stared into the flames, the voices above me pleasant and meaningless until I heard my name mentioned. My mother was telling Mrs. Avery about our walk around the university. She said it was a beautiful campus.

'Beautiful?' Dr. Avery said. 'What do you mean by beautiful?'

My mother looked at him. She didn't answer.

'I assume you're referring to the buildings.'

'Sure. The buildings, the grounds. The general layout.'

'Pseudo-Gothic humbug,' Dr. Avery said. 'A movie set.'

'Dr. Avery believes that the university pays too much attention to appearances,' Mrs. Avery said.

'That's all they pay attention to,' Dr. Avery said.

'I wouldn't know about that,' my mother said. 'I'm not an expert on architecture. It looked nice enough to me.'

'Yes, well that's the whole point, isn't it?' Dr. Avery said. 'It *looks* like a university. The same with the so-called education they're selling. It's a counterfeit experience from top to bottom. Utterly hollow. All *materia*, no *anima*.'

He lost me there, and I went back to looking at the flames. Dr. Avery rumbled on. He had been quiet before, but once he got started he didn't stop, and I wouldn't have wanted him to. The sound of his voice made me drowsy with assurance, like the drone of a car engine when you're lying on the backseat, going home from a long trip. Now and then Mrs. Avery spoke up, expressing concord with something the Doctor had said, making her complete agreement known; then he resumed. Sister shifted beside me. She yawned, turned a page. The logs settled in the fireplace, very softly, like some old sleeping dog adjusting his bones.

Dr. Avery talked for quite a while. Then my mother spoke my name. Nothing more, only my name. Dr. Avery went on as if he hadn't heard. He was leaning forward, one finger wagging to the cadence of his words, glasses glinting as his great head shook. I looked at my mother. She sat stiffly in the rocker, her hands kneading the purse in her lap. Her face was bleak, frozen. It was the expression she wore when she got trapped by some diehard salesman or a pair of Mormons who wouldn't go away. She wanted to leave.

I did not want to leave. Nodding by the fire, torpid and content, I had forgotten that this was not my home. The heat and the firelight worked on me like Dr. Avery's voice, lulling me into a state of familial serenity such as these people seemed to enjoy. I even managed to forget they were not my family, and that they too would soon be moving on. I made them part of my story without any sense that they had their own to live out.

What that was, I don't know. We never saw them again. But now, so many years later, I can venture a guess. My guess is that Dr. Avery had been denied tenure by the university, and that this wasn't the first to prove itself unequal to him, nor the last. I see him carrying his fight against mere appearances from one unworthy institution to the next, each of them refusing, with increasing vehemence, his call to spiritual greatness. Dr. Avery's colleagues, small minds joined to small hearts, ridicule him as a nuisance and a bore. His high-mindedness, they imply, is a cover for lack of distinction in his field, whatever that may be. Again and again they send him packing. Mrs. Avery consoles his wounded *anima* with unfailing loyalty, and ministers to his swelling *materia* with larger and larger batches of brownies. She believes in him. Her faith, whatever its foundation, is heroic. Not once does she imagine, as a lesser woman might, that her chances for common happiness—old friends, a place of her own, a life rooted in community— have been sacrificed not to some higher truth but to vanity and arrogance.

No, that part belongs to Sister. Sister will be the heretic. She has no choice, being their child. In time, not many years after this night, she will decide that the disappointments of her life can be traced to their failings. Who knows those failings better than Sister? There are scenes. Dr. Avery is accused of being himself, Mrs. Avery of being herself. The visits home from Barnard or Reed or wherever Sister's scholarship takes her, and then from the distant city where she works, become theatrical productions. Angry whispers in the kitchen, shouts at the dinner table, early departure. This goes on for years, but not forever. Sister makes peace with her parents. She even comes to cherish what she has resented, their refusal to talk and act as others do, their endless moving on, the bright splash of their oddity in the muddy flow. She finds she has no choice but to love them, and who can love them better than Sister?

It might have gone this way, or another way. I have made these people part of my story without knowing anything of theirs, just as I did that night, dreaming myself one of them. We were strangers. I'd spent maybe forty-five minutes in their apartment, just long enough to get warm and lose sight of the facts.

My mother spoke my name again. I stayed where I was. Usually I would have gotten to my feet without being prodded, not out of obedience but because it pleased me to anticipate her, to show off our teamwork. This time I just stared at her sullenly. She looked wrong in the rocking chair; she was too glamorous for it. I could see her glamor almost as a thing apart, another presence, a brassy impatient friend just dying to get her out of here, away from all this domesticity.

She said we ought to think about getting home. Sister raised her head and looked at me. I still didn't move. I could see my mother's surprise. She waited for me to do something, and when I didn't she rocked forward slowly and stood up. Everyone stood with her except me. I felt foolish and bratty sitting on the floor all by myself, but I stayed there anyway while she made the final pleasantries. When she moved toward the door, I got up and mumbled my good-byes, then followed her outside.

Dr. Avery held the door for us.

'I still think it's a pretty campus,' my mother said.

He laughed—*Ho ho ho*. 'Well, so be it,' he said. 'To each his own.' He waited until we reached the sidewalk, then turned the light off and closed the door. It made a solid bang behind us.

'What was all that about?' my mother said.

I didn't answer.

'Are you feeling okay?'

'Yes.' Then I said, 'I'm a little cold.'

'Cold? Why didn't you say something?' She tried to look concerned but I could see that she was glad to have a simple answer for what had happened back in the house.

She took off her suit jacket. 'Here.'

'That's okay.'

'Put it on.'

'Really, Mom. I'll be okay.'

'Put it on, dimwit!'

I pulled the coat over my shoulders. We walked for a while. 'I look ridiculous,' I said.

'So . . . who cares?'

'I do.'

'Okay, you do. *Sorry*. Boy, you're a regular barrel of laughs tonight.'

'I'm not wearing this thing on the bus.'

'Nobody said you had to wear it on the bus. You want to grab something to eat before we head back?'

I told her sure, fine, whatever she wanted.

'Maybe we can find a pizza place. Think you could eat some pizza?'

I said I thought I could.

A black dog with gleaming eyes crossed the street in our direction.

'Hello, sport,' my mother said.

The dog trotted along beside us for a while, then took off.

I turned up the jacket collar and hunched my shoulders.

'Are you still cold?'

'A little.' I was shivering like crazy. It seemed to me I'd never been so cold, and I blamed my mother for it, for taking me outside again, away from the fire. I knew it wasn't her fault but I blamed her anyway—for this and the wind in my face and for every nameless thing that was not as it should be.

'Come here.' She pulled me over and began to rub her hand up and down my arm. When I leaned away she held on and kept rubbing. It felt good. I wasn't really warm, but I was as warm as I was going to get.

'Just out of curiosity,' my mother said, 'what did you think of the campus? Honestly.'

'I liked it.'

'I thought it was great,' she said.

'So did I.'

'That big blowhard,' she said. 'Where does he get off?'

I have my own fireplace now. Where we live the winters are long and cold. The wind blows the snow sideways, the house creaks, the windows glaze over with ferns of ice. After dinner I lay the fire, building four walls of logs like a roofless cabin. That's the best way. Only greenhorns use the teepee method. My children wait behind me, jockeying for position, furiously arguing their right to apply the match. I tell them to do it together. Their hands shake with eagerness as they strike the matches and hold them to the crumpled paper, torching as many spots as they can before the kindling starts to crackle. Then they sit back on their heels and watch the flame engulf the cabin walls. Their faces are reverent.

My wife comes in and praises the fire, knowing the pride it gives me. She lies on the couch with her book but doesn't read it. I don't read mine, either. I watch the fire, watch the changing light on the faces of my family. I try to feel at home, and I do, almost entirely. This is the moment I dream of when I am far away; this is my dream of home. But in the very heart of it I catch myself bracing a little, as if in fear of being tricked. As if to really believe in it will somehow make it vanish, like a voice waking me from sleep.

THE CUSTODIAN

Deborah Eisenberg

For years after Isobel left town (was sent from town, to live with an aunt in San Francisco) Lynnie would sometimes see her at a distance, crossing a street or turning a corner. But just as Lynnie started after her Isobel would vanish, having been replaced by a substitute, some long-legged stranger with pale, floaty hair. And while Lynnie might have been just as happy, by and large, not to see Isobel, at those moments she was felled by a terrible sorrow, as though somewhere a messenger searching for her had been waylaid, or was lost.

It was sixteen years after Lynnie had watched Isobel disappearing from view in the back seat of her father's car when Lynnie really did see her again. And then, although Isobel walked right into Lynnie's shop, several long, chaotic moments elapsed before Lynnie understood who Isobel was. 'Isobel,' she said, and, as the well-dressed customer browsing meditatively among the shelves and cases of expensive food turned to look full at Lynnie, the face that Lynnie had known so well— a girl's face that drew everything toward it and returned nothing— came forward in the woman's.

'Oh,' Isobel said. 'It's you. But Mother wrote me you were living in Boston. Or did I make that up?'

'You didn't make it up,' Lynnie said.

'Well, then,' Isobel said, and hesitated. 'You're back.'

'That about sums it up,' Lynnie said. She let her hand bounce lightly against the counter, twice. 'I hear you're still in San Francisco,' she said, relenting—they were adults now.

'Mmm,' Isobel said. 'Yes.' She frowned.

Lynnie cleared her throat. 'And someone told me you have a baby.'

'Oh, yes,' Isobel said. 'Two. And a husband, of course. All that sort of thing.' She and Lynnie smiled at one another—an odd, formal equilibrium.

'And you,' Isobel said, disengaging. 'What are you doing these days?'

'This—' Lynnie gestured. 'Of course, I have help now.'

'Heavens,' Isobel remarked unheatedly.

'"Heavens,"' Lynnie said. 'I know.' But either more of a reaction from Isobel or less would have been just as infuriating. 'Heavens' or 'How nice' was all that anyone had said when Lynnie retreated from Boston and managed, through effort born of near-panic, to open the store. All her life Lynnie had been assumed to be inadequate to any but the simplest endeavor; then, from the moment the store opened, that was something no one remembered. No one but her, Lynnie thought; she remembered it perfectly.

'Isn't it funny?' Isobel was saying. 'I drove by yesterday, and I thought, How nice that there's a place like that up here now. I'll have to stop in and get something for Mother, to cheer her up.'

'I'm sorry about your father,' Lynnie said.

'Yes,' Isobel said. 'God. I was just at the hospital. They say the operation was successful, but I don't know what that's supposed to mean. It seemed they might mean successful in the sense that he didn't die during it.' Her flat green glance found Lynnie, then moved away.

'Hard to think of him . . . in a hospital,' Lynnie said. 'He always seemed so—' He'd seemed so big.

'Strong,' Isobel said. 'Yes, he's strong all right. He and I are still on the most horrible terms, if you can believe it. It's simply idiotic. I suppose he has to keep it up to justify himself. All these years! You know, this is the first time I've been back, Lynnie—he came out for my wedding, and Mother's made him come with her twice to see the boys, but I haven't been back once. Not once. And there I was today— obviously I'd decided to get here before he died. But did he say anything—like he was glad I'd come? Of course not. Lynnie, he's riddled with tumors, he can't weigh more than a hundred pounds, but he behaved as though he were still sitting in that huge chair of his, telling me what I'd done to him.'

Lynnie shook her head. How easily Isobel was talking about these things.

'So,' Isobel said.

'Well,' Lynnie said.

'Yes,' Isobel said.

'I'll wrap up some things for your mother if you want,' Lynnie said. 'I've got a new pâté I think she'll like. And her favorite crackers have come in.'

'Lovely,' Isobel said. 'Thanks.' She pushed back a curving lock of hair and scanned the shelves as though waiting for some information to appear on them. 'So Mother comes into your store.'

'Oh, yes,' Lynnie said.

'Funny,' Isobel said. Isobel looked like anyone else now, Lynnie understood with a little shock. Very pretty, but like anyone else. Only her hair, with its own marvelous life, was still extraordinary. 'How's your mother, by the way?' Isobel said.

'All right,' Lynnie said, and glanced at her. 'So far.'

'That's good,' Isobel said opaquely.

'And at least she's not such a terror anymore,' Lynnie said. 'She's living up north with Frank now.'

'Frank . . .' Isobel said.

'Frank,' Lynnie said. She reached up to the roll of thick waxed paper and tore a piece off thunderously. 'My brother. The little one.'

'Oh, yes,' Isobel said. 'Of course. You know, this feels so peculiar— being here, seeing you. The whole place stopped for me, really, when I went away.'

'I'm sure,' Lynnie said, flushing. 'Well, we still exist. Our lives keep going on. I have the store, and people come into it. Your mother comes in. Cissy Haddad comes in. Ross comes in, Claire comes in. All six of their children come in . . .'

'*Six*—' Isobel stared at Lynnie; her laugh was just a breath. 'Well, I guess that means they stayed together, anyway.'

'Mostly,' Lynnie said. But Isobel only waited, and looked at her. 'There was a while there, a few years ago, when he moved in with an ex-student of his. Claire got in the van with the four youngest—Emily and Bo were already at school— and took off. It didn't last too long, of course, the thing with the girl, and of course Claire came back. After that they sold the stone house. To a broker, I heard.'

'Oh,' Isobel said. Absently she picked up an apple from a mound on the counter and looked into its glossy surface as though it were a mirror.

'They're renovating a farmhouse now,' Lynnie said. 'It's much smaller.'

'Too bad,' Isobel said, putting down the apple.

'Yes.'

'Was she pretty?' Isobel asked.

'Who?' Lynnie said. 'Ross's girl? Not especially.'

'Ah,' Isobel said, and Lynnie looked away, ashamed of herself.

Isobel started to speak but didn't. She scanned the shelves again vaguely, then smiled over at Lynnie. 'You know what else is funny?' she said. 'When I woke up this morning, I looked across the street. And I saw this woman going out the door of your old house, and just for an instant I thought, There's Lynnie. And then I thought, No, it can't be that person's all grown up.'

For a long time after Isobel had left town, Lynnie would do what she could to avoid running into Ross or Claire; and eventually when she saw them it would seem to her not only that her feeling about them had undergone an alteration but that they themselves were different in some way. Over the years it became all too clear that this was true: their shine had been tarnished by a slight fussiness—they had come to seem like people who were anxious about being rained on.

Newcomers might have been astonished to learn that there was a time when people had paused in their dealings with one another to look as Ross walked down the street with Claire or the children. Recent arrivals to the town—additions to the faculty of the college, the businessmen and bankers who were now able to live in country homes and still work in their city offices from computer terminals—what was it they saw when Ross and Claire passed by? Fossil forms, Lynnie thought. Museum reproductions. It was the Claire and Ross of years ago who were vivid, living. A residual radiance clung to objects they'd handled and places where they'd spent time. The current Ross and Claire were lightless, their own aftermath.

Once in a while, though—it happened sometimes when she encountered one of them unexpectedly—Lynnie would see them as they had been. For an instant their sleeping power would flash, but then their dimmed present selves might greet Lynnie, with casual and distant politeness, and a breathtaking pain would cauterize the exquisitely reworked wound.

It is summer when Lynnie snd Isobel first come upon Ross and Claire. Lynnie and Isobel live across the street from one another, but Isobel is older and has better things to do with her time than see Lynnie. And because Lynnie's mother works at the plant for unpredictable stretches, on unpredictable shifts, Lynnie frequently must look after her younger brothers. Still, when Lynnie is free, she is often able to persuade Isobel to do something, particularly in the summers, when Isobel is bored brainless.

They take bicycle expeditions then, during those long summers, often along the old highway. The highway is silent, lined with birchwoods, and has several alluring and mysterious features—among them a dark, green wooden restaurant with screened windows, and a motel, slightly shabby, where there are always, puzzlingly, several cars parked. Leading from the highway is a wealth of dirt roads, on one of which Lynnie and Isobel find a wonderful house.

The house is stone, and stands empty on a hill. Clouds float by it, making great black shadows swing over the sloping meadows below with their cows and barns and wildflowers. Inside, in the spreading coolness, the light flows as variously clear and shaded as water. Trees seem to crowd in the dim recesses. The house is just there, enclosing part of the world: the huge fireplace could be the site of gatherings that take place once every hundred, or once every thousand, years. The girls walk carefully when they visit, fearful of churning up the delicate maze of silence.

For several summers, the house has been theirs, but one day, the summer that Lynnie is twelve and Isobel is just turning fourteen, there is a van parked in front. Lynnie and Isobel wheel their bicycles stealthily into the woods across the road and walk as close as they dare, crouching down opposite the house, well hidden, to watch.

Three men and a woman carry bundles and cartons into the house. Bundles and cartons and large pieces of furniture sit outside, where two small children tumble around among them, their wisps of voices floating high into the birdcalls and branches above Lynnie and Isobel. The woman is slight, like a child herself, with a shiny braid of black hair down her back, and there is no question about which of the men she, the furniture, and the children belong to.

Lynnie squints, and seems to draw closer, hovering just too far off to see his face. Then, for just a fraction of a second, she penetrates the distance.

The sun moves behind Lynnie and Isobel, and the man to whom

everything belongs waves the others inside, hoisting up the smaller child as he follows. Just as Lynnie and Isobel reach cautiously for their bicycles, the man looks out again, shading his eyes. They freeze, and for a moment he stands there peering out toward them.

Neither Lynnie nor Isobel suggests going on—to town, or to the gorge, or anywhere. They ride back the way they've come, and, without discussion, go upstairs to Isobel's room.

Isobel lies down across her flounced bed while Lynnie wanders around absently examining Isobel's things, which she knows so well: Isobel's books, her stuffed animals, her china figurines.

'Do you think we're the first people to see them?' Lynnie says.

'The first people *ever*?' Isobel says, flopping over onto her side.

Lynnie stares out Isobel's window at her own house. She doesn't know what to do when Isobel's in a bad mood. She should just leave, she thinks.

From here, her house looks as though it were about to slide to the ground. A large aluminum cannister clings to its side like a devouring space monster. 'Do you want to go back out and do something?' she asks.

'What would we do?' Isobel says, into her pillow. 'There's nothing to do. There's not one single thing to do here. And now would you mind sitting down, please, Lynnie? Because you happen to be driving me insane.'

As she leaves Isobel's, Lynnie pauses before crossing the street to watch her brothers playing in front of the house. They look weak and bony, but the two older boys fight savagely. A plastic gun lies near them on the ground. Frank, as usual, is playing by himself, but he is just as banged up as they are. His skin is patchy and chapped— summer and winter he breathes through his mouth, and even this temperate sun is strong enough to singe the life out of his fine, almost white hair. She looks just like him, Lynnie thinks. Except chunky. 'Chunky' is the word people use.

Inside, Lynnie's mother is stationed in front of the TV. At any hour Lynnie's mother might be found staring at the television, and beyond it, through the front window, as though something of importance were due to happen out on the street. The television is almost always on, and when men friends come to visit, Lynnie's mother turns up the volume, so that other noises bleed alarmingly through the insistent rectangle of synthetic sound.

Lynnie brings a paper napkin from the kitchen and inserts it between her mother's glass of beer and the table. 'May I inquire . . .?' her mother says.

'Isobel's mother says you should never leave a glass on the furniture,' Lynnie says. 'It makes a ring.'

Lynnie's mother looks at her, then lifts the glass and crumples the napkin. 'Thank you,' she says, turning back to her program. 'I'll remember that.' A thin wave of laughter comes from the TV screen, and little shapes jump and throb there, but Lynnie is thinking about the people from the stone house.

Lynnie's mother can be annoyed when she knows that Lynnie has been playing with Isobel; Isobel's father works for the same company Lynnie's mother works for, but not in the plant. He works in the office, behind a big desk. Whenever Lynnie is downstairs in Isobel's house and Isobel's father walks in, Lynnie scuttles as though she might be trodden underfoot. In fact, Isobel's father hardly notices her; perhaps he doesn't even know from one of her visits to the next that she is the same little girl. But he booms down at Isobel, scrutinizing her from his great height, and sometimes even lifts her way up over his head.

Isobel's mother is tall and smells good and dresses in neat wool. Sometimes when she sees Lynnie hesitating at the foot of the drive she opens the door, with a bright, special smile. 'Lynnie, dear,' she says, 'would you like to come in and see Isobel? Or have a snack?' But sometimes, when Lynnie and Isobel are playing, Isobel's mother calls Isobel away for a whispered conference, from which Isobel returns to say that Lynnie has to go now, for this reason or that.

When Lynnie looks out the window of the room she shares with Frank, she can see Isobel's large, arched window, and if the light is just right she can see Isobel's bed, too, with its white flounces, and a heavenly blue haze into which, at this distance, the flowers of Isobel's wallpaper melt.

One day, doing errands for her mother in town, Lynnie sees the woman from the stone house coming out of the bakery with the children, each of whom carefully holds a large, icing-covered cookie. The woman bends down and picks up one of the children, smiling—unaware, Lynnie observes, that people are noticing her.

Lynnie sees the woman several times, and then one day she sees the man.

She has anticipated his face exactly. But when he smiles at her, the little frown line between his eyes stays. And the marvelousness of this surprise causes a sensation across the entire surface of her skin, like the rippling of leaves that demonstrates a subtle shift of air.

When Lynnie sees Isobel she can't help talking about the people from the stone house. She describes variations in their clothing or demeanor, compiling a detailed body of knowledge while Isobel lies on her bed, her eyes closed. 'Should we give them names?' Lynnie says one afternoon.

'No,' Isobel says.

But Lynnie can't stop. 'Why not?' she says, after a moment.

'"Why not?"' Isobel says.

'Don't, Isobel,' Lynnie pleads.

'"Don't, Isobel,"' Isobel says, making her hands into a tube to speak through. Her voice is hollow and terrifying.

Lynnie breathes heavily through her mouth. 'Why not?' she says.

'Why *not*,' Isobel says, sitting up and sighing, 'is because they already have names.'

'I know,' Lynnie says, mystified.

'Their names,' Isobel says, 'are Ross and Claire.'

Lynnie stares at her.

'They had dinner at Cissy Haddad's house one night,' Isobel says. 'Ross is going to be teaching medieval literature at the college. He's in Cissy's father's department.'

'"Department"?' Lynnie says.

'Yes,' Isobel says.

Lynnie frowns. 'How do you know?' she asks. How *long* has Isobel known?

Isobel shrugs. 'I'm just telling you what Cissy said.' She looks at Lynnie. 'I think Cissy has a crush on him.'

'What else did Cissy say?' Lynnie asks unhappily.

'Nothing,' Isobel says. 'Oh. Except that he's thirty-five and Claire's only twenty-three. She used to be one of his students.'

'One of his students?' Lynnie says.

'"One of his—"' Isobel begins, and then flops down on the bed again. 'Oh, Lynnie.'

One day Lynnie sees Cissy Haddad in the drugstore. Lynnie hurries to select the items on her mother's list, then waits until Cissy goes to the counter. 'Hi,' she says, getting into line behind Cissy. She feels herself turning red.

'Oh, hi, Lynnie,' Cissy says, and smiles wonderfully. 'Are you having a fun summer?'

'Yes,' Lynnie says.

'What're you doing?' Cissy says.

'Just mostly looking after my brothers,' Lynnie says. She feels bewildered by Cissy's dazzling smile, her pretty sundress. 'And riding around and things with Isobel.'

'That's good,' Cissy says. And then, instead of saying something useful about Isobel, which might lead to Ross and Claire, she asks, 'Are you coming to high school this year? I can't remember.'

'No,' Lynnie says. 'Isobel is.'

Cissy peers into Lynnie's basket of embarrassing purchases.

'What are you getting?' she asks.

'Things for my mother,' Lynnie says, squirming. 'What about you?'

'Oh,' Cissy says. 'Just lipstick.'

One fall day when Lynnie gets home from school, her mother summons her over the noise from the TV. 'You got a phone call,' she says shortly. 'The lady wants you to call her back.' And Lynnie knows, while her mother is still speaking, whom the call was from.

Lynnie dials, and the soft, dark shadow of Claire's voice answers. She is looking for someone to help with the children on a regular basis, she explains, several afternoons a week. She got Lynnie's name from Tom Haddad's daughter. She knows that Lynnie is very young, but this is nothing difficult—just playing with the children upstairs or outside so that she can have a couple of hours to paint. 'I thought I would be able to do so much here,' she says, as though Lynnie were an old friend, someone her own age, 'but there's never enough time, is there?'

'I'll need you just as much with the boys,' Lynnie's mother says later. 'And you'd better remember your homework.'

'I will,' Lynnie says, though, actually, beyond a certain point, it scarcely matters; however hard she tries, she lags far behind in school, and her teachers no longer try to stifle their exclamations of impatience. 'I'll do my homework.' And her mother makes no further objections; Lynnie will be earning money.

Claire leads Lynnie around in the house that used to be Lynnie and Isobel's. Now it is all filled up with the lives of these people.

Everywhere there is a regal disorder of books, and in the biggest room downstairs, with its immense fireplace, there are sofas and, at one end, a vast table. A thicket of canvases and brushes has sprung up in a corner, and Lynnie sees pictures of the table on whose surface objects are tensely balanced, and sketch after sketch of Ross and the children. 'What do you think?' Claire says, and it is a moment before Lynnie realizes what Claire is asking her.

'I like them,' Lynnie says. But in fact they frighten her—the figures seem caught, glowing in a webby dimness.

In the kitchen huge pots and pans flash, and a great loaf of brown bread lies out on a counter. Claire opens the door to Ross's study; stacks and stacks of paper, more books than Lynnie has ever seen breed from its light-shot core.

Upstairs Bo and Emily are engrossed in a sprawling project of blocks. Emily explains the dreamlike construction to Lynnie, gracefully accepting Bo's effortful elaborations, and when Lynnie leaves both children reach up to her with their tanned little arms.

Twice a week Lynnie goes to the stone house. Bo and Emily have big, bright, smooth wooden toys, some of which were made by Ross. Lynnie strokes the toys; she runs her hand over them like a blind person; she runs her hand over the pictures in Bo and Emily's beautiful storybooks. But then Claire counts out Lynnie's money, and Lynnie is to go. And at the first sight of her own house she is slightly sickened, as upon disembarkation—not by the firm ground underfoot but by a ghostly rocking of water.

When Claire finishes painting for the afternoon, she calls Lynnie and Bo and Emily into the kitchen. For a while, although Bo and Emily chatter and nuzzle against her, Claire seems hardly to know where she is. But gradually she returns, and makes for herself and Lynnie a dense, sweet coffee in a little copper pot, which must be brought to the boil three times. They drink it from identical cups, and Lynnie marvels, looking at Claire, that she herself is there.

Some afternoons Ross is around. He announces that he will be in his study, working, but sooner or later he always appears in the kitchen, and talks about things he is reading for his book.

'What do you think, Lynnie?' he asks once. He has just proposed an idea for a new chapter, to which Claire's response was merely 'Possible.'

Lynnie can feel herself blush. 'I don't know,' she says.

Amusement begins to spread from behind his eyes. 'Do you think it's a good idea?' he asks.

'Yes,' she says, wary.

'Why?' he says.

'Because you just said it was,' Lynnie says, turning a deeper red.

He laughs happily and gives Lynnie a little hug. 'You see?' he says to Claire.

When the snow lies in great drifts around the stone house, students begin to come, too, and sit around the kitchen. They drink beer, and the girls exclaim over Bo and Emily while the boys shyly answer Claire's gentle questions and Lynnie holds her coffee cup tightly in misery. Now and again, as he talks to them, Ross touches the students lightly on the wrist or shoulder.

Late one Saturday afternoon, Lynnie is washing dishes in her own house when her mother walks in with several large grocery bags. 'I was just in town,' she announces unnecessarily, and grins an odd, questioning grin at Lynnie. 'Now, who do you think I saw there?'

'I don't know who you saw,' Lynnie says, reaching for a dishcloth.

'The man you work for,' her mother says.

'How do you know who he is?' Lynnie says.

'Everybody knows who he is,' her mother says. 'He was in the stationery store. I just went in to get some tape, but I stuck around to watch. Muriel Furman was waiting on him. She almost went into a

trance. That poor thing.' Lynnie's mother shakes her head and begins
to unload groceries. 'Homeliest white woman I ever saw.'

'Mother,' Lynnie says. She stares unhappily out the little window
over the sink.

'I've seen the wife around a few times, too,' Lynnie's mother says.
'She's a pretty girl, but I wish her luck with him.'

Lynnie has not been to Isobel's house once this year. Isobel comes and
goes with Cissy Haddad and other high-school friends. From across
the street Lynnie can sometimes see their shapes behind the film of
Isobel's window. At night, when Isobel's light is on and her window is
transparent, Lynnie watches Isobel moving back and forth until the
curtain closes.

One afternoon as Lynnie is arriving home, she almost walks into Isobel.
'Wake up, Lynnie,' Isobel says. And then, 'Want to come over?'

'Lynnie, dear,' Isobel's mother says as Lynnie and Isobel go upstairs.
'How *nice* to see you.'

It has been so long since Lynnie has been in Isobel's room that
Isobel's things—the flouncy bed and the china figurines and the stuffed
animals she used to see so often—have a new, melancholy luster.
'How's high school?' she asks.

'It's hard,' Isobel says. 'You won't believe it.'

But Lynnie will. She does. Almost every day she remembers that
that is where she is going next fall—to the immense, tentacled building
that looks like a factory. She has reason to suspect that she will be
divided from most of her classmates there, and put into the classes for
people who won't be going on to college—the stupid people—with all
the meanest teachers. No one has threatened her with this, but
everybody knows how it works. Everybody knows what goes on in
that building.

Lynnie picks up a stuffed turtle and strokes its furry shell.

'How's school?' Isobel asks. 'How's old Miss Fisher?'

'She doesn't like me,' Lynnie says. 'Miss Fish Face.'

'Oh, well,' Isobel says. 'So what? Soon you'll never have to see her
again.' She looks at Lynnie and smiles. 'What else have you been up
to?'

Lynnie feels slightly weak because of what she is about to tell Isobel.

She has been saving it up, she realizes, a long time. 'Well,' she says slowly, 'I've been babysitting for the kids at the stone house.'

'Have you?' Isobel says, but as she says it Lynnie understands that Isobel already knew, and although Isobel is waiting, Lynnie cannot speak.

'You know what—' Isobel says after a moment. 'Lynnie, what are you doing to that poor turtle? But do you know what Cissy's father said about that man, Ross? Cissy's father said he's an arrogant son of a bitch.' She looks at Lynnie, hugging her pillow expectantly. 'I heard him.'

Lynnie and Claire and three students watch as Ross describes various arguments concerning a matter that has come up in class. The students look at him with hazy, hopeful smiles. But not Lynnie—she is ashamed to have heard what Isobel said to her.

Ross glances down at her unhappy face. 'Apparently Lynnie disagrees,' he says, stroking a strand of her pale, flossy hair behind her ear. 'Apparently Lynnie feels that Heineman fails to account for the Church's influence over the emerging class of tradesmen.'

The students laugh, understanding his various points, and Ross smiles at Lynnie. But Lynnie is ashamed again—doubly ashamed—and leans for comfort into the treacherous hand that still strokes her hair.

Lynnie has two Rosses who blend together and diverge unpredictably. Many mornings begin drowsily encircled in the fleecy protection of one, but sometimes, as Lynnie continues to wake, the one is assumed into the other. He strokes Lynnie's hair, inflicting injury and healing it in this one motion, and she opens her eyes to see her own room, and Frank curled up in the other bed, breathing laboriously, susceptible himself to the devious assaults of dreams.

In the fall, Lynnie is put, as she had feared, into the classes for the slowest students. Had anyone entertained hopes for her, this would have been the end of them.

A few of her old schoolmates are confined to her classes, but most have sailed into classes from which they will sail out again into college, then marriage and careers. She sees them only in the halls and the lunchroom and on the athletic fields. Every day they look taller, more powerful, more like strangers.

Most of those in her classes really are strangers. But in some ways they are as familiar as cousins met for the first time. Their clothes, for instance, are not right, and they are the worst students from all the elementary schools in the area. The boys are rough or sly or helpless, or all three, like her brothers, and the girls are ungainly and bland-looking. They stand in clumps in the halls, watching girls like Isobel and Cissy Haddad with a beleaguered envy, and trading accounts of the shocking things such girls have been known to do.

Oddly, Isobel is friendlier to Lynnie at school, in full view of everyone, than she is out of school, despite Lynnie's stigma. 'Hi, Lynnie,' she calls out with a dewy showpiece of a smile, not too different from her mother's.

'Hi,' Lynnie answers, facing a squadron of Isobel's friends.

One afternoon as Lynnie approaches her house a silence reaches for her like a suction. Her brothers are not outside, and the television is not on. No one is in the kitchen or upstairs. She sits without moving while the winter sky goes dark. Across the street Isobel turns on the light in her room and sits down at her little desk. After a while she leaves, turning off the light, but Lynnie continues to stare at the blank window. By the time Lynnie hears her mother's car, her arms and legs feel stiff. She waits for a moment before going downstairs to be told what has happened.

Frank is in the hospital with a ruptured appendix, her mother says; her face has a terrible jellylike look. If she could see her own face, Lynnie wonders, would it look like that?

There will be no more going to the stone house; she will be needed at home, her mother is saying, staring at Lynnie as though Lynnie were shrinking into a past of no meaning—the way a dying person might look at an enemy.

The next day, Lynnie seeks out Isobel in the lunchroom. 'A ruptured appendix,' Isobel says. 'That's really dangerous, you know.'

'My mother says Frank is going to be all right,' Lynnie says doggedly.

'Poor Lynnie,' Isobel says. 'So what are you going to do if Ross and Claire hire someone else?'

Lynnie puts her head down on the lunch table and closes her eyes. The sweet, unpleasant smell of the lunchroom rises up, and the din of the students, talking and laughing, folds around her.

'Poor Lynnie,' Isobel says again.

Later that week, Lynnie brings Isobel to the stone house. Claire makes coffee, and when she brings out a third tiny china cup, Lynnie is unable to hear anything for several seconds.

Ross comes in, whistling, and lets the door slam behind him. 'What's this?' he asks, indicating Isobel. 'Invader or captive?'

'Friendly native,' Claire says. 'Isobel's going to be our new Lynnie.'

'What's the matter with our old Lynnie?' Ross says. He looks at Isobel for a moment. 'Our old Lynnie's fine with me.'

'Oh, Ross.' Claire sighs. 'I told you. Lynnie's brother is sick.'

'Hmm,' Ross says.

'He's in the hospital, Ross,' Claire says.

'Oh, God,' Ross says. 'Yes, I'm sorry to hear that, Lynnie.'

'First day of the new semester,' Claire says to Lynnie. 'He's always disgusting the first day. How are your new students, my love?'

'Unspeakable,' Ross says.

'Truly,' Claire says. She smiles at Isobel.

'Worse than ever,' Ross says, taking a beer from the refrigerator. 'There isn't *one*. Well, one, maybe. A possibility. A real savage, but she has an interesting quality. Potential, at least.'

'I used to have potential,' Claire says, 'but look at me now.'

Ross raises his beer to her. 'Look at you now,' he says.

Ross holds the door as Lynnie and Isobel leave. 'I've seen you in town,' he says to Isobel. 'You're older than I thought.'

She glances up at him and then turns back to Claire. 'Goodbye,' she says. 'See you soon.'

'See you soon,' Claire says, coming to join them at the door. 'I do appreciate this. I'm going to have another baby, and I want to get in as much painting as I can first.'

'You're going to have another baby?' Lynnie says, staring.

'We're going to have hundreds of babies,' Ross says, putting his arms around Claire from behind. 'We're going to have hundreds and hundreds of babies.'

*

Afterward, Lynnie would become heavy and slow whenever she even thought of the time when Frank was sick. Their room was desolate while he was in the hospital; when he returned she felt how cramped it had always been before. Frank was testy all the time then, and cried easily. Her family deserved their troubles, she thought. Other people looked down on them, looked down and looked down, and then when they got tired of it they went back to their own business. But her family—and she—were the same whether anyone was looking or not.

Isobel's mother stops Lynnie on the sidewalk to ask after Frank. The special, kind voice she uses makes Lynnie's skin jump now. How could she ever have thought she adored Isobel's mother, Lynnie wonders, shuddering with an old, sugared hatred.

At night Lynnie can see Isobel in her room, brushing her hair, or sometimes, even, curled up against her big white pillows, reading. Has Isobel seen Ross and Claire that day? Lynnie always wonders. Did they talk about anything in particular? What did they do?

At school, Isobel sends her display of cheery waves and smiles in Lynnie's direction, and it is as though Ross and Claire had never existed. But once in a while she and Isobel meet on the sidewalk, and then they stop to talk in their ordinary way, without any smiles or fuss at all. 'Claire's in a good mood,' Isobel tells Lynnie one afternoon. 'She loves being pregnant.'

Pregnant. What a word. 'How's Ross?' Lynnie says.

'He's all right.' Isobel shrugs. 'He's got an assistant now, some student of his. Mary Katherine. She's always around.'

Lynnie feels herself beginning to blush. 'Don't you like him?'

'I like him.' Isobel shrugs again. 'He lends me books.'

'Oh.' Lynnie looks at Isobel wonderingly. 'What books?' she says without thinking.

'Just books he tells me to read,' Isobel says.

'Oh,' Lynnie says.

It is spring when Lynnie returns to the stone house. She is hugged and exclaimed over, and Emily and Bo perform for her, but she looks around as though it were she who had just come out of a long illness.

The big, smooth toys, the wonderful picture books no longer inspire her longing, or even her interest.

'We've missed you,' Claire says. Lynnie rests her head against the window frame, and the pale hills outside wobble.

But Claire has asked Isobel to sit for a portrait, so Isobel is at the stone house all the time now. The house is full of people—Lynnie upstairs with Emily and Bo, and Ross in his study with Mary Katherine, and Isobel and Claire in the big room among Claire's canvases.

In the afternoons they all gather in the kitchen. Sometimes Mary Katherine's boyfriend, Derek, joins them and watches Mary Katherine with large, mournful eyes while she smokes cigarette after cigarette and talks cleverly with Ross about his work. 'Doesn't he drive you crazy?' Mary Katherine says once to Claire. 'He's so opinionated.'

'Is he?' Claire says, smiling.

'Oh, Claire,' Mary Katherine says. 'I wish I were like you. You're *serene*. And you can *do* everything. You can paint, you can cook . . .'

'Claire can do everything,' Ross says. 'Claire can paint, Claire can cook, Claire can fix a carburetor . . .'

'What a useful person to be married to,' Mary Katherine says.

Claire laughs, but Derek looks up at Mary Katherine unhappily.

'*I* can't do anything,' Mary Katherine says. 'I'm hopeless. Aren't I, Ross?'

'Hopeless,' Ross says, and Lynnie's eyes cloud mysteriously. 'Truly hopeless.'

Now and again Ross asks Isobel's opinion about something he has given her to read. She looks straight ahead as she answers, as though she were remembering, and Ross nods soberly. Once Lynnie sees Ross look at Mary Katherine during Isobel's recitation. For a moment Mary Katherine looks back at him from narrow gray eyes, then makes her red mouth into an O from which blossoms a series of wavering smoke rings.

One day in April, when several students have dropped by, the temperature plummets and the sky turns into a white, billowing cloth that hides the trees and farmhouses. 'We'd better go now,' one of the students says, 'or we'll be snowed in forever.'

'Can you give me and Lynnie a lift?' Isobel asks. 'We're on bikes.'

'Stay for the show,' Ross says to her. 'It's going to be sensational up here.'

'Coming?' the student says to Isobel. 'Staying? Well, O.K., then.' Lynnie sees the student raise her eyebrows to Mary Katherine before, holding her coat closed, she goes out with her friends into the blowing wildness.

'We should go, too,' Derek says to Mary Katherine.

'Why?' Mary Katherine says. 'We've got four-wheel drive.'

'Stick around,' Ross says. 'If you feel like it.' Mary Katherine stares at him for a moment, but he goes to the door, squinting into the swarming snow where the students are disappearing. Behind him a silence has fallen.

'Yes,' Claire says suddenly. 'Everybody stay. There's plenty of food—we could live for months. Besides, I want to celebrate. I finished Isobel today.'

Isobel frowns. 'You finished?'

'With your part, at least,' Claire says. 'The rest I can do on my own. So you're liberated. And we should have a magnificent ceremonial dinner, don't you think, everybody? For the snow.' She stands, her hands together as though she has just clapped, looking at each of them in turn. Claire has a fever, Lynnie thinks.

'Why not?' Mary Katherine says. She closes her eyes. 'We can give you two a ride home later, Isobel.'

Bo and Emily are put to bed, and Lynnie, Isobel, Ross, Claire, Mary Katherine, and Derek set about making dinner. Although night has come, the kitchen glimmers with the snow's busy whiteness.

Ross opens a bottle of wine and everyone except Claire drinks. 'This is delicious!' Lynnie says, dazed with happiness, and the others smile at her, as though she has said something original and charming.

Even when they must chop and measure, no one turns on the lights. Claire finds candles, and Lynnie holds her glass up near a flame. A clear patch of red shivers on the wall. 'Feel,' Claire says, taking Lynnie's hand and putting it against her hard, round stomach, and Lynnie feels the baby kick.

'Why are we whispering?' Ross whispers, and then laughs. Claire moves vaporously within the globe of smeary candlelight.

Claire and Derek make a fire in the huge fireplace while Ross gets out the heavy, deep-colored Mexican dishes and opens another bottle of wine. 'Ross,' Claire says. But Ross fills the glasses again.

Lynnie wanders out into the big room to look at Claire's portrait of Isobel. Isobel stares back from the painting, not at her. At what? Staring out, Isobel recedes, drowning, into the darkness behind her.

What a meal they have produced! Chickens and platters of vegetables and a marvelously silly-looking peaked and scroll-rimmed pie. They sit at the big table eating quietly and appreciatively while the fire snaps and breathes. Outside, the brilliant white earth curves against a black sky, and black shadows of the snow-laden trees and telephone wires lie across it; there is light everywhere—a great, white moon, and stars flung out, winking.

Derek leans back in his chair, closing his eyes and letting one arm fall around Mary Katherine's chair. She casts a ruminating, regretful glance over him; when she looks away again it is as though he has been covered with a sheet.

Isobel gets up from the table and stretches. A silence falls around her like petals. She goes to the rug in front of the fire and lies down, her hair fanning out around her. Lynnie follows groggily and curls up on one of the sofas.

'That was perfect,' Claire says. 'Ideal. And now I'm going upstairs.' She burns feverishly for a moment as she pauses in the doorway, but then subsides into her usual smoky softness.

'Good night,' Lynnie calls, and for full seconds after Claire has disappeared from view the others stare at the tingling darkness where she was.

Ross pushes his chair back from the table and walks over to the rug where Isobel lies. 'Who's for a walk?' he says, looking down at her.

Mary Katherine stubs out a cigarette. 'Come on,' Ross says, prodding Isobel with his foot. Isobel looks at his foot, then away.

Ross is standing just inches from Lynnie; she can feel his outline—a little extra density of air.

'Derek,' Mary Katherine says softly. 'It's time to go. Lynnie? Isobel?'

'I can run the girls home later,' Ross says.

'Right,' Mary Katherine says after a moment. She goes to the closet for her coat.

'Come on, you two,' Ross says. 'Up. Isobel? This is not going to last—' He gestures toward the window. 'It's tonight only. Out of the cave, lazy little bears. Into the refreshing night.'

Ross reaches a hand down to Isobel. She considers it, then looks up at him. 'I hate to be refreshed,' she says, still looking at him, and shifts slightly on the rug.

'I don't believe this,' Mary Katherine says quietly.

Lynnie sits up. The stars move back, then forward. The snow flashes, pitching her almost off balance. 'Wait, wait,' Isobel says, scrambling to her feet as Mary Katherine goes to the door. 'We're coming.'

In the car Derek makes a joke, but no one laughs. Next to Lynnie, Isobel sits in a burnished silence. Branches support a canopy of snow over them as they drive out onto the old highway. Three cars are parked in front of the motel. They are covered with snow; no tire tracks are visible. All the motel windows are dark except one, where a faint aureole escapes from behind the curtain. Isobel breathes—just a feather of a sigh—and leans back against the seat.

Lynnie wakes up roughly, crying out as though she were being dragged through a screen of sleep into the day. Frank is no longer in his bed, and the room is bright. Lynnie sits up, shivering, exhausted from the night, and sees that the sun is already turning the snow to a glaze.

'You got in late enough,' Lynnie's mother says when Lynnie comes downstairs.

'I tried not to wake you,' Lynnie says.

'I can imagine,' her mother says. 'You were knocking things over left and right. I suppose those people gave you plenty to drink.'

'I wasn't drunk, Mother,' Lynnie says.

'No,' her mother says. 'Good. Well, I don't want you staying late with those people again. You can leave that sort of thing to Isobel. She looked fairly steady on her feet last night going up the drive.'

Lynnie looks at her mother.

'I wonder what Isobel's parents think,' Lynnie's mother says.

'Isobel's parents trust her, Mother,' Lynnie says.

'Well that's *their* problem, isn't it?' her mother says.

Isobel has stopped coming to the stone house, and her portrait leans against the wall, untouched since she left. But one day, at the beginning of summer, she goes along with Lynnie to see the new baby.

'He's strange, isn't he?' Claire says as Isobel picks him up. 'They're always so strange at the beginning—much easier to believe a stork brings them. Did a stork bring you, Willie? A stork?'

Through the window they can see Ross outside, working, and Lynnie listens to the rhythmic striking of his spade and the earth sliding off it in a little pile of sound. 'We're planting a lilac,' she hears Claire say. Claire's voice slides, silvery, through the gold day, and Ross looks up, shading his eyes.

The sun melts into the sky. Lynnie hears Claire and Isobel talking behind the chinking of the spade, but then once, when there should be the spade, there is no sound, and Lynnie looks up to see Ross taking off his shirt. When had Claire and Isobel stopped talking?

Isobel stands up, transferring Willie to Lynnie.

'Don't go,' Claire commands quietly.

'No . . .' Isobel says. Her voice is sleepy, puzzled, and she sits back down.

The room is silent again, but then the door bangs and Ross comes in, holding his crumpled shirt. 'Hello, everyone,' he says, going to the sink to slap cold water against his face. 'Hello, Isobel.' He tosses back dripping hair.

'Hello,' Isobel says.

Lynnie looks up at Claire, but Claire's eyes are half closed as she gazes down at her long, graceful hands lying on the table. 'Yes,' Claire says, although no one has spoken.

'Ross,' Isobel says, standing, 'I brought back your book.' She hands Ross a small, faded book with gold on the edges of the pages.

He takes the book and looks at it for a moment, at the shape of it in his hand. 'Ah,' he says. 'Maybe I'll find something else for you one of these days.'

'Mm,' Isobel says, pushing her hair back.

Willie makes a little smacking sound, and the others look at him.

'When's good to drop things by?' Ross says.

'Anytime,' Isobel says. 'Sometime.' She pivots childishly on one foot. 'Saturdays are all right.'

Claire puts her hands against her eyes, against her forehead. 'Would anybody like iced tea?' she asks.

'Not I,' Isobel says. 'I have to go.'

*

The students have left town for the summer—even Derek. At least, Lynnie has not seen him since the night it snowed. And Mary Katherine herself is hardly in evidence. She comes over once in a while, but when she finishes her work, instead of sitting around the kitchen, she leaves.

Lynnie might be alone in the house, except for Bo and Emily. Claire is so quiet now, sealed off in a life with Willie, that sometimes Lynnie doesn't realize that she is standing right there. And when Lynnie and the children are outside, the children seem to disappear into the net of gold light. They seem far away from her—little motes—and barely audible; the quiet from the house muffles their voices.

Ross is frequently out, doing one thing and another, and his smiles for Lynnie have become terribly kind—self-deprecating and sudden, as though she had become, overnight, fragile or precious. Now that Isobel has finally gone away, Ross and Claire seem to have gone with her; her absence is a vacuum into which they have disappeared. Day after day, nothing changes. Day after day, the sky sheds gold, and nothing changes. The house is saturated with absences.

Now Lynnie sees Isobel only as she streaks by in the little green car she has been given for her sixteenth birthday, or from the window in her room at night before she draws the curtain. One Saturday afternoon when Lynnie is outside with her brothers, Ross pulls up across the street. He waves to Lynnie as he walks up Isobel's drive and knocks on the door. Lynnie watches as Isobel opens the door and accepts a book he holds out to her. Ross disappears inside. A few minutes later he reemerges, waves again to Lynnie, and drives off.

These days Lynnie's mother is more irritable than usual. There have been rumors of layoffs at the plant. Once, when Lynnie is watching TV with her they see Isobel's father drive up across the street. 'Look at that fat bastard,' Lynnie's mother says. 'Now, there's a man who knows how to run a tight ship.'

Even years and years later, just the thought of the school building could still call up Lynnie's dread, from that summer, of going back to school. Still, there is some relief in finally having to do it, and by the third or fourth day Lynnie finds she is comforted by the distant roaring of the corridors, and the familiar faces that at last sight were the faces of strangers.

One afternoon the first week, she sees Cissy Haddad looking in her direction, and she waves shyly. But then she realizes that Cissy is staring at something else. She turns around and there is Isobel, looking back at Cissy. Nothing reflects from Isobel's flat green eyes.

'Isobel—' Lynnie says.

'Hello, Lynnie,' Isobel says slowly, and only then seems to see her. Lynnie turns back in confusion to Cissy, but Cissy is gone.

'Do you want a ride?' Isobel asks, looking straight ahead. 'I've got my car.'

'How was your summer?' Isobel asks on the way home.

'All right,' Lynnie says. 'The sky is a deep, open blue again. Soon the leaves will change. 'I was sorry you weren't around the stone house.'

'Thank you, Lynnie,' Isobel says seriously, and Lynnie remembers the way Cissy had been staring at Isobel. 'That means a lot to me.'

Lynnie's mother looks up when Lynnie comes into the house. 'Hanging around with Isobel again?' she says. 'I thought she'd dropped you.'

Lynnie stands up very straight. 'Isobel's my friend,' she says.

'Isobel is not your friend,' her mother says. 'I want you to understand that.'

On Saturday, Lynnie goes back to her room after breakfast, and lies down in her unmade bed. Outside it is muggy and hot. She has homework to do, and chores, but she can't force herself to get up. The sounds of the television, and of her brothers playing outside, wash over her.

A car door slams, and Lynnie gets up to look out the window—maybe Isobel is going somewhere and will want company.

But it is not Isobel. It is Ross. Lynnie watches as Ross goes up Isobel's front walk and knocks on the door. The sound of brass on brass echoes up to Lynnie's room.

Isobel's car is in the driveway, but her mother's and father's are gone. Lynnie watches as Isobel appears at the front door and lets Ross in, and then as dim shapes spread in Isobel's room.

Lynnie returns to her bed and lies there. The room bears down on her, and the noise; one of her brothers is crying. She turns violently into the pillow, clenched and stiff, and for a while she tries to cry, but every effort is false, and unsatisfactory. At certain moments she can feel her heart beating rapidly.

Later, when she gets up again, Ross's car is gone. She turns back to the roiling ocean of sheets on her own bed, and reaches out, anticipating a wave rising to her, but it is enragingly inert. She grabs the unresisting top sheet and tries to hurl it to the floor, but it folds around her before it falls, slack and disgusting. The bottom sheet comes loose more satisfyingly, tearing away from the mattress and streaming into her arms like clouds, but a tiny sound bores into the clamor in her ears, and she wheels around to see Frank standing in the doorway with his hand on the knob. He looks at her, breathing uncomfortably through his mouth, before he turns away, closing the door behind him.

That night Lynnie's mother sits in front of the television in the dark, like a priestess. The cold, pale light flattens out her face, and craterlike shadows collect around her eyes, her mouth, in the hollows of her cheeks. 'And what do you think of your employer visiting Isobel?' she says.

Across the street, Isobel's window blazes. 'He lends Isobel books,' Lynnie says.

'I see,' her mother says. 'Quite the little scholar.'

The next day, Lynnie rides her bicycle to the stone house to say that she will not be working there any longer. Pedaling with all her strength, she is not even aware of reaching the edge of town, though afterward she can see every branch of the birchwood along the old highway as it flashes by, every cinder block of the motel, even the paint peeling from its sign.

Claire stands in the doorway while Lynnie talks loudly, trying to make herself heard through the static engulfing her. She has too much homework, she tries to explain; she is sorry, but her mother needs her. Her bicycle lies where she dropped it in her frenzy to get to the door, one wheel still spinning, and while she talks she sees dim forms shifting behind Isobel's window, a brief tumbling of entwined bodies on the damp leaves under the birches, the sad, washed light inside the old motel, where a plain chest of drawers with a mirror above it stands against the wall. In the mirror is a double bed with a blue cover on which Ross lies, staring up at the ceiling.

'Yes . . .' Claire is saying, and she materializes in front of Lynnie. 'I understand . . .' From inside, behind Claire, comes the sound of Ross whistling.

It is the following week that Isobel leaves. Lynnie watches from her window as Isobel and her mother and father load up her father's car and get into it. They are taking a trip, Lynnie thinks; they are just taking a trip, but still she runs down the stairs as fast as she can, and then, as the car pulls out into the street, Isobel twists around in the back seat. Her face is waxy with an unhealthy glow, and her hair ripples out around her. Lynnie raises her hand, perhaps imperceptibly, but in any case Isobel only looks.

So nothing has to be explained to Lynnie the next day or the next or the next, when Isobel does not appear at school. And she is not puzzled by the groups of girls who huddle in the corridor whispering, or by Cissy Haddad's strange, tight greetings, or by the rumor, which begins to circulate almost immediately, of an anonymous letter to Isobel's parents.

And when, one day soon after Isobel's departure, Isobel's mother passes her on the sidewalk with nothing beyond a rapid glance of distaste, Lynnie sees in an instant what Isobel's mother must always have seen: an impassive, solid, limp-haired child, an inconveniently frequent visitor, breathing noisily, hungry for a smile—a negligible girl, utterly unlike her own daughter. And then Lynnie sees Isobel, vanishing brightly all over again as she looks back from her father's car, pressing into Lynnie's safekeeping everything that should have vanished along with her.

THE RABBIT HOLE AS LIKELY EXPLANATION

Ann Beattie

My mother does not remember being invited to my first wedding. This comes up in conversation when I pick her up from the lab, where blood has been drawn to see how she's doing on her medication. She's sitting in an orange plastic chair, giving the man next to her advice I'm not sure he asked for about how to fill out forms on a clipboard. Apparently, before I arrived, she told him that she had not been invited to either of my weddings.

'I don't know why you sent me to have my blood drawn,' she says.

'The doctor asked me to make an appointment. I did not send you.'

'Well, you were late. I sat there waiting and waiting.'

'You showed up an hour before your appointment, Ma. That's why you were there so long. I arrived fifteen minutes after the nurse called me.' It's my authoritative but cajoling voice. One tone negates the other and nothing much gets communicated.

'You sound like Perry Mason,' she says.

'Ma, there's a person trying to get around you.'

'Well, I'm very sorry if I'm holding anyone up. They can just honk and get into the other lane.'

A woman hurries around my mother in the hospital corridor, narrowly missing an oncoming wheelchair brigade: four chairs, taking up most of the hallway.

'She drives a sports car, that one,' my mother says. 'You can always tell. But look at the size of her. How does she fit in the car?'

I decide to ignore her. She has on dangling hoop earrings, and there's a scratch on her forehead and a Band-Aid on her cheekbone. Her face looks a little like an obstacle course. 'Who is going to get our car for us?' she asks.

'Who do you think? Sit in the lobby, and I'll turn in to the driveway.'

'A car makes you think about the future all the time, doesn't it?' she says. 'You have to do all that imagining: how you'll get out of the garage and into your lane and how you'll deal with all the traffic, and then one time, remember, just as you got to the driveway a man and a woman stood smack in the center, arguing, and they wouldn't move so you could pull in.'

'My life is a delight,' I say

'I don't think your new job agrees with you. You're such a beautiful seamstress—a real, old-fashioned talent—and what do you do but work on computers and leave that lovely house in the country and drive into this . . . this crap five days a week.'

'Thank you, Ma, for expressing even more eloquently than I—'

'Did you finish those swordfish costumes?'

'Starfish. I was tired, and I watched TV last night. Now, if you sit in that chair over there you'll see me pull in. It's windy. I don't want you standing outside.'

'You always have some reason why I can't be outside. You're afraid of the bees, aren't you? After that bee stung your toe when you were raking, you got desperate about yellow jackets—that's what they're called. You shouldn't have had on sandals when you were raking. Wear your hiking boots when you rake leaves, if you can't find another husband to do it for you.'

'Please stop lecturing me and—'

'Get your car! What's the worst that can happen? I have to stand up for a few minutes? It's not like I'm one of those guards outside Buckingham Palace who has to look straight ahead until he loses consciousness.'

'Okay You can stand here and I'll pull in.'

'What car do you have?'

'The same car I always have.'

'If I don't come out, come in for me.'

'Well, of course, Ma. But why wouldn't you come out?'

'SUVs can block your view. They drive right up, like they own the curb. They've got those tinted windows like Liz Taylor might be inside, or a gangster. That lovely man from Brunei—why did I say that? I must have been thinking of the Sultan of Brunei. Anyway, that man I was talking to said that in New York City he was getting out of a cab at a hotel at the same exact moment that Elizabeth Taylor got out of a limousine. He said she just kept handing little dogs out the door to everybody. The doorman. The bellhop. Her hairdresser had one under each arm. But they weren't hers—they were his own dogs! He didn't have a free hand to help Elizabeth Taylor. So that desperate man—'

'Ma, we've got to get going.'

'I'll come with you.'

'You hate elevators. The last time we tried that, you wouldn't walk—'

'Well, the stairs didn't kill me, did they?'

'I wasn't parked five flights up. Look, just stand by the window and—'

'I know what's happening. You're telling me over and over!'

I raise my hands and drop them. 'See you soon,' I say.

'Is it the green car? The black car that I always think is green?'

'Yes, Ma. My only car.'

'Well, you don't have to say it like that. I hope you never know what it's like to have small confusions about things. I understand that your car is black. It's when it's in strong sun that it looks a little green.'

'Back in five,' I say, and enter the revolving door. A man ahead of me, with both arms in casts, pushes on the glass with his forehead. We're out in a few seconds. Then he turns and looks at me, his face crimson.

'I didn't know if I pushed, whether it might make the door go too fast,' I say.

'I figured there was an explanation,' he says dully, and walks away.

The fat woman who passed us in the hallway is waiting on the sidewalk for the light to change, chatting on her cell phone. When the light blinks green, she moves forward with her head turned to the side, as if the phone clamped to her ear were leading her. She has on an ill-fitting blazer and one of those long skirts that everybody wears, with sensible shoes and a teeny purse dangling over her shoulder. 'Right behind you,' my mother says distinctly, catching up with me halfway to the opposite curb.

'Ma, there's an elevator.'

'You do enough things for your mother! It's desperate of you to do this on your lunch hour. Does picking me up mean you won't get any food? Now that you can see I'm fine, you could send me home in a cab.'

'No, no, it's no problem. But last night you asked me to drop you at the hairdresser. Wasn't that where you wanted to go?'

'Oh, I don't think that's today.'

'Yes. The appointment is in fifteen minutes. With Eloise.'

'I wouldn't want to be named for somebody who caused a commotion at the Plaza. Would you?'

'No. Ma, why don't you wait by the ticket booth, and when I drive—'

'You're full of ideas! Why won't you just let me go to the car with you?'

'In an elevator? You're going to get in an elevator? All right. Fine with me.'

'It isn't one of those glass ones, is it?'

'It does have one glass wall.'

'I'll be like those other women, then. The ones who've hit the glass ceiling.'

'Here we are.'

'It has a funny smell. I'll sit in a chair and wait for you.'

'Ma, that's back across the street. You're here now. I can introduce you to the guy over there in the booth, who collects the money. Or you can just take a deep breath and ride up with me. Okay?'

A man inside the elevator, wearing a suit, holds the door open. 'Thank you,' I say 'Ma?'

'I like your suggestion about going to that chapel,' she says. 'Pick me up there.'

The man continues to hold the door with his shoulder, his eyes cast down.

'Not a chapel, a booth. Right there? That's where you'll be?'

'Yes. Over there with that man.'

'You see the man—' I step off the elevator and the doors close behind me.

'I did see him. He said that his son was getting married in Las Vegas. And I said, "I never got to go to my daughter's weddings." And he said, "How many weddings did she have?" and of course I answered honestly. So he said, "How did that make you feel?" and I said that a dog was at one of them.'

'That was the wedding you came to. My first wedding. You don't remember putting a bow on Ebeneezer's neck? It was your idea.' I take her arm and guide her toward the elevator.

'Yes, I took it off a beautiful floral display that was meant to be inside the church, but you and that man wouldn't go inside. There was no flat place to stand. If you were a woman wearing heels, there was no place to stand anywhere, and it was going to rain.'

'It was a sunny day.'

'I don't remember that. Did Grandma make your dress?'

'No. She offered, but I wore a dress we bought in London.'

'That was just desperate. It must have broken her heart.'

'Her arthritis was so bad she could hardly hold a pen, let alone a needle.'

'You must have broken her heart.'

'Well, Ma, this isn't getting us to the car. What's the plan?'

'The Marshall Plan.'

'What?'

'The Marshall Plan. People of my generation don't scoff at that.'

'Ma, maybe we'd better give standing by the booth another try. You don't even have to speak to the man. Will you do it?'

'Do you have some objection if I get on the elevator with you?'

'No, but this time if you say you're going to do it you have to do it. We can't have people holding doors open all day. People need to get where they're going.'

'Listen to the things you say! They're so obvious, I don't know why you say them.'

She is looking through her purse. Just below the top of her head, I can see her scalp through her hair. 'Ma,' I say.

'Yes, yes, coming,' she says. 'I thought I might have the card with that hairstylist's name.'

'It's Eloise.'

'Thank you, dear. Why didn't you say so before?'

I call my brother, Tim. 'She's worse,' I say. 'If you want to visit her while she's still more or less with it, I'd suggest you book a flight.'

'You don't know,' he says. 'The fight for tenure. How much rides on this one article.'

'Tim. As your sister. I'm not talking about your problems I'm—'

'She's been going downhill for some time. And God bless you for taking care of her! She's a wonderful woman. And I give you all the credit. You're a patient person.'

'Tim. She's losing it by the day. If you care—if you care, see her now.'

'Let's be honest: I don't have deep feelings, and I wasn't her favorite. That was the problem with René: Did I have any deep feelings? I mean, kudos! Kudos to you! Do you have any understanding of why Mom and Dad got together? He was a recluse, and she was such a party animal. She never understood a person turning to books for serious study, did she? Did she? Maybe I'd be the last to know.'

'Tim, I suggest you visit before Christmas.'

'That sounds more than a little ominous. May I say that? You call when I've just gotten home from a day I couldn't paraphrase, and you tell me—as you have so many times—that she's about to die, or lose her marbles entirely and then you say—'

'Take care, Tim,' I say, and hang up.

I drive to my mother's apartment to kill time while she gets her hair done, and go into the living room and see that the plants need watering. Two are new arrivals, plants that friends brought her when she was in the hospital, having her foot operated on: a kalanchoe and a miniature chrysanthemum. I rinse out the mug she probably had her morning coffee in and fill it under the faucet. I douse the plants, refilling the mug twice. My brother is rethinking Wordsworth at a university in Ohio, and for years I have been back in this small town in Virginia where we grew up, looking out for our mother. Kudos, as he would say.

'Okay,' the doctor says. 'We've known the time was coming. It will be much better if she's in an environment where her needs are met. I'm only talking about assisted living. If it will help, I'm happy to meet with her and explain that things have reached a point where she needs a more comprehensive support system.'

'She'll say no.'

'Regardless,' he says. 'You and I know that if there was a fire she wouldn't be capable of processing the necessity of getting out. Does she eat dinner? We can't say for sure that she eats, now, can we? She needs to maintain her caloric intake. We want to allow her to avail herself of resources structured so that she can best meet her own needs.'

'She'll say no,' I say again.

'May I suggest that you let Tim operate as a support system?'

'Forget him. He's already been denied tenure twice.'

'Be that as it may if your brother knows she's not eating—'

'Do you know she's not eating?'

'Let's say she's not eating,' he says. 'It's a slippery slope.'

'Pretending that I have my brother as a "support system" has no basis in reality. You want me to admit that she's thin? Okay. She's thin.'

'Please grant my point, without—'

'Why? Because you're a doctor? Because you're pissed off that she misbehaved at some cashier's stand in a parking lot?'

'You told me she pulled the fire alarm,' he says. 'She's out of control! Face it.'

'I'm not sure,' I say, my voice quivering.

'I am. I've known you forever. I remember your mother making chocolate-chip cookies, my father always going to your house to see if she'd made the damned cookies. I know how difficult it is when a parent isn't able to take care of himself. My father lived in my house, and Donna took care of him in a way I can never thank her enough for, until he . . . well, until he died.'

'Tim wants me to move her to a cheap nursing home in Ohio.'

'Out of the question.'

'Right. She hasn't come to the point where she needs to go to Ohio. On the other hand, we should put her in the slammer here.'

'The slammer. We can't have a serious discussion if you pretend we're talking to each other in a comic strip.'

I bring my knees to my forehead, clasp my legs, and press the kneecaps hard into my eyes.

'I understand from Dr. Milrus that you're having a difficult time,' the therapist says. Her office is windowless, the chairs cheerfully mismatched. 'Why don't you fill me in?'

'Well, my mother had a stroke a year ago. It did something . . . Not that she didn't have some confusions before, but after the stroke she thought my brother was ten years old. She still sometimes says things about him that I can't make any sense of, unless I remember that she often, really quite often, thinks he's still ten. She also believes that I'm sixty. I mean, she thinks I'm only fourteen years younger than she is! And, to her, that's proof that my father had another family. Our family was an afterthought, my father had had another family and I'm a child of the first marriage. I'm sixty years old, whereas she herself was only seventy-four when she had the stroke and fell over on the golf course.'

The therapist nods.

'In any case, my brother is forty-four—about to be forty-five—and lately it's all she'll talk about.'

'Your brother's age?'

'No, the revelation. That they—you know, the other wife and children—existed. She thinks the shock made her fall down at the fourth tee.'

'Were your parents happily married?'

'I've shown her my baby album and said, "If I was some other family's child, then what is this?" And she says, "More of your father's chicanery." That is the exact word she uses. The thing is, I am not sixty. I'll be fifty-one next week.'

'It's difficult, having someone dependent upon us, isn't it?'

'Well, yes. But that's because she causes herself so much pain by thinking that my father had a previous family.'

'How do you think you can best care for your mother?'

'She pities me! She really does! She says she's met every one of them: a son and a daughter, and a woman, a wife, who looks very much like her, which seems to make her sad. Well, I guess it would make her sad. Of course it's fiction, but I've given up trying to tell her that, because in a way I think it's symbolically important. It's necessary to her that she think what she thinks, but I'm just so tired of what she thinks. Do you know what I mean?'

'Tell me about yourself,' the therapist says. 'You live alone?'

'Me? Well, at this point I'm divorced, after I made the mistake of not marrying my boyfriend, Vic, and married an old friend instead. Vic and I talked about getting married, but I was having a lot of trouble taking care of my mother, and I could never give him enough attention. When we broke up, Vic devoted all his time to his secretary's dog, Banderas. If Vic was grieving, he did it while he was at the dog park.'

'And you work at Cosmos Computer, it says here?'

'I do. They're really very family-oriented. They understand absolutely that I have to take time off to do things for my mother. I used to work at an interior-design store, and I still sew. I've just finished some starfish costumes for a friend's third-grade class.'

'Jack Milrus thinks your mother might benefit from being in assisted living.'

'I know, but he doesn't know—he really doesn't know—what it's like to approach my mother about anything.'

'What is the worst thing that might happen if you did approach your mother?'

'The worst thing? My mother turns any subject to the other family, and whatever I want is just caught up in the whirlwind of complexity of this thing I won't acknowledge, which is my father's previous life, and, you know, she omits my brother from any discussion because she thinks he's a ten-year-old child.'

'You feel frustrated.'

'Is there any other way to feel?'

'You could say to yourself, "My mother has had a stroke and has certain confusions that I can't do anything about."'

'You don't understand. It is absolutely necessary that I acknowledge this other family. If I don't, I've lost all credibility.'

The therapist shifts in her seat. 'May I make a suggestion?' she says. 'This is your mother's problem, not yours. You understand something that your mother, whose brain has been affected by a stroke, cannot understand. Just as you would guide a child, who does not know how to function in the world, you are now in a position where—whatever your mother believes—you must nevertheless do what is best for her.'

'You need a vacation,' Jack Milrus says. 'If I weren't on call this weekend, I'd suggest that you and Donna and I go up to Washington and see that show at the Corcoran where all the figures walk out of the paintings.'

'I'm sorry I keep bothering you with this. I know I have to make a decision. It's just that when I went back to look at the Oaks and that woman had mashed an eclair into her face—'

'It's funny. Just look at it as funny. Kids make a mess. Old people make a mess. Some old biddy pushed her nose into a pastry.'

'Right,' I say, draining my gin and tonic. We are in his backyard. Inside, Donna is making her famous osso buco. 'You know, I wanted to ask you something. Sometimes she says "desperate." She uses the word when you wouldn't expect to hear it.'

'Strokes,' he says.

'But is she trying to say what she feels?'

'Does it come out like a hiccup or something?' He pulls up a weed.

'No, she just says it, instead of another word.'

He looks at the long taproot of the dandelion he's twisted up. 'The South,' he says. 'These things have a horribly long growing season.' He drops it in a wheelbarrow filled with limp things raked up from the yard. 'I am desperate to banish dandelions,' he says.

'No, she wouldn't use it like that. She'd say something like, "Oh, it was desperate of you to ask me to dinner."'

'It certainly was. You weren't paying any attention to me on the telephone.'

'Just about ready!' Donna calls out the kitchen window. Jack raises a hand in acknowledgment. He says, 'Donna's debating whether to tell you that she saw Vic and Banderas having a fight near the dog park. Vic was knocking Banderas on the snout with a baseball cap, Donna says, and Banderas had squared off and was showing teeth. Groceries all over the street.'

'I'm amazed. I thought Banderas could do no wrong.'

'Well, things change.'

In the yard next door, the neighbor's strange son faces the street lamp and, excruciatingly slowly, begins his many evening sun salutations.

Cora, my brother's friend, calls me at midnight. I am awake, watching *Igby Goes Down* on the VCR. Susan Sarandon, as the dying mother, is a wonder. Three friends sent me the tape for my birthday. The only other time such a thing has happened was years ago, when four friends sent me *Play It as It Lays* by Joan Didion.

'Tim thinks that he and I should do our share and have Mom here for a vacation, which we could do in November, when the college has a reading break,' Cora says. 'I would move into Tim's condominium, if it wouldn't offend Mom.'

'That's nice of you,' I say. 'But you know that she thinks Tim is ten years old? I'm not sure that she'd be willing to fly to Ohio to have a ten-year-old take care of her.'

'What?'

'Tim hasn't told you about this? He wrote her a letter, recently, and she saved it to show me how good his penmanship was.'

'Well, when she gets here she'll see that he's a grown-up.'

'She might think it's a Tim impostor, or something. She'll talk to you constantly about our father's first family.'

'I still have some Ativan from when a root canal had to be redone,' Cora says.

'Okay, look—I'm not trying to discourage you. But I'm also not convinced that she can make the trip alone. Would Tim consider driving here to pick her up?'

'Gee. My nephew is eleven, and he's been back and forth to the West Coast several times.'

'I don't think this is a case of packing snacks in her backpack and giving her a puzzle book for the plane,' I say.

'Oh, I am not trying to infantilize your mother. Quite the opposite: I think that if she suspects there's doubt about whether she can do it on her own she might not rise to the occasion, but if we just . . .'

'People never finish their sentences anymore,' I say.

'Oh, gosh, I can finish,' Cora says. 'I mean, I was saying that she'll take care of herself if we assume that she *can* take care of herself.'

'Would a baby take care of itself if we assumed that it could?'

'Oh, my goodness!' Cora says. 'Look what time it is! I thought it was nine o'clock! Is it after midnight?'

'Twelve-fifteen.'

'My watch stopped! I'm looking at the kitchen clock and it says twelve-ten.'

I have met Cora twice: once she weighed almost two hundred pounds, and the other time she'd been on Atkins and weighed a hundred and forty. *Bride's* magazine was in the car when she picked me up at the airport. During the last year, however, her dreams have not been fulfilled.

'Many apologies,' Cora says.

'Listen,' I say. 'I was awake. No need to apologize. But I don't feel that we've settled anything.'

'I'm going to have Tim call you tomorrow, and I am really sorry!'

'Cora, I didn't mean anything personal when I said that people don't finish sentences anymore. I don't finish my own.'

'You take care, now!' she says, and hangs up.

'She's where?'

'Right here in my office. She was on a bench in Lee Park. Someone saw her talking to a woman who was drunk—a street person—just before the cops arrived. The woman was throwing bottles she'd gotten out of a restaurant's recycling at the statue. Your mother said she was keeping score. The woman was winning, the statue losing. The woman had blood all over her face, so eventually somebody called the cops.'

'Blood all over her face?'

'She'd cut her fingers picking up glass after she threw it. It was the other woman who was bloody.'

'Oh, God, my mother's okay?'

'Yes, but we need to act. I've called the Oaks. They can't do anything today, but tomorrow they can put her in a semiprivate for three nights, which they aren't allowed to do, but never mind. Believe me: once she's in there, they'll find a place.'

'I'll be right there.'

'Hold on,' he says. 'We need to have a plan. I don't want her at your place: I want her hospitalized tonight, and I want an MRI. Tomorrow morning, if there's no problem, you can take her to the Oaks.'

'What's the point of scaring her to death? Why does she have to be in a hospital?'

'She's very confused. It won't be any help if you don't get to sleep tonight.'

'I feel like we should—'

'You feel like you should protect your mother, but that's not really possible, is it? She was picked up in Lee Park. Fortunately she had my business card and her beautician's card clipped to a shopping list that contains—it's right in front of me—items such as Easter eggs and arsenic.'

'Arsenic? Was she going to poison herself?'

There is a moment of silence. 'Let's say she was,' he says, 'for the sake of argument. Now, come and pick her up, and we can get things rolling.'

Tim and Cora were getting married by a justice of the peace at approximately the same time that 'Mom' was tracking bottles in Lee Park; they converge on the hospital room with Donna Milrus, who whispers apologetically that her husband is 'playing doctor' and avoiding visiting hours.

Cora's wedding bouquet is in my mother's water pitcher. Tim cracks his knuckles and clears his throat repeatedly. 'They got upset that I'd been sitting in the park. Can you imagine?' my mother says suddenly to the assembled company. 'Do you think we're going to have many more of these desperate fall days?'

The next morning, only Tim and I are there to get her into his rental car and take her to the Oaks. Our mother sits in front, her purse on her lap, occasionally saying something irrational, which I finally figure out is the result of her reading vanity license plates aloud.

From the backseat, I look at the town like a visitor. There's much too much traffic. People's faces inside their cars surprise me: no one over the age of twenty seems to have a neutral, let alone happy, expression. Men with jutting jaws and women squinting hard pass by. I find myself wondering why more of them don't wear sunglasses, and whether that might not help. My thoughts drift: the Gucci sunglasses I lost in London; the time I dressed as a skeleton for Halloween. In childhood, I appeared on Halloween as Felix the Cat, as Jiminy Cricket (I still have the cane, which I often pull out of the closet, mistaking it for an umbrella), and as a tomato.

'You know,' my mother says to my brother, 'your father had an entire family before he met us. He never mentioned them, either. Wasn't that cruel? If we'd met them, we might have liked them, and vice versa. Your sister gets upset if I say that's the case, but everything you read now suggests that it's better if the families meet. You have a ten-year-old brother from that first family. You're too old to be jealous of a child, aren't you? So there's no reason why you wouldn't get along.'

'Mom,' he says breathlessly.

'Your sister tells me every time we see each other that she's fifty-one. She's preoccupied with age. Being around an old person can do that. I'm old, but I forget to think about myself that way. Your sister is in the backseat right now thinking about mortality, mark my words.'

My brother's knuckles are white on the wheel.

'Are we going to the hairdresser?' she says suddenly. She taps the back of her neck. Her fingers move up until they encounter small curls. When Tim realizes that I'm not going to answer, he says, 'Your hair looks lovely, Mom. Don't worry about it.'

'Well, I always like to be punctual when I have an appointment,' she says.

I think how strange it is that I was never dressed up as Cleopatra, or as a ballerina. What was wrong with me that I wanted to be a tomato?

'Ma, on Halloween, was I ever dressed as a girl?'

In the mirror, my brother's eyes dart to mine. For a second, I remember Vic's eyes as he checked my reactions in the rearview mirror, those times I had my mother sit up front so the two of them could converse more easily.

'Well,' my mother says, 'I think one year you thought about being a nurse, but Joanne Willoughby was going to be a nurse. I was in the grocery store, and there was Mrs. Willoughby, fingering the costume we'd thought about the night before. It was wrong of me not to be more decisive. I think that's what made you impulsive as a grown-up.'

'You think I'm impulsive? I think of myself as somebody who never does anything unexpected.'

'I wouldn't say that,' my mother says. 'Look at that man you married when you didn't even really know him. The first husband. And then you married that man you knew way back in high school. It makes me wonder if you didn't inherit some of your father's fickle tendencies.'

'Let's not fight,' my brother says.

'What do you think other mothers would say if I told them both my children got married without inviting me to their weddings? I think some of them would think that must say something about me. Maybe it was my inadequacy that made your father consider us second-best. Tim, men tell other men things. Did your father tell you about the other family?'

Tim tightens his grip on the wheel. He doesn't answer. Our mother pats his arm. She says, 'Tim wanted to be Edgar Bergen one year. Do you remember? But your father pointed out that we'd have to buy one of those expensive Charlie McCarthy dolls, and he wasn't about to do that. Little did we know, he had a whole other family to support.'

Everyone at the Oaks is referred to formally as 'Mrs.' You can tell when the nurses really like someone, because they refer to her by the less formal 'Miz.'

Miz Banks is my mother's roommate. She has a tuft of pure white hair that makes her look like an exotic bird. She is ninety-nine.

'Today is Halloween, I understand,' my mother says. 'Are we going to have a party?'

The nurse smiles. 'Whether or not it's a special occasion, we always have a lovely midday meal,' she says. 'And we hope the family will join us.'

'It's suppertime?' Miz Banks says.

'No, ma'am, it's only ten a.m. right now,' the nurse says loudly. 'But we'll come get you for the midday meal, as we always do.'

'Oh, God,' Tim says. 'What do we do now?'

The nurse frowns. 'Excuse me?' she says.

'I thought Dr. Milrus was going to be here,' he says. He looks around the room, as if Jack Milrus might be hiding somewhere. Not possible, unless he's wedged himself behind the desk that is sitting at an odd angle in the corner. The nurse follows his gaze and says, 'Miz Banks's nephew has feng-shuied her part of the room.'

Nearest the door—in our part of the room—there is white wicker furniture. Three pink bears teeter on a mobile hung from an air vent in the ceiling. On a bulletin board is a color picture of a baby with one tooth, grinning. Our mother has settled into a yellow chair and looks quite small. She eyes everyone, and says nothing.

'Would this be a convenient time to sign some papers?' the nurse asks. It is the second time that she has mentioned this—both times to my brother, not me.

'Oh, my God,' he says. 'How can this be happening?' He is not doing very well.

'Let's step outside and let the ladies get to know each other,' the nurse says. She takes his arm and leads him through the door. 'We don't want to be negative,' I hear her say.

I sit on my mother's bed. My mother looks at me blankly. It is as if she doesn't recognize me in this context. She says, finally, 'Whose Greek fisherman's cap is that?'

She is pointing to the Sony Walkman that I placed on the bed, along with an overnight bag and some magazines.

'That's a machine that plays music, Ma.'

'No, it isn't,' she says. 'It's a Greek fisherman's cap.'

I pick it up and hold it out to her. I press 'play,' and music can be heard through the dangling earphones. We both look at it as if it were the most curious thing in the world. I adjust the volume to low and put the earphones on her head. She closes her eyes. Finally she says, 'Is this the beginning of the Halloween party?'

'I threw you off, talking about Halloween,' I say. 'Today's just a day in early November.'

'Thanksgiving is next,' she says, opening her eyes.

'I suppose it is,' I say. I notice that Miz Banks's head has fallen forward.

'Is that thing over there the turkey?' my mother says, pointing.

'It's your roommate.'

'I was joking,' she says.

I realize that I am clenching my hands only when I unclench them. I try to smile, but I can't hold up the corners of my mouth.

My mother arranges the earphones around her neck as if they were a stethoscope. 'If I'd let you be what you wanted that time, maybe I'd have my own private nurse now. Maybe I wasn't so smart, after all.'

'This is just temporary,' I lie.

'Well, I don't want to go to my grave thinking you blame me for things that were out of my control. It's perfectly possible that your father was a bigamist. My mother told me not to marry him.'

'Gramma told you not to marry Daddy?'

'She was a smart old fox. She sniffed him out.'

'But he never did what you accuse him of. He came home from the war and married you, and you had us. Maybe we confused you by growing up so fast or something. I don't want to make you mad by mentioning my age, but maybe all those years that we were a family so long ago, were like one long Halloween: we were costumed as children, and then we outgrew the costumes and we were grown.'

She looks at me. 'That's an interesting way to put it,' she says.

'And the other family—maybe it's like the mixup between the man dreaming he's a butterfly or the butterfly dreaming he's a man. Maybe you were confused after your stroke, or it came to you in a dream and it seemed real, the way dreams sometimes linger. Maybe you couldn't understand how we'd all aged, so you invented us again as young people. And for some reason Tim got frozen in time. You said the other wife looked like you. Well, maybe she *was* you.'

'I don't know,' my mother says slowly 'I think your father was just attracted to the same type of woman.'

'But nobody ever met these people. There's no marriage license. He was married to you for almost fifty years. Don't you see that what I'm saying is a more likely explanation?'

'You really do remind me of that detective. Desperate Mason. You get an idea, and your eyes get big, just the way his do. I feel like you're about to lean into the witness stand.'

Jack Milrus, a towel around his neck, stands in the doorway. 'In a million years, you'll never guess why I'm late,' he says. 'A wheel came off a truck and knocked my car off the road, into a pond. I had to get out through the window and wade back to the highway.'

A nurse comes up behind him with more towels and some dry clothes.

'Maybe it's just raining out, but it feels to him like he was in a pond,' my mother says, winking at me.

'You understand!' I say.

'Everybody has his little embellishments,' my mother says. 'There wouldn't be any books to read to children and there would be precious few to read to adults if storytellers weren't allowed a few embellishments.'

'Ma! That is absolutely true.'

'Excuse me while I step into the bathroom and change my clothes.'

'Humor him,' my mother whispers to me behind her hand. 'When he comes out, he'll think he's a doctor, but you and I will know that Jack is only hoping to go to medical school.'

You think you understand the problem you're facing, only to find out there is another, totally unexpected problem.

There is much consternation and confusion among the nurses when Tim disappears and has not reappeared after nearly an hour. Jack Milrus weighs in: Tim is immature and irresponsible, he says. Quite possibly a much more severe problem than anyone suspected. My mother suggests slyly that Tim decided to fall down a rabbit hole and have an adventure. She says, 'The rabbit hole's a more likely explanation,' smiling smugly.

Stretched out in bed, her tennis shoes neatly arranged on the floor, my mother says, 'He always ran away from difficult situations. Look at you and Jack, with those astonished expressions on your faces! Mr. Mason will find him,' she adds. Then she closes her eyes.

'You see?' Jack Milrus whispers, guiding me out of the room. 'She's adjusted beautifully. And it's hardly a terrible place, is it?' He answers his own question: 'No, it isn't.'

'What happened to the truck?' I ask.

'Driver apologized. Stood on the shoulder talking on his cell phone. Three cop cars were there in about three seconds. I got away by pointing to my MD plates.'

'Did Tim tell you he just got married?'

'I heard that. During visiting hours, his wife took Donna aside to give her the happy news and to say that we weren't to slight him in any way, because he was ready, willing, and able—that was the way she said it to Donna—to assume responsibility for his mother's well-being. She also went to the hospital this morning just after you left and caused a commotion because they'd thrown away her wedding bouquet.'

The phone call the next morning comes as a surprise. Like a telemarketer, Tim seems to be reading from a script: 'Our relationship may be strained beyond redemption. When I went to the nurses' desk and saw that you had included personal information about me on a form you had apparently already filled out elsewhere, in collusion with your doctor friend, I realized that you were yet again condescending to me and subjecting me to humiliation. I was very hurt that you had written both of our names as "Person to be notified in an emergency," but then undercut that by affixing a Post-it note saying, "Call me first. He's hard to find." How would you know? How would you know what my teaching schedule is when you have never expressed the slightest interest? How do you know when I leave my house in the morning and when I return at night? You've always wanted to come first. It is also my personal opinion that you okayed the throwing out of my wife's nosegay, which was on loan to Mom. So go ahead and okay everything. Have her euthanized, if that's what you want to do, and see if I care. Do you realize that you barely took an insincere second to congratulate me and my wife? If you have no respect for me, I nevertheless expect a modicum of respect for my wife.'

Of course, he does not know that I'm joking when I respond, 'No, thanks. I'm very happy with my AT&T service.'

When he slams down the phone, I consider returning to bed and curling into a fetal position, though at the same time I realize that I cannot miss one more day of work. I walk into the bathroom, wearing Vic's old bathrobe, which I hang on the back of the door. I shower and brush my teeth. I call the Oaks, to see if my mother slept through the night. She did, and is playing bingo. I dress quickly, comb my hair, pick up my purse and keys, and open the front door. A FedEx letter leans against the railing, with Cora's name and return address on it. I take a step back, walk inside, and open it. There is a sealed envelope with my name on it. I stare at it.

The phone rings. It is Mariah Roberts, 2003 Virginia Teacher of the Year for Grade Three, calling to say that she is embarrassed but it has been pointed out to her that children dressed as starfish and sea horses, dancing in front of dangling nets, represent species that are endangered, and often 'collected' or otherwise 'preyed upon,' and that she wants to reimburse me for materials, but she most certainly does not want me to sew starfish costumes. I look across the bedroom, to the pointy costumes piled on a chair, only the top one still awaiting its zipper. They suddenly look sad—deflated, more than slightly absurd. I can't think what to say and am surprised to realize that I'm too choked up to speak. 'Not to worry,' I finally say. 'Is the whole performance canceled?' 'It's being reconceived,' she says. 'We want sea life that is empowered.' 'Barracuda?' I say. 'I'll run that by them,' she says.

When we hang up, I continue to examine the sealed envelope. Then I pick up the phone and dial. To my surprise, Vic answers on the second ring.

'Hey, I've been thinking about you,' he says. 'Really. I was going to call and see how you were doing. How's your mother?'

'Fine,' I say. 'There's something that's been bothering me. Can I ask you a quick question?'

'Shoot.'

'Donna Milrus said she saw you and Banderas having a fight.'

'Yeah,' he says warily.

'It's none of my business, but what caused it?'

'Jumped on the car and his claws scratched the paint.'

'You said he was the best-trained dog in the world.'

'I know it. He always waits for me to open the door, but that day, you tell me. He jumped up and clawed the hell out of the car. If he'd been scared by something, I might have made an allowance. But there was nobody. And then as soon as I swatted him, who gets out of her Lexus but Donna Milrus, and suddenly the grocery bag slips out of my hands and splits open ... all this stuff rolling toward her, and she points the toe of one of those expensive shoes she wears and stops an orange.'

'I can't believe that about you and Banderas. It shakes up all my assumptions.'

'That's what happened,' he says.

'Thanks for the information.'

'Hey, wait. I really was getting ready to call you. I was going to say maybe we could get together and take your mother to the Italian place for dinner.'

'That's nice,' I say, 'but I don't think so.'

There is a moment's silence.

'Bye, Vic,' I say.

'Wait,' he says quickly. 'You really called about the dog?'

'Uh-huh. You talked about him a lot, you know. He was a big part of our lives.'

'There was and is absolutely nothing between me and my secretary, if that's what you think,' he says. 'She's dating a guy who works in Baltimore. I've got this dream that she'll marry him and leave the dog behind, because he's got cats.'

'I hope for your sake that happens. I've got to go to work.'

'How about coffee?' he says.

'Sure,' I say. 'We'll talk again.'

'What's wrong with coffee right now?'

'Don't you have a job?'

'I thought we were going to be friends. Wasn't that your idea? Ditch me because I'm ten years younger than you, because you're such an ageist, but we can still be great friends, you can even marry some guy and we'll still be friends, but you never call, and when you do it's with some question about a dog you took a dislike to before you ever met him, because you're a jealous woman. The same way you can like somebody's kid, and not like them, I like the dog.'

'You love the dog.'

'Okay, so I'm a little leery about that word. Can I come over for coffee tonight, if you don't have time now?'

'Only if you agree in advance to do me a favor.'

'I agree to do you a favor.'

'Don't you want to know what it is?'

'No.'

'It calls on one of your little-used skills.'

'Sex?'

'No, not sex. Paper cutting.'

'What do you want me to cut up that you can't cut up?'

'A letter from my sister-in-law.'

'You don't have a sister-in-law. Wait: Your brother got married? I'm amazed. I thought he didn't much care for women.'

'You think Tim is gay?'

'I didn't say that. I always thought of the guy as a misanthrope. I'm just saying I'm surprised. Why don't you rip up the letter yourself?'

'Vic, don't be obtuse. I want you to do one of those cutout things with it. I want you to take what I'm completely sure is something terrible and transform it. You know—that thing your grandmother taught you.'

'Oh,' he says. 'You mean, like the fence and the arbor with the vine?'

'Well, I don't know. It doesn't have to be that.'

'I haven't practiced in a while,' he says. 'Did you have something particular in mind?'

'I haven't read it,' I say. 'But I think I know what it says. So how about a skeleton with something driven through its heart?'

'I'm afraid my grandmother's interest was landscape.'

'I bet you could do it.'

'Sailboat riding on waves?'

'My idea is better.'

'But out of my field of expertise.'

'Tell me the truth,' I say. 'I can handle it. Did you buy groceries to cook that woman dinner?'

'No,' he says. 'Also, remember that you dumped me, and then for a finale you married some jerk so I'd be entitled to do anything I wanted. Then you call and want me to make a corpse with a stake through its heart because you don't like your new sister-in-law, either. Ask yourself: Am I so normal myself?'

Banderas nearly topples me, then immediately begins sniffing, dragging the afghan off the sofa. He rolls on a corner as if it were carrion, snorting as he rises and charges toward the bedroom.

'That's the letter?' Vic says, snatching the envelope from the center of the table. He rips it open. 'Dear Sister-in-law,' he reads, holding the paper above his head as I run toward him. He looks so different with his stubbly beard, and I realize with a pang that I don't recognize the shirt he's wearing. He starts again: 'Dear Sister-in-law.' He whirls sideways, the paper clutched tightly in his hand. 'I know that Tim will be speaking to you, but I wanted to personally send you this note. I think that families have differences, but everyone's viewpoint is important. I would very much like—' He whirls again, and this time Banderas runs into the fray, rising up on his back legs as if he, too, wanted the letter.

'Let the dog eat it! Let him eat the thing if you have to read it out loud!' I say.

'—to invite you for Thanksgiving dinner, and also to offer you some of our frequent-flier miles, if that might be helpful, parenthesis, though it may be a blackout period, end paren.'

Vic looks at me. 'Aren't you embarrassed at your reaction to this woman? Aren't you?'

The dog leaps into the afghan and rolls again, catching a claw in the weave. Vic and I stand facing each other. I am panting, too shocked to speak.

'Please excuse Tim for disappearing when I came to the door of the Oaks. I was there to see if I could help. He said my face provoked a realization of his newfound strength.' Vic sighs. He says, 'Just what I was afraid of—some New Ager as crazy as your brother. "I'm sure you understand that I was happy to know that I could be helpful to Tim in this trying time. We must all put the past behind us and celebrate our personal Thanksgiving, parenthesis, our wedding, end paren, and I am sure that everything can be put right when we get together. Fondly, your sister-in-law, Cora."'

There are tears in my eyes. The afghan is going to need major repair. Vic has brought his best friend into my house to destroy it, and all he will do is hold the piece of paper above his head, as if he'd just won a trophy.

'I practiced this afternoon,' he says finally, lowering his arm. 'I can do either a train coming through the mountains or a garland of roses with a butterfly on top.'

'Great,' I say, sitting on the floor, fighting back tears. 'The butterfly can be dreaming it's a man, or the man can be dreaming he's . . .' I change my mind about what I was going to say: 'Or the man can be dreaming he's desperate.'

Vic doesn't hear me; he's busy trying to get Banderas to drop a starfish costume he's capering with.

'Why do you think it would work?' I say to Vic. 'We were never right for each other. I'm in my fifties. It would be my third marriage.'

Carefully, he creases the letter a second, then a third time. He lifts the scissors out of their small plastic container, fumbling awkwardly with his big fingers. He frowns in concentration and begins to cut. Eventually, from the positive cuttings, I figure out that he's decided on the tram motif. Cutting air away to expose a puff of steam, he says, 'Let's take it slow, then. You could invite me to go with you to Thanksgiving.'

THE MIRACLE AT BALLINSPITTLE

T. C. Boyle

There they are, the holybugs, widows in their weeds and fat-ankled mothers with palsied children, all lined up before the snotgreen likeness of the Virgin, and McGahee and McCarey among them. This statue, alone among all the myriad three-foot-high snotgreen likenesses of the Virgin cast in plaster by Finnbar Finnegan & Sons, Cork City, was seen one grim March afternoon some years back to move its limbs ever so slightly, as if seized suddenly by the need of a good sinew-cracking stretch. Nuala Nolan, a young girl in the throes of Lenten abnegation, was the only one to witness the movement—a gentle beckoning of the statue's outthrust hand—after a fifteen-day vigil during which she took nothing into her body but Marmite and soda water. Ever since, the place has been packed with tourists.

Even now, in the crowd of humble countrymen in shit-smeared boots and knit skullcaps, McGahee can detect a certain number of Teutonic or Manhattanite faces above cableknit sweaters and pendant cameras. Drunk and in debt, on the run from a bad marriage, two DWI convictions, and the wheezy expiring gasps of his moribund mother, McGahee pays them no heed. His powers of concentration run deep. He is forty years old, as lithe as a boxer though he's done no hard physical labor since he took a construction job between semesters at college twenty years back, and he has the watery eyes and doleful, doglike expression of the saint. Twelve hours ago he was in New York, at Paddy Flynn's, pouring out his heart and enumerating his woes for McCarey, when McCarey said, 'Fuck it, let's go to Ireland.' And now here he is at Ballinspittle, wearing the rumpled Levi's and Taiwanese sportcoat he'd pulled on in his apartment yesterday morning, three hours off the plane from Kennedy and flush with warmth from the venerable Irish distillates washing through his veins.

McCarey—plump. stately McCarey—stands beside him, bleary-eyed and impatient, disdainfully scanning the crowd. Heads are bowed. Infants snuffle. From somewhere in the distance come the bleat of a lamb and the mechanical call of the cuckoo. McGahee checks his watch: they've been here seven minutes already and nothing's happened. His mind begins to wander. He's thinking about orthodontia—thinking an orthodontist could make a fortune in this country—when he looks up and spots her, Nuala Nolan, a scarecrow of a girl, an anorectic, bones-in-a-sack sort of girl, kneeling in front of the queue and reciting the Mysteries in a voice parched for food and drink. Since the statue moved she has stuck to her diet of Marmite and soda water until the very synapses of her brain have become encrusted with salt and she raves like a mariner lost at sea. McGahee regards her with awe. A light rain has begun to fall.

And then suddenly, before he knows what's come over him, McGahee goes limp. He feels lightheaded, transported, feels himself sinking into another realm, as helpless and cut adrift as when Dr. Beibelman put him under for his gallbladder operation. He breaks out in a sweat. His vision goes dim. The murmur of the crowd, the call of the cuckoo, and the bleat of the lamb all meld into a single sound—a voice—and that voice, ubiquitous, timeless, all-embracing, permeates his every cell and fiber. It seems to speak through him, through the broad-beamed old hag beside him, through McCarey, Nuala Nolan, the stones and birds and fishes of the sea. 'Davey,' the voice calls in the sweetest tones he ever heard, 'Davey McGahee, come to me, come to my embrace.'

As one, the crowd parts, a hundred stupefied faces turned toward him, and there she is, the Virgin, snotgreen no longer but radiant with the aquamarine of actuality, her eyes glowing, arms beckoning. McGahee casts a quick glance around him. McCarey looks as if he's been punched in the gut, Nuala Nolan's skeletal face is clenched with hate and jealousy, the humble countrymen and farmwives stare numbly from him to the statue and back again . . . and then, as if in response to a subconscious signal, they drop to their knees in a human wave so that only he, Davey McGahee, remains standing. 'Come to me,' the figure implores, and slowly, as if his feet were encased in cement, his head reeling and his stomach sour, he begins to move forward, his own arms outstretched in ecstasy.

The words of his catechism, forgotten these thirty years, echo in his head: 'Mother Mary, Mother of God, pray for us sinners now and at the hour of our—'

'Yesssss!' the statue suddenly shrieks, the upturned palm curled into a fist, a fist like a weapon. 'And you think it's as easy as that, do you?'

McGahee stops cold, hovering over the tiny effigy like a giant, a troglodyte, a naked barbarian. Three feet high, grotesque, shaking its fists up at him, the thing changes before his eyes. Gone is the beatific smile, gone the grace of the eyes and the faintly mad and indulgent look of the transported saint. The face is a gargoyle's, a shrew's, and the voice, sharpening, probing like a dental tool, suddenly bears an uncanny resemblance to his ex-wife's. 'Sinner!' the gargoyle hisses. 'Fall on your knees!'

The crowd gasps. McGahee, his bowels turned to ice, pitches forward into the turf. 'No, no, no!' he cries, clutching at the grass and squeezing his eyes shut. 'Hush,' a new voice whispers in his ear, 'look. You must look.' There's a hand on his neck, bony and cold. He winks open an eye. The statue is gone and Nuala Nolan leans over him, her hair gone in patches, the death's-head of her face and suffering eyes, her breath like the loam of the grave. 'Look, up there,' she whispers.

High above them, receding into the heavens like a kite loosed from a string, is the statue. Its voice comes to him faint and distant— 'Behold ... now ... your sins ... and excesses ...'—and then it dwindles away like a fading echo.

Suddenly, behind the naked pedestal, a bright sunlit vista appears, grapevines marshaled in rows, fields of barley, corn, and hops, and then, falling from the sky with thunderous crashes, a succession of vats, kegs, hogsheads, and buckets mounting up in the foreground as if on some phantom pier piled high with freight. *Boom, boom, ka-boom, boom,* down they come till the vista is obscured and the kegs mount to the tops of the trees. McGahee pushes himself up to his knees and looks around him. The crowd is regarding him steadily, jaws set, the inclemency of the hanging judge sunk into their eyes. McCarey, kneeling too now and looking as if he's just lurched up out of a drunken snooze to find himself on a subway car on another planet, has gone steely-eyed with the rest of them. And Nuala Nolan, poised over him, grins till the long naked roots of her teeth gleam beneath the skirts of her rotten gums.

'Your drinking!' shrieks a voice from the back of the throng, his wife's voice, and there she is, Fredda, barefoot and in a snotgreen robe and hood, wafting her way through the crowd and pointing her long accusatory finger at his poor miserable shrinking self. 'Every drop,' she booms, and the vast array of vats and kegs and tumblers swivels to reveal the signs hung from their sweating slats—GIN, BOURBON, BEER, WHISKEY, SCHNAPPS, PERNOD—and the crowd lets out a long exhalation of shock and lament.

The keg of gin. Tall it is and huge, its contents vaguely sloshing. You could throw cars into it, buses, tractor trailers. But no, never, he couldn't have drunk that much gin, no man could. And beside it the beer, frothy and bubbling, a cauldron the size of a rest home. 'No!' he cries in protest. 'I don't even like the taste of the stuff.'

'Yes, yes, yes,' chants a voice beside him. The statue is back, Fredda gone. It speaks in a voice he recognizes, though the wheezy, rheumy deathbed rasp of it has been wiped clean. 'Ma?' he says, turning to the thing.

Three feet tall, slick as a seal, the robes flowing like the sea, the effigy looks up at him out of his mother's face in miniature. 'I warned you,' the voice leaps out at him, high and querulous, 'out behind the 7-11 with Ricky Reitbauer and that criminal Tommy Capistrano, cheap wine and all the rest.'

'But Mom, *Pernod*?' He peers into the little pot of it, a pot so small you couldn't boil a good Safeway chicken in it. There it is. Pernod. Milky and unclean. It turns his stomach even to look at it.

'Your liver, son,' the statue murmurs with a resignation that brings tears to his eyes, 'just look at it.'

He feels a prick in his side and there it is, his liver—a poor piece of cheesy meat, stippled and striped and purple—dangling from the plaster fingers. 'God,' he moans, 'God Almighty.'

'Rotten as your soul,' the statue says.

McGahee, still on his knees, begins to blubber. Meaningless slips of apology issue from his lips—'I didn't mean . . . it wasn't . . . how could I know?'—when all of a sudden the statue shouts 'Drugs!' with a voice of iron.

Immediately the scene changes. The vats are gone, replaced with bales of marijuana, jars of pills in every color imaginable, big, overbrimming tureens of white powder, a drugstore display of airplane glue. In the background, grinning Laotians, Peruvian peasants with hundreds of scrawny children propped like puppets on their shoulders.

'But, but—' McGahee stutters, rising to his feet to protest, but the statue doesn't give him a chance, won't, can't, and the stentorian voice—his wife's, his mother's, no one's and everyone's, he even detects a trace of his high-school principal's in there—the stentorian voice booms: 'Sins of the Flesh!'

He blinks his eyes and the Turks and their bales are gone. The backdrop now is foggy and obscure, dim as the mists of memory. The statue is silent. Gradually the poor sinner becomes aware of a salacious murmur, an undercurrent of moaning and panting, and the lubricious thwack and whap of the act itself. 'Davey,' a girl's voice calls, tender, pubescent, 'I'm scared.' And then his own voice, bland and reassuring: 'I won't stick it in, Cindy, I won't, I swear . . . or maybe, maybe just . . . just an inch . . .'

The mist lifts and there they are, in teddies and negligees, in garter belts and sweat socks, naked and wet and kneading their breasts like dough. 'Davey,' they moan, 'oh, Davey, fuck me, fuck me, fuck me,' and he knows them all, from Cindy Lou Harris and Betsy Butler in the twelfth grade to Fredda in her youth and the sad and ugly faces of his one-night stands and chance encounters, right on up to the bug-eyed woman with the doleful breasts he'd diddled in the rest room on the way out from Kennedy. And worse. Behind them, milling around in a mob that stretches to the horizon, are all the women and girls he'd ever lusted after, even for a second, the twitching behinds and airy bosoms he'd stopped to admire on the street, the legs he'd wanted to stroke and lips to press to his own. McCarey's wife, Beatrice, is there and Fred Dolby's thirteen-year-old daughter, the woman with the freckled bosom who used to sunbathe in the tiger-skin bikini next door when they lived in Irvington, the girl from the typing pool, and the outrageous little shaven-headed vixen from Domino's Pizza. And as if that weren't enough, there's the crowd from books and films too. Linda Lovelace, Sophia Loren, Emma Bovary, the Sabine women and Lot's wife, even Virginia Woolf with her puckered foxy face and the eyes that seem to beg for a good slap on the bottom. It's too much—all of them murmuring his name like a crazed chorus of Molly Blooms, and yes, she's there too—and the mob behind him hissing, hissing.

He glances at the statue. The plaster lip curls in disgust, the adamantine hand rises and falls, and the women vanish. 'Gluttony!' howls the Virgin and all at once he's surrounded by forlornly mooing herds of cattle, sad-eyed pigs and sheep, funereal geese and clucking

ducks, a spill of scuttling crabs and claw-waving lobsters, even the odd
dog or two he'd inadvertently wolfed down in Tijuana burritos and
Cantonese stir-fry. And the scales—scales the size of the Washington
Monument—sunk under pyramids of ketchup, peanut butter, tortilla
chips, truckloads of potatoes, onions, avocados, peppermint candies
and after-dinner mints, half-eaten burgers and fork-scattered peas, the
whole slithering wasteful cornucopia of his secret and public
devouring. 'Moooooo,' accuse the cows. 'Stinker!' 'Pig!' 'Glutton!' cry
voices from the crowd.

Prostrate now, the cattle hanging over him, letting loose with their
streams of urine and clots of dung, McGahee shoves his fists into his
eyes and cries out for mercy. But there is no mercy. The statue, wicked
and glittering, its tiny twisted features clenching and unclenching like
the balls of its fists, announces one after another the unremitting
parade of his sins: 'Insults to Humanity, False Idols, Sloth, Unclean
Thoughts, The Kicking of Dogs and Cheating at Cards!'

His head reels. He won't look. The voices cry out in hurt and
laceration and he feels the very ground give way beneath him. The rest,
mercifully, is a blank.

When he comes to, muttering in protest—'False idols, I mean like an
autographed picture of Mickey Mantle, for christ's sake?'—he finds
himself in a cramped mud-and-wattle hut that reeks of goat dung and
incense. By the flickering glow of a bank of votary candles, he can
make out the bowed and patchy head of Nuala Nolan. Outside it is
dark and the rain drives down with a hiss. For a long moment,
McGahee lies there, studying the fleshless form of the girl, her bones
sharp and sepulchral in the quavering light. He feels used up, burned
out, feels as if he's been cored like an apple. His head screams. His
throat is dry. His bladder is bursting.

He pushes himself up and the bony demi-saint levels her tranced
gaze on him, 'Hush,' she says, and the memory of all that's happened
washes over him like a typhoon.

'How long have I—?'

'Two days.' Her voice is a reverent whisper, the murmur of the
acolyte, the apostle. 'They say the Pope himself is on the way.'

'The Pope?' McGahee feels a long shiver run through him.

Nods the balding death's-head. The voice is dry as husks, wheezy, but a girl's voice all the same, and an enthusiast's. 'They say it's the greatest vision vouchsafed to man since the time of Christ. Two hundred and fifteen people witnessed it, every glorious moment, from the cask of gin to the furtive masturbation to the ace up the sleeve.' She's leaning over him now, inching forward on all fours, her breath like chopped meat gone bad in the refrigerator; he can see, through the tattered shirt, where her breasts used to be. 'Look,' she whispers, gesturing toward the hunched low entranceway.

He looks and the sudden light dazzles him. Blinking in wonder, he creeps to the crude doorway and peers out. Immediately a murmur goes up from the crowd—hundreds upon hundreds of them gathered in the rain on their knees—and an explosion of flash cameras blinds him. Beyond the crowd he can make out a police cordon, vans and video cameras, CBS, BBC, KDOG, and NPR, a face above a trenchcoat that could only belong to Dan Rather himself. 'Holy of holies!' cries a voice from the front of the mob—he knows that voice—and the crowd takes it up in a chant that breaks off into the Lord's Prayer. Stupefied, he wriggles out of the hut and stands, bathed in light. It's McCarey there before him, reaching out with a hundred others to embrace his ankles, kiss his feet, tear with trembling devoted fingers at his Levi's and Taiwanese tweed—Michael McCarey, adulterer, gambler, drunk and atheist, cheater of the IRS and bane of the Major Deegan—hunkered down in the rain like a holy supplicant. And there, not thirty feet away, is the statue, lit like Betelgeuse and as inanimate and snotgreen as a stone of the sea.

Rain pelts McGahee's bare head and the chill seizes him like a claw jerking hard and sudden at the ruined ancient priest-ridden superstitious root of him. The flashbulbs pop in his face, a murmur of Latin assaults his ears, Sister Mary Magdalen's unyielding face rises before him out of the dim mists of eighth-grade math . . . and then the sudden imperious call of nature blinds him to all wonder and he's staggering round back of the hut to relieve himself of his two days' accumulation of salts and uric acid and dregs of whiskey. Stumbling, fumbling for his zipper, the twin pains in his groin like arrows driven through him, he jerks out his poor pud and lets fly.

'Piss!' roars a voice behind him, and he swivels his head in fright, helpless before the stream that issues from him like a torrent. The crowd falls prostrate in the mud, cameras whir, voices cry out. It is the statue, of course, livid, jerking its limbs and racking its body like the image of the Führer in his maddest denunciation. 'Piss on sacred ground, will you,' rage the plaster lips in the voice of his own father, that mild and pacifistic man, 'you unholy insect, you whited sepulcher, you speck of dust in the eye of your Lord and maker!'

What can he do? He clutches himself, flooding the ground, dissolving the hut, befouling the bony scrag of the anchorite herself.

'Unregenerate!' shrieks the Virgin. 'Unrepentant! Sinner to the core!'

And then it comes.

The skies part, the rain turns to popcorn, marshmallows, English muffins, the light of seven suns scorches down on that humble crowd gathered on the sward, and all the visions of that first terrible day crash over them in hellish simulcast. The great vats of beer and gin and whiskey fall to pieces and the sea of booze floats them, the cattle bellowing and kicking, sheep bleating and dogs barking, despoiled girls and hardened women clutching for the shoulders of the panicked communicants as for sticks of wood awash in the sea, Sophia Loren herself and Virginia Woolf, Fredda, Cindy Lou Harris, and McCarey's wife swept by in a blur, the TV vans overturned, the trenchcoat torn from Dan Rather's back, and the gardai sent sprawling—'Thank God he didn't eat rattlesnake,' someone cries—and then it's over. Night returns. Rain falls. The booze sinks softly into the earth, food lies rotting in clumps. A drumbeat of hoofs thunders off into the dark while fish wriggle and escargots creep, and Fredda, McCarey, the shaven-headed pizza vixen, and all the gap-toothed countrymen and farmwives and palsied children pick themselves up from the ground amid the curses of the men cheated at cards, the lament of the fallen women, and the mad frenzied chorus of prayer that speaks over it all in the tongue of terror and astonishment.

But oh, sad wonder, McGahee is gone.

Today the site remains as it was that night, fenced off from the merely curious, combed over inch by inch by priests and parapsychologists, blessed by the Pope, a shrine as reverenced as Lourdes and the Holy See itself. The cattle were sold off at auction after intensive study proved them ordinary enough, though brands were traced to Montana, Texas, and the Swiss Alps, and the food—burgers and snowcones, rib roasts, fig newtons, extra dill pickles, and all the rest—was left where it fell, to feed the birds and fertilize the soil. The odd rib or T-bone, picked clean and bleached by the elements, still lies there on the ground in mute testimony to those three days of tumult. Fredda McGahee Meyerowitz, Herb Bucknell and others cheated at cards, the girl from the pizza parlor and the rest were sent home via Aer Lingus, compliments of the Irish government. What became of Virginia Woolf, dead forty years prior to these events, is not known, nor the fate of Emma Bovary either, though one need only refer to Flaubert for the best clue to this mystery. And of course, there are the tourism figures— up a whopping 672 percent since the miracle.

McCarey has joined an order of Franciscan monks, and Nuala Nolan, piqued no doubt by her supporting role in the unfolding of the miracle, has taken a job in a pastry shop, where she eats by day and prays for forgiveness by night. As for Davey McGahee himself, the prime mover and motivator of all these enduring mysteries, here the lenses of history and of myth and miracology grow obscure. Some say he descended into a black hole of the earth, others that he evaporated, while still others insist that he ascended to heaven in a blaze of light, Saint of the Common Sinner.

For who hasn't lusted after woman or man or drunk his booze and laid to rest whole herds to feed his greedy gullet? Who hasn't watched them starve by the roadside in the hollows and waste places of the world and who among us hasn't scoffed at the credulous and ignored the miracle we see outside the window every day of our lives? Ask not for whom the bell tolls—unless perhaps you take the flight to Cork City, and the bus or rented Nissan out to Ballinspittle by the Sea, and gaze on the halfsize snotgreen statue of the Virgin, mute and unmoving all these many years.

WORK

Denis Johnson

I'd been staying at the Holiday Inn with my girlfriend, honestly the most beautiful woman I'd ever known, for three days under a phony name, shooting heroin. We made love in the bed, ate steaks at the restaurant, shot up in the john, puked, cried, accused one another, begged of one another, forgave, promised, and carried one another to heaven.

But there was a fight. I stood outside the motel hitchhiking, dressed up in a hurry, shirtless under my jacket, with the wind crying through my earring. A bus came. I climbed aboard and sat on the plastic seat while the things of our city turned in the windows like the images in a slot machine,

Once, as we stood arguing at a streetcorner, I punched her in the stomach. She doubled over and broke down crying. A car full of young college men stopped beside us.

'She's feeling sick,' I told them.

'Bullshit,' one of them said. 'You elbowed her right in the gut.'

'He did, he did, he did,' she said, weeping.

I don't remember what I said to them. I remember loneliness crushing first my lungs, then my heart, then my balls. They put her in the car with them and drove away.

But she came back.

This morning, after the fight, after sitting on the bus for several blocks with a thoughtless, red mind, I jumped down and walked into the Vine.

The Vine was still and cold. Wayne was the only customer. His hands were shaking. He couldn't lift his glass.

I put my left hand on Wayne's shoulder, and with my right, opiated and steady, I brought his shot of bourbon to his lips.

'How would you feel about making some money?' he asked me.

'I was just going to go over here in the corner and nod out,' I informed him.

'I decided,' he said, 'in my mind, to make some money.'

'So what?' I said.

'Come with me,' he begged.

'You mean you need a ride.'

'I have the tools,' he said. 'All we need is that sorry-ass car of yours to get around in.'

We found my sixty-dollar Chevrolet, the finest and best thing I ever bought, considering the price, in the streets near my apartment. I liked that car. It was the kind of thing you could bang into a phone pole with and nothing would happen at all.

Wayne cradled his burlap sack of tools in his lap as we drove out of town to where the fields bunched up into hills and then dipped down toward a cool river mothered by benevolent clouds.

All the houses on the riverbank—a dozen or so—were abandoned. The same company, you could tell, had built them all, and then painted them four different colors. The windows in the lower stories were empty of glass. We passed alongside them and I saw that the ground floors of these buildings were covered with silt. Sometime back a flood had run over the banks, cancelling everything. But now the river was flat and slow. Willows stroked the waters with their hair.

'Are we doing a burglary?' I asked Wayne.

'You can't burgulate a forgotten, empty house,' he said, horrified at my stupidity.

I didn't say anything.

'This is a salvage job,' he said. 'Pull up to that one, right about there.'

The house we parked in front of just had a terrible feeling about it. I knocked.

'Don't do that,' Wayne said. 'It's stupid.'

Inside, our feet kicked up the silt the river had left here. The watermark wandered the walls of the downstairs about three feet above the floor. Straight, stiff grass lay all over the place in bunches, as if someone had stretched them there to dry.

Wayne used a pry bar, and I had a shiny hammer with a blue rubber grip. We put the pry points in the seams of the wall and started tearing away the Sheetrock. It came loose with a noise like old men coughing. Whenever we exposed some of the wiring in its white plastic jacket, we ripped it free of its connections, pulled it out, and bunched it up. That's what we were after. We intended to sell the copper wire for scrap.

By the time we were on the second floor, I could see we were going to make some money. But I was getting tired. I dropped the hammer, went to the bathroom. I was sweaty and thirsty. But of course the water didn't work.

I went back to Wayne, standing in one of two small empty bedrooms, and started dancing around and pounding the walls, breaking through the Sheetrock and making a giant racket, until the hammer got stuck. Wayne ignored this misbehavior.

I was catching my breath.

I asked him, 'Who owned these houses, do you think?'

He stopped doing anything. 'This is my house.'

'It is?'

'It was.'

He gave the wire a long, smooth yank, a gesture full of the serenity of hatred, popping its staples and freeing it into the room.

We balled up big gobs of wire in the center of each room, working for over an hour. I boosted Wayne through the trapdoor into the attic, and he pulled me up after him, both of us sweating and our pores leaking the poisons of drink, which smelled like old citrus peelings, and we made a mound of white-jacketed wire in the top of his former home, pulling it up out of the floor.

I felt weak. I had to vomit in the corner—just a thimbleful of grey bile. 'All this work,' I complained, 'is fucking with my high. Can't you figure out some easier way of making a dollar?'

Wayne went to the window. He rapped it several times with his pry bar, each time harder, until it was loudly destroyed. We threw the stuff out there onto the mud-flattened meadow that came right up below us from the river.

It was quiet in this strange neighborhood along the bank except for the steady breeze in the young leaves. But now we heard a boat coming upstream. The sound curlicued through the riverside saplings like a bee, and in a minute a flat-nosed sports boat cut up the middle of the river going thirty or forty, at least.

This boat was pulling behind itself a tremendous triangular kite on a rope. From the kite, up in the air a hundred feet or so, a woman was suspended, belted in somehow, I would have guessed. She had long red hair. She was delicate and white, and naked except for her beautiful hair. I don't know what she was thinking as she floated past these ruins.

'What's she doing?' was all I could say, though we could see that she was flying.

'Now, that is a beautiful sight,' Wayne said.

On the way to town, Wayne asked me to make a long detour onto the Old Highway. He had me pull up to a lopsided farmhouse set on a hill of grass.

'I'm not going in but for two seconds,' he said. 'You want to come in?'

'Who's here?' I said.

'Come and see,' he told me.

It didn't seem anyone was home when we climbed the porch and he knocked. But he didn't knock again, and after a full three minutes a woman opened the door, a slender redhead in a dress printed with small blossoms. She didn't smile. 'Hi,' was all she said to us.

'Can we come in?' Wayne asked.

'Let me come onto the porch,' she said, and walked past us to stand looking out over the fields.

I waited at the other end of the porch, leaning against the rail, and didn't listen. I don't know what they said to one another. She walked down the steps, and Wayne followed. He stood hugging himself and talking down at the earth. The wind lifted and dropped her long red hair. She was about forty, with a bloodless, waterlogged beauty. I guessed Wayne was the storm that had stranded her here.

In a minute he said to me, 'Come on.' He got in the driver's seat and started the car—you didn't need a key to start it.

I came down the steps and got in beside him. He looked at her through the windshield. She hadn't gone back inside yet, or done anything at all.

'That's my wife,' he told me, as if it wasn't obvious.

I turned around in the seat and studied Wayne's wife as we drove off.

What word can be uttered about those fields? She stood in the middle of them as on a high mountain, with her red hair pulled out sideways by the wind, around her the green and grey plains pressed down flat, and all the grasses of Iowa whistling one note.

I knew who she was.

'That was her, wasn't it?' I said.

Wayne was speechless.

There was no doubt in my mind. She was the woman we'd seen flying over the river. As nearly as I could tell, I'd wandered into some sort of dream that Wayne was having about his wife, and his house. But I didn't say anything more about it.

Because, after all, in small ways, it was turning out to be one of the best days of my life, whether it was somebody else's dream or not. We turned in the scrap wire for twenty-eight dollars—each—at a salvage yard near the gleaming tracks at the edge of town, and went back to the Vine.

Who should be pouring drinks there but a young woman whose name I can't remember. But I remember the way she poured. It was like doubling your money. She wasn't going to make her employers rich. Needless to say, she was revered among us.

'I'm buying,' I said.

'No way in hell,' Wayne said.

'Come on.'

'It is,' Wayne said, 'my sacrifice.'

Sacrifice? Where had he gotten a word like sacrifice? Certainly I had never heard of it.

I'd seen Wayne look across the poker table in a bar and accuse—I do not exaggerate—the biggest, blackest man in Iowa of cheating, accuse him for no other reason than that he, Wayne, was a bit irked by the run of the cards. That was my idea of sacrifice, tossing yourself away, discarding your body. The black man stood up and circled the neck of a beer bottle with his fingers. He was taller than anyone who had ever entered that barroom.

'Step outside,' Wayne said.

And the man said, 'This ain't school.'

'What the goddamn fucking piss-hell,' Wayne said, 'is that suppose to mean?'

'I ain't stepping outside like you do at school. Make your try right here and now.'

'This ain't a place for our kind of business,' Wayne said, 'not inside here with women and children and dogs and cripples.'

'Shit,' the man said. 'You're just drunk.'

'I don't care,' Wayne said. 'To me you don't make no more noise than a fart in a paper bag.'

The huge, murderous man said nothing.

'I'm going to sit down now,' Wayne said, 'and I'm going to play my game, and fuck you.'

The man shook his head. He sat down too. This was an amazing thing. By reaching out one hand and taking hold of it for two or three seconds, he could have popped Wayne's head like an egg.

And then came one of those moments. I remember living through one when I was eighteen and spending the afternoon in bed with my first wife, before we were married. Our naked bodies started glowing, and the air turned such a strange color I thought my life must be leaving me, and with every young fiber and cell I wanted to hold on to it for another breath. A clattering sound was tearing up my head as I staggered upright and opened the door on a vision I will never see again: Where are my women now, with their sweet wet words and ways, and the miraculous balls of hail popping in a green translucence in the yards?

We put on our clothes, she and I, and walked out into a town flooded ankle-deep with white, buoyant stones. Birth should have been like that.

That moment in the bar, after the fight was narrowly averted, was like the green silence after the hailstorm. Somebody was buying a round of drinks. The cards were scattered on the table, face up, face down, and they seemed to foretell that whatever we did to one another would be washed away by liquor or explained away by sad songs.

Wayne was a part of all that.

The Vine was like a railroad club car that had somehow run itself off the tracks into a swamp of time where it awaited the blows of the wrecking ball. And the blows really were coming. Because of Urban Renewal, they were tearing up and throwing away the whole downtown.

And here we were, this afternoon, with nearly thirty dollars each, and our favorite, our very favorite, person tending bar. I wish I could remember her name, but I remember only her grace and her generosity.

All the really good times happened when Wayne was around. But this afternoon, somehow, was the best of all those times. We had money. We were grimy and tired. Usually we felt guilty and frightened, because there was something wrong with us, and we didn't know what it was; but today we had the feeling of men who had worked.

The Vine had no jukebox, but a real stereo continually playing tunes of alcoholic self-pity and sentimental divorce. 'Nurse,' I sobbed. She poured doubles like an angel, right up to the lip of a cocktail glass, no measuring. 'You have a lovely pitching arm.' You had to go down to them like a hummingbird over a blossom. I saw her much later, not too many years ago, and when I smiled she seemed to believe I was making advances. But it was only that I remembered. I'll never forget you. Your husband will beat you with an extension cord and the bus will pull away leaving you standing there in tears, but you were my mother.

NOTHING TO ASK FOR

Dennis McFarland

Inside Mack's apartment, a concentrator—a medical machine that looks like an elaborate stereo speaker on casters—sits behind an orange swivel chair, making its rhythmic, percussive noise like ocean waves, taking in normal filthy air, humidifying it, and filtering out everything but oxygen, which it sends through clear plastic tubing to Mack's nostrils. He sits on the couch, as usual, channel grazing, the remote-control button under his thumb, and he appears to be scrutinizing the short segments of what he sees on the TV screen with Zenlike patience. He has planted one foot on the beveled edge of the long oak coffee table, and he dangles one leg—thinner at the thigh than my wrist—over the other. In the sharp valley of his lap, Eberhardt, his old long-haired dachshund, lies sleeping. The table is covered with two dozen medicine bottles, though Mack has now taken himself off all drugs except cough syrup and something for heartburn. Also, stacks of books and pamphlets—though he has lost the ability to read—on how to heal yourself, on Buddhism, on Hinduism, on dying. In one pamphlet there's a long list that includes most human ailments, the personality traits and character flaws that cause these ailments, and the affirmations that need to be said in order to overcome them. According to this well-intentioned misguidedness, most disease is caused by self-hatred, or rejection of reality, and almost anything can be cured by learning to love yourself—which is accomplished by saying, aloud and often, 'I love myself.' Next to these books are pamphlets and Xeroxed articles describing more unorthodox remedies—herbal brews, ultrasound, lemon juice, urine, even penicillin. And, in a ceramic dish next to these, a small, waxy envelope that contains 'ash'—a very fine, gray-white, spiritually enhancing powder materialized out of thin air by Swami Lahiri Baba.

As I change the plastic liner inside Mack's trash can, into which he throws his millions of Kleenex, I block his view of the TV screen—which he endures serenely, his head perfectly still, eyes unaverted. 'Do you remember old Dorothy Hughes?' he asks me. 'What do you suppose ever happened to her?'

'I don't know,' I say. 'I saw her years ago on the nude beach at San Gregorio. With some black guy who was down by the surf doing cartwheels. She pretended she didn't know me.'

'I don't blame her,' says Mack, making bug-eyes. 'I wouldn't like to be seen with any grown-up who does cartwheels, would you?'

'No,' I say.

Then he asks, 'Was everybody we knew back then crazy?'

What Mack means by 'back then' is our college days, in Santa Cruz, when we judged almost everything in terms of how freshly it rejected the status quo: the famous professor who began his twentieth-century-philosophy class by tossing pink rubber dildos in through the classroom window; Antonioni and Luis Buñuel screened each weekend in the dormitory basement; the artichokes in the student garden, left on their stalks and allowed to open and become what they truly were—enormous, purple-hearted flowers. There were no paving-stone quadrangles or venerable colonnades—our campus was the redwood forest, the buildings nestled among the trees, invisible one from the other—and when we emerged from the woods at the end of the school day, what we saw was nothing more or less than the sun setting over the Pacific. We lived with thirteen other students, in a rented Victorian mansion on West Cliff Drive, and at night the yellow beacon from the nearby lighthouse invaded our attic windows; we drifted to sleep listening to the barking of seals. On weekends we had serious softball games in the vacant field next to the house—us against a team of tattooed, long-haired townies—and afterward, keyed up, tired and sweating, Mack and I walked the north shore to a place where we could watch the waves pound into the rocks and send up sun-ignited columns of water twenty-five and thirty feet tall. Though most of what we initiated 'back then' now seems to have been faddish and wrongheaded, our friendship was exceptionally sane and has endured for twenty years. It endured the melodramatic confusion of Dorothy Hughes, our beautiful shortstop—I loved her, but she loved Mack. It endured the subsequent revelation that Mack was gay—any tension on that count managed by him with remarks about what a homely bastard I was. It endured his fury and frustration over my low-bottom alcoholism, and my sometimes raging (and enraging) process of getting clean and sober. And it has endured the onlooking fish-eyes of his long string of lovers and my two wives. Neither of us had a biological brother—that could account for something—but at recent moments when I have felt most frightened, now that Mack is so ill, I've thought that we persisted simply because we couldn't let go of the sense of *thoroughness* our friendship gave us; we constantly reported to each other on our separate lives, as if we knew that by doing so we were getting more from life than we would ever have been entitled to individually.

In answer to his question—was everybody crazy back then—I say, 'Yes, I think so.'

He laughs, then coughs. When he coughs these days—which is often—he goes on coughing until a viscous, bloody fluid comes up, which he catches in a Kleenex and tosses into the trash can. Earlier, his doctors could drain his lungs with a needle through his back— last time they collected an entire liter from one lung— but now that Mack has developed the cancer, there are tumors that break up the fluid into many small isolated pockets, too many to drain. Radiation or chemotherapy would kill him; he's too weak even for a flu shot. Later today, he will go to the hospital for another bronchoscopy; they want to see if there's anything they can do to help him, though they have already told him there isn't. His medical care comes in the form of visiting nurses, physical therapists, and a curious duo at the hospital: one doctor who is young, affectionate, and incompetent but who comforts and consoles, hugs and holds hands; another—old, rude, brash, and expert—who says things like 'You might as well face it. You're going to die. Get your papers in order.' In fact, they've given Mack two weeks to two months, and it has now been ten weeks.

'Oh, my God,' cries Lester, Mack's lover, opening the screen door, entering the room, and looking around. 'I don't recognize this hovel. And what's that wonderful smell?'

This morning, while Lester was out, I vacuumed and generally straightened up. Their apartment is on the ground floor of a building like all the buildings in this southern California neighborhood—a two-story motel-like structure of white stucco and steel railings. Outside the door are an X-rated hibiscus (blood red, with its jutting, yellow, powder-tipped stamen), a plastic macaw on a swing, two enormous yuccas; inside, carpet, and plainness. The wonderful smell is the turkey I'm roasting; Mack can't eat anything before the bronchoscopy, but I figure it will be here for them when they return from the hospital, and they can eat off it for the rest of the week.

Lester, a South Carolina boy in his late twenties, is sick, too—twice he has nearly died of pneumonia—but he's in a healthy period now. He's tall, thin, and bearded, a devotee of the writings of Shirley MacLaine—an unlikely guru, if you ask me, but my wife, Marilyn, tells me I'm too judgmental. Probably she is right.

The dog, Eberhardt, has woken up and waddles sleepily over to where Lester stands. Lester extends his arm toward Mack, two envelopes in his hand, and after a moment's pause Mack reaches for them. It's partly this typical hesitation of Mack's—a slowing of the mind, actually—that makes him appear serene, contemplative these days. Occasionally, he really does get confused, which terrifies him. But I can't help thinking that something in there has sharpened as well— maybe a kind of simplification. Now he stares at the top envelope for a full minute, as Lester and I watch him. This is something we do: we watch him. 'Oh-h-h,' he says, at last. 'A letter from my mother.'

'And one from Lucy, too,' says Lester. 'Isn't that nice?'

'I guess,' says Mack. Then: 'Well, yes. It is.'

'You want me to open them?' I ask.

'Would you?' he says, handing them to me. 'Read 'em to me, too.'

They are only cards, with short notes inside, both from Des Moines. Mack's mother says it just makes her sick that he's sick, wants to know if there's anything he needs. Lucy, the sister, is gushy, misremembers a few things from the past, says she's writing instead of calling because she knows she will cry if she tries to talk. Lucy, who refused to let Mack enter her house at Christmastime one year—actually left him on the stoop in sub-zero cold—until he removed the gold earring from his ear. Mack's mother, who waited until after the funeral last year to let Mack know that his father had died; Mack's obvious illness at the funeral would have been an embarrassment.

But they've come around, Mack has told me in the face of my anger.

I said better late than never.

And Mack, all forgiveness, all humility, said that's exactly right: much better.

'Mrs. Mears is having a craft sale today,' Lester says. Mrs. Mears, an elderly neighbor, lives out back in a cottage with her husband. 'You guys want to go?'

Eberhardt, hearing 'go,' begins leaping at Lester's shins, but when we look at Mack, his eyelids are at half-mast—he's half asleep.

We watch him for a moment, and I say, 'Maybe in a little while, Lester.'

Lester sits on the edge of his bed reading the newspaper, which lies flat on the spread in front of him. He has his own TV in his room, and a VCR. On the dresser, movies whose cases show men in studded black leather jockstraps, with gloves to match—dungeon masters of startling handsomeness. On the floor, a stack of gay magazines. Somewhere on the cover of each of these magazines the word 'macho' appears; and inside some of them, in the personal ads, men, meaning to attract others, refer to themselves as pigs. 'Don't putz,' Lester says to me as I straighten some things on top of the dresser. 'Enough already.'

I wonder where he picked up 'putz'—surely not in South Carolina. I say, 'You need to get somebody in. To help. You need to arrange it now. What if you were suddenly to get sick again?'

'I know,' he says. 'He's gotten to be quite a handful, hasn't he? Is he still asleep?'

'Yes,' I answer. 'Yes and yes.'

The phone rings and Lester reaches for it. As soon as he begins to speak I can tell, from his tone, that it's my four-year-old on the line. After a moment Lester says, 'Kit,' smiling, and hands me the phone, then returns to his newspaper.

I sit on the other side of the bed, and after I say hello, Kit says, 'We need some milk.'

'O.K.,' I say. 'Milk. What are you up to this morning?'

'Being angry mostly,' she says.

'Oh?' I say. 'Why?'

'Mommy and I are not getting along very well.'

'That's too bad,' I say. 'I hope you won't stay angry for long.'

'We won't,' she says. 'We're going to make up in a minute.'

'Good,' I say.

'When are you coming home?'

'In a little while.'

'After my nap?'

'Yes,' I say. 'Right after your nap.'

'Is Mack very sick?'

She already knows the answer, of course. 'Yes,' I say.

'Is he going to die?'

This one, too. 'Most likely,' I say. 'He's that sick.'

'Bye,' she says suddenly—her sense of closure always takes me by surprise—and I say, 'Don't stay angry for long, O.K.?'

'You already said that,' she says, rightly, and I wait for a moment, half expecting Marilyn to come on the line; ordinarily she would, and hearing her voice right now would do me good. After another moment, though, there's the click.

Marilyn is back in school, earning a Ph.D. in religious studies. I teach sixth grade, and because I'm faculty adviser for the little magazine the sixth graders put out each year, I stay late many afternoons. Marilyn wanted me home this Saturday morning. 'You're at work all week,' she said, 'and then you're over there on Saturday. Is that fair?'

I told her I didn't know—which was the honest truth. Then, in a possibly dramatic way, I told her that fairness was not my favorite subject these days, given that my best friend was dying.

We were in our kitchen, and through the window I could see Kit playing with a neighbor's cat in the back yard. Marilyn turned on the hot water in the kitchen sink and stood still while the steam rose into her face. 'It's become a question of where you belong,' she said at last. 'I think you're too involved.'

For this I had no answer, except to say, 'I agree'—which wasn't really an answer, since I had no intention of staying home, or becoming less involved, or changing anything.

Now Lester and I can hear Mack's scraping cough in the next room. We are silent until he stops. 'By the way,' Lester says at last, taking the telephone receiver out of my hand, 'have you noticed that he *listens* now?'

'I know,' I say. 'He told me he'd finally entered his listening period.'

'Yeah,' says Lester, 'as if it's the natural progression. You blab your whole life away, ignoring other people, and then right before you die you start to listen.'

The slight bitterness in Lester's tone makes me feel shaky inside. It's true that Mack was always a better talker than a listener, but I suddenly feel that I'm walking a thin wire, and that anything like collusion would throw me off balance. All I know for sure is that I don't want to hear any more. Maybe Lester reads this in my face, because what he says next sounds like an explanation: he tells me that his poor old backwoods mother was nearly deaf when he was growing up, that she relied almost entirely on reading lips. 'All she had to do when she wanted to turn me off,' he says, 'was to just turn her back on me. Simple,' he says, making a little circle with his finger. 'No more Lester.'

'That's terrible,' I say.

'I was a terrible coward,' he says. 'Can you imagine Kit letting you get away with something like that? She'd bite your kneecaps.'

'Still,' I say, 'that's terrible.'

Lester shrugs his shoulders, and after another moment I say, 'I'm going to the K mart. Mack needs a padded toilet seat. You want anything?'

'Yeah,' he says. 'But they don't sell it at K mart.'

'What is it?' I ask.

'It's a *joke*, Dan, for Chrissake,' he says. 'Honestly, I think you've completely lost your sense of humor.'

When I think about this, it seems true.

'Are you coming back?' he asks.

'Right back,' I answer. 'If you think of it, baste the turkey.'

'How could I not think of it?' he says, sniffing the air.

In the living room, Mack is lying with his eyes open now, staring blankly at the TV. At the moment, a shop-at-home show is on, but he changes channels, and an announcer says, 'When we return, we'll talk about tree pruning,' and Mack changes the channel again. He looks at me, nods thoughtfully, and says, 'Tree pruning. Interesting. It's just like the way they put a limit on your credit card, so you don't spend too much.'

'I don't understand,' I say.

'Oh, you know,' he says. 'Pruning the trees. Didn't the man just say something about pruning trees?' He sits up and adjusts the plastic tube in one nostril.

'Yes,' I say.

'Well, it's like the credit cards. The limit they put on the credit cards is . . .' He stops talking and looks straight into my eyes, frightened. 'It doesn't make any sense, does it?' he says. 'Jesus Christ. I'm not making sense.'

Way out east on University, there is a video arcade every half mile or so. Adult peepshows. Also a McDonald's, and the rest. Taverns—the kind that are open at eight in the morning—with clever names: Tobacco Rhoda's, the Cruz Inn. Bodegas that smell of cat piss and are really fronts for numbers games. Huge discount stores. Lester, who is an expert in these matters, has told me that all these places feed on addicts. 'What do you think—those peepshows stay in business on the strength of the occasional customer? No way. It's a steady clientele of people in there every day, for hours at a time, dropping in quarters. That whole strip of road is *made* for addicts. And all the strips like it. That's what America's all about, you know. You got your alcoholics in the bars. Your food addicts sucking it up at Jack-in-the-Box—you ever go in one of those places and count the fat people? You got your sex addicts in the peepshows. Your shopping addicts at the K mart. Your gamblers running numbers in the bodegas and your junkies in the alleyways. We're all nothing but a bunch of addicts. The whole fucking addicted country.'

In the arcades, says Lester, the videos show myriad combinations and arrangements of men and women, men and men, women and women. Some show older men being serviced by eager, selfless young women who seem to live for one thing only, who can't get enough. Some of these women have put their hair into pigtails and shaved themselves—they're supposed to look like children. Inside the peepshow booths there's semen on the floor. And in the old days, there were glory holes cut into the wooden walls between some of the booths, so, if it pleased you, you could communicate with your neighbor. Not anymore. Mack and Lester tell me that some things have changed. The holes have been boarded up. In the public men's rooms you no longer read, scribbled in the stalls, 'All faggots should die.' You read, 'All faggots should die of AIDS.' Mack rails against the moratorium on fetal-tissue research, the most promising avenue for a cure. 'If it was Legionnaires dying, we wouldn't have any moratorium,' he says. And he often talks about Africa, where governments impede efforts to teach villagers about condoms: a social worker, attempting to explain their use, isn't allowed to remove the condoms from their foil packets; in another country, with a slightly more liberal government, a field nurse stretches a condom over his hand, to show how it works, and later villagers are found wearing the condoms like mittens, thinking this will protect them from disease. Lester laughs at these stories but shakes his head. In our own country, something called 'family values' has emerged with clarity. 'Whose family?' Mack wants to know, holding out his hands palms upward. 'I mean we *all* come from families, don't we? The dizziest queen comes from a family. The ax murderer. Even Dan *Quayle* comes from a family of some kind.'

But Mack and Lester are dying, Mack first. As I steer my pickup into the parking lot at the K mart, I almost clip the front fender of a big, deep-throated Chevy that's leaving. I have startled the driver, a young Chicano boy with four kids in the back seat, and he flips me the bird—aggressively, his arm out the window—but I feel protected today by my sense of purpose: I have come to buy a padded toilet seat for my friend.

When he was younger, Mack wanted to be a cultural anthropologist, but he was slow to break in after we were out of graduate school—never landed anything more than a low-paying position assisting someone else, nothing more than a student's job, really. Eventually, he began driving a tour bus in San Diego, which not only provided a steady income but suited him so well that in time he was managing the line and began to refer to the position not as his job but as his calling. He said that San Diego was like a pretty blond boy without too many brains. He knew just how to play up its cultural assets while allowing its beauty to speak for itself. He said he liked being 'at the controls.' But he had to quit work over a year ago, and now his hands have become so shaky that he can no longer even manage a pen and paper.

When I get back to the apartment from my trip to the K mart, Mack asks me to take down a letter for him to an old high school buddy back in Des Moines, a country-and-western singer who has sent him a couple of her latest recordings. '*Whenever I met a new doctor or nurse,*' he dictates, '*I always asked them whether they believed in miracles.*'

Mack sits up a bit straighter and rearranges the pillows behind his back on the couch. 'What did I just say?' he asks me.

'"I always asked them whether they believed in miracles."'

'Yes,' he says, and continues. '*And if they said no, I told them I wanted to see someone else. I didn't want them treating me. Back then, I was hoping for a miracle, which seemed reasonable.* Do you think this is too detailed?' he asks me.

'No,' I say. 'I think it's fine.'

'I don't want to depress her.'

'Go on,' I say.

'But now I have lung cancer,' he continues. *'So now I need not one but two miracles. That doesn't seem as possible somehow.* Wait. Did you write "possible" yet?'

'No,' I say. '"That doesn't seem as . . ."'

'Reasonable,' he says. 'Didn't I say "reasonable" before?'

'Yes,' I say. '"That doesn't seem as reasonable somehow."'

'Yes,' he says. 'How does that sound?'

'It sounds fine, Mack. It's not for publication, you know.'

'It's not?' he says, feigning astonishment. 'I thought it was: "Letters of an AIDS Victim."' He says this in a spooky voice and makes his bug-eyes. Since his head is a perfect skull, the whole effect really is a little spooky.

'What else?' I say.

'Thank you for your nice letter,' he continues, *'and for the tapes.'* He begins coughing—a horrible, rasping seizure. Mack has told me that he has lost all fear; he said he realized this a few weeks ago, on the skyride at the zoo. But when the coughing sets in, when it seems that it may never stop, I think I see terror in his eyes: he begins tapping his breastbone with the fingers of one hand, as if he's trying to wake up his lungs, prod them to do their appointed work. Finally he does stop, and he sits for a moment in silence, in thought. Then he dictates: *'It makes me very happy that you are so successful.'*

At Mrs. Mears's craft sale, in the alley behind her cottage, she has set up several card tables: Scores of plastic dolls with hand-knitted dresses, shoes, and hats. Handmade doll furniture. Christmas ornaments. A whole box of knitted bonnets and scarves for dolls. Also, some baked goods. Now, while Lester holds Eberhardt, Mrs. Mears, wearing a large straw hat and sunglasses, outfits the dachshund in one of the bonnets and scarves. 'There now,' she says. 'Have you ever seen anything so *precious*? I'm going to get my camera.'

Mack sits in a folding chair by one of the tables; next to him sits Mr. Mears, also in a folding chair. The two men look very much alike, though Mr. Mears is not nearly as emaciated as Mack. And of course Mr. Mears is eighty-seven. Mack, on the calendar, is not quite forty. I notice that Mack's shoelaces are untied, and I kneel to tie them. 'The thing about reincarnation,' he's saying to Mr. Mears, 'is that you can't remember anything and you don't recognize anybody.'

'Consciously,' says Lester, butting in. '*Sub*consciously you do.'

'Subconsciously,' says Mack. 'What's the point? I'm not the least bit interested.'

Mr. Mears removes his houndstooth-check cap and scratches his bald, freckled head. 'I'm not, either,' he says with great resignation.

As Mrs. Mears returns with the camera, she says, 'Put him over there, in Mack's lap.'

'It doesn't matter whether you're interested or not,' says Lester, dropping Eberhardt into Mack's lap.

'Give me good old-fashioned heaven and hell,' says Mr. Mears.

'I should think you would've had enough of that already,' says Lester.

Mr. Mears gives Lester a suspicious look, then gazes down at his own knees. 'Then give me nothing,' he says finally.

I stand up and step aside just in time for Mrs. Mears to snap the picture. 'Did you ever *see* anything?' she says, all sunshades and yellow teeth, but as she heads back toward the cottage door, her face is immediately serious. She takes me by the arm and pulls me along, reaching for something from one of the tables—a doll's bed, white with a red strawberry painted on the headboard. 'For your little girl,' she says aloud. Then she whispers, 'You better get him out of the sun, don't you think? He doesn't look so good.'

But when I turn again, I see that Lester is already helping Mack out of his chair. 'Here—let me,' says Mrs. Mears, reaching an arm toward them, and she escorts Mack up the narrow, shaded sidewalk, back toward the apartment building. Lester moves alongside me and says, 'Dan, do you think you could give Mack his bath this afternoon? I'd like to take Eberhardt for a walk.'

'Of course,' I say, quickly.

But a while later—after I have drawn the bath, after I've taken a large beach towel out of the linen closet, refolded it into a thick square, and put it into the water to serve as a cushion for Mack to sit on in the tub; when I'm holding the towel under, against some resistance, waiting for the bubbles to stop surfacing, and there's something horrible about it, like drowning a small animal—I think Lester has tricked me into this task of bathing Mack, and the saliva in my mouth suddenly seems to taste of Scotch, which I have not actually tasted in nine years.

There is no time to consider any of this, however, for in a moment Mack enters the bathroom, trailing his tubes behind him, and says, 'Are you ready for my Auschwitz look?'

'I've seen it before,' I say.

And it's true. I have, a few times, helping him with his shirt and pants after Lester has bathed him and gotten him into his underwear. But that doesn't feel like preparation. The sight of him naked is like a powerful, scary drug: you forget between trips, remember only when you start to come on to it again. I help him off with his clothes now and guide him into the tub and gently onto the underwater towel. 'That's nice,' he says, and I begin soaping the hollows of his shoulders, the hard wash-board of his back. This is not human skin as we know it but something already dead—so dry, dense, and pleasantly brown as to appear manufactured. I soap the cage of his chest, his stomach—the hard, depressed abdomen of a greyhound—the steep vaults of his armpits, his legs, his feet. Oddly, his hands and feet appear almost normal, even a bit swollen. At last I give him the slippery bar of soap. 'Your turn,' I say.

'My poor cock,' he says as he begins to wash himself.

When he's done, I rinse him all over with the hand spray attached to the faucet. I lather the feathery white wisps of his hair—we have to remove the plastic oxygen tubes for this—then rinse again. 'You know,' he says, 'I know it's irrational, but I feel kind of turned off to sex.'

The apparent understatement of this almost takes my breath away. 'There are more important things,' I say.

'Oh, I know,' he says. 'I just hope Lester's not too unhappy.' Then, after a moment, he says, 'You know, Dan, it's only logical that they've all given up on me. And I've accepted it mostly. But I still have days when I think I should at least be given a chance.'

'You can ask them for anything you want, Mack,' I say.

'I know,' he says. 'That's the problem—there's nothing to ask for.'

'Mack,' I say. 'I think I understand what you meant this morning about the tree pruning and the credit cards.'

'You do?'

'Well, I think your mind just shifted into metaphor. Because I can see that pruning trees is like imposing a limit—just like the limit on the credit cards.'

Mack is silent, pondering this. 'Maybe,' he says at last, hesitantly—a moment of disappointment for us both.

I get him out and hooked up to the oxygen again, dry him off, and begin dressing him. Somehow I get the oxygen tubes trapped between his legs and the elastic waistband of his sweatpants—no big deal, but I suddenly feel panicky—and I have to take them off his face again to set them to rights. After he's safely back on the living room couch and I've returned to the bathroom, I hear him: low, painful-sounding groans. 'Are you all right?' I call from the hallway.

'Oh, yes,' he says, 'I'm just moaning. It's one of the few pleasures I have left.'

The bathtub is coated with a crust of dead skin, which I wash away with the sprayer. Then I find a screwdriver and go to work on the toilet seat. After I get the old one off, I need to scrub around the area where the plastic screws were. I've sprinkled Ajax all around the rim of the bowl and found the scrub brush when Lester appears at the bathroom door, back with Eberhardt from their walk. 'Oh, Dan, really,' he says. 'You go too far. Down on your knees now, scrubbing our toilet.'

'Lester, leave me alone,' I say.

'Well, it's true,' he says. 'You really do.'

'Maybe I'm working out my survivor's guilt,' I say, 'if you don't mind.'

'You mean because your best buddy's dying and you're not?'

'Yes,' I say. 'It's very common.'

He parks one hip on the edge of the sink, and after a moment he says this: 'Danny boy, if you feel guilty about surviving . . . that's not irreversible, you know. I could fix that.'

We are both stunned. He looks at me. In another moment, there are tears in his eyes. He quickly closes the bathroom door, moves to the tub and turns on the water, sits on the side, and bursts into sobs. 'I'm sorry,' he says. 'I'm so sorry.'

'Forget it,' I say.

He begins to compose himself almost at once. 'This is what Jane Alexander did when she played Eleanor Roosevelt,' he says. 'Do you remember? When she needed to cry she'd go in the bathroom and turn on the water, so nobody could hear her. Remember?'

*

In the pickup, on the way to the hospital, Lester—in the middle, between Mack and me—says, 'Maybe after they're down there you could doze off, but on the *way* down, they want you awake.' He's explaining the bronchoscopy to me—the insertion of the tube down the windpipe—with which he is personally familiar: 'They reach certain points on the way down where they have to ask you to swallow.'

'*He's* not having the test, is he?' Mack says, looking confused.

'No, of course not,' says Lester.

'Didn't you just say to him that he had to swallow?'

'I meant *anyone*, Mac,' says Lester.

'Oh,' says Mack. 'Oh, yeah.'

'The general "you,"' Lester says to me. 'He keeps forgetting little things like that.'

Mack shakes his head, then points at his temple with one finger. 'My mind,' he says.

Mack is on tank oxygen now, which comes with a small caddy. I push the caddy, behind him, and Lester assists him along the short walk from the curb to the hospital's front door and the elevators. Nine years ago, it was Mack who drove *me* to a different wing of this same hospital—against my drunken, slobbery will—to dry out. And as I watch him struggle up the low inclined ramp toward the glass and steel doors, I recall the single irrefutable thing he said to me in the car on the way. 'You stink,' he said. 'You've puked and probably pissed your pants and you *stink*,' he said—my loyal, articulate, and best friend, saving my life, and causing me to cry like a baby.

Inside the clinic upstairs, the nurse, a sour young blond woman in a sky-blue uniform who looks terribly overworked, says to Mack, 'You know better than to be late.'

We are five minutes late to the second. Mack looks at her incredulously. He stands with one hand on the handle of the oxygen-tank caddy. He straightens up, perfectly erect—the indignant, shockingly skeletal posture of a man fasting to the death for some holy principle. He gives the nurse the bug-eyes and says, 'And you know better than to keep me waiting every time I come over here for some goddamn procedure. But get over yourself: shit happens.'

He turns and winks at me.

Though I've offered to return for them afterward, Lester has insisted on taking a taxi, so I will leave them here and drive back home, where again I'll try—successfully, this time—to explain to my wife how all this feels to me, and where, a few minutes later, I'll stand outside the door to my daughter's room, comforted by the music of her small high voice as she consoles her dolls.

Now the nurse gets Mack into a wheelchair and leaves us in the middle of the reception area; then, from the proper position at her desk, she calls Mack's name, and says he may proceed to the laboratory.

'Dan,' Mack says, stretching his spotted, broomstick arms toward me. 'Old pal. Do you remember the Christmas we drove out to Des Moines on the motorcycle?'

We did go to Des Moines together, one very snowy Christmas—but of course we didn't go on any motorcycle, not in December.

'We had fun,' I say and put my arms around him, awkwardly, since he is sitting.

'Help me up,' he whispers confidentially—and I begin to lift him.

GRIT

Tom Franklin

Chugging and clinging among the dark pine trees north of Mobile, Alabama, the Black Beauty Minerals plant was a rickety green hull of storage tanks, chutes and conveyor belts. Glen, the manager, felt like the captain of a ragtag spaceship that had crashlanded, a prison barge full of poachers and thieves, smugglers and assassins.

The owners, Ernie and Dwight, lived far away, in Detroit, and when the Black Beauty lost its biggest client—Ingalls Shipbuilding—to government budget cuts, they ordered Glen to lay off his two-man night shift. One of the workers was a long-haired turd Glen enjoyed letting go, a punk who would've likely failed his next drug test. But the other man, Roy Jones, did some bookmaking on the side, and Glen had been in a betting slump lately. So when Roy, who'd had a great year as a bookie, crunched over the gritty black yard to the office, Glen owed him over four thousand dollars.

Roy, a fat black man, strode in without knocking and wedged himself into the chair across from Glen's desk, probably expecting more stalling of the debt.

Glen cleared his throat. 'I've got some bad news, Roy—'

'Chill, baby,' Roy said. He removed his hard hat, which left its imprint in his hair. 'I know I'm fixing to get laid off, and I got a counteroffer for you.' He slid a cigar from his hat lining and smelled it.

Glen was surprised. The Ingalls announcement hadn't come until a few hours ago. Ernie and Dwight had just released him from their third conference call of the afternoon, the kind where they both yelled at him at the same time.

'How'd you find that out, Roy?' he asked.

Roy lit his cigar. 'One thing you ain't learned yet is how to get the system doggie-style. Two of my associates work over at Ingalls, and one of 'em been fucking the bigwig's secretary.'

'Well—'

'Hang on, Glen. I expect E and D done called you and told you to lay my big fat ass off. But that's cool, baby.' He tipped his ashes into his hard hat. "Cause I got other irons in the fire.'

He said he had an 'independent buyer' for some Black Beauty sandblasting grit. Said he had, in fact, a few lined up. What he wanted was to run an off-the-books night shift for a few hours a night, three nights a week. He said he had an associate who'd deliver the stuff. The day-shifters could be bought off. Glen could doctor the paperwork so the little production wouldn't be noticed by Ernie and Dwight.

'But don't answer now,' Roy said, replacing his hard hat. 'Sleep on it tonight, baby. Mull it over.'

Glen—a forty-two-year-old, ulcer-ridden, insomniac, half-alcoholic chronic gambler—mulled Roy's idea over in his tiny apartment that evening by drinking three six-packs of Bud Light. He picked up the phone and placed a large bet with Roy on the upcoming Braves–Giants game, taking San Francisco because Barry Bonds was on fire. Then he dialed the number of the Pizza Hut managed by his most recent ex-wife's new boyfriend, placed an order for five extra-large thick-crust pies with pineapple and double anchovies, and had it delivered to another of his ex-wives' houses for her and her boyfriend. Glen had four ex-wives in all, and he was still in love with each of them. Every night as he got drunk it felt like somebody had shot him in the chest with buckshot and left four big airy holes in his heart, holes that grew with each beer, as if—there was no other way he could think of it— his heart were being sandblasted.

The Braves rallied in the eighth and Bonds's sixteen-game hitting streak was snapped, so when Roy came by the next day, Glen owed him another eight hundred dollars and change.

Roy sat down. 'You made up your mind yet?'

'Impossible,' Glen said. 'Even if I wanted to, I couldn't go along. Ernie and Dwight'd pop in out of nowhere and we'd all be up the creek.'

Today Roy wore tan slacks and a brown silk shirt. Shiny brown shoes and, when he crossed his legs, thin argyle socks. A brown fedora in his lap. The first time Glen had seen him in anything but work clothes.

Roy shook a cigar from its box and lit it. 'Glen, you the most gullible motherfucker ever wore a hard hat. Don't you reckon I know when them tight-asses is coming down here?'

'How? Got somebody fucking their wives?'

Roy hesitated. 'My cousin's daughter work in the Detroit airport.'

Glen's mind flashed a quick slideshow of Ernie and Dwight's past disastrous visits. 'You might've mentioned that four years ago.'

'Baby,' Roy said, 'I'll cut you for ten percent of every load we sell.'

'There's a recession, Roy. I can't unload this grit to save my life, and if I can't, you sure as hell can't.'

Roy chuckled. 'Got-damn, boy.' He pulled out a wad of hundred-dollar bills. 'This is what I done presold. I got friends all up and down the coast. They got some rusty-ass shit needs sandblasting. You ain't no salesman, Glen. You couldn't sell a whore on a battleship.'

'Roy, it's illegal.'

'Go look out yonder.' Roy pointed to the window overlooking the black-grit parking lot.

Glen obeyed. A big white guy with a little head was leaning against Roy's cream-colored El Dorado, carving at his fingernails with a long knife.

'That's my associate, Snakebite,' Roy said. 'He'll be delivering the stuff. He also collect for me, if you know what I mean.'

Glen knew.

'Up till now,' Roy said, 'you been getting off easy 'cause you was the boss. Now that that's changed . . .'

Glen looked at him. 'You threatening me, Roy?'

'Naw, baby. I'm a businessman.' Roy took out his pocket ledger. 'As of now, I'm forgetting every got-damn cent you owe me.' Glen watched Roy write *paid* by the frighteningly high red figure he would've been having nightmares about, had he been able to sleep.

Roy started running his phantom night shift Monday through Wednesday nights. To keep the four day-shifters quiet, he gave them a slight payoff—a 'taste'—each week. So they clocked in in the mornings and pretended the machinery wasn't hot, that the plant hadn't run all night. And Glen, hungover, took his clipboard and measuring tape out and stared at the dwindling stockpiles of raw grit where Roy had taken material. Then he went back across the yard into his office, locked the door, rubbed his eyes, doctored his paperwork and—some days—threw up.

Staring out the window, he worried that the day shift would rat to Ernie and Dwight. He'd never been close to the workers— in his first week as manager, four years before, he'd confiscated the radio they kept in the control room. Instead of spending afternoons in his office making sales calls the way the previous manager had, Glen had stayed out in the heat with the men, cracking the whip, having the plant operator retake grit samples, watching the millwright repair leaks, making sure the payloader's fittings were well-greased. He timed the guys' breaks, stomped into the break room if they stayed a minute past their half hour. If someone got a personal phone call, Glen would go to another extension and pick up and say, 'Excuse me,' in an icy tone and wait for them to hang up.

In the plant, they were supposed to wear hard hats, safety glasses, steel-toe boots, leather gloves, earplugs and, depending on where they worked, a dust mask or respirator. Glen struck here, too, because his predecessor had let the guys grow lax. In those first months, Glen had stepped on their toes to check for steel and yelled in their ears to check for plugs. He'd written them up for the tiniest safety violation and put it in their permanent files.

So they hated him. They took orders sullenly and drew a finger across their throats as a warning signal when he approached. They never invited him to participate in their betting pools or asked him to get a beer after work.

Now Glen swore to give up gambling. He locked himself in the office during the day and made halfhearted sales calls: 'The unique thing about our sandblasting grit,' he'd say wearily, 'is that no piece, no matter how small, has a round edge.' At night, he stayed home and watched sitcoms and nature shows instead of baseball. When cabin fever struck, he went to the movies instead of the dog track or the casino boats in Biloxi. He even managed to curb his drinking on weeknights.

Until early July. There was an Independence Day weekend series between Atlanta and the Cards in St. Louis and the plant had a four-day weekend. A drunk Glen, who when lonely sometimes called 1-900 handicapping lines, got a great tip from Lucky Dave Rizetti—'A sure by-God thing,' Lucky Dave promised. 'Take the Bravos, take 'em for big money.' And Glen took them, betting almost two grand over the four games. But the series was filled with freaky incidents, relief pitchers hitting home runs, Golden-Glovers making stupid two-base throwing errors, etc.

So on Tuesday, the holiday over, Glen was back in debt. Then add the fact that the lawyers of exes two and three had been sending letters threatening lawsuits if Glen didn't pay his alimony. The lawyers said they'd get a court order and garnish his wages. Christ, if Ernie and Dwight got wind of that, they'd fly down and can him for sure.

They came twice a year or so, the old bastards, for spot inspections, speaking in their Yankee accents and wearing polished hard hats on their prim gray crew cuts. They would fly in from Detroit, first class, and rent a Caddy and get suites at the top of the Riverview downtown. They'd bring rolled-up plans to the plant and walk around frowning and making notes. Glen always felt ill when they were on-site—they constantly grumbled about lack of production or low sales figures or how an elevator wasn't up to spec. They'd peer into his red eyes and sniff his breath. He would follow them around the plant's perimeter, his chin nicked from shaving, and he'd nod and hold his stomach.

On Tuesday, after Independence Day, Glen sat in his office staring at the electric bill—he would have to account for the extra power the phantom night shift was using—when Roy stuck his head in the door. He smiled, smoking a cigar, and sat down across from Glen's desk.

'Just come by to tell you we fixing to start running four nights a week,' Roy said.

Glen started to object, but there was a shrill noise.

'Hang on.' Roy brought a slim cellular phone out of his pocket.

Glen shrugged and doodled (man dangling by noose) on his desk calendar while Roy took another order for grit.

When Roy snapped the phone shut, Glen said, 'No. You can't go to four nights. Who the hell was that? They want *two* loads? Never mind. Your night shift's gotta stop altogether, end of story.'

'Impossible,' Roy said.

'Impossible?'

'Look out the window.'

Glen obeyed, saw a cute young woman in Roy's car. She was frowning.

'You see that pretty little thing?' Roy asked. 'You know how old she is? Nineteen, Glen. *Nineteen*. She the freshest thing in the world, too. She go jogging every morning, and when she come back she don't even smell bad. Her breath don't stink in the morning.' Roy coughed. 'I wake up my breath smell like burnt tar.'

'Roy—'

'You think a fresh little girl like that's with me 'cause she love me? Hell no. She with me 'cause I'm getting rich. So no, baby, we can't stop. Business just too damn good. Which remind me—' He opened his ledger. 'You back up in four figures again.'

'Roy, just stick to the subject at hand. I'm not asking you to stop. I'm ordering you to stop.'

'Baby,' Roy said quietly, 'you ain't exactly in a strong bargaining position. Who's E and D gonna hold responsible if they hear about our little operation? You the manager. You the one been falsifying records. Naw, baby. The "subject" ain't whether or not old Roy's gonna stop making grit. The "subject" is what to do about all that money you owe me.'

What they did was compromise. Roy said he'd been too busy to make grit and look after his bookmaking business. So Glen would go to work for him, at night. Roy would forget about the two grand and pay Glen ten bucks an hour to work nine hours a night, four nights a week.

'I bet you can use the extra bread,' Roy said. 'That alimony can eat a man up.'

Then Roy said he needed Glen's office; the phones were better. It was quieter, he said. He could think. So that night Glen worked in the plant and Roy used the air-conditioned office. Sweating under the tanks, Glen saw Roy's fat silhouette behind the curtains, and he uncapped his flask and toasted the irony. He spent the night in the hot, claustrophobic control room, watching gauges, adjusting dials and taking samples; climbing into the front end loader once an hour and filling the hopper with raw material; on top of the tanks measuring the amount of grit they'd made; and standing by the loading chute, filling Snakebite's big purple Peterbilt.

At six that morning, with the plant shut down and Roy gone, Glen slogged to the office before the day-shifters clocked in. The room smelled like cigars, and Glen made a mental note to start smoking them in case Ernie and Dwight popped in. He locked the door behind him and pulled off his shoes and poured out little piles of grit. He lay back on his desk, exhausted, put his hands over his face, shut his eyes, and got his first good sleep in months.

Snakebite, six foot five, also slept during the day, in his Peterbilt, in the cab behind the seat, the truck parked among the pines near the plant. He showered every other day in the break room and ate canned pork and beans and Vienna sausages that he speared with his pocketknife. He had a tattoo on his left biceps, a big diamondback rattler with its mouth opened, tongue and fangs extended. He wore pointed snakeskin cowboy boots but no cowboy hat because adult hat sizes swallowed his tiny head. To Glen, he looked like a football player wearing shoulder pads but no helmet. He said he 'hailed' from El Paso, Texas, but he'd 'vamoosed' because his wife, a 'mean little filly' who'd once stabbed him, had discovered that he was 'stepping out' with a waitress in Amarillo.

Glen knew this and much more because Snakebite never stopped talking. One night, as the truck loaded, Snakebite showed Glen a rare World War I trench knife, a heavy steel blade with brass knuckles for a handle.

'I collect knives,' Snakebite said. 'Looky here.' He bent and pulled up a tight jeans leg over his boot, revealing a white-handled stiletto.

'My Mississippi Gambler,' Snakebite said. 'It's a throwing knife. See this quick unhitching gadget on the holster?' He flipped a snap and the knife came right out of his boot into his hand. 'This is the one my wife stabbed me with,' he said. He showed Glen the scar, a white line on his left forearm. Glen didn't have any scars from his ex-wives that he could show, so he uncapped his flask and knocked back a swig. He offered the flask to Snakebite, who took it.

'Don't mind if I do, Slick,' he said, winking.

'Where's this load going?' Glen asked, nodding toward the black stream of grit falling into the truck. He'd been curious about Roy's clients, thinking he might try to steal the business.

Snakebite grinned and punched him in the shoulder. 'Shit, boy. You oughta know that's classified. You find out old Roy's secrets and he's outta business. Then I'm outta business.'

'So.' Glen swallowed. 'I hear you do a little, um, collecting for Roy.'

Snakebite drained the flask. 'Don't worry about that, Slick. Old Roy

ain't never sicced me on anybody I liked. And even if he did, hell, it
ain't ever as bad as you see in the movies.'

Working nights for Roy Jones Grit, Inc., Glen wore a ratty T-shirt, old
sneakers, a Braves cap and short pants. He turned off every breaker
and light he could spare to keep the electric bill low, so the place was
dark and dangerous. He began carrying a flashlight hooked to his belt.
He tried to cut power during the day, too. He adjusted all the electrical
and mechanical equipment to their most efficient settings. He even
turned the temperature dial in the break-room refrigerator to 'warmer'
and stole the microwave (supposedly a great wattage-drainer) from its
shelf and pawned it, then called the day-shifters in for a meeting where
he gave the 'thief' a chance to confess. No one did, and the meeting
became a lecture where Glen urged the men to 'conserve energy, not
just for the good of the plant, but for the sake of the whole fucking
environment.' To set an example, he told them, he would stop using
the air conditioner in the office.

But not Roy: Roy ran the AC full-blast all night so that the office was
ice-cold. Not that Glen had a lot of time to notice. Typically it took one
man to operate the plant and another the loader. Doing both, as well
as loading Snakebite's truck, Glen found himself run ragged by
morning, so covered with sweat, grit and dust that the lines in his face
and the corners of his eyes and the insides of his ears were black, and
his snot, when he blew his nose, even that was black.

One evening in mid-July Glen trudged to the office to complain. He
opened the door and came face-to-face with the young woman from
Roy's car. She had lovely black skin and round brown eyes. Rich dark
hair in cornrow braids that would've hung down except for her
headband. She wore bright green spandex pants and a sports bra.

'Hello,' Glen said.

'Right.' She flounced into the bathroom.

Glen hurried to Roy's desk. 'What the hell's she doing here?'

Roy had his feet and a portable television on the desk. He was
watching the Yankees. 'Your new assistant,' he said. 'You just keep
your got-damn hands off her.'

'She can't work here.' Glen glanced at the TV. 'What's the score?
What if she gets hurt? She's just a girl.'

'Woman,' she said from the door.

'Tied up,' Roy said.

'Sorry,' Glen said. 'Miss . . .?'

'Ms.'

Roy cranked the volume without looking at them. 'You been whining about having too much work every night,' he told Glen, 'so Jalalieh gonna start driving the loader for you.'

Jalalieh

Ja-LA-lee-ay.

As Glen instructed her in the operation of the Caterpillar 950 front-end loader, she stayed quiet. It was crowded in the cab and he had to hang on the stepladder to allow her room to work the levers that raised, lowered and swiveled the bucket. She smelled good, even over the diesel odor of the payloader, and he soon found himself staring at her thighs and biceps.

'You work out a lot?' he asked.

'Careful big bad Roy don't see you making small talk,' she said.

'Pull back on the bucket easy,' he said. 'You'll spill less.'

'That's better, little man. Keep it professional.'

So with great patience and fear he instructed her on how to gain speed when heading in to scoop raw material, how to drop the bucket along the ground and dig from the bottom of a pile, locking the raise lever and working the swivel lever back and forth as it rose to get the fullest bucket. He showed her how to hold a loaded bucket high and peer beneath it to see, how to roll smoothly over the rough black ground and up the ramp behind the plant to the hopper. How to dump the bucket while shifting into reverse so the material fell evenly onto the hopper grate, and how to back down the ramp while lowering the bucket. She caught on quickly and within a few nights was a much better loader operator than most of the day shift guys. Glen watched from the ground with pride as she tore giant bulging bucketfuls from the piles and carried them safely over the yard. And as he noticed the way her breasts bounced when she passed, he felt the hot, gritty wind swirling and whistling through the caves of his heart.

*

A few night later, while Glen and Snakebite watched the truck load, Snakebite explained about his tiny head.

'Everybody on my daddy's side's got little bitty heads,' he said. 'It's kinda like our trademark. We ain't got no butts, either. Look.' He turned and, sure enough, there was all this spare material in the seat of his blue jeans. Snakebite laughed. 'But me, I make up for it with my dick.'

'Pardon?' Glen said.

'Well, I ain't fixing to whip it out, but I got the biggest durn cock-a-doodle-doo you liable to see on a white man. Yes sir,' he said, lowering his voice so it was hard to hear over the roar of the plant, 'when I get a hard-on, I ain't got enough loose skin left to close my eyes.'

Glen, whose penis was average, took out his flask. He was unscrewing the lid when Jalalieh thundered past in the loader. When Glen glanced at Snakebite, the truck driver was looking after her with his eyes wide open.

The next night, as the truck loaded, something clattered behind them. Glen unclipped his flashlight and Snakebite followed him around a dark corner to the garbage cans. An armadillo had gotten into the trash, one of its feet in an aluminum pie-plate.

'Well, hello there, you old armored dildo,' Snakebite said. When it tried to dart away, he cornered it. 'Tell you what, Slick'—he winked at Glen—'you keep an eye on our friend and I'll be right back.'

He trotted toward his truck and Glen kept the flashlight aimed at the armadillo—gray, the size of a football, just squatting there, white icing on its snout. Soon Snakebite reappeared with a briefcase. He set it on a garbage can and opened it and rummaged around, finally coming out with something bundled in a towel. He unwrapped it and Glen saw several different-colored knives.

Snakebite grinned. 'I bought 'em offa circus Indian chief used to chuck 'em at a squaw that spun on a big old wagon wheel.'

He took a knife by its wide blade and flicked it. The armadillo jumped straight up and landed running, the handle poking out of its side. Snakebite fired another knife which ricocheted off the armadillo's back. Another stuck in its shoulder. A fourth knife bounced off the concrete. Glen glanced away, ashamed for not stopping Snakebite. When he looked again the armadillo lay on its side, inflating and deflating with loud rasps.

'I hate them sum-bitches,' Snakebite said. He stepped forward and drew back his foot to punt the armadillo.

Suddenly a light flared, catching the two men like the headlights of night hunters: Jalalieh, in the loader, bore down on them, the bucket scraping the ground, igniting sparks. Glen dove one way and Snakebite the other as she plowed in like a freight train, sweeping up the armadillo, the garbage cans, the knives. In a second she was gone, disappearing around the plant, leaving them flat on their bellies with their heads covered like survivors of an explosion.

'That's a hot little honey,' Snakebite said once he was back on his feet. He dusted off his jeans. 'You reckon old Roy'd sell me a piece of that? Add it to my bill?'

It wasn't Glen's jealousy that surprised him. 'You owe Roy money?'

'Yep. Borrowed it to get my truck painted.'

'Roy's a loan shark too?'

'You ever see *Jaws*?' Snakebite asked.

Glen said he had.

'How 'bout *The Godfather*?'

'Yeah.'

'Well, if Michael Corleone waded out in the ocean and fucked that shark, then you'd have old Roy.'

Later, as Jalalieh climbed out of the loader, Glen stood waiting in the shadows.

'A what?'

'Tour,' he repeated. 'See, the Black Beauty, it's a state-of-the-art facility.'

'This dump?'

'With cutting-edge technology.' He grinned. 'Get it?'

She folded her arms.

'Okay,' Glen said. 'The unique thing about our grit is that no piece—'

'Has a round edge. So what?'

Nevertheless, she allowed Glen to lead her around the plant, explaining how the raw material from the loader fell onto a conveyor belt, then into a machine similar to a grain elevator. From there it rode up into the dryer, a tall cylindrical oven which used natural gas to burn the moisture out. Next, the dry grit flowed into the crusher, a wide centrifuge that spun the grit at high speeds and smashed the grains against iron walls, pulverizing any outsized rock into smaller pieces. Finally atop the plant, Glen showed her the shaker, a jingling, vibrating box the size of a coffin. Raising his voice to be heard, he explained how the shaker housed several screens and sifted the grit down through them, distributing it by size into the storage tanks under their feet.

Staring at the shaker, Jalalieh said, 'It's like one of those motel beds you put a quarter in.'

Every night and day the dryer dried and the crusher crushed and the shaker shook, sifting grit down through the screens into their proper tanks. To keep pieces from clogging the screens, rubber balls were placed between the layers when the screens were built. Little by little, the grit eroded the balls, so they'd gradually be whittled from the size of handballs down to marbles, then BBs, and finally they'd just disappear so that, every two weeks or so, Glen's day-shift guys would have to build new screens, add new balls. Since Glen had begun sleeping during the day, the workers had gotten lax again. While the grit clogged the shaker and gnawed holes in chutes and pipes and elevators and accumulated in piles that grew each hour, the day shift played poker in the control room, sunbathed on top of the tanks; had king-of-the-mountain contests on the stockpiles.

One morning, Glen was snoring on his desk when he heard something thump against the side of the office.

He rolled over, rubbing his eyes, squinting in the bright light, and he looked out the window at the plant shimmering against the hot white sky. Then he saw his entire four-man day crew and some tall guy playing baseball with an old shovel handle. There was a pitcher on a mound of grit with a box of the rubber screen balls open beside him. There were two fielders trying to shag the flies. There was a catcher wearing a respirator, hard hat and welding sleeves for protection. The batter was Snakebite, and he was whacking the pitched balls clear over the mountains of grit, nearly to the interstate.

Glen closed his eyes and went back to sleep.

Every night Glen scaled that ladder up between the storage tanks— quite a climb in the dark, over a hundred feet with no protection against gravity but the metal cage around the ladder. At the top, catwalks joined the tanks. Out past the handrails, darkness stretched all around, and in the distance blinked the lights of radio towers and chemical-plant smokestacks. The Black Beauty had its own blinking yellow beacon on a pole high above, a warning to low-flying aircraft, the one light Glen feared shutting off—certainly that would be illegal. It blinked every few seconds, illuminating the dusty air, and Glen followed his flashlight beam from tank to tank, prying open the heavy metal lids and unspooling over each an ancient measuring tape with a big iron bolt on its end.

A few nights after Jalalieh's tour, Glen climbed the ladder to take measurements. It was nearly dawn, and he'd just finished when he saw her. Hugging her knees, Jalalieh sat overhead, atop the tallest elevator platform, appearing and vanishing in the light. Glen crept over and scaled the short ladder beside her, the first faint smear of sunrise spreading below them.

'Pretty,' he said.

She shrugged. 'Don't tell that asshole you saw me here.'

'Snakebite?'

'Roy.'

Glen gripped the ladder hopefully. 'You love Roy?'

She shook her head.

'So you're with him because he . . . buys you things?'

'What things? My little brother owes him money. Roy and I came up with this arrangement.'

Glen felt a rush of horror and glee. Her affection suddenly seemed plausible. He hung there, trying to say the right thing. He wanted to explain why he hadn't stood up for the armadillo—because pissing Snakebite off might be dangerous—but that made him sound cowardly. Instead he said, 'What would Roy do to your brother if you didn't honor your arrangement?'

Jalalieh glanced at him. 'He's already done it.'

'Done what?'

'He had that truck driver cut the toes off his foot with wire cutters.'

Glen was about to change the subject, but she'd already swung to the tank below. By the time he descended, she was gone. He thought of the armadillo again, the knives, how Jalalieh had barreled in and taken control. It reminded him of the first time he'd accompanied his second ex-wife's father to a cockfight, which was illegal in Alabama. What had unsettled Glen wasn't the violence of the roosters pecking and spurring each other—he actually enjoyed betting on the bloody matches—but that several hippie-looking spectators had been smoking joints, right out in the open. Later he attributed his discomfort to that being his first and only experience outside the law.

Until now. Now the Black Beauty was a place with power up for grabs, a world where you fought for what you wanted, where you plotted, used force.

It was just getting light, time to shut down the plant, but Glen stood under the tanks, watching the dark office across the yard, where no doubt Roy slept like a king.

'Got-damn it, Glen,' Roy said. 'Ain't I told you to get some damn cable in here?'

Glen stood in his sneakers and baseball cap, Jalalieh behind him in the office door. 'This is a business, not a residence,' Glen said. 'There's problems getting it installed.'

'Then you better nigger-rig something by tomorrow night.' Roy rose from his chair behind the desk, which had two portable TVs on it. 'What?' he said to Jalalieh. 'The little girl don't like that word? "Nigger"?'

'Try "African American,"' she said stiffly.

'Fuck that,' he said. 'I ain't no got-damn African American. I'm *American* American!'

She turned in a clatter of braids and vanished.

'And you,' Roy said, 'you got to clean this pigsty up.'

Glen went cold. 'Oh, Christ,' he said. 'When?'

'They flying in Wednesday night. Be here first thing Thursday.'

Ernie and Dwight.

So in addition to his other work, Glen spent the night cleaning his plant. He patched holes and leaks with silicon. He welded, shoveled, sandblasted. Replaced filters and built new shaker screens and greased bone-dry fittings and paid Jalalieh fifty bucks to straighten the stockpiled material with the loader. By daybreak the place was in sterling shape and a solid black, grimy Glen trudged over to the office. He hid Roy's TVs in the closet. Sprayed Pledge and vacuumed the carpet and Windexed the windows and emptied an entire can of Lysol into the air. He flipped the calendar to—what month was it?—August.

No time to go home, so Glen showered in the break room, using

Snakebite's motel bar of Ivory soap and his sample-sized Head &
Shoulders. When he stepped out, cinching his tie, it was seven, nearly
time for the day shift to begin. He hurried to the plant to see things in
the light. Perfect. Not a stray speck of grit. Gorgeous. In the office, he
took out the ledgers and began to fudge. An hour later he looked up,
his hand numb from erasing. Eight o'clock. They'd be here any second.

By ten they still hadn't arrived. The day-shifters had clocked in and,
seeing the plant clean, understood there was an inspection and were
working like they used to. For a moment, staring out the window at the
humming plant and the legitimately loading trucks and the men doing
constructive things in their safety equipment, Glen felt nostalgic and
sad. He grabbed the phone.

'I said don't be calling this early,' Roy growled.

'Where the hell are they?'

'Chill, baby. I had 'em met at the airport.'

Images of Ernie and Dwight fingerless, mangled, swam before
Glen's eyes. 'My God.' He sat down.

'Naw, baby.' Roy chuckled. 'I told a couple of my bitches to meet
'em. Them two old white mens ain't been treated this good they whole
life.'

'Hookers?' Glen switched ears. 'So Ernie and Dwight aren't
coming?'

'I expect they'll drop by for a few minutes,' Roy said. 'But Glen, if I
was you, I wouldn't sweat E and D. If I was you, baby, I'd be scared of
old Roy. I'd be coming up with some got-damn money and I'd be
doing it fast.'

True to Roy's word, Ernie and Dwight showed up in the afternoon,
unshaven, red-eyed, smelling of gin and smiling, their ties loose,
wedding rings missing. They stayed at the plant for half an hour,
complimenting Glen on his appearance and on how spic-and-span his
operation was. Keep up the good work, they said, falling back into
their Caddy, and standing in the parking lot as they drove away, Glen
saw a pink garter hanging from the rearview mirror.

Glen spent the rest of the day and most of his checking account bribing
one of his ex-wives' old boyfriends, a cable installer, to run a line to the
office. Then he went to apply for a home-improvement loan. Sitting

across from the banker, who looked ten years younger, Glen stopped listening as soon as the guy said, '*Four* alimonies?'

Back at the plant, he hoped the new cable (including HBO and Cinemax) would ease Roy's temper. He filled the hopper and fired the plant up early. From behind the crusher he saw Roy drive up, saw him and Jalalieh get out. They didn't speak: Roy went into the office, carrying another TV, and Jalalieh stalked across the yard to the loader. She climbed in and started the engine, raced it to build air pressure. She goosed the levers, wiggling the bucket the way some people jingle keys. Catching Glen's eye, she drew a finger across her throat.

Just after dusk Snakebite's Peterbilt rumbled into the yard. It paused on the scales, then pulled next to the plant and stopped beneath the loading chute. Glen had the grit flowing before Snakebite's boots touched the ground. He stuffed his trembling hands into his pockets as the trucker shambled toward him.

'I'm real sorry, Slick,' Snakebite mumbled, his eyes down. 'It's nothing personal. Have you got the money? Any of it?'

Glen shook his head in disbelief, which also answered the question.

'I'll give you a few minutes,' Snakebite said, 'if you wanna get drunk. That helps a little.'

Glen glanced at the dark office window—Roy would be there, watching.

'It won't be too bad,' Snakebite said. 'Roy needs you. He only wants me to take one of your little fingers, at the first knuckle. You even get to pick which one.' He jerked a thumb behind him. 'I keep some rubbing alcohol in the truck, and some Band-Aids. We can get you fixed up real quick. You better go on take you a swig, though.' Snakebite had moved so close that Glen could smell Head & Shoulders shampoo.

He pointed toward the control room, and when Snakebite looked, Glen bolted for the ladder and shot up through the roaring darkness.

It was breezy at the top, warm fumes in the air from nearby insecticide plants. Backing away from the edge, Glen slipped and fell to one knee. He felt warm blood running down his bare leg.

'Jalalieh?' he whispered. '*You up here?*' Searching for a weapon, he found the measuring tape with the bolt on the end. He scrambled to his feet and watched the side of the tank as it lit and faded, lit and faded.

In one flash of light a hand appeared, then another, then Snakebite's tiny head. His wide shoulders surfaced next, rubbing the ladder cage. On the tank, he wobbled uncertainly in his boots. He looked behind him, a hundred feet down, where his truck purred, still loading.

Glen let out a few feet of the measuring tape. Began swinging the bolt over his head like a mace.

'Slick!' Snakebite called. 'Let's just get it over with. It won't even hurt till a few seconds after I do it. Just keep your hand elevated above your heart, and that'll help the throbbing.'

He took a tentative step as a gust of hot, acrid wind swirled. He bent to roll up his pants leg, then disappeared as the light faded. When he appeared again, he held the Mississippi Gambler. 'It's real sharp, Slick. Ain't no sawing involved. Just a quick cut and it's all over.'

Glen moved back, swinging his mace, the shaker rattling beside him, the tank humming beneath his sneakers. He stepped onto the metal gridwork of a catwalk and the ground appeared for a moment, far below, then vanished. When the light came again Snakebite loomed in front of him. Glen yelled and the mace flew wildly to the right.

Snakebite struck him in the chest with a giant forearm that sent Glen skidding across the catwalk, his cap fluttering away. He tried to rise, but the truck driver pinned him flat on his belly, his right arm twisted behind him.

'Hold your breath, Slick,' Snakebite grunted.

Glen fisted his left hand and felt hot grit. With his teeth clenched, he slung it over his shoulder.

Snakebite yelled, let him go. Glen rolled and saw the big man staggering backward, clawing at his eyes.

There was only the one ladder down, and Snakebite had it blocked, so Glen began to circle the shaker. A glint of something white bounced off the rail by his hand—the Mississippi Gambler—and Snakebite charged, the trench knife gleaming.

Glen dodged and, running for the ladder, got pegged in the shoulder by the shaker. He spun, grabbing his arm, and fell, kicking at Snakebite, who swiped halfheartedly with the trench knife. Glen scrabbled to his feet and feinted, but the truck driver moved with him, and Glen was cornered. Snakebite, pulsing in and out of the darkness, lifted his giant hand as if someone had just introduced them.

Glen slowly raised his right hand, balled in a fist. 'How could you cut off her brother's toes?' he yelled.

'Whose brother?' Snakebite grabbed Glen's hand and forced the pinky out. 'Don't watch,' he said.

Glen closed his eyes, expecting the cut to be ice-cold at first.

But the howl in the air was not, he thought, coming from him. He opened one eye and put his fist (pinky intact) down. The truck driver, clutching his tiny head with both hands, still had the trench knife hooked to his fingers. Behind him, Jalalieh was backing away with an iron pipe in her fist. Snakebite dropped the trench knife and fell to his knees. He rolled on his side and curled into a ball.

Glen picked up the knife.

'Come on,' Jalalieh hissed. 'Roy's on his way!'

They hurried across the tanks and the spotlights flared, as if the Black Beauty were about to lift off into the night. Glen knew Roy had flipped the master breaker below. Jalalieh took his arm and they crept to the rail. Roy was pulling himself up, sweaty, scowling, a snub-nosed pistol in one hand. Glen began to kick grit off the edge to slow him.

'Got-damn it!' Roy yelled, and a bullet sang straight up into the night, a foot from Glen's chin.

'Jesus!' He pushed Jalalieh behind him and they stumbled back. Glen remembered a proposal he'd sent Ernie and Dwight a year ago— one that called for another access way to the top, stairs or a caged elevator.

A long minute passed before Roy finally hoisted himself onto the tanks, grit glittering on his cheeks and forehead. Breathing hard, he transferred the pistol to the hand holding the rail and with the other removed his fedora and dusted himself off. He took a cigar from his shirt pocket and chomped on it but didn't try lighting it.

'Girl,' he said to Jalalieh. 'Get over here.'

She left Glen, careful of the shaker, more careful of Roy.

'Get your ass down there and fill up that got-damn hopper,' he ordered. 'It's fixing to run out.'

She shot Glen a look he couldn't identify, then disappeared down the ladder.

'Snakebite!' Roy yelled.

The big driver stirred, grit pouring off him. He rubbed the back of his head with one hand and his eyes with the other. There was blood on his collar and fingers. He blinked at Roy.

'Shit, baby,' Roy laughed, 'we wear hard hats in the plant for a reason, right, Glen?'

Snakebite, his eyes lowered, limped across the catwalk and stuffed himself into the ladder cage.

Holding the pistol loosely at his side, Roy watched Glen. 'You want something done right,' he muttered, 'don't send no stupid-ass Texas redneck.' He slipped the gun into his pants pocket and turned, walked toward the ladder. 'I'm gonna garnish your salary,' he called over his shoulder, 'till your debt's paid off.'

Glen followed him, his heart rattling in his chest. When he lifted his hand to cover his eyes, he saw the trench knife.

Roy was crossing the catwalk, holding the rails on either side, when Glen lunged and hit him in the back of the neck with the brass knuckles. The cigar shot from his mouth and Roy was surprisingly easy—a hand on his belt, one on his collar—to offset and shove over the rail. Falling, Roy opened his mouth but no sound came out. With eyes that looked incredibly hurt, he dropped, arms wheeling, legs running. He was screaming now, shrinking, turning an awkward somersault. Glen looked away before he hit the concrete.

On the ground, Glen could feel the tanks vibrating in his legs. He took deep breaths, hugging himself, and felt better. His heart was still there, hanging on, antique maybe, shot full of holes and eroded nearly to nothing, but still, by God, pumping. He went to a line of breakers and flipped one. The spotlights died.

He heard footsteps, and Jalalieh ran past him in the dark. Glen reached for her but she was gone. He followed. They found Snakebite standing by Roy's body. He'd thrown a tarp over him.

'He slipped,' Glen said.

'Right.' Jalalieh ran her brown eyes over Glen, then looked up into the darkness. 'He must've.'

'God almighty,' Snakebite said. He rubbed his nose. For a moment Glen thought the truck driver was crying, but it was just grit in his eyes.

Jalalieh knelt and pulled back the tarp. There was blood. Without flinching, she went through Roy's pockets and found his gun, the keys to his car, his roll of money and his ledger. She stood, and Glen and Snakebite followed her into the control room. Inside, she studied the ledger. Looking over her shoulder, Glen saw an almost illegible list that must have been Roy's grit clients. He strained to read them but Jalalieh flipped to a list of names and numbers. Glen's own debt, he noticed, was tiny in comparison to Snakebite's, and to Jalalieh's.

Jalalieh's?

Glen frowned. 'What about your little brother?'

'What brother?' She licked her thumb and began counting the money. Behind her, Snakebite sat heavily in a chair.

'So, wait,' Glen said, 'you were paying Roy by, by—'

'By fucking, Glen.' She glanced at him. 'You want it spelled out, little man? He was fucking you one way and me another way. And the truth is, you were getting the better deal.'

'What now?' Snakebite asked, his voice like gravel.

'You deliver, same as always,' Jalalieh said. 'And keep quiet. Nothing's changed.'

With the truck driver gone, Glen grew suddenly nauseated. He crossed the room and took a hard hat from the rack and filled it with a colorless liquid. He closed his eyes and breathed through his nose.

At the control panel, Jalalieh tapped the dryer's temperature gauge. 'How hot does this thing get?'

Glen had cold sweats. 'Thousand degrees Fahrenheit,' he said, which didn't seem nearly enough to warm him.

She smiled. 'Shut the plant down.'

Half an hour later things were very quiet, only the fiddling of crickets from nearby trees. Jalalieh came in the loader. Glen looked away while she scooped Roy, tarp and all, off the ground.

He walked through the plant, pausing to kick open a cutoff valve that released a hissing cloud of steam. At the dryer, Jalalieh lowered the bucket and dumped Roy's body. One of his shoes had come off. In heavy gloves, Glen turned the wheel that opened the furnace door. It took them both to lift the fat man and, squinting against the heat, to cram him into the chamber. Jalalieh pitched his fedora in, then sent Glen after the shoe. By the time they'd closed the door and locked the wheel, they could see through the thick yellowed porthole that Roy's clothes and hair had caught fire.

Jalalieh followed Glen into the control room and watched him press buttons and adjust dials, the plant puffing and groaning as it stirred to life. She said she wanted to ignite the dryer, and when it came time to set the temperature she cranked the knob into the red. For an hour they sat quietly, passing Glen's flask back and forth, while Roy burned in the dryer, while his charred bones were pounded to dust in the crusher and dumped into the shaker, which clattered madly, sifting the remains of Roy Jones through the screens and sending him through various chutes and depositing the tiny flecks, according to size, into the storage tanks.

Two weeks later Jalalieh called the plant, collect. She told Glen that Ernie and Dwight were slated for another surprise inspection on September fifth. She gave him the phone numbers of two reliable hookers. Then shc read him her account number in the bank where Glen was to deposit her cut. She wouldn't give her location, but said she lived alone, in a cabin, and there was snow. That she jogged every day up mountains, through tall trees. That she'd taken a part-time job at a logging plant, for the fun of it, driving a front-end loader. 'Only here they call it a skidder,' she told him.

'Ja—' he said, but she'd hung up.

He replaced the phone and leaned back in his chair. Propped his feet on his desk. It was time to throw himself head, body and heart into work. He speed-dialed Snakebite on the cellular phone and told him to be at the plant by eight. Tonight would be busy. You'd think, from all the sandblasting grit they were selling, that the entire hull of the world was caked and corroded with rust, barnacles and scum, and that somebody, somewhere, was finally cleaning things up.

A NEW MAN

Edward P. Jones

One day in late October, Woodrow L. Cunningham came home early with his bad heart and found his daughter with the two boys. He was then fifty-two years old, a conscientious deacon at Rising Star AME Zion, a paid-up lifetime member of the NAACP and the Urban League, a twenty-five year member of the Elks. For ten years he had been the chief engineer at the Sheraton Park Hotel, where practically every employee knew his name. For longer than he could recall, his friends and lodge members had been telling him that he was capable of being more than just the number-one maintenance man. But he always told them that he was contented in the job, that it was all he needed, and this was true for the most part. He would be in that same position some thirteen years later, when death happened upon him as he bent down over a hotel bathroom sink, about to do a job a younger engineer claimed he could not handle.

The afternoon he came home early and discovered his daughter with the boys, he found a letter in the mailbox from his father in Georgia. He read the letter while standing in the hall of the apartment building. He expected nothing of importance, as usual, and that was what he found. 'Alice took me to Buddy Wilson funeral just last week,' Woodrow read. 'I loaned him the shirt they buried him in. And that tie he had on was one that I give him too. I thought I would miss him but I do not miss him very much. Checkers was never Buddy Wilsons game.' As he read, he massaged the area around his heart, an old habit, something he did even when his heart was not giving him trouble. 'I hope you and the family can come down before the winter months set in. Company is never the same after winter get here.'

He put the letter back in the envelope, and as he absently looked at the upside-down stamp taped in the vicinity of the corner, the pain in his heart eased. He could picture his father sitting at the kitchen table, writing the letter, occasionally touching the pencil point to his tongue. A new mongrel's head would be resting across his lap, across thin legs that could still carry the old man five miles down the road and back.

Woodrow, feeling better, considered returning to work, but he knew his heart was deceitful. He folded the envelope and stuck it in his back pocket, and out of the pocket it would fall late that night as he prepared for bed after returning from the police station.

Several feet before he reached his apartment door he could hear the boys' laughter and bits and pieces of their man-child conquer-the-world talk. He could not hear his daughter at first. He stopped at his door and listened for nearly five minutes, and in that time he became so fascinated by what the boys were saying that he would not have cared if someone walking in the hall found him listening. It was only when he heard his daughter's laughter, familiar, known, that he put his key in the door. She stood just inside the door when he entered, her eyes accusing but her mouth set in a small O of surprise. Beyond her he could see the boys with their legs draped over the arms of the couch and gray smoke above their heads wafting toward the open window.

He asked his daughter, 'Why ain't you in school?'

'They let us out early today,' she said. 'The teachers had some kinda meetin.'

He did not listen to her, because he had found that she lived to lie. Woodrow watched the boys as they took their time straightening themselves up, and he knew that their deliberateness was the result of something his daughter had said about him. Without taking his eyes from the boys, he asked his daughter again why she wasn't in school. When he finally looked at her, he saw that she was holding the stump of a thin cigarette. The smoke he smelled was unfamiliar, and at first he thought that they were smoking very stale cigarettes, or cigarettes that had gotten wet and been dried. He slapped her. 'I told you not to smoke in my house,' he said.

She was fifteen, and up until six months or so before, she would have collapsed into the chair, collapsed into a fit of crying. But now she picked up the fallen cigarette from the floor and stamped it out in the ashtray on the tiny table beside the easy chair. Her hand shook, the only reminder of the old days. 'We just talkin. We ain't doin nothin wrong,' she said quietly.

He shouted to the boys, 'Get outta my house!' They stood up quickly, and Woodrow could tell that whatever she had told them about him, such anger was not part of it. They looked once at the girl.

'They my guests, Daddy,' she said, sitting in the easy chair and crossing her legs. 'I invited em over here.'

Woodrow took two steps to the boy nearest him—the tall light-skinned one he would spot from a bus window a year or so later—and grabbed him with one hand by the jacket collar, shook him until the boy raised his hands as if to protect his face from a blow. The boy's eyes widened and Woodrow shook him some more. He had been living a black man's civilized life in Washington and had not felt so coiled and bristled since the days when he worked with wild men in the turpentine camps in Florida. 'I ain't done nothin,' the boy said. The words sounded familiar, similar to those of a wild man ready to slink away into his cabin with his tail between his legs. Woodrow relaxed. 'I swear. I don't want no trouble, Mr. Cunningham.' The boy had no other smell but that peculiar cigarette smoke, and it was a shock to Woodrow that a body with that smell should know something that seemed as personal as his name. The other, smaller boy had tiptoed around Woodrow and was having trouble opening the door. After the small boy had gone out, Woodrow flung the light-skinned boy out behind him. Woodrow locked the door, and the boys stood for several minutes, pounding on the door, mouthing off.

'Why you treat my guests like that?' Elaine Cunningham had not moved from the chair.

'Clean up this mess,' he told her, 'and I don't wanna see one ash when you done.'

She said nothing more, but busied herself tidying the couch cushions. Then Woodrow, after flicking the cushions a few times with his handkerchief, sat in the middle of the couch, and the couch sagged with the familiarity of this weight.

When Elaine had returned the room to what it was, her father said, 'I want to know what you was doin in here with them boys.'

'Nothin. We wasn't doin nothin. Just talkin, thas all, Daddy.' She sat in the easy chair, leaned toward him with her elbows on her knees.

'You can do your talkin down on the stoop,' he said.

'Why don't you just say you tryin to cuse me a somethin? Why don't you just come out and say it?'

'If you didn't do things, you wouldn't get accused,' he said. He talked without thought, because those words and words like them had been spoken so much to her that he was able to parrot himself. 'If you start actin like a young lady should, start studyin and what not, and tryin to make somethin of yourself . . .' Woodrow L. Cunningham bein Woodrow L. Cunningham, he thought.

She stood up quickly, and he was sickened to see her breasts bounce. 'I could study them stupid books half the damn day and sit in church the other half, and I'd still get the same stuff thrown in my face bout how I ain't doin right.'

'Okay, thas anough a that.' He felt a familiar rumbling in his heart. 'I done heard anough.'

'I wanna go out.' She stood with her arms folded. 'I wanna go out.'

'Go on back to your room. Thas the only goin out you gonna be doin. I don't wanna hear another word outta your mouth till your mother get home.' He closed his eyes to wait her out, for he knew she was now capable of standing there till doomsday to sulk. When he heard her going down the hall, he waited for the door to slam. But there was no sound and he gradually opened his eyes. He put a cushion at one end of the couch and took off his shoes and lay down, his hands resting on the large mound that was his stomach. All his friends told him that if he lost thirty or forty pounds he would be a new man, but he did not think that was true. He considered asking Elaine to bring his pills from his bedroom, for he had left the vial he traveled with at work. But he suffered the pain rather than suffer her stirring about. He watched his wife's curtains flap gently with the breeze and the movement soothed him.

'I would not say anything bad about mariage,' his father had written to Woodrow after Woodrow called to say he was considering marrying Rita Hadley. 'It is easier to pick up and walk away from a wife and a family if you don't like it then you can walk away from your own bad cooking.' Woodrow had never been inclined to marry anyone, was able, as he would tell his lodge brothers, to get all the trim he wanted without buying some woman a ring and walking down the aisle with her. 'Doin it to a woman for a few months was all right,' he would say, sounding like his father, 'cause that only put the idea of marryin in their heads. Doin it to them any more than that and the idea take root.'

It had never crossed his mind to sleep with any of the women at Rising Star AME, for he had discovered in Georgia that the wrath of church women was greater than that of all others, even old whores. He only went out with Rita because the preacher took him aside one

Sunday and told him it was unnatural to go about unmarried and that he should give some thought to promenading with Sister Rita sometime. And, too, he was thirty-six and it was beginning to occur to him that women might not go on forever laying down and opening their legs for him. The second time they went out, he put his arm around Rita and pulled her to him there in the Booker-T Theater. She smacked his hand and that made his johnson hard. 'I ain't like that, Mr. Cunningham.' He had heard those words before. But when he pulled her to him again, she twisted his finger until it hurt. And that was something he had not experienced before.

His father suffered a mild stroke a week before the wedding. 'Do not take this sickness to mean that I do not send my blessing to your mariage to Miss Rita Hadley,' his father said in a letter he had dictated to Alice, his oldest daughter. 'God took pity on you when he send her your way.' Even in the unfamiliarity of Alice's handwriting, the familiarity of his father was there in all the lines, right down to the misspelled words. Until some of his father's children learned in their teens, his father had been the only one in the family who could read and write. 'This,' he said of his reading and writing, 'makes me as good as a white man.' And before some of his children learned, discovered there was no magic to it, he enjoyed reading aloud at the supper table to his family, his voice stringing out a long monotone of words that often meant nothing to him and even less to his family because the man read so quickly.

His father read anything he could get his hands on—the words on feed bags, on medicine bottles, on years-old magazine pages they used for wallpaper, just about everything except the Bible. He had a fondness for weeks-old newspapers he would find in the streets when he went to town. No one—not even the squirming small kids—was allowed to move from the supper table until he had finished reading, hooking one word to another until it all became babble. Indeed, it was such a babble that some of his sons would joke behind his back that he was lying about knowing how to read. 'Few white men can do what I'm doin right now,' he would say. 'You go bring ten white men in here and I bet nine couldn't read this. Couldn't read it if God commanded em to.' Sometimes, to torment his wife, he would hold a scrap of newspaper close to her face and tell her to read the headlines. 'I cain't,' she would say. 'You know I cain't.' No matter how many times he did this, his father would laugh with the pleasure of the very first time. Then he would pass the newspaper among his children and tell them to read him the headlines, and each one would hold it uncomfortably and repeat what their mother had said.

When Woodrow woke, it was nearly five o'clock and his wife was sitting on the side of the couch, asking where Elaine was. 'She ain't in her room,' his wife said and kissed his forehead. A school cafeteria worker, Rita was a very thin woman who, before she met Woodrow, had lived only for her job and her church activities. She was five years older than he was and had resigned herself to the fact that she was not the type of woman men wanted to marry. 'I've put it all in God's hands,' she once said to a friend before Woodrow came along, 'and left it there.'

Rita waited until seven o'clock before she began calling her daughter's friends. 'Stop worryin,' Woodrow told her after the tenth call, 'you know how that girl is.' At eight-thirty, they put on light coats and went in search, visiting the same houses and apartments that Rita had called. They returned home about ten and waited until eleven, when they put on their coats again and went to the police station at 16th and V Northwest. They did not call the station because somewhere Woodrow had heard that the law wouldn't begin to hear a complaint unless you stood before it in person.

At the station, the man at the front desk did not look up until they had been standing there for some two minutes. Woodrow wanted to tell him that the police chief and the mayor were now black men and that they couldn't be ignored, but when the man behind the desk looked up, Woodrow could see in his eyes that none of that would have mattered to him.

'Our daughter is missing,' Rita said.

'How long?' said the man, a sergeant with an unpronounceable name on his name tag. He pulled a form from a pile to his left and then he took up a pen, loudly clicking out the point to write.

'We haven't seen her since this afternoon,' Woodrow says.

The sergeant clicked the pen again and set it on the desk, then put the form back on top with the others. 'Not long enough,' he said. 'Has to be gone forty-eight hours. Till then she's missing, but she's not a missing person.'

'She only a baby.'

'How old?'

'Fifteen,' Woodrow said.

'She's just a runaway,' the sergeant said.

'She never run away before,' Woodrow said. 'This ain't like her, sergeant.' Woodrow felt that like all white men, the man enjoyed having attention paid to his rank.

'Don't matter. She's probably waiting for you at home right now, wondering where you two buggied off to. Go home. If she isn't home, then come back when she's a missing person.'

Woodrow took Rita's arm as they went back, because he sensed that she was near collapsing. 'What happened?' she asked as they turned the corner of U and 10th streets. 'Did you say somethin bad to her?'

He told her everything that he could remember, even what Elaine was wearing when he last saw her. Answering was not difficult because no blame had yet been assigned. Despite the time nearing midnight, they became confident with each step that Elaine was just at a friend's they did not know about, that the friend's mother, like any good mother, would soon send their daughter home. Rita, in the last blocks before their apartment, leaned into her husband and his warmth helped to put her at ease.

They waited up until about four in the morning, and then they undressed without words in the dark. Rita began to cry the moment her head hit the pillow, for she was afraid to see the sun come up and find that a new day had arrived without Elaine being home. She asked him again what happened, and he told her again, even things that he had forgotten—the logo of the football team on the light-skinned boy's jacket, the fact that the other boy was bald except for a half-dollar-sized spot of hair carved on the back of his head. He was still talking when she dozed off with him holding her.

Before they had coffee later that morning, about seven thirty, they called their jobs to say they would not be in. Work had always occupied a place at the center of their lives, and there was initially something eerie about being home when it was not a holiday or the weekend. They spent the rest of the morning searching the streets together, and in the afternoon, they separated to cover more ground. They did the same thing after dinner, each spreading out farther and farther from their apartment on R Street. That evening, they called neighbors and friends, church and lodge members, to tell them that their child was missing and that they needed their help and their prayers. Their friends and neighbors began searching that evening, and a few went with Woodrow and Rita the next day to the police station to file a missing person's report. A different sergeant was at the desk, and though he was a white man, Woodrow felt that he understood their trouble.

For nearly three months, Woodrow and Rita searched after they came from work, and each evening after they and their friends had been out, the pastor of Rising Star spoke to a small group that gathered in the Cunninghams' living room. 'The world is cold and not hospitable,' he would conclude, holding his hat in both hands, 'but we know our God to be a kind God and that he has provided our little sister with a place of comfort and warmth until she returns to her parents and to all of us who love and treasure her.'

In the kitchen beside the refrigerator, Rita tacked up a giant map of Washington, on which she noted where she and others had searched. 'I didn't know the city was this big,' she said the day she put it up, her fingertips touching the neighborhoods that she had never heard of or had heard of only in passing—foreign lands she thought she would never set eyes on. Petworth. Anacostia. Lincoln Park. And in the beginning, the very size of the city lifted her spirits, for in a place so big, there was certainly a spot that held something as small as her child, and if they just kept looking long enough, they would come upon that place.

'What happened?' Rita would ask as they prepared for bed. What he told her and her listening replaced everything they had ever done in that bed—discussing what future they wanted for Elaine, lovemaking, sharing what the world had done to them that workday. 'What happened?' It was just about the only thing she ever asked Woodrow as the months grew colder. 'What happened? Whatcha say to her?' By late February, when fewer and fewer people were going out to search, he had told the whole story, but then he began to tell her things that had not happened. There were three boys, he said at one point, for example. Or, he could see a gun sticking out of the jacket pocket of the light-skinned one, and he could see the outline of a knife in the back pants pocket of the third. Or he would say that the record player was playing so loudly he could hear it from the street. They were small embellishments at first, and if his wife noticed that the story of what happened was changing, she said nothing. In time, with winter disappearing, he was adding more and more so that it was no longer a falseness here and there that was embedded in the whole of the truth, but the truth itself, an ever-diminishing kernel, that was contained in the whole of falseness. And, like some kind of bedtime story, she listened and drifted with his words into a sleep where the things he was telling her were sometimes happening.

By March, Woodrow had written countless letters to his father telling the old man it was not necessary to come to Washington to help look for the girl. 'I got a sign from God,' the old man kept writing, 'that I could help find her.' Then, with spring, he began writing that he had received signs that he was not long for the world, that finding the girl was the last thing God wanted him to do. In the longest letters the old man had ever written to the one child of his who responded, he would go on and on about the signs he saw signaling his own death: The mongrel would no longer take food from his hand; the dead visited him at night, sitting down on the side of his bed and telling him things about himself; the rising sun now touched his house last in the morning, though there were houses to the left and right of his.

'You keep telling me that I'll be hurt or lost,' the old man wrote Woodrow. 'But I know the way that Washington, D.C. is set up. I came there once maybe twice. How could I get lost. Take a chance on me, and we'll have that child home before you can blink one eye. I can bring Sparky he got some bloodhound in him.'

In late April, Rita took down the map in the kitchen. The tacks fell to the floor and she left them there. She put the map in the bottom drawer of her daughter's dresser, among the blouses and blue jeans and a diary she would not find the strength to read for another three months. Her days of searching during the week dwindled down to two, then to one. She returned the car a church member had lent her to drive around the city in. Each evening when she got home, Woodrow would be out and she left his dinner in the oven to stay warm. Every now and again, when the hour was late, she went out to look for him, often for no other reason than that there was nothing worth watching on the television. As she put on more and more weight, it became difficult for her to stand and dish out food to the students at lunchtime.

Her supervisor and fellow workers sympathized, and, after a week of perfunctory training, she was allowed to sit and work at the cash register.

As he continued going about the city, sometimes on foot, Woodrow told himself and everyone else that he was hunting for his daughter, but this was only a piece of the truth. 'I'm lookin for my daughter, who's run away,' he said to those opening the doors where he knocked. 'She's been gone a long time, and her mama and me are about to lose our minds.' He sometimes presented a picture of his daughter, smiling radiantly, that was taken only months before she disappeared. But just as often, he would pull out a photograph of the girl when she was five, standing one Easter between her parents in front of Rising Star. All who looked at the photograph, even the drunks half-blind with alcohol, were touched by the picture of the little girl in her Easter dress who had now gone away from her parents, parents who were now worried sick. Many people invited Woodrow into their homes.

The Easter picture became a passport, and the more places he visited the more places he wanted to see. On U Street, a woman of twenty-five or so with three children put down the child she was holding to get a better look at the picture of the five-year-old girl. Woodrow, in the doorway, noted just over her shoulder that on her wall there was a calendar with a snow-covered mountain, hung with the prominence others would have given a landscape painting. An old woman on Harvard Street, tsk-tsking as she looked at the picture, invited him in for coffee and cake. 'My prayers go out to you.' Nearly everything in her apartment was covered in plastic, even the pictures on the walls. The old woman sat him on her plastic-covered couch and placed the food on a coffee table covered with a plastic cloth. 'And such a sweet-lookin child, too, son.' When he asked to use the bathroom (more out of curiosity than for relief), she pointed to a plastic path leading away down the hall. 'Stay on the mat, son.'

A tottering man in a place on 21st Street just off Benning Road began to cry when Woodrow told him his story. 'Dora, Dora,' the man called to a woman. 'Come see this little angel.' The woman, who was also tottering, pulled Woodrow into their house with one hand, while the other hand pressed the picture to her bosom. The man and Woodrow sat on the couch. The woman stood in front of them, swaying trancelike, her eyes closed, the picture still pressed to her. The man put his arm around Woodrow and breathed a sour wine smell into his face. 'Let's me and you pray about this situation,' he said.

One April evening, a little more than a year and a half after their daughter disappeared, Rita was standing in front of their building, waiting for him. 'We have fish tonight. It's in the stove waitin,' she said, in the same way she would have said, 'I know what you been doin. And who you been doin it with.' 'We have fish to eat,' she said again. She turned around and went back inside. 'We have fish, and we have to move from this place,' she said.

Woodrow's father died nearly seven years after Elaine Cunningham disappeared. Of the eight children he had had with Woodrow's mother and the five he had had with other women, only Woodrow, Alice, and a half-brother who lived down the road from the old man came to the funeral. It was a frozen day in January, and the gravediggers broke two picks before they had even gone down one foot. They labored seven hours to make a hole for the old man. 'Even the ground don't want him,' said one of the old man's friends standing at the gravesite.

There was not much in the old man's place to divide among his heirs. In a wooden trunk in one of the back rooms, Woodrow found several pictures of his mother. He had been kneeling down, going through the trunk, and when he saw the pictures, he cried out as if he had been struck. He had not seen his mother's face in more than forty years, had thought his father had destroyed all the pictures of her. 'You always looked like her,' Alice said, coming up behind him. 'Even when you sat at the right hand of the father, you looked like her.'

Though he was younger than three other brothers, Woodrow had worked hardest of his father's children. At first, his father had sat his children about the supper table according to their ages, but then he began to seat them according to who did the most work. His best workers sat closest to him, and by the time he was seven, Woodrow had worked his way to the right hand of his father. Woodrow's mother sat at the far end of the table, between two of her daughters. Most of his brothers and sisters, unable to pick the amount of cotton Woodrow could, never forgave him for living only to be close to their father. But he learned to pay them no mind and even learned to enjoy their hostility. He never moved from that right-hand place until the day he went off down the road to work in the turpentine camps.

He also found in the trunk some letters he wrote his father from the camps and from railroad yards and from the places he worked as he made his way up to Washington. They were all of one page or less, and they were all about work, work from sunup to sundown. There were no friends mentioned, there were no descriptions of places where he lived, there were no names of women courted, loved. 'I got a two-week job tanning hides,' he wrote from a nameless place in South Carolina. 'I got work cureing tobacco. I may stay on after the season,' he wrote from somewhere near Raleigh. 'I have been working in the stables outside Charlotesvile. The pay is good. I got used to the smell, and the work goes easy.'

Woodrow and Rita took the train back to Washington, bringing back a few of the pictures and none of the letters, which he burned in a barrel outside his father's house. Everything along the way back to D.C. was as frozen as Georgia. It was as if the cold had separated the world into three unrelated and distinct parts—the earth, what was on the earth, and the sky above. Nothing moved. Flying birds seemed to freeze in midair, and then the cold would nail them there.

Rita and Woodrow were back in the apartment on Independence Avenue in Southeast by ten o'clock that night. Rita took her usual place at an easy chair near the window. On a table beside the chair was all she needed—the television guide, snacks, the telephone. The chair was very large and had had to be specially ordered, because she could not fit into the regular ones in the store.

Woodrow, even though the hour was late and the weather people were predicting even colder temperatures, quietly put on his heaviest coat and left the apartrnent. He said nothing to Rita, and she did not look up when the door locked behind him. At the corner of Independence and 15th, Woodrow looked into the grocery store window at the owner he had become friends with since moving to Southeast. No customers went into the store, and the owner was dozing behind the counter, his head back, his mouth open. Woodrow watched him for a very long time. By now he knew everything about the man and his store and the sons who helped the man, and there was no urgency to be inside with him. Having lost so much weight, Woodrow felt that even more of the world had opened up to him. And so he wondered if he should go on down 15th Street, try to find a house he had not visited before, and bring out the picture of the child in her Easter dress.

BLUE BOY

Kevin Canty

High on his aluminum stand, stoned at ten-thirty in the morning, Kenny studied the day's crop of girls and women from behind his dark glasses and waited for Mrs. Jordan to arrive.

The usual moms were spread out with their kids and Garfield towels on the grass next to the patio. They always had this scatter of crap around them, Kenny noticed: toys and clothes and radios and suntan lotion. And the kids were always trying to crawl away and drown themselves. Some of the moms were not bad, the ones who had zipped their bodies back into shape. They wore the sexiest bathing suits so everyone could see their tight little trampoline bellies. Something slightly frightening about them, though, pretending that their kids didn't exist. Something better about the regular moms in the one-piece suits with the weight they couldn't quite hide. Better, Kenny thought, but not sexy.

The other side of the pool, next to the snack bar, was for the girls, the 'teens,' as they were known around the country club. Teen dances, teen Ping-Pong tournaments. These girls were Kenny's age but that was as far as it went. They saw right through him when they bothered to look at all. Lack of money made him invisible. So he watched them instead, their hard, smooth bodies like car fenders, straight hair and good teeth. They were trying to be sexy but really they weren't and Kenny, staring at them, couldn't figure out why. They lay face-down on their towels on the concrete deck in tiny unstrung bikinis, never moving a muscle, not even lifting their heads to talk to their friends inside the shade of the snack bar. Everybody was friends here, everybody had money except Kenny.

This lifeguard job was a going-away present from his girlfriend. Her dad was on the board of the country club. It was as easy as that. Two days into the summer, everybody figured out that he didn't belong here, Kenny included. He lived in a yellow-brick apartment with his father, near downtown, a thirty-minute bike ride from here. This summer his father had taken to falling asleep on the couch every night with the TV on and a last highball on the floor beside him. Kenny would find him in the morning and cover him up, like a piece of furniture. Some of these girls must have problems, he thought. He wondered what they were, hoped they were serious.

Invisible in his dark sunglasses, part of the patio furniture, Kenny spent his days imagining what it would be like to fuck all the wives and all the daughters of the country club. The only thing they would let him have was skin, and he stole as much of it as he could. He loved to see the pale side of a woman's breast as she lay stretched, top undone, arms over her head, or the pale skin at the edge of her swimsuit bottom, like a promise. He lived for the revealing moment, accidents of skin when a bathing suit was being adjusted or a T-shirt put on, or when a woman would emerge from the water, blind and dripping, and if her suit was made of a certain kind of material, Kenny would see her outlined in every detail, as if she stood naked in front of him. I got you, he thought. Kenny stared and stared.

Not that any of them were possible. Not the girls, not the women. This was just something to do while he was stoned in the big lifeguard chair.

One in particular, though. Her name was Mrs. Jordan and she wasn't a mom and she wasn't a daughter. Every morning at eleven o'clock, when the last shade of the trees was passing from the deck, Mrs. Jordan would arrive alone, press her blond hair into an aqua cap—the exact shade of the blue-tile bottom—and swim fifty laps. Kenny counted, every morning. When she was done she would towel herself carefully dry, then coat herself with sunblock and lie down on one of the lounges, loosening her hair so that it shone different shades of gold and silver in the morning sunlight. Kenny knew it was fake; he wondered sometimes what color her hair was really, but he didn't mind. This was beautiful. This was sexy.

This particular morning she came as usual at eleven and swam her fifty laps and then laid her body carefully down on the chaise lounge. She would stay there, face-down and unmoving, until one-thirty, when she would rise, swim thirty more laps and leave, as she did every day. Every day the same. She lay as still as any of the money kids but she was thinking something, there was something going on inside her head, and Kenny wondered what it was. He made up special stories about her while she lay there. She was waiting to go to prison for drugs, for a long time, and she would be old when she got out. She was dying a slow and painless death, some made-for-TV disease without symptoms, and in her hours on the chaise lounge she was remembering the good years of her life, all spent at poolside. She had time for a last romance, a poolside lover, and Kenny, with his sun-blond hair and his flat, tanned stomach and his vague eyes, would …

Suddenly she startled straight upright, looked everywhere, rose to her feet and dove headlong into the deep end of the pool.

This sudden dive filled Kenny with fear: things were happening, things were changing, had he been caught? He looked around the pool and saw only the usual scatter of moms and children and teenage girls; looked into the deep end, following the movement of Mrs. Jordan's dive and saw, tiny and self-contained, bundled into itself, a small child sleeping on the bottom of the water. It can't be sleeping, he thought. It looked so blue through the lapping water, the little bundled child, like an Indian papoose. He watched the broken, refracted line of Mrs. Jordan's body in her black bathing suit.

Before Kenny could move, before he could make up his mind, she was wading out of the shallow end with the drowned child pressed to her chest.

'Jesus!' yelled one of the mothers. 'Oh, Jesus, Johnny, what happened to you?' She ran to Mrs. Jordan, screaming, eyes of a wounded horse, while Mrs. Jordan patted the child on the back, as if it had a little cough.

'Johnny!' yelled the mother, ripping him from Mrs. Jordan's arms.

Kenny, who had somehow come to life, took the boy from his mother's arms. He probed the boy's throat, as he had been taught, then laid the blue boy down on a blue-striped towel, tilted his head back, pinched his nose shut and began to try to breathe life back into him. A kiss, he thought, feeling the tiny cold lips against his own. Nothing.

Nothing.

And then, a slow stirring, water boiling out of the boy's lungs, a slow convulsion, then Kenny tasted chlorine, and a gout of water spilled out of the boy's mouth, staining the concrete dark in a spreading pool, and the boy began to breathe again, and he began to sputter and wail. Kenny handed him to his mother. All the money kids were watching, all the moms. The wind was shaking the tops of the trees, showing both the pale undersides of the leaves and the deep green, glossy tops, casting scattered shadows at the edge of the concrete deck. The manager was shouting as he half-ran down the hill from the courts in his hard black shoes, a money kid fluttering behind him.

'Should I call the firemen?' the manager shouted. 'Should I call the police?'

'Everything is fine,' Mrs. Jordan called out to him, the first words Kenny had ever heard her say. He was startled to hear that she had a Southern accent: Texas Tennessee? The boy subsided into quiet sobs, pressed against his mother, little pigeon-sounds.

Kenny broke through the circle of watchers and started toward his stand again. His knee hurt deep inside. What did he do to himself? When he looked down it was bleeding freely: he must have banged it on the lifeguard stand, or when he knelt down on the concrete. He couldn't remember how he got from the chair to the boy. There was a slice of time missing. The marijuana haze had left him, and everything was very clear. He sat on a bench near the fence at the deep end and watched them tell their stories to the manager, each in turn, with gestures: headshakes, swooping movements of the hands. In the center of the circle stood Mrs. Jordan, her hair turned dull brown by the water, scattered streaks of fool's gold. She stood flat-footed and troubled in her wet black bathing suit, trying to understand. Her eyes were soft, tired-looking, and the line of her chin was looser than it had once been. Kenny felt his heart pull toward her for reasons he didn't understand. She wasn't perfect anymore. I could hurt her, Kenny thought. I could touch her.

The manager clattered toward him in his black shoes, and the others trailed behind, leaving a group around the mother and child. 'What's wrong with your knee? the manager asked.

'I don't know,' Kenny said. 'It hurts a little, probably nothing serious.' He straightened his leg out experimentally and winced at the grinding inside his kneecap. Something was loose in there.

'Do you want to see a doctor?'

I ought to, Kenny thought, I seem to be damaged. But he couldn't bring himself to ask. He said, 'I'm all right, I think.'

'Why don't you take today off?' the manager asked. 'We can cover for you.'

Mrs. Jordan had disappeared somehow.

'Am I in trouble?' Kenny asked.

'I don't know,' the manager said. He didn't really want to talk about it. 'I don't think so,' he finally said. 'Why don't you just go home? We'll talk about this tomorrow.'

'He saved that boy's life,' one of the money kids said, just like she was on television. 'That little boy would have died.'

'Right, right,' the manager said, then turned back to Kenny. 'I'm not saying you didn't do the right thing, I'm just, you know, I'm sure you're a little keyed up. We're all a little keyed up. Why don't you go?'

'All right,' Kenny said, though when he thought of his father's apartment, he didn't want to go there. The wing of the angel of death has brushed my shoulder, he thought. I don't want to explain to my father.

He felt the eyes of the swimmers on his back as he limped into the locker room. He sat on the bench and looked at his knee, which didn't tell him anything. He was still bleeding from the scraped skin but the real problem was someplace inside where he couldn't see it. He stared at it, waiting for something to happen, but it kept on being his knee, incommunicado. And then he remembered that he had saved a baby's life, and also that he'd almost lost him. Mrs. Jordan, at least, knew he'd almost missed the whole thing. The boy should have died. Who else knew this? But it seemed to matter so little, next to the memory of those cold, tiny lips, the porcelain emptiness of the boy's dead eyes.

In the dim employee's locker room, he showered the chlorine off and changed into his street clothes. He looked around the room and wondered if he would see it again if he was fired. It was a nothing place but Kenny was superstitious about saying good-bye. Too many things in his life—his mother, New Jersey—had disappeared without warning. Good-bye, dead place, unloved rooms. I have fucked your daughters for long enough, or maybe I'll see you tomorrow.

'You're bleeding,' Mrs. Jordan said.

'It's nothing much,' Kenny said. Then wondered what she was doing there in the driveway of the employee entrance, where his bike was locked to the fence. She wore white loose shorts, a purple top that emphasized her deep, even tan, and tiny gold-strapped sandals. Her hair was nearly dry, beginning to sparkle again. She had a little lipstick on and something to make her eyes look bright and Kenny liked the artifice, though it put her out of reach. Kenny was an inch or two taller but she was looking down at him.

'I think you ought to see a doctor,' she said. 'I saw you were limping.'

'I just banged up my knee a little.'

'You don't know what might be going on in there,' she said. Her tone implied something reprehensible, a wild party or a Communist cell meeting. She said, 'I damaged my knee six years ago from trying to run a marathon and it has never been right since.'

'This isn't that bad,' Kenny said.

'I didn't feel a thing at the time it happened,' Mrs. Jordan said. 'Didn't feel a thing.'

There didn't seem to be any place for Kenny to put his eyes: he looked down and there were her legs, looked up and there were her breasts under the purple silk and her eyes, which were soft and dangerous. Kenny thought of the dozens of times he had fucked her, and the dozens of ways, and he was ashamed of himself, standing this close. He wanted to escape, wanted to be rid of her.

'I tell you what,' he said. 'If it still feels bad tomorrow, I'll get to the clinic.'

'Rice,' she said. 'Rest, ice, compression, elevation. The important thing is to ice it down as quickly as you can to keep the swelling down, because the swelling is what does the real damage sometimes. How were you going to get home?'

What did she want from him? Kenny wished he could snap his fingers and she'd be gone, click the heels of his sneakers together three times and poof! He liked her better as a body, a place for him to put his thoughts, but there she was. 'I've got my bike,' he said.

'Where do you live?' she asked. 'How far?'

'Look, I'm going to be fine,' he said.

'I'm sorry,' Mrs. Jordan said. And for a moment they were the same. It was the blue baby, Kenny thought, remembering how she looked by the side of the pool with her hair down in wet strings and her face naked and worn. He felt a little surge of sympathy for her, though he knew it was misplaced. Adults didn't need his sympathy, at least adults with money. Still there she was.

She said, 'I'm sorry, I'm being pushy, aren't I? You go ahead and do whatever you want. I just thought that was a fine thing you did back there and it was like nobody even noticed.'

'That's all right.'

She shrugged her shoulders. 'Well, it bothered me. Sure you don't want a ride home?'

Kenny was about to say no but he thought for a minute: how would he get home otherwise? Maybe there was nothing too wrong with his knee but he wasn't looking forward to riding his bike. And there was this other thing, a vague memory of Mrs. Jordan when she was still in his imagination, before she started to talk, before she turned into an adult. It wasn't much, like a faint perfume. He said, 'I guess I could use a ride, if you don't mind.'

'I'd be delighted to,' she said, smiling, getting her way. He followed her up the gravel drive, shoving his bike. It fit without fuss into the trunk of her Crown Victoria, dark blue with a cream interior. The locks unlocked automatically, the windows all rolled down. Everything was obeying Mrs. Jordan. She swung the big Ford out into the noonday traffic and the cars seemed to part, to make way for her. In her good clean clothes, in her confident driving, she was an adult now, powerful. Kenny felt like what he was: a kid in dirty shorts clutching a Kleenex to his knee. Kiss it, make it better. His own weakness irritated Kenny.

'That blue boy,' Mrs. Jordan said, and Kenny knew what she meant, exactly, his smallness and the strange, wrong color of his skin. He seemed so quiet and self-contained. In Kenny's memory, the child sleeping under the water would fit inside a teacup. Then he understood: she wanted to talk it, needed to put it together in her mind. She had held the little cold body too, and the two of them were the only ones who knew.

'What happened back there?' Mrs. Jordan asked. 'How did that happen?'

Fuck it, Kenny thought. He said, 'I was stoned. I didn't even see him.'

'Hmmm,' Mrs. Jordan said, then drove calmly onward for a few blocks. Kenny, beside her, was terrified at his own confession. What if she turned him in? The manager wouldn't be happy till he was behind bars. He didn't feel stoned at all, he hadn't since Mrs. Jordan's dive.

'Stoned on what?' she asked at a stoplight, eyes forward.

'Just smoking dope.'

'That's not too good of an idea, is it?' A brief glance, enough for him to see she wasn't angry. 'This is a disappointment.'

'Why?'

She considered a moment. 'It's one thing to save a child from circumstance,' she said. 'It seems like another thing entirely when it's just carelessness, right? I really want to believe that I saved that child's life.'

'You did.'

'But only from you.' She smiled brightly at him, then pulled away late from the green light realized that her words, her manners, were as well thought out and as artificial as her clothes, or her hair. He admired this, too, stuck as he was in sincerity. Brightly, Mrs. Jordan said, 'You're bleeding on my upholstery, there.'

'Shit,' Kenny said, cupping his hand over the wound, wishing away the red-brown stain that had already dried onto the car seat. 'Shoot, I mean. I'm sorry.'

'No, it's OK, say what you want,' Mrs. Jordan said. 'You know what I'm going to do?'

Kenny didn't reply but she went on anyway: 'I'm going to stop by my house if that's all right, put a bandage on that and then get you some ice. I'm afraid it's going to start to swell up on you if you don't look out. Is that OK?'

'Sure,' Kenny said, dirty jokes running through his head, *Playboy* cartoons about grocery boys. What did she have in mind? Nothing, he knew: she was doing him a favor and nothing more. But he couldn't be sure. There was always that other possibility and she looked fine driving down the avenue with her hair all gold again. Mrs. Jordan was sort of coming and going, fading in and out. Kenny found himself looking at the outside of another person, wondering what was going on inside that skin. What was it like to be Mrs. Jordan, what was she thinking? Or: what did she do when she was 'thinking'? Was it the same thing that Kenny did, or was it another thing altogether? Kenny thought of the inside of his own mind as a small deserted island, well-worn paths through the tired bushes. The mental landscape of Mrs. Jordan, on the other hand, he imagined as dense with foliage and flowers, a perfumed jungle roamed by wild and dangerous animals, bright eyes glittering elusively.

'Here we are,' she said, pulling the Crown Victoria into the drive of a big bland colonial, an exploded doll-house. As they crawled up the blinding white dean concrete driveway, the garage door rolled obediently open, into the gasoline darkness, and then shut again behind them.

'Would you like a lemonade, or a Coke, or a cup of coffee? We have everything,' she said. 'Would you like a beer?'

A beer, he thought immediately, something to calm him down. But he lacked the nerve. 'Iced tea, if you have any.'

'We do,' she said. 'Of course we do.'

She left him bleeding in the backyard, an even carpet of green punctuated by flowering shrubs, like covered chairs. Beyond the yard rose the edge of a deep, tangled forest. No one could see in, they couldn't see out. Dappled sunlight, a cool intermittent breeze. Kenny knew this place in dreams: the place of no excuses, no explanations. Everything was perfect. In a moment Mrs. Jordan would come out barefoot and she would stand at the edge of the grass and take her earrings off and then loosen her white shorts and let them fall to the grass and she would step gracefully out of them. Or she would call to him from the upstairs bedroom. Or he would be walking down a hallway, for some reason he couldn't figure out, and accidentally see her through a half-open door, half-naked, changing out of her damp bathing suit, and she would look up and see that he caught her and look at him with that same open look he had seen at the poolside and then she would open the door and take him by the hand, her own hand still damp from the bathing suit, the white flesh where the sun didn't reach … Kenny wondered: where does the shit in my head come from?

'Lemonade,' said Mrs. Jordan, and poured him a glass, though he seemed to remember that he'd asked for something different. Next to the pitcher of lemonade she set a metal roll of adhesive tape and a couple of gauze pads in aromatic waxy envelopes that smelled like Band-Aids, that made him feel like a small child again.

'I'm terrible at first aid,' Mrs. Jordan said. 'I'll try my best but I flunked my merit badge, I'm afraid.'

The fragrance of Band-Aids: Kenny remembered an ordinary afternoon, home from school, contagious but not really sick, eight years old, ears buzzing with fever, reading at the kitchen table—reading a Superman comic book, with Mr. MXYZPTLK as the villain—and his mother boiling hot dogs for their lunch and his father calling, some trivial reminder, and his mother hanging up the phone and sitting silently at the table for a moment, raging, and then standing up and dashing the pan of hot dogs against the wall, splattering the kitchen with boiling water, burning her own hand badly—he remembered the scarlet stretched-tight texture of her skin as she rubbed butter into the burn, not looking at him. Kenny was unhurt, a few tiny droplets landing on the skin of his arm, in places he could still feel: there and there and there. The opposite of this orderly, sunlit yard. I'm not one of you, he thought, looking at Mrs. Jordan's golden head.

'All done,' she said. A spotless square of gauze was fastened to his leg with tidy strips of tape, a haze of antiseptic school-nurse aroma. 'All better,' she said.

'Thank you,' he said, trying to will his attention away from her body. But he had fucked her so many times in his thoughts that it was hard to stop, and she wasn't wearing much, and she was right there.

'It wasn't that bad to start with,' she said. 'Jesus, I can't stop thinking about it.'

'What?'

'That boy, the way he almost drowned.' She eased into a chair, across the glass-topped table from him, and stared off into the woods at the edge of the lawn, thinking. Kenny stole intimate glances of her body while she was unaware. Assuming she was unaware.

She said, 'It's just so many million-to-one shots: if I hadn't happened to look, if you hadn't known how to do that breathing thing, if he'd been down there a minute longer. It makes you wonder how anything ever happens at all.'

'It makes me wonder why his mother wasn't watching him,' Kenny said.

'Or the lifeguard, Kenny,' she said, with a little cold smile.

'How did you know that?'

'What?'

'My name? How did you know my name?'

'I don't know,' she said. 'I heard it at the club, I suppose, or you told me. Why? What's so strange about that?'

'Well, I don't know yours,' he said, a little amazed at his own audacity, fearful. He was asking for more than a name. Mrs. Jordan seemed to know this, too; she hesitated for a moment before answering.

'Linda,' she said. 'Linda Lavinia Jordan. I'm very pleased to meet you.' She extended her hand across the table, formally, and Kenny shook it. Her hand was small, soft, vaguely perfumed.

'Lavinia?' he asked.

'After an aunt,' she said. She seemed to have explained this many times before. 'Everybody's got to have some kind of middle name. What's yours?'

'Milton,' he said ashamedly. 'Kenneth Milton Kolodny. My mother was an English teacher.'

'Was?' asked Mrs. Jordan. 'She's passed away?'

'Oh, no,' Kenny said, then found that he couldn't go on. His mother was in the hospital, on that day, at that hour while Kenny sat enjoying his lemonade in the clear light of Mrs. Jordan's patio. He thought of the hallways more than anything else, pale green linoleum, smells of rubbing alcohol and old clothes and vomit. Where she was likely to remain. The man in the next room would scream as if he were being murdered, any hour of the day or night. Kenny felt like an imposter, like any words he cared to say would be a lie, anything but the unsayable truth: I am the son of people in trouble, I carry this sickness with me.

'It's all right,' Mrs. Jordan said, looking at him curiously. 'I shouldn't have asked.'

'It's complicated,' Kenny said. He felt the distance between them again, two lives, two silences. At the same time, he felt an obscure victory: this confusion was at least his own, it was something Mrs. Jordan couldn't know. It was one thing he was better at. For the first time since he had breathed the boy back to life, Kenny felt that he had his own shape, a person after all. He was learning something here. At least his problems were his own.

'We should get going,' Mrs. Jordan said. 'I have some errands to run this afternoon, and I'm sure you need to get going. You're all fixed up.' She didn't seem anxious to go, though. Her drink was only half-finished, she stayed in her chair. Kenny wanted to ask her why she had brought him here, though he suspected there was nothing like a reason. He imagined himself moving to touch her, standing behind her chair and letting his hand caress the soft skin of her neck, her shoulders, while she bent her head to welcome him.

She said, 'That was a remarkable thing today, wasn't it?'

'That was amazing,' he said. 'You were amazing.'

'It wasn't much,' she said, ducking her head, pleased. 'I just don't know how I managed to see him. I don't know what made me look up.'

'You were awake?'

'Oh yes,' she said, 'I'm always awake.'

The questions sprang to his mind but he didn't dare ask them: What are you thinking? What are you doing? He saw her on the chaise lounge, every curve of her gold bathing suit, every line of skin, like a photograph in front of him. The face that was turned toward him now seemed superimposed on that memory, so that he saw two sides of her at once. How many Mrs. Jordans?

'A remarkable thing,' she said again, softly, like a door closing. Then, in a sudden burst of energy, she drained her drink and assembled everything onto the tray again: tape, scissors, disinfectant, lemonade. 'Time to get going,' she said, rising. 'But thanks for coming by. I'm going to remember this day, I think.'

'Me, too,' Kenny said, following her into the bland interior of her house, sofas and coasters and pictures of relatives in elaborate frames. Purse, telephone, refrigerator.

'I'll be back in a second,' she said, and disappeared upstairs.

Kenny stood in the kitchen next to the winter coats, men's and women's woolen overcoats hanging on their pegs like abandoned persons. In the dead of summer these coats seemed exotic as sponge divers' outfits. There was a man's good gray overcoat hanging on the rack, a husband's coat. Kenny felt an obscure jealousy, as if he were married to Mrs. Jordan, as if the child sleeping under the water had been their own child, born into the air again. On an impulse, Kenny put his hand into the pocket of the overcoat, a soft, solid pocket meant for a bigger hand than his, and brought out a passcard for the Washington subway, a white cotton handkerchief, a scrap of gum wrapper and seven dollars, two singles and a five. Kenny kept the money and the passcard and stuffed the handkerchief back into the coat pocket, the yellow gum wrapper fluttering to the floor in his hurry. Now this ordinary hallway felt dangerous, as if it had suddenly been raised fifty feet off the ground, so that walking it required care. Kenny didn't know why he had taken the money. He wasn't a thief. The money was part of something that belonged to him. He wasn't stealing so much as taking his own back. Mine, mine, mine.

'All set?' asked Mrs. Jordan, sweeping into the room, bending by the coats to pick up the yellow, guilty scrap of gum wrapper. Kenny felt his throat close, certain he was caught, but she only dropped it carelessly into the wastebasket. She held the door to the garage open for him, then locked it behind her while he stood in the half-lit darkness, not sure what to do with himself. The motor of Mrs. Jordan's big Ford was ticking as it cooled. The stolen money felt hot in his pocket and he was getting away with it and he knew something that he didn't know before: that all you had to do was reach out your hand and try for it. Kenny fell out of his childhood in an instant, as soon as he saw that all the rules and all the things you were supposed to do were made-up things for children. That was what his father knew, and Mrs. Jordan, and now Kenny: that you just did what you wanted, you opened your hand and tried to grab for it and the rules didn't matter.

'Linda,' he said.

She turned away from the door and stood uncertainly, as if she were trying to remember something, put something together. She was standing maybe two feet away from him, cans of ancient paint and weed killer and hose attachments on the shelves behind her. The bare skin of her arms, the curve of her neck. Kenny stretched his hand toward her and touched behind her neck.

He raised his eyes to her face and knew at once that he had mistaken her. Surprise, then fear, crossed her face as she edged away from him. 'What are you doing?' Mrs. Jordan said, stepping back away from him. 'What did you think …'

Her mouth was open, she couldn't understand. In an instant Kenny moved from inside to outside, a camera zooming out too fast. He saw who they were, where they were: a boy, a woman, a Ford. He saw the fear plainly on her face and thought, for the second time that day, I could hurt you. I could fuck you if I wanted to. She was trying to unlock the car but she kept looking back at him and she couldn't find the lock with her hand and he understood that he had the power if he wanted it.

'I don't mean to hurt you,' he said.

But this only made her more scared, scared of Kenny. He could see it in her face as she backed toward the car, trying to make herself small, invisible. And Kenny thought, if that's the way you want it. He didn't have the thought for long, just for a second, but it was long enough to remember, long enough so he couldn't deny it: if I can't get it any other way, I'll just take it. As long as I'm nothing now, nothing but a fear, I'll just take it. And this was the thing that scared him, that made him drop his arms to his sides and walk backward away from her toward the kitchen door. 'I'm sorry,' he said. 'I didn't mean anything by it.'

'That's all right but it's time for you to go,' she said quickly, not looking at him. She got the car door open and then the garage door was rising up by itself and the daylight came flooding into the spidery darkness and it was gone. She was starting the car.

'Wait a minute,' Kenny said. 'My bike. It's in the trunk.'

She looked up at him, suspicious, wondering if this was a trick. Then she put the car into reverse and for a moment Kenny thought she was driving away with his bike; she backed the big car out of the garage and into the street and turned. Then she stopped the car and got out and opened the trunk and got back into the car before Kenny could reach her. He heard the garage door rolling shut behind him as he wrestled the ten-speed out of the trunk. When he slammed it shut she was driving away instantly, around the corner and gone, leaving him alone with his bike on the street of big blank houses. He tried to pedal the bike but it was no use with his bad knee—the bandage got in the way and the gravel inside was burning and grinding. He turned back for one last look at Mrs. Jordan's big white house shining in the sunlight. It was a house without a face, without an expression. You couldn't even tell if anyone was home or not. All the houses on this street. He felt like they were staring at him as he started for home, pushing his bike, limping down the asphalt on his swelling, bleeding knee.

Smoking cigarettes on the porch in the cool night, the river sound of traffic on the avenue two blocks away, Kenny watched the streetlight shadows on the sidewalk. Taxis and cats. The smoke curling out into the light from under the eaves of the porch gave his eyes something to rest on. Kenny loved to smoke, but usually he didn't let himself. He had drunk two of his father's Ballantines, had thought about drinking four or five more—he wouldn't get in trouble for it—but being drunk would only fill him with big useless emotions. Kenny had learned that much from his father.

If I can't get it any other way, I'll just take it. Her face in the light of the one bulb in the garage, the fear on it, over and over.

Kenny heard his father whistling before he saw him, 'Sentimental Journey' from a block away. A little after two, closing time at the Moon Palace, the only tolerable bar in walking distance according to Kenny's father. He was an expert whistler, a virtuoso. The plain melody of the song was broken and turned inside out, embellished with trilling melodic runs and odd accents, derived, Kenny knew, from the show-off jazz pianists his father loved, Art Tatum especially. He seemed to be walking all right. He hauled himself into one of the porch chairs and took a deep breath of the night air, shaking his head. Then turned to Kenny. 'Get me a beer, would you?'

Kenny hesitated. Normally he wouldn't, not when his father was already drunk, they both knew that, but this was a day when all regular bets had been canceled. 'For Christ sake, Kenny,' his father said. 'Just a beer, OK?'

Kenny fetched the beer for him. Though he wanted one himself, he decided against it, not wanting to go along with his father. Not wanting to be his father's son, he got himself a glass of water. The beer could wait; his father wouldn't last long. He was smoking one of Kenny's cigarettes when Kenny came outside again.

'Did you hear about this Miss America thing?' his father asked. 'They caught her, I guess she was in one of these dirty magazines fooling around with another girl, I mean, Jesus. Everybody's cheating.' He stubbed his cigarette out and lit another from Kenny's pack. 'People cheat on their taxes,' he said, 'people cheat on their marriages. Everybody wants something for nothing, you ever think of that?'

It occurred to Kenny that the cigarette his father was smoking was bought with one of the dollars he'd stolen from Mrs. Jordan's house. An intricate balance of right and wrong and just plain taking. You wanted something and you reached your hand out and took it. Kenny knew he had learned something that day he would not forget.

'Don't ever go to law school,' his father said, and settled back into the chair.

There was nothing Kenny wanted to talk about with his father. He didn't even know how he would put it into words: I saved a life today and then something happened ... Something was taking shape inside him, his own life, his own life story. He felt restless, ready to move on, but he knew that his life would burst out of him when the time came, and not before. Still, he was restless, restless.

'That was really something,' the manager said. 'You saved that boy's life.'

Kenny wished he would go away. The night before had never quite ended, the day felt stillborn, hot and sluggish. His knee was swollen and bruise-purple and it hurt. The money kids gathered, as if around an accident. The manager said, 'The board would like to give you this, and also to thank you for a tremendous service.'

He beamed at Kenny and offered his big hand, like congratulating a banjo, and the money kids broke into fake applause. Kenny smiled until they all went away, then climbed his chair to watch the morning sun crawl across the deck and wait for Mrs. Jordan. After a while it occurred to him to open the envelope that the manager had pressed into his hand, where he found a check from the club for twenty-five dollars, which seemed like the exact wrong sum of money. It should have been more or it should have been nothing.

The blue baby, he thought, the image already fading from his mind, like the sample photographs in drugstore windows, smiling faces disappearing into monochromatic blue. Our child. Nothing had really happened, it was just a misunderstanding. The waiting was killing him. The minutes before eleven o'clock, when Mrs. Jordan would or wouldn't come, when she would or wouldn't ask to speak to the manager, the minutes crept by like palsied old men. Something needed to happen. Wreckage would suit him as well as anything else. He wanted some definite action, some release, that moment when the wave takes and tumbles you underwater and you either come up into the air or you don't, but this day seemed stuck in a perpetual sunlit middle. Two teenage girls reclining on silvery air-mattresses, the smell of cocoa butter, the snack bar radio playing stale sixties hits: 'My Guy,' 'Crosstown Traffic,' 'Ride My See-Saw.'

Eleven came and went without her.

She could not do this to him. If she was at the manager's office, fine, if she was at the police station, if her husband—if she had a husband— was on his way down to the club. But to leave him like this, in between, Kenny would split open and spill his insides on the dean cement of the deck. This nothing.

A few minutes later, though, a few minutes late, she came out of the women's changing room in her usual suit and her usual sandals. She swam her usual fifty laps and then arranged herself, without a word to Kenny or a look at him, on the usual chaise lounge and began to do whatever she did, which Kenny would never know. No managers, no police, no husbands. Things were just going on. Kenny's mother was alive, his father, Mrs. Jordan was alive. Instead, this emptiness inside him, growing to fill his skin. The sunlight seemed hollow, slanting down on the empty patio, slanting toward September. From behind his dark glasses he stared down at Mrs. Jordan, her legs, her hips, the lovely line of her arms, her hair that sparkled artificial gold and silver in the sun. Useless anger boiled inside his chest. There were still six weeks of summer left.

ANTHROPOLOGY

Andrea Lee

(My cousin says: Didn't you think about what they would think, that they were going to read it, too? Of course Aunt Noah and her friends would read it, if it were about them, the more so because it was in a fancy Northern magazine. They can read. You weren't dealing with a tribe of Mbuti Pygmies.)

It is bad enough and quite a novelty to be scolded by my cousin, who lives in a dusty labyrinth of books in a West Village artists' building and rarely abandons his Olympian bibliotaph's detachment to chide anyone face-to-face. But his chance remark about Pygmies also punishes me in an idiosyncratic way. It makes me remember a girl I knew at Harvard, a girl with the unlikely name of Undine Loving, whom everybody thought was my sister, the way everybody always assumes that young black women with light complexions and middle-class accents are close relations, as if there could be only one possible family of us. Anyway, this Undine—who was, I think, from Chicago and was prettier than I, with a pair of bright hazel eyes in a round, merry face that under cropped hair suggested a boy chorister, and an equally round, high-spirited backside in the tight Levi's she always wore—this Undine was a grad student, the brilliant protégé of a famous anthropologist, and she went off for a year to Zaire to live among Pygmies. They'll think she's a goddess, my boyfriend at the time annoyed me by remarking. After that I was haunted by an irritating vision of Undine: tall, fair, and callipygian among reverent little brown men with peppercorn hair: an African-American Snow White. I lost sight of her after that, but I'm certain that, in the Ituri Forest, Undine was as dedicated a professional who ever took notes—abandoning toothpaste and toilet paper and subjecting herself to the menstrual hut, clear and scientific about her motives. Never even fractionally disturbing the equilibrium of the Lilliputian society she had chosen to observe. Not like me.

Well, of course, I never had a science, never had a plan. (That's obvious, says my cousin.) Two years ago, the summer before I moved to Rome, I went to spend three weeks with my great-aunt Noah, in Ball County, North Carolina. It was a freak impulse: a last-minute addressing of my attention to the country I was leaving behind. I hadn't been there since I was a child. I was prompted by a writer's vague instinct that there was a thread to be grasped, a strand, initially finer than spider silk, that might grow firmer and more solid in my hands, might lead to something that for the want of a better term I call *of interest*. I never pretended—

(You wanted to investigate your *roots*, says my cousin flatly.) He extracts a cigarette from a red pack bearing the picture of a clove and the words *Kretek Jakarta* and lights it with the kind of ironic flourish that I imagine he uses to intimidate his students at NYU. The way he says *roots*—that spurious seventies term—is so shaming. It brings back all the jokes we used to make in college about fat black American tourists in polyester dashikis trundling around Senegal in Alex Haley tour buses. Black intellectuals are notorious for their snobbish reverence toward Africa—as if crass human nature didn't exist there, too. And, from his West Village aerie, my cousin regards with the same aggressive piety the patch of coastal North Carolina that, before the diaspora north and west, was home to five generations of our family.

We are sitting at his dining table, which is about the length and width of the Gutenberg Bible, covered with clove ash and Melitta filters and the corrected proofs of his latest article. The article is about the whitewashed 'magic houses' of the Niger tribe and how the dense plaster arabesques that ornament their facades, gleaming like cake icing, are echoed faintly across the ocean in the designs of glorious, raucous Bahia. He is very good at what he does, my cousin. And he is the happiest of scholars, a minor celebrity in his field, paid royally by obscure foundations to rove from hemisphere to hemisphere, chasing artistic clues that point to a primeval tropical unity. Kerala, Cameroon, Honduras, the Phillipines. Ex-wife, children, a string of overeducated girlfriends left hovering wistfully in the dust behind him. He is always traveling, always alone, always vaguely belonging, always from somewhere else. Once he sent me a postcard from Cochin, signed, 'Affectionately yours, The Wandering Negro.'

Outside on Twelfth Street, sticky acid-green buds are bursting in a March heat wave. But no weather penetrates this studio, which is as close as a confessional and has two computer screens glowing balefully in the background. As he reprimands me I am observing with fascination that my cousin knows how to smoke like a European. I'm the one who lives in Rome, dammit, and yet it is he who smokes with one hand drifting almost incidentally up to his lips and then flowing bonelessly down to the tabletop. And the half-sweet smell of those ridiculous clove cigarettes has permeated every corner of his apartment, giving it a vague atmosphere of stale festivity as if a wassail bowl were tucked away on his overstuffed bookshelves.

I'd be more impressed by all this exotic intellectualism if I didn't remember him as a boy during the single summer we both spent with Aunt Noah down in Ball County. A sallow bookworm with a towering forehead that now in middle age has achieved a mandarin distinction but was then cartoonish. A greedy solitary boy who stole the crumbling syrupy crust off fruit cobblers and who spent the summer afternoons shut in Aunt Noah's unused living room fussily drawing ironclad ships of the Civil War. The two of us loathed each other, and all that summer we never willingly exchanged a word, except insults as I tore by him with my gang of scabby-kneed girlfriends from down the road.

The memory gives me courage to defend myself. All I did, after all, was write a magazine article.

(An article about quilts and superstitions! A fuzzy folkloristic excursion. You made Aunt Noah and the others look cute and rustic and backward like a mixture of *Amos 'n' Andy* and *The Beverly Hillbillies*. Talk about quilts—you embroidered your information. And you mortally offended them—you called them black.)

But they *are* black.

(They don't choose to define themselves that way, and if anybody knows that, you do. We're talking about a group of old people who don't look black and who have always called themselves, if anything, colored. People whose blood has been mixed for so many generations that their lives have been constructed on the idea of being a separate caste. Like in Brazil, or other sensible countries where they accept nuances. Anyway, in ten years Aunt Noah and all those people you visited will be dead. What use was it to upset them by forcing your definitions on them? It's not your place to tell them who they are.)

I nearly burst out laughing at this last phrase, which I haven't heard for a long time. It's not your place to do this, to say that. My cousin used it primly and deliberately as an allusion to the entire structure of family and tradition he thinks I flouted. The phrase is a country heirloom, passed down from women like our grandmother and her sister Eleanora and already sounding archaic on the lips of our mothers in the suburbs of the North. It evokes those towns on the North Carolina–Virginia border, where our families still own land: villages marooned in the tobacco fields, where—as in every other rural community in the world—'place,' identity, whether defined by pigmentation, occupation, economic rank, or family name, forms an invisible web that lends structure to daily life. In Ball County everyone knows everyone's place. There, the white-white people, the white-black people like Aunt Noah, and the black-black people all keep to their own niches, even though they may rub shoulders every day and even though they may share the same last names and the same ancestors. Aunt Eleanora became Aunt Noah—Noah as in *know*—because she is a phenomenal chronicler of place, and can recite labyrinthine genealogies with the offhand fluency of a bard. When I was little I was convinced that she was called Noah because she had actually been aboard the Ark. And that she had stored in her head—perhaps on tiny pieces of parchment, like the papers in fortune cookies—the name of every child born since the waters receded from Ararat.

I was scared to death when I went down to Ball County after so many years. Am I thinking this or speaking aloud? Something of each. My cousin's face grows less bellicose as he listens. We actually like each other, my cousin and I. Our childhood hostility has been transmogrified into a bond that is nothing like the instinctive understanding that flows between brothers and sisters: it is more a deeply buried iron link of formal respect. When I was still living in Manhattan we rarely saw each other, but we knew we were snobs about the same occult things. That's why I allow him to scold me. That's why I have to try to explain things to him.

I was scared, I continue. The usual last-minute terrors you get when you're about to return to a place where you've been perfectly happy. I was convinced it would be awful: ruin and disillusion, not a blade of grass the way I remembered it. I was afraid above all that I wouldn't be able to sleep. That I would end up lying awake in a suffocating Southern night contemplating a wreath of moths around a lightbulb, and listening to an old woman thumping around in the next bedroom like a revenant in a coffin. I took medication with me. Strong stuff.

(Very practical, says my cousin.)

But the minute I got there I knew I wouldn't need it. You know I hate driving, so I took an overnight bus from the Port Authority. There isn't a plane or a train that goes near there. And when I got off the bus in front of Ball County Courthouse at dawn, the air was like milk. Five o'clock in the morning at the end of June and 90 percent humidity. White porches and green leaves swimming in mist. Aunt Noah picked me up and drove me down Route 14 in the Oldsmobile that Uncle Pershing left her. A car as long and slow as Cleopatra's barge. And I just lay back, waking up, and sank into the luxurious realization that you can go home again. From vertical New York, life had turned horizontal as a mattress: tobacco, corn, and soybeans spreading out on either side. And you know the first thing I remembered?

(What?)

What it was like to pee in the cornfields. You know I used to run races through the rows with those girls from down the road, and very often we used to stop and pee, not because we had to, but for the fun of it. I remembered the exact feeling of squatting down in that long corridor of leaves, our feet sinking into the sides of the furrow as we pulled down our Carter's cotton underpants, the heat from the ground blasting up onto our backsides as we pissed lakes into the black dirt.

The last time before my visit that I had seen Aunt Noah was two years earlier at my wedding in Massachusetts. There she elicited great curiosity from my husband's family, a studious clan of New England Brahmins who could not digest the fact that the interracial marriage to which they had agreed with such eager tolerance had allied them with a woman who appeared to be an elderly white Southern housewife. She looked the same as she had at the wedding and very much as she had when we were kids. Eighty-three years old, with smooth graying hair colored intermittently with Loving Care and styled in a precise nineteen fifties helmet that suited her crisp pastel shirtwaist dresses and flat shoes. The same crumpled pale-skinned face of an aged belle, round and girlish from the front but the profile displaying a blunt leonine nose and calm predator's folds around the mouth—she was born, after all, in the magisterial solar month of July. The same blue-gray eyes, shrewd and humorous, sometimes alight with the intense love of a childless woman for her nieces and nephews but never sentimental, never suffering a fool. And, at odd moments, curiously remote.

Well, you look beautiful, she said, when she saw me get off the bus.

And the whole focus of my life seemed to shift around. At the close of my twenties, as I was beginning to feel unbearably adult, crushed by the responsibilities of a recently acquired husband, apartment, and job, here I was offered the brief chance to become a young girl again. Better than being a pampered visiting daughter in my mother's house: a pampered visiting niece.

Driving to her house through the sunrise, she said: I hear you made peace with those in-laws of yours.

Things are okay now, I said, feeling my face get hot. She was referring to a newlywed spat that had overflowed into the two families and brought out all the animosity that had been so dutifully concealed at the wedding.

They used excuses to make trouble between you and your husband. He's a nice boy, so I don't lay blame on your marrying white. But you have to watch out for white folks. No matter how friendly they act at first, you can't trust them.

As always it seemed funny to hear this from the lips of someone who looked like Aunt Noah. Who got teased up North by kids on the street when she walked through black neighborhoods. Until she stopped, as she always did, and told them what was what.

The sky was paling into tropical heat, the mist chased away by the brazen song of a million cicadas. The smell of fertilizer and drying earth flowed through the car windows, and I could feel my pores starting to pump out sweat, as if I'd parachuted into equatorial Africa.

Aunt Noah, I said, just to tweak her, you wouldn't have liked it if I'd married a black-black man.

Oh Lord, honey, no, she said. She put on the blinker and turned off the highway into the gravel driveway. We passed beneath the fringes of the giant willow that shaded the brick ranch house Uncle Pershing built fifty years ago as a palace for his beautiful childless wife. The house designed to rival the houses of rich white people in Ball County. Built and air-conditioned with the rent of dark-skinned tenants who cultivated the acres of tobacco that have belonged to Noah and Pershing's families for two hundred years. They were cousins, Noah and Pershing, and they had married both for love and because marrying cousins was what one did among their people at that time. A nigger is just as bad as white trash, she said, turning off the engine. But, honey, there were still plenty of boys you could have chosen from our own kind.

(You stayed two weeks, my cousin says, jealously.)

I was researching folkways, I tell him, keeping a straight face. I was hoping to find a mother lode of West African animism, pithy backwoods expressions, seventeenth-century English thieves' cant, poetic upwellings from the cyclic drama of agriculture, as played out on the Southeastern tidal plain. I wanted to be ravished by the dying tradition of the peasant South, like Jean Toomer.

(My cousin can't resist the reference. *Fecund Southern night, a pregnant Negress*, he declaims, in the orotund voice of a Baptist preacher.)

What I really did during my visit was laze around and let Aunt Noah spoil me. Every morning scrambled eggs, grits, country ham, and hot biscuits with homemade peach preserves. She was up for hours before me, working in her garden. A fructiferous Eden of giant pea vines, prodigious tomato plants, squash blossoms like Victrola horns. She wore a green sun hat that made her look like an elderly infant, blissfully happy. Breakfast over and the house tidy, we would set out on visits where she displayed me in the only way she knew how, as an ornamental young sprig on the family tree. I fell into the gratifying role of the cherished newlywed niece, passed around admiringly like a mail-order collectible doll. Dressing in her frilly pink guest room, I put on charming outfits: long skirts, flowery blouses. I looked like a poster girl for *Southern Living*. Everyone we visited was enchanted. My husband, who telephoned me every night, began to seem very far away: a small white boy's voice sounding forlornly out of Manhattan.

The people we called on all seemed to be distant relatives of Aunt Noah's and mine, and more than once I nearly fell asleep in a stuffy front room listening to two old voices tracing the spiderweb of connections. I'd decided to write about quilts, and that gave us an excuse to go chasing around Ball County peering at old masterpieces dragged out of mothballs, and new ones stitched out of lurid polyester. Everybody had quilts, and everybody had some variation of the same four family names. Hopper, Osborne, Amiel, Mills. There was Gertie Osborne, a little freckled woman with the diction of a Victorian schoolmistress, who contributed the 'Rambling Reader' column to the *Ball County Chronicle*. The tobacco magnate and head deacon P. H. Mills, tall and rich and silent in his white linen suits. Mary Amiel, who lived up the road from Aunt Noah and wrote poetry privately printed in a volume entitled *The Flaming Depths*. Aunt Noah's brother-in-law Hopper Mills, who rode a decrepit motorbike over to check up on her every day at dawn.

I practiced pistol-shooting in the woods and went to the tobacco auction and rode the rope-drawn ferry down at Crenshaw Crossing. And I attended the Mount Moriah Baptist church, where years before I had passed Sunday mornings in starched dresses and cotton gloves. The big church stood unchanged under the pines: an air-conditioned Williamsburg copy in brick as vauntingly prosperous as Aunt Noah's ranch house.

After the service, they were all together outside the church, chatting in the pine shade: the fabled White Negroes of Ball County. An enterprising *Ebony* magazine journalist had described them that way once, back in 1955. They were a group who defied conventional logic: Southern landowners of African descent who had pale skins and generations of free ancestors. Republicans to a man. People who'd fought to desegregate Greensboro and had marched on Washington yet still expected their poorer, blacker tenants to address them as Miss Nora or Mr. Fred. Most of them were over seventy: their sons and daughters had escaped years ago to Washington or Atlanta or Los Angeles or New York. To them I was the symbol of all those runaway children, and they loved me to pieces.

(But then you went and called them black. In print, which to people raised on the Bible and the McGuffey Readers is as definitive as a set of stone tablets. And you did it not in some academic journal but in a magazine that people buy on newsstands all over the country. To them it was the worst thing they could have read about themselves—)

I didn't—

(Except perhaps being called white.)

I didn't mean—

(It was the most presumptuous thing you could have done. They're old. They've survived, defining themselves in a certain way. We children and grandchildren can call ourselves Afro-American or African-American or black or whatever the week's fashion happens to be.)

You—

(And of course you knew this. We all grew up knowing it. You're a very smart woman, and the question is why you allowed yourself to be so careless. So breezy and destructive. Maybe to make sure you couldn't go back there.)

I say: That's enough. Stop it.

And my cousin, for a minute, does stop. I never noticed before how much he looks like Uncle Pershing. The same mountainous brow and reprobative eyes of a biblical patriarch that look out of framed photographs in Aunt Noah's living room. A memory reawakens of being similarly thundered at, in the course of that childhood summer, when I lied about borrowing Uncle Pershing's pocketknife.

We sit staring at each other across this little cluttered table in Greenwich Village. I am letting him tell me off as I would never allow my brother or my husband—especially my husband. But the buried link between my cousin and me makes the fact that I actually sit and take it inevitable. As I do, it occurs to me that fifty years ago, in the moribund world we are arguing about, it would have been an obvious choice for the two of us to get married. As Ball County cousins always did. And how far we have flown from it all, as if we were genuine emigrants, energetically forgetful of some small, dire old-world country plagued by dictators, drought, locusts, and pogroms. Years ago yet another of our cousins, a dentist in Atlanta, was approached by Aunt Noah about moving his family back to Ball County and taking over her house and land. I remember him grimacing with incredulity about it as we sat over drinks once in an airport bar. Why did the family select him for this honor? he asked, with a strained laugh. The last place anyone would ever want to be, he said.

I don't know what else to do but stumble on with my story.

Aunt Noah was having a good time showing me off. On one of the last days of my visit, she drove me clear across the county to the house where she grew up. I'd never been there, though I knew that was where it had all begun. It was on this land, in the seventeen forties, before North Carolina statutes about slavery and mixing of races had grown hard and fast, that a Scotch-Irish settler—a debtor or petty thief deported to the pitch-pine wilderness of the penal colony—allowed his handsome half-African, half-Indian bond servant to marry his only daughter. The handsomeness of the bond servant is part of the tradition, as is the pregnancy of the daughter. Their descendants took the land and joined the group of farmers and artisans who managed to carve out an independent station between the white planters and the black slaves until after the Civil War. Dissertations and books have been written about them. The name some scholars chose for them has a certain lyricism: Tidewater Free Negroes.

My daddy grew tobacco and was the best blacksmith in the county, Aunt Noah told me. There wasn't a man, black or white, who didn't respect him.

We had turned onto a dirt road that led through fields of tobacco and corn farmed by the two tenant families who divided the old house. It was a nineteenth-century farmhouse, white and green with a rambling porch and fretwork around the eaves. I saw with a pang that the paint was peeling and that the whole structure had achieved the undulating organic shape that signals imminent collapse.

I can't keep it up, and, honey, the tenants just do enough to keep the roof from falling in, she said. Good morning, Hattie, she called out, stopping the car and waving to a woman with cornrowed hair and skin the color of dark plums, who came out of the front door.

Good morning, Miss Nora, said Hattie.

Mama's flower garden was over there, Aunt Noah told me. You never saw such peonies. We had a fishpond and a greenhouse and an icehouse. Didn't have to buy anything except sugar and coffee and flour. And over there was a paddock for trotting horses. You know there was a fair every year where Papa and other of our kind of folks used to race their sulkies. Our own county fair.

She collected the rent, and we drove away. On the road, she stopped and showed me her mother's family graveyard, a mound covered with Amiel and Hopper tombstones rising in the middle of a tobacco field. She told me she paid a boy to clean off the brush.

You know it's hard to see the old place like that, she said. But I don't see any use in holding on to things just for the sake of holding on. You children are all off in the North, marrying your niggers or your white trash—honey, I'm just fooling, you know how I talk—and pretty soon we ugly old folks are going to go. Then there will just be some bones out in the fields and some money in the bank.

That was the night that my husband called from New York with the news we had hoped for: His assignment in Europe was for Rome.

(You really pissed them off, you know, says my cousin, continuing where he left off. You were already in Italy when the article was published, and your mother never told you, but it was quite an item for the rest of the family. There was that neighbor of Aunt Noah's, Dan Mills, who was threatening to sue. They said he was ranting: *I'm not African-American like they printed there! I'm not black!*)

Well, God knows I'm sorry about it now. But really—what could I have called them? The quaint colored folk of the Carolina lowlands? Mulattos and octoroons, like something out of *Mandingo*?

(You could have thought more about it, he says, his voice softening. You could have considered things before plunging into the quilts and the superstitions.)

You know, I tell him, I did talk to Aunt Noah just after the article came out. She said: Oh, honey, some of the folks around here got worked up about what you wrote, but they calmed right down when the TV truck came around and put them on the evening news.

My cousin drums his fingers thoughtfully on the table as I look on with a certain muted glee. I can tell that he isn't familiar with this twist in the story.

(Well—he says.) Rising to brew us another pot of coffee. Public scourging finished; case closed. By degrees he changes the subject to a much-discussed new book on W.E.B. Du Bois in Germany. Have I read about that sojourn in the early nineteen thirties? Dubois's weirdly prescient musings on American segregation and the National Socialist racial laws?

We talk about this and about his ex-wife and his upcoming trip to Celebes and the recent flood of Nigerian Kok statues on the London art market. Then, irresistibly, we turn again to Ball County. I surprise my cousin by telling him that if I can get back to the States this fall, I may go down there for Thanksgiving. With my husband. Aunt Noah invited us. That's when they kill the pigs, and I want to taste some of that fall barbecue. Why don't you come too? I say.

(Me? I'm not a barbecue fan, he says. Having the grace to flush slightly on the ears. Aren't you afraid that they're going to burn a cross in front of your window? he adds with a smile.)

I'll never write about that place again, I say. Just one thing, though—

(What?)

What would you have called them?

He takes his time lighting up another Kretek Jakarta. His eyes, through the foreign smoke, grow as remote as Aunt Noah's, receding in the distance like a highway in a rearview mirror. And I have a moment of false nostalgia. A quick glimpse of an image that never was: a boy racing me down a long corridor of July corn, his big flat feet churning up the dirt where we'd peed to mark our territory like two young dogs, his skinny figure tearing along ahead of me, both of us breaking our necks to get to the vanishing point where the green rows come together and geometry begins. Gone.

His cigarette lit, my cousin shakes his head and gives a short exasperated laugh. (In the end, it doesn't make a damn bit of dlfference, does it? he says.)

THE PLAGUE OF DOVES

Louise Erdrich

Some years before the turn of the last century, my great-uncle, one of
the first Catholic priests of aboriginal blood, put the call out to his
congregation, telling everyone to gather at St. Gabriel's, wearing
scapulars and holding missals. From that place, they would proceed to
walk the fields in a long, sweeping row, and with each step loudly pray
away the doves. My great-uncle's human flock had taken up the plow
and farmed among Norwegian settlers. Unlike the French, who
mingled with my ancestors, the Norwegians took little interest in the
women native to the land and did not intermarry. In fact, they
disregarded everybody but themselves and were quite clannish. But
the doves ate their crops just the same. They ate the wheat seedlings
and the rye and started on the corn. They ate the sprouts of new
flowers and the buds of apples and the tough leaves of oak trees and
even last year's chaff. The doves were plump, and delicious smoked,
but one could wring the necks of hundreds or even thousands and
effect no visible diminishment of their number. The pole-and-mud
houses of the mixed-bloods and the skin tents of the blanket Indians
were crushed by the weight of the birds. When they descended, both
Indians and whites set up great bonfires and tried to drive them into
nets. The birds were burned, roasted, baked in pies, stewed, salted
down in barrels, or clubbed to death with sticks and left to rot. But the
dead only fed the living, and each morning when the people woke it
was to the scraping and beating of wings, the murmurous susurration,
the awful cooing babble, and the sight of the curious and gentle faces
of those creatures.

My great-uncle had hastily constructed crisscrossed racks of sticks
to protect the rare glass windows of what was grandly called the
rectory. In a corner of that one-room cabin, his twelve-year-old
brother, whom he had saved from a life of excessive freedom, slept on
a pallet of cottonwood branches and a mattress stuffed with grass.
This was the softest bed the boy had ever had, and he did not want to
leave it, but my great-uncle thrust a choirboy surplice at him and

ordered him to polish up the candelabra that he would carry in the procession.

This boy would be my grandfather's father, my Mooshum, and since he lived to be over a hundred I was able to hear him tell and retell the story of the most momentous day of his life—which began with this attempt to vanquish the plague of doves. Sitting on a hard chair, between our first television and the small alcove of bookshelves set into the wall of our government-owned house on the Bureau of Indian Affairs school campus, he told us how he'd heard the scratching of the doves' feet as they climbed all over the screens of sticks that his brother had made. He dreaded going to the outhouse, because some of the birds had got mired in the filth beneath the hole and set up a screeching clamor of despair that caused others of their kind to throw themselves against the hut in rescue attempts. But he did not dare relieve himself anywhere else. So through a flurry of wings, shuffling so as not to step on the birds, he made his way to the outhouse and completed the necessary actions with his eyes shut. Leaving, he tied the door closed so that no other doves would be trapped.

The outhouse drama, always the first scene in Mooshum's story of that momentous day, was filled with the sort of details that my brother and I found interesting; the outhouse—which was an exotic but not unfamiliar feature—and the horror of the birds' death by excrement gripped our attention. Mooshum was our second-favorite indoor entertainment. Television was the first. But our father had removed the television's knobs and hidden them. Despite constant efforts, we couldn't find the knobs, and we came to believe that he carried them on his person at all times. So instead we listened to our Mooshum. While he talked, we sat on kitchen chairs and twisted our hair. Our mother had given him a red Folgers coffee can for spitting snoose. He wore soft, worn green Sears work clothes, a pair of battered brown lace-up boots, and a twill cap, even in the house. His eyes shone from slits cut deep into his face. He was hunched and dried-out, with random wisps of white hair falling over his ears and neck. From time to time, as he spoke, we glimpsed the murky scraggle of his teeth. Still, such was his conviction in the telling of this story that it wasn't hard at all to imagine him at twelve.

My great-uncle put on his vestments, hand-me-downs from a Minneapolis parish. Since real incense was impossible to obtain, he stuffed the censer with dry sage rolled up in balls. Then he wet a comb at the cabin's iron hand pump and slicked back his hair and his little brother's hair. The church cabin was just across the yard, and wagons had been pulling up for the past hour or so, each with a dog or two tied in the box to keep the birds and their droppings off the piled hay where people would sit. The constant movement of the birds made some of the horses skittish. Many wore blinders and had bouquets of calming chamomile tied to their harnesses. As our Mooshum walked across the yard, he saw that the roof of the church was covered with birds that repeatedly—in play, it seemed—flew up and knocked one another off the holy cross that marked the cabin as a church. Great-Uncle was more than six feet tall, an imposing man, whose melodious voice carried over the confusion of sounds as he organized his parishioners into a line. The two brothers stood at the center, and with the faithful congregants spread out on either side they made their way slowly down the hill toward the first of the fields they hoped to clear.

The sun was dull that day, thickly clouded over, and the air was oppressively still, so that pungent clouds of sage smoke hung all around the metal basket on its chain as it swung in each direction. In the first field, the doves were packed so tightly on the ground that there was a sudden agitation among the women, who could not move forward without sweeping the birds into their skirts. In panic, the birds tangled themselves in the cloth. The line halted suddenly as the women erupted in a raging dance, each twirling, stamping, beating, and flapping her skirts. So vehement was the dance that the birds all around them popped into flight, frightening other birds, and within moments the entire field was a storm of birds that roared and blasted down upon the people, who nonetheless stood firm with splayed missals on their heads. To move forward, the women forsook their modesty. They knotted their skirts up around their thighs, held out their rosaries or scapulars, and chanted the Hail Mary into the wind of beating wings. Mooshum, who had rarely seen a woman's lower limbs, dropped behind, delighted. As he watched the women's naked round brown legs thrash through the field, he lowered the candelabra that his brother had given him to protect his face. Instantly, he was struck on the forehead by a bird that hurtled from the sky with such force that it seemed to have been flung directly by God, to smite and blind him before he carried his sin of appreciation any further.

At this point in the story, Mooshum often became so agitated that he acted out the smiting and, to our pleasure, mimed his collapse, throwing himself upon the floor. Then he opened his eyes and lifted his head and stared into space, clearly seeing, even now, the vision of the Holy Spirit, which appeared to him not in the form of a white bird among the brown doves but as the earthly body of a girl.

Our family has something of a historical reputation for romantic encounters. My aunt Philomena, struck by the smile of a man on a passenger train, raised her hand from the ditch where she stood picking berries, and was unable to see his hand wave in return. But something made her stay there until nightfall and then camp there overnight, and wait quietly for another whole day until the man came walking back to her from the next stop, sixty miles ahead. My oldest cousin, Curtis, dated the Haskell Indian Princess, who cut her braids off and gave them to him the night she died of tuberculosis. He remained a bachelor, in her memory, until his fifties. My aunt Agathe left the convent for a priest. My cousin Eugene reformed a small-town stripper. Even my sedate-looking father was swept through the Second World War by one promising glance from my mother. And so on.

These tales of extravagant encounter contrasted with the modesty of the subsequent marriages and occupations of my relatives. We are a tribe of office workers, bank tellers, booksellers, and bureaucrats. The wildest of us (Eugene) owns a restaurant, and the most heroic of us (my father) teaches seventh grade. Yet this current of drama holds together the generations, I think, and my brother and I listened to Mooshum not only to find out what had happened but also because we hoped for instructions on how to behave when our own moment of recognition, or romantic trial, should arrive.

In truth, I thought that mine had probably already come, for even as I sat there listening to Mooshum my fingers obsessively spelled out the name of my beloved on my arm or in my hand or on my knee. I believed that if I wrote his name on my body a million times he would kiss me. I knew that he loved me, and he was safe in the knowledge that I loved him, but we attended a Roman Catholic grade school in the early nineteen-sixties, when boys and girls who were known to be in love hardly talked to each other and certainly never touched. We played softball and kickball together, and acted and spoke through other children who were eager to deliver messages. I had copied a series of these secondhand love statements into my tiny leopard-print diary, which had a golden lock. The key was hidden in the hollow knob of my bedstead. Also, I had written the name of my beloved, in blood from a scratched mosquito bite, along the inner wall of my closet. His name held for me the sacred resonance of those Old Testament words written in fire by an invisible hand. *Mene, mene, tekel, upharsin.* I could not say his name aloud. I could only write it with my fingers on my skin, until my mother feared I'd got lice and coated my hair with mayonnaise, covered my head with a shower cap, and told me to sit in a bath that was as hot as I could stand until my condition should satisfy her.

I locked the bathroom door, controlled the hot water with my toe, and, since I had nothing else to do, decided to advance my name-writing total by several thousand. As I wrote, I found places on myself that changed and warmed in response to the repetition of those letters, and without an idea in the world what I was doing I gave myself successive alphabetical orgasms so shocking in their intensity and delicacy that the mayonnaise must have melted off my head. I then stopped writing on myself. I believed that I had reached the million mark, and didn't dare try the same thing again.

Ash Wednesday passed, and I was reminded that I was made of dust only and would return to dust as soon as life was done with me. My body, inscribed everywhere with the holy name Merlin Koppin (I can say it now), was only a temporary surface, soon to crumble like a leaf. As always, we entered the Lenten season aware that our hunger for sweets or salted pretzels or whatever we had given up was only a phantom craving. The hunger of the spirit alone was real. It was my good fortune not to understand that writing my boyfriend's name on myself had been an impure act, so I felt that I had nothing worse to atone for than my collaboration with my brother's discovery that pliers from the toolbox worked as well as knobs on the television. As soon as my parents were gone, we could watch 'The Three Stooges'—our and Mooshum's favorite, and a show that my parents thought abominable. It was Palm Sunday before my father happened to come home from an errand and rest his hand on the hot surface of the television and then fix us with the foxlike suspicion that his students surely dreaded. He got the truth out of us quickly. The pliers were hidden, along with the knobs, and Mooshum's story resumed.

The girl who would become my great-grandmother had fallen behind the other women in the field, because she was too shy to knot up her skirts. Her name was Junesse, and she, too, was twelve years old. The trick, she found, was to walk very slowly so that the birds had time to move politely aside instead of starting upward. Junesse wore a long white Communion dress made of layers of filmy muslin. She had insisted on wearing this dress, and the aunt who cared for her had given in but had promised to beat her if she returned with a rip or a stain. This threat, too, had deterred Junesse from joining in the other women's wild dance. But now, finding herself alone with the felled candelabra-bearer, she perhaps forced their fate in the world by kneeling in a patch of bird slime to revive him, and then sealed it by using her sash to blot away the wash of blood from his forehead, where the bird had wounded him.

And there she was! Mooshum paused in his story. His hands opened and the hundreds of wrinkles in his face folded into a mask of unsurpassable happiness. Her black hair was tied with a white ribbon. Her white dress had a bodice embroidered with white flower petals and white leaves. And she had the pale, heavy skin and slanting black eyes of the Métis women in whose honor a bishop of that diocese had written a warning to his priests, advising them to pray hard and to remember that although women's forms could be inordinately fair, they were also savage and permeable. The Devil came and went in them at will. Of course, Junesse Malaterre was innocent, but she was also sharp of mind. Her last name, which came down to us from some French *voyageur*, refers to the cleft furrows of godless rock, the barren valleys, striped outcrops, and mazelike configurations of rose, gray, tan, and purple stone that characterize the Badlands of North Dakota. To this place Mooshum and Junesse eventually made their way.

'We seen into each udder's dept,' was how my Mooshum put it, in his gentle reservation accent. There was always a moment of silence among the three of us as the scene played out. Mooshum saw what he described. I don't know what my brother saw—perhaps another boy. (He eventually came out to everyone at my parents' silver-anniversary dinner party.) Or perhaps he saw that, after a whirl of experience and a minor car accident, he, too, would settle into the dull happiness of routine with his insurance-claims adjuster. As for me, I saw two beings—the boy shaken, frowning, the girl in white kneeling over him pressing the sash of her dress to the wound on his head, stanching the flow of blood. Most important, I saw their dark, mutual gaze. The Holy Spirit hovered between them. Her sash reddened, His blood defied gravity and flowed up her arm. Then her mouth opened. Did they kiss? I couldn't ask Mooshum. She hadn't had time to write his name on her body even once, and, besides, she didn't know his name. They had seen into each other's being, therefore names were irrelevant. They ran away together, Mooshum said, before either had thought to ask what the other was called. And then they decided not to have names for a while—all that mattered was that they had escaped, slipped their knots, cut the harnesses that their relatives had tightened. Junesse fled her aunt's beating and the endless drudgery of caring for six younger cousins, who would all die the following winter of a choking cough. Mooshum fled the sanctified future that his brother had picked out for him.

The two children in white clothes melted into the wall of birds. Their robes soon became as dark as the soil, and so they blended into the earth as they made their way along the edges of fields, through open country, to where the farmable land stopped and the ground split open and the beautifully abraded knobs and canyons of the Badlands began. Although it took them several years to physically consummate their feelings (Mooshum hinted at this but never came right out and said it), they were in love. And they were survivors. They knew how to make a fire from scratch, and for the first few days they were able to live on the roasted meat of doves. It was too early in the year for there to be much else to gather in the way of food, but they stole birds' eggs and dug up weeds. They snared rabbits, and begged what they could from isolated homesteads.

On the Monday that we braided our blessed palms in school, braces were put on my teeth. Unlike now, when every other child undergoes some sort of orthodonture, braces were rare then. It is really extraordinary that my parents, in such modest circumstances, decided to correct my teeth at all. Our dentist was old-fashioned, and believed that to protect the enamel of my front teeth from the wires he should cap them in gold. So one day I appeared in school with two long, resplendent front teeth and a mouth full of hardware. It hadn't occurred to me that I'd be teased, but then somebody whispered, 'Easter Bunny!' By noon recess, boys swirled around me, poking, trying to get me to smile. Suddenly, as if a great wind had blown everyone else off the bare gravel yard, there was Merlin Koppin. He shoved me and laughed right in my face. Then the other boys swept him away. I took refuge in the only sheltered spot on the playground, an alcove in the brick on the southern side facing the littered hulks of cars behind a gas station. I stood in a silent bubble, rubbing my collarbone where his hands had pushed, wondering. What had happened to our love? It was in danger, maybe finished. Because of golden teeth. Even then, such a radical change in feeling seemed impossible to bear. Remembering our family history, though, I rallied myself to the challenge. Included in the romantic tales were episodes of reversals. I had justice on my side, and, besides, when my braces came off I would be beautiful. Of this I had been assured by my parents. So as we were entering the classroom in our usual parallel lines, me in the girls' line, he in the boys', I maneuvered myself across from Merlin, punched him in the arm, hard, and said, 'Love me or leave me.' Then I marched away. My knees were weak, my heart pounded. My act had been wild and unprecedented. Soon everyone had heard about it, and I was famous, even among the eighth-grade girls, one of whom, Tenny McElwayne, offered to beat Merlin up for me. Power was mine, and it was Holy Week.

The statues were shrouded in purple except for our church's exceptionally graphic Stations of the Cross. Nowadays, the Stations of the Cross are carved in tasteful wood or otherwise abstracted. But our church's version was molded of plaster and painted with bloody relish. Eyes rolled to the whites. Mouths contorted. Limbs flailed. It was all there. The side aisles of the church were wide, and there was plenty of room for schoolchildren to kneel on the aggregate stone floor and contemplate the hard truths of torture. The most sensitive of the girls, and one boy, destined not for the priesthood but for a spectacular musical career, wept openly and luxuriantly. The rest of us, soaked in guilt or secretly admiring the gore, tried to sit back unobtrusively on our bottoms and spare our kneecaps. At some point, we were allowed into the pews, where, during the three holiest hours of the afternoon on Good Friday, with Christ slowly dying underneath his purple cape, we were supposed to maintain silence. During that time, I decided to begin erasing Merlin's name from my body by writing it backward a million times: Nippok Nilrem. I began my task in the palm of my hand, then moved to my knee. I'd managed only a hundred when I was thrilled to realize that Merlin was trying frantically to catch my eye, a thing that had never happened before. As I've said, our love affair had been carried out by intermediaries. But my fierce punch seemed to have hot-wired his emotions. That he should be so impetuous, so desperate, as to seek me out directly! I was overcome with a wash of shyness and terror. I wanted to acknowledge Merlin, but I couldn't now. I stayed frozen in place until we were dismissed.

Easter Sunday. I am dressed in blue dotted nylon swiss. The seams prickle and the neck itches, but the over-all effect, I think, is glorious. I own a hat that has fake lilies of the valley on it and a stretchy band that digs into my chin. At the last moment, I beg to wear my mother's lace mantilla instead, the one like Jackie Kennedy's, headgear that only the most fashionable older girls wear. Nevertheless, I am completely unprepared for what happens when I return from taking Holy Communion. I am kneeling at the end of the pew. We are instructed to remain silent and to allow Christ's presence to diffuse in us. I do my best. But then I see Merlin in the line for Communion on my side of the church, which means that on the way back to his seat he will pass only inches from me. I can keep my head demurely down, or I can look up. The choice dizzies me. And I do look up. He rounds the first pew. I hold my gaze steady. He sees that I am looking at him—freckles, dark slicked-back hair, narrow brown eyes—and he does not look away. With the Host of the Resurrection in his mouth, my first love gives me a glare of anguished passion that suddenly ignites the million invisible names.

For one whole summer, my great-grandparents lived off a bag of contraband pinto beans. They killed the rattlesnakes that came down to the streambed to hunt, roasted them, used salt from a little mineral wash to season the meat. They managed to find some berry bushes and to snare a few gophers and rabbits. But the taste of freedom was eclipsed now by their longing for a good, hot dinner. Though desolate, the Badlands were far from empty; they were peopled in Mooshum's time by unpurposed miscreants and outlaws as well as by honest ranchers. One day, Mooshum and Junesse heard an inhuman shrieking from some bushes deep in a draw where they'd set snares. Upon cautiously investigating, they found that they had snared a pig by its hind leg. While they were debating how to kill it, there appeared on a rise the silhouette of an immense person wearing a wide fedora and seated on a horse. They could have run, but as the rider approached them they were too amazed to move, or didn't want to, for the light now caught the features of a giant woman dressed in the clothing of a man. Her eyes were small and shrewd, her nose and cheeks pudgy, her lip a narrow curl of flesh. One long braid hung down beside a large and motherly breast. She wore twill trousers, boots, chaps, leather gauntlets, and a cowhide belt with silver conchas. Her wide-brimmed hat was banded with the skin of a snake. Her brown bloodstock horse stopped short, polite and obedient. The woman spat a stream of tobacco juice at a quiet lizard, laughed when it jumped and skittered, then ordered the two children to stand still while she roped her hog. With swift and expert motions, she dismounted and tied the pig to the pommel of her saddle, then released its hind leg.

'Climb on,' she commanded, gesturing at the horse, and when the children did she grasped the halter and started walking. The roped pig trotted along behind. By the time they reached the woman's ranch, which was miles off, the two had fallen asleep. The woman had a ranch hand take them down, still sleeping, and lay them in a bedroom in her house, which was large and ramshackle, partly sod and partly framed. There were two little beds in the room, plus a trundle where she herself sometimes slept, snoring like an engine, when she was angry with her husband, the notorious Ott Black. In this place my Mooshum and his bride-to-be would live until they turned sixteen.

In Erling Nicolai Rolfsrud's compendium of memorable women and men from North Dakota, 'Mustache' Maude Black is described as not unwomanly, though she smoked, drank, was a crack shot and a hard-assed camp boss. These things, my Mooshum said, were all true, as was the mention of both her kind ways and her habit of casual rustling. The last was just a sport to her, Mooshum said; she never meant any harm by it. Mustache Maude sometimes had a mustache, and sometimes, when she plucked it out, she didn't. She kept a neat henhouse and a tidy kitchen. She grew very fond of Mooshum and

Junesse, taught them to rope, ride, shoot, and make an unbeatable chicken-and-dumpling stew. Divining their love, she quickly banished Mooshum to the men's bunkhouse, where he soon learned the many ways in which he could make children in the future with Junesse. He practiced in his mind, and could hardly wait. But Maude forbade their marriage until both were sixteen. When that day came, she threw a wedding supper that was talked about for years, featuring several delectably roasted animals that seemed to be the same size and type as those which had gone missing from the farms of the dinner guests. This caused a stir, but Maude kept the liquor flowing, and most of the ranchers shrugged it off.

What was not shrugged off, what was truly resented, was the fact that Maude had thrown an elaborate shindig for a couple of Indians. Or half-breeds. It didn't matter which. These were uncertain times in North Dakota. People's nerves were still shot over what had happened to Custer, and every few years there occurred a lynching. Just a few years before, the remains of five men had been found, still strung from trees, supposedly the victims of a vigilante party led by Flopping Bill Cantrell. Some time later, an entire family was murdered and three Indians were caught by a mob and hanged for maybe doing it, including a boy named Paul Holy Track, who was only thirteen.

The foul murder of a woman on a farm just to the west of Maude's place caused the neighbors to disregard, in their need for immediate revenge, the sudden absence of that woman's husband and to turn their thoughts to the nearest available Indian. There I was, Mooshum said. One night, the yard of pounded dirt between the bunkhouse and Maude's sleeping quarters filled with men hoisting torches of flaring pitch. Their howls rousted Maude from her bed. As a precaution, she had sent Mooshum down to her kitchen cellar to sleep the night. So he knew what happened only through the memory of his wife, for he heard nothing and dreamed his way through the danger.

'Send him out to us,' they bawled, 'or we will take him ourselves.'

Maude stood in the doorway in her nightgown, her holster belted on, a cocked pistol in either hand. She never liked to a be woken from sleep.

'I'll shoot the first two of youse that climbs down off his horse,' she said, then gestured to the sleepy man beside her, 'and Ott Black will plug the next!'

The men were very drunk and could hardly control their horses. One fell off, and Maude shot him in the leg. He started screaming worse than the snared pig.

'Which one of you boys is next?' Maude roared.

'Send out the goddam Indian!' they called. But the yell had less conviction, punctuated, as it was, by the shot man's hoarse shrieks.

'What Indian?'

'That boy!'

'He ain't no Indian,' Maude said. 'He's a Jew from the land of Galilee! One of the lost tribe of Israel!'

Ott Black nearly choked at his wife's wit.

The men laughed nervously, and called for the boy again.

'I was just having fun with you,' Maude said. 'Fact is, he's Ott Black's trueborn son.'

This threw the men back in their saddles. Ott blinked, then caught on and bellowed, 'You men never knowed a woman till you knowed Maude Black!'

The men fell back into the night and left their fallen would-be lyncher kicking in the dirt and pleading to God for mercy. Maybe Maude's bullet had hit a nerve or a bone, for the man seemed to be in an unusual amount of pain for just a gunshot wound to the leg. He began to rave and foam at the mouth, so Maude tied him to his saddle and set out for the doctor's. He died on the way from loss of blood. Before dawn, Maude came back, gave my great-grandparents her two best horses, and told them to ride hard back the way they had come. Which was how they ended up on their home reservation in time to receive their allotments, where they farmed using government-issue seed and plows and reared their six children, one of whom was my grandfather, and where my parents took us every summer just after the wood ticks had settled down.

The story may have been true, for, as I have said, there really was a Mustache Maude Black who had a husband named Ott. Only the story changed. Sometimes Maude was the one to claim Mooshum as her son in the story and sometimes she went on to claim that she'd had an affair with Chief Gall. And sometimes she plugged the man in the gut. But if there was embellishment it had to do only with facts. St. Gabriel's Church was named for God's messenger, the archangel who currently serves as the patron saint of telecommunications workers. Those doves were surely the passenger pigeons of legend and truth, whose numbers were such that nobody thought they could ever be wiped from the earth.

As Mooshum grew frailer and had trouble getting out of his chair, our parents relaxed their television boycott. More often now, our father fixed the magic circles of plastic onto their metal posts and twiddled them until the picture cleared. We sometimes all watched 'The Three Stooges' together. The black-haired one looked a lot like the woman who had saved his life, Mooshum said, nodding and pointing at the set. I remember imagining his gnarled brown finger as the hand of a strong young man gripping the candelabra, which, by the way, my great-grandparents had lugged all the way down to the Badlands, where it had come in handy for killing snakes and gophers. They had given their only possession to Maude as a gesture of their gratitude. She had thrust it back at them the night they escaped.

That tall, seven-branched silver-plated instrument, with its finish worn down to tin in some spots, now stood in a place of honor in the center of our dining-room table. It held beeswax tapers, which had been lit during Easter dinner. A month later, in the little alcove on the school playground, I kissed Merlin Koppin. Our kiss was hard, passionate, strangely mature. Afterward, I walked home alone. I walked very slowly. Halfway there, I stopped and stared at a piece of the sidewalk that I'd crossed a thousand times and knew intimately. There was a crack in it—deep, long, jagged, and dark. It was the day when the huge old cottonwood trees shed cotton. Their heart-shaped leaves ticked and hissed high above me. The air was filled with falling down, and the gutters were plump with a snow of light. I had expected to feel joy, but instead I felt a confusion of sorrow, or maybe fear, for it suddenly seemed that my life was a hungry story and I its source and with this kiss I had begun to deliver myself to the words.

A ROMANTIC WEEKEND

Mary Gaitskill

She was meeting a man she had recently and abruptly fallen in love with. She was in a state of ghastly anxiety. He was married, for one thing, to a Korean woman whom he described as the embodiment of all that was feminine and elegant. Not only that, but a psychic had told her that a relationship with him could cripple her emotionally for the rest of her life. On top of this, she was tormented by the feeling that she looked inadequate. Perhaps her body tilted too far forward as she walked, perhaps her jacket made her torso look bulky in contrast to her calves and ankles, which were probably skinny. She felt like an object unraveling in every direction. In anticipation of their meeting, she had not been able to sleep the night before; she had therefore eaten some amphetamines and these had heightened her feeling of disintegration.

When she arrived at the comer he wasn't there. She stood against a building, trying to arrange her body in the least repulsive configuration possible. Her discomfort mounted. She crossed the street and stood on the other corner. It seemed as though everyone who walked by was eating. A large, distracted businessman went by holding a half-eaten hot dog. Two girls passed, sharing cashews from a white bag. The eating added to her sense that the world was disorderly and unbeautiful. She became acutely aware of the garbage on the street. The wind stirred it; a candy wrapper waved forlornly from its trapped position in the mesh of a jammed public wastebasket. This was all wrong, all horrible. Her meeting with him should be perfect and scrap-free. She couldn't bear the thought of flapping trash. Why wasn't he there to meet her? Minutes passed. Her shoulders drew together.

She stepped into a flower store. The store was clean and white, except for a few smudges on the linoleum floor. Homosexuals with low voices stood behind the counter. Arranged stalks bearing absurd blossoms protruded from sedate round vases and bristled in the aisles. She had a paroxysm of fantasy. He held her, helpless and swooning, in his arms. They were supported by a soft ball of puffy blue stuff. Thornless roses surrounded their heads. His gaze penetrated her so thoroughly, it was as though he had thrust his hand into her chest and begun feeling her ribs one by one. This was all right with her. 'I have never met anyone I felt this way about,' he said. 'I love you.' He made her do things she'd never done before, and then they went for a walk and looked at the new tulips that were bound to have grown up somewhere. None of this felt stupid or corny, but she knew that it was. Miserably, she tried to gain a sense of proportion. She stared at the flowers. They were an agony of bright, organised beauty. She couldn't help it. She wanted to give him flowers. She wanted to be with him in a room full of flowers. She visualised herself standing in front of him, bearing a handful of blameless flowers trapped in the ugly pastel paper the florist would staple around them. The vision was brutally embarrassing, too much so to stay in her mind for more than seconds.

She stepped out of the flower store. He was not there. Her anxiety approached despair. They were supposed to spend the weekend together.

He stood in a cheap pizza stand across the street, eating a greasy slice and watching her as she stood on the corner. Her anxiety was visible to him. It was at once disconcerting and weirdly attractive. Her appearance otherwise was not pleasing. He couldn't quite put his finger on why this was. Perhaps it was the suggestion of meekness in her dress, of a desire to be inconspicuous, or worse, of plain thoughtlessness about how clothes looked on her.

He had met her at a party during the previous week. She immediately reminded him of a girl he had known years before, Sharon, a painfully serious girl with a pale, gentle face whom he had tormented off and on for two years before leaving for his wife. Although it had gratified him enormously to leave her, he had missed hurting her for years, and had been half-consciously looking for another woman with a similarly fatal combination of pride, weakness and a foolish lust for something resembling passion. On meeting Beth, he was astonished at how much she looked, talked and moved like his former victim. She was delicately morbid in all her gestures, sensitive, arrogant, vulnerable to flattery. She veered between extravagant outbursts of opinion and sudden, uncertain halts, during which she seemed to look to him for approval. She was in love with the idea of intelligence, and she overestimated her own. Her sense of the world, though she presented it aggressively, could be, he sensed, snatched out from under her with little or no trouble. She said, 'I hope you are a savage.'

He went home with her that night. He lay with her on her sagging, lumpy single mattress, tipping his head to blow smoke into the room. She butted her forehead against his chest. The mattress squeaked with every movement. He told her about Sharon. 'I had a relationship like that when I was in college,' she said. 'Somebody opened me up in a way that I had no control over. He hurt me. He changed me completely. Now I can't have sex normally.'

The room was pathetically decorated with postcards, pictures of huge-eyed Japanese cartoon characters, and tiny, maddening toys that she had obviously gone out of her way to find, displayed in a tightly arranged tumble on her dresser. A frail model airplane dangled from the light above her dresser. Next to it was a pasted-up cartoon of a pink-haired girl cringing open-mouthed before a spike-haired boy-villain in shorts and glasses. Her short skirt was blown up by the force of his threatening expression, and her panties showed. What kind of person would put crap like this up on her wall?

'I'm afraid of you,' she murmured.

'Why?'

'Because I just am.'

'Don't worry. I won't give you any more pain than you can handle.'

She curled against him and squeezed her feet together like a stretching cat. Her socks were thick and ugly, and her feet were large for her size. Details like this could repel him, but he felt tenderly toward the long, grubby, squeezed-together feet. He said, 'I want a slave.'

She said, 'I don't know. We'll see.'

He asked her to spend the weekend with him three days later.

It had seemed like a good idea at the time, but now he felt an irritating combination of guilt and anxiety. He thought of his wife, making breakfast with her delicate, methodical movements, or in the bathroom, painstakingly applying kohl under her huge eyes, flicking away the excess with pretty, birdlike finger gestures, her thin elbows raised, her eyes blank with concentration. He thought of Beth, naked and bound, blindfolded and spread-eagled on the floor of her cluttered apartment. Her cartoon characters grinned as he beat her with a whip. Welts rose on her breasts, thighs, stomach and arms. She screamed and twisted, wrenching her neck from side to side. She was going to be scarred for life. He had another picture of her sitting across from him at a restaurant, very erect, one arm on the table, her face serious and intent. Her large glasses drew her face down, made it look somber and elegant. She was smoking a cigarette with slow, mournful intakes of breath. These images lay on top of one another, forming a hideously confusing grid. How was he going to sort them out? He managed to separate the picture of his wife and the original picture of blindfolded Beth and hold them apart. He imagined himself traveling happily between the two. Perhaps, as time went on, he could bring Beth home and have his wife beat her too. She would do the dishes and serve them dinner. The grid closed up again and his stomach went into a moil. The thing was complicated and potentially exhausting. He looked at the anxious girl on the corner. She had said that she wanted to be hurt, but he suspected that she didn't understand what that meant.

He should probably just stay in the pizza place and watch her until she went away. It might be entertaining to see how long she waited. He felt a certain pity for her. He also felt, from his glassed-in vantage point, as though he were torturing an insect. He gloated as he ate his pizza.

At the height of her anxiety she saw him through the glass wall of the pizza stand. She immediately noticed his gloating countenance. She recognised the coldly scornful element in his watching and waiting as opposed to greeting her. She suffered, but only for an instant; she was then smitten by love. She smiled and crossed the street with a senseless confidence in the power of her smile.

'I was about to come over,' he said. 'I had to eat first. I was starving.' He folded the last of his pizza in half and stuck it in his mouth.

She noticed a piece of bright orange pizza stuck between his teeth, and it endeared him to her.

They left the pizza stand. He walked with wide steps, and his heavy black overcoat swung rakishly, she thought, above his boots. He was a slight, slender boy with a pale, narrow face and blond hair that wisped across one brow. In the big coat he looked like the young pet of a budding secret police force. She thought he was beautiful.

He hailed a cab and directed the driver to the airport. He looked at her sitting beside him. 'This is going to be a disaster,' he said. 'I'll probably wind up leaving you there and coming back alone.'

'I hope not,' she said. 'I don't have any money. If you left me there, I wouldn't be able to get back by myself.'

'That's too bad. Because I might.' He watched her face for a reaction. It showed discomfort and excitement and something that he could only qualify as foolishness, as if she had just dropped a tray full of glasses in public. 'Don't worry, I wouldn't do that,' he said. 'But I like the idea that I could.'

'So do I.' She was terribly distressed. She wanted to throw her arms around him.

He thought: There is something wrong. Her passivity was pleasing, as was her silence and her willingness to place herself in his hands. But he sensed another element present in her that he could not define and did not like. Her tightly folded hands were nervous and repulsive. Her public posture was brittle, not pliant. There was a rigidity that if cracked would yield nothing. He was disconcerted to realise that he didn't know if he could crack it anyway. He began to feel uncomfortable. Perhaps the weekend would be a disaster.

They arrived at the airport an hour early. They went to a bar and drank. The bar was an open-ended cube with a red neon sign that said 'Cocktails.' There was no sense of shelter in it. The furniture was spindly and exposed, and there were no doors to protect you from the sight of dazed, unattractive passengers wandering through the airport with their luggage. She ordered a Bloody Mary.

'I can't believe you ordered that,' he said.

'Why not?'

'Because I want a bloody Beth.' He gave her a look that made her think of a neurotic dog with its tongue hanging out, waiting to bite someone.

'Oh,' she said.

He offered her a cigarette.

'I don't smoke,' she said. 'I told you twice.'

'Well, you should start.'

They sat quietly and drank for several minutes.

'Do you like to look at people?' she asked.

She was clearly struggling to talk to him. He saw that her face had become very tense. He could've increased her discomfort, but for the moment he had lost the energy to do so.

'Yes,' he said. 'I do.'

They spent some moments regarding the people around them. They were short on material. There were only a few customers in the bar; most of them were men in suits who sat there seemingly enmeshed in a web of habit and accumulated rancor that they called their personalities, so utterly unaware of their entanglement that they clearly considered themselves men of the world, even though they had long ago stopped noticing it. Then a couple walked through the door, carrying luggage. The woman's bright skirt flashed with each step. The man walked ahead of her. He walked too fast for her to keep up. She looked harried. Her eyes were wide and dark and clotted with makeup; there was a mole on her chin. He paused, as though considering whether he would stop for a drink. He decided not to and strode again. Her earrings jiggled as she followed. They left a faint trail of sex and disappointment behind them.

Beth watched the woman's hips move under her skirt. 'There was something unpleasant about them,' she said.

'Yes, there was.'

It cheered her to find this point of contact. 'I'm sorry I'm not more talkative,' she said.

'That's all right.' His narrow eyes became feral once again. 'Women should be quiet.' It suddenly struck her that it would seem completely natural if he lunged forward and bit her face.

'I agree,' she said sharply. 'There aren't many men around worth talking to.'

He was nonplussed by her peevish tone. Perhaps, he thought, he'd imagined it.

He hadn't.

They had more drinks on the plane. They were served a hunk of white-frosted raisin pastry in a red paper bag. He wasn't hungry, but the vulgar cake appealed to him so he stuck it in his baggage.

They had a brief discussion about shoes, from the point of view of expense and aesthetics. They talked about intelligence and art. There were large gaps of silence that were disheartening to both of them. She began talking about old people, and how nice they could be. He had a picture of her kneeling on the floor in black stockings and handcuffs. This picture became blurred, static-ridden, and then obscured by their conversation. He felt a ghastly sense of longing. He called back the picture, which no longer gave him any pleasure. He superimposed it upon a picture of himself standing in a nightclub the week before, holding a drink and talking to a rather combative girl who wanted his number.

'Some old people are beautiful in an unearthly way,' she continued. 'I saw this old lady in the drugstore the other day who must've been in her nineties. She was so fragile and pretty, she was like a little elf.'

He looked at her and said, 'Are you going to start being fun to be around or are you going to be a big drag?'

She didn't answer right away. She didn't see how this followed her comment about the old lady. 'I don't know.'

'I don't think you're very sexual,' he said. 'You're not the way I thought you were when I first met you.'

She was so hurt by this that she had difficulty answering. Finally, she said, 'I can be very sexual or very unsexual depending on who I'm with and in what situation. It has to be the right kind of thing. I'm sort of a cerebral person. I think I respond to things in a cerebral way, mostly.'

'That's what I mean.'

She was struck dumb with frustration. She had obviously disappointed him in some fundamental way, which she felt was completely due to misunderstanding. If only she could think of the correct thing to say, she was sure she could clear it up. The blue puffball thing unfurled itself before her with sickening power. It was the same image of him holding her and gazing into her eyes with bone-dislodging intent, thinly veiling the many shattering events that she anticipated between them. The prospect made her disoriented with pleasure. The only problem was, this image seemed to have no connection with what was happening now. She tried to think back to the time they had spent in her apartment, when he had held her and said, 'You're cute.' What had happened between then and now to so disappoint him?

She hadn't yet noticed how much he had disappointed her.

He couldn't tell if he was disappointing her or not. She completely mystified him, especially after her abrupt speech on cerebralism. It was now impossible to even have a clear picture of what he wanted to do to this unglamorous creature, who looked as though she bit her nails and read books at night. Dim, half-formed pictures of his wife, Sharon, Beth and a sixteen-year-old Chinese hooker he'd seen a month before crawled aimlessly over each other. He sat and brooded in a bad-natured and slightly drunken way.

She sat next to him, diminished and fretful, with idiot radio songs about sex in her head.

They were staying in his grandmother's deserted apartment in Washington, DC. The complex was a series of building blocks seemingly arranged at random, stuck together and painted the least attractive colors available. It was surrounded by bright green grass and a circular driveway, and placed on a quiet highway that led into the city. There was a drive-in bank and an insurance office next to it. It was enveloped in the steady, continuous noise of cars driving by at roughly the same speed.

'This is a horrible building,' she said as they traveled up in the elevator.

The door slid open and they walked down a hall carpeted with dense brown nylon. The grandmother's apartment opened before them. Beth found the refrigerator and opened it. There was a crumpled package of French bread, a jar of hot peppers, several lumps covered with aluminum foil, two bottles of wine and a six-pack. 'Is your grandmother an alcoholic?' she asked.

'I don't know.' He dropped his heavy leather bag and her white canvas one in the living room, took off his coat and threw it on the bags. She watched him standing there, pale and gaunt in a black leather shirt tied at his waist with a leather belt. That image of him would stay with her for years for no good reason and with no emotional significance. He dropped into a chair, his thin arms flopping lightly on its arms. He nodded at the tray of whiskey, Scotch and liqueurs on the coffee table before him. 'Why don't you make yourself a drink?'

She dropped to her knees beside the table and nervously played with the bottles. He was watching her quietly, his expression hooded. She plucked a bottle of thick chocolate liqueur from the cluster, poured herself a glass and sat in the chair across from his with both hands around it. She could no longer ignore the character of the apartment. It was brutally ridiculous, almost sadistic in its absurdity. The couch and chairs were covered with a floral print. A thin maize carpet zipped across the floor. There were throw rugs. There were artificial flowers. There was an abundance of small tables and shelves housing a legion of figures; grinning glass maidens in sumptuous gowns bore baskets of glass roses, ceramic birds warbled from the ceramic stumps they clung to, glass horses galloped across teak-wood pastures. A ceramic weather poodle and his diamond-eyed kitty-cat companions silently watched the silent scene in the room.

'Are you all right?' he asked.

'I hate this apartment. It's really awful.'

'What were you expecting? Jesus Christ. It's a lot like yours, you know.'

'Yes. That's true, I have to admit.' She drank her liqueur.

'Do you think you could improve your attitude about this whole thing? You might try being a little more positive.'

Coming from him, this question was preposterous. He must be so pathologically insecure that his perception of his own behavior was thoroughly distorted. He saw rejection everywhere, she decided; she must reassure him. 'But I do feel positive about being here,' she said. She paused, searching for the best way to express the extremity of her positive feelings. She invisibly implored him to see and mount their blue puffball bed. 'It would be impossible for you to disappoint me. The whole idea of you makes me happy. Anything you do will be all right.'

Her generosity unnerved him. He wondered if she realised what she was saying. 'Does anybody know you're here?' he asked. 'Did you tell anyone where you were going?'

'No.' She had in fact told several people.

'That wasn't very smart.'

'Why not?'

'You don't know me at all. Anything could happen to you.'

She put her glass on the coffee table, crossed the floor and dropped to her knees between his legs. She threw her arms around his thighs. She nuzzled his groin with her nose. He tightened. She unzipped his pants. 'Stop,' he said. 'Wait.' She took his shoulders—she had a surprisingly strong grip—and pulled him to the carpet. His hovering brood of images and plans was suddenly upended, as though it had been sitting on a table that a rampaging crazy person had flipped over. He felt assaulted and invaded. This was not what he had in mind, but to refuse would make him seem somehow less virile than she. Queasily, he stripped off her clothes and put their bodies in a viable position. He fastened his teeth on her breast and bit her. She made a surprised noise and her body stiffened. He bit her again, harder. She screamed. He wanted to draw blood. Her screams were short and stifled. He could tell that she was trying to like being bitten, but that she did not. He gnawed her breast She screamed sharply. They screwed. They broke apart and regarded each other warily. She put her hand on his tentatively. He realised what had been disturbing him about her. With other women whom he had been with in similar situations, he had experienced a relaxing sense of emptiness within them that had made it easy for him to get inside them and, once there, smear himself all over their innermost territory until it was no longer theirs but his. His wife did not have this empty quality yet the gracious way in which she emptied herself for him made her submission, as far as it went, all the more poignant This exasperating girl, on the other hand, contained a tangible somethingness that she not only refused to expunge, but that seemed to willfully expand itself so that he banged into it with every attempt to invade her. He didn't mind the somethingness; he rather liked it, in fact, and had looked forward to seeing it demolished. But she refused to let him do it. Why had she told him she was a masochist? He looked at her body Her limbs were muscular and alert. He considered taking her by the neck and bashing her head against the floor.

He stood abruptly. 'I want to get something to eat I'm starving.'

She put her hand on his ankle. Her desire to abase herself had been completely frustrated. She had pulled him to the rug certain that if only they could fuck, he would enter her with overwhelming force and take complete control of her. Instead she had barely felt him, and what she had felt was remote and cold. Somewhere on her exterior he'd been doing some biting thing that meant nothing to her and was quite unpleasant. Despairing, she held his ankle tighter and put her forehead on the carpet. At least she could stay at his feet, worshiping He twisted free and walked away. 'Come on,' he said.

*

The car was in the parking lot. It was because of the car that this weekend had come about. It was his wife's car an expensive thing that her ex-husband had given her. It had been in Washington for over a year; he was here to retrieve it and drive it back to New York.

Beth was appalled by the car. It was a loud yellow monster with a narrow, vicious shape and absurd doors that snapped up from the roof and out like wings. In another setting it might have seemed glamorous, but here, behind this equally monstrous building in her unsatisfactory clothing, the idea of sitting in it with him struck her as comparable to putting on a clown nose and wearing it to dinner.

They drove down a suburban highway lined with small businesses, malls and restaurants. It was twilight; several neon signs blinked consolingly.

'Do you think you could make some effort to change your mood?' he said.

'I'm not in a bad mood,' she said wearily. 'I just feel blank.'

Not blank enough, he thought.

He pulled into a Roy Rogers fast food cafeteria. She thought: He is not even going to take me to a nice place. She was insulted. It seemed as though he was insulting her on purpose. The idea was incredible to her.

She walked through the line with him but did not take any of the shiny dishes of food displayed on the fluorescent-lit aluminum shelves. He felt a pang of worry. He was no longer angry, and her drawn white face disturbed him.

'Why aren't you eating?'

'I'm not hungry.'

They sat down. He picked at his food, eyeing her with veiled alarm. It occurred to her that it might embarrass him to eat in front of her while she ate nothing. She asked if she could have some of his salad. He eagerly passed her the entire bowl of pale leaves strewn with orange dressing. 'Have it all.'

He huddled his shoulders orphanlike as he ate; his blond hair stood tangled like pensive weeds. 'I don't know why you're not eating,' he said fretfully. 'You're going to be hungry later on.'

Her predisposition to adore him was provoked. She smiled.

'Why are you staring at me like that?' he asked.

'I'm just enjoying the way you look. You're very airy.'

Again, his eyes showed alarm.

'Sometimes when I look at you, I feel like I'm seeing a tank of small, quick fish, the bright darting kind that go every which way.'

He paused, stunned and dangle-forked over his pinched, curled-up steak. 'I'm beginning to think you're out of your fucking mind.'

Her happy expression collapsed.

'Why can't you talk to me in a half-normal fucking way?' he continued. 'Like the way we talked on the plane. I liked that. That was a conversation.' In fact, he hadn't liked the conversation on the plane either, but compared to this one, it seemed quite all right.

When they got back to the apartment, they sat on the floor and drank more alcohol. 'I want you to drink a lot,' he said. 'I want to make you do things you don't want to do.'

'But I won't do anything I don't want to do. You have to make me want it.'

He lay on his back in silent frustration.

'What are your parents like?' she asked.

'What?'

'Your parents. What are they like?'

'I don't know. I don't have that much to do with them. My mother is nice. My father's a prick. That's what they're like.' He put one hand over his face; a square-shaped album-style view of his family presented itself. They were all at the breakfast table, talking and reaching for things. His mother moved in the background, a slim, worried shadow in her pink robe. His sister sat next to him, tall, blond and arrogant, talking and flicking at toast crumbs in the corners of her mouth. His father sat at the head of the table, his big arms spread over everything, leaning over his plate as if he had to defend it, gnawing his breakfast. He felt unhappy and then angry. He thought of a little Italian girl he had met in a go-go bar a while back, and comforted himself with the memory of her slim haunches and pretty high-heeled feet on either side of his head as she squatted over him.

'It seems that way with my parents when you first look at them. But in fact my mother is much more aggressive and, I would say, more cruel than my father, even though she's more passive and soft on the surface.'

She began a lengthy and, in his view, incredible and unnecessary history of her family life, including descriptions of her brother and sister. Her entire family seemed to have a collectively disturbed personality characterised by long brooding silences, unpleasing compulsive sloppiness (unflushed toilets, used Kleenex abandoned everywhere, dirty underwear on the floor) and outbursts of irrational, violent anger. It was horrible. He wanted to go home.

He poked himself up on his elbows. 'Are you a liar?' he asked. 'Do you lie often?'

She stopped in midsentence and looked at him. She seemed to consider the question earnestly. 'No,' she said. 'Not really. I mean, I can lie, but I usually don't about important things. Why do you ask?'

'Why did you tell me you were a masochist?'

'What makes you think I'm not?'

'You don't act like one.'

'Well, I don't know how you can say that. You hardly know me. We've hardly done anything yet.'

'What do you want to do?'

'I can't just come out and tell you. It would ruin it.'

He picked up his cigarette lighter and nicked it, picked up her shirt and stuck the lighter underneath. She didn't move fast enough. She screamed and leapt to her feet.

'Don't do that! That's awful!'

He rolled over on his stomach. 'See. I told you. You're not a masochist.'

'Shit! That wasn't erotic in the least. I don't come when I stub my toe either.'

In the ensuing silence it occurred to her that she was angry, and had been for some time.

'I'm tired,' she said. I want to go to bed.' She walked out of the room.

He sat up. 'Well, we're making decisions, aren't we?'

She reentered the room. 'Where are we supposed to sleep, anyway?'

He showed her the guest room and the fold-out couch. She immediately began dismantling the couch with stiff, angry movements. Her body seemed full of unnatural energy and purpose. She had, he decided, ruined the weekend, not only for him but for herself. Her willful, masculine, stupid somethingness had obstructed their mutual pleasure and satisfaction. The only course of action left was hostility. He opened his grandmother's writing desk and took out a piece of paper and a Magic Marker. He wrote the word 'stupid' in thick black letters. He held it first near her chest, like a placard, and then above her crotch. She ignored him.

'Where are the sheets?' she asked.

'How'd you get so tough all of a sudden?' He threw the paper on the desk and took a sheet from a dresser drawer.

'We'll need a blanket too, if we open the window. And I want to open the window.'

He regarded her sarcastically. 'You're just keeping yourself from getting what you want by acting like this.'

'You obviously don't know what I want.'

They got undressed. He contemptuously took in the muscular, energetic look of her body. She looked more like a boy than a girl, in spite of her pronounced hips and round breasts. Her short, spiky red hair was more than enough to render her masculine. Even the dark bruise he had inflicted on her breast and the slight burn from his lighter failed to lend her a more feminine quality.

She opened the window. They got under the blanket on the fold-out couch and lay there, not touching, as though they really were about to sleep. Of course, neither one of them could.

'Why is this happening?' she asked.

'You tell me.'

'I don't know. I really don't know.' Her voice was small and pathetic.

'Part of it is that you don't talk when you should, and then you talk too much when you shouldn't be saying anything at all.'

In confusion, she reviewed the various moments they had spent together, trying to classify them in terms of whether or not it had been appropriate to speak, and to rate her performance accordingly. Her confusion increased. Tears floated on her eyes. She curled her body against his.

'You're hurting my feelings,' she said, 'but I don't think you're doing it on purpose.'

He was briefly touched. 'Accidental pain,' he said musingly. He took her head in both hands and pushed it between his legs. She opened her mouth compliantly. He had hurt her after all, he reflected. She was confused and exhausted, and at this instant, anyway, she was doing what he wanted her to do. Still, it wasn't enough. He released her and she moved upward to lie on top of him, resting her head on his shoulder. She spoke dreamily. 'I would do anything with you.'

'You would not. You would be disgusted.'

'Disgusted by what?'

'You would be disgusted if I even told you.'

She rolled away from him. 'It's probably nothing.'

'Have you ever been pissed on?'

He gloated as he felt her body tighten.

'No.'

'Well, that's what I want to do to you.'

'On your grandmother's rug?'

'I want you to drink it. If any got on the rug, you'd clean it up.'

'Oh.'

'I knew you'd be shocked.'

'I'm not. I just never wanted to do it.'

'So? That isn't any good to me.'

In fact, she was shocked. Then she was humiliated, and not in the way she had planned. Her seductive puffball cloud deflated with a flaccid hiss, leaving two drunken, bad-tempered, incompetent, malodorous people blinking and uncomfortable on its remains. She stared at the ugly roses with their heads collapsed in a dead wilt and slowly saw what a jerk she'd been. Then she got mad.

'Do you like people to piss on you?' she asked.

'Yeah. Last month I met this great girl at Billy's Topless. She pissed in my face for only twenty bucks.'

His voice was high-pitched and stupidly aggressive, like some weird kid who would walk up to you on the street and offer to take care of your sexual needs. How, she thought miserably, could she have mistaken this hostile moron for the dark, brooding hero who would crush her like an insect and then talk about life and art?

'There's a lot of other things I'd like to do too,' he said with odd self-righteousness. 'But I don't think you could handle it.'

'It's not a question of handling it.' She said these last two words very sarcastically. 'So far everything you've said to me has been incredibly banal. You haven't presented anything in a way that's even remotely attractive.' She sounded like a prim, prematurely adult child complaining to her teacher about someone putting a worm down her back.

He felt like an idiot. How had he gotten stuck with this prissy, reedy-voiced thing with a huge forehead who poked and picked over everything that came out of his mouth? He longed for a dim-eyed little slut with a big, bright mouth and black vinyl underwear. What had he had in mind when he brought this girl here, anyway? Her serious, desperate face, panicked and tear-stained. Her ridiculous air of sacrifice and abandonment as he spread-eagled and bound her. White skin that marked easily. Frightened eyes. An exposed personality that could be yanked from her and held out of reach like . . . oh, he could see it only in scraps; his imagination fumbled and lost its grip. He looked at her hatefully self-possessed, compact little form. He pushed her roughly. 'Oh, I'd do anything with you,' he mimicked. 'You would not.'

She rolled away on her side, her body curled tightly. He felt her trembling. She sniffed.

'Don't tell me I've broken your heart.'

She continued crying.

'This isn't bothering me at all,' he said. 'In fact, I'm rather enjoying it.'

The trembling stopped. She sniffed once, turned on her back and looked at him with puzzled eyes. She blinked. He suddenly felt tired. I shouldn't be doing this, he thought. She is actually a nice person. For a moment he had an impulse to embrace her. He had a stronger impulse to beat her. He looked around the room until he saw a light wood stick that his grandmother had for some reason left standing in the corner. He pointed at it.

'Get me that stick. I want to beat you with it.'

'I don't want to.'

'Get it. I want to humiliate you even more.'

She shook her head, her eyes wide with alarm. She held the blanket up to her chin.

'Come on,' he coaxed. 'Let me beat you. I'd be much nicer after I beat you.'

'I don't think you're capable of being as nice as you'd have to be to interest me at this point.'

'All right. I'll get it myself.' He got the stick and snatched the blanket from her body.

She sat, her legs curled in a kneeling position. 'Don't,' she said. 'I'm scared.'

'You should be scared,' he said. 'I'm going to torture you.' He brandished the stick, which actually felt as though it would break on the second or third blow. They froze in their positions, staring at each other.

She was the first to drop her eyes. She regarded the torn-off blanket meditatively. 'You have really disappointed me,' she said. 'This whole thing has been a complete waste of time.'

He sat on the bed, stick in lap. 'You don't care about my feelings.'

'I think I want to sleep in the next room.'

They couldn't sleep separately any better than they could sleep together. She lay curled up on the couch pondering what seemed to be the ugly nature of her life. He lay wound in a blanket, blinking in the dark, as a dislocated, manic and unpleasing revue of his sexual experiences stumbled through his memory in a queasy scramble.

In the morning they agreed that they would return to Manhattan immediately. Despite their mutual ill humor, they fornicated again, mostly because they could more easily ignore each other while doing so.

They packed quickly and silently.

'It's going to be a long drive back,' he said. 'Try not to make me feel like too much of a prick, okay?'

'I don't care what you feel like.'

He would have liked to dump her at the side of the road somewhere, but he wasn't indifferent enough to societal rules to do that. Besides, he felt vaguely sorry that he had made her cry, and while this made him view her grudgingly, he felt obliged not to worsen the situation. Ideally she would disappear, taking her stupid canvas bag with her. In reality, she sat beside him in the car with more solidity and presence than she had displayed since they met on the corner in Manhattan. She seemed fully prepared to sit in silence for the entire six-hour drive. He turned on the radio.

'Would you mind turning that down a little?'

'Anything for you.'

She rolled her eyes.

Without much hope, he employed a tactic he used to pacify his wife when they argued. He would give her a choice and let her make it. 'Would you like something to eat?' he asked. 'You must be starving.'

She was. They spent almost an hour driving up and down the available streets trying to find a restaurant she wanted to be in. She finally chose a small, clean egg-and-toast place. Her humor visibly improved as they sat before their breakfast. 'I like eggs,' she said. 'They are so comforting.'

He began to talk to her out of sheer curiosity. They talked about music, college, people they knew in common and drugs they used to take as teenagers. She said that when she had taken LSD, she had often lost her sense of identity so completely that she didn't recognise herself in the mirror. This pathetic statement brought back her attractiveness in a terrific rush. She noted the quick dark gleam in his eyes.

'You should've let me beat you,' he said. 'I wouldn't have hurt you too much.'

'That's not the point. The moment was wrong. It wouldn't have meant anything.'

'It would've meant something to me.' He paused. 'But you probably would've spoiled it. You would've started screaming right away and made me stop.'

The construction workers at the next table stared at them quizzically. She smiled pleasantly at them and returned her gaze to him. 'You don't know that.'

He was so relieved at the ease between them that he put his arm around her as they left the restaurant. She stretched up and kissed his neck.

'We just had the wrong idea about each other,' she said. 'It's nobody's fault that we're incompatible.'

'Well, soon we'll be in Manhattan, and it'll be all over. You'll never have to see me again.' He hoped she would dispute this, but she didn't.

They continued to talk in the car, about the nature of time, their parents and the injustice of racism.

She was too exhausted to extract much from the pedestrian conversation, but the sound of his voice, the position of his body and his sudden receptivity were intoxicating. Time took on a grainy, dreamy aspect that made impossible conversations and unlikely gestures feasible, like a space capsule that enables its inhabitants to happily walk up the wall. The peculiar little car became a warm, humming cocoon, like a miniature house she had, as a little girl, assembled out of odds and ends for invented characters. She felt as if she were a very young child, when every notion that appeared in her head was new and naked of association and thus needed to be expressed carefully so it didn't become malformed. She wanted to set every one of them before him in a row, as she had once presented crayon drawings to her father in a neat many-colored sequence. Then he would shift his posture slightly or make a gesture that suddenly made him seem so helpless and frail that she longed to protect him and cosset him away, like a delicate pet in a matchbox filled with cotton. She rested her head on his shoulder and lovingly regarded the legs that bent at the knee and tapered to the booted feet resting on the brakes or the accelerator. This was as good as her original fantasy, possibly even better.

'Can I abuse you some more now?' he asked sweetly. 'In the car?'

'What do you want to do?'

'Gag you? That's all, I'd just like to gag you.'

'But I want to talk to you.'

He sighed. 'You're really not a masochist, you know.'

She shrugged. 'Maybe not. It always seemed like I was.'

'You might have fantasies, but I don't think you have any concept of a real slave mentality. You have too much ego to be part of another person.'

'I don't know, I've never had the chance to try it. I've never met anyone I wanted to do that with.'

'If you were a slave, you wouldn't make the choice.'

'All right, I'm not a slave. With me it's more a matter of love.' She was just barely aware that she was pitching her voice higher and softer than it was naturally, so that she sounded like a cartoon girl. 'It's like the highest form of love.'

He thought this was really cute. Sure it was nauseating, but it was feminine in a radio-song kind of way.

'You don't seem interested in love. It's not about that for you.'

'That's not true. That's not true at all. Why do you think I was so rough back there? Deep down, I'm afraid I'll fall in love with you, that I'll need to be with you and fuck you . . . forever.' He was enjoying himself now. He was beginning to see her as a locked garden that he could sneak into and sit in for days, tearing the heads off the flowers.

On one hand, she was beside herself with bliss. On the other, she was scrutinising him carefully from behind an opaque facade as he entered her pasteboard scene of flora and fauna. Could he function as a character in this landscape? She imagined sitting across from him in a Japanese restaurant, talking about anything. He would look intently into her eyes . . .

He saw her apartment and then his. He saw them existing a nice distance apart, each of them blocked off by cleanly cut boundaries. Her apartment bloomed with scenes that spiraled toward him in colorful circular motions and then froze suddenly and clearly in place. She was crawling blindfolded across the floor. She was bound and naked in an S&M bar. She was sitting next to him in a taxi, her skirt pulled up, his fingers in her vagina.

. . . and then they would go back to her apartment. He would beat her and fuck her mouth.

Then he would go home to his wife, and she would make dinner for him. It was so well balanced, the mere contemplation of it gave him pleasure.

The next day he would send her flowers.

He let go of the wheel with one hand and patted her head. She gripped his shirt frantically.

He thought: This could work out fine.

TWO DOGS

Steve Yarbrough

Prior to the end of World War II, the area had been part of Germany. In the '20s and '30s, the village was a well-known resort. Then the war started, and after the Nazis attacked Russia, Hitler established his eastern command post at Wolf's Lair just a few kilometers away—and Krutyn was turned into a recuperation center. My brother-in-law says that by 1943, German pilots were going crazy in droves; the Luftwaffe sent them here for a few weeks to calm them down.

We're sitting on a pier that juts out into the Krutynia River. Our kayaks, all ten of them, are stacked on the bank a few feet away. We're on a guided tour that ends tomorrow. I'm the only non-Pole in our group.

Tomek is a member of the new entrepreneurial class, a textile trader who owns warehouses in several countries and does business all over the world. His English has a few holes in it, but it's still more solid than my Polish. And anyway, he's been my brother-in-law for fifteen years. There are things we both know so well that we never need to say them.

We know, for instance, that our wives, who are sisters, both had difficult childhoods, that their mother used to disappear and go on drinking binges that lasted for days at a time, and when their father came home and found her gone he would always ask my wife Anna— who is three years older than Basia—why she hadn't kept her mother at home. Today Anna doesn't drink at all, while Basia never goes twenty-four hours without having at least five or six shots of vodka— and often, she has a good many more. Anna hates nothing so much as a loud party, whereas Basia, if she had her way, would have one every day.

Tomek and I both know that a special bond exists between my sister-in-law and me. Years ago, when Anna and I first started living together, Basia came to California to visit. She and I hit it off really well. In fact, she probably talked Anna into marrying me. I had created a favorable impression because each evening, after Anna went to bed, I'd sit up with Basia, drinking vodka and talking. She has a wonderful way of mixing several languages together in the same sentence: a Polish subject, a German verb, an English object.

Sometimes, during those conversations that took place so many years ago, we'd get a little tipsy, and once or twice the talk turned risky. 'I very love sex,' she said late one night, giving herself a body rub. 'Anna too?'

I did my best not to gag. 'Anna too.'

'*Wunderbar!*' she said. '*To jest very gut!*' Then she gave me the body rub. And to tell the truth, I rubbed back.

This kind of behavior has continued from time to time, whenever we come to Poland or they come to California. Last night, when we were walking through the bushes toward our respective cottages, she and I stumbled into one another, and the next thing I knew she was in my arms and I was kissing her. I realized we should stop, because there was no telling who else might be wandering around out there, but we kept at it a pretty good while. I even put my hands on her bottom.

I gesture at the canopy of limbs and leaves that keeps the river in constant shade. 'I can see why they'd send crazy people here,' I tell Tomek. 'It's a calm, peaceful place.'

'Peaceful,' he agrees. '*Tak. Bardzo.*'

We sit there for a while, our feet dangling in the water. Across the river, a couple of swans idle near their flock; every time a canoeist passes, the bigger of the two swans sticks its neck out and hisses.

This seems as good a time as any to bring up something that's been on my mind. I recently acquired a large sum of money: a studio in Hollywood made a movie out of one of my books. I'm thinking of quitting my teaching job and buying something here, because even after fifteen years in California, Anna still hasn't quite adapted to American life. 'If you had to do what I've had to do,' she's told me more times than I can count, 'you would go as crazy as a June bug.'

'Crazy as a *betsy*bug.'

'See what I mean? Can you imagine how humiliating it is to bungel a simple cliche?'

Poland is a different country now than it was fifteen years ago—I've been telling myself that lately. They've got ATMs now. They've got billboards and faxes, CNN and KFC. I could do it for her—I love my wife that much. All I need is a cell phone and a reliable internet server.

Tomek is not an excitable man; he's the kind of guy who thinks about things long and hard, who considers all actions carefully. He listens quietly while I tell him that in addition to being relatives, we might soon become countrymen. He continues to dangle his feet in the water and keeps looking at the opposite shore. When I've finished, he's silent for a couple of minutes. Then he says, 'Do you remember my friend Sikala?'

I met Sikala years ago. I remember him partly because he and his wife owned the biggest, meanest-looking Rottweiler I had ever seen. I also remember him because one room of his tiny apartment down in Warsaw had been turned into a library, and the library contained about three thousand books, including Polish translations of all Graham Greene's novels. Sikala and I engaged in a spirited argument about the character Pyle in *The Quiet American*. Sikala maintained that whatever his flaws, Pyle had gone to Vietnam to do good. I said he was just there trying to stir up enough trouble to keep himself entertained. Sikala finally called me a cynic, and I said yes, and what was Graham Greene?

'Yeah, I remember Sikala,' I say. 'He's that lawyer I met down in Warsaw.' Tomek nods.

'So,' I say, 'what about him?'

There on the pier jutting out into the Krutynia, while canoeists float past, their oars gently rowing the water, in this place where all those young Germans—those young blond Aryans who dished out so much death—knew their own last moments of peace, my brother-in-law begins to tell me a story.

During the last years of the Jaruzelski regime, Sikala and his wife Danusia, who is also an attorney, spent a lot of their time representing Solidarity activists. They became close friends of Adam Michnik and Jacek Kuron, the intellectual heart and soul of the Solidarity movement, and they even had some dealings with Lech Walesa. They served as informal counsel for the family of Jerzy Popieluszko, the priest who was murdered by the secret police back in 1984.

Doing legal work for dissidents caused the Sikalas no small amount of trouble. One day their car disappeared. About a week later Sikala received a package; when he unwrapped the heavy box, he discovered that it contained a metal cube that had lots of jagged edges; a note attached to the cube said *Thanks for joining the campaign to conserve parking space*. One day he came home to find that all his books had been removed from their shelves and thrown on the floor and doused in gasoline. This time the note said *We would have burned them, but even we can't get around the fact that the stores are out of matches*. One night, while they slept, someone entered their apartment, removed the doorknob, then left and locked them in. *You could fly out*, the voice on the telephone said. *The landing pad's only fifteen floors down*.

They had never been dog-lovers. They bought Heifetz as an act of self-defense. He was six weeks old when they got him, just a small dun-colored pup, but within a year he had grown into a full-sized Rottweiler. He spent most of his time in Sikala's library, standing at the window, his paws up on the sill, as he monitored motion down below. Whenever anyone entered the building, he would turn and dash into the living room. He'd wait there, listening for the lift, and if it stopped at the fifteenth floor, he would begin barking before the doors had even opened. The barking sounded amplified, as if Heifetz had been plugged into a massive sound system with the reverb turned on. There were no more attacks on the Sikalas' property, no more notes, no visits at night.

Unwanted guests annoyed Heifetz, just as they had annoyed Sikala himself. But it would take another dog to drive them both mad.

When the Jaruzelski government crumbled and former dissidents began to assume power, Sikala was in a uniquely good position. By the mid '90s he had become Warsaw's top prosecuting attorney. His wife Danusia, meanwhile, had gone to work for Coca-Cola. They both earned large salaries. They sold their apartment and bought a six-bedroom house near Lazienki Park, in Warsaw's most exclusive area; they made several smart investments, took trips to Japan, Hawaii, Crete, the Carribean. And then, after Sikala convinced Danusia they needed a place to get away to on weekends and holidays, they bought a badly rundown cottage in the village of Spychowo, about forty kilometers from Olsztyn.

Sikala had been born in Warsaw, and Danusia had grown up in Gdansk. Neither one of them had ever lived in the country, though Sikala had always been interested in Polish folk music and had actually spent some money in recent years collecting folk art. He had filled his new house in Warsaw with wood carvings, woven carpets, black madonnas, and lots of other items he'd bought in village marketplaces:

an old milk churn, an iron kettle, a chopping block stained with the blood of countless chickens.

At first glance it might seem strange that a man who'd spent most of his life in the city would crave a country dwelling. But it made sense, my brother-in-law said, if you knew Sikala's tastes—especially if you remembered that in addition to liking folk art he was a voracious reader and that while his intellect was hard enough to appreciate Graham Greene, his heart was the heart of a romantic. For instance, he loved the novels of Henryk Sienkiewicz.

At the end of the nineteenth century, when Poland was still partitioned between Prussia, the Austro-Hungarian Empire and Russia, Sienkiewicz wrote a series of historical novels depicting the struggles of Polish heroes against foreign aggressors. Sikala's favorite of these novels was *Krzyzacy*—or *The Teutonic Knights*. One of the more memorable characters in the book is a man named Jurand, a great Polish warrior who, as luck would have it, lived in the village of Spychowo—the very place where Sikala bought his cottage more than five hundred years later. Jurand fought and won many battles against the knights of the Teutonic order. Finally, in an effort to punish him for his successes, the knights kidnapped his daughter Danusia. They carried her away to their fortress at Marienburg. Jurand mounted up and went to get her, but the knights would only let him see her if he first agreed to dress as a penitent. Draped in beggars' rags, he entered her cell. Her hair was wild-looking, her eyes unfocused. Captivity had driven her insane.

Seeing the mad look in Danusia's eyes, unfortunately, was not the end of Jurand's punishment. The knights blinded him and cut out his tongue. Then they dragged him from their fortress and threw him in the dirt. For weeks he wandered through the forest, unable to see or speak, his hair completely white now. Finally a former servant saw him and asked him the most famous question in Polish literature:

'Are *thou* the great Jurand of Spychowo?'

A group of German tourists is standing at the far end of the pier: three plump couples in their mid to late seventies—they are, as Poles say, the *right* age. They're all wearing knee shorts. One of them, a bald man who has a pipe in his shirt pocket, gestures at the river and says something to the others.

My brother-in-law is generally open-minded, but when he hears that guttural speech, a look of distaste appears on his face. If translated literally, the Polish word for *German—Niemiec*—means 'the one who can't speak.' Their language is not exactly music to the Polish ear. Yet at the same time Poles want their marks. Earlier today, at the marketplace in Krutyn, I noticed that all the guidebooks for sale were in German. There was even one guide to Wolf's Lair; all the pictures of Hitler looked heroic.

I nod in the direction of the couples. 'You think that guy's telling them about a fish he caught the last time he was here, back in '43?'

Tomek shrugs. 'It's possible.'

The Germans eventually wander off, looking as if they're sizing the place up for purchase.

'So,' I say, 'you're telling me that Sikala bought this little rundown house in some godforsaken village because he fancied himself the reincarnation of a mythical Polish knight?'

'I didn't say that.'

'But you implied it.'

'How?'

'Well, I mean, after all—his wife has the same name as Jurand's daughter. '

'Danusia is a common Polish name.'

'Plus, he'd made a career of defending Polish patriots against the puppets of a foreign power.'

'If you called Marek Sikala a patriot, I am sure that he would cringe.'

'So what's the point of the story?'

'You know,' Tomek says, 'you are a little bit like Basia.'

I'm a lot like Basia, that's no secret, but it's one of those things I didn't think we'd ever say. He's a lot like Anna, as far as that goes, but I don't plan to point it out.

'How am I like Basia?'

'You are very eager to find out certain things.'

This line of talk is worrisome, but we've got a dialogue going, and it can't be abandoned. 'For instance?' I say.

'For instance, you want to know the *point* of the story.'

'Yeah,' I say, relieved. 'What's wrong with that?'

'Maybe it has no point. Maybe I tell it to kill time.'

'You wouldn't do that.'

'Why not?'

'You're a businessman. Time's money.'

'Well,' he says, 'that is certainly true.'

'So what's the point of the story?'

Tomek pulls his feet out of the water and sits crosslegged on the pier. He says, 'It all has to do with Heifetz.'

Sikala was not a bad businessman. He had seen the cottage in Spychowo before he bought it, and he knew it needed remodeling. But when he and Danusia spent their first weekend there, he learned that it was one thing to look at a fixer-upper and an altogether different thing to live in it. The wiring had apparently been done shortly after the discovery of electricity; if you tried to listen to the radio while you were working on your laptop, the power would go off. Flushing more than one piece of paper down the toilet at a time would leave you in dire need of a plumber, and a gas mask might come in handy too because somewhere in the kitchen there was a leak. In the attic a territorial dispute was being waged between the rats and the birds.

The more serious problem, though, was external. The cottage stood at the edge of town, on a dirt lane. Directly behind it, on yet another dirt lane, was a similar cottage. That cottage, which was separated from Sikala's by a rickety fence about one-and-a-half meters high, belonged to an old peasant and his wife.

They owned a flock of chickens that walked around the back yard doing what chickens do. They owned a cow which they kept in the back yard, too, and the cow drew flies by the thousands. The chickens and the cow must have been there when Sikala examined the cottage before making his offer, but for some reason he hadn't seen them.

'You know how it is when you go to the theater,' he told Danusia that Saturday night as they lay in the bedroom sweltering—they'd closed their window to keep out the flies and the smell of manure. 'How much attention do you really pay to the background scenery?'

'Not too much,' she conceded. 'But when I go to the theater I'm not thinking of buying the stage.'

It was right then—while the word *stage* hung in the air—that they first became aware of Burek's existence. It was as if, having somehow understood that a conversation about theatrical matters was taking place just a few meters away, he had picked this moment to make a dramatic entry into their lives. He emitted a single howl, long and drawn-out, a whole note that he held for what seemed a million measures.

Heifetz had been sleeping in the kitchen. Long before the howl died away, he'd switched on the megabass, rocking the walls as only a Rottweiler can. They heard a chair go over, a plate crashing to the floor. A pair of heavy paws smacked the kitchen door.

Sikala leapt out of bed. 'Hurry up!' Danusia said. 'The fool'll throw himself through the window!'

Heifetz hadn't thought of that yet—he was too busy trying to throw himself through the door. It took a lot of begging and pleading and no small amount of wrestling to get him calmed down. Periodically, throughout the night, the neighbor's dog howled, and Heifetz went nuts all over again.

The next morning, when Sikala, who had scarcely slept, took him out into the back yard to pee, he almost broke loose: the other dog was visible through a crack in the boards.

He was just a small brown mutt; if you'd wanted to find anything aristocratic in that dog's background, Sikala told Tomek, you would have needed the help of a medievalist. The mutt just stood there at the fence, looking through the boards at Heifetz, who was pawing the ground and growling, spit flying from his mouth.

'Burek!' It was the voice of the old man. 'Get back here!'

The dog disappeared. A few seconds later there was a loud yelp, followed by the sound of jangling chain links.

'Stay away from that fence today!' the old man hollered, loud enough for the whole village to hear. 'This time tomorrow that big fancy son of a bitch'll be prancing around on the subway.'

Heifetz was not prancing around on the subway the next day; instead he was prancing through Lazienki Park on a leash. But it occurred to Sikala, as he followed along behind, that if the old peasant could see the two of them now, he would consider his point proven. They were in their element, and they had left him and Burek in theirs.

Sikala had imagined that the cottage in Spychowo would be a place where he and Danusia cou!d go for peace and quiet. Somehow he had never asked himself how he would get along with the locals. He had not, in all honesty, even considered their possible presence, so there had been no reason for him to wonder what his neighbors might be like.

It was true that if he'd thought about those possible neighbors, he might have idealized them as hardworking, honest farm people. He'd been guilty in the past of idealizing simple people. Years ago, right after the end of martial law, he had defended several Solidarity activists who worked at the Ursus Tractor factory. They had been accused of sedition, and he had gotten the charge dismissed, probably because the government wasn't really interested in prosecuting the workers but in scaring them. Two or three days after he represented the men, he went to dinner at a friend's apartment. The friend lived in Ursynow, which was near the factory. On his way across the parking lot, Sikala saw one of the men he'd represented—a tall blond kid named Zenek, who'd been courageous enough not to inform on other trade unionists, even after the secret police had beaten the bottoms of his feet with rubber truncheons. He'd been the defendent Sikala felt closest to, the one he told everybody about.

Zenek was roaring drunk now, brandishing an empty vodka bottle at a young woman who had her back against somebody's car. When Sikala yelled his name, he spun around. Seeing a chance to flee, the girl ran off.

Zenek grinned and dropped the bottle on the ground. It shattered. 'No loss,' he said. 'It was empty. She was too.' His eyes tried to focus. 'Hey—you're my lawyer.' He threw his head back and laughed. 'My lawyer's met my whore. That makes me feel real special.'

It had not made Sikala feel special, and he did not feel special now, trudging through the park behind Heifetz. He felt like a man who had not slept much on the weekend, a man whose wife was unhappy with a decision he alone had made. 'I told you we didn't need this cottage,' Danusia had said yesterday, when they were driving home. 'We simply don't belong there. It was foolish to buy it, and it's even more foolish not to sell it right now.'

Sikala had locked his hands around the steering wheel. 'This is the new Poland,' he said. 'We have the right to be *whatever* and *wherever* we want to.'

This belief that the world was newly filled with possibility, that a place like Spychowo could and should open its arms to outsiders, was sorely tested by the events of the next few weekends. Sikala and Danusia would leave Warsaw on Friday afternoon in their new Mercedes wagon. After the first couple of Fridays Danusia rode silently, her face more often than not averted. Sikala, teeth gritted, drove at increasingly high speeds, almost as if he were afraid that Spychowo was in the act of erecting a barrier to keep him out. Heifetz sat in back, emitting low-pitched growls.

Every night Burek howled. You never knew exactly when he would start, though it was usually after ten o'clock. They lay in bed, stiff as corpses, waiting for him to crank up. As soon as he did, Heifetz would growl and throw himself at the door, and Sikala would have to get up and try to calm him.

During the day Burek stayed chained, and even though the little dog was so still and quiet he seemed to be an inanimate object, as befitted an animal whose name meant 'small brown thing,' Heifetz was anything but placid. He ran along the fence, barking, snarling, hitting the boards with his paws. The old man on the other side never yelled at him, but they could hear him walking around his yard, muttering curses against city folks who thought milk and eggs were produced by cartons rather than cows and chickens.

'Sooner or later,' Danusia said at the breakfast table one Sunday morning, 'Heifetz is going to go over that fence or through it, and when he does he'll turn that poor little mutt into a hand towel.'

Sikala laid down the slice of bread he'd been eating. It tasted stale. Nothing he bought in this village tasted right to him. The butter was rancid, the farmer's cheese was dry, the sausage contained huge chunks of bone and gristle. It was as if the entire community—men, women, children and domestic animals—had conspired to drive him out.

And who were the people of Spychowo? A bunch of peasants that he'd stood up for when it was dangerous to do so. Had it not been for him and others like him, they'd still be begging the government to buy their eggs and milk for a fraction of the market price. They'd be sucking up to the manager of the nearest collective farm, hoping he'd deign to sell them a few sacks of surplus fodder.

'If Heifetz goes through the fence and makes a meal out of Burek,' he told Danusia, 'you won't see tears from me.' He pushed his plate aside. From now on, he promised himself, he'd bring food from the city. 'Maybe while he's at it, he can take a leg off the bastard's owner.'

The following weekend Danusia attended a meeting in Helsinki. Sikala had decided not to go to Spychowo, but as he lounged around the house Saturday morning, he began to feel like a quitter. And since he was not the kind of man who could easily admit defeat—did not indeed want to become that kind of man—he finally threw a sander and a few gallons of varnish in the Mercedes, put Heifetz on a leash and led him out to the car.

When they reached Spychowo, it was almost three o'clock. He took Heifetz out back and turned him loose, then went inside and plugged in the sander. He'd been meaning to sand the floors, and this seemed as good a time as any.

He lost himself as always in the noisy, mindless work. It was after eight before he thought of taking a break. He turned the machine off, walked over to the refrigerator and opened a beer. He sat down in the living room and started drinking it, enjoying the cold bitter taste; he was halfway through the bottle before it occurred to him to wonder why Heifetz wasn't barking.

He opened the kitchen door and stepped into the back yard. Heifetz was gone. He hurried over to the fence and peeked through the gap in the boards. Burek's chain lay stretched out on the ground. The cow stood nearby, chewing her cud, and a couple of chickens were scampering around, but Burek was nowhere in sight.

Sikala turned and ran across the yard. There was a gate on one side of the house, and it was still locked. But Rottweilers are flexible, and the fence was only chest high. He must have thrown himself over it, Sikala figured. Either that or he'd jumped directly over the fence in back.

Sikala unlocked the gate and swung it open. He'd taken a step or two before he saw Heifetz coming across the yard toward him.

Sikala did not believe in God—he hadn't attended mass since the days of Solidarity, at which time going to church was seen as an act of defiance. Nonetheless he said 'Oh, Jesus' and crossed himself when he saw the object—small, brown and limp—dangling from the big dog's jaws.

*

Marek Sikala was not a weave-and-feint type—he was the kind of man who came straight at you. He had stood up in a court of law and accused government ministers of lying at a time when those same ministers were causing people to disappear. So he would never be able to explain to his own satisfaction why he had done what he did that night. He knew, though, that it had something to do with an awareness that for once words would fail him—that in the end, he could not have sat down with the old man, told him what had happened and apologized. It was as if he'd suddenly been struck dumb, as if someone had cut out his tongue.

After locking Heifetz in the hall closet, where instead of raising hell he barely whimpered, Sikala carried Burek into the bathroom and examined him. Apparently Heifetz had broken his neck: he didn't have a mark on him, and there was no blood to be seen, though his fur was caked with dirt; it looked as if he'd been dragged through the mud for a kilometer or two.

Sikala filled the bathub. Gently, regretfully, he laid Burek's body in the water. With great care he shampooed him, then rinsed him off and lifted him out.

Danusia had left a blowdryer in the bathroom cabinet. Sikala pulled it out, hooked it up and blow-dried Burek. While he worked, he ran a comb through the dog's hair, pulling out the tangles. When he had finished, Burek, smelling now of herbal shampoo, looked considerably better than he'd ever looked alive.

Sikala knew the peasant and his wife went to bed at dusk; he was going to have to gamble that they hadn't yet missed Burek. He waited until it was pitch dark, then he carried the body outside.

Sweating badly, he squatted down beside the fence and pulled at a rotten board. He had to twist it back and forth, but the nails soon came loose. Clutching the blow-dried body, he stepped into his neighbor's back yard.

The cow paid him no mind as he tiptoed past. He knelt down and laid Burek on the ground and fastened the chain around his neck.

Within three hours Sikala was in Warsaw, sitting on the sofa in his living room—across the street from Lazienki Park, where kings and queens had summered—drinking shot after shot of vodka.

Our wives are upon us. A few minutes ago, when Tomek saw them coming toward us, he quit telling the story. It may be that Basia already knows the story and he doesn't want to bore her with it, or it may be that he doesn't want her to hear it. It may be that he doesn't want anybody to hear it but me. The other possibility—that the story is over—is one l can't countenance. All actions—especially deceitful actions—are supposed to come with consequences attached. That's the way narrative works.

The women are both wearing backpacks. *'Moja siostra ist gut influence,'* Basia says. 'She ask me to go for a walk.'

She looks like she could stand a walk: her eyes are red from last night's drinking, and she's perspiring, though it's a cool day. Before too long, if she's not careful, she's going to put on weight. In fact, I realize, it's already starting. She's bigger than she was last summer when they came to California. I ought to know, because I spent a lot of time sneaking peeks at her when she was wearing her bathing suit. And one evening, while Tomek and Anna were at the airport, trying to iron out some problem with Tomek's return ticket, we actually threw our clothes off and crawled into the jacuzzi. Tomek and Anna came back before we thought they would, but they didn't find us, because they remained in the house, enabling us to get our clothes on and skip out the side gate. When we came through the front door, claiming we'd been strolling around the neighborhood, they didn't act suspicious; they were sitting together at the kitchen table, slicing vegetables for kebabs.

I'm surprised now to hear that the idea to take a walk through the woods originated with Anna. Walking through the woods with your sister means you'll have to talk to her, and Anna has never found it easy to talk to Basia. She says they might as well be speaking different languages. All Basia does is tell her jokes, most of them dirty, or prattle on and on about some bash she went wild at.

I try to catch Anna's eye, to flash her a look and ask what's up, but she's staring at the water as if she's trying to see all the way to the bottom of the river. It looks as if she's facing a task she doesn't relish.

After telling us they'll see us at dinner, Basia steps off toward a trailhead, with Anna following along about half-a-step behind. There's a nature preserve nearby, and as they walk away, Basia turns and hollers, 'We now go to watch little birds mate!'

I laugh, but Tomek doesn't. Sitting there beside him, I wonder, for the first time, what it would be like to live with Basia—to do more than exchange a few words here and a few words there and steal a hug or a kiss in the bushes. I've got a feeling it's not a constant party.

I've got a feeling, too, that if I want to know the rest of Sikala's story, I'll have to ask. My brother-in-law has lapsed from the storytellng mode.

'So,' I say, 'what happened?'

'What happened?' He sounds confused.

'Yeah. What happened?'

'To whom?'

'Sikala. You know—after he carried the dog's body back and put the chain around his neck.'

'Oh, that,' Tomek says. He looks at me now in a way that makes me uncomfortable—it's almost as if he thinks I know what happened but I'm trying to make him say it. 'Well,' he says, 'I will tell you.'

For two or three days he could not bring himself to tell Danusia what had happened in Spychowo. Because now he knew that if Heifetz had killed the dog and he, Sikala, had simply gone to the neighbors, admitted it, and offered his apologies, no shame would be attached to the incident. As it was, he'd done what he had so often accused others of doing. He'd slipped around at night and committed despicable acts. For the first time in his life, he'd betrayed his own principles.

When he finally told Danusia what he'd done, she confirmed his worst fears: 'You must have lost your mind.'

He couldn't meet her gaze.

He couldn't meet his own gaze, either. For a couple of weeks he wouldn't look at himself in the mirror, not even when he shaved; he nicked his face so many times he began to look as if he'd been involved in a knife fight. At night, instead of getting in bed when Danusia did, he sat up late, staring out the window, looking away from it barely long enough to locate the vodka bottle.

In the end he understood that his identity was at risk. He'd bested General Jaruzelski and the secret police, he'd struck fears into the hearts of the Warsaw mafia. But if he was not careful, a brown mutt and an old man who probably couldn't write his own name would rob him, Marek Sikala, crusader for justice, of all that he was and had ever hoped to be.

And so, two weeks after he'd planted a blow-dried body in his neighbor's back yard, he headed for Spychowo alone.

He stopped in the village to buy a bottle of vodka. As he left the store, he saw the old man's wife walking past. She carried a basket, as if she were headed for the market. He got back in the car and drove on.

He'd never actually seen the front of the other man's house, but when he parked before it, he discovered that the front, if anything, was even more of an eyesore than the back. Broken windowpanes had been covered with brown paper and taped up, and the front door looked as if it were in a state of dry-rot. Over in one corner of the yard, there was a black patch where a pile of junk had been set on fire. Bits of broken glass and scorched metal littered the ground.

Holding the bottle, Sikala got out of the car and walked across the yard. Chickens scattered before him. He took a deep breath and knocked on the door.

The old man opened it. He wore a pair of muddy-looking pants and a badly stained workshirt; his boots wreaked of cowshit. He must have been eating berries, because purple juice was oozing from one corner of his mouth.

'I'm your neighbor,' Sikala said. 'Marek Sikala.'

He had thought the man might snarl at him, that he might even turn and grab a weapon. Instead, with an air of panic, he looked at the floor. A dirty rag lay there, just to one side of the door. He stooped over, picked it up, and quickly wiped his mouth. Then he stuck the rag in his pocket, wiped his palm on his pants, and offered his hand.

'Jan Karolak,' he said.

Sikala shook hands with him. 'I thought maybe we could have a drink together,' he said, lifting the vodka bottle.

If the old man thought it an odd suggestion, he didn't let on. He gestured at a pair of rickety chairs pulled up before a television that looked as if it had been made during the Stalinist period. 'I'll get us some glasses,' he said.

After the old man disappeared into the kitchen, Sikala looked around the living room. It was full of religious icons: a manger scene, a plaster statue of the Virgin, a cheap copy of Raphael's madonna, and, above the front door, an unusally large wooden cross with nail holes where Christ's hands would have been. Given the way he'd heard the old man swearing, Sikala figured his wife was the devout one.

The old man returned with two glasses, a plate of bread and a salt shaker. Sikkala opened the bottle and filled both glasses, and the old man sat down beside him. 'Well,' Sikala said, 'to your health.'

The old man nodded and solemnly downed his vodka.

Sikala filled the glasses again. He knew what he wanted to say; he'd rehearsed his speech off and on for the last two weeks. He would tell the old man that Heifetz had been bought as an act of self-defense. The dog was loyal, he'd always protected them, back at a time when they needed protecting from those who would do them harm. For whatever reason, he must have believed that Burek represented a threat to them. 'And so,' Sikala would say, 'he trespassed on your property and killed your dog. And in my own fear, I caused you more suffering by bringing your dog back, after he was dead, and leaving his body for you to find.'

He wouldn't stop there. He would say that in a strange way Heifetz had been right: Burek was a threat. He was a threat simply because his presence had shown Sikala that he'd come to a place where he didn't belong. He'd acted as if the whole world was his home, or ought to be, and he was here now to apologize not only for the death of Burek but also for his own arrogance.

'Your dog . . .' he began.

To his amazement, the old man made the sign of the cross. 'Did you hear about it?'

'Hear about what?'

'That's right—you haven't been here for a few weeks.'

Without bothering to say 'to your health,' the old man turned his glass up and tossed the vodka down.

He wiped his mouth on the back of his hand. 'I'm not a good man,' he said. 'When I was in my thirties, I beat my son so badly that he ran away, and we never found out what had happened to him. I've stolen things, I've lied, I used to sleep with other men's wives. My own wife, she always told me that one day the veil which had covered my eyes and kept me in darkness and ignorance for so long would finally be stripped away and I would see a sight that might blind me or might frighten me so badly it would kill me. She said that if neither of those things happened, it would mean that for some reason God had not given up on me, and I would finally see the world as He intended. And she was right.'

He said that about three weeks ago, Burek, who'd been acting strange for several days, walked into the front yard, made a funny noise, then flipped onto his side and died.

'So I dragged him out into the woods,' he said, 'and buried him.'

Instantly Sikala sized things up. He understood that he'd been granted the opportunity to come here and gracefully fufill a simple task. That task was to maintain a completely straight face, to swallow the laughter that threatened to bubble up into his throat, to receive the forthcoming news with the air of respect and reverence the occasion demanded.

'Go on,' he said. 'Tell me what happened.'

The old man looked at the statue of the Virgin, closed his eyes for a few seconds, then crossed himself again. 'During the night,' he said, 'Burek had risen from the dead.'

You've seen them—you must have. Those old strays that square off against one another, circling, pawing the ground, neither one quite willing to get down to business?

It seems to me now, as I sit in California writing this all down in a house which has become so still and quiet it might as well be a mausoleum, that my brother-in-law and I were like that. There we sit on that pier in Krutyn, a place where the crazy came to rest before flying off to kill or be killed. He's got his feet up under him. Mine are still dangling in the water. Neither one of us wants to address the most obvious question. Why has he told me this story?

You've probably concluded, just as I had, that he'd told it to illustrate the danger of taking up residence in a place where you don't belong, that he wanted me to realize how crazy my plans were. You've probably thought how perfect it was that those Germans came by, so that I could bring up the etymology of the word 'Niemiec': the one who can't speak. You've noticed how nicely that set up the moment when Sikala—unable to imagine explaining what had happened to a man so different from him that he might as well have spoken another language—goes temporarily insane and blow-dries Burek. But have you had time to realize that by making a fool of himself, Sikala helped another man find peace?

My brother-in-law rises, so that he's looking down on me. Somehow I know that his English will be flawless, that he's rehearsed what he plans to say. 'When our tour ends tomorrow,' he says, 'I'm leaving Basia. That's the beginning of what I have to tell you.'

The chill I feel is not the result of the breeze off the river. 'What's the rest of it?' I ask him.

He lays his hand on my shoulder and finishes the story.

PEOPLE LIKE THAT ARE THE ONLY PEOPLE HERE: CANONICAL BABBLING IN PEED ONK

Lorrie Moore

A beginning, an end: there seems to be neither. The whole thing is like a cloud that just lands and everywhere inside it is full of rain. A start: the Mother finds a blood clot in the Baby's diaper. What is the story? Who put this here? It is big and bright, with a broken khaki-colored vein in it. Over the weekend, the Baby had looked listless and spacey, clayey and grim. But today he looks fine—so what is this thing, startling against the white diaper, like a tiny mouse heart packed in snow? Perhaps it belongs to someone else. Perhaps it is something menstrual, something belonging to the Mother or to the Babysitter, something the Baby has found in a wastebasket and for his own demented baby reasons stowed away here. (Babies: they're crazy! What can you do?) In her mind, the Mother takes this away from his body and attaches it to someone else's. There. Doesn't that make more sense?

Still, she phones the clinic at the children's hospital. 'Blood in the diaper,' she says, and, sounding alarmed and perplexed, the woman on the other end says, 'Come in now.'

Such pleasingly instant service! Just say 'blood.' Just say 'diaper.' Look what you get!

In the examination room, pediatrician, nurse, head resident—all seem less alarmed and perplexed than simply perplexed. At first, stupidly, the Mother is calmed by this. But soon, besides peering and saying 'Hmmmm,' the pediatrician, nurse, and head resident are all drawing their mouths in, bluish and tight—morning glories sensing noon. They fold their arms across their white-coated chests, unfold them again and jot things down. They order an ultrasound. Bladder and kidneys. 'Here's the card. Go downstairs; turn left.'

In Radiology, the Baby stands anxiously on the table, naked against the Mother as she holds him still against her legs and waist, the

Radiologist's cold scanning disc moving about the Baby's back. The Baby whimpers, looks up at the Mother. *Let's get out of here*, his eyes beg. *Pick me up!* The Radiologist stops, freezes one of the many swirls of oceanic gray, and clicks repeatedly, a single moment within the long, cavernous weather map that is the Baby's insides.

'Are you finding something?' asks the Mother. Last year, her uncle Larry had had a kidney removed for something that turned out to be benign. These imaging machines! They are like dogs, or metal detectors: they find everything, but don't know what they've found. That's where the surgeons come in. They're like the owners of the dogs. 'Give me that,' they say to the dog. 'What the heck is that?'

'The surgeon will speak to you,' says the Radiologist.

'Are you finding something?'

'The surgeon will speak to you,' the Radiologist says again. 'There seems to be something there, but the surgeon will talk to you about it.'

'My uncle once had something on his kidney,' says the Mother. 'So they removed the kidney and it turned out the something was benign.'

The Radiologist smiles a broad, ominous smile. 'That's always the way it is,' he says. 'You don't know exactly what it is until it's in the bucket.'

'"In the bucket,"' the Mother repeats.

The Radiologist's grin grows scarily wider—is that even possible? 'That's doctor talk,' he says.

'It's very appealing,' says the Mother. 'It's a very appealing way to talk.' Swirls of bile and blood, mustard and maroon in a pail, the colors of an African flag or some exuberant salad bar: *in the bucket*—she imagines it all.

'The Surgeon will see you soon,' he says again. He tousles the Baby's ringletty hair. 'Cute kid,' he says.

'Let's see now,' says the Surgeon in one of his examining rooms. He has stepped in, then stepped out, then come back in again. He has crisp, frowning features, sharp bones, and a tennis-in-Bermuda tan. He crosses his blue-cottoned legs. He is wearing clogs.

The Mother knows her own face is a big white dumpling of worry. She is still wearing her long, dark parka, holding the Baby, who has pulled the hood up over her head because he always thinks it's funny to do that. Though on certain windy mornings she would like to think she could look vaguely romantic like this, like some French Lieutenant's Woman of the Prairie, in all of her saner moments she knows she doesn't. Ever. She knows she looks ridiculous—like one of those animals made out of twisted party balloons. She lowers the hood and slips one arm out of the sleeve. The Baby wants to get up and play with the light switch. He fidgets, fusses, and points.

'He's big on lights these days,' explains the Mother.

'That's okay,' says the Surgeon, nodding toward the light switch. 'Let him play with it.' The Mother goes and stands by it, and the Baby begins turning the lights off and on, off and on.

'What we have here is a Wilms' tumor,' says the Surgeon, suddenly plunged into darkness. He says 'tumor' as if it were the most normal thing in the world.

'Wilms'?' repeats the Mother. The room is quickly on fire again with light, then wiped dark again. Among the three of them here, there is a long silence, as if it were suddenly the middle of the night. 'Is that apostrophe s or s apostrophe?' the Mother says finally. She is a writer and a teacher. Spelling can be important—perhaps even at a time like this, though she has never before been at a time like this, so there are barbarisms she could easily commit and not know.

The lights come on: the world is doused and exposed.

'S apostrophe,' says the Surgeon. 'I think.' The lights go back out, but the Surgeon continues speaking in the dark. 'A malignant tumor on the left kidney.'

Wait a minute. Hold on here. The Baby is only a baby, fed on organic applesauce and soy milk—a little prince!—and he was standing so close to her during the ultrasound. How could he have this terrible thing? It must have been *her* kidney. A fifties kidney. A DDT kidney. The Mother clears her throat. 'Is it possible it was my kidney on the scan? I mean, I've never heard of a baby with a tumor, and, frankly, I was standing very close.' She would make the blood hers, the tumor hers, it would all be some treacherous, farcical mistake.

'No, that's not possible,' says the Surgeon. The light goes back on.

'It's not?' says the Mother. Wait until it's *in the bucket*, she thinks. Don't be so sure. *Do we have to wait until it's in the bucket to find out a mistake has been made?*

'We will start with a radical nephrectomy,' says the Surgeon, instantly thrown into darkness again. His voice comes from nowhere and everywhere at once. 'And then we'll begin with chemotherapy after that. These tumors usually respond very well to chemo.'

'I've never heard of a baby having chemo,' the Mother says. *Baby and Chemo*, she thinks: they should never even appear in the same sentence together, let alone the same life. In her other life, her life before this day, she had been a believer in alternative medicine. Chemotherapy? Unthinkable. Now, suddenly, alternative medicine seems the wacko maiden aunt to the Nice Big Daddy of Conventional Treatment. How quickly the old girl faints and gives way, leaves one just standing there. Chemo? Of course: chemo! Why by all means: chemo. Absolutely! Chemo!

The Baby flicks the switch back on, and the walls reappear, big wedges of light checkered with small framed watercolors of the local lake. The Mother has begun to cry: all of life has led her here, to this moment. After this, there is no more life. There is something else, something stumbling and unlivable, something mechanical, something for robots, but not life. Life has been taken and broken, quickly, like a stick. The room goes dark again, so that the Mother can cry more freely. How can a baby's body be stolen so fast? How much can one heaven-sent and unsuspecting child endure? Why has he not been spared this inconceivable fate?

Perhaps, she thinks, she is being punished: too many babysitters too early on. ('Come to Mommy! Come to Mommy-Baby-sitter!' she used to say. But it was a joke!) Her life, perhaps, bore too openly the marks and wigs of deepest drag. Her unmotherly thoughts had all been noted: the panicky hope that his nap would last longer than it did; her occasional desire to kiss him passionately on the mouth (to make out with her baby!); her ongoing complaints about the very vocabulary of motherhood, how it degraded the speaker ('Is this a poopie onesie! Yes, it's a very poopie onesie!'). She had, moreover, on three occasions used the formula bottles as flower vases. She twice let the Baby's ears get fudgy with wax. A few afternoons last month, at snacktime, she placed a bowl of Cheerios on the floor for him to eat, like a dog. She let him play with the Dustbuster. Just once, before he was born, she said, 'Healthy? I just want the kid to be rich.' A joke, for God's sake! After he was born she announced that her life had become a daily sequence of mind-wrecking chores, the same ones over and over again, like a novel by Mrs. Camus. Another joke! These jokes will kill you! She had told too often, and with too much enjoyment, the story of how the Baby had said 'Hi' to his high chair, waved at the lake waves, shouted 'Goody-goody-goody' in what seemed to be a Russian accent, pointed at his eyes and said 'Ice.' And all that nonsensical baby talk: wasn't it a stitch? 'Canonical babbling,' the language experts called it. He recounted whole stories in it—totally made up, she could tell. He embroidered; he fished; he exaggerated. What a card! To friends, she spoke of his eating habits (carrots yes, tuna no). She mentioned, too much, his sidesplitting giggle. Did she have to be so boring? Did she have no consideration for others, for the intellectual demands and courtesies of human society? Would she not even attempt to be more interesting? It was a crime against the human mind not even to try.

Now her baby, for all these reasons—lack of motherly gratitude, motherly judgment, motherly proportion—will be taken away.

The room is fluorescently ablaze again. The Mother digs around in her parka pocket and comes up with a Kleenex. It is old and thin, like a mashed flower saved from a dance; she dabs it at her eyes and nose.

'The Baby won't suffer as much as you,' says the Surgeon.

And who can contradict? Not the Baby, who in his Slavic Betty Boop voice can say only *mama, dada, cheese, ice, bye-bye, outside, boogie-boogie, goody-goody, eddy-eddy*, and *car*. (Who is Eddy? They have no idea.) This will not suffice to express his mortal suffering. Who can say what babies do with their agony and shock? Not they themselves. (Baby talk: isn't it a stitch?) They put it all no place anyone can really see. They are like a different race, a different species: they seem not to experience pain the way we do. Yeah, that's it: their nervous systems are not as fully formed, and *they just don't experience pain the way we do*. A tune to keep one humming through the war. 'You'll get through it,' the Surgeon says.

'How?' asks the Mother. 'How does one get through it?'

'You just put your head down and go,' says the Surgeon. He picks up his file folder. He is a skilled manual laborer. The tricky emotional stuff is not to his liking. The babies. The babies! What can be said to console the parents about the babies? 'I'll go phone the oncologist on duty to let him know,' he says, and leaves the room.

'Come here, sweetie,' the Mother says to the Baby, who has toddled off toward a gum wrapper on the floor. 'We've got to put your jacket on.' She picks him up and he reaches for the light switch again. Light, dark. Peekaboo: where's baby? Where did baby go?

At home, she leaves a message—'Urgent! Call me!'—for the Husband on his voice mail. Then she takes the Baby upstairs for his nap, rocks him in the rocker. The Baby waves good-bye to his little bears, then looks toward the window and says, 'Bye-bye, outside.' He has, lately, the habit of waving good-bye to everything, and now it seems as if he senses an imminent departure, and it breaks her heart to hear him. *Bye-bye!* She sings low and monotonously, like a small appliance, which is how he likes it. He is drowsy, dozy, drifting off. He has grown so much in the last year, he hardly fits in her lap anymore; his limbs dangle off like a pietà. His head rolls slightly inside the crook of her arm. She can feel him falling backward into sleep, his mouth round and open like the sweetest of poppies. All the lullabies in the world, all the melodies threaded through with maternal melancholy now become for her—abandoned as a mother can be by working men and napping babies—the songs of hard, hard grief. Sitting there, bowed and bobbing, the Mother feels the entirety of her love as worry and heartbreak. A quick and irrevocable alchemy: there is no longer one unworried scrap left for happiness. 'If you go,' she keens low into his soapy neck, into the ranunculus coil of his ear, 'we are going with you. We are nothing without you. Without you, we are a heap of rocks. We are gravel and mold. Without you, we are two stumps, with nothing any longer in our hearts. Wherever this takes you, we are following. We will be there. Don't be scared. We are going, too. That is that.'

'Take Notes,' says the Husband, after coming straight home from work, midafternoon, hearing the news, and saying all the words out loud— *surgery, metastasis, dialysis, transplant*—then collapsing in a chair in tears. 'Take notes. We are going to need the money.'

   'Good God,' cries the Mother. Everything inside her suddenly begins to cower and shrink, a thinning of bones. Perhaps this is a soldier's readiness, but it has the whiff of death and defeat. It feels like a heart attack, a failure of will and courage, a power failure: a failure of everything. Her face, when she glimpses it in a mirror, is cold and bloated with shock, her eyes scarlet and shrunk. She has already started to wear sunglasses indoors, like a celebrity widow. From where will her own strength come? From some philosophy? From some frigid little philosophy? She is neither stalwart nor realistic and has trouble with basic concepts, such as the one that says events move in one direction only and do not jump up, turn around, and take themselves back.

The Husband begins too many of his sentences with 'What if.' He is trying to piece everything together like a train wreck. He is trying to get the train to town.

'We'll just take all the steps, move through all the stages. We'll go where we have to go. We'll hunt; we'll find; we'll pay what we have to pay. What if we can't pay?'

'Sounds like shopping.'

'I cannot believe this is happening to our little boy,' he says, and starts to sob again. 'Why didn't it happen to one of us? It's so unfair. Just last week, my doctor declared me in perfect health: the prostate of a twenty-year-old, the heart of a ten-year-old, the brain of an insect—or whatever it was he said. What a nightmare this is.'

What words can be uttered? You turn just slightly and there it is: the death of your child. It is part symbol, part devil, and in your blind spot all along, until, if you are unlucky, it is completely upon you. Then it is a fierce little country abducting you; it holds you squarely inside itself like a cellar room—the best boundaries of you are the boundaries of it. Are there windows? Sometimes aren't there windows?

The Mother is not a shopper. She hates to shop, is generally bad at it, though she does like a good sale. She cannot stroll meaningfully through anger, denial, grief, and acceptance. She goes straight to bargaining and stays there. How much? she calls out to the ceiling, to some makeshift construction of holiness she has desperately, though not uncreatively, assembled in her mind and prayed to; a doubter, never before given to prayer, she must now reap what she has not sown; she must assemble from scratch an entire altar of worship and begging. She tries for noble abstractions, nothing too anthropomorphic, just some Higher Morality, though if this particular Highness looks something like the manager at Marshall Field's, sucking a Frango mint, so be it. Amen. Just tell me what you want, requests the Mother. And how do you want it? More charitable acts? A billion starting now.

Charitable thoughts? Harder, but of course! Of course! I'll do the
cooking, honey; I'll pay the rent. Just tell me. *Excuse me?* Well, if not to
you, to whom do I speak? Hello? To whom do I have to speak around
here? A higher-up? A superior? Wait? I can wait. I've got all day. I've
got the whole damn day.

The Husband now lies next to her in bed, sighing. 'Poor little guy
could survive all this, only to be killed in a car crash at the age of
sixteen,' he says.

The wife, bargaining, considers this. 'We'll take the car crash,' she
says.

'What?'

'Let's Make a Deal! Sixteen Is a Full Life! We'll take the car crash.
We'll take the car crash, in front of which Carol Merrill is now
standing.'

Now the Manager of Marshall Field's reappears. 'To take the
surprises out is to take the life out of life,' he says.

The phone rings. The Husband gets up and leaves the room.

'But I don't want these surprises,' says the Mother. 'Here! You take
these surprises!'

'To know the narrative in advance is to turn yourself into a
machine,' the Manager continues. 'What makes humans human is
precisely that they do not know the future. That is why they do the
fateful and amusing things they do: who can say how anything will
turn out? Therein lies the only hope for redemption, discovery, and—
let's be frank—fun, fun, fun! There might be things people will get
away with. And not just motel towels. There might be great illicit loves,
enduring joy, faith-shaking accidents with farm machinery. But you
have to not know in order to see what stories your life's efforts bring
you. The mystery is all.'

The Mother, though shy, has grown confrontational. 'Is this the kind
of bogus, random crap they teach at merchandising school? We would
like fewer surprises, fewer efforts and mysteries, thank you. K through
eight; can we just get K through eight?' It now seems like the luckiest,
most beautiful, most musical phrase she's ever heard: K through eight.
The very lilt. The very thought.

The Manager continues, trying things out. 'I mean, the whole
conception of "the story," of cause and effect, the whole idea that
people have a clue as to how the world works is just a piece of

laughable metaphysical colonialism perpetrated upon the wild country of time.'

Did they own a gun? The Mother begins looking through drawers.

The Husband comes back into the room and observes her. 'Ha! The Great Havoc that is the Puzzle of all Life!' he says of the Marshall Field's management policy. He has just gotten off a conference call with the insurance company and the hospital. The surgery will be Friday. 'It's all just some dirty capitalist's idea of a philosophy.'

'Maybe it's just a fact of narrative and you really can't politicize it,' says the Mother. It is now only the two of them.

'Whose side are you on?'

'I'm on the Baby's side.'

'Are you taking notes for this?'

'No.'

'You're not?'

'No. I can't. Not this! I write fiction. This isn't fiction.'

'Then write nonfiction. Do a piece of journalism. Get two dollars a word.'

'Then it has to be true and full of information. I'm not trained. I'm not that skilled. Plus, I have a convenient personal principle about artists not abandoning art. One should never turn one's back on a vivid imagination. Even the whole memoir thing annoys me.'

'Well, make things up, but pretend they're real.'

'I'm not that insured.'

'You're making me nervous '

'Sweetie, darling, I m not that good. I can't *do this*. I can do—what can I do? I can do quasi-amusing phone dialogue. I can do succinct descriptions of weather. I can do screwball outings with the family pet. Sometimes I can do those. Honey, I only do what I can. I do *the careful ironies of daydream*. I do *the marshy ideas upon which intimate life is built*. But this? Our baby with cancer? I'm sorry. My stop was two stations back. This is irony at its most gaudy and careless. This is a Hieronymus Bosch of facts and figures and blood and graphs. This is a nightmare of narrative slop. This cannot be designed. This cannot even be noted in preparation for a design—'

'We're going to need the money.'

'To say nothing of the moral boundaries of pecuniary recompense in a situation such as this—'

'What if the other kidney goes? What if he needs a transplant? Where are the moral boundaries there? What are we going to do, have bake sales?'

'We can sell the house. I hate this house. It makes me crazy.'

'And we'll live—where again?'

'The Ronald McDonald place. I hear it's nice. It's the least McDonald's can do.'

'You have a keen sense of justice.'

'I try. What can I say?' She pauses. 'Is all this really happening? I keep thinking that soon it will be over—the life expectancy of a cloud is supposed to be only twelve hours—and then I realize something has occurred that can never ever be over.'

The Husband buries his face in his hands: 'Our poor baby. How did this happen to him?' He looks over and stares at the bookcase that serves as the nightstand. 'And do you think even one of these baby books is any help?' He picks up the Leach, the Spock, the *What to Expect*. 'Where in the pages or index of any of these does it say 'chemotherapy' or 'Hickman catheter' or 'renal sarcoma'? Where does it say 'carcinogenesis'? You know what these books are obsessed with? *Holding a fucking spoon*.' He begins hurling the books off the night table and against the far wall.

'Hey,' says the Mother, trying to soothe. 'Hey, hey, hey.' But compared to his stormy roar, her words are those of a backup singer—a Shondell, a Pip—a doo-wop ditty. Books, and now more books, continue to fly.

Take Notes.

Is *fainthearted* one word or two? Student prose has wrecked her spelling.

It's one word. Two words—*Faint Hearted*—what would that be? The name of a drag queen.

Take Notes. In the end, you suffer alone. But at the beginning you suffer with a whole lot of others. When your child has cancer, you are instantly whisked away to another planet: one of bald-headed little boys. Pediatric Oncology. Peed Onk. You wash your hands for thirty seconds in antibacterial soap before you are allowed to enter through the swinging doors. You put paper slippers on your shoes. You keep your voice down. A whole place has been designed and decorated for your nightmare. Here is where your nightmare will occur. We've got a room all ready for you. We have cots. We have refrigerators. 'The children are almost entirely boys,' says one of the nurses. 'No one knows why. It's been documented, but a lot of people out there still don't realize it.' The little boys are all from sweet-sounding places— Janesville and Appleton—little heartland towns with giant landfills, agricultural runoff, paper factories, Joe McCarthy's grave (Alone, a site of great toxicity, thinks the Mother. The soil should be tested).

All the bald little boys look like brothers. They wheel their IVs up and down the single corridor of Peed Onk. Some of the lively ones, feeling good for a day, ride the lower bars of the IV while their large, cheerful mothers whiz them along the halls. *Wheee!*

The Mother does not feel large and cheerful. In her mind, she is scathing, acid-tongued, wraith-thin, and chain-smoking out on a fire escape somewhere. Beneath her lie the gentle undulations of the Midwest, with all its aspirations to be—to be what? To be Long Island. How it has succeeded! Strip mall upon strip mall. Lurid water, poisoned potatoes. The Mother drags deeply, blowing clouds of smoke out over the disfigured cornfields. When a baby gets cancer, it seems stupid ever to have given up smoking. When a baby gets cancer, you think, Whom are we kidding? Let's all light up. When a baby gets cancer, you think, Who came up with *this* idea? What celestial abandon gave rise to *this*? Pour me a drink, so I can refuse to toast.

The Mother does not know how to be one of these other mothers, with their blond hair and sweatpants and sneakers and determined pleasantness. She does not think that she can be anything similar. She does not feel remotely like them. She knows, for instance, too many people in Greenwich Village. She mail-orders oysters and tiramisu from a shop in SoHo. She is close friends with four actual homosexuals. Her husband is asking her to Take Notes.

Where do these women get their sweatpants? She will find out.

She will start, perhaps, with the costume and work from there.

She will live according to the bromides. Take one day at a time. Take a positive attitude. *Take a hike!* She wishes that there were more interesting things that were useful and true, but it seems now that it's only the boring things that are useful and true. *One day at a time.* And *at least we have our health.* How ordinary. How obvious. One day at a time. You need a brain for that?

While the Surgeon is fine-boned, regal, and laconic—they have correctly guessed his game to be doubles—there is a bit of the mad, overcaffeinated scientist to the Oncologist. He speaks quickly. He knows a lot of studies and numbers. He can do the math. Good! Someone should be able to do the math! 'It's a fast but wimpy tumor,' he explains. 'It typically metastasizes to the lung.' He rattles off some numbers, time frames, risk statistics. Fast but wimpy: the Mother tries to imagine this combination of traits, tries to think and think, and can only come up with Claudia Osk from the fourth grade, who blushed and almost wept when called on in class, but in gym could outrun everyone in the quarter-mile fire-door-to-fence dash. The Mother thinks now of this tumor as Claudia Osk. They are going to get Claudia Osk, make her sorry. All right! Claudia Osk must die. Though it has never been mentioned before, it now seems clear that Claudia Osk should have died long ago. Who was she anyway? So conceited: not letting anyone beat her in a race. Well, hey, hey, hey: don't look now, Claudia!

The Husband nudges her. 'Are you listening?'

'The chances of this happening even just to one kidney are one in fifteen thousand. Now given all these other factors, the chances on the second kidney are about one in eight.'

'One in eight,' says the Husband. 'Not bad. As long as it's not one in fifteen thousand.'

The Mother studies the trees and fish along the ceiling's edge in the Save the Planet wallpaper border. Save the Planet. Yes! But the windows in this very building don't open and diesel fumes are leaking into the ventilating system, near which, outside, a delivery truck is parked. The air is nauseous and stale.

'Really,' the Oncologist is saying, 'of all the cancers he could get, this is probably the best.'

'We win,' says the Mother.

'Best, I know, hardly seems the right word. Look, you two probably need to get some rest. We'll see how the surgery and histology go. Then we'll start with chemo the week following. A little light chemo: vincristine and—'

'Vincristine?' interrupts the Mother. 'Wine of Christ?'

'The names are strange, I know. The other one we use is actinomycin-D. Sometimes called 'dactinomycin.' People move the *D* around to the front.'

'They move the *D* around to the front,' repeats the Mother.

'Yup!' the Oncologist says. 'I don't know why—they just do!'

'Christ didn't survive his wine,' says the Husband.

'But of course he did,' says the Oncologist, and nods toward the Baby, who has now found a cupboard full of hospital linens and bandages and is yanking them all out onto the floor. 'I'll see you guys tomorrow, after the surgery.' And with that, the Oncologist leaves.

'Or, rather, Christ *was* his wine,' mumbles the Husband. Everything he knows about the New Testament, he has gleaned from the sound track of *Godspell*. 'His blood was the wine. What a great beverage idea.'

'A little light chemo. Don't you like that one?' says the Mother. '*Eine kleine* dactinomycin. I'd like to see Mozart write that one up for a big wad o' cash.'

'Come here, honey,' the Husband says to the Baby, who has now pulled off both his shoes.

'It's bad enough when they refer to medical science as "an inexact science,"' says the Mother. 'But when they start referring to it as "an art," I get extremely nervous.'

Yeah. If we wanted art, Doc, we'd go to an art museum.' The Husband picks up the Baby. 'You're an artist,' he says to the Mother, with the taint of accusation in his voice. 'They probably think you find creativity reassuring.'

The Mother sighs. 'I just find it inevitable. Lets go get something to eat.' And so they take the elevator to the cafeteria, where there is a high chair, and where, not noticing, they all eat a lot of apples with the price tags still on them.

Because his surgery is not until tomorrow, the Baby likes the hospital. He likes the long corridors, down which he can run. He likes everything on wheels. The flower carts in the lobby! ('Please keep your boy away from the flowers,' says the vendor. 'We'll buy the whole display,' snaps the Mother, adding, 'Actual children in a children's hospital—unbelievable, isn't it?') The Baby likes the other little boys. Places to go! People to see! Rooms to wander into! There is Intensive

Care. There is the Trauma Unit. The Baby smiles and waves. What a little Cancer Personality! Bandaged citizens smile and wave back. In Peed Onk, there are the bald little boys to play with. Joey, Eric, Tim, Mort, and Tod (Mort! Tod!). There is the four-year-old, Ned, holding his little deflated rubber ball, the one with the intriguing curling hose. The Baby wants to play with it. 'It's mine. Leave it alone,' says Ned. 'Tell the Baby to leave it alone.'

'Baby, you've got to share,' says the Mother from a chair some feet away.

Suddenly, from down near the Tiny Tim Lounge, comes Ned's mother, large and blond and sweatpanted. 'Stop that! Stop it!' she cries out, dashing toward the Baby and Ned and pushing the Baby away. 'Don't touch that!' she barks at the Baby, who is only a Baby and bursts into tears because he has never been yelled at like this before.

Ned's mom glares at everyone. 'This is drawing fluid from Neddy's liver!' She pats at the rubber thing and starts to cry a little.

'Oh my God,' says the Mother. She comforts the Baby, who is also crying. She and Ned, the only dry-eyed people, look at each other. 'I'm so sorry,' she says to Ned and then to his mother. 'I'm so stupid. I thought they were squabbling over a toy.'

'It does look like a toy,' agrees Ned. He smiles. He is an angel. All the little boys are angels. Total, sweet, bald little angels, and now God is trying to get them back for himself. Who are they, mere mortal women, in the face of this, this powerful and overwhelming and inscrutable thing, God's will? They are the mothers, that's who. You can't have him! they shout every day. You dirty old man! *Get out of here! Hands off!*

'I'm so sorry,' says the Mother again. 'I didn't know.'

Ned's mother smiles vaguely. 'Of course you didn't know,' she says, and walks back to the Tiny Tim Lounge.

The Tiny Tim Lounge is a little sitting area at the end of the Peed Onk corridor. There are two small sofas, a table, a rocking chair, a television and a VCR. There are various videos: *Speed*, *Dune*, and *Star Wars*. On one of the lounge walls there is a gold plaque with the singer Tiny Tim's name on it: his son was treated once at this hospital and so, five years ago, he donated money for this lounge. It is a cramped little lounge, which, one suspects, would be larger if Tiny Tim's son had actually lived. Instead, he died here, at this hospital and now there is this tiny room which is part gratitude, part generosity, part *fuck-you*.

Sifting through the videocassettes, the Mother wonders what science fiction could begin to compete with the science fiction of cancer itself—a tumor with its differentiated muscle and bone cells, a clump of wild nothing and its mad, ambitious desire to be something: something inside you, instead of you, another organism, but with a monster's architecture, a demon's sabotage and chaos. Think of leukemia, a tumor diabolically taking liquid form, better to swim about incognito in the blood. George Lucas, direct that!

Sitting with the other parents in the Tiny Tim Lounge, the night before the surgery, having put the Baby to bed in his high steel crib two rooms down, the Mother begins to hear the stories: leukemia in kindergarten, sarcomas in Little League, neuroblastomas discovered at summer camp. 'Eric slid into third base, but then the scrape didn't heal.' The parents pat one another's forearms and speak of other children's hospitals as if they were resorts. 'You were at St. Jude's last winter? So were we. What did you think of it? We loved the staff.' Jobs have been quit, marriages hacked up, bank accounts ravaged; the parents have seemingly endured the unendurable. They speak not of the *possibility* of comas brought on by the chemo, but of the *number* of them. 'He was in his first coma last July,' says Ned's mother. 'It was a scary time, but we pulled through.'

Pulling through is what people do around here. There is a kind of bravery in their lives that isn't bravery at all. It is automatic, unflinching, a mix of man and machine, consuming and unquestionable obligation meeting illness move for move in a giant even-steven game of chess—an unending round of something that looks like shadowboxing, though between love and death, which is the shadow? 'Everyone admires us for our courage,' says one man. 'They have no idea what they're talking about.'

I could get out of here, thinks the Mother. I could just get on a bus and go, never come back. Change my name. A kind of witness relocation thing.

'Courage requires options,' the man adds.

The Baby might be better off.

'There are options,' says a woman with a thick suede headband. 'You could give up. You could fall apart.'

'No, you can't. Nobody does. I've never seen it,' says the man. 'Well, not *really* fall apart.' Then the lounge falls quiet. Over the VCR someone has taped the fortune from a fortune cookie. 'Optimism,' it says, 'is what allows a teakettle to sing though up to its neck in hot water.' Underneath, someone else has taped a clipping from a summer horoscope. 'Cancer rules!' it says. Who would tape this up? Somebody's twelve-year-old brother. One of the fathers—Joey's father—gets up and tears them both off, makes a small wad in his fist.

There is some rustling of magazine pages.

The Mother clears her throat. 'Tiny Tim forgot the wet bar,' she says.

Ned, who is still up, comes out of his room and down the corridor, whose lights dim at nine. Standing next to her chair, he says to the Mother, 'Where are you from? What is wrong with your baby?'

In the tiny room that is theirs, she sleeps fitfully in her sweatpants, occasionally leaping up to check on the Baby. This is what the sweatpants are for: leaping. In case of fire. In case of anything. In case the difference between day and night starts to dissolve, and there is no difference at all, so why pretend? In the cot beside her, the Husband, who has taken a sleeping pill, is snoring loudly, his arms folded about his head in a kind of origami. How could either of them have stayed back at the house, with its empty high chair and empty crib? Occasionally the Baby wakes and cries out, and she bolts up, goes to him, rubs his back, rearranges the linens. The clock on the metal dresser shows that it is five after three. Then twenty to five. And then it is really morning, the beginning of this day, nephrectomy day. Will she be glad when it's over, or barely alive, or both? Each day this week has arrived huge, empty, and unknown, like a spaceship, and this one especially is lit a bright gray.

'He'll need to put this on,' says John, one of the nurses, bright and early, handing the Mother a thin greenish garment with roses and teddy bears printed on it. A wave of nausea hits her; this smock, she thinks, will soon be splattered with—with what?

The Baby is awake but drowsy. She lifts off his pajamas. 'Don't forget, *bubeleh*,' she whispers, undressing and dressing him. 'We will be with you every moment, every step. When you think you are asleep and floating off far away from everybody, Mommy will still be there.' If she hasn't fled on a bus. 'Mommy will take care of you. And Daddy, too.' She hopes the Baby does not detect her own fear and uncertainty, which she must hide from him, like a limp. He is hungry, not having been allowed to eat, and he is no longer amused by this new place, but worried about its hardships. Oh, my baby, she thinks. And the room starts to swim a little. The Husband comes in to take over. 'Take a break,' he says to her. 'I'll walk him around for five minutes.'

She leaves but doesn't know where to go. In the hallway, she is approached by a kind of social worker, a customer-relations person, who had given them a video to watch about the anesthesia: how the parent accompanies the child into the operating room, and how gently, nicely the drugs are administered.

'Did you watch the video?'

'Yes,' says the Mother.

'Wasn't it helpful?'

'I don't know,' says the Mother.

'Do you have any questions?' asks the video woman. 'Do you have any questions?' asked of someone who has recently landed in this fearful, alien place seems to the Mother an absurd and amazing little courtesy. The very specificity of a question would give a lie to the overwhelming strangeness of everything around her.

'Not right now,' says the Mother. 'Right now, I think I'm just going to go to the bathroom.'

When she returns to the Baby's room, everyone is there: the surgeon, the anesthesiologist, all the nurses, the social worker. In their blue caps and scrubs, they look like a clutch of forget-me-nots, and forget them, who could? The Baby, in his little teddy-bear smock, seems cold and scared. He reaches out and the Mother lifts him from the Husband's arms, rubs his back to warm him.

'Well, it's time!' says the Surgeon, forcing a smile.

'Shall we go?' says the Anesthesiologist.

What follows is a blur of obedience and bright lights. They take an elevator down to a big concrete room, the anteroom, the greenroom, the backstage of the operating room. Lining the walls are long shelves full of blue surgical outfits. 'Children often become afraid of the color blue,' says one of the nurses. But of course. Of course! 'Now, which one of you would like to come into the operating room for the anesthesia?'

'I will,' says the Mother.

'Are you sure?' asks the Husband.

'Yup.' She kisses the Baby's hair. 'Mr. Curlyhead,' people keep calling him here, and it seems both rude and nice. Women look admiringly at his long lashes and exclaim, 'Always the boys! Always the boys!'

Two surgical nurses put a blue smock and a blue cotton cap on the Mother. The Baby finds this funny and keeps pulling at the cap. 'This way,' says another nurse, and the Mother follows. 'Just put the Baby down on the table.'

In the video, the mother holds the baby and fumes are gently waved under the baby's nose until he falls asleep. Now, out of view of camera or social worker, the Anesthesiologist is anxious to get this under way and not let too much gas leak out into the room generally. The occupational hazard of this, his chosen profession, is gas exposure and nerve damage, and it has started to worry him. No doubt he frets about it to his wife every night. Now he turns the gas on and quickly clamps the plastic mouthpiece over the baby's cheeks and lips.

The Baby is startled. The Mother is startled. The Baby starts to scream and redden behind the plastic, but he cannot be heard. He thrashes. 'Tell him it's okay,' says the nurse to the Mother.

Okay? 'It's okay,' repeats the Mother, holding his hand, but she knows he can tell it's not okay, because he can see not only that she is still wearing that stupid paper cap but that her words are mechanical and swallowed, and she is biting her lips to keep them from trembling. Panicked, he attempts to sit. He cannot breathe; his arms reach up. *Bye-bye, outside.* And then, quite quickly, his eyes shut; he untenses and has fallen not *into* sleep but aside to sleep, an odd, kidnapping kind of sleep, his terror now hidden someplace deep inside him.

'How did it go?' asks the social worker, waiting in the concrete outer room. The Mother is hysterical. A nurse has ushered her out.

'It wasn't at all like the filmstrip!' she cries. 'It wasn't like the filmstrip at all!'

'The filmstrip? You mean the video?' asks the social worker.

'It wasn't like that at all! It was brutal and unforgivable.'

'Why that's terrible,' she says, her role now no longer misinformational but janitorial, and she touches the Mother's arm, though the Mother shakes it off and goes to find the Husband.

She finds him in the large mulberry Surgery Lounge, where he has been taken and where there is free hot chocolate in small Styrofoam cups. Red cellophane garlands festoon the doorways. She has totally forgotten it is as close to Christmas as this. A pianist in the corner is playing 'Carol of the Bells,' and it sounds not only unfestive but scary, like the theme from *The Exorcist*.

There is a giant clock on the far wall. It is a kind of porthole into the operating room, a way of assessing the Baby's ordeal: forty-five minutes for the Hickman implant; two and a half hours for the nephrectomy. And then, after that, three months of chemotherapy The magazine on her lap stays open at a ruby-hued perfume ad.

'Still not taking notes,' says the Husband.

'Nope.'

'You know, in a way, this is the kind of thing you've always written about.'

'You are really something, you know that? This is life. This isn't a "kind of thing."'

'But this is the kind of thing that fiction is: it's the unlivable life, the strange room tacked onto the house, the extra moon that is circling the earth unbeknownst to science.'

'I told you that.'

'I'm quoting you.'

She looks at her watch, thinking of the Baby. 'How long has it been?'

'Not long. Too long. In the end, maybe those're the same things.'

'What do you suppose is happening to him right this second?'

Infection? Slipping knives? 'I don't know. But you know what? I've gotta go. I've gotta just walk a bit.' The Husband gets up, walks around the lounge, then comes back and sits down.

The synapses between the minutes are unswimmable. An hour is thick as fudge. The Mother feels depleted; she is a string of empty tin cans attached by wire, something a goat would sniff and chew, something now and then enlivened by a jolt of electricity.

She hears their names being called over the intercom. 'Yes? Yes?' She stands up quickly. Her words have flown out before her, an exhalation of birds. The piano music has stopped. The pianist is gone. She and the Husband approach the main desk, where a man looks up at them and smiles. Before him is a xeroxed list of patients' names. 'That's our little boy right there,' says the Mother, seeing the Baby's name on the list and pointing at it. 'Is there some word? Is everything okay?'

'Yes,' says the man. 'Your boy is doing fine. They've just finished with the catheter, and they are moving on to the kidney.'

'But it's been two hours already! Oh my God, did something go wrong? What happened? What went wrong?'

'Did something go wrong?' The Husband tugs at his collar.

'Not really. It just took longer than they expected. I'm told everything is fine. They wanted you to know.'

'Thank you,' says the Husband. They turn and walk back toward where they were sitting.

'I'm not going to make it.' The Mother sighs, sinking into a fake leather chair shaped somewhat like a baseball mitt. 'But before I go, I'm taking half this hospital out with me.'

'Do you want some coffee?' asks the Husband.

'I don't know,' says the Mother. 'No, I guess not. No. Do you?'

'Nah, I don't, either, I guess,' he says.

'Would you like part of an orange?'

'Oh, maybe, I guess, if you're having one.' She takes an orange from her purse and just sits there peeling its difficult skin, the flesh rupturing beneath her fingers, the juice trickling down her hands, stinging the hangnails. She and the Husband chew and swallow, discreetly spit the seeds into Kleenex, and read from photocopies of the latest medical research, which they begged from the intern. They read, and underline, and sigh and close their eyes, and after some time, the surgery is over. A nurse from Peed Onk comes down to tell them.

'Your little boy's in recovery right now. He's doing well. You can see him in about fifteen minutes.'

How can it be described? How can any of it be described? The trip and the story of the trip are always two different things. The narrator is the one who has stayed home, but then, afterward, presses her mouth upon the traveler's mouth, in order to make the mouth work, to make the mouth say, say, say. One cannot go to a place and speak of it; one cannot both see and say, not really. One can go, and upon returning make a lot of hand motions and indications with the arms. The mouth itself, working at the speed of light, at the eye's instructions, is necessarily struck still; so fast, so much to report, it hangs open and dumb as a gutted bell. All that unsayable life! That's where the narrator comes in. The narrator comes with her kisses and mimicry and tidying up. The narrator comes and makes a slow, fake song of the mouth's eager devastation.

It is a horror and a miracle to see him. He is lying in his crib in his room, tubed up, splayed like a boy on a cross, his arms stiffened into cardboard 'no-no's' so that he cannot yank out the tubes. There is the bladder catheter, the nasal-gastric tube, and the Hickman, which, beneath the skin, is plugged into his jugular, then popped out his chest wall and capped with a long plastic cap. There is a large bandage taped over his abdomen. Groggy, on a morphine drip, still he is able to look at her when, maneuvering through all the vinyl wiring, she leans to hold him, and when she does, he begins to cry, but cry silently, without motion or noise. She has never seen a baby cry without motion or noise. It is the crying of an old person: silent, beyond opinion, shattered. In someone so tiny, it is frightening and unnatural. She wants to pick up the Baby and run—out of there, out of there. She wants to whip out a gun: *No-no's, eh? This whole thing is what I call a no-no.* Don't you touch him! she wants to shout at the surgeons and the needle nurses. Not anymore! No more! No more! She would crawl up and lie beside him in the crib if she could. But instead, because of all his intricate wiring, she must lean and cuddle, sing to him, songs of peril and flight: 'We gotta get out of this place, if it's the last thing we ever do. We gotta get out of this place . . . there's a better life for me and you.'

Very 1967. She was eleven then and impressionable.

The Baby looks at her, pleadingly, his arms splayed out in surrender. To where? Where is there to go? Take me! Take me!

That night, postop night, the Mother and Husband lie afloat in the cot together. A fluorescent lamp near the crib is kept on in the dark. The Baby breathes evenly but thinly in his drugged sleep. The morphine in its first flooding doses apparently makes him feel as if he were falling backward—or so the Mother has been told—and it causes the Baby to jerk, to catch himself over and over, as if he were being dropped from a tree. 'Is this right? Isn't there something that should be done?' The nurses come in hourly, different ones—the night shifts seem strangely short and frequent. If the Baby stirs or frets, the nurses give him more morphine through the Hickman catheter, then leave to tend to other patients. The Mother rises to check on him in the low light. There is gurgling from the clear plastic suction tube coming out of his mouth. Brownish clumps have collected in the tube. What is going on?

The Mother rings for the nurse. Is it Renée or Sarah or Darcy? She's forgotten.

'What, what is it?' murmurs the Husband, waking up.

'Something is wrong,' says the Mother. 'It looks like blood in his N-G tube.'

'What?' The Husband gets out of bed. He, too, is wearing sweatpants.

The nurse—Valerie—pushes open the heavy door to the room and enters quietly. 'Everything okay?'

'There's something wrong here. The tube is sucking blood out of his stomach. It looks like it may have perforated his stomach and that now he's bleeding internally. Look!'

Valerie is a saint, but her voice is the standard hospital saint voice: an infuriating, pharmaceutical calm. It says, Everything is normal here. Death is normal. Pain is normal. Nothing is abnormal. So there is nothing to get excited about. 'Well now, let's see.' She holds up the plastic tube and tries to see inside it. 'Hmmm,' she says. 'I'll call the attending physician.'

Because this is a research and teaching hospital, all the regular doctors are at home sleeping in their Mission-style beds. Tonight, as is apparently the case every weekend night, the attending physician is a medical student. He looks fifteen. The authority he attempts to convey, he cannot remotely inhabit. He is not even in the same building with it. He shakes everyone's hands, then strokes his chin, a gesture no doubt gleaned from some piece of dinner theater his parents took him to once. As if there were an actual beard on that chin! As if beard growth on that chin were even possible! *Our Town*! *Kiss Me Kate*! *Barefoot in the Park*! He is attempting to convince, if not to impress.

'We're in trouble,' the Mother whispers to the Husband. She is tired, tired of young people grubbing for grades. 'We've got Dr. "Kiss Me Kate," here.'

The Husband looks at her blankly, a mix of disorientation and divorce.

The medical student holds the tubing in his hands. 'I don't really see anything,' he says.

He flunks! 'You don't?' The Mother shoves her way in, holds the clear tubing in both hands. 'That,' she says. 'Right here and here.' Just this past semester, she said to one of her own students, 'If you don't see how this essay is better than that one, then I want you just to go out into the hallway and stand there until you do.' Is it important to keep one's voice down? The Baby stays asleep. He is drugged and dreaming, far away.

'Hmmm,' says the medical student. 'Perhaps there's a little irritation in the stomach.'

'A little irritation?' The Mother grows furious. 'This is blood. These are clumps and clots. This stupid thing is sucking the life right out of him!' Life! She is starting to cry.

They turn off the suction and bring in antacids, which they feed into the Baby through the tube. Then they turn the suction on again. This time on low.

'What was it on before?' asks the Husband.

'High,' says Valerie. 'Doctor's orders, though I don't know why. I don't know why these doctors do a lot of the things they do.'

'Maybe they're . . . not all that bright?' suggests the Mother. She is feeling relief and rage simultaneously: there is a feeling of prayer and litigation in the air. Yet essentially, she is grateful. Isn't she? She thinks she is. And still, and still: look at all the things you have to do to protect a child, a hospital merely an intensification of life's cruel obstacle course.

The Surgeon comes to visit on Saturday morning. He steps in and nods at the Baby, who is awake but glazed from the morphine, his eyes two dark unseeing grapes. 'The boy looks fine,' the Surgeon announces. He peeks under the Baby's bandage. 'The stitches look good,' he says. The Baby's abdomen is stitched all the way across like a baseball. 'And the other kidney, when we looked at it yesterday face-to-face, looked fine. We'll try to wean him off the morphine a little, and see how he's doing on Monday.' He clears his throat. 'And now,' he says, looking about the room at the nurses and medical students, 'I would like to speak with the Mother, alone.'

The Mother's heart gives a jolt. 'Me?'

'Yes,' he says, motioning, then turning.

She gets up and steps out into the empty hallway with him, closing the door behind her. What can this be about? She hears the Baby fretting a little in his crib. Her brain fills with pain and alarm. Her voice comes out as a hoarse whisper. 'Is there something—'

'There is a particular thing I need from you,' says the Surgeon, turning and standing there very seriously.

'Yes?' Her heart is pounding. She does not feel resilient enough for any more bad news.

'I need to ask a favor.'

'Certainly,' she says, attempting very hard to summon the strength and courage for this occasion, whatever it is; her throat has tightened to a fist.

From inside his white coat, the surgeon removes a thin paperback book and thrusts it toward her. 'Will you sign my copy of your novel?'

The Mother looks down and sees that it is indeed a copy of a novel she has written, one about teenaged girls.

She looks up. A big, spirited grin is cutting across his face. 'I read this last summer,' he says, 'and I still remember parts of it! Those girls got into such trouble!'

Of all the surreal moments of the last few days, this, she thinks, might be the most so.

'Okay,' she says, and the Surgeon merrily hands her a pen.

'You can just write "To Dr.—" Oh, I don't need to tell you what to write.'

The Mother sits down on a bench and shakes ink into the pen. A sigh of relief washes over and out of her. Oh, the pleasure of a sigh of relief, like the finest moments of love; has anyone properly sung the praises of sighs of relief? She opens the book to the title page. She breathes deeply. What is he doing reading novels about teenaged girls, anyway? And why didn't he buy the hardcover? She inscribes something grateful and true, then hands the book back to him.

'Is he going to be okay?'

'The boy? The boy is going to be fine,' he says, then taps her stiffly on the shoulder. 'Now you take care. It's Saturday. Drink a little wine.'

Over the weekend, while the Baby sleeps, the Mother and Husband sit together in the Tiny Tim Lounge. The Husband is restless and makes cafeteria and sundry runs, running errands for everyone. In his absence, the other parents regale her further with their sagas. Pediatric cancer and chemo stories: the children's amputations, blood poisoning, teeth flaking like shale, the learning delays and disabilities caused by chemo frying the young, budding brain. But strangely optimistic codas are tacked on—endings as stiff and loopy as carpenter's lace, crisp and empty as lettuce, reticulate as a net—ah, words. 'After all that business with the tutor, he's better now, and fitted with new incisors by my wife's cousin's husband, who did dental school in two and a half years, if you can believe that. We hope for the best. We take things as they come. Life is hard.'

'Life's a big problem,' agrees the Mother. Part of her welcomes and invites all their tales. In the few long days since this nightmare began, part of her has become addicted to disaster and war stories. She wants only to hear about the sadness and emergencies of others. They are the only situations that can join hands with her own; everything else bounces off her shiny shield of resentment and unsympathy. Nothing else can even stay in her brain. From this, no doubt, the philistine world is made, or should one say recruited? Together, the parents huddle all day in the Tiny Tim Lounge—no need to watch *Oprah*. They leave Oprah in the dust. Oprah has nothing on them. They chat matter-of-factly, then fall silent and watch *Dune* or *Star Wars*, in which there are bright and shiny robots, whom the Mother now sees not as robots at all but as human beings who have had terrible things happen to them.

Some of their friends visit with stuffed animals and soft greetings of 'Looking good' for the dozing baby, though the room is way past the stuffed-animal limit. The Mother arranges, once more, a plateful of Mint Milano cookies and cups of take-out coffee for guests. All her nutso pals stop by—the two on Prozac, the one obsessed with the word *penis* in the word *happiness*, the one who recently had her hair foiled green. 'Your friends put the *de* in *fin de siècle*,' says the Husband. Overheard, or recorded, all marital conversation sounds as if someone must be joking, though usually no one is.

She loves her friends, especially loves them for coming, since there are times they all fight and don't speak for weeks. Is this friendship? For now and here, it must do and is, and is, she swears it is. For one, they never offer impromptu spiritual lectures about death, how it is part of life, its natural ebb and flow, how we all must accept that, or other such utterances that make her want to scratch out some eyes. Like true friends, they take no hardy or elegant stance loosely choreographed from some broad perspective. They get right in there and mutter 'Jesus Christ!' and shake their heads. Plus, they are the only people who not only will laugh at her stupid jokes but offer up stupid ones of their own. *What do you get when you cross Tiny Tim with a pit bull?* A child's illness is a strain on the mind. They know how to laugh in a fluty, desperate way—unlike the people who are more her husband's friends and who seem just to deepen their sorrowful gazes, nodding their heads with Sympathy. How exiling and estranging are everybody's Sympathetic Expressions! When anyone laughs, she thinks, Okay! Hooray: a buddy. In disaster as in show business.

Nurses come and go; their chirpy voices both startle and soothe. Some of the other Peed Onk parents stick their heads in to see how the Baby is and offer encouragement.

Green Hair scratches her head. 'Everyone's so friendly here. Is there someone in this place who isn't doing all this airy, scripted optimism—or are people like that the only people here?'

'It's Modern Middle Medicine meets the Modern Middle Family,' says the Husband. 'In the Modern Middle West.'

Someone has brought in take-out lo mein, and they all eat it out in the hall by the elevators.

Parents are allowed use of the Courtesy Line.

'You've got to have a second child,' says a different friend on the phone, a friend from out of town. 'An heir and a spare. That's what we did. We had another child to ensure we wouldn't off ourselves if we lost our first.'

'Really?'

'I'm serious.'

'A formal suicide? Wouldn't you just drink yourself into a lifelong stupor and let it go at that?'

'Nope. I knew how I would do it even. For a while, until our second came along, I had it all planned.'

'What did you plan?'

'I can't go into too much detail, because—Hi, honey!—the kids are here now in the room. But I'll spell out the general idea: R-O-P-E.'

Sunday evening, she goes and sinks down on the sofa in the Tiny Tim Lounge next to Frank, Joey's father. He is a short, stocky man with the currentless, flatlined look behind the eyes that all the parents eventually get here. He has shaved his head bald in solidarity with his son. His little boy has been battling cancer for five years. It is now in the liver, and the rumor around the corridor is that Joey has three weeks to live. She knows that Joey's mother, Heather, left Frank years ago, two years into the cancer, and has remarried and had another child, a girl named Brittany. The Mother sees Heather here sometimes with her new life—the cute little girl and the new, young, full-haired husband who will never be so maniacally and debilitatingly obsessed with Joey's illness the way Frank, her first husband, was. Heather comes to visit Joey, to say hello and now good-bye, but she is not Joey's main man. Frank is.

Frank is full of stories—about the doctors, about the food, about the nurses, about Joey. Joey, affectless from his meds, sometimes leaves his room and comes out to watch TV in his bathrobe. He is jaundiced and bald, and though he is nine, he looks no older than six. Frank has devoted the last four and a half years to saving Joey's life. When the cancer was first diagnosed, the doctors gave Joey a 20 percent chance of living six more months. Now here it is, almost five years later, and Joey's still here. It is all due to Frank, who, early on, quit his job as vice president of a consulting firm in order to commit himself totally to his son. He is proud of everything he's given up and done, but he is tired. Part of him now really believes things are coming to a close, that this is the end. He says this without tears. There are no more tears.

'You have probably been through more than anyone else on this corridor,' says the Mother.

'I could tell you stories,' he says. There is a sour odor between them, and she realizes that neither of them has bathed for days.

'Tell me one. Tell me the worst one.' She knows he hates his ex-wife and hates her new husband even more.

'The worst? They're all the worst. Here's one: one morning, I went out for breakfast with my buddy—it was the only time I'd left Joey alone ever; left him for two hours is all—and when I came back, his N-G tube was full of blood. They had the suction on too high, and it was sucking the guts right out of him.'

'Oh my God. That just happened to us,' said the Mother.

'It did?'

'Friday night.'

'You're kidding. They let that happen again? I gave them such a chewing-out about that!'

'I guess our luck is not so good. We get your very worst story on the second night we're here.'

'It's not a bad place, though.'

'It's not?'

'Naw. I've seen worse. I've taken Joey everywhere.'

'He seems very strong.' Truth is, at this point, Joey seems like a zombie and frightens her.

'Joey's a fucking genius. A biological genius. They'd given him six months, remember.'

The Mother nods.

'Six months is not very long,' says Frank. 'Six months is nothing. He was four and a half years old.'

All the words are like blows. She feels flooded with affection and mourning for this man. She looks away, out the window, out past the hospital parking lot, up toward the black marbled sky and the electric eyelash of the moon. 'And now he's nine,' she says. 'You're his hero.'

'And he's mine,' says Frank, though the fatigue in his voice seems to overwhelm him. 'He'll be that forever. Excuse me,' he says, 'I've got to go check. His breathing hasn't been good. Excuse me.'

'Good news and bad,' says the Oncologist on Monday. He has knocked, entered the room, and now stands there. Their cots are unmade. One wastebasket is overflowing with coffee cups. 'We've got the pathologist's report. The bad news is that the kidney they removed had certain lesions, called 'rests,' which are associated with a higher risk for disease in the other kidney. The good news is that the tumor is stage one, regular cell structure, and under five hundred grams, which qualifies you for a national experiment in which chemotherapy isn't done but your boy is monitored with ultrasound instead. It's not all that risky, given that the patient's watched closely, but here is the literature on it. There are forms to sign, if you decide to do that. Read all this and we can discuss it further. You have to decide within four days.'

Lesions? Rests? They dry up and scatter like M&M's on the floor. All she hears is the part about no chemo. Another sigh of relief rises up in her and spills out. In a life where there is only the bearable and the unbearable, a sigh of relief is an ecstasy.

'No chemo?' says the Husband. 'Do you recommend that?'

The Oncologist shrugs. What casual gestures these doctors are permitted! 'I know chemo. I like chemo,' says the Oncologist. 'But this is for you to decide. It depends how you feel.'

The Husband leans forward. 'But don't you think that now that we have the upper hand with this thing, we should keep going? Shouldn't we stomp on it, beat it, smash it to death with the chemo?'

The Mother swats him angrily and hard. 'Honey, you're delirious!' She whispers, but it comes out as a hiss. 'This is our lucky break!' Then she adds gently, 'We don't want the Baby to have chemo.'

The Husband turns back to the Oncologist. 'What do you think?'

'It could be,' he says, shrugging. 'It could be that this is your lucky break. But you won't know for sure for five years.'

The Husband turns back to the Mother. 'Okay,' he says. 'Okay.'

The Baby grows happier and strong. He begins to move and sit and eat. Wednesday morning, they are allowed to leave, and leave without chemo. The Oncologist looks a little nervous. 'Are you nervous about this?' asks the Mother.

'Of course I'm nervous.' But he shrugs and doesn't look that nervous. 'See you in six weeks for the ultrasound,' he says, waves and then leaves, looking at his big black shoes as he does.

The Baby smiles, even toddles around a little, the sun bursting through the clouds, an angel chorus crescendoing. Nurses arrive. The Hickman is taken out of the Baby's neck and chest; antibiotic lotion is dispensed. The Mother packs up their bags. The Baby sucks on a bottle of juice and does not cry.

'No chemo?' says one of the nurses. 'Not even a *little* chemo?'

'We're doing watch and wait,' says the Mother.

The other parents look envious but concerned. They have never seen any child get out of there with his hair and white blood cells intact.

'Will you be okay?' asks Ned's mother.

'The worry's going to kill us,' says the Husband.

'But if all we have to do is worry,' chides the Mother, 'every day for a hundred years, it'll be easy. It'll be nothing. I'll take all the worry in the world, if it wards off the thing itself.'

'That's right,' says Ned's mother. 'Compared to everything else, compared to all the actual events, the worry is nothing.'

The Husband shakes his head. 'I'm such an amateur,' he moans.

'You're both doing admirably,' says the other mother. 'Your baby's lucky, and I wish you all the best.'

The Husband shakes her hand warmly. 'Thank you,' he says. 'You've been wonderful.'

Another mother, the mother of Eric, comes up to them. 'It's all very hard,' she says, her head cocked to one side. 'But there's a lot of collateral beauty along the way.'

Collateral beauty? Who is entitled to such a thing? A child is ill. No one is entitled to any collateral beauty!

'Thank you,' says the Husband.

Joey's father, Frank, comes up and embraces them both. 'It's a journey,' he says. He chucks the Baby on the chin. 'Good luck, little man.'

'Yes, thank you so much,' says the Mother. 'We hope things go well with Joey.' She knows that Joey had a hard, terrible night.

Frank shrugs and steps back. 'Gotta go,' he says. 'Good-bye!'

'Bye,' she says, and then he is gone. She bites the inside of her lip, a bit tearily, then bends down to pick up the diaper bag, which is now stuffed with little animals; helium balloons are tied to its zipper. Shouldering the thing, the Mother feels she has just won a prize. All the parents have now vanished down the hall in the opposite direction. The Husband moves close. With one arm, he takes the Baby from her; with the other, he rubs her back. He can see she is starting to get weepy.

'Aren't these people nice? Don't you feel better hearing about their lives?' he asks.

Why does he do this, form clubs all the time; why does even this society of suffering soothe him? When it comes to death and dying, perhaps someone in this family ought to be more of a snob.

'All these nice people with their brave stories,' he continues as they make their way toward the elevator bank, waving good-bye to the nursing staff as they go, even the Baby waving shyly. *Bye-bye! Bye-bye!* 'Don't you feel consoled, knowing we're all in the same boat, that we're all in this together?'

But who on earth would want to be in this boat? the Mother thinks. This boat is a nightmare boat. Look where it goes: to a silver-and-white room, where, just before your eyesight and hearing and your ability to touch or be touched disappear entirely, you must watch your child die.

Rope! Bring on the rope.

'Let's make our own way,' says the Mother, 'and not in this boat.'

Woman Overboard! She takes the Baby back from the Husband, cups the Baby's cheek in her hand, kisses his brow and then, quickly, his flowery mouth. The Baby's heart—she can hear it—drums with life. 'For as long as I live,' says the Mother, pressing the elevator button—up or down, everyone in the end has to leave this way—'I never want to see any of these people again.'

There are the notes.

Now where is the money?

CIVILWARLAND IN BAD DECLINE

George Saunders

Whenever a potential big investor comes for the tour the first thing I do is take him out to the transplanted Erie Canal Lock. We've got a good ninety feet of actual Canal out there and a well-researched dioramic of a coolie campsite. Were our faces ever red when we found out it was actually the Irish who built the Canal. We've got no budget to correct, so every fifteen minutes or so a device in the bunkhouse gives off the approximate aroma of an Oriental meal.

Today my possible Historical Reconstruction Associate is Mr. Haberstrom, founder of Burn'n'Learn. Burn'n'Learn is national. Their gimmick is a fully stocked library on the premises and as you tan you call out the name of any book you want to these high-school girls on roller skates. As we walk up the trail he's wearing a sweatsuit and smoking a cigar and I tell him I admire his acumen. I tell him some men are dreamers and others are doers. He asks which am I and I say let's face it, I'm basically the guy who leads the dreamers up the trail to view the Canal Segment. He likes that. He says I have a good head on my shoulders. He touches my arm and says he's hot to spend some reflective moments at the Canal because his great-grandfather was a barge guider way back when who got killed by a donkey. When we reach the clearing he gets all emotional and bolts off through the gambling plaster Chinese. Not to be crass but I sense an impending sizable contribution.

When I come up behind him however I see that once again the gangs have been at it with their spray cans, all over my Lock. Haberstrom takes a nice long look. Then he pokes me with the spitty end of his cigar and says not with his money I don't, and storms back down the trail.

I stand there alone a few minutes. The last thing I need is some fat guy's spit on my tie. I think about quitting. Then I think about my last degrading batch of résumés. Two hundred send-outs and no nibbles. My feeling is that prospective employers are put off by the fact that I was a lowly Verisimilitude Inspector for nine years with no promotions. I think of my car payment. I think of how much Marcus and Howie love the little playhouse I'm still paying off. Once again I decide to eat my pride and sit tight.

So I wipe off my tie with a leaf and start down to break the Haberstrom news to Mr. Alsuga.

Mr. A's another self-made man. He cashed in on his love of history by conceptualizing CivilWarLand in his spare time. He started out with just a settler's shack and one Union costume and now has considerable influence in Rotary.

His office is in City Hall. He agrees that the gangs are getting out of hand. Last month they wounded three Visitors and killed a dray horse. Several of them encircled and made fun of Mrs. Dugan in her settler outfit as she was taking her fresh-baked bread over to the simulated Towne Meeting. No way they're paying admission, so they're either tunneling in or coming in over the retaining wall.

Mr. Alsuga believes the solution to the gang problem is Teen Groups. I tell him that's basically what a gang is, a Teen Group. But he says how can it be a Teen Group without an adult mentor with a special skill, like whittling? Mr. Alsuga whittles. Once he gave an Old Tyme Skills Seminar on it in the Blacksmith Shoppe. It was poorly attended. All he got was two widowers and a chess-club type no gang would have wanted anyway. And myself. I attended. Evelyn called me a bootlicker, but I attended. She called me a bootlicker, and I told her she'd better bear in mind which side of the bread her butter was on. She said whichever side it was on it wasn't enough to shake a stick at. She's always denigrating my paystub. I came home from the Seminar with this kind of whittled duck. She threw it away the next day because she said she thought it was an acorn. It looked nothing like an acorn. As far as I'm concerned she threw it away out of spite. It made me livid and twice that night I had to step into a closet and perform my Hatred Abatement Breathing.

But that's neither here nor there.

Mr. Alsuga pulls out the summer stats. We're in the worst attendance decline in ten years. If it gets any worse, staff is going to be let go in droves. He gives me a meaningful look. I know full well I'm not one of his key players. Then he asks who we have that might be willing to fight fire with fire.

I say: I could research it.

He says: Why don't you research it?
So I go research it.

Sylvia Loomis is the queen of info. It's in her personality. She enjoys
digging up dirt on people. She calls herself an S&M buff in training.
She's still too meek to go whole hog, so when she parties at the Make
Me Club on Airport Road she limits herself to walking around talking
mean while wearing kiddie handcuffs. But she's good at what she
does, which is Security. It was Sylvia who identified the part-timer
systematically crapping in the planters in the Gift Acquisition Center
and Sylvia who figured out it was Phil in Grounds leaving obscene
messages for the Teen Belles on MessageMinder. She has access to all
records. I ask can she identify current employees with a history of
violence. She says she can if I buy her lunch.

We decide to eat in-Park. We go over to Nate's Saloon. Sylvia says
don't spread it around but two of the nine cancan girls are knocked up.
Then she pulls out her folder and says that according to her review of
the data, we have a pretty tame bunch on our hands. The best she can
do is Ned Quinn. His records indicate that while in high school he once
burned down a storage shed. I almost die laughing. Quinn's an
Adjunct Thespian and a world-class worry-wart. I can't count the times
I've come upon him in Costuming, dwelling on the gory details of his
Dread Disease Rider. He's a failed actor who won't stop trying. He says
this is the only job he could find that would allow him to continue to
develop his craft. Because he's ugly as sin he specializes in roles that
require masks, such as Humpty-Dumpty during Mother Goose Days.

I report back to Mr. Alsuga and he says Quinn may not be much but
he's all we've got. Quinn's dirt-poor with six kids and Mr. A says that's
a plus, as we'll need someone between a rock and a hard place. What
he suggests we do is equip the Desperate Patrol with live ammo and
put Quinn in charge. The Desperate Patrol limps along under
floodlights as the night's crowning event. We've costumed them to
resemble troops who've been in the field too long. We used actual
Gettysburg photos. The climax of the Patrol is a re-enacted partial
rebellion, quelled by a rousing speech. After the speech the boys take
off their hats and put their arms around each other and sing 'I Was Born
Under a Wandering Star.' Then there's fireworks and the Parade of Old-
Fashioned Conveyance. Then we clear the place out and go home.

'Why not confab with Quinn?' Mr. A says. 'Get his input and feelings.'

'I was going to say that,' I say.

I look up the Thespian Center's SpeedDial extension and a few minutes later Quinn's bounding up the steps in the Wounded Grizzly suit.

'Desperate Patrol?' Mr. A says as Quinn sits down. 'Any interest on your part?'

'Love it,' Quinn says. 'Excellent.' He's been trying to get on Desperate Patrol for years. It's considered the pinnacle by the Thespians because of the wealth of speaking parts. He's so excited he's shifting around in his seat and getting some of his paw blood on Mr. A's nice cane chair.

'The gangs in our park are a damn blight,' Mr. A says. 'I'm talking about meeting force with force. Something in it for you? Oh yes.'

'I'd like to see Quinn give the rousing speech myself,' I say.

'Societal order,' Mr. A says. 'Sustaining the lifeblood of this goddamned park we've all put so much of our hearts into.'

'He's not just free-associating,' I say.

'I'm not sure I get it,' Quinn says.

'What I'm suggesting is live ammo in your weapon only,' Mr. A says. 'Fire at your discretion. You see an unsavory intruder, you shoot at his feet. Just give him a scare. Nobody gets hurt. An additional two bills a week is what I'm talking.'

'I'm an actor,' Quinn says.

'Quinn's got kids,' I say. 'He knows the value of a buck.'

'This is acting of the highest stripe,' Mr. A says. 'Act like a mercenary.'

'Go for it on a trial basis,' I say.

'I'm not sure I get it,' Quinn says. 'But jeez, that's good money.'

'Superfantastic,' says Mr. A.

Next evening Mr. A and I go over the Verisimilitude Irregularities List. We've been having some heated discussions about our bird-species percentages. Mr. Grayson, Staff Ornithologist, has recently recalculated and estimates that to accurately approximate the 1865 bird population we'll need to eliminate a couple hundred orioles or so. He suggests using air guns or poison. Mr. A says that, in his eyes, in fiscally troubled times, an ornithologist is a luxury, and this may be the perfect time to send Grayson packing. I like Grayson. He went way overboard on Howie's baseball candy. But I've got me and mine to think of. So I call Grayson in. Mr. A says did you botch the initial calculation or were you privy to new info. Mr. Grayson admits it was a botch. Mr. A sends him out into the hall and we confab.

'You'll do the telling,' Mr. A says. 'I'm getting too old for cruelty.'

He takes his walking stick and beeper and says he'll be in the Great Forest if I need him.

I call Grayson back in and let him go, and hand him Kleenexes and fend off a few blows and almost before I know it he's reeling out the door and I go grab a pita.

Is this the life I envisioned for myself? My God no. I wanted to be a high jumper. But I have two of the sweetest children ever born. I go in at night and look at them in their fairly expensive sleepers and think: There are a couple of kids who don't need to worry about freezing to death or being cast out to the wolves. You should see their little eyes light up when I bring home a treat. They may not know the value of a dollar, but it's my intention to see that they never need to.

I'm filling out Grayson's Employee Retrospective when I hear gunshots from the perimeter. I run out and there's Quinn and a few of his men tied to the cannon. The gang guys took Quinn's pants and put some tiny notches in his penis with their knives. I free Quinn and tell him to get over to the Infirmary to guard against infection. He's absolutely shaking and can hardly walk, so I wrap him up in a Confederate flag and call over a hay cart and load him in.

When I tell Mr. A he says: Garbage in, garbage out, and that we were idiots for expecting a milquetoast to save our rears.

We decide to leave the police out of it because of the possible bad PR. So we give Quinn the rest of the week off and promise to let him play Grant now and then, and that's that.

When visitors first come in there's this cornball part where they sit in this kind of spaceship and supposedly get blasted into space and travel faster than the speed of light and end up in 1865. The unit's dated. The helmets we distribute look like bowls and all the paint's peeling off. I've argued and argued that we need to update. But in the midst of a budget crunch one can't necessarily hang the moon. When the tape of space sounds is over and the walls stop shaking, we pass out the period costumes. We try not to offend anyone, liability law being what it is. We distribute the slave and Native American roles equitably among racial groups. Anyone is free to request a different identity at any time. In spite of our precautions, there's a Herlicher in every crowd. He's the guy who sued us last fall for making him hangman. He claimed that for weeks afterwards he had nightmares and because he wasn't getting enough sleep botched a big contract by sending an important government buyer a load of torn pool liners. Big deal, is my feeling. But he's suing us for fifty grand for emotional stress because the buyer ridiculed him in front of his co-workers. Whenever he comes in we make him sheriff but he won't back down an inch.

Mr. A calls me into his office and says he's got bad news and bad news, and which do I want first. I say the bad news. First off, he says, the gangs have spraypainted a picture of Quinn's notched penis on the side of the Everly Mansion. Second, last Friday's simulated frontier hunt has got us in hot water, because apparently some of the beef we toughen up to resemble buffalo meat was tainted, and the story's going in the Sunday supplement. And finally, the verdict's come in on the Herlicher case and we owe that goofball a hundred grand instead of fifty because the pinko judge empathized.

I wait for him to say I'm fired but instead he breaks down in tears. I pat his back and mix him a drink. He says why don't I join him. So I join him.

'It doesn't look good,' he says, 'for men like you and I.'

'No it doesn't,' I say.

'All I wanted to do,' he says, 'was to give the public a meaningful perspective on a historical niche I've always found personally fascinating.'

'I know what you mean,' I say.

At eleven the phone rings. It's Maurer in Refuse Control calling to say that the gangs have set fire to the Anglican Church. That structure cost upwards of ninety thousand to transport from Clydesville and refurbish. We can see the flames from Mr. A's window.

'Oh Christ!' Mr. A says. 'If I could kill those kids I would kill those kids. One shouldn't desecrate the dream of another individual in the fashion in which they have mine.'

'I know it,' I say.

We drink and drink and finally he falls asleep on his office couch.

On the way to my car I keep an eye out for the ghostly McKinnon family. Back in the actual 1860s all this land was theirs. Their homestead's long gone but our records indicate that it was located near present-day Information Hoedown. They probably never saw this many buildings in their entire lives. They don't realize we're chronically slumming, they just think the valley's prospering. Something bad must have happened to them because their spirits are always wandering around at night looking dismayed.

Tonight I find the Mrs. doing wash by the creek. She sees me coming and asks if she can buy my boots. Machine stitching amazes her. I ask how are the girls. She says Maribeth has been sad because no appropriate boy ever died in the valley so she's doomed to loneliness forever. Maribeth is a homely sincere girl who glides around mooning and pining and reading bad poetry chapbooks. Whenever we keep the Park open late for high-school parties, she's in her glory. There was one kid who was able to see her and even got a crush on her, but when he finally tried to kiss her near Hostelry and found out she was spectral it just about killed him. I slipped him a fifty and told him to keep it under wraps. As far as I know he's still in therapy. I realize I should have come forward but they probably would have nut-hutted me, and then where would my family be?

The Mrs. says what Maribeth needs is choir practice followed by a nice quilting bee. In better times I would have taken the quilting-bee idea and run with it. But now there's no budget. That's basically how I finally moved up from Verisimilitude Inspector to Special Assistant, by lifting ideas from the McKinnons. The Mrs. likes me because after she taught me a few obscure 1800s ballads and I parlayed them into Individual Achievement Awards, I bought her a Rubik's Cube. To her, colored plastic is like something from Venus. The Mr. has kind of warned me away from her a couple of times. He doesn't trust me. He thinks the Rubik's Cube is the devil's work. I've brought him lighters and *Playboys* and once I even dragged out Howie's little synth and the mobile battery pak. I set the synth for carillon and played it from behind a bush. I could tell he was tickled, but he stonewalled. It's too bad I can't make an inroad because he was at Antietam and could be a gold mine of war info. He came back from the war and a year later died in his cornfield, which is now Parking. So he spends most of his time out there calling the cars Beelzebubs and kicking their tires.

Tonight he's walking silently up and down the rows. I get out to my KCar and think oh jeez, I've locked the keys in. The Mr. sits down at the base of the A3 lightpole and asks did I see the fire and do I realize it was divine retribution for my slovenly moral state. I say thank you very much. No way I'm telling him about the gangs. He can barely handle the concept of women wearing trousers. Finally I give up on prying the window down and go call Evelyn for the spare set. While I wait for her I sit on the hood and watch the stars. The Mr. watches them too. He says there are fewer than when he was a boy. He says that even the heavens have fallen into disrepair. I think about explaining smog to him but then Evelyn pulls up.

She's wearing her bathrobe and as soon as she gets out starts with the lip. Howie and Marcus are asleep in the back. The Mr. says it's part and parcel of my fallen state that I allow a woman to speak to me in such a tone. He suggests I throttle her and lock her in the woodshed. Meanwhile she's going on and on so much about my irresponsibility that the kids are waking up. I want to get out before the gangs come swooping down on us. The Parking Area's easy pickings. She calls me a thoughtless oaf and sticks me in the gut with the car keys.

Marcus wakes up all groggy and says: Hey, our daddy.

Evelyn says: Yes, unfortunately he is.

Just after lunch next day a guy shows up at Personnel looking so completely Civil War they immediately hire him and send him out to sit on the porch of the old Kriegal place with a butter churn. His name's Samuel and he doesn't say a word going through Costuming and at the end of the day leaves on a bike. I do the normal clandestine New Employee Observation from the O'Toole gazebo and I like what I see. He seems to have a passable knowledge of how to pretend to churn butter. At one point he makes the mistake of departing from the list of Then-Current Events to discuss the World Series with a Visitor, but my feeling is, we can work with that. All in all he presents a positive and convincing appearance, and I say so in my review.

Sylvia runs her routine check on him and calls me at home that night and says boy do we have a hot prospect on our hands if fucking with the gangs is still on our agenda. She talks like that. I've got her on speakerphone in the rec room and Marcus starts running around the room saying fuck. Evelyn stands there with her arms crossed, giving me a drop-dead look. I wave her off and she flips me the bird.

Sylvia's federal sources indicate that Samuel got kicked out of Vietnam for participating in a bloodbath. Sylvia claims this is oxymoronic. She sounds excited. She suggests I take a nice long look at his marksmanship scores. She says his special combat course listing goes on for pages.

I call Mr. A and he says it sounds like Sam's our man. I express reservations at arming an alleged war criminal and giving him free rein in a family-oriented facility. Mr. A says if we don't get our act together there won't be any family-oriented facility left in a month. Revenues have hit rock bottom and his investors are frothing at the mouth. There's talk of outright closure and liquidation of assets.

He says: Now get off your indefensible high horse and give me Sam's home phone.

So I get off my indefensible high horse and give him Sam's home phone.

Thursday after we've armed Samuel and sent him and the Patrol out, I stop by the Worship Center to check on the Foley baptism. Baptisms are an excellent revenue source. We charge three hundred dollars to rent the Center, which is the former lodge of the Siala utopian free-love community. We trucked it in from downstate, a redbrick building with a nice gold dome. In the old days if one of the Sialians was overeating to the exclusion of others or excessively masturbating, he or she would be publicly dressed down for hours on end in the lodge. Now we put up white draperies and pipe in Stephen Foster and provide at no charge a list of preachers of various denominations.

The Foleys are an overweight crew. The room's full of crying sincere large people wishing the best for a baby. It makes me remember our own sweet beaners in their little frocks. I sit down near the wood-burning heater in the Invalid area and see that Justin in Prep has forgotten to remove the mannequin elderly couple clutching rosaries. Hopefully the Foleys won't notice and withhold payment.

The priest dips the baby's head into the fake marble basin and the door flies open and in comes a racially mixed gang. They stroll up the aisle tousling hair and requisition a Foley niece, a cute redhead of about sixteen. Her dad stands up and gets a blackjack in the head. One of the gang guys pushes her down the aisle with his hands on her breasts. As she passes she looks right at me. The gang guy spits on my shoe and I make my face neutral so he won't get hacked off and drag me into it.

The door slams and the Foleys sit there stunned. Then the baby starts crying and everyone runs shouting outside in time to see the gang dragging the niece into the woods. I panic. I try to think of where the nearest pay phone is. I'm weighing the efficiency of running to Administration and making the call from my cubicle when six fast shots come from the woods. Several of the oldest Foleys assume the worst and drop weeping to their knees in the churchyard.

I don't know the first thing about counseling survivors, so I run for Mr. A.

He's drinking and watching his bigscreen. I tell him what happened and he jumps up and calls the police. Then he says let's go do whatever little we can for these poor people who entrusted us with their sacred family occasion only to have us drop the ball by failing to adequately protect them.

When we get back to the churchyard the Foleys are kicking and upbraiding six gang corpses. Samuel's having a glass of punch with the niece. The niece's dad is hanging all over Sam trying to confirm his daughter's virginity. Sam says it wasn't even close and goes on and on about the precision of his scope.

Then we hear sirens.

Sam says: I'm going into the woods.

Mr. A says: We never saw you, big guy.

The niece's dad says: Bless you, sir.

Sam says: Adios.

Mr. A stands on the hitching post and makes a little speech, the gist of which is, let's blame another gang for killing these dirtbags so Sam can get on with his important work.

The Foleys agree.

The police arrive and we all lie like rugs.

The word spreads on Sam and the gangs leave us alone. For two months the Park is quiet and revenues start upscaling. Then some high-school kid pulls a butter knife on Fred Moore and steals a handful of penny candy from the General Store. As per specs, Fred alerts Mr. A of a Revenue-Impacting Event. Mr. A calls Security and we perform Exit Sealage. We look everywhere, but the kid's gone. Mr. A says what the hell, Unseal, it's just candy, profit loss is minimal. Sam hears the Unseal Tone on the PA and comes out of the woods all mad with his face painted and says that once the word gets out we've gone soft the gangs will be back in a heartbeat. I ask since when do gangs use butter knives. Sam says a properly trained individual can kill a wild boar with a butter knife. Mr. A gives me a look and says why don't we let Sam run this aspect of the operation since he possesses the necessary expertise. Then Mr. A offers to buy him lunch and Sam says no, he'll eat raw weeds and berries as usual.

I go back to my Verisimilitude Evaluation on the Cimarron Brothel. Everything looks super. As per my recommendations they've replaced the young attractive simulated whores with uglier women with a little less on the ball. We were able to move the ex-simulated whores over to the Sweete Shoppe, so everybody's happy, especially the new simulated whores, who were for the most part middle-aged women we lured away from fast-food places via superior wages.

When I've finished the Evaluation I go back to my office for lunch. I step inside and turn on the fake oil lamp and there's a damn human hand on my chair, holding a note. All around the hand there's penny candy. The note says: Sir, another pig disciplined who won't mess with us anymore and also I need more ammo. It's signed: Samuel the Rectifier.

I call Mr. A and he says Jesus. Then he tells me to bury the hand in the marsh behind Refreshments. I say shouldn't we call the police. He says we let it pass when it was six dead kids, why should we start getting moralistic now over one stinking hand?

I say: But sir, he killed a high-schooler for stealing candy.

He says: That so-called high-schooler threatened Fred Moore, a valued old friend of mine, with a knife.

A butter knife, I say.

He asks if I've seen the droves of unemployed huddled in front of Personnel every morning.

I ask if that's a threat and he says no, it's a reasonable future prognostication.

'What's done is done,' he says. 'We're in this together. If I take the fall on this, you'll eat the wienie as well. Let's just put this sordid ugliness behind us and get on with the business of providing an enjoyable living for those we love.'

I hang up and sit looking at the hand. There's a class ring on it.

Finally I knock it into a garbage sack with my phone and go out to the marsh.

As I'm digging, Mr. McKinnon glides up. He gets down on his knees and starts sniffing the sack. He starts talking about bloody wagon wheels and a boy he once saw sitting in a creek slapping the water with his own severed arm. He tells how the dead looked with rain on their faces and of hearing lunatic singing from all corners of the field of battle and of king-sized rodents gorging themselves on the entrails of his friends.

It occurs to me that the Mr.'s a loon.

I dig down a couple feet and drop the hand in. Then I backfill and get out of there fast. I look over my shoulder and he's rocking back and forth over the hole mumbling to himself.

As I pass a sewer cover the Mrs. rises out of it. Seeing the Mr. enthralled by blood she starts shrieking and howling to beat the band. When she finally calms down she comes to rest in a tree branch. Tears run down her see-through cheeks. She says there's been a horrid violent seed in him since he came home from the war. She says she can see they're going to have to go away. Then she blasts over my head elongate and glowing and full of grief and my hat gets sucked off.

All night I have bad dreams about severed hands. In one I'm eating chili and a hand comes out of my bowl and gives me the thumbs-down. I wake up with a tingling wrist. Evelyn says if I insist on sleeping uneasily would I mind doing it on the couch, since she has a family to care for during the day and this requires a certain amount of rest. I think about confessing to her but then I realize if I do she'll nail me.

The nights when she'd fall asleep with her cheek on my thigh are certainly long past.

I lie there awhile watching her make angry faces in her sleep. Then I go for a walk. As usual Mr. Ebershom's practicing figure-skating moves in his foyer. I sit down by our subdivision's fake creek and think. First of all, burying a hand isn't murder. It doesn't say anywhere thou shalt not bury some guy's hand. By the time I got involved the kid was dead. Where his hand ended up is inconsequential.

Then I think: What am I saying? I did a horrible thing. Even as I sit here I'm an accomplice and an obstructor of justice.

But then I see myself in the penitentiary and the boys waking up scared in the night without me, and right then and there with my feet in the creek I decide to stay clammed up forever and take my lumps in the afterlife.

Halloween's special in the Park. Our brochure says: Lose Yourself in Eerie Autumnal Splendor. We spray cobwebs around the Structures and dress up Staff in ghoul costumes and hand out period-authentic treats. We hide holograph generators in the woods and project images of famous Americans as ghosts. It's always a confusing time for the McKinnons. Last year the Mr. got in a head-to-head with the image of Jefferson Davis. He stood there in the woods yelling at it for hours while the Mrs. and the girls begged him to come away. Finally I had to cut power to the unit.

I drive home at lunch and pick the boys up for trick-or-treating. Marcus is a rancher and Howie's an accountant. He's wearing thick fake lips and carrying a ledger. The Park's the only safe place to trick-or-treat anymore. Last year some wacko in a complex near our house laced his Snickers with a virus. I drove by the school and they were CPRing this little girl in a canary suit. So forget it.

I take them around to the various Structures and they pick up their share of saltwater taffy and hard tasteless frontier candy and wooden whistles and toy soldiers made of soap.

Then just as we start across the Timeless Green a mob of teens bursts out of the Feinstein Memorial Conifer Grove.

'Gangs!' I yell to the boys. 'Get down!'

I hear a shot and look up and there's Samuel standing on a stump at tree line. Thank God, I think. He lets loose another round and one of the teens drops. Marcus is down beside me whimpering with his nose in my armpit. Howie's always been the slow one. He stands there with his mouth open, one hand in his plastic pumpkin. A second teen drops. Then Howie drops and his pumpkin goes flying.

I crawl over and beg him to be okay. He says there's no pain. I check him over and check him over and all that's wrong is his ledger's been shot. I'm so relieved I kiss him on the mouth and he yells at me to quit.

Samuel drops a third teen, then runs yipping into the woods.

The ambulance shows up and the paramedics load up the wounded teens. They're all still alive and one's saying a rosary. I take the boys to City Hall and confront Mr. A. I tell him I'm turning Sam in. He asks if I've gone daft and suggests I try putting food on the table from a jail cell while convicts stand in line waiting to have their way with my rear.

At this point I send the boys out to the foyer.

'He shot Howie,' I say. 'I want him put away.'

'He shot Howie's ledger,' Mr. A says. 'He shot Howie's ledger in the process of saving Howie's life. But whatever. Let's not mince hairs. If Sam gets put away, we get put away. Does that sound to you like a desirable experience? '

'No,' I say.

'What I'm primarily saying,' he says, 'is that this is a time for knowledge assimilation, not backstabbing. We learned a lesson, you and I. We personally grew. Gratitude for this growth is an appropriate response. Gratitude, and being careful never to make the same mistake twice.'

He gets out a Bible and says let's swear on it that we'll never hire a crazed maniac to perform an important security function again. Then the phone rings. Sylvia's cross-referenced today's Admissions data and found that the teens weren't a gang at all but a bird-watching group who made the mistake of being male and adolescent and wandering too far off the trail.

'Ouch,' Mr. A says. 'This could be a serious negative.'

In the foyer the kids are trying to get the loaches in the corporate tank to eat bits of Styrofoam. I phone Evelyn and tell her what happened and she calls me a butcher. She wants to know how on earth I could bring the boys to the Park knowing what I knew. She says she doesn't see how I'm going to live with myself in light of how much they trusted and loved me and how badly I let them down by leaving their fates to chance.

I say I'm sorry and she seems to be thinking. Then she tells me just get them home without putting them in further jeopardy, assuming that's within the scope of my mental powers.

*

At home she puts them in the tub and sends me out for pizza. I opt for Melvin's Pasta Lair. Melvin's a religious zealot who during the Depression worked five jobs at once. Sometimes I tell him my troubles and he says I should stop whining and count my blessings. Tonight I tell him I feel I should take some responsibility for eliminating the Samuel problem but I'm hesitant because of the discrepancy in our relative experience in violence. He says you mean you're scared. I say not scared, just aware of the likelihood of the possibility of failure. He gives me a look. I say it must have been great to grow up when men were men. He says men have always been what they are now, namely incapable of coping with life without the intervention of God the Almighty. Then in the oven behind him my pizza starts smoking and he says case in point.

He makes me another and urges me to get in touch with my Lord personally. I tell him I will. I always tell him I will.

When I get home they're gone.

Evelyn's note says: I could never forgive you for putting our sons at risk. Goodbye forever, you passive flake. Don't try to find us. I've told the kids you sent us away in order to marry a floozy.

Like an idiot I run out to the street. Mrs. Schmidt is prodding her automatic sprinkler system with a rake, trying to detect leaks in advance. She asks how I am and I tell her not now. I sit on the lawn. The stars are very near. The phone rings. I run inside prepared to grovel, but it's only Mr. A. He says come down to the Park immediately because he's got big horrific news.

When I get there he's sitting in his office half-crocked. He tells me we're unemployed. The investors have gotten wind of the bird-watcher shootings and withdrawn all support. The Park is no more. I tell him about Evelyn and the kids. He says that's the least of his worries because he's got crushing debt. He asks if I have any savings he could have. I say no. He says that just for the record and my own personal development, he's always found me dull and has kept me around primarily for my yes-man capabilities and because sometimes I'm so cautious I'm a hoot.

Then he says: Look, get your ass out, I'm torching this shithole for insurance purposes.

I want to hit or at least insult him, but I need this week's pay to find my kids. So I jog off through the Park. In front of Information

Hoedown I see the McKinnons cavorting. I get closer and see that they're not cavorting at all, they've inadvertently wandered too close to their actual death site and are being compelled to act out again and again the last minutes of their lives. The girls are lying side by side on the ground and the Mr. is whacking at them with an invisible scythe. The Mrs. is belly-up with one arm flailing in what must have been the parlor. The shrieking is mind-boggling. When he's killed everyone the Mr. walks out to his former field and mimes blowing out his brains. Then he gets up and starts over. It goes on and on, through five cycles. Finally he sits down in the dirt and starts weeping. The Mrs. and the girls backpedal away. He gets up and follows them, pitifully trying to explain.

Behind us the Visitor Center erupts in flames.

The McKinnons go off down the hill, passing through bushes and trees. He's shouting for forgiveness. He's shouting that he's just a man. He's shouting that hatred and war made him nuts. I start running down the hill agreeing with him. The Mrs. gives me a look and puts her hands over Maribeth's ears. We're all running. The Mrs. starts screaming about the feel of the scythe as it opened her up. The girls bemoan their unborn kids. We make quite a group. Since I'm still alive I keep clipping trees with my shoulders and falling down.

At the bottom of the hill they pass through the retaining wall and I run into it. I wake up on my back in the culvert. Blood's running out of my ears and a transparent boy's kneeling over me. I can tell he's no McKinnon because he's wearing sweatpants.

'Get up now,' he says in a gentle voice. 'Fire's coming.'

'No,' I say. 'I'm through. I'm done living.'

'I don't think so,' he says. 'You've got amends to make.'

'I screwed up,' I say. 'I did bad things.'

'No joke,' he says, and holds up his stump.

I roll over into the culvert muck and he grabs me by the collar and sits me up.

'I steal four jawbreakers and a Slim Jim and your friend kills and mutilates me?' he says.

'He wasn't my friend,' I say.

'He wasn't your enemy,' the kid says.

Then he cocks his head. Through his clear skull I see Sam coming out of the woods. The kid cowers behind me. Even dead he's scared of

Sam. He's so scared he blasts straight up in the air shrieking and vanishes over the retaining wall.

Sam comes for me with a hunting knife.

'Don't take this too personal,' he says, 'but you've got to go. You know a few things I don't want broadcast.'

I'm madly framing calming words in my head as he drives the knife in. I can't believe it. Never again to see my kids? Never again to sleep and wake to their liquid high voices and sweet breaths?

Sweet Evelyn, I think, I should have loved you better.

Possessing perfect knowledge I hover above him as he hacks me to bits. I see his rough childhood. I see his mother doing something horrid to him with a broomstick. I see the hate in his heart and the people he has yet to kill before pneumonia gets him at eighty-three. I see the dead kid's mom unable to sleep, pounding her fists against her face in grief at the moment I was burying her son's hand. I see the pain I've caused. I see the man I could have been, and the man I was, and then everything is bright and new and keen with love and I sweep through Sam's body, trying to change him, trying so hard, and feeling only hate and hate, solid as stone.

ISSUES I DEALT WITH IN THERAPY

Matthew Klam

We were on a preppy East Coast resort island, in the middle of summer, we just flew in for the wedding of my incredible friend Bob. We were here on vacation, away from the hot city; I was so glad to be out of that fucking house. The simple fact that it's a plane trip away and you're staying in a hotel on this fake, preppy island, and because you're not married and yet you're at a wedding together, because you're too cheap to go on decent vacations, because your own day-to-day life could use some tuning up and like any sane person you've already erected an invisible barrier between yourself and that life back there and you're now pretending that it isn't real, and because Bob is suddenly this big deal, your most skyrocketing friend, and Bob's wedding weekend has finally arrived—well, it's a new beginning. I could feel the excitement.

We got to the hotel and parked the rental car and walked down to the water in our street clothes. People passed by with beach umbrellas and L. L. Bean canvas tote bags, floating in the heat. Kids ran happily in the wet patch left by the outgoing tide as seagulls hovered rigidly in the air above us, screaming into the wind. We walked back up through the mushy sand to the steps of the hotel parking lot, Phylida's long white translucent sundress blowing in front of me. We passed the advance team for Gore, fifteen blond-haired women in their early twenties wearing hairbands talking on cell phones on the little patch of grass bordering some brown split-wood railings in front of the hotel. I was looking at everything: the people getting out of the rental cars, the bracelets on the women, the sunshine brightly beaming. It was Bob's sunshine, you were on his island now. I looked back at Phylida; she smiled. The wind lifted her dress all the way up in the front before she could catch it. A guy struggled to pull out his golf clubs from the trunk, and a valet half his age whisked the bag away like a feather. The wife laughed. Who were they? I think every room in the hotel was rented to the four hundred people invited to the wedding.

It was an old wooden hotel, the charming kind, creaking stairway, crooked floors. Our room was small, antique crap in it, a jingling glass lampshade on a side table, a queen-size bed raised to an enormous height, a frilly cover, a cheap, modern glass door on sliders leading out to a wooden balcony that gave you splinters and, as promised, looked out on a downwind stretch of the same beach where Bob and Niloo would be getting married, a mile away.

They'd been hyping us with stuff in the mail for six months. The 'Set this date aside' card. The letter that began, 'Tell us exactly what you eat,' with rows of boxes to check off: 'Are you dairy-tolerant?' 'Do you like sushi or do you eat it to be polite?' 'Our chef will not cook with peanuts.' The six-piece engraved invitation. Lists of the island's golf courses. A note about where they registered—'Sheetmaker to the Earl of Windsor.' A special mailing to the lady guests—'We hope you'll start shopping for that perfect full-length formal summer gown to wear to our summer wedding on the shore.' Another list for me because I was an usher—what kind of tux shirt collar they (Bob) wanted us to get, suggested books for preparing your toast. A sheet of facts on the island, how great Americans retired here, how it played a part in the Revolutionary War, how the something of democracy was born here— the letter Bob typed up said—'to help free our nation of tyranny evermore and make America the most wonderful country in the world.'

The freak-show element of the wedding was like a side thing: Madeleine Albright would be here tomorrow; Ruth Bader Ginsburg insisted on performing the ceremony; that advance team for Gore was trying to figure out whether the rain would hold off so Al could helicopter in for an appearance.

What was I doing here?

Bob and I met during graduate school at a food drive for torture victims of repressive regimes; Bob was in charge of cans. He was silly and fun, a goofy guy in a baseball hat. He studied civil-rights law. He said he wanted to help black people straighten out the mess. I was getting a master's in international relations. Our friendship was based on leaving each other messages in fake Spanish accents, discussing girls' private areas, pretending we were rich. The next semester we became roommates. He came home at eleven o'clock and inhaled vats of popcorn.

We graduated. Bob moved out to be closer to the Justice

Department. He worked in civil rights; he desegregated a poor school district in Mississippi that was secretly being run by the Klan. Bob jailed them. I sort of worshipped him. I thought he was Superman.

I worked at a nonprofit that attacked the military-industrial complex, but I'll tell you right now it did nothing. I might as well have been talking into a phone flipped upside down. It would be hard to explain exactly what we accomplished in our self-justifying fantasy of left-wing liberal dogshit.

I'd stop by and see him working and even the tiniest tic, the way his leg shook when he spoke, the way he filed papers by throwing them on the floor, seemed magnified, intentional, smart.

They won a big case and he got to be in the televised press conference. He sat up tall and straight. He'd cut his hair short for it. Every answer out of his mouth was like a perfectly fired javelin. The camera refused to move from him. He'd starved himself on those long trips to Mississippi, and now with no hair he looked like an astronaut.

Soon he was having chats with Janet Reno, riding with her over to Congress. He wasn't lawyering as much. He'd moved up. 'It's titular.' What's titular? 'We do planning.' They had some sticky problems in Immigration and Naturalization: They were trying to figure out how to throw Haitians back in the water. When I phoned him at work he could only whisper. He gave the impression that things were hectic and constantly needed his attention. We still talked about our old plans to do good—we wanted to open a soup kitchen in a motor home and drive it around—but he liked seeing himself on the news, and the next time we were together he did a long analysis reworking the performance I saw on TV. He went to events at the White House, standing in for the attorney general. 'After Memorial Day,' he explained, 'you wear the white dinner jacket.'

Time passed. He met everybody. He called Barbara Walters at her home. He had four thousand names in his handheld electronic Rolodex. I swung by his apartment. He stuck handwritten notes from King Hussein on his refrigerator, photos of himself coming down the staircase of *Air Force One*, looking pale and tired. He'd become important, and I was hypnotized and gladly took what he handed me, a box of candies, an opened bottle of peach schnapps, outpourings of guilt he felt at the sight of me.

He quit Justice and went to work on a guy's campaign. He ran it and won. You saw Bob on TV on election night, dancing in a hat he made out of a dinner napkin. He became a 'media catastrophe consultant'— what's that? He 'befriended politicians under fire.' He sat in on meetings. Alone, just the two of us, he entertained me with their indiscretions: the congressman accused of photocopying his testicles, the federal judge who fell into fetal position when women said no. He needed somebody to be his friend, to help him grasp what he'd become, but I also got the feeling he went in and out of remembering I was there.

He bought a nice house. He got a smaller cell phone, a full-time squirrelly assistant cutting into our lunches to tell Bob he had to go. He went to work for Senator Sheslow, whose wife had just had a stroke, she was an invalid; Sheslow thought he might run for president. Bob was flying to Dallas and Japan, talking to folks. 'It's like fund-raising.' And Al Gore was calling to consider him for a job. These jobs didn't have names anymore. 'I'll be the youngest member of Gore's top guys,' he told me in his monotone robotic rambling into the speaker phone as he drove alone somewhere, exhausted. 'It'll be outstanding,' he said.

He had other distinctions. A booming voice, big hands, thick fingers, brown-colored dents on his car from backing into trees, pouchy bags under his bloodshot eyes, a colossal memory—he could produce anything ever said in passing, the name of my childhood pet turtle, how Sheslow voted on a tax bill fifteen years before, it all sat front row in his mind, it was all immediate. He knew George W's weak spots, the trajectory of Chinese rocketry. He had constant weight problems. He shrunk and ballooned and went on diets. He was hungry. He kept popcorn in a lunch bag in his suit-coat pocket. He bit his fingernails till they bled like they'd been shoved inside a sink disposal. I felt for him, but he didn't need my sympathy. I'd wonder, What's he going to do next? Why did he like me? Why was Bill Clinton calling this guy for advice when he couldn't park his car without hanging two wheels on the curb?

The way he spoke now had changed; he used the word *outstanding*, the word *sequentially*. The last time I saw him was at this brunch fund-raiser he made me go to; he'd been bingeing on wheat-grass pills for four days and had stomach cramps and diarrhea but he said he felt 'fantastic.' And the way he acted now—in the last year and a half he went from a young power-hungry sellout to, like, my uncle Denny with the fat gut and the sweaty sheen, wetting his shirts, singing corny show tunes into my answering machine. 'I'm sorry I called at such a late hour, the next time I do I'll bring you a flower.'

Seeing him, the rare times I got together with him now, passing by his office at the Capitol, stopping at his house to be yawned at, or snored at, was like visiting his grave. Niloo would watch his snoring nostrils—he looked like a gorilla—and go, 'He flies pretty high, doesn't he?' or 'Guess who phoned us last night.' In the old days I could get up and go home. Now I had to listen to his bullshit from her too, swallow it twice.

Phylida and I stepped out on the balcony. White-painted wicker chairs with cushions, a table warped by weather, suspended on three legs. Two guys stood on the balcony next to ours, doing what we were doing, feeling the air. They were Italians, friends of Bob and Niloo's, also just arrived. Both guys were tan, had facial hair, wore mirrored lenses. They'd changed into swimming stuff and were ready to go down to the beach. They looked like a couple. One guy wore a very fine loosely woven shiny multicolor sweater in the zillion-degree sun. He fingered his webbed beach purse. The other guy had clean-shaven legs which were flawless and brown. The guy with the purse said, 'We met them vacationing at a place like this in Lisbon.' He said this to the air in front of him. I had a panicky urge to figure out when Bob and Niloo had been to Lisbon, but I couldn't picture what continent Lisbon was on so I said, 'What kind of place was that?' Both guys smiled at once. I'd been holding Phylida's hand, and brought it up and kissed it.

On the balcony on the other side a woman sat alone having a beer on her wicker loveseat. Her name was Sebastian. She had a long, washed-out-green dress unwrinkling on a hanger, and the ocean breeze kept tipping it into her face as she sat, looking pale and basically dead, squinting into the hot sun reflecting off the ocean. Phylida leaned across the railing and asked, 'Did you and Niloo grow up together in New Jersey?' Sebastian knew Niloo from college. She offered Phylida a beer. Already, the first lonely person Phylida saw she befriended. The gay guys stood muscularly in belted swim trunks. I went back inside and hung up my suit.

I lay down on the bed and listened to the women chat. They told each other where they'd come from. Phylida worked into her intro that

Bob and I no longer knew each other. Sebastian said, 'I can't believe I got invited to this thing.' Phylida was leaning on the balcony divider, moving her weight back and forth, her butt aimed at the opening in the doorway at my feet. I felt myself relaxing. Phylida's butt had become the focal point of our life together. It was soft and circular and amazing. I wanted to crawl inside it. I got comfort knowing it was there. She was explaining her medical residency to Sebastian. Now it was swinging. I shut my eyes and began twitching, conking out like the overworked dead person with foul breath I'd become.

After a while Phylida came in and closed the sliding glass door and the see-through curtain, not the heavier, room-darkening drape, and lay down next to me and explained that Sebastian hadn't rented a car and wanted to ride over with us to the rehearsal dinner. Then she fell asleep. She hadn't slept all week. She hadn't slept in seven months and four years. Medical residents are sleep-deprived. On call for three surgical rotations this week, she slept through her beeper one night, what they call a 'no-hitter,' got clobbered the next two nights with huge repair jobs, came home in a black cloud, unable to talk.

I said, 'Are you asleep?' She didn't move. 'How can somebody name a girl Sebastian?'

Phylida and I never fought. We also never saw each other. Our life consisted of lengths of days, with nothing fun in the middle, grinding. We got together and listed what had happened since the last time we spoke, became sad and fell asleep. I kissed her canted hipbone. I ran my finger along her 'zipper,' the scar that went from her sternum to her crotch, open heart surgery as a kid, what got her interested in medicine back then, coarctation of the aorta—a narrow, collapsing aorta, congenitally smushed. I weighed her chest. She let me. I said, 'Should I let you sleep?'

She said, 'Did I sleep on the plane?' I said yes. She turned toward me exhaling. 'This'll be us someday.'

'What?'

'You and me.'

Phylida and I were on the verge of something. Picture us picturing ourselves as next in line for our own wedding weekend. (We'd already talked about what kind of ring I would get her—the stone, the setting.) Picture us wondering: Why does this feel like nothing? Picture us thinking the same thing separately and not talking about it and coming up empty. She was trying to be nice, waiting for that fucking ring now for months and months; she did this imitation of an adoring girlfriend, holding my Coke in the car, but it made her furious and we both wanted to get this over with.

I went for her chest, unbuttoning as fast as I could, opening up her bra. She looked in my eyes and waited.

I ran my hands all over her body. Phylida let out a breath and smiled. Her flaxen hair fell in a spiral shape across a pillow. I kissed her nipples. She liked that. She did a noise with her tongue against her teeth—*tchk*—as I moved my hands around her silky cream mountains. I'd always been attracted to her, although sometimes she walked down the street like John Wayne with his dungarees shoved up his ass in *Stagecoach*.

'They're yours,' she said.

'What is?'

'This is the last pair of tits you'll ever squeeze,' she said, and giggled.

'Why do you have to talk as if you just got out of an insane asylum?' I said. She smiled. Why didn't I understand where she was going with any particular thought?

I licked her ribs. She took her dress off. She had a face that held all the mysteries of Ireland. She had a single blond hair coming out of her chin I never saw before. She wore old blue cotton panties with just a slight fume of musk and salt. She let me pull them all the way down. She had a twat. It was pink and twat-shaped and smelled like roses. What else? She had a mother and a father. Her mother was the garden-variety kind, antihistamines, uppers, soda can in the hand, surprising cotton-ball-white pageboy hairdo. Her father left the family every year on Christmas; he mailed us refrigerator-size boxes of furniture out of guilt. She made a bubble noise in her sleep. She lived for running late; she drove fast, ran people over in crosswalks. She smelled like saddle soap. She had a cowlick on her forehead. She had microscribbled blue capillaries beneath the furry softness on the back of her neck. Her hair looked like corn silk. Her lips were a cornfield. She lay between the rows of corn on the bedspread and let me touch her and wanted more.

'I like that,' she said, pulling at me.

It terrified me when she acted like a slut. I said, 'Let me get unbuckled.'

Bob's fantastic wedding weekend, plane ride from Boston, dry in-flight peanuts, mysterious hotel on the ocean, the grooved tracks of nauseating similarities between us and every other person in this hotel, in the world.

I stared at her. I wanted to get married, too. I wanted to be swept away. Phylida and I had talked about our whole lives—where to live, how to live; we met the other's family, everybody loved everybody, yabba blabba—the only thing left was, like, pull the trigger, get that ring!

She said, 'Your winky is starting to get a little small.' She said this in a bright voice, ashamed of herself. She held it at the base—the outline of her lips was white—and tried blowing me.

I could feel myself spiraling away from sex toward all my fears and anxieties. I tried to 'get metaphysical' with my fears, to keep with my psychologist's urging (she, of the fluffy, Native American 'dream catcher' on her gray office wall) so they didn't overtake me. I looked down at Phylida, beautifully pumping away, and the face of Steven Spielberg floated into my mind, expressionless, bearded, dumb-founded. I thought of how much money he had. He had a private jet with customized woodwork interior, a daybed with a nightstand and a cup holder. A friend of Bob's, some jackass named Dan who helped me plan the order of who gave what toasts this weekend, also had a private jet. Shares of Dan's amazing start-up company cost twenty-six cents apiece two years ago. At this moment they're worth forty-seven dollars. Some of the other invitees were in on Dan's first stock offering; they had names like Lafayette and Sky. I didn't have enough money to be showing my face around this crowd. Sometimes when I traveled for work I pretended I was a foreign spy. I wasn't a spy. Dan would be arriving in his jet today; in a half hour, in fact. I knew that because Bob once suggested I pick Dan up with my personal chauffeuring services but I actually wouldn't be able to because Dan could go fuck himself.

What was with the old, baggy, stained underwear Phylida wore? They looked like something from a nursing home. And what about that chin hair? What about the Italian woman in my office with the extremely high-heeled black suede boots, who did this little secret cha-cha with her legs whenever she came and stood by my desk?

Phylida. If there was any way on earth for me to make her happy, make her laugh, make her feel better, I would find it. But I didn't love her. Not a little. Nothing. I didn't *not* love her. This had nothing to do with love. This was a life arrangement, for all time. What could that mean? Being married forever, living in timeless eternity. Not a joyous eternity, not that basketball-shaped baloney with no ends—slice and slice and there's still a ton left—but the other eternity of Christian-fundamentalist kooks, floating around dead in a pink nightie with a dopey look on your face and a gold banjo, trying to be good.

Happiness. Half penis. I didn't have the slightest interest in fooling around.

I pushed Phylida off me. She looked up, smiling, trying to keep the mood upbeat. Her red mouth, her beautiful face. I would've liked to chop my dick off and fling it from the balcony. 'It's not gonna work,' I said.

'Don't get hysterical.'

'It happened last week. That's twice in a row.'

'It happens to you every time we try to have sex away from home.' That placid look, that flat-lipped smile. She touched her lips. Her eyelashes were like a foot long. They flapped through the air. Her eyes sparkled so wet and clear and blue like the soaring heart of Bob's tumescent sky groaning with sunlight outside our windows that I had to stop looking or die. Why do married people have to live together in our society? Why can't they get houses next door to each other, shoot semen through the window? Why did she like to kick me in her sleep? Why did I feel like strangling her flutelike pinkish throat when she did?

I said, 'I fucked you in Mexico.'

'You fucked me in Mexico.'

'Right.'

'Don't get all penis-focused.'

'Could we not talk about it and make me feel even worse?'

'You're thinking about getting married, our life together. You're worried about eternity.'

'I'm not thinking about anything.'

'You're still my hero. I believe in you.'

'Oh Christ.'

'I'm trying to help.'

I stood, wearing just my underwear, and walked to the bathroom.

'You're rushing. You're tired.'

'Thank you.'

'You have a wedgie.'

The bathroom had a full set of amenities in a wicker basket packed in tissue paper. French soap in a plastic case, English shampoo, a thing to shine shoes. I felt humiliated. A highly detailed advertisement for blackheads stared back at me. I ran some water. I heard her speaking to someone about her outfit for tonight. 'It's blue and it has an A line.' I couldn't hear what else she said. She giggled.

'What's so funny?'

'I'm telling my mother how fat I look in my dress.' I gargled with the complimentary mouthwash and went back out. Phylida lay naked, propped on the bed and put her hand over the receiver.

'My mother said the problem is in your mind and you have nothing to worry about.' Ha! Good one! She switched from me back to the phone to me again and said, 'She said I should get you some of those pills and you'll be fine.' I thought she was kidding. She said good-bye.

'Was there really somebody on the other end?'

'Relax,' she said. 'Anyway, that medication's not what it's cracked up to be.'

'Is that what you told your mother?'

'It's a joke. Lighten up. We're on vacation.' She said something about absorption problems inhibiting blood flow. 'Worse-case scenario, science can do things for this now.' She looked at me with her earnest bullshit doctor face. She started dialing another number.

'Hang up the phone.'

'I have to check my messages.' She rested the phone on her pubic bone. 'There's a procedure; they make a two-millimeter incision at the base of the phallus and slide a lubricated sterile tube inside. It explodes and stiffens when you activate the prosthetic device.' Phylida was in the surgery unit in her residency and showed real talent for it and liked the ability to both scalpel living people and pretend to be saving them.

'You don't mean *explode*,' I said. 'That word would be *expand*.' I didn't want anyone exploding my dick.

'They implant a piece of polyethylene, it's an outpatient procedure and it can be filled with either sterile salt water or air, I believe.'

'Are you dialing direct?'

'Why?'

'Because hotels rip you off.'

'You're not the boss of my money.' She sat there, now sadly looking at the neatly spiraled phone cord lying along her small flat belly, the phone covering her nice vagina.

Phylida placed her makeup bag on the bed, ready to go. She looked like a suffocating powdered mannequin. I felt the same but looked worse. Sebastian knocked and came in and stood by the television cabinet. She'd somehow found a greenish eye shadow to match her dress, and the added touches of it along her cheekbones made her face look skinless. With the acne and veins visible on her arms, she radiated pulsing green blood. On closer inspection she smelled of sour panic sweat. I smiled at her and she touched her jaw.

Phylida read the premailed directions ('Unscheduled toasts may come after dessert and coffee') as I drove through town to the restaurant. Every inch of street was jammed with traffic and sunburned people in salmon-colored shorts shoving past each other, licking melting ice cream off their wrists. Sebastian talked nonstop: 'I wonder if Bibbity Blob is coming.' She talked about Niloo's college days: 'She bought a new purse every time she went to New York City. She slept with what's-his-name.' When we pulled in line for the car valet, Sebastian asked if I had a tissue and cleared her throat and served up a morsel of vomit. 'I hate this kind of thing,' she said. Phylida leaned backward with her arm through the slit in the front seats, the dark-blue matte cloth of her dress pulling taut across her front, highlighting her individuated teardrop-shaped braless tits that I'd felt before, and patted Sebastian's knee.

The women walked behind me as I strode through the restaurant, trying to think of a way to tell people I'd been to London twice for work in the last six months. There was a patio where people stood drinking. The dining area was out back under a tent. We said hello to Bob's parents and met Niloo's parents, Mr. and Mrs. Niyangoda, and Mr. Niyangoda's new wife, Naomi. Phylida looked around and said it all seemed nice, and I nodded and she said, 'At my wedding the bridesmaids will wear metallic scarves, very little makeup, full-length illusion skirts. The cake will be made to look like Wedgewood.'

Sebastian was wondering what Niloo's hair would be like. Sebastian's own hair was short and so greasy and frail it looked like it had been waxed to her head. Something about events like these made people appear either acceptable or pathetic. I got us another round. I'd actually had one more up at the bar, which made three. Was my drinking maybe becoming something? Had it blossomed over these last few months, at home at night, waiting for Phylida, alone until 2 or 3 A.M., foggy and secretly seething? It was a question.

Phylida and Sebastian moved off to find food. A man with a foreign accent came up to me and said I was not to worry: even though he'd lost ten million dollars when he consolidated his businesses, the former premier of France was on his new executive board. He then drank his drink, said nothing, and stared at me. Another man joined us, holding a cigarette. His face had fine lines like an apple going soft. He said he thought the island was beautiful. People chatted. An older woman pulled on the skin of her throat and said, 'I'm going to have this done.' At the other end of the lawn I spotted Phylida chewing; her mouth was full and she waved her hand furiously through the air at me in an exaggerated gleeful way—there was no sorrow in her jaw. I didn't have the money to marry that girl. Originally I liked her because she looked dumb. I didn't know she was a doctor. She swam some delicacy in front of her mouth to taunt me before popping it, and a bullfrog bellowed sadly nearby, similar to the noise my dad made when he let one go; my heart felt like an anvil, it was pulling me down.

Candles were being lit inside the tent. I picked up the scent of pipe tobacco and gardenias. The moon came out. I spotted Bob in a blue tie and red silk pocket square and a straw-colored coat that was already damply dark under the arms and along the back from sweat. The last time I spoke to him was three months earlier when he left me waiting at a Thai restaurant until I gave up, because on the way over Sheslow beeped him. 'Well,' he said. The deep voice. He shook hands with everyone and then gave me a slap on the back, a broad, thick hand with rock-hard fingers kneading into my trapezius muscle like it was about to tear it off the bone. He sucked in air. 'It's terrific to see you.'

'Yeah?'

'Come with me.'

I wondered if Bob was taking me aside to explain why he'd chosen me as an usher and to give me a Tiffany sterling-silver fountain pen with my initials. I wondered if maybe he was flipping out and needed to talk seriously right now about marrying Niloo. He pulled out a set of keys. The sky was dusky and you could see fireflies.

He said, 'My father-in-law brought some wine in his car. Would you just give me a hand?'

As we looked for the car in an open field beside the patio I reminded Bob we hadn't spoken in months. He tried to remember our last talk. 'I'm at a loss,' he said, smiling. He asked me about work.

I shifted my coat and nothing occurred to me. I shrugged.

'Don't worry.' He laughed, and hit me again; Bob language for trying to be reassuring. 'It'll get better.' For such an unfeeling, pompous dick, he'd often come through with ways to help—calling an editor at the op-ed page of the *Times*, introducing me to a scientist at one of his campaign fund-raisers who later testified for us on the Hill. He'd actually spent hours of his spare time last winter finding a job for one of our interns who wanted to work as a legislative aide. Why?

'Where do you go for your honeymoon?' I asked.

'A tiny island nation near Sri Lanka.' He said he knew the king.

As we got to the trunk of Mr. Niyangoda's black Mercedes I noticed that Bob's sweat stains had spread up to his chest below his chin.

How was *his* work going?

'Fantastic.' This was the most incredible week of his life. He put his finger in my face: 'Sheslow will be the next president of the United States. I have no doubt.' They'd just been tacitly endorsed by this one slob, things were zooming. 'We will make our nation strong and safe, and ethnic violence will be eradicated by prosperity.' He was going on C-SPAN on Monday. His shirt collar pinched his neck just slightly, so an arc of flesh hung from his chin. 'We're bringing slot machines to highway rest stops.'

I said, 'How does C-SPAN decide—'

He grabbed his beeper and called in to work while I listened to the tones of his tiny flip phone, waiting.

No word yet from Gore. 'If he comes tomorrow,' he said, 'I've got the job.'

What about the senator's presidency? I asked.

'Staying where I am would be a lateral move.' He thought more and said, 'In my heart I know he's a freak.'

I said, 'Bob, you're going to the White House.'

He said, 'I can't believe my life!' He was so excited he dropped the keys on the ground trying to open the lock.

In the trunk there were four cases of wine. The cases were made of wood. He said, 'Do you know about *premier cru*?' He gave it his disgusting French accent. He lifted one up and read the name off the box. 'Stuff like this goes right to the collectors,' he said. He slid the case toward me on the lip of the trunk and sighed, grinning widely as the light from the restaurant caught the sheen off his temples, and whispered, 'I feel like a god right now, you know?'—he was having a kind of galaxial moment—as the case began falling between us like some terrible tipped boulder and we both lunged for it, trying to stop it with our knees, and failing, as it slipped down the bumper, and there was a miserable gnashing of sound, the unmistakable sound of glass breaking.

Bob came up with his teeth set across his open mouth. I froze. 'Are you crazy?' he said.

I said, 'You had it.'

'You're such an idiot,' he said. He tore a panel off the top of the crate and very carefully checked each bottle, setting them neatly on the grass. The neck of one was cracked beneath the foil and the top came off when he touched it, gushing wine. 'Convenient twist-off,' he said, staring at me insanely. He poured the rest on the grass in front of me and turned and fired the bottle out of sight. It went through some trees and smashed.

'That's five hundred dollars,' he said. 'It's a lot of money for a guy like you to be wasting.'

I pointed to the red stain on his blazer. I couldn't stop myself.

'Oh no,' he said. 'Look at my—look at my coat!' He held his elbow up in the air and then spotted his shirt cuff, also stained. 'You got my cuff, too!' In fact, I hadn't spilled anything anywhere. My gaze fell to the ground—but there, on his shoes—

'My Cole Haan! You got it on my shoe!' We both reached down at the same time to wipe the wine off his *leche*-colored shoe and banged heads. He stood up, going loony now, gripping his brow, and in the split second in which he appeared to be deciding whether to punch me out or laugh, he suddenly poked me in the head with his nail-hard poking finger and said, 'That's using the old noggin!' He went on, trying to be as lighthearted and fun as possible. 'Your brain,' he said, searching for something clever, 'is like the surface of Mars, a red rocky place where scientists believe there is life'—he kept poking, poke poke—'But there's no life, right?' They had not yet found life on Mars, yes, I had to agree. Then he laughed and shook me as though the whole thing was a joke: 'You almost wasted a case worth six thousand dollars!' I laughed, too. I try to laugh as much as possible.

When I got back to the tent, I spotted Phylida waving a seating card at me. The banquet had been divided into sections named after the countries of antiquity. We were in Flanders. Next over was Gaul, then Mesopotamia.

Phylida's face was flushed deep bluish red, as she gestured toward Sebastian, 'We've been glugging too much.' Sleep deprivation combined with the many substances that swam inside her—she'd self-prescribed medications for everything from dry inner-eyelid lining to mood swings to clenched jaw muscles—along with drinking a gallon of wine made her brain tilt slightly, causing her to combine or invent words. Sebastian held a stricken, catlike pose. Then she left, having been assigned to Bavaria.

Appetizers arrived. Bob's dad gave the first speech, and I felt a funny gurgle down inside me like a warm gastric balloon rising. From that moment on, each time someone stood up, I experienced a slight cramping gut, kind of needing to poop, while assembling and abandoning thoughts for the toast I was about to give; I'd feel in my pocket for the notes I'd made on the plane in case my speech flopped; then the speaker would finish and the balloon would—deflate.

I said to Phylida, 'Can you see a mark on my forehead?' She shrugged, but I felt it; it stung where he'd doinked me as if he was doinking me still.

She said, 'I'm sunburned.' She put her hand on the bare skin above the scooped-out back of her dress and made a red flash burn. Ouch. She'd sat out on the porch at the height of the afternoon with Sebastian, bare-shouldered in her flimsy sundress, while I napped.

Bob's brother made a toast.

A bird flew into the tent and got trapped. It came closer, pounding the air above me. I seemed to be the only one who noticed. My colon felt distended. Dan, the guy with his own private jet, was standing at the microphone, his glass raised. 'They are today's dream, tomorrow's hope.' It sounded like an illiterate campaign speech. But the toast that followed Dan's was worse. I racked my brain to think of something to say to two hundred people. I burped, and it smelled like an egg that had turned rotten.

Suddenly Phylida pulled both shoulders of her dress down and put some ice from the butter dish on her neck. When I asked what was going on she said, 'My wine's completely dranken. Drinken.' She had a selective intelligence. She looked around. 'We need the guy.' I waved at him. Maybe it was simply the release after so much hard work at the hospital. Without the support of the shoulder straps, her tits suddenly shuddered and fell down. 'Hello,' my girlfriend-slash-fiancée-slash-bulb-headed alien then said to the folks across from us. 'I already got a hangover.'

Why was everything starting to suck?

I studied the face of Wayne, Bob's closest longtime buddy, as he carefully picked his way along Bob's first kiss in summer camp, their car accident in drivers' ed, how glad but also sorry he was to see Bob getting hitched.

Bob stood and toasted Niloo, a 'great great person.' She sat looking up at him uncomfortably as he spoke. 'How on earth do you put up with me?'

He had, I now realized, completely accepted his fate: to go through life as a humorless douchebag for whom everything came too easily. He showed no sign of effort, his voice broke, he paced himself. 'This woman,' he said, 'is the love of my life.'

Phylida was now sweating. I said, 'What's wrong with you?'

She said, 'When is this gonna end?' She said she'd slept four hours total since Wednesday (though that didn't count drooling all down her blouse on the airplane) and started telling me about the last patient she'd admitted this morning, a homeless guy. She said there's a certain kind of fungus that only grows on a person's anus, and he had it. It eats skin. She gave me her saintly look of pain.

I said, 'You knew this would be a late night,' and she started to cry. She put her hand up to her throat and took her pulse and put the other hand in the middle of her chest.

She said, 'I'm having an arrhythmic palpitation.' Her kind of aortic problem had been fixed with surgery. This was only a murmur. She started tapping her cheek.

'What are you doing?'

'It's a test for hypocalcemia.'

I said, 'Call a taxi. Just go.' She said she had to wait until I made my toast.

Niles was solemnly reading the exact figures of the landslide election Bob won running for seventh-grade class president from the original newspaper he'd saved when a woman in the seat next to me looked over and sighed. I smiled back—I was next. On the far end of the tent guys were talking very loudly, smoking cigarettes. The gay guys from the hotel balcony pressed by, saying *ciao*. It was almost eleven. Phylida wasn't the only one with her head on the table. People were croaking. We'd all traveled a long way today, flown to this island, and we'd toasted and drunk. The woman introduced herself—she was actually seated in Gaul and had to lean over because of the gap between tables.

I hadn't seen her before. I said, 'You're a friend of Niloo's?' She said no. Her name was Anne. I said, 'How do you know Bob?'

'He's a new friend.'

'What does that mean?'

Leaning toward me caused the front of her dress to fall open; the tops of her tits were tanned and between her white-satin bra cups was a tiny miniature bow the size of a snowflake, and I wondered if some person had tied that bow by hand. 'Actually I work for Gore.'

I said, 'Oh.' She nodded. I said, 'Were you with that group by the hotel this afternoon?'

She said, 'I work on his senior staff in fund-raising.' Across the tent Niles was winding up. My gut bubbled.

'Is Al coming tomorrow?' She didn't know. Her dress was white with black S-shaped vines across the front. A sizeable chunk of her tit came exposed when she moved her arm. In order not to stare I looked down at my hands meditatively, but the glow of her high-cut panties came through the body-hugging front of her dress. I said, 'Are you going to hire Bob?'

She said, 'We think he's amazing.'

People had been saying that all night. I still couldn't figure out what they meant. 'Like what parts, exactly?'

'His intelligence, his loyalty, his experience, his values.' She had the serious determination of a nine-year-old girl burning army ants with a match.

'Yeah?'

'We admire his belief system.'

Belief system? Based on what—liking people with money? The great wines of Burgundy? Gorging himself on chicken tikka masala and then sticking his finger down his throat in the restaurant parking lot and puking between the headlights of my car? The belief system that let him zip money into a certain fund during his last campaign from this other giant account ('A gift, really, from a very dear friend') out of which he paid himself?

'Oh,' I said. 'What belief system?'

Phylida, meanwhile, had woken up. I'm not sure how long she'd been staring at me. My future soul mate-slash-fever blister-slash-sleeping beauty had a string bean imprinted on her cheek. With her giant eyes and her pink face she looked like an unborn squirrel.

I said, 'This is Anne.'

Phylida said, 'Did you enjoy looking down her dress?'

People cheered. Niles was done.

I took forever pushing between chairs to get to the spot with the mike. My legs felt like two thick rusty chains. I tested the microphone. There was suddenly an audience, staring.

I took out the note in my pocket and silently read it. The night Bob phoned, in tears, about leading the polls. Hmm. I paused solemnly. Bob rose up in his chair and keyed in on me. He had that stupid set to his eyes and mouth—picture Donald Trump—of always waiting to be looked at. I gazed over the crowd. What I was going to say? 'Well.' The skin of my face felt like it had been stretched on a coat hanger in front of an oven that was my head. The next line on the piece of paper said, 'Story about landlady.' I thought for a second. It was something about a pizza box catching fire on the stove.

I cleared my throat. My legs: heavy. My face: hot. I thought of FDR, the late-afternoon stiffness in his joints, the onset of polio. I sputtered. 'You've had a lot of jobs, Bob.' I really should've read this over on the plane.

'Quite a few.' I couldn't speak. 'Big jobs.' There's no funny or clever metaphor for what I was failing to do up there. I had lost my air of assumed normalness. I should've figured I'd flip out and written down every word. I was dying. I wanted to sit. I gritted my teeth and clenched my ass up and tried to go forward. 'You're smart.' I couldn't breathe. 'Very smart.' My small lungs shot puffs of white gas—performance anxiety. 'An incredible guy.' The people closest to me looked as if an asteroid was coming over my shoulder and about to crush them.

'Unfortunately, I'm blanking on some of your successes.' A couple of the smokers were laughing at me. Well, wouldn't you? 'I'm sure they'll come to me in a moment.' I reached down and quietly drank an entire glass of water. 'Why couldn't I have been at some loser's wedding now?' I said, to myself, out loud, into the microphone. 'I wouldn't have to remember so much.' Bob's head looked like a fire engine, his nostrils flaring, and his glare made the noise of a fire engine horn. Niloo was grinning. 'Can't you stop and give somebody else a chance, for Christ's sake?' I put the water down and gripped the mike stand. I'm going to faint, I thought. No. I'm going to explode from my bowels. And then I'll faint.

It began as a queasy chuckle or two, and then the entire room erupted in a wave of laughter. In fact they'd been laughing for a while. All night everyone had been dying just to crack a smile—the natural tendency is to want to laugh at events like this—but no one had given them a chance. Now they had me: the buffoon. I pulled the mike from the stand and reached up to wipe the sweat off my face and they laughed at that too, the most uproarious laugh so far. What the hell?

'Anyway, standing up here talking to you,' I said, feeling more confident suddenly, 'is actually the most time we've spent together in a year and a half, you big pain in the ass.' They roared like a beer-hall crowd as Bob watched me, and I found myself remembering him working his cell phone earlier in the night, and pictured shoving it down his throat with a toilet plunger. The smokers had joined in, they were yelling at Bob now, mocking me; one called him a pain in the ass. I stepped forward, trying to keep the momentum with me, and said, 'After Bob moves to the Oval Office,' pointing to them, 'he'll send you guys some interns.' More yuks, far out of proportion to the dopiness of the joke. I raised my right hand and in a lame Clinton drawl said, 'I, Bob, solemnly swear to set aside interns who can suck a bowling ball through a Krazy Straw for my dearest former roommate.' They yelled. Niloo had leaned into Bob's shoulder, she had her hand over her mouth, her face was twisted frozen as she cracked up. I made one of those fists politicians use when they're trying to be emphatic. Niloo couldn't control herself. I said, 'Is this funny to you, Niloo? Do you know what you're in for?' Her face was crimped and she was sort of nodding. 'Can I give you some advice?' I paused—why had I been screaming?—and continued, quietly this time. 'Stand up and start running and never look back.'

I began shaking my head cornily. 'You're a nice person, Niloo. It's such a shame.' More hilarity, a monsoon. 'But if you're going to live your life together'—I started doing a bad televangelist Southern idiot—'you must never stand directly in front of him after he has eaten a large meal. It's very dangerous. And do not worry your pretty self about his latest diet, O.K.?' I made a puking, retching motion. 'Don't be surprised if he sticks his finger down his throat and throws up all over your car.' I took a breath and pointed at him. 'I don't know if anybody told you, Bob, vomiting and diarrhea are not the best answer to weight gain.' I was on autopilot. 'Try Richard Simmons's *Sweatin' to the Oldies*.' I did a little dance move. People were really letting go now; one guy slipped out of his chair and a waiter had to dodge him. Bob was staring at me, immobile, his large mind turning.

Bob wasn't going to be introducing me to Al Gore tomorrow.

Over in Flanders, Phylida bent over suddenly and the people seated by her jumped backward out of their chairs. Phylida, I realized, had either just thrown up or had knocked something over or had fallen comatose onto the ground. That's my woman. I was marrying Drankenstein. I was the bride of Drankenstein. What a wonderful couple we'd make. How fun we were at a party. What a future we had. Phylida reared her head after a moment, eyeballs rolling high into her forehead, with her sweaty brown-rooted old hair plastered against it, and I imagined my being up here again—next year? the summer after?—toasting her at our own wedding, and I thought: I might as well kill myself. 'Bob,' I said, and waited for his expression to change. No change. He was looking at me like I was a stain on your carpet that you scrubbed and it got worse. Ah, what the hell. I raised my empty glass and the place got silent. 'How come you never call me back anymore, you fat, pusillanimous, popcorn-eating, obsequious, spermy, whoring, curry-barfing ass licker?'

Had I gone too far?

'That,' Phylida said, looking up at me when I returned to the table, her face gaunt and sculpted, 'was a disaster.'

I said, 'We can go now.' The party started breaking up then. We stood and got ready to leave.

Anne opened her mouth wide and laughed when our eyes met. 'That was quite a testimonial,' she said. 'What else do you know about Bob?' I felt a haze, like mucus, covering my eyes. I watched her as she stood and moved closer, clearly excited.

'What else do I know?'

She had one of those high waists with hips that were just a bit too wide so her dress sat up there like a slipcover hanging on a sofa pillow. 'Tell us something really juicy.' I thought I'd said enough.

Back at the hotel, Phylida pulled her dress up over her head and threw it in the corner under the desk, kicked her shoes off, pulled down her nylons, and sat on the edge of the bed in her underwear, groaning. Even hunched over like that, there wasn't a blip of fat on her. She put on her spaghetti-strap camisole. I stared at her long torso, her strong shoulders, her long neck. She looked like she was made out of rubber. I waited for her to look at me. 'Are you gonna go right to sleep?' I said.

I was trying to be nice, trying not to want her. The night's debacle had left me charged. Why was her arm skin so soft? We were here together in this perfect glimpse of unreal time in a fancy hotel, and I wanted to keep it that way. I looked at her and she yawned, which made her shiver so her tits shuddered. 'I'm going to bed.' She was so beautiful our whole life threatened to devolve into my headless worship of her hot beauty. My dick, of course, was hard. Not like that egg-yolk dick from earlier today. It now lay in my pants like a stunned fish. I loved her so much I couldn't think. I loved her because I was horny. I was horny because I was sad, because the night had been awful, because it was almost over. I thought back to that shocked look on Bob's face during my toast, the crowd laughing all around him.

'I thought we might go down to the beach,' I said. She looked in her makeup bag and got out some pills. She threw them down dry and pulled out her sleep mask from her makeup bag. She shook the strap out.

'I love you,' I said. I asked her if she wanted to take her top off. She put the mask on her head. The sound of my voice was deep and nasal, the way it had been when it carried across the crowd, amplified, when it shook the crowd.

'O.K.,' she said. She pulled my hand off her arm. 'Don't touch me.'

'That's it?'

'You're wired about your toast. You feel like you put one over on Bob, don't ask me why.' She lay back on top of the bedspread and pulled her eye mask down. Her panties were whisper-weight, see-through orange lace. I put my nose next to her foot and sniffed it. I pictured giving it to her as she bit me and seizured and sobbed, loving it. I felt so released after all that worrying—so overjoyed. I pictured ramming that wine bottle up Bob's ass, breaking off the shattered stem while he's whooping and screaming. I pictured Richard Nixon getting shot, red wine splashing, trying to hold the lapels of his suit closed as he fell. I saw Bill Clinton, floating in space, docking headfirst into the space station. She lifted the edge of her mask and looked at me for a long moment with one eye. 'If you want to do it,' she said, 'go ahead.'

I thought for a second. Something about it seemed wrong. 'Forget it.' She pulled the mask back down and moved her nose once and was gone.

I found Sebastian out on her wicker loveseat. I climbed over the partition and sat next to her. The smell of her in the moonlight. I smelled pee; late-night sour wine breath? I don't know, something bitter—mixed with sweat. She was smoking a cigarette and said she came a long way not to talk to anybody the whole night. She said Niloo's other college friends had been seated together, away from her. 'They see each other anyway because they all live in Boston.' She had an elbow on her knee with the cigarette in that hand; it looked like she'd done this position most nights. She said the trip cost her a thousand dollars. Her lips jutted out stiffly when she tried to smoke. It wasn't just the pee-pee smell that made talking to her so tricky. She was unsure and furious about the whole world around her. (On top of everything else, in my haste to get Phylida back to our room, we'd ditched Sebastian and I didn't know how she'd gotten back.) I wanted to say to her, 'What did you expect?' She looked at me, shaking her head with her mouth open, and ran out of gas. She tried again, 'Do you think she intended for me not to come?' A steady drip fell from the balcony above us, from a wet bathing suit. I said no. The moonlight caught her eyelashes and from here she looked like a lonesome, long-nosed, greasy teenage boy. There was so little moonlight I couldn't figure out what her face was doing. I said, 'You don't have to invite her to yours.'

Her arm that had been propped on her knee fell into her her lap, and her head went to that angle the librarian's would go to when I stopped at the med school and asked if she'd seen Phylida. She said, 'Invite her to my what?'

'What?'

She said, 'You're so fucking lucky you got somebody else. You're so lucky.' She was waiting to take another puff.

What did I have to say about that?

Phylida lay on her side on the bedspread in her underwear, the table lamp on beside her. I saw her lips moving as her eyebrows jumped under her eye mask. I saw that damned chin hair still, some soft lines on her throat; her long neck, her strong round shoulder knob, the line down to her hollow waist, the bump up over her hip that's so unbelievably beautiful it proves God's a perverted ass freak. I kissed her bare white inner forearm again and again, I heard the click of my lips against her skin. Loving anybody is different from impaling anybody or getting something to own and have. It's like trying to hug your favorite painting, or talk to or waltz with the perfect time of day, the memory of the most beautiful tree you ever saw.

I slep hard and woke up in such blackness. I didn't know where I was; a hotel room is like the bottom of a well. The air conditioner had come on during the night and the air felt parched and dead. I tripped on the suitcase, pissed dizzily, stood on the carpet behind the drape looking out the window at a silver ocean and a steel-colored beach, coal-colored sky. I lay back down, wide awake. For the next hour or two I had the sudden profound feeling of remembering Bob, out of nowhere, completely. This random onslaught of memories: Bob in his bathrobe, imitating Queen Elizabeth; moving through the supermarket, spent, in slow motion, his enormous hard-soled shoes slapping the shiny floor; a lame nothing good-bye when I volunteered to drive him to the airport for a six-month trip down south; the sight of his retarded handwriting on a scrap in the kitchen we shared. Ironing his pants in the morning, trying to get the crotch flat. He went through an entire can of spray starch just to make me laugh. I started laughing to myself there again, years after the fact, amazed at how Phylida could sleep and at the same time sigh so loudly there beside me.

It was light out. Phylida was shoving the bed, talking.

'Did you know Ally Sheedy has a house on this island?' The doors had been thrown open and the room was filling with ocean air, the lace canopy thing above me blowing, lit with sunshine. All the humidity that had been in the air yesterday was gone. You could feel the lightness of the air. I looked out the window and saw clear to the horizon. Phylida kept talking. She'd walked around the town. She bought this hat. She just ate breakfast, and charged it to the room. She had square sunglasses under the hat on her small square nose, soft fat morning lips. Her thighs were firm, smooth vanilla hanging out of the untied white bathrobe. Underneath the robe she had her blue-flowered stretchy bikini. I saw her belly button, the giant freckle on her hip.

She took off the sunglasses to reveal two bloodshot eyes, maroon bags beneath them that reminded me of nothing so much as testicles, and said, 'I don't think I slept last night.'

The beginning of the end.

'I kept thinking someone was going to come into the room and kill us.'

Phylida was falling apart. She was one rotation away from a seventy-two-hour-long crying jag. When these cycles ended we were both a mess, and she was always a little more nuts, a little less reachable, than when they began.

'I kept hearing people on the beach.'

'You thought they wanted to kill you?'

'I thought they wanted to kill you for that speech you made last night.' She was about to cry. 'I'm scared I'll never be able to sleep again.'

'You will.' I loved her, even more when she was going crazy. Now what? We had big problems. I, on the one hand, couldn't live on a wage from a bankrupt think tank. She, on the other hand, had messed her sleep rhythm up irrevocably. A surgical resident who can't sleep on command won't make it.

She said, 'Are you mad at me because of last night?'

'I didn't say a thing.'

'Because I didn't let you screw me?'

'Phylida, what good is any of it?'

I looked at the clock. I said I had to be at the country club two hours before her, for photos for the wedding party.

She said, 'I just think we should have separate beds at home so we can sleep.'

'Do what?'

Phylida shoved a towel from the bathroom into her knapsack. 'Your ugly girlfriend was down there at breakfast. She asked about you.' I sat up. She meant Anne, and then I remembered talking to her at dinner as she wondered if she could get more dirt from me on Bob.

'The only reason she talked to me was because I know Bob.'

'Come get me on the beach before you leave. I don't want to fry.'

I'm running toward the bathroom, tripping out of my underwear, smelling my armpits. I put on shorts and am down at the restaurant in forty seconds. A gray wooden porch overlooking a field leading down to a marsh. Anne sat alone, drinking juice. Her coffee looked cold and bitter. She had very thin arms that she raised up, hostagelike, because I was standing above her in the sun. Her voice was all gravelly. She kept clearing her throat. 'You have the nerve to show your face in public after last night?' She laughed. Yuk yuk. I acted surprised that she recognized me. She did have an abrupt set of gaping nostrils that were a little hard to look at. 'Did you get all the information you needed?'

'Oh.' She laughed and gestured at the other chair. 'I didn't come here for that.' Anyway, she said, Bob had a superb network of friends, and they'd all been saying wonderful things. She waved her hand as though, there beside her, was the network: twenty-five-year-old World Bank vice presidents, *New York Times* bureau chiefs, hedge-fund stock pickers, rich fucks who had been campaigning since they were five years old and got everything on a silver platter, lived in unbelievable apartments with wide doorways and African carpets, and took turns powdering each other's bungholes. She said he was up for a job that was tremendously important for the Democratic party. 'We're in a formula-one race. We've got to keep the distance between us and the guy behind us.' She spoke as if she were reading the directions off a box of cake mix. She said Bob could make the difference. 'He's brilliant.'

'Keep saying that and it'll come true.'

'You're obsessed with him.'

I thought back to when Bob worked at INS, Immigration and Naturalization, at Justice, how he had whole families, Rwandans who were here seeking asylum, removed from the homes where relief agencies had put them, shipped back to Africa for sure death. I asked if she knew why the U.S. stood by and watched the Hutus slaughter a million defenseless women and children with machetes.

She asked what I had against him. I said, nothing. She asked what I did for a living. 'I'm a midlevel analyst at a nongovernmental research institute whose aim is to demilitarize the Western conglomerates.' When I told her where, she'd never heard of it. 'It's nothing. We're not important.' She nodded.

I said, 'When does a person stop doing what they're doing because they believe in it, and start doing it for some other cockamamie reason?'

She said, 'I think it happens when you turn thirty.'

It was a sunny day, Bob's special day. A breeze flicked across the tables, boats sailed silently by. I said whatever came to my head. I told her Bob and I used to work at the Boys Club on weekends, volunteering; he quit doing that. He spent his free weekends collecting antique garbage, statues, fake Louis XIV chairs, that's why he carried all that debt on his credit cards. She nodded slowly. The last time I ran into him downtown, he stood looking at me—a pin glowed on his lapel I'd never seen before. He put out his hand but couldn't come up with my name for his friends. What a piece of shit. Why did I remember everything about him? The look on his face walking past me, at his uncle's funeral; the way he jogged, chest high, when he first got fat; the smell of the apartment he moved into with Niloo, when nothing inside it belonged to him—the couches, the fringed ottoman—and he didn't care, he didn't feel guilty, and didn't treat any of it with respect. Everything seemed to belong to Bob. Everything seemed like a joke. Anne began looking in her purse. She didn't care about what I remembered about Bob.

She said, 'I once sat in the Democratic National Committee headquarters and watched Bob raise a quarter of a million dollars in forty-five minutes. He had people calling back from airplanes, from the golf course, from Australia—$10,000, $25,000, $40,000. Whatever he asked.' She was glowing, her hair had come down and swept around her face suddenly and she shook her head and her nostrils filled. 'It was beautiful,' she said. I said nothing.

'Can you think of any possible way he'd embarrass the vice president? Drinking and driving? Smoking marijuana?' She was absolutely serious. I said no. This *was* serious—I couldn't think of any other word for it—it was soul murder. 'Soul murder,' I said, half audible. She blinked for a second. 'Has he ever said anything derogatory or off-color about the president or Mrs. Clinton, or the vice president or Mrs. Gore?'

'He thinks Tipper's got a fat ass.'

'He's very loyal.'

'Don't ask me.'

'You could learn a few things about loyalty from him.'

'I'm sure.'

'If he's bulimic—most bulimic people I know are thin.'

'Yeah, well.'

'The FBI did a background check. His credit-card debt is all paid off.'

Anne got up. It was a quarter to eleven. I ordered a beer. It was his wedding day, after all. I had to be at the country club at eleven-thirty. I drank it in one gulp and ordered another and barely touched it. I didn't see her again till later. I sat there for a minute and thought.

Dan, the rich guy, came toward me. I thought he wanted to shake hands. He simply pointed. 'I can't believe you're here.' Eyes narrowing, he moved away. Like many of the men in the wedding party, he wore a tuxedo that was a kind of custom job. Everyone else ignored me. We were waiting. Bob stood in his asinine four-button European tux with his hair greased back, shredding the lid of a coffee cup with his teeth. Niles and Wayne were staying in a rented house on the other side of the island, and they were late.

'Why do all my friends hate me?' Bob said. This was a last vestige of his powerful charm, these moments of lucidity. 'And people say I'm selfish.'

They arrived and we pinned our flowers on and pictures were taken as we cooked in the sun in our tuxes. I overheard Bob saying that the senator was here and Madeleine Albright had arrived last night with Justice Ginsburg and that certain parts of the lawn would be secured for a landing area by Secret Service in case the weather held. But the predicted weather—terrible fog by three o'clock, scaled back from rain—would make a helicopter visit impossible. Bob sounded relieved—he was selling us on the fog, embracing the weather so something larger than himself could take the fall. 'It comes in off the ocean, it looks just like smoke.' Later he stood in the kitchen while I drank some ice water. 'The island is transformed,' he told Niles, who nodded stupidly. 'All you hear is the foghorn blowing.'

Bob left to change his sweat-stained shirt. Niloo told me he'd been up since five, calling everybody he knew connected to Gore. 'I told him he'd better relax and forget about this business or he'd miss his whole day. He'd miss everything for what?' Her eyebrows bore down heavily and crossed. She had beautiful cinnamon-colored skin. Her eye shadow was bluish silver, and her mouth was dark cranberry red. 'He just gets nuts!' I could see her thinking; the years lay before her and she saw the loneliness and wasted effort in a flash and erased it all, and I saw her chest fall. She looked worried. I said, 'I'm sure he knows you're right.' Maybe I was seeing things, but there appeared to be a tiny pink mark in the center of her forehead, a flushed circle of irritated skin, with a crescent-shaped indentation inside it. Her mother came up and asked if she was ready, and they looked at each other, all perturbed. 'Well,' Niloo said. It might've been a scar from before.

The grounds of the country club were on a promontory, many acres jutting out into the water, with immense visibility of the western half of the island. It was a clear, crisp day. As people began to arrive you could see Bob looking up and down the coast.

Phylida was walking funny in that long dress. I could see from this distance how red she was, sunburned. 'I fell asleep on the beach,' she said. I had forgotten to come back to get her. Up close her face held patches of rouge. She said, 'I wish I was dead.' I started to apologize. She said, 'This isn't your fault.' She didn't actually remember applying sunblock. She said, 'It hurts to have these clothes on.' She was in bad shape. I asked if she wanted to have a seat. She said, 'I can't bend.' I asked how she got here. She made a motion to indicate she'd been lying down in the taxi. 'I hate myself so much.'

I said, 'It's O.K.' We backed into the shade and stood there, and she looked at me and whispered something. There were tears in her eyes.

'I can't believe I did this,' she said. I wanted to hold her. 'I'm responsible,' I said. 'I'll never leave you again.' I told her I loved her, and I kissed the ends of her fingers because I didn't want to harm her burns. I ignored people who wanted to be seated, I let the other guys do it, and then we watched the ceremony standing. We couldn't hear any of it because the wind was blowing. She switched her weight from one foot to the other. Even her ankle was white skin striped with bright red. Afterward waiters came through with hors d'oeuvres and champagne. 'Should I drink?' she said. When she'd arrived her face was flushed. Now it was pale and sweaty.

A helicopter, just a speck at first, came chopping along toward us—you could barely hear it over the surf until it was upon us. I guess the trained eye could tell from way off, this was not the vice president's official green-and-white airship. Then it hovered, knocking in the air above us, and Bob stood staring up, standing by his mom and dad, sun blazing in his copper-bristled hair.

'Paparazzi?' he said.

No. It was just some guy having a closer look at our festivities before flying away.

Phylida didn't last much longer. She asked me to take her back to the hotel. We stopped at a pharmacy and she loaded up on drugs and popped them, got some cortisone lotion, and I helped her out of those clothes and under some cool wet towels. Sometime between spreading the lotion all over her body and taking off all my clothes and trying to lie on top of her, I was overcome by her frail beauty, and my mind raced through her troubled world, anything I could think of to help restore her: I said, 'I'll move the bed for you, I'll find black shades, I'll buy that sound machine that mimics the rhythm of a mother's heart.' I tried to think of a way she wouldn't be disturbed when I got dressed in the morning. She said, 'Thank you. You're sweet.'

I kissed every part of her. I realized that she was exactly what I wanted in a woman: sparkling eyes, springy hindquarters, the ability to save her own life. I felt for her then what I feel now, and knew without thinking anymore that we'd made it. Her nude hip, the most elegant line on earth, was staring me in the face. I touched her unburned parts and she smiled. We struggled to find a way I could hold her, and then suddenly it seemed we both were breathing harder.

I was unclothed and her skin burned against my unclothed body. She turned onto her stomach—I was above her, as careful as I could be—we found this to be the only angle. With her burns and loveliness and all, she pulled me in. I felt like a giant fishhook and I had her on the line and we were both rocking. I was like the Fonz with my dick right then. I tried not to touch anything except her peachy, scrumptious pillowy ass, but we were grinding and eventually I knew I was rubbing against the burned spots. She'd gotten ridden down into the bedspread and it must've felt like sandpaper against her burns but she said nothing, making sweet painful noises and laying low and going with it; she fought me while yielding.

Afterward we ate the apples we'd brought for the plane. We found a movie on TV about a princess riding a motorcycle. As the afternoon passed I knew then that I was missing this great event, with no way of predicting who might've flown in by now. Bibi Netanyahu? Marlon Brando riding a llama? I didn't feel like I should be at one place or the other. It didn't feel like a lateral move. It felt good. We ordered crab sandwiches from town and had them delivered to the room. Sebastian returned with cake on a platter. We had a party.

THE TOUGHEST INDIAN IN THE WORLD

Sherman Alexie

Being a Spokane Indian, I only pick up Indian hitchhikers.

I learned this particular ceremony from my father, a Coeur d'Alene, who always stopped for those twentieth-century aboriginal nomads who refused to believe the salmon were gone. I don't know what they believed in exactly, but they wore hope like a bright shirt.

My father never taught me about hope. Instead, he continually told me that our salmon—our hope—would never come back, and though such lessons may seem cruel, I know enough to cover my heart in any crowd of white people.

'They'll kill you if they get the chance,' my father said. 'Love you or hate you, white people will shoot you in the heart. Even after all these years, they'll still smell the salmon on you, the dead salmon, and that will make white people dangerous.'

All of us, Indian and white, are haunted by salmon.

When I was a boy, I leaned over the edge of one dam or another—perhaps Long Lake or Little Falls or the great gray dragon known as the Grand Coulee—and watched the ghosts of the salmon rise from the water to the sky and become constellations.

For most Indians, stars are nothing more than white tombstones scattered across a dark graveyard.

But the Indian hitchhikers my father picked up refused to admit the existence of sky, let alone the possibility that salmon might be stars. They were common people who believed only in the thumb and the foot. My father envied those simple Indian hitchhikers. He wanted to change their minds about salmon; he wanted to break open their hearts and see the future in their blood. He loved them.

In 1975 or '76 or '77, driving along one highway or another, my father would point out a hitchhiker standing beside the road a mile or two in the distance.

'Indian,' he said if it was an Indian, and he was never wrong, though I could never tell if the distant figure was male or female, let alone Indian or not.

If a distant figure happened to be white, my father would drive by without comment.

That was how I learned to be silent in the presence of white people.

The silence is not about hate or pain or fear. Indians just like to believe that white people will vanish, perhaps explode into smoke, if they are ignored enough times. Perhaps a thousand white families are still waiting for their sons and daughters to return home, and can't recognize them when they float back as morning fog.

'We better stop,' my mother said from the passenger seat. She was one of those Spokane women who always wore a purple bandanna tied tightly around her head.

These days, her bandanna is usually red. There are reasons, motives, traditions behind the choice of color, but my mother keeps them secret.

'Make room,' my father said to my siblings and me as we sat on the floor in the cavernous passenger area of our blue van. We sat on carpet samples because my father had torn out the seats in a sober rage not long after he bought the van from a crazy white man.

I have three brothers and three sisters now. Back then, I had four of each. I missed one of the funerals and cried myself sick during the other one.

'Make room,' my father said again—he said everything twice—and only then did we scramble to make space for the Indian hitchhiker.

Of course, it was easy enough to make room for one hitchhiker, but Indians usually travel in packs. Once or twice, we picked up entire all-Indian basketball teams, along with their coaches, girlfriends, and cousins. Fifteen, twenty Indian strangers squeezed into the back of a blue van with nine wide-eyed Indian kids.

Back in those days, I loved the smell of Indians, and of Indian hitchhikers in particular. They were usually in some stage of drunkenness, often in need of soap and a towel, and always ready to sing.

Oh, the songs! Indian blues bellowed at the highest volumes. We called them '49s,' those cross-cultural songs that combined Indian lyrics and rhythms with country-and-western and blues melodies. It seemed that every Indian knew all the lyrics to every Hank Williams song ever recorded. Hank was our Jesus, Patsy Cline was our Virgin

Mary, and Freddy Fender, George Jones, Conway Twitty, Loretta Lynn, Tammy Wynette, Charley Pride, Ronnie Milsap, Tanya Tucker, Marty Robbins, Johnny Horton, Donna Fargo, and Charlie Rich were our disciples.

We all know that nostalgia is dangerous, but I remember those days with a clear conscience. Of course, we live in different days now, and there aren't as many Indian hitchhikers as there used to be.

Now, I drive my own car, a 1998 Toyota Camry, the best-selling automobile in the United States, and therefore the one most often stolen. *Consumer Reports* has named it the most reliable family sedan for sixteen years running, and I believe it.

In my Camry, I pick up three or four Indian hitchhikers a week. Mostly men. They're usually headed home, back to their reservations or somewhere close to their reservations. Indians hardly ever travel in a straight line, so a Crow Indian might hitchhike west when his reservation is back east in Montana. He has some people to see in Seattle, he might explain if I ever asked him. But I never ask Indians their reasons for hitchhiking. All that matters is this: They are Indians walking, raising their thumbs, and I am there to pick them up.

At the newspaper where I work, my fellow reporters think I'm crazy to pick up hitchhikers. They're all white and never stop to pick up anybody, let alone an Indian. After all, we're the ones who write the stories and headlines: HITCHHIKER KILLS HUSBAND AND WIFE, MISSING GIRL'S BODY FOUND, RAPIST STRIKES AGAIN. If I really tried, maybe I could explain to them why I pick up any Indian, but who wants to try? Instead, if they ask I just give them a smile and turn back to my computer. My coworkers smile back and laugh loudly. They're always laughing loudly at me, at one another, at themselves, at goofy typos in the newspapers, at the idea of hitchhikers.

I dated one of them for a few months. Cindy. She covered the local courts: speeding tickets and divorces, drunk driving and embezzlement. Cindy firmly believed in the who-what-where-when-why-and-how of journalism. In daily conversation, she talked like she was writing the lead of her latest story. Hell, she talked like that in bed.

'How does that feel?' I asked, quite possibly the only Indian man who has ever asked that question.

'I love it when you touch me there,' she answered. 'But it would help if you rubbed it about thirty percent lighter and with your thumb instead of your middle finger. And could you maybe turn the radio to a different station? KYZY would be good. I feel like soft jazz will work better for me right now. A minor chord, a C or G-flat, or something like that. Okay, honey?'

During lovemaking, I would get so exhausted by the size of her erotic vocabulary that I would fall asleep before my orgasm, continue pumping away as if I were awake, and then regain consciousness with a sudden start when I finally did come, more out of reflex than passion.

Don't get me wrong. Cindy is a good one, cute and smart, funny as hell, a good catch no matter how you define it, but she was also one of those white women who date only brown-skinned guys. Indians like me, black dudes, Mexicans, even a few Iranians. I started to feel like a trophy, or like one of those entries in a personal ad. I asked Cindy why she never dated pale boys.

'White guys bore me,' she said. 'All they want to talk about is their fathers.'

'What do brown guys talk about?' I asked her.

'Their mothers,' she said and laughed, then promptly left me for a public defender who was half Japanese and half African, a combination that left Cindy dizzy with the interracial possibilities.

Since Cindy, I haven't dated anyone. I live in my studio apartment with the ghosts of two dogs, Felix and Oscar, and a laptop computer stuffed with bad poems, the aborted halves of three novels, and some three-paragraph personality pieces I wrote for the newspaper.

I'm a features writer, and an Indian at that, so I get all the shit jobs. Not the dangerous shit jobs or the monotonous shit jobs. No. I get to write the articles designed to please the eye, ear, and heart. And there is no journalism more soul-endangering to write than journalism that aims to please.

So it was with reluctance that I climbed into my car last week and headed down Highway 2 to write some damn pleasant story about some damn pleasant people. Then I saw the Indian hitchhiker standing beside the road. He looked the way Indian hitchhikers usually look. Long, straggly black hair. Brown eyes and skin. Missing a couple of teeth. A bad complexion that used to be much worse. Crooked nose that had been broken more than once. Big, misshapen ears. A few whiskers masquerading as a mustache. Even before he climbed into my car I could tell he was tough. He had some serious muscles that threatened to rip through his blue jeans and denim jacket. When he was in the car, I could see his hands up close, and they told his whole story. His fingers were twisted into weird, permanent shapes, and his knuckles were covered with layers of scar tissue.

'Jeez,' I said. 'You're a fighter, enit?'

I threw in the 'enit,' a reservation colloquialism, because I wanted the fighter to know that I had grown up on the rez, in the woods, with every Indian in the world.

The hitchhiker looked down at his hands, flexed them into fists. I could tell it hurt him to do that.

'Yeah,' he said. 'I'm a fighter.'

I pulled back onto the highway, looking over my shoulder to check my blind spot.

'What tribe are you?' I asked him, inverting the last two words in order to sound as aboriginal as possible.

'Lummi,' he said. 'What about you?'

'Spokane.'

'I know some Spokanes. Haven't seen them in a long time.'

He clutched his backpack in his lap like he didn't want to let it go for anything. He reached inside a pocket and pulled out a piece of deer jerky. I recognized it by the smell.

'Want some?' he asked.

'Sure.'

It had been a long time since I'd eaten jerky. The salt, the gamy taste. I felt as Indian as Indian gets, driving down the road in a fast car, chewing on jerky, talking to an indigenous fighter.

'Where you headed?' I asked.

'Home. Back to the rez.'

I nodded my head as I passed a big truck. The driver gave us a smile as we went by. I tooted the horn.

'Big truck,' said the fighter.

I haven't lived on my reservation for twelve years. But I live in Spokane, which is only an hour's drive from the rez. Still, I hardly ever go home. I don't know why not. I don't think about it much, I guess, but my mom and dad still live in the same house where I grew up. My brothers and sisters, too. The ghosts of my two dead siblings share an apartment in the converted high school. It's just a local call from Spokane to the rez, so I talk to all of them once or twice a week. Smoke signals courtesy of U.S. West Communications. Sometimes they call me up to talk about the stories they've seen that I've written for the newspaper. Pet pigs and support groups and science fairs. Once in a while, I used to fill in for the obituaries writer when she was sick. Then she died, and I had to write her obituary.

'How far are you going?' asked the fighter, meaning how much closer was he going to get to his reservation than he was now.

'Up to Wenatchee,' I said. 'I've got some people to interview there.'

'Interview? What for?'

'I'm a reporter. I work for the newspaper.'

'No,' said the fighter, looking at me like I was stupid for thinking he was stupid. 'I mean, what's the story about?'

'Oh, not much. There's two sets of twins who work for the fire department. Human-interest stuff, you know?'

'Two sets of twins, enit? That's weird.'

He offered me more deer jerky, but I was too thirsty from the salty meat, so l offered him a Pepsi instead.

'Don't mind if I do,' he said.

'They're in a cooler on the backseat,' I said. 'Grab me one, too.'

He maneuvered his backpack carefully and found room enough to reach into the backseat for the soda pop. He opened my can first and handed it to me. A friendly gesture for a stranger. I took a big mouthful and hiccupped loudly.

'That always happens to me when I drink cold things,' he said.

We sipped slowly after that. I kept my eyes on the road while he stared out the window into the wheat fields. We were quiet for many miles.

'Who do you fight?' I asked as we passed through another anonymous small town.

'Mostly Indians,' he said. 'Money fights, you know? I go from rez to rez, fighting the best they have. Winner takes all.'

'Jeez, I never heard of that.'

'Yeah, I guess it's illegal.'

He rubbed his hands together. I could see fresh wounds.

'Man,' I said. 'Those fights must be rough.'

The fighter stared out the window. I watched him for a little too long and almost drove off the road. Car horns sounded all around us.

'Jeez,' the fighter said. 'Close one, enit?'

'Close enough,' I said.

He hugged his backpack more tightly, using it as a barrier between his chest and the dashboard. An Indian hitchhiker's version of a passenger-side air bag.

'Who'd you fight last?' I asked, trying to concentrate on the road.

'Some Flathead,' he said. 'In Arlee. He was supposed to be the toughest Indian in the world.'

'Was he?'

'Nah, no way. Wasn't even close. Wasn't even tougher than me.'

He told me how big the Flathead kid was, way over six feet tall and two hundred and some pounds. Big buck Indian. Had hands as big as this and arms as big as that. Had a chin like a damn buffalo. The fighter told me that he hit the Flathead kid harder than he ever hit anybody before.

'I hit him like he was a white man,' the fighter said. 'I hit him like he was two or three white men rolled into one.'

But the Flathead kid would not go down, even though his face swelled up so bad that he looked like the Elephant Man. There were no referees, no judge, no bells to signal the end of the round. The winner was the Indian still standing. Punch after punch, man, and the kid would not go down.

'I was so tired after a while,' said the fighter, 'that I just took a step back and watched the kid. He stood there with his arms down, swaying from side to side like some toy, you know? Head bobbing on his neck like there was no bone at all. You couldn't even see his eyes no more. He was all messed up.'

'What'd you do?' I asked.

'Ah, hell, I couldn't fight him no more. That kid was planning to die before he ever went down. So I just sat on the ground while they counted me out. Dumb Flathead kid didn't even know what was happening. I just sat on the ground while they raised his hand. While all the winners collected their money and all the losers cussed me out. I just sat there, man.'

'Jeez,' I said. 'What happened next?'

'Not much. I sat there until everybody was gone. Then I stood up and decided to head for home. I'm tired of this shit. I just want to go home for a while. I got enough money to last me a long time. I'm a rich Indian, you hear? I'm a rich Indian.'

The fighter finished his Pepsi, rolled down his window, and pitched the can out. I almost protested, but decided against it. I kept my empty can wedged between my legs.

'That's a hell of a story,' I said.

'Ain't no story,' he said. 'It's what happened.'

'Jeez,' I said. 'You would've been a warrior in the old days, enit? You would've been a killer. You would have stolen everybody's goddamn horses. That would've been you. You would've been it.'

I was excited. I wanted the fighter to know how much I thought of him. He didn't even look at me.

'A killer,' he said. 'Sure.'

We didn't talk much after that. I pulled into Wenatchee just before sundown, and the fighter seemed happy to be leaving me.

'Thanks for the ride, cousin,' he said as he climbed out. Indians always call each other cousin, especially if they're strangers.

'Wait,' I said.

He looked at me, waiting impatiently.

I wanted to know if he had a place to sleep that night. It was supposed to get cold. There was a mountain range between Wenatchee and his reservation. Big mountains that were dormant volcanoes, but that could all blow up at any time. We wrote about it once in the newspaper. Things can change so quickly. So many emergencies and disasters that we can barely keep track. I wanted to tell him how much I cared about my job, even if I had to write about small-town firemen. I wanted to tell the fighter that I pick up all Indian hitchhikers, young and old, men and women, and get them a little closer to home, even if l can't get them all the way. I wanted to tell him that the night sky was a graveyard. I wanted to know if he was the toughest Indian in the world.

'It's late,' I finally said. 'You can crash with me, if you want.'

He studied my face and then looked down the long road toward his reservation.

'Okay,' he said. 'That sounds good.'

We got a room at the Pony Soldier Motel, and both of us laughed at the irony of it all. Inside the room, in a generic watercolor hanging above the bed, the U.S. Cavalry was kicking the crap out of a band of renegade Indians.

'What tribe you think they are?' I asked the fighter.

'All of them,' he said.

The fighter crashed on the floor while I curled up in the uncomfortable bed. I couldn't sleep for the longest time. I listened to the fighter talk in his sleep. I stared up at the water-stained ceiling. I don't know what time it was when I finally drifted off, and I don't know what time it was when the fighter got into bed with me. He was naked and his penis was hard. I felt it press against my back as he snuggled up close to me, reached inside my underwear, and took my penis in his hand. Neither of us said a word. He continued to stroke me as he rubbed himself against my back. That went on for a long time. I had never been that close to another man, but the fighter's callused fingers felt better than I would have imagined if I had ever allowed myself to imagine such things.

'This isn't working,' he whispered. 'I can't come.'

Without thinking, I reached around and took the fighter's penis in my hand. He was surprisingly small.

'No,' he said. 'I want to be inside you.'

'I don't know,' I said. 'I've never done this before.'

'It's okay,' he said. 'I'll be careful. I have rubbers.'

Without waiting for my answer, he released me and got up from the bed. I turned to look at him. He was beautiful and scarred. So much brown skin marked with bruises, badly healed wounds, and tattoos. His long black hair was unbraided and hung down to his thin waist. My slacks and dress shirt were folded and draped over the chair near the window. My shoes were sitting on the table. Blue light filled the room. The fighter bent down to his pack and searched for his condoms. For reasons I could not explain then and cannot explain now, I kicked off my underwear and rolled over on my stomach. I could not see him, but I could hear him breathing heavily as he found the condoms, tore open a package, and rolled one over his penis. He crawled onto the bed, between my legs, and slid a pillow beneath my belly.

'Are you ready?' he asked.

'I'm not gay,' I said.

'Sure,' he said as he pushed himself into me. He was small but it hurt more than I expected, and I knew that I would be sore for days afterward. But I wanted him to save me. He didn't say anything. He just pumped into me for a few minutes, came with a loud sigh, and then pulled out. I quickly rolled off the bed and went into the bathroom. I locked the door behind me and stood there in the dark. I smelled like salmon.

'Hey,' the fighter said through the door. 'Are you okay?'

'Yes,' I said. 'I'm fine.'

A long silence.

'Hey,' he said. 'Would you mind if I slept in the bed with you?' I had no answer to that.

'Listen,' I said. 'That Flathead boy you fought? You know, the one you really beat up? The one who wouldn't fall down?'

In my mind, I could see the fighter pummeling that boy. Punch after punch. The boy too beaten to fight back, but too strong to fall down.

'Yeah, what about him?' asked the fighter.

'What was his name?'

'His name?'

'Yeah, his name.'

'Elmer something or other.'

'Did he have an Indian name?'

'I have no idea. How the hell would I know that?'

I stood there in the dark for a long time. I was chilled. I wanted to get into bed and fall asleep.

'Hey,' I said. 'I think, I think maybe—well, I think you should leave now.'

'Yeah,' said the fighter, not surprised. I heard him softly singing as he dressed and stuffed all of his belongings into his pack. I wanted to know what he was singing, so I opened the bathroom door just as he was opening the door to leave. He stopped, looked at me, and smiled.

'Hey, tough guy,' he said. 'You were good.'

The fighter walked out the door, left it open, and walked away. I stood in the doorway and watched him continue his walk down the highway, past the city limits. I watched him rise from earth to sky and become a new constellation. I closed the door and wondered what was going to happen next. Feeling uncomfortable and cold, I went back into the bathroom. I ran the shower with the hottest water possible. I stared at myself in the mirror. Steam quickly filled the room. I threw a few shadow punches. Feeling stronger, I stepped into the shower and searched my body for changes. A middle-aged man needs to look for tumors. I dried myself with a towel too small for the job. Then I crawled naked into bed. I wondered if I was a warrior in this life and if I had been a warrior in a previous life. Lonely and laughing, I fell asleep. I didn't dream at all, not one bit. Or perhaps I dreamed but remembered none of it. Instead, I woke early the next morning, before sunrise, and went out into the world. I walked past my car. I stepped onto the pavement, still warm from the previous day's sun. I started walking. In bare feet, I traveled upriver toward the place where I was born and will someday die. At that moment, if you had broken open my heart you could have looked inside and seen the thin white skeletons of one thousand salmon.

A TEMPORARY MATTER

Jhumpa Lahiri

The notice informed them that it was a temporary matter: for five days their electricity would be cut off for one hour, beginning at eight P.M. A line had gone down in the last snowstorm, and the repairmen were going to take advantage of the milder evenings to set it right. The work would affect only the houses on the quiet tree-lined street, within walking distance of a row of brick-faced stores and a trolley stop, where Shoba and Shukumar had lived for three years.

'It's good of them to warn us,' Shoba conceded after reading the notice aloud, more for her own benefit than Shukumar's. She let the strap of her leather satchel, plump with files, slip from her shoulders, and left it in the hallway as she walked into the kitchen. She wore a navy blue poplin raincoat over gray sweatpants and white sneakers, looking, at thirty-three, like the type of woman she'd once claimed she would never resemble.

She'd come from the gym. Her cranberry lipstick was visible only on the outer reaches of her mouth, and her eyeliner had left charcoal patches beneath her lower lashes. She used to look this way sometimes, Shukumar thought, on mornings after a party or a night at a bar, when she'd been too lazy to wash her face, too eager to collapse into his arms. She dropped a sheaf of mail on the table without a glance. Her eyes were still fixed on the notice in her other hand. 'But they should do this sort of thing during the day.'

'When I'm here, you mean,' Shukumar said. He put a glass lid on a pot of lamb, adjusting it so only the slightest bit of steam could escape. Since January he'd been working at home, trying to complete the final chapters of his dissertation on agrarian revolts in India. 'When do the repairs start?'

'It says March nineteenth. Is today the nineteenth?' Shoba walked over to the framed corkboard that hung on the wall by the fridge, bare except for a calendar of William Morris wallpaper patterns. She looked at it as if for the first time, studying the wallpaper pattern carefully on the top half before allowing her eyes to fall to the numbered grid on the bottom. A friend had sent the calendar in the mail as a Christmas gift, even though Shoba and Shukumar hadn't celebrated Christmas that year.

'Today then,' Shoba announced. 'You have a dentist appointment next Friday, by the way.'

He ran his tongue over the tops of his teeth; he'd forgotten to brush them that morning. It wasn't the first time. He hadn't left the house at all that day, or the day before. The more Shoba stayed out, the more she began putting in extra hours at work and taking on additional projects, the more he wanted to stay in, not even leaving to get the mail, or to buy fruit or wine at the stores by the trolley stop.

Six months ago, in September, Shukumar was at an academic conference in Baltimore when Shoba went into labor, three weeks before her due date. He hadn't wanted to go to the conference, but she had insisted; it was important to make contacts, and he would be entering the job market next year. She told him that she had his number at the hotel, and a copy of his schedule and flight numbers, and she had arranged with her friend Gillian for a ride to the hospital in the event of an emergency. When the cab pulled away that morning for the airport, Shoba stood waving good-bye in her robe, with one arm resting on the mound of her belly as if it were a perfectly natural part of her body.

Each time he thought of that moment, the last moment he saw Shoba pregnant, it was the cab he remembered most, a station wagon, painted red with blue lettering. It was cavernous compared to their own car. Although Shukumar was six feet tall, with hands too big ever to rest comfortably in the pockets of his jeans, he felt dwarfed in the back seat. As the cab sped down Beacon Street, he imagined a day when he and Shoba might need to buy a station wagon of their own, to cart their children back and forth from music lessons and dentist appointments. He imagined himself gripping the wheel, as Shoba turned around to hand the children juice boxes. Once, these images of parenthood had troubled Shukumar, adding to his anxiety that he was still a student at thirty-five. But that early autumn morning, the trees still heavy with bronze leaves, he welcomed the image for the first time.

A member of the staff had found him somehow among the identical convention rooms and handed him a stiff square of stationery. It was only a telephone number, but Shukumar knew it was the hospital. When he returned to Boston it was over. The baby had been born dead. Shoba was lying on a bed, asleep, in a private room so small there was barely enough space to stand beside her, in a wing of the hospital they hadn't been to on the tour for expectant parents. Her placenta had weakened and she'd had a cesarean, though not quickly enough. The doctor explained that these things happen. He smiled in the kindest way it was possible to smile at people known only professionally. Shoba would be back on her feet in a few weeks. There was nothing to indicate that she would not be able to have children in the future.

These days Shoba was always gone by the time Shukumar woke up. He would open his eyes and see the long black hairs she shed on her pillow and think of her, dressed, sipping her third cup of coffee already, in her office downtown, where she searched for typographical errors in textbooks and marked them, in a code she had once explained to him, with an assortment of colored pencils. She would do the same for his dissertation, she promised, when it was ready. He envied her the specificity of her task, so unlike the elusive nature of his. He was a mediocre student who had a facility for absorbing details without curiosity. Until September he had been diligent if not dedicated, summarizing chapters, outlining arguments on pads of yellow lined paper. But now he would lie in their bed until he grew bored, gazing at his side of the closet which Shoba always left partly open, at the row of the tweed jackets and corduroy trousers he would not have to choose from to teach his classes that semester. After the baby died it was too late to withdraw from his teaching duties. But his adviser had arranged things so that he had the spring semester to himself. Shukumar was in his sixth year of graduate school. 'That and the summer should give you a good push,' his adviser had said. 'You should be able to wrap things up by next September.'

But nothing was pushing Shukumar. Instead he thought of how he and Shoba had become experts at avoiding each other in their three-bedroom house, spending as much time on separate floors as possible. He thought of how he no longer looked forward to weekends, when she sat for hours on the sofa with her colored pencils and her files, so that he feared that putting on a record in his own house might be rude.

He thought of how long it had been since she looked into his eyes and smiled, or whispered his name on those rare occasions they still reached for each other's bodies before sleeping.

In the beginning he had believed that it would pass, that he and Shoba would get through it all somehow. She was only thirty-three. She was strong, on her feet again. But it wasn't a consolation. It was often nearly lunchtime when Shukumar would finally pull himself out of bed and head downstairs to the coffeepot, pouring out the extra bit Shoba left for him, along with an empty mug, on the countertop.

Shukumar gathered onion skins in his hands and let them drop into the garbage pail, on top of the ribbons of fat he'd trimmed from the lamb. He ran the water in the sink, soaking the knife and the cutting board, and rubbed a lemon half along his fingertips to get rid of the garlic smell, a trick he'd learned from Shoba. It was seven-thirty. Through the window he saw the sky, like soft black pitch. Uneven banks of snow still lined the sidewalks, though it was warm enough for people to walk about without hats or gloves. Nearly three feet had fallen in the last storm, so that for a week people had to walk single file, in narrow trenches. For a week that was Shukumar's excuse for not leaving the house. But now the trenches were widening, and water drained steadily into grates in the pavement.

'The lamb won't be done by eight,' Shukumar said. 'We may have to eat in the dark.'

'We can light candles,' Shoba suggested. She unclipped her hair, coiled neatly at her nape during the days, and pried the sneakers from her feet without untying them. 'I'm going to shower before the lights go,' she said, heading for the staircase. 'I'll be down.'

Shukumar moved her satchel and her sneakers to the side of the fridge. She wasn't this way before. She used to put her coat on a hanger, her sneakers in the closet, and she paid bills as soon as they came. But now she treated the house as if it were a hotel. The fact that the yellow chintz armchair in the living room clashed with the blue-and-maroon Turkish carpet no longer bothered her. On the enclosed porch at the back of the house, a crisp white bag still sat on the wicker chaise, filled with lace she had once planned to turn into curtains.

While Shoba showered, Shukumar went into the downstairs bathroom and found a new toothbrush in its box beneath the sink.

The cheap, stiff bristles hurt his gums, and he spit some blood into the basin. The spare brush was one of many stored in a metal basket. Shoba had bought them once when they were on sale, in the event that a visitor decided, at the last minute, to spend the night.

It was typical of her. She was the type to prepare for surprises, good and bad. If she found a skirt or a purse she liked she bought two. She kept the bonuses from her job in a separate bank account in her name. It hadn't bothered him. His own mother had fallen to pieces when his father died, abandoning the house he grew up in and moving back to Calcutta, leaving Shukumar to settle it all. He liked that Shoba was different. It astonished him, her capacity to think ahead. When she used to do the shopping, the pantry was always stocked with extra bottles of olive and corn oil, depending on whether they were cooking Italian or Indian. There were endless boxes of pasta in all shapes and colors, zippered sacks of basmati rice, whole sides of lambs and goats from the Muslim butchers at Haymarket, chopped up and frozen in endless plastic bags. Every other Saturday they wound through the maze of stalls Shukumar eventually knew by heart. He watched in disbelief as she bought more food, trailing behind her with canvas bags as she pushed through the crowd, arguing under the morning sun with boys too young to shave but already missing teeth, who twisted up brown paper bags of artichokes, plums, gingerroot, and yams, and dropped them on their scales, and tossed them to Shoba one by one. She didn't mind being jostled, even when she was pregnant. She was tall, and broad-shouldered, with hips that her obstetrician assured her were made for childbearing. During the drive back home, as the car curved along the Charles, they invariably marveled at how much food they'd bought.

It never went to waste. When friends dropped by, Shoba would throw together meals that appeared to have taken half a day to prepare, from things she had frozen and bottled, not cheap things in tins but peppers she had marinated herself with rosemary, and chutneys that she cooked on Sundays, stirring boiling pots of tomatoes and prunes. Her labeled mason jars lined the shelves of the kitchen, in endless sealed pyramids, enough, they'd agreed, to last for their grandchildren to taste. They'd eaten it all by now. Shukumar had been going through their supplies steadily, preparing meals for the two of them, measuring out cupfuls of rice, defrosting bags of meat day after day. He combed through her cookbooks every afternoon, following her penciled instructions to use two teaspoons of ground coriander seeds instead of one, or red lentils instead of yellow. Each of the recipes was dated, telling the first time they had eaten the dish together. April 2, cauliflower with fennel. January 14, chicken with almonds and sultanas. He had no memory of eating those meals, and yet there they were, recorded in her neat proofreader's hand. Shukumar enjoyed cooking now. It was the one thing that made him feel productive. If it weren't for him, he knew, Shoba would eat a bowl of cereal for her dinner.

Tonight, with no lights, they would have to eat together. For months now they'd served themselves from the stove, and he'd taken his plate into his study, letting the meal grow cold on his desk before shoving it into his mouth without pause, while Shoba took her plate to the living room and watched game shows, or proofread files with her arsenal of colored pencils at hand.

At some point in the evening she visited him. When he heard her approach he would put away his novel and begin typing sentences. She would rest her hands on his shoulders and stare with him into the blue glow of the computer screen. 'Don't work too hard,' she would say after a minute or two, and head off to bed. It was the one time in the day she sought him out, and yet he'd come to dread it. He knew it was something she forced herself to do. She would look around the walls of the room, which they had decorated together last summer with a border of marching ducks and rabbits playing trumpets and drums. By the end of August there was a cherry crib under the window, a white changing table with mint-green knobs, and a rocking chair with checkered cushions. Shukumar had disassembled it all before bringing Shoba back from the hospital, scraping off the rabbits and ducks with a spatula. For some reason the room did not haunt him the way it haunted Shoba. In January, when he stopped working at his carrel in the library, he set up his desk there deliberately, partly because the room soothed him, and partly because it was a place Shoba avoided.

Shukumar returned to the kitchen and began to open drawers. He tried to locate a candle among the scissors, the eggbeaters and whisks, the mortar and pestle she'd bought in a bazaar in Calcutta, and used to pound garlic cloves and cardamom pods, back when she used to cook. He found a flashlight, but no batteries, and a half-empty box of birthday candles. Shoba had thrown him a surprise birthday party last May. One hundred and twenty people had crammed into the house— all the friends and the friends of friends they now systematically avoided. Bottles of vinho verde had nested in a bed of ice in the bathtub. Shoba was in her fifth month, drinking ginger ale from a martini glass. She had made a vanilla cream cake with custard and spun sugar. All night she kept Shukumar's long fingers linked with hers as they walked among the guests at the party.

Since September their only guest had been Shoba's mother. She came from Arizona and stayed with them for two months after Shoba returned from the hospital. She cooked dinner every night, drove herself to the supermarket, washed their clothes, put them away. She was a religious woman. She set up a small shrine, a framed picture of a lavender-faced goddess and a plate of marigold petals, on the bedside table in the guest room, and prayed twice a day for healthy grandchildren in the future. She was polite to Shukumar without being friendly. She folded his sweaters with an expertise she had learned from her job in a department store. She replaced a missing button on his winter coat and knit him a beige and brown scarf, presenting it to him without the least bit of ceremony, as if he had only dropped it and hadn't noticed. She never talked to him about Shoba; once, when he mentioned the baby's death, she looked up from her knitting, and said, 'But you weren't even there.'

It struck him as odd that there were no real candles in the house. That Shoba hadn't prepared for such an ordinary emergency. He looked now for something to put the birthday candles in and settled on the soil of a potted ivy that normally sat on the windowsill over the sink. Even though the plant was inches from the tap, the soil was so dry that he had to water it first before the candles would stand straight. He pushed aside the things on the kitchen table, the piles of mail, the unread library books. He remembered their first meals there, when they were so thrilled to be married, to be living together in the same house at last, that they would just reach for each other foolishly, more eager to make love than to eat. He put down two embroidered place mats, a wedding gift from an uncle in Lucknow, and set out the plates and wineglasses they usually saved for guests. He put the ivy in the middle, the white-edged, star-shaped leaves girded by ten little candles. He switched on the digital clock radio and tuned it to a jazz station.

'What's all this?' Shoba said when she came downstairs. Her hair was wrapped in a thick white towel. She undid the towel and draped it over a chair, allowing her hair, damp and dark, to fall across her back. As she walked absently toward the stove she took out a few tangles with her fingers. She wore a clean pair of sweatpants, a T-shirt, an old flannel robe. Her stomach was flat again, her waist narrow before the flare of her hips, the belt of the robe tied in a floppy knot.

It was nearly eight. Shukumar put the rice on the table and the lentils from the night before into the microwave oven, punching the numbers on the timer.

'You made *rogan josh*,' Shoba observed, looking through the glass lid at the bright paprika stew.

Shukumar took out a piece of lamb, pinching it quickly between his fingers so as not to scald himself. He prodded a larger piece with a serving spoon to make sure the meat slipped easily from the bone. 'It's ready,' he announced.

The microwave had just beeped when the lights went out, and the music disappeared.

'Perfect timing,' Shoba said.

'All I could find were birthday candles.' He lit up the ivy, keeping the rest of the candles and a book of matches by his plate.

'It doesn't matter,' she said, running a finger along the stem of her wineglass. 'It looks lovely.'

In the dimness, he knew how she sat, a bit forward in her chair, ankles crossed against the lowest rung, left elbow on the table. During his search for the candles, Shukumar had found a bottle of wine in a crate he had thought was empty. He clamped the bottle between his knees while he turned in the corkscrew. He worried about spilling, and so he picked up the glasses and held them close to his lap while he filled them. They served themselves, stirring the rice with their forks, squinting as they extracted bay leaves and cloves from the stew. Every few minutes Shukumar lit a few more birthday candles and drove them into the soil of the pot.

'It's like India,' Shoba said, watching him tend his makeshift candelabra. 'Sometimes the current disappears for hours at a stretch.

I once had to attend an entire rice ceremony in the dark. The baby just cried and cried. It must have been so hot.'

Their baby had never cried, Shukumar considered. Their baby would never have a rice ceremony, even though Shoba had already made the guest list, and decided on which of her three brothers she was going to ask to feed the child its first taste of solid food, at six months if it was a boy, seven if it was a girl.

'Are you hot?' he asked her. He pushed the blazing ivy pot to the other end of the table, closer to the piles of books and mail, making it even more difficult for them to see each other. He was suddenly irritated that he couldn't go upstairs and sit in front of the computer.

'No. It's delicious,' she said, tapping her plate with her fork. 'It really is.'

He refilled the wine in her glass. She thanked him.

They weren't like this before. Now he had to struggle to say something that interested her, something that made her look up from her plate, or from her proofreading files. Eventually he gave up trying to amuse her. He learned not to mind the silences.

'I remember during power failures at my grandmother's house, we all had to say something,' Shoba continued. He could barely see her face, but from her tone he knew her eyes were narrowed, as if trying to focus on a distant object. It was a habit of hers.

'Like what?'

'I don't know. A little poem. A joke. A fact about the world. For some reason my relatives always wanted me to tell them the names of my friends in America. I don't know why the information was so interesting to them. The last time I saw my aunt she asked after four girls I went to elementary school with in Tucson. I barely remember them now.'

Shukumar hadn't spent as much time in India as Shoba had. His parents, who settled in New Hampshire, used to go back without him. The first time he'd gone as an infant he'd nearly died of amoebic dysentery. His father, a nervous type, was afraid to take him again, in case something were to happen, and left him with his aunt and uncle in Concord. As a teenager he preferred sailing camp or scooping ice cream during the summers to going to Calcutta. It wasn't until after his father died, in his last year of college, that the country began to interest him, and he studied its history from course books as if it were any other subject. He wished now that he had his own childhood story of India.

'Let's do that,' she said suddenly.

'Do what?'

'Say something to each other in the dark.'

'Like what? I don't know any jokes.'

'No, no jokes.' She thought for a minute. 'How about telling each other something we've never told before.'

'I used to play this game in high school,' Shukumar recalled. 'When I got drunk.'

'You're thinking of truth or dare. This is different. Okay, I'll start.' She took a sip of wine. 'The first time I was alone in your apartment, I looked in your address book to see if you'd written me in. I think we'd known each other two weeks.'

'Where was I?'

'You went to answer the telephone in the other room. It was your mother, and I figured it would be a long call. I wanted to know if you'd promoted me from the margins of your newspaper.'

'Had I?'

'No. But I didn't give up on you. Now it's your turn.'

He couldn't think of anything, but Shoba was waiting for him to speak. She hadn't appeared so determined in months. What was there left to say to her? He thought back to their first meeting, four years earlier at a lecture hall in Cambridge, where a group of Bengali poets were giving a recital. They'd ended up side by side, on folding wooden chairs. Shukumar was soon bored; he was unable to decipher the literary diction, and couldn't join the rest of the audience as they sighed and nodded solemnly after certain phrases. Peering at the newspaper folded in his lap, he studied the temperatures of cities around the world. Ninety-one degrees in Singapore yesterday, fifty-one in Stockholm. When he turned his head to the left, he saw a woman next to him making a grocery list on the back of a folder, and was startled to find that she was beautiful.

'Okay,' he said, remembering. 'The first time we went out to dinner, to the Portuguese place, I forgot to tip the waiter. I went back the next morning, found out his name, left money with the manager.'

'You went all the way back to Somerville just to tip a waiter?'

'I took a cab.'

'Why did you forget to tip the waiter?'

The birthday candles had burned out, but he pictured her face clearly in the dark, the wide tilting eyes, the full grape-toned lips; the fall at age two from her high chair still visible as a comma on her chin. Each day, Shukumar noticed, her beauty, which had once overwhelmed him, seemed to fade. The cosmetics that had seemed superfluous were necessary now, not to improve her but to define her somehow.

'By the end of the meal I had a funny feeling that I might marry you,' he said, admitting it to himself as well as to her for the first time. 'It must have distracted me.'

The next night Shoba came home earlier than usual. There was lamb left over from the evening before, and Shukumar heated it up so that they were able to eat by seven. He'd gone out that day, through the melting snow, and bought a packet of taper candles from the corner store, and batteries to fit the flashlight. He had the candles ready on the countertop, standing in brass holders shaped like lotuses, but they ate under the glow of the copper-shaded ceiling lamp that hung over the table.

When they had finished eating, Shukumar was surprised to see that Shoba was stacking her plate on top of his, and then carrying them over to the sink. He had assumed she would retreat to the living room, behind her barricade of files.

'Don't worry about the dishes,' he said, taking them from her hands.

'It seems silly not to,' she replied, pouring a drop of detergent onto a sponge. 'It's nearly eight o'clock.'

His heart quickened. All day Shukumar had looked forward to the lights going out. He thought about what Shoba had said the night before, about looking in his address book. It felt good to remember her as she was then, how bold yet nervous she'd been when they first met, how hopeful. They stood side by side at the sink, their reflections fitting together in the frame of the window. It made him shy, the way he felt the first time they stood together in a mirror. He couldn't recall the last time they'd been photographed. They had stopped attending parties, went nowhere together. The film in his camera still contained pictures of Shoba, in the yard, when she was pregnant.

After finishing the dishes, they leaned against the counter, drying their hands on either end of a towel. At eight o'clock the house went black. Shukumar lit the wicks of the candles, impressed by their long, steady flames.

'Let's sit outside,' Shoba said. 'I think it's warm still.'

They each took a candle and sat down on the steps. It seemed strange to be sitting outside with patches of snow still on the ground. But everyone was out of their houses tonight, the air fresh enough to make people restless. Screen doors opened and closed. A small parade of neighbors passed by with flashlights.

'We're going to the bookstore to browse,' a silver-haired man called out. He was walking with his wife, a thin woman in a windbreaker, and holding a dog on a leash. They were the Bradfords, and they had tucked a sympathy card into Shoba and Shukumar's mailbox back in September. 'I hear they've got their power.'

'They'd better,' Shukumar said. 'Or you'll be browsing in the dark.'

The woman laughed, slipping her arm through the crook of her husband's elbow. 'Want to join us?'

'No thanks,' Shoba and Shukumar called out together. It surprised Shukumar that his words matched hers.

He wondered what Shoba would tell him in the dark. The worst possibilities had already run through his head. That she'd had an affair. That she didn't respect him for being thirty-five and still a student. That she blamed him for being in Baltimore the way her mother did. But he knew those things weren't true. She'd been faithful, as had he. She believed in him. It was she who had insisted he go to Baltimore. What didn't they know about each other? He knew she curled her fingers tightly when she slept, that her body twitched during bad dreams. He knew it was honeydew she favored over cantaloupe. He knew that when they returned from the hospital the first thing she did when she walked into the house was pick out objects of theirs and toss them into a pile in the hallway: books from the shelves, plants from the windowsills, paintings from walls, photos from tables, pots and pans that hung from the hooks over the stove. Shukumar had stepped out of her way, watching as she moved methodically from room to room. When she was satisfied, she stood there staring at the pile she'd made, her lips drawn back in such distaste that Shukumar had thought she would spit. Then she'd started to cry.

He began to feel cold as he sat there on the steps. He felt that he needed her to talk first, in order to reciprocate.

'That time when your mother came to visit us,' she said finally. 'When I said one night that I had to stay late at work, I went out with Gillian and had a martini.'

He looked at her profile, the slender nose, the slightly masculine set of her jaw. He remembered that night well; eating with his mother, tired from teaching two classes back to back, wishing Shoba were there to say more of the right things because he came up with only the wrong ones. It had been twelve years since his father had died, and his mother had come to spend two weeks with him and Shoba, so they could honor his father's memory together. Each night his mother cooked something his father had liked, but she was too upset to eat the dishes herself, and her eyes would well up as Shoba stroked her hand. 'It's so touching,' Shoba had said to him at the time. Now he pictured Shoba with Gillian, in a bar with striped velvet sofas, the one they used to go to after the movies, making sure she got her extra olive, asking Gillian for a cigarette. He imagined her complaining, and Gillian sympathizing about visits from in-laws. It was Gillian who had driven Shoba to the hospital.

'Your turn,' she said, stopping his thoughts.

At the end of their street Shukumar heard sounds of a drill and the electricians shouting over it. He looked at the darkened facades of the houses lining the street. Candles glowed in the windows of one. In spite of the warmth, smoke rose from the chimney.

'I cheated on my Oriental Civilization exam in college,' he said. 'It was my last semester, my last set of exams. My father had died a few months before. I could see the blue book of the guy next to me. He was an American guy, a maniac. He knew Urdu and Sanskrit. I couldn't remember if the verse we had to identify was an example of a *ghazal* or not. I looked at his answer and copied it down.'

It had happened over fifteen years ago. He felt relief now, having told her.

She turned to him, looking not at his face, but at his shoes—old moccasins he wore as if they were slippers, the leather at the back permanently flattened. He wondered if it bothered her, what he'd said. She took his hand and pressed it. 'You didn't have to tell me why you did it,' she said, moving closer to him.

They sat together until nine o'clock, when the lights came on. They heard some people across the street clapping from their porch, and televisions being turned on. The Bradfords walked back down the street, eating ice-cream cones and waving. Shoba and Shukumar waved back. Then they stood up, his hand still in hers, and went inside.

Somehow, without saying anything, it had turned into this. Into an exchange of confessions—the little ways they'd hurt or disappointed each other, and themselves. The following day Shukumar thought for hours about what to say to her. He was torn between admitting that he once ripped out a photo of a woman in one of the fashion magazines she used to subscribe to and carried it in his books for a week, or saying that he really hadn't lost the sweater-vest she bought him for their third wedding anniversary but had exchanged it for cash at Filene's, and that he had gotten drunk alone in the middle of the day at a hotel bar. For their first anniversary, Shoba had cooked a ten-course dinner just for him. The vest depressed him. 'My wife gave me a sweater-vest for our anniversary,' he complained to the bartender, his head heavy with cognac. 'What do you expect?' the bartender had replied. 'You're married.'

As for the picture of the woman, he didn't know why he'd ripped it out. She wasn't as pretty as Shoba. She wore a white sequined dress, and had a sullen face and lean, mannish legs. Her bare arms were raised, her fists around her head, as if she were about to punch herself in the ears. It was an advertisement for stockings. Shoba had been pregnant at the time, her stomach suddenly immense, to the point where Shukumar no longer wanted to touch her. The first time he saw the picture he was lying in bed next to her, watching her as she read. When he noticed the magazine in the recycling pile he found the woman and tore out the page as carefully as he could. For about a week he allowed himself a glimpse each day. He felt an intense desire for the woman, but it was a desire that turned to disgust after a minute or two. It was the closest he'd come to infidelity.

He told Shoba about the sweater on the third night, the picture on the fourth. She said nothing as he spoke, expressed no protest or reproach. She simply listened, and then she took his hand, pressing it as she had before. On the third night, she told him that once after a lecture they'd attended, she let him speak to the chairman of his department without telling him that he had a dab of pâté on his chin. She'd been irritated with him for some reason, and so she'd let him go on and on, about securing his fellowship for the following semester, without putting a finger to her own chin as a signal. The fourth night, she said that she never liked the one poem he'd ever published in his life, in a literary magazine in Utah. He'd written the poem after meeting Shoba. She added that she found the poem sentimental.

Something happened when the house was dark. They were able to talk to each other again. The third night after supper they'd sat together on the sofa, and once it was dark he began kissing her awkwardly on her forehead and her face, and though it was dark he closed his eyes, and knew that she did, too. The fourth night they walked carefully upstairs, to bed, feeling together for the final step with their feet before the landing, and making love with a desperation they had forgotten. She wept without sound, and whispered his name, and traced his eyebrows with her finger in the dark. As he made love to her he wondered what he would say to her the next night, and what she would say, the thought of it exciting him. 'Hold me,' he said, 'hold me in your arms.' By the time the lights came back on downstairs, they'd fallen asleep.

The morning of the fifth night Shukumar found another notice from the electric company in the mailbox. The line had been repaired ahead of schedule, it said. He was disappointed. He had planned on making shrimp *malai* for Shoba, but when he arrived at the store he didn't feel like cooking anymore. It wasn't the same, he thought, knowing that the lights wouldn't go out. In the store the shrimp looked gray and thin. The coconut milk tin was dusty and overpriced. Still, he bought them, along with a beeswax candle and two bottles of wine.

She came home at seven-thirty. 'I suppose this is the end of our game,' he said when he saw her reading the notice.

She looked at him. 'You can still light candles if you want.' She hadn't been to the gym tonight. She wore a suit beneath the raincoat. Her makeup had been retouched recently.

When she went upstairs to change, Shukumar poured himself some wine and put on a record, a Thelonius Monk album he knew she liked.

When she came downstairs they ate together. She didn't thank him or compliment him. They simply ate in a darkened room, in the glow of a beeswax candle. They had survived a difficult time. They finished off the shrimp. They finished off the first bottle of wine and moved on to the second. They sat together until the candle had nearly burned away. She shifted in her chair, and Shukumar thought that she was about to say something. But instead she blew out the candle, stood up, turned on the light switch, and sat down again.

'Shouldn't we keep the lights off?' Shukumar asked.

She set her plate aside and clasped her hands on the table. 'I want you to see my face when I tell you this,' she said gently.

His heart began to pound. The day she told him she was pregnant, she had used the very same words, saying them in the same gentle way, turning off the basketball game he'd been watching on television. He hadn't been prepared then. Now he was.

Only he didn't want her to be pregnant again. He didn't want to have to pretend to be happy.

'I've been looking for an apartment and I've found one,' she said, narrowing her eyes on something, it seemed, behind his left shoulder. It was nobody's fault, she continued. They'd been through enough. She needed some time alone. She had money saved up for a security deposit. The apartment was on Beacon Hill, so she could walk to work. She had signed the lease that night before coming home.

She wouldn't look at him, but he stared at her. It was obvious that she'd rehearsed the lines. All this time she'd been looking for an apartment, testing the water pressure, asking a Realtor if heat and hot water were included in the rent. It sickened Shukumar, knowing that she had spent these past evenings preparing for a life without him. He was relieved and yet he was sickened. This was what she'd been trying to tell him for the past four evenings. This was the point of her game.

Now it was his turn to speak. There was something he'd sworn he would never tell her, and for six months he had done his best to block it from his mind. Before the ultrasound she had asked the doctor not to tell her the sex of their child, and Shukumar had agreed. She had wanted it to be a surprise.

Later, those few times they talked about what had happened, she said at least they'd been spared that knowledge. In a way she almost took pride in her decision, for it enabled her to seek refuge in a mystery. He knew that she assumed it was a mystery for him, too. He'd arrived too late from Baltimore—when it was all over and she was lying on the hospital bed. But he hadn't. He'd arrived early enough to see their baby, and to hold him before they cremated him. At first he had recoiled at the suggestion, but the doctor said holding the baby might help him with the process of grieving. Shoba was asleep. The baby had been cleaned off, his bulbous lids shut tight to the world.

'Our baby was a boy,' he said. 'His skin was more red than brown. He had black hair on his head. He weighed almost five pounds. His fingers were curled shut, just like yours in the night.'

Shoba looked at him now, her face contorted with sorrow. He had cheated on a college exam, ripped a picture of a woman out of a magazine. He had returned a sweater and got drunk in the middle of the day instead. These were the things he had told her. He had held his son, who had known life only within her, against his chest in a darkened room in an unknown wing of the hospital. He had held him until a nurse knocked and took him away, and he promised himself that day that he would never tell Shoba, because he still loved her then, and it was the one thing in her life that she had wanted to be a surprise.

Shukumar stood up and stacked his plate on top of hers. He carried the plates to the sink, but instead of running the tap he looked out the window. Outside the evening was still warm, and the Bradfords were walking arm in arm. As he watched the couple the room went dark, and he spun around. Shoba had turned the lights off. She came back to the table and sat down, and after a moment Shukumar joined her. They wept together, for the things they now knew.

AURORA

Junot Díaz

Earlier today me and Cut drove down to South River and bought us
some more smoke. The regular pick-up, enough to last us the rest of the
month. The Peruvian dude who hooks us up gave us a sampler of his
superweed (jewel luv it, he said) and on the way home, past the
Hydrox factory, we could have sworn we smelled cookies baking right
in the back seat. Cut was smelling chocolate chip but I was smoothed
out on those rocky coconut ones we used to get at school.

Holy shit, Cut said. I'm drooling all over myself.

I looked over at him but the black stubble on his chin and neck was
dry. This shit is potent, I said.

That's the word I'm looking for. Potent.

Strong, I said.

It took us four hours of TV to sort, weigh and bag the smoke. We
were puffing the whole way through and by the time we were in bed
we were gone. Cut's still giggling over the cookies and me, I'm just
waiting for Aurora to show up. Fridays are good days to expect her.
Fridays are smoke days and she knows it.

We haven't seen each other for a week. Not since she put some
scratches on my arm. Fading now, like you could rub them with spit
and they'd go away but when she first put them there, with her sharp-
ass nails, they were long and swollen.

Around midnight I hear her tapping on the basement window. She
calls my name maybe four times before I say, I'm going out to talk to
her.

Don't do it, Cut says. Just leave it alone.

He's not a fan of Aurora, never gives me the messages she leaves
with him. I've found these notes in his pockets and under our couches.
Bullshit mostly but every now and then she leaves one that makes me
want to treat her better. I lie in bed some more, listening to our
neighbors flush parts of themselves down a pipe. She stops tapping,
maybe to smoke a cigarette or just to listen for my breathing.

Cut rolls over. Leave it bro.

I'm going, I say.

She meets me at the door of the utility room, a single bulb lit behind her. I shut the door behind us and we kiss, once, on the lips, but she keeps them closed, first-date style. A few months ago Cut broke the lock to this place and now the utility room's ours, like an extension, an office. Concrete with splotches of oil. A drain hole in the corner where we throw our cigs and condoms.

She's skinny—six months out of juvie and she's skinny like a twelve-year-old.

I want some company, she says.

Where are the dogs?

You know they don't like you. She looks out the window, all tagged over with initials and fuck yous. It's going to rain, she says.

It always looks like that.

Yeah, but this time it's going to rain for real.

I put my ass down on the old mattress, which stinks of pussy.

Where's your partner? she asks.

He's sleeping.

That's all that nigger does. She's got the shakes—even in this light I can see that. Hard to kiss anyone like that, hard even to touch them—the flesh moves like it's on rollers. She yanks open the drawstrings on her knapsack and pulls out cigarettes. She's living out of her bag again, on cigarettes and dirty clothes. I see a T-shirt, a couple of tampons and those same green shorts, the thin high-cut ones I bought her last summer.

Where you been? I ask. Haven't seen you around.

You know me. Yo ando más que un perro.

Her hair is dark with water. She must have gotten herself a shower, maybe at a friend's, maybe in an empty apartment. I know that I should dis her for being away so long, that Cut's probably listening, but I take her hand and kiss it.

Come on, I say.

You ain't said nothing about the last time.

I can't remember no last time. I just remember you.

She looks at me like maybe she's going to shove my smooth-ass line back down my throat. Then her face becomes smooth. Do you want to jig?

Yeah, I say. I push her back on that mattress and grab at her clothes. Go easy, she says.

I can't help myself with her and being blunted makes it worse. She has her hands on my shoulder blades and the way she pulls on them I think maybe she's trying to open me.

Go easy, she says.

We all do shit like this, stuff that's no good for you. You do it and then there's no feeling positive about it afterward . When Cut puts his salsa on the next morning, I wake up, alone, the blood doing jumping jacks in my head. I see that she's searched my pockets, left them hanging out of my pants like tongues. She didn't even bother to push the fuckers back in.

A Working Day

Raining this morning. We hit the crowd at the bus stop, pass by the trailer park across Route 9, near the Audio Shack. Dropping rocks all over. Ten here, ten there, an ounce of weed for the big guy with the warts, some H for his coked-up girl, the one with the bloody left eye. Everybody's buying for the holiday weekend. Each time I put a bag in a hand I say, Pow, right there, my man.

Cut says he heard us last night, rides me the whole time about it. I'm surprised the AIDS ain't bit your dick off yet, he says.

I'm immune, I tell him. He looks at me and tells me to keep talking. Just keep talking, he says.

Four calls come in and we take the Pathfinder out to South Amboy and Freehold. Then it's back to the Terrace for more foot action. That's the way we run things, the less driving, the better.

None of our customers are anybody special. We don't have priests or abuelas or police officers on our lists. Just a lot of kids and some older folks who haven't had a job or a haircut since the last census. I have friends in Perth Amboy and New Brunswick who tell me they deal to whole families, from the grandparents down to the fourth graders. Things around here aren't like that yet, but more kids are dealing and bigger crews are coming in from out of town, relatives of folks who live here. We're still making mad paper but it's harder now and Cut's already been sliced once and me, I'm thinking it's time to grow, to incorporate but Cut says, Fuck no. The smaller the better.

We're reliable and easy-going and that keeps us good with the older people, who don't want shit from anybody. Me, I'm tight with the kids, that's my side of the business. We work all hours of the day and when Cut goes to see his girl I keep at it, prowling up and down Westminister, saying wassup to everybody. I'm good for solo work. I'm edgy and don't like to be inside too much. You should have seen me in school. Olvidate.

One of Our Nights

We hurt each other too well to let it drop. She breaks everything I own, yells at me like it might change something, tries to slam doors on my fingers. When she wants me to promise her a love that's never been seen anywhere I think about the other girls. The last one was on Kean's women's basketball team, with skin that made mine look dark. A college girl with her own car, who came over right after her games, in her uniform, mad at some other school for a bad lay-up or an elbow in the chin.

Tonight me and Aurora sit in front of the TV and split a case of Budweiser. This is going to hurt, she says, holding her can up. There's H too, a little for her, a little for me. Upstairs my neighbors have their own long night going and they're laying out all their cards about one another. Big cruel loud cards.

Listen to that romance, she says.

It's all sweet talk, I say. They're yelling because they're in love.

She picks off my glasses and kisses the parts of my face that almost never get touched, the skin under the glass and frame.

You got those long eyelashes that make me want to cry, she says. How could anybody hurt a man with eyelashes like this?

I don't know, I say, though she should. She once tried to jam a pen in my thigh, but that was the night I punched her chest black and blue so I don't think it counts.

I pass out first, like always. I catch flashes from the movie before I'm completely gone. A man pouring too much Scotch into a plastic cup. A couple running toward each other. I wish I could stay awake through a thousand bad shows the way she does, but it's OK as long as she's breathing past the side of my neck.

Later I open my eyes and catch her kissing Cut. She's pumping her hips into him and he's got his hairy-ass hands in her hair. Fuck, I say but then I wake up and she's snoring on the couch. I put my hand on her side. She's barely nineteen, too skinny for anybody but me. She has her pipe right on the table, waited for me to fall out before hitting it. I have to open the porch door to kill the smell. I go back to sleep and when I wake up in the morning I'm laying in the tub and I've got blood on my chin and I can't remember how in the world that happened. This is no good, I tell myself. I go into the sala, wanting her to be there but she's gone again and I punch myself in the nose just to clear my head.

Love

We don't see each other much. Twice a month, four times maybe. Time don't flow right with me these days but I know it ain't often. I got my own life now, she tells me but you don't need to be an expert to see that she's flying again. That's what she's got going on, that's what's new.

We were tighter before she got sent to juvie, much tighter. Every day we chilled and if we needed a place we'd find ourselves an empty apartment, one that hadn't been rented yet. We'd break in. Smash a window, slide it up, wiggle on through. We'd bring sheets, pillows, and candles to make the place less cold. Aurora would color the walls, draw different pictures with crayons, splatter the red wax from the candles into patterns, beautiful patterns. You got talent, I told her and she laughed. I used to be real good at art. Real good. We'd have these apartments for a couple of weeks, until the supers came to clean for the next tenants and then we'd come by and find the window fixed and the lock on the door.

On some nights—especially when Cut's fucking his girl in the next bed—I want us to be like that again. I think I'm one of those guys who lives too much in the past. Cut'll be working his girl and she'll be like, Oh yes, dámelo duro, Papi, and I'll just get dressed and go looking for her ass. She still does the apartment thing but hangs out with a gang of crackheads, one of two girls there, sticks with this boy Harry. She says he's like her brother but I know better. Harry's a little pato, a cabrón, twice beat by Cut, twice beat by me. On the nights I find her she clings to him like she's his other nut, never wants to step outside for a minute. The others ask me if I have anything, giving me bullshit looks like they're hard or something. Do you have anything? Harry's moaning, his head caught between his knees like a big ripe coconut.

Anything? I say No, and grab onto her bicep, lead her into the bedroom. She slumps against the closet door. I thought maybe you'd want to get something to eat, I say.

I ate. You got cigarettes?

I give her a fresh pack. She holds it lightly, debating if she should smoke a few or sell the pack to somebody.

I can give you another, I say and she asks why I have to be such an ass.

I'm just offering.

Don't offer me anything with that voice.

Just go easy, nena.

We smoke a couple, her hissing out smoke, and then I close the plastic blinds. Sometimes I have condoms but not every time and while she says she ain't with anybody else, I don't kid myself. Harry's yelling, What the fuck are you doing? but he doesn't touch the door, doesn't even knock. After, when she's picking at my back and the others in the next room have started talking again, I'm amazed at how nasty I feel, how I want to put my fist in her face.

I don't always find her; she spends a lot of time at the Hacienda, with the rest of her fucked-up friends. I find unlocked doors and Dorito crumbs, maybe an unflushed toilet. Always puke, in a closet or on a wall. Sometimes folks take craps right on the living room floor; I've learned not to walk around until my eyes get used to the dark. I go from room to room, hand out in front of me, wishing that maybe just this once I'll feel her soft face on the other side of my fingers instead of some fucking plaster wall. Once that actually happened, a long time ago.

The apartments are all the same, no surprises whatsoever. I wash my hands in the sink, dry them on the walls and head out.

Corner

You watch anything long enough and you can become an expert at it. Get to know how it lives, what it eats. Tonight the corner is cold and nothing is really going on. You can hear the dice clicking on the curb and every truck and souped-up shitmobile that rolls in from the highway announces itself with bass.

The corner's where you smoke, eat, fuck, where you play selo. Selo games like you've never seen. I know brothers who make two, three hundred a night on the dice. Always somebody losing big. But you have to be careful with that. Never know who'll lose and then come back with a 9 or a machete, looking for the rematch. I follow Cut's advice and do my dealing nice and tranquilo, no flash, not a lot of talking. I'm cool with everybody and when folks show up they always give me a pound, knock their shoulder into mine, ask me how it's been. Cut talks to his girl, pulling her long hair, messing with her little boy but his eyes are always watching the road for cops, like minesweepers.

We're all under the big street lamps, everyone's the color of day-old piss. When I'm fifty this is how I'll remember my friends: tired and yellow and drunk. Eggie's out here too. Homeboy's got himself an afro and his big head looks ridiculous on his skinny-ass neck. He's way-out high tonight. Back in the day, before Cut's girl took over, he was Cut's gunboy but he was an irresponsible motherfucker, showed it around too much and talked amazing amounts of shit. He's arguing with some of the tígueres over nonsense and when he doesn't back down I can see that nobody's happy. The corner's hot now and I just shake my head. Nelo, the nigger Eggie's talking shit to, has had more PTI than most of us have had traffic tickets. I ain't in the mood for this shit.

I ask Cut if he wants burgers and his girl's boy trots over and says, Get me two.

Come back quick, Cut says, all about business. He tries to hand me bills but I laugh, tell him it's on me.

The Pathfinder sits in the next parking lot, crusty with mud but still a slamming ride. I'm in no rush; I take it out behind the apartments, onto the road that leads to the dump. This was our spot when we were younger, where we started fires we sometimes couldn't keep down. Whole areas around the road are still black. Everything that catches in my headlights—the stack of old tires, signs, shacks—has a memory scratched onto it. Here's where I shot my first pistol. Here's where we stashed our porn magazines. Here's where I kissed my first girl.

I get to the restaurant late; the lights are out but I know the girl in the front and she lets me in. She's heavy but has a good face, makes me think of the one time we kissed, when I put my hand in her pants and felt the pad she had on. I ask her about her mother and she says, Regular. The brother? Still down in Virginia with the Navy. Don't let him turn into no pato. She laughs, pulls at the nameplate around her neck. Any woman who laughs as dope as she does won't ever have trouble finding men. I tell her that and she looks a little scared of me. She gives me what she has under the lamps for free and when I get back to the corner Eggie's out cold on the grass. A couple of older kids stand around him, pissing hard streams into his face. Come on, Eggie, somebody says. Open that mouth. Supper's coming. Cut's laughing too hard to talk to me and he ain't the only one. Brothers are falling over with laughter and some grab onto their boys, pretend to smash their heads against the curb. I give the boy his hamburgers and he goes between two bushes, where no one will bother him. He squats down and unfolds the oily paper, careful not to stain his Carhardt. Why don't you give me a piece of that? some girl asks him.

Because I'm hungry, he says, taking a big bite out.

Lucero

I would have named it after you, she said. She folded my shirt and put it on the kitchen counter. Nothing in the apartment, only us naked and some beer and half a pizza, cold and greasy. You're named after a star.

This was before I knew about the kid. She kept going on like that and finally I said, What the fuck are you talking about?

She picked the shirt up and folded it again, patting it down like this had taken her some serious effort. I'm telling you something. Something about me. What you should be doing is listening.

I Could Save You

I find her outside the Quick Check, hot with a fever. She wants to go to the Hacienda but not alone. Come on, she says, her palm on my shoulder.

Are you in trouble?

Fuck that. I just want company.

I know I should just go home. The cops bust the Hacienda about twice a year, like it's a holiday. Today could be my lucky day. Today could be our lucky day.

You don't have to come inside. Just hang with me a little.

If something inside of me is saying no, why do I say Yeah, sure?

We walk up to Route 9 and wait for the other side to clear. Cars buzz past and a new Pontiac swerves towards us, a scare, streetlights flowing back over its top, but we're too lifted to flinch. The driver's blond and laughing and we give him the finger. We watch the cars and above us the sky has gone the color of pumpkins. I haven't seen her in ten days, but she's steady, her hair combed back straight, like she was back in school or something. My mom's getting married, she says.

To that radiator guy?

No, some other guy. Owns a carwash.

That's real nice. She's lucky for her age.

You want to come with me to the wedding?

I put my cigarette out. Why can't I see us there? Her smoking in the bathroom and me dealing to the groom. I don't know about that.

My mom sent me money to buy a dress.

You still got it?

Of course I got it. She looks and sounds hurt so I kiss her. Maybe next week I'll go look at dresses. I want something that'll make me look good. Something that'll make my ass look good.

We head down a road for utility vehicles, where beer bottles grow out of the weeds like squashes. The Hacienda is past this road, a house with orange tiles on the roof and yellow stucco on the walls. The boards across the windows are as loose as old teeth, the bushes around the front big and mangy like old school afros. When the cops nailed her here last year she told them she was looking for me, that we were supposed to be going to a movie together. I wasn't within ten miles of the place. Those pigs must have laughed their asses off. A movie. Of course. When they asked her what movie she couldn't even come up with one.

I want you to wait out here, she says.

That's fine by me. The Hacienda's not my territory.

Aurora rubs a finger over her chin. Don't go nowhere. Just hurry your ass up.

I will. She put her hands in her purple windbreaker.

Make it fast Aurora.

I just got to have a word with somebody, she says and I'm thinking how easy it would be for her to turn around and say, Hey, let's go home. I'd put my arm around her and I wouldn't let her go for like fifty years, maybe not ever. I know people who quit just like that, who wake up one day with bad breath and say, No more, I've had enough. She smiles at me and jogs around the corner, the ends of her hair falling up and down on her neck. I make myself a shadow against the bushes and listen for the Dodges and the Chevies that stop in the next parking lot, for the walkers that come rolling up with their hands in their pockets. I hear everything. A bike chain rattling. TVs snapping on in nearby apartments, squeezing ten voices into a room. After an hour the traffic on Route 9 has slowed and you can hear the cars roaring on from as far up as the Ernston light. Everybody knows about this house; people come from all over.

I'm sweating. I walk down to the utility road and come back. Come on, I say. An old fuck in a green sweatsuit comes out of the Hacienda, his hair combed up into a salt and pepper torch. An abuelo type, the sort who yells at you for spitting on his sidewalk. He has this smile on his face—big, wide, shit-eating. I know all about the nonsense that goes on in these houses, the ass that gets sold, the beasting.

Hey, I say and when he sees me, short, dark, unhappy, he breaks. He throws himself against his car door. Come here, I say. I walk over to him slow, my hand out in front of me like I'm armed. I just want to ask you something. He slides down to the ground, his arms out, fingers spread, hands like starfishes. I step on his ankle but he doesn't yell. He has his eyes closed, his nostrils wide. I grind down hard but he doesn't make a sound.

While You Were Gone

She sent me three letters from juvie and none of them said much, three pages of bullshit. She talked about the food and how rough the sheets were, how she woke up ashy in the morning, like it was winter. Three months and I still haven't had my period. The doctor here tells me it's my nerves. Yeah, right. I'd tell you about the other girls (there's a lot to tell) but they rip those letters up. I hope you doing good. Don't think bad about me. And don't let anybody sell my dogs either.

Her tía Fresa held onto the first letters for a couple of weeks before turning them over to me, unopened. Just tell me if she's OK or not, Fresa said. That's about as much as I want to know.

She sounds OK to me.

Good. Don't tell me anything else.

You should at least write her.

She put her hands on my shoulders and leaned down to my ear. You write her.

I wrote but I can't remember what I said to her, except that the cops had come after her neighbor for stealing somebody's car and that the gulls were shitting on everything. After the second letter I didn't write anymore and it didn't feel wrong or bad. I had a lot to keep me busy.

She came home in September and by then we had the Pathfinder in the parking lot and a new Zenith in the living room. Stay away from her, Cut said. Luck like that don't get better.

No sweat, I said. You know I got the iron will.

People like her got addictive personalities. You don't want to be catching that.

We stayed apart a whole weekend but on Monday I was coming home from Pathmark with a gallon of milk when I heard, Hey macho. I turned around and there she was, out with her dogs. She was wearing a black sweater, black stirrup pants and old black sneakers. I thought she'd come out messed-up but she was just thinner and couldn't keep still, her hands and face restless, like kids you have to watch.

How are you? I kept asking and she said, Just put your hands on me. We started to walk and the more we talked the faster we went.

Do this, she said. I want to feel your fingers.

She had mouth-sized bruises on her neck. Don't worry about them. They ain't contagious.

I can feel your bones.

She laughed. I can feel them too.

If I had half a brain I would have done what Cut told me to do. Dump her sorry ass. When I told him we were in love he laughed. I'm the King of Bullshit, he said, and you just hit me with some, my friend.

We found an empty apartment out near the highway, left the dogs and the milk outside. You know how it is when you get back with somebody you've loved. It felt better than it ever was, better than it ever could be again. After, she drew on the walls with her lipstick and her nail polish, stick men and stick women boning.

What was it like in there? I asked. Me and Cut drove past one night and it didn't look good. We honked the horn for a long time, you know, thought maybe you'd hear.

She sat up and looked at me. It was a cold-ass stare.

We were just hoping.

I hit a couple of girls, she said. Stupid girls. That was a big mistake. The staff put me in the Quiet Room. Eleven days the first time. Fourteen after that. That's the sort of shit that you can't get used to, no matter who you are. She looked at her drawings. I made up this whole new life in there. You should have seen it. The two of us had kids, a big blue house, hobbies, the whole fucking thing.

She ran her nails over my side. A week from then she would be asking me again, begging actually, telling me all the good things we'd do and after a while I hit her and made the blood come out of her ear like a worm but right then, in that apartment, we seemed like we were normal folks. Like maybe everything was better.

THE TUMBLERS

Nathan Englander

Who would have thought that a war of such proportions would bother to turn its fury against the fools of Chelm? Never before, not by smallpox or tax collectors, was the city intruded upon by the troubles of the outside world.

The Wise Men had seen to this when the town council was first founded. They drew up a law on a length of parchment, signed it, stamped on their seal, and nailed it, with much fanfare, to a tree: Not a wind, not a whistle, not the shadow from a cloud floating outside city limits, was welcome in the place called Chelm.

These were simple people with simple beliefs, who simply wanted to be left to themselves. And they were for generations, no one going in and only stories coming out, as good stories somehow always do. Tales of the Wise Men's logic, most notably of Mendel's grandfather, Gronam the Ox, spread, as the war later would, to the far corners of the earth.

In the Fulton Street Fish Market the dockworkers laughed with Yiddish good humor upon hearing how Gronam had tried to drown a carp. At a dairy restaurant in Buenos Aires, a customer was overcome with hiccups as his waiter recounted the events of the great sour cream shortage, explaining how Gronam had declared that water was sour cream and sour cream water, single-handedly saving the Feast of Weeks from complete and total ruin.

How the stories escaped is no great mystery, for though outsiders were unwelcome, every few years someone would pass through. There had been, among the trespassers, one vagrant and one vamp, one troubadour lost in a blizzard and one horse trader on a mule. A gypsy tinker with a friendly face stayed a week. He put new hinges on all the doors while his wife told fortunes to the superstitious in the shade of the square. Of course, the most famous visit of all was made by the circus troupe that planted a tent and put on for three days show after show. Aside from these few that came through the center of town, there was also, always, no matter what some say, a black market thriving on the outskirts of Chelm. For where else did the stores come up with their delicacies? Even the biggest deniers of its existence could be seen eating a banana now and then.

Gronam's logic was still employed when the invaders built the walls around a corner of the city, creating the Ghetto of Chelm. There were so many good things lacking and so many bad in abundance that the people of the ghetto renamed almost all that they had: they called their aches 'mother's milk,' and darkness became 'freedom'; filth they referred to as 'hope'—and felt for a while, looking at each other's hands and faces and soot-blackened clothes, fortunate. It was only death that they could not rename, for they had nothing to put in its place. This is when they became sad and felt their hunger and when some began to lose their faith in God. This is when the Mahmir Rebbe, the most pious of them all, sent Mendel outside the walls.

It was no great shock to Mendel, for the streets outside the cramped ghetto were the streets of their town, the homes their homes, even if others now lived in them. The black market was the same except that it had been made that much more clandestine and greedy by the war. Mendel was happy to find that his grandfather's wisdom had been adopted among the peasants with whom he dealt. Potatoes were treated as gold, and a sack of gold might as well have been potatoes. Mendel traded away riches' worth of the latter (now the former) for as much as he could conceal on his person of the former (now the latter). He took the whole business to be a positive sign, thinking that people were beginning to regain their good sense.

The successful transaction gave Mendel a touch of real confidence. Instead of sneaking back the way he came, he ventured past the front of the icehouse and ignored the first signs of a rising sun. He ran through the alley behind Cross-eyed Bilha's store and skirted around the town square, keeping on until he arrived at his house. It was insanity—or suicide—for him to be out there. All anyone would need was a glimpse of him to know, less than that even, their senses had become so sharp. And what of the fate of the potatoes? They surely wouldn't make it to the ghetto if Mendel were caught and strung up from the declaration tree with a sign that said SMUGGLER hung around his neck. Those precious potatoes that filled his pockets and lined his long underwear from ankles to elbows would all go to waste, softening up and sprouting eyes. But Mendel needed to see his front gate and strip of lawn and the shingles he had painted himself only two summers before. It was then that the shutters flew open on his very own bedroom window. Mendel turned and ran with all his might, having seen no more of the new resident than a fog of breath. On the next street he found a sewer grate and, with considerable force, yanked it free. A rooster crowed and Mendel heard it at first as a call for help and a siren and the screeching of a bullet. Lowering himself underground and replacing the grate, he heard the rooster's call again and understood what it was— nature functioning as it should. He took it to be another positive sign.

Raising himself from the sewer, Mendel was unsure onto which side of the wall he had emerged. The Ghetto of Chelm was alive with hustle and bustle. Were it not for the ragged appearance of each individual Jew, the crowd could have belonged to any cosmopolitan street.

'What is this? Has the circus returned to Chelm? Have they restocked all the sweetshops with licorice?' Mendel addressed the orphan Yocheved, grabbing hold of her arm and cradling in his palm a tiny potato, which she snatched away. She looked up at him, her eyes wet from the wind.

'We are all going to live on a farm and must hurry not to miss the train.'

'A farm you say.' He pulled at his beard and bent until his face was even with the child's. 'With milking cows?'

'And ducks,' said Yocheved before running away.

'Roasted? Or glazed in the style of the Chinese?' he called after her, though she had already disappeared into the crowd, vanishing with the finesse that all the remaining ghetto children had acquired. He had never tasted glazed duck, only knew that there was somewhere in existence such a thing. As he wove through the scrambling ghettoites Mendel fantasized about such a meal, wondered if it was like biting into a caramel-coated apple or as tender and dark as the crust of yolk-basted bread. His stomach churned at the thought of it as he rushed off to find the Rebbe.

The decree was elementary: only essential items were to be taken on the trains. Most packed their meager stores of food, some clothing, and a photograph or two. Here and there a diamond ring found its way into a hunk of bread, or a string of pearls rolled itself into a pair of wool socks.

For the Hasidim of Chelm, interpreting such a request was far from simple. As in any other town where Hasidim live, two distinct groups had formed. In Chelm they were called the Students of the Mekyl and the Mahmir Hasidim. The Students of the Mekyl were a relaxed bunch, taking their worship lightly while keeping within the letter of the law. Due to the ease of observance and the Epicurean way in which they relished in the Lord, they were a very popular group, numbering into the thousands.

The Mahmir Hasidim, on the other hand, were extremely strict. If a fast was to last one day, they would cease eating the day before and starve themselves a day later, guarding against the possibility that in setting their lunar calendars they had been fooled by the phases of the moon. As with the fasts went every requirement in Jewish law. Doubling was not enough, so they tripled, often passing out before pouring the twelfth glass of wine required of the Passover seders. Such zealousness takes much dedication. And considering the adjusted length of the holidays—upward of three weeks at a shot—not any small time commitment either. The Mahmir Hasidim, including children, numbered fewer than twenty on the day the ghetto was dissolved.

Initially circulating as rumor, the edict sparked mass confusion. The inhabitants of the ghetto tried to make logical decisions based on whispers and the skeptical clucking of tongues. Heads of households rubbed their temples and squeezed shut their eyes, struggling to apply their common sense to a situation anything but common.

To ease the terror spreading among his followers, the leader of the Mekyls was forced to make a decree of his own. Hoisted atop a boxcar, balancing on the sawed-off and lovingly sanded broomstick that had replaced his mahogany cane, he defined 'essential items' as everything one would need to stock a summer home. In response to a query called out from the crowd of his followers, he announced that the summer home was to be considered unfurnished. He bellowed the last word and slammed down the broomstick for emphasis, sending an echo through the empty belly of the car below.

Off went the Mekyls to gather bedsteads and bureaus, hammocks

and lawn chairs—all that a family might need in relocation. The rabbi
of the Mahmir Hasidim, in his infinite strictness (and in response to the
shameful indulgence of the Mekyls), understood 'essential' to exclude
anything other than one's long underwear, for all else was excess
adornment.

'Even our ritual fringes?' asked Feitel, astonished.

'Even the hair of one's beard,' said the Rebbe, considering the grave
nature of their predicament. This sent a shudder through his followers,
all except Mendel, who was busy distributing potatoes amid the
humble gathering. No one ate. They were waiting for the Rebbe to
make the blessing. But the Rebbe refused his share. 'Better to give it to
a Mekyl who is not so used to doing without.'

They all, as if by reflex, stuck out their hands so Mendel should take
back theirs too. 'Eat, eat!' said the Rebbe. 'You eat yours and give me
the pleasure of watching.' He smiled at his followers. 'Such loyal
students even Rebbe Akiva, blessed be his memory, would've been
honored to have.'

The Mahmirim rushed back to their cramped flats, the men
shedding their gaberdines and ritual fringes, the women folding their
frocks and slipping them into drawers. Feitel, his hand shaking, the
tears streaming down his face, began to cut at his beard, bit by bit, inch
by inch. 'Why not in one shot?' his wife, Zahava, asked. 'Get it over
with.' But he couldn't. So he trimmed at his beard like a barber, as if
putting on finishing touches that never seemed right. Zahava paced the
floor, stepping through the clumps of hair and the long, dusty
rectangles of sunshine that, relentless, could not be kept from the
ghetto. For the first time in her married life Zahava left her kerchief at
home, needlessly locking the door behind her.

They returned to the makeshift station to find the students of the
Mekyl lugging mattresses and dishes and suitcases so full they leaked
sleeves and collars from every seam. One little girl brought along her
pet dog, its mangy condition made no less shocking by the fact that it
looked healthier than its mistress. The Mahmirim turned their faces
away from this laxity of definition. An earthly edict, even one coming
from their abusers, should be translated strictly lest the invaders think
that Jews were not pious in their observance.

The Mahmir Rebbe ordered his followers away from that mass of
heathens in case—God forbid—one of the Mahmirim, shivering in long

underwear and with naked scalp, should be mistaken for a member of that court. They trudged off in their scanty dress, the women feeling no shame, since the call for such immodesty had come from their teacher's mouth.

Not even the last car of the train was far enough away for the Rebbe. 'Come,' he said, pushing through the crowd toward the tunnel that was and was not Chelm.

Though there was a track and a tunnel, and a makeshift station newly constructed by the enemy, none of it was actually part of town. Gronam had seen to this himself when the railroad first laid track along the edge of the woods. He had sworn that the train would not pass through any part of Chelm (swore, he thought, safely—sure it wasn't an issue). Checking over maps and deeds and squabbling over whether to pace the distances off heel-toe or toe-heel, the Wise Men discovered that the hill through which the workers were tunneling was very much part of Chelm. They panicked, argued, screamed themselves hoarse in a marathon meeting. It was almost midnight when Gronam came up with a plan.

Tapping on doors, whispering into sleep-clogged ears, the Wise Men roused every able body from bed, and together they sneaked down to the site armed with chisels and kitchen knives, screwdrivers and hoes. It was the only time any of them had been, though only by a few feet, outside of Chelm. Taking up bricks destined for tunnel walls, they waited for Gronam's signal. He *hoo-hoo*ed like an owl and they set to work etching a longitudinal line around each one. Before dawn, before the workers returned to find the bricks stacked as they were at quitting time the day before and a fine snow of dust around the site, Gronam made a declaration. The top half of every brick was to be considered theirs, and the bottom half, everything below the line, belonged to the railroad. In this way, when the train would enter the tunnel it would not actually pass through Chelm. They reveled in Gronam's wisdom, having kept the railroad out of town and also made its residents richer in the bargain—for they were now the proud owners of so many top halves of bricks which they hadn't had before.

Mendel recalled that morning. He had stood in his nightshirt in the street outside his parents' home and watched his grandfather—the massive Gronam—being carried back to the square on the shoulders of neighbors and friends. Simple times, he thought. Even the greatest of challenges, the battle against the railroad, all seemed so simple now.

The memory left him light-headed (so grueling was the journey from that morning as a child back to the one that, like a trap, bit into their lives with iron teeth). He stumbled forward into the wedge of Mahmirim, nearly knocking little Yocheved to the ground. He steadied himself and then the girl as they moved slowly forward, forging their way across the current of Jews that swirled, rushed, and finally broke against the hard floors of the cattle cars.

Mendel did not understand how the Rebbe planned to reach the tunnel alive, though he believed they would succeed. The darkness had been getting closer for so long, it seemed only just that it should finally envelop them, pull them into its vacuum—the tunnel ready to swallow them up like so many coins dropped into a pocket.

And that is how it felt to Mendel, like they were falling away from an open hand, plunging, as they broke away from the crowd.

In the moment that two guards passed the entrance to the tunnel in opposite directions, their shepherds straining on their leashes, in the moment when the sniper on the top of the train had his attention turned the other way, in the moment before Mendel followed the Rebbe into the tunnel, Yocheved spotted her uncle Misha and froze. Mendel did not bump into her again, though he would, until his death, wish he had.

Yocheved watched her uncle being shoved, brutalized, beaten into a boxcar, her sweet uncle who would carve her treats out of marzipan: flowers, and fruits, and peacocks whose feathers melted on her tongue.

'Come along, Yocheved,' the Rebbe called from the tunnel without breaking stride. But the darkness was so uninviting and there was Uncle Misha—a car length away—who always had for her a gift.

Her attention was drawn to the sound of a healthy bark, an angry bark, not the type that might have come from the sickly Jewish dog which had already been put down. It was the bark of a dog that drags its master. Yocheved turned to see the beast bolting along the perimeter of the crowd.

Before the dog could reach her and tear the clothes from her skin and the skin from her bones, the sniper on the train put a single bullet through her neck. The bullet left a ruby hole that resembled a charm an immodest girl might wear. Yocheved touched a finger to her throat and turned her gaze toward the sky, wondering from where such a strange gift had come.

Only Mendel looked back at the sound of the shot; the others had learned the lessons of Sodom.

The Mahmirim followed the tracks around a bend where they found, waiting for them, a passenger train. Maybe a second train waited outside every ghetto so that Mahmirim should not have to ride with Mekylim. The cars were old, a patchwork of relics from the last century. The locomotive in the distance looked too small for the job. Far better still, Mendel felt, than the freight wagons and the chaos they had left on the other side of the tunnel. Mendel was sure that the conductor waited for the next train at the next ghetto to move on with its load. There had never been enough travel or commerce to warrant another track and suddenly there was traffic, so rich was the land with Jews.

'Nu?' the Rebbe said to Mendel. 'You are the tallest. Go have a look.'

At each car, Mendel placed his foot on the metal step and pulled himself up with the bar bolted alongside. His hands were huge, befitting his lineage. Gronam's own were said to have been as broad as a shovel's head. Mendel's—somewhat smaller—had always been soft, ungainly but unnoticed. The ghetto changed that. It turned them hard and menacing. There was a moment as he grabbed hold of the bar when the Mahmirim wondered if Mendel would rise up to meet the window or pull the train over on their heads.

Leaning right, peering in, Mendel announced his findings. 'Full,' he said. 'Full.' Then 'Full, again.' Pressed together as one, the Rebbe and his followers moved forward after each response.

On the fourth attempt the car was empty and Mendel pushed open the door. The Mahmirim hurried aboard, still oblivious to their good fortune and completely unaware that it was a gentile train.

On any other transport the Mahmirim wouldn't have gotten even that far. But this happened to be a train of showmen, entertainers waiting for clear passage to a most important engagement. These were worldly people traveling about during wartime. Very little in the way of oddities could shock them—something in which they took great pride. And, of course, as Mendel would later find out, there had been until most recently the Romanian and his bear. Because of him— and the bear—those dozing in the last few cars, those who saw the flash of Mendel's head and the pack of identically clad fools stumbling behind, were actually tickled at the sight. Another lesson in fate for Mendel. The difference between the sniper's bullet and survival fell somewhere between a little girl's daydream and a fondness for bears.

The Romanian had been saddled with a runtish secondhand bear that would not dance or step up on a ball or growl with fake ferociousness. Useless from a life of posing with children in front of a slack-shuttered camera, the bear refused to do anything but sit. From this the Romanian concocted a routine. He would dress the bear as a wounded soldier and lug his furry comrade around the stage, setting off firecrackers and spouting political satire. It brought audiences to hysterics. A prize act! From this he came up with others: the fireman, the side-splitting Siamese twins, and—for the benefit of the entertainers themselves—the bride. When the train was chugging slowly up a hill, the Romanian would dress the bear in bridal gown and veil. He'd get off the front car cradling his bride and pretend they'd just missed their honeymoon train to the mountains. The entertainers howled with joy as he ran alongside the tracks crying out for a conductor and tripping over a giant tin pocket watch tied to his waist and dragging behind. A funny man, that Romanian. And strong. A very strong man it takes to run with a bear.

When the Mahmirim appeared at the back of the train, all who saw them remembered their friend. How they all missed his antics after he was taken away. And how the little bear had moped. Like a real person. Yes, it would be good to have a new group of wiseacres. And they turned in their seats, laughing out loud at these shaved-headed fools, these clowns without makeup—no, not clowns, acrobats. They could only be acrobats in such bland and colorless attire—and so skinny, too. Just the right builds for it. Lithe for the high wire.

In this way, the Mahmirim successfully boarded the train.

They busied themselves with choosing compartments, seeing that Raizel the widow had space to prop up her feet, separating the women from the men, trying to favor husbands and wives and to keep the youngest, Shraga, a boy of eleven, with his mother. In deference to King Saul's having numbered the people with lambs, the Rebbe, as is the fashion, counted his followers with a verse of Psalms, one word for each person, knowing already that he would fall short without Yocheved. This is the curse that had befallen them. Always one less word.

Mendel, who had once been a Mekyl but overcome by the wisdom of the Mahmirim had joined their small tribe, still hadn't lost his taste for excessive drink. He found his way to the bar car—well stocked for wartime—without even a pocket, let alone a złoty, with which he might come by some refreshment. Scratching at the wool of his long underwear, he stared at the bottles, listening as they rocked one against the other, tinkling lightly like chimes. He was especially taken with a leaded-crystal decanter. Its smooth single-malt contents rode up and down its inner walls, caressing the glass and teasing Mendel in a way that he considered cruel.

Dismissing the peril to which he was exposing the others, Mendel sought out a benefactor who might sport him a drink. It was in this way—in which only God can turn a selfish act into a miracle—that Mendel initially saved all of their lives.

An expert on the French horn complimented Mendel on the rustic simplicity of his costume and invited him to join her in a drink. It was this tippler who alerted Mendel to the fact that the Mahmirim were assumed to be acrobats. Talking freely, and intermittently cursing the scheduling delays caused by the endless transports, she told him of the final destinations of those nuisance-causing trains.

'This,' she said, 'was told to me by Günter the Magnificent—who was never that magnificent considering that Druckenmüller always outclassed him with both the doves and the rings.' She paused and ordered two brandies. Mendel put his hand out to touch her arm, stopping short of contact.

'If you wouldn't mind, if it's not too presumptuous.' He pointed to the decanter, blushing, remembering the Rebbe's lectures on gluttony.

'Fine choice, fine choice. My pleasure.' She knocked an empty snifter against the deep polished brown of the table (a color so rich it seemed as if the brandy had seeped through her glass and distilled into the table's surface). Not since the confiscation of the Mekyl Rebbe's cane had Mendel seen such opulence. 'Barman, a scotch as well. Your finest.' The barman served three drinks and the musician poured the extra brandy into her glass. She drank without a word. Mendel toasted her silently and, after the blessing, sipped at his scotch, his first in so very long. He let its smoky flavor rise up and fill his head, hoping that if he drank slowly enough, if he let the scotch rest on his tongue long enough and roll gradually enough down his throat, then maybe he could cure his palate like the oak slats of a cask. Maybe then he could keep the warmth and the comfort with him for however much longer God might deem that they should survive.

'Anyway, Günter came to us directly from a performance for the highest of the high where his beautiful assistant Leine had been told in the powder room by the wife of an official of unmatched feats of magic being performed with the trains. They go away full—packed so tightly that babies are stuffed in over the heads of the passengers when there's no room for another full grown—and come back empty, as if never before used.'

'And the Jews?' asked Mendel. 'What trick is performed with the Jews?'

'Sleight of hand,' she said, splashing the table with her drink and waving her fingers by way of demonstration. 'A classic illusion. First they are here, and then they are gone.

'According to the wife of the official, those who witness it faint dead away, overcome by the grand scale of the illusion. For a moment the magician stands, a field of Jews at his feet, then nothing.' She paused for dramatic effect, not unaccustomed to life in the theater. 'The train sits empty. The magician stands alone on the platform. Nothing remains but the traditional puff of smoke. This trick he performs, puff after puff, twenty-four hours a day.

'After Günter heard, he forgot all about Druckenmüller and his doves and became obsessed with what Leine had told him. He would sit at the bar and attempt the same thing with rabbits, turning his ratty bunnies into colored bursts of smoke, some pink, some purple, occasionally plain gray. He swore he wouldn't give up until he had perfected his magic. Though he knew, you could tell, that it would never match the magnitude of a trainload of Jews. I told him myself when he asked my opinion. Günter, I said, it takes more than nimble fingers to achieve the extraordinary.' With that Mendel felt a hand on his knee.

Pausing only to finish his drink, Mendel ran back to the car full of Mahmirim and relayed to the Rebbe the tales of horror he had heard.

Mendel was the Rebbe's favorite. Maybe not always so strict in his service of the Lord, Mendel was full of His spirit; this the Rebbe could see. For that reason he ignored the prohibition against gossip and took into consideration his student's most unbelievable report.

'It can't be, Mendele!' said the Rebbe.

'Their cruelty knows no bounds,' cried Raizel the widow.

The Rebbe sat in silence for some minutes, considering the events of the last years and the mystery of all those who had disappeared before them. He decided that what Mendel told them must be so.

'I'm afraid,' he said, 'that the gossip Mendel repeats is true. Due to its importance, in this instance there can be no sin in repeating such idle talk.' The Rebbe glanced at the passing scenery and pulled at the air where once had been his beard. 'No other choice,' he said. 'A solitary option. Only one thing for us to do . . .' The followers of the Mahmir Rebbe hung on his words.

'We must tumble.'

Mendel had been to the circus as a boy. During the three-day engagement, Mendel had sneaked into the tent for every performance, hiding under the bowed pine benches and peering out through the space beneath all the legs too short to reach the hay-strewn ground.

Though he did not remember a single routine or feat of daring, he did recall, in addition to the sparkling of some scandalously placed sequins, the secret to convincing the other performers that they were indeed acrobats. The secret was nothing more than an exclamation. It was, simply, a 'Hup!' Knowing this, the Mahmirim lined the corridor and began to practice.

'You must clap your hands once in a while as well,' Mendel told them. The Rebbe was already nearing old age and therefore clapped and hupped far more than he jumped.

Who knew that Raizel the widow had double-jointed arms, or that Shmuel Berel could scurry about upside down on hands and feet mocking the movements of a crab. Falling from a luggage rack from which he had tried to suspend himself, Mendel, on his back, began to laugh. The others shared the release and laughed along with him. In their car near the end of the train, there was real and heartfelt delight. They were giddy with the chance God had granted them. They laughed as the uncondemned might, as free people in free countries do.

The Rebbe interrupted this laughter. 'Even in the most foreign situation we must adhere to the laws,' he said. Therefore, as in the laws of singing, no woman was to tumble unless accompanied by another woman, and no man was to catch a woman—though husbands were given a dispensation to catch their airborne wives.

Not even an hour had gone by before it was obvious what state they were in: weak with hunger and sickness, never having asked of their bodies such rigors before—all this on top of their near-total ignorance of acrobatics and the shaking of the train. At the least, they would need further direction. A tip or two on which to build.

Pained by the sight of it, the Rebbe called a stop to their futile flailing about.

'Mendel,' he said, 'back to your drunks and gossips. Bring us the secrets to this act. As is, not even a blind man would be tricked by the sounds of such graceless footfalls.'

'Me!' Mendel said, with the mock surprise of Moses, as if there were some other among them fit to do the job.

'Yes, you,' the Rebbe said, shooing him away. 'Hurry off.'

Mendel did not move.

He looked at the Mahmirim as he thought the others might. He saw that it was only by God's will that they had gotten that far. A ward of the insane or of consumptives would have been a far better misperception in which to entangle this group of uniformly clad souls. Their acceptance as acrobats was a stretch, a first-glance guess, a benefit of the doubt granted by circumstance and only as valuable as their debut would prove. It was an absurd undertaking. But then again, Mendel thought, no more unbelievable than the reality from which they'd escaped, no more unfathomable than the magic of disappearing Jews. If the good people of Chelm could believe that water was sour cream, if the peasant who woke up that first morning in Mendel's bed and put on Mendel's slippers and padded over to the window could believe, upon throwing back the shutters, that the view he saw had always been his own, then why not pass as acrobats and tumble across the earth until they found a place where they were welcome?

'What am I to bring back?' Mendel said.

'The secrets,' answered the Rebbe, an edge in his voice, no time left for hedging or making things clear. 'There are secrets behind everything that God creates.'

'And a needle and thread,' said Raizel the widow. 'And a pair of scissors. And anything, too.'

'Anything?' Mendel said.

'Yes, anything,' Raizel said. 'Bits of paper or string. Anything that a needle can prick or thread can hold.'

Mendel raised his eyebrows at the request. The widow talked as if he were heading off to Cross-eyed Bilha's general store.

'They will have,' she said. 'They are entertainers—forever losing buttons and splitting seams.' She clucked her tongue at Mendel, who still had his eyebrows raised. 'These costumes, as is, will surely never do.'

It was the horn gleaming on the table next to the slumped form of its player that first caught Mendel's attention. He rushed over and sat down next to her. He stared out the window at the forest rushing by. He tried to make out secluded worlds cloaked by the trees. Little Yocheved's farm must be out there somewhere, a lone homestead hidden like Eden in the woods. It would be on the other side of a broad and rushing river where the dogs would lose scent of a Jewish trail.

Mendel knocked on the table to rouse the musician and looked up to find gazes focused upon him from around the bar. The observers did not appear unfriendly, only curious, travel weary, interested—Mendel assumed—in a new face who already knew a woman so well.

'You?' she said, lifting her head and smiling. 'My knight in bedclothes has returned.' The others went back to their drinks as she scanned the room in half consciousness. 'Barman,' she called. 'A drink for my knight.' She rested her head on the crook of her arm and slid the horn over so she could see Mendel with an uninterrupted view. 'You were in my dream,' she said. 'You and Günter. I mustn't tell such stories anymore, they haunt me so.'

'I've torn my costume,' Mendel said, 'the only one I have. And in a most embarrassing place.'

Shielded by the table, she walked her fingers up Mendel's leg.

'I can't imagine where,' she said, attempting a flutter of alcohol-deadened lids.

'Thread,' Mendel said, 'and a needle. You wouldn't happen to have—'

'Of course,' she said. She tried to push herself up. 'In my compartment, come along. I'll sew you up there.'

'No,' he said. 'You go, I'll stay here—and if you could, if you wouldn't mind making an introduction, I'm in desperate need of advice.'

'After I sew you,' she said. She curled her lip into a pout, accentuating an odd mark left by years of playing. 'It's only two cars away.'

'You go,' Mendel said. 'And then we'll talk. And maybe later tonight I'll come by and you can reinforce the seams.' Mendel winked.

The horn player purred and went off, stumbling against the rhythm of the train so that she actually appeared balanced. Mendel spied the open horn case under the table. Rummaging through it, he found a flowered cotton rag, damp with saliva. Looking about, nonchalant, he tucked it into his sleeve.

'It's called a Full Twisting Voltas,' Mendel said, trying to approximate the move as he had understood it. Aware that, as much as had been lost during a half demonstration in a smoke-filled bar car, twice that was again lost in his return to the Mahmirim, and another twice that lost again in his body's awkward translation of the move.

Shmuel Berel, intent and driven, attempted the move first, proving—as he would throughout the afternoon—to be almost completely useless when it came to anything where timing was involved. Under protest, for he wanted to do his share, Shmuel was told to scuttle about the stage continuously during the performance doing his upside-down backward walk. Coordination proved to be a problem for Raizel the widow and Shraga's mother, and—not surprisingly—the Rebbe as well. For them Mendel returned again to the bar car in search of simpler, less challenging moves. For Shraga, a live wire and a natural performer, he inquired about some more complicated combinations on which to work.

Mendel paused between cars, pondering the rush of track and tie and the choices it raised. How would it be if he were to jump off and roll, in faulty acrobatic form, down an embankment and into a stretch of field? What if he were to start himself off on another tributary of the nightmare, to seek out a scheme as random and hopeless as the one of which he was a part; and what of the wheels and the possibility of lowering himself underneath, thrusting himself into some new hell that would at least guarantee a comfort in its permanence—how much easier to face an eternity without wonder? Over and over again, Mendel chose neither, feeling the rush of wind and moving on into the next car, passing and excusing, smiling his way along, his senses sharpened like a nesting bird's, eagle-eyed and watching for scraps of cotton or lost ribbon, anything to bring back to Raizel and her needle.

Two men, forever at the same window and smoking a ransom's worth of cigars, had come to recognize Mendel and begun to make friendly jokes at his expense. The pair particularly relished the additions to his costume. 'The Ragdoll Review,' one would say. And the other, rotating the cigar, puff, puff, puffing away at it like a locomotive himself, would yank it from his mouth and say, 'How many of you are there, each adorned with one more scrap?'

As many as the cars, Mendel thought, and the trains, and the lengths of track. As many as have been taken and wait at the stations and right now move toward another place. As plentiful as the drops of rain that puddle the world over, except in Chelm, where they gather in the gutters into torrents of sour cream.

Each time Mendel returned to the Mahmirim, he found the car seemingly empty. At most he'd catch a rustling of curtains, or find Raizel smiling sheepishly—too slow to seal herself into a compartment before his entrance. It reminded him of the center of town when strangers stumbled through. All the townspeople would disappear, including Cross-eyed Bilha, who also ran the inn. (The inn was a brainchild of the Wise Men—for whether or not strangers were welcome, no one should be able to say that Chelm was so provincial as to lack accommodations.) Eventually, out of curiosity or terror, a resident who could stand the suspense no longer would venture a look outside. The circus, prepared for a three-day extravaganza, whip and chair already in the ring and tigers poised on overturned tubs, had sat three times three days until one of the Wise Men first dared peer into the tent.

'Open up,' Mendel called, 'it gets dark and there's work to be done.' Compartment doors opened and Mendel told everyone to remain in their seats. 'Just Shraga,' he said, 'and Feitel and Zahava. We are going to break the routine down into sections, and each will learn his own part.'

'No,' the Rebbe said. 'There isn't time. What if we should arrive in an hour before all have learned what it is they are to do?'

'There is time,' Mendel said. 'The train barely moves now. Up front they get off and walk alongside only to climb on a few lengths back. We will have the whole of tomorrow morning and up until noon. The horn player told me—we are headed to an evening performance.'

'It sounds like they are trying to make a fool of you,' Feitel said. 'As if maybe they know.'

'Do they know?' Zahava asked.

'What is it they know?' Little Shraga came out of his compartment, frightened.

'No one knows,' Mendel said. 'If they knew it would be over and done with—of that you can be sure. As for practicing, there is great wisdom in the sections. They will allow you to rest, Rebbe, and for Raizel to sew.' Mendel smiled at Raizel as she fastened a cork to Feitel's chest. Feitel chewed on a bit of thread to keep away the Angel of Death, for only the dead wear their garments while they are sewn. 'It is called choreography, Rebbe. It is the way such things are done.'

That understood, they worked on the choreography in the aisle that ran the length of the car. Those watching sat in their compartments with the doors slid open and tried to pick up the moves from the quick flicker of a body in motion passing before them. It was like learning how to dance by thumbing through a flip book, page by page.

While some worked on cartwheels and somersaults, rolling in a line first one way and then the other, Shraga, reckless and with more room in which to move his spindly body, actually showed a great deal of promise. So much that the Rebbe said, 'In another world, my son, who knows what might have become of you.'

The Mahmirim worked until they could work no more. That night they rolled in their sleep while the engineer up front tugged his whistle in greeting to the engines pulling the doomed the other way.

Shraga was the first to rise, an hour before dawn. He woke each of the others with a gentle touch on the shoulder. Each one, snapping awake, looked around for a moment, agitated and confused.

They began to practice right off, doing the best they could in the darkness. The Rebbe interrupted as the sky began to lighten. 'Come up from there,' the Rebbe said to Raizel. She was on the floor tearing bits of upholstery from under the seats, from where the craftsmen had cinched the corners. These she would sew into a moon over Zahava's heart. 'Come along,' the Rebbe said. Mendel, who was fiddling with a spoon Raizel had fastened to a sleeve and advising Shraga on the length of his leap, came with the others to crowd around the Rebbe's compartment.

'More than one kind of dedication is required if we are to survive this ordeal.' The Rebbe looked out the window as he spoke.

They separated the men from the women and began to say their morning prayers. It was not a matter of disregarding the true peril to which it exposed them but an instance in which the danger was not considered. They called out to the heavens in full voices. When they had finished there was a pause, a moment of silence. It was as if they were waiting for an answer from the Lord.

The train stopped.

Feitel was in the air when it did. He landed with a momentum greater than the train's and rolled pell-mell into the hardness of a wall.

'I've broken my back,' he said. The others ignored him. There wasn't the urgency of truth in his voice. And outside the windows there were tracks upon tracks and platform after platform and the first uncountable stories of a building, higher, surely, than the Tower of Babel was ever meant to be.

By the time Feitel got to his feet, the performers had already begun to pour out onto the platform, lugging trunks and valises, garment bags and makeup cases with rounded edges and silver clasps.

The door to the car slammed open and a head and shoulders popped in. On the face was a thin mustache that, like a rain gutter, diverted the sweat away from pale lips. And how the sweat ran; in that very first moment the face reddened noticeably and new beads of perspiration drove on the last.

'Who are you?' the man asked. 'What might this ragtag bunch perform?'

Mendel stepped forward.

'We are the tumblers.'

'Have you tumbled off the garbage heap?'

Feitel felt the ridiculousness of his costume and put his hand over the five-pointed star of champagne corks fastened to his chest.

'No matter,' the man said. 'How much prep time do you need?'

'Prep?' Mendel was at a loss.

'I've no patience for this. We're three hours late already. They'll have my head, not yours.' A hand plunged through the door. The man looked at the watch on the wrist and wiped the sweat from his brow as best he could. The hand appeared an odd match, as if this intruder were constructed of loose parts. His face reddened further and he puffed out his cheeks. 'Prep time,' he said. 'Trampolines, pommel horses, trapezes. What needs be set up?'

'Nothing,' Mendel said.

'As plain as you look, eh? Fine. Then, good.' He appeared to calm slightly ever so slightly. 'Then you're on first. Now get down there and help the others lug their chattel to the theater.'

The Mahmirim rushed out the door, Mendel's mouth opening wide as he followed the rest of the building into the sky. He let out a whistle and then continued to gape. It was beautiful and menacing. The whole place was menacing, for every wonder was in some way marred, every thing of beauty stained gray with war. To try to escape from it, to schedule galas and dress for balls, was farcical even for the enemy. The gray mood was all pervading. The performers hurried along with their preshow expressions, looking dyspeptic. Impostors, one and all. Their stage smiles, Mendel knew, would sparkle.

Raizel the widow led a monkey on a leash. The monkey held a banana, the first any had seen in years. The widow would pick up her pace and then stop suddenly. The monkey did the same. Her crooked fingers were bunched into a single claw, ready to snatch the prize away at first chance. Mendel stood behind her, a trunk on his head, watching Raizel try to trick a banana from a monkey. He was surprised, as always, to witness a new degradation, to find another display of wretchedness original enough to bring tears to his eyes. He took a deep breath and ignored his sense of injustice, a rich man's emotion, a feeling Mendel had given up the liberty of experiencing horrors and horrors before.

It was only a short time until they reached their destination, a building as wide as the train was long. The interior promised to be grand. But the Mahmirim didn't get to see any of the trompe l'oeil or gold leaf that adorned the lobby. They were ushered backstage through double doors.

As the procession filed in, the mood of the entertainers transformed. There was a newfound energy, a heightened professionalism. Even the drinkers from the bar car and the tired smokers Mendel had shuffled past in the passageways moved with a sudden precision. Mendel took note of it as a juggler grabbed the monkey and began, with detached brutality, to force the animal into trousers. He noted it as the aging dancers hid their heads behind the lids of mirrored cases, only to look up again having created an illusion of youth that, from any seat in the house, would go unchallenged. Mendel went cold with terror, watching, trying to isolate what in these innocuous preparations was so disturbing.

As the stage manager hurried by, his shirt transparent with perspiration, his arms full of tin swords, and screaming 'Schnell' at anyone whose idle gaze he caught, Mendel understood to what his great terror was due. It was the efficiency displayed by each and every one, the crack hop-to-it-ness, the discipline and order. He had seen it from the start, from the day the intruders marched into town and, finding the square empty, began kicking down doors, from the instant meticulousness demanded that a war of such massive scope make time to seek out a happily isolated dot-on-the-map hamlet-called-city where resided the fools of Chelm. It was this efficiency, Mendel knew, that would catch up with them.

'It's like we are in the bowels of the earth,' Raizel said, motioning to the catwalk and the sandbags and the endless ropes and pegs.

'Which one to pull for rain?' Feitel said. 'And which for a good harvest?'

'And which for redemption?' the Rebbe said—his tone forlorn and as close as he came to despair.

'You did a wonderful job,' Mendel said. He, against all they had been taught, put a hand to Raizel's cheek. 'The costumes are most imaginative.' He knocked his elbows together, and the spoons clinked like a dull chime.

'A wonder with a needle and thread. It's true.' This from Zahava in a breastplate of cigarette boxes and with pipe cleaners sewn to her knees.

The widow slipped an arm around Zahava's waist—always such a trim girl, even before—and pulled her close as she used to do Sabbath mornings on the way out of the shtibl. Raizel squeezed her as tightly as she could, and Zahava, more gently, squeezed back. Both held their eyes closed. It was obvious that they were together in another place, back outside the shtibl when the dogwoods were in bloom, both in new dresses, modest and lovely.

Mendel and the Rebbe and Feitel, all the Mahmirim who could not join in the embrace or the escape to better times, looked away. It was too much to bear unopaqued by any of the usual defenses. They raised their eyes as Zahava planted a kiss on the old woman's head, a kiss so sincere that Mendel tried to cut the gravity by half:

'You know,' he said, 'never has so much been made of the accidental boarding of a second-class train.'

His observation, a poor joke, did not get a single smile. It only set the Mahmirim to looking about once again, desperate for a place on which to rest their gazes.

It may have come from a leaky pipe, a hole in the roof, or off the chin of the stage manager darting about, but most likely it was a tear abandoned by an anonymous eye. It hit the floor, a single drop, immediately to the right of the Rebbe.

'What is this?' the Rebbe said. 'I won't have it. Not for a minute!'

Mendel and the others put on expressions as if they did not know to what he referred, as if they did not sense the somberness and the defeat rising up around them.

'Come, come,' said the Rebbe. 'We are on first, and Shraga has not yet perfected his Full Twisting Voltas.' He tapped out a four beat with his foot. 'Hup,' he said. 'From the top,' he said, exhausting all of the vocabulary that he had learned.

They made a space for themselves and ran through the routine, the Rebbe not letting them rest for a moment and Mendel loving him with all his heart.

The manager came for them at five minutes to curtain. It was then, from the wings, that they got to see it all. The red carpets and festooned gold braids, the chandelier and frescoed ceiling—full of heroes and maidens and celestial rays—hemmed in by elaborate moldings. And the moldings themselves were bedecked with rosy-cheeked cherubim carved from wood. There was also the audience—the women in gowns and hair piled high, the men in their uniforms, pinned heavy with medals for efficiency and bravery and strength. An important audience, just the kind to make a nervous man sweat. There was also a box up and off to the left; in it sat a leader and his escort, a man of great power on whom, Mendel could tell, a part of everyone was focused. The chandelier was turned down and the stage lights came up and the manager whispered 'Go' so that Shraga stepped out onto the stage. The others followed. It was as plain as that. They followed because there was nothing else to do.

For a moment, then two, then three, they all stood at the back of the stage, blinded. Raizel put a hand up to her eyes. There was a cough and then a chuckle. The echo had not yet come to rest when the Rebbe called out:

'To your marks!'

Lifting their heads, straightening their postures, they spread out across the hard floor.

'Hup,' cried the Rebbe, and the routine commenced. Shraga cartwheeled and flipped. The widow Raizel jumped once and then stood off to the side with her double-jointed arms turned inside out. Mendel, glorious Mendel, actually executed a springing Half-Hanlon and, with Shmuel Berel's assistance (his only real task), ended in a Soaring Angel. Feitel, off his mark, missed his wife as she came toward him in a leap. Zahava landed on her ankle, which let out a crisp, clear crack. She did not whimper, quickly standing up. Though it was obvious even from the balcony that her foot was not on right. There was, after a gasp from the audience, silence. Then from above, from off to the left, a voice was heard. Mendel knew from which box it came. He knew it was the most polished, the most straight and tall, a maker of magic, to be sure. Of course, this is conjecture, for how could he see?

'Look,' said the voice. 'They are as clumsy as Jews.' There was a pause and then singular and boisterous laughter. The laughter echoed and was picked up by the audience, who laughed back with lesser glee—not wanting to overstep their bounds. Mendel looked back to the Rebbe, and the Rebbe shrugged. Young Shraga, a natural survivor, took a hop-step as if to continue. Zahava moved toward the widow Raizel and rested a hand on her shoulder.

'More,' called the voice. 'The farce can't have already come to its end. More!' it said. Another voice, that of a woman, came from the same place and barely carried to the stage.

'Yes, keep on,' it said. 'More of the Jewish ballet.' The fatuous laugh that followed, as with the other, was picked up by the audience and the cavernous echo so that it seemed even the wooden cherubim laughed from above.

The Rebbe took a deep breath and began to tap with his foot.

Mendel waved him off and stepped forward, moving downstage, the spotlight harsh and unforgiving against his skin. He reached out past the footlights into the dark, his hands cracked and bloodless, gnarled and intrusive.

Mendel turned his palms upward, benighted.

But there were no snipers, as there are for hands that reach out of the ghettos; no dogs, as for hands that reach out from the cracks in boxcar floors; no angels waiting, as they always do, for hands that reach out from chimneys into ash-clouded skies.

DEVOTION

Adam Haslett

Through the open French doors, Owen surveyed the garden. The day was hot for June, a pale sun burning in a cloudless sky, wilting the last of the irises, the rhododendron blossoms drooping. A breeze moved through the laburnum trees, carrying a sheet of the Sunday paper into the rose border. Mrs. Giles's collie yapped on the other side of the hedge. With his handkerchief, Owen wiped sweat from the back of his neck.

His sister, Hillary, stood at the counter sorting strawberries. She'd nearly finished the dinner preparations, though Ben wouldn't arrive for hours yet. She wore a beige linen dress he'd never seen on her before. Her black-and-gray hair, usually kept up in a bun, hung down to her shoulders. For a woman in her mid-fifties, she had a slender, graceful figure.

'You're awfully dressed up,' he said.

'The wine,' she said. 'Why don't you open a bottle of the red? And we'll need the tray from the dining room.'

'We're using the silver, are we?'

'Yes, I thought we would.'

'We didn't use the silver at Christmas.'

He watched Hillary dig for something in the fridge.

'It should be on the right under the carving dish,' she said. Raising himself from his chair, Owen walked through into the dining room. From the sideboard he removed the familiar gravy boats and serving dishes until he found the tarnished platter. The china and silver had come from their parents' when their father died, along with the side tables and sitting chairs and the pictures on the walls.

'It'd take an hour to clean this,' he called into the kitchen. 'There's polish in the cabinet.'

'We've *five* perfectly good trays in the cupboard.'

'It's behind the drink, on the left.'

He gritted his teeth. She could be so bloody imperious.

'This is some production,' he muttered, seated again at the kitchen table. He daubed a cloth in polish and drew it over the smooth metal. They weren't in the habit of having people in to dinner. Aunt Philippa from Shropshire, their mother's sister, usually came at Christmas and stayed three or four nights. Now and again, Hillary had Miriam Franks, one of her fellow teachers from the comprehensive, in on a Sunday. They'd have coffee in the living room afterward and talk about the students. Occasionally they'd go out if a new restaurant opened on the High Street, but they'd never been gourmets. Most of Owen's partners at the firm had professed to discover wine at a certain age and now took their holidays in Italy. He and Hillary rented a cottage in the Lake District the last two weeks of August. They had been going for years and were perfectly happy with it. A nice little stone house that caught all the afternoon light and had a view of Lake Windermere.

He pressed the cloth harder onto the tray, rubbing at the tarnished corners. Years ago he'd gone to dinners, up in Knightsbridge and Mayfair. Richard Stallybrass, an art dealer, gave private gentlemen's parties, as he called them, at his flat on Belgrave Place. All very civilized. Solicitors, journalists, the odd duke or MP, there with the implicit and, in the 1970s, safe assumption that nothing would be said. Half of them had wives and children. Saul Thompson, an old friend from school, had introduced Owen to this little world and for several years Owen had been quite taken with it. He'd looked at flats in central London, encouraged by Saul to leave the suburbs and enjoy the pleasures of the city.

But there had always been Hillary and this house. She and Owen had lost their mother when they were young and it had driven them closer than many siblings were. He couldn't see himself leaving her here in Wimbledon. The idea of his sister's loneliness haunted him. One year to the next he'd put off his plans to move.

Then Saul was dead, one of the first to be claimed by the epidemic. A year later Richard Stallybrass died. Owen's connection to the gay life had always been tenuous. AIDS severed it. His work for the firm went on, work he enjoyed. And despite what an observer might assume, he hadn't been miserable. Not every fate was alike. Not everyone ended up paired off in love.

'The wine, Owen? Aren't you going to open it?'

But then he'd met Ben, and things had changed.

'Sorry?' he said.

'The wine. It's on the sideboard.'

Hillary held a glass to the light, checking for smudges.

'We're certainly pulling out all the stops,' he said. When she made no reply, he continued. 'Believe it or not, I commented on your dress earlier but you didn't hear me. I haven't seen that one before. Have you been shopping?'

'You didn't comment on my dress, Owen. You said I was awfully dressed up.'

She looked out the window over the kitchen sink. They both watched another sheet of the *Sunday Times* tumble gently into the flower beds.

'I thought we'd have our salad outside,' she said. 'Ben might like to see the garden.'

Standing in stockinged feet before the open door of his wardrobe, Owen pushed aside the row of gray pinstripe suits, looking for a green summer blazer he remembered wearing the year before to a garden party the firm had given out in Surrey. Brushing the dust off the shoulders, he put it on over his white shirt.

On the shelf above the suits was a boater hat—he couldn't imagine what he'd worn that to—and just behind it, barely visible, the shoe box. He paused a moment, staring at the corner of it. Ben would be here in a few hours. His first visit since he'd gone back to the States, fifteen years ago. Why now? Owen had asked himself all weekend.

'I'll be over for a conference,' he'd said when Owen took the call Thursday. And yet he could so easily have come and gone from London with no word to them.

As he had each of the last three nights, Owen reached behind the boater hat and took down the shoe box. Fourteen years it had sat there untouched. Now the dust on the lid showed his fingerprints again. He listened for the sound of Hillary downstairs, then crossed the room and closed the door. Perching on the edge of the side chair, he removed the lid of the box and unfolded the last of the four letters.

November 4, 1985
Boston

Dear Hillary,

It's awkward writing when I haven't heard back from my other letters. I suppose I'll get the message soon enough. Right now I'm still bewildered. My only thought is you've decided my leaving was my own choice and not the *Globe*'s, that I have no intention of trying to get back there. I'm not sure what more I can say to convince you. I've told my editor I'll give him six months to get me reassigned to London or I'm quitting. I've been talking to people there, trying to see what might be available. It would be a lot easier if I thought this all had some purpose.

I know things got started late, that we didn't have much time before I had to leave. Owen kept you a secret for too long. But for me those were great months. I feel like a romantic clown to say I live on the memory of them, but it's not altogether untrue. I can't settle here again. I feel like I'm on a leash, everything so depressingly familiar. I'm tempted to write out all my recollections of our weekends, our evenings together, just so I can linger on them a bit more, but that would be maudlin, and you wouldn't like that—which is, of course, why I love you.

If this is over, for heaven's sake just let me know.

Yours,
   Ben

Owen slid the paper back into its envelope and replaced it in the box on his lap. Dust floated in the light by the window. The rectangle of sun on the floor crept over the red pile carpet.

For most of his life he'd hated Sundays. Their gnawing stillness, the faint memories of religion. A day loneliness won. But in these last years that quiet little dread had faded. He and Hillary made a point of cooking a big breakfast and taking a walk on the common afterward. In winter they read the paper together by the fire in the front room and often walked into the town for a film in the evening. In spring and summer they spent hours in the garden. They weren't unhappy people.

From the pack on his bedside table he took a cigarette. He rolled it idly between thumb and forefinger. Would it be taken away, this life of theirs? Was Ben coming here for an answer?

He smoked the cigarette down to the filter, then returned the shoe box to its shelf and closed the door of his wardrobe. Ben was married now, had two children. That's what he'd said on the phone; they'd spoken only a minute or two. Did he still wonder why he'd never heard?

Through the window Owen could see his sister clearing their tea mugs from the garden table. There had been other men she'd gone out to dinner with over the years. A Mr. Kreske, the divorced father of a sixth-form student, who'd driven down from Putney. The maths teacher, Mr. Hamilton, had taken her to several plays in the city before returning to Scotland. Owen had tried to say encouraging things about these evenings of hers, but then the tone of her voice had always made it clear that that's all they were, evenings.

In the kitchen Hillary stood by the sink, arranging roses in a vase.

'I see you made up the guest room,' he said.

She looked directly at him, failing to register the comment. He could tell she was trying to remember something. They did that: rested their eyes on each other in moments of distraction, as you might stare at a ring on your finger.

'The guest bed. You made it up.'

'Oh, yes. I did,' she said, drawn back into the room. 'I thought if dinner goes late and he doesn't feel like taking a train . . .'

'Of course.'

Sitting again at the table, Owen picked up the tray. In it he could see his reflection, his graying hair. What would Ben look like now? he wondered.

'Chives,' she said. 'I forgot the chives.'

They'd met through the firm, of all places. The *Globe* had Ben working on a story about differences between British and American lawyers. They went to lunch and somehow the conversation wandered. 'You ask all sorts of questions,' Owen could remember saying to him. And it was true. Ben had no hesitation about inquiring into Owen's private life, where he lived, how he spent his time. All in the most guileless manner, as though such questions were part of his beat.

'I hope he hasn't become allergic to anything,' Hillary said, setting the chives down on the cutting board.

Though Ben had been in London nearly a year, he hadn't seen much of the place. Owen offered himself as a guide. On weekends they traveled up to Hampstead or Camden Town, or out to the East End, taking long walks, getting lunch along the way. They talked about all sorts of things. It turned out Ben too had lost a parent at a young age. When Owen heard that, he understood why he'd been drawn to Ben: he seemed to comprehend a certain register of sadness intuitively. Other than Hillary, Owen had never spoken to anyone about the death of his mother.

'I come up with lots of analogies for it,' he could remember Ben saying. 'Like I was burned and can't feel anything again until the flame gets that hot. Or like people's lives are over and I'm just wandering through an abandoned house. None of them really work. But you have to think the problem somehow.'

Not the sort of conversation Owen had with colleagues at the office.

He picked up the cloth and wiped it again over the reflective center of the tray. Owen and his sister were so alike. Everyone said that. From the clipped tone of their voice, their gestures, right down into the byways of thought, the way they considered before speaking, said only what was needed. That she too had been attracted to Ben made perfect sense.

Hillary crossed the room and stood with her hands on Owen's shoulders. He could feel the warmth of her palms through his cotton blazer. Unusual, this: the two of them touching.

'It'll be curious, won't it?' she said. 'To see him so briefly after all this time.'

'Yes.'

Twenty-five years ago he and Hillary had moved into this house together. They'd thought of it as a temporary arrangement. Hillary was doing her student teaching; he'd just started with the firm and had yet to settle on a place. It seemed like the beginning of something.

'I suppose his wife couldn't come because of the children.' Her thumbs rested against his collar.

She was the only person who knew of his preference for men, now that Saul and the others were gone. She'd never judged him, never raised an eyebrow.

'Interesting he should get in touch after such a gap,' Owen said.

She removed her hands from his shoulders. 'It strikes you as odd, does it?'

'A bit.'

'I think it's thoughtful of him,' she said.

'Indeed.'

In the front hall, the doorbell rang.

'Goodness,' Hillary said, 'he's awfully early.'

He listened to her footsteps as she left the room, listened as they stopped in front of the hall mirror.

'I've been with a man once myself,' Ben had said on the night Owen finally spoke to him of his feelings. Like a prayer answered, those words were. Was it such a crime he'd fallen in love?

A few more steps and then the turning of the latch.

'Oh,' he heard his sister say. 'Mrs. Giles. Hello.'

Owen closed his eyes, relieved for the moment. Her son lived in Australia; she'd been widowed the year before. After that she'd begun stopping by on the weekends, first with the excuse of borrowing a cup of something but later just for the company.

'You're doing all right in the heat, are you?' she asked.

'Yes, we're managing,' Hillary said.

Owen joined them in the hall. He could tell from the look on his sister's face she was trying to steel her courage to say they had company on the way.

'Hello there, Owen,' Mrs. Giles said. 'Saw your firm in the paper today.'

'Did you?'

'Yes, something about the law courts. There's always news of the courts. So much of it on the telly now. Old Rumpole.'

'Right,' he said.

'Well . . . I was just on my way by . . . but you're occupied, I'm sure.'

'No, no,' Hillary said, glancing at Owen. 'Someone's coming later . . . but I was just putting a kettle on.'

'Really, you don't have to,' Mrs. Giles said.

'Not at all.'

*

They sat in the front room, Hillary glancing now and again at her watch. A production of *Les Misérables* had reached Perth, and Peter Giles had a leading role.

'Amazing story, don't you think?' Mrs. Giles said, sipping her tea.

The air in the room was close and Owen could feel sweat soaking the back of his shirt.

'Peter plays opposite an Australian girl. Can't quite imagine it done in that accent, but there we are. I sense he's fond of her, though he doesn't admit it in his letters.'

By the portrait of their parents over the mantel, a fly buzzed. Owen sat motionless on the couch, staring over Mrs. Giles's shoulder.

His sister had always been an early riser. Up at five-thirty or six for breakfast and to prepare for class. At seven-thirty she'd leave the house in time for morning assembly. As a partner, he never had to be at the firm until well after nine. He read the *Financial Times* with his coffee and looked over whatever had come in the post. There had been no elaborate operation, no fretting over things. A circumstance had presented itself. The letters from Ben arrived. He took them up to his room. That's all there was to it.

'More tea?'

'No, thank you,' Owen said.

The local council had decided on a one-way system for the town center and Mrs. Giles believed it would only make things worse. 'They've done it down in Winchester. My sister says it's a terrible mess.'

'Right,' Owen said.

They had kissed only once, in the small hours of an August night, on the sofa in Ben's flat, light from the streetlamps coming through the high windows. Earlier, strolling back over the bridge from Battersea, Owen had told him the story of him and Hillary being sent to look for their mother: walking out across the fields to a wood where she sometimes went in the mornings; the rain starting up and soaking them before they arrived under the canopy of oaks, and looked up to see their mother's slender frame wrapped in her beige overcoat, her face lifeless, her body turning in the wind. And he'd told Ben how his sister—twelve years old—had taken him in her arms right then and there, sheltering his eyes from the awful sight, and whispered in his ear, 'We will survive this, we will survive this.' A story he'd never told anyone before. And when he and Ben had finished another bottle of wine, reclining there on the sofa, they'd hugged, and then they'd kissed, their hands running through each other's hair.

'I can't do this,' Ben had whispered as Owen rested his head against Ben's chest.

'Smells wonderful, whatever it is you're cooking,' Mrs. Giles said. Hillary nodded.

For that moment before Ben had spoken, as he lay in his arms, Owen had believed in the fantasy of love as the creator, your life clay in its hands.

'I should check the food. Owen, why don't you show Mrs. Giles a bit of the garden. She hasn't seen the delphiniums, I'm sure.'

'Of course,' he said, looking into his sister's taut smile.

'I suspect I've mistreated my garden,' Mrs. Giles said as the two of them reached the bottom of the lawn. 'John it was who had the green thumb. I'm just a bungler really.'

The skin of her hands was mottled and soft looking. The gold ring she still wore hung rather loosely on her finger.

'I think Ben and I might have a weekend away,' Hillary had said one evening in the front room as they watched the evening news. The two of them had only met a few weeks before. An accident really, Hillary in the city on an errand, coming to drop something by for Owen, deciding at the last minute to join them for dinner. When the office phoned the restaurant in the middle of the meal, Owen had to leave the two of them alone.

A weekend at the cottage on Lake Windermere is what they had.

Owen had always thought of himself as a rational person, capable of perspective. As a school boy, he'd read *Othello*. *O, beware, my lord, of jealousy! It is the green-eyed monster, which doth mock the meat it feeds on.* What paltry aid literature turned out to be when the feelings were yours and not others'.

'Funny, I miss him in the most peculiar ways,' Mrs. Giles said. 'We'd always kept the chutney over the stove, and as we only ever had it in the evenings, he'd be there to fetch it. Ridiculous to use a stepladder for the chutney, if you think about it. Does just as well on the counter.'

'Yes,' Owen said.

They stared together into the blue flowers.

'I expect it won't be long before I join him,' she said.

'No, you're in fine shape, surely.'

'Doesn't upset me—the idea. It used to, but not anymore. I've been very lucky. He was a good person.'

Owen could hear the telephone ringing in the house.

'Could you get that?' Hillary called from the kitchen.

'I apologize, I—'

'No, please, carry on,' Mrs. Giles said.

He left her there and passing through the dining room, crossed the hall to the phone.

'Owen, it's Ben Hansen.'

'Ben.'

'Look, I feel terrible about this, but I'm not going to be able to make it out there tonight.'

'Oh.'

'Yeah, the meetings are running late here and I'm supposed to give this talk, it's all been pushed back. Horrible timing, I'm afraid.'

Owen could hear his sister closing the oven door, the water coming on in the sink.

'I'm sorry about that. It's a great pity. I know Hillary was looking forward to seeing you. We both were.'

'I was looking forward to it myself, I really was,' he said. 'Have you been well?'

Owen laughed. 'Me? Yes. I've been fine. Everything's very much the same on this end . . . It does seem awfully long ago you were here.'

For a moment, neither of them spoke.

Standing there in the hall, Owen felt a sudden longing. He imagined Ben as he often saw him in his mind's eye, tall and thin, half a step ahead on the Battersea Bridge, hands scrunched into his pockets. And he pictured the men he sometimes saw holding hands in Soho or Piccadilly. In June, perhaps on this very Sunday, thousands marched. He wanted to tell Ben what it felt like to pass two men on the street like that, how he had always in a sense been afraid.

'You're still with the firm?'

'Yes,' Owen said. 'That's right.' And he wanted to say how frightened he'd been watching his friend Saul's ravaged body die, how the specter of disease had made him timid. How he, Ben, had seemed a refuge.

'And with you, things have been well?'

He listened as Ben described his life—columnist now for the paper, the children beginning school; he heard the easy, slightly weary tone in his voice—a parent's fatigue. And he wondered how Ben remembered them. Were Hillary and Owen Simpson just two people he'd met on a year abroad ages ago? Had he been coming here for answers, or did he just have a free evening and a curiosity about what had become of them?

What did it matter now? There would be no revelation tonight. He was safe again.

'Might you be back over at some point?' he asked. He sensed their conversation about to end and felt on the edge of panic.

'Definitely. It's one of the things I wanted to ask you about. Judy and I were thinking of bringing the kids—maybe next summer—and I remembered you rented that place up north. Is there a person to call about getting one of those?'

'The cottages? . . . Yes, of course.'

'Yeah, that would be great. I'll try to give you a call when we're ready to firm up some plans.'

'And Judy? She's well?'

'Sure, she's heard all about you, wants to meet you both sometime.'

'That would be terrific,' Owen said, the longing there again.

'Ben?'

'Yes?'

'Who is it?' Hillary asked, stepping into the hall, drying her hands with a dishcloth. A red amulet their mother had worn hung round her neck, resting against the front of her linen dress.

'Ben,' he mouthed.

Her face stiffened slightly.

'Hillary's just here,' he said into the phone. 'Why don't you have a word?' He held the receiver out to her.

'He can't make it.'

'Is that right?' she said, staring straight through him. She took the phone. Owen walked back into the dining room; by the sideboard, he paused.

'No, no, don't be silly,' he heard his sister say. 'It's quite all right.'

'A beautiful evening, isn't it?' Mrs. Giles said as he stepped back onto the terrace. The air was mild now, the sun beginning to shade into the trees. Clouds like distant mountains had appeared on the horizon.

'Yes,' he said, imagining the evening view of the lake from the garden of their cottage, the way they checked the progress of the days by which dip in the hills the sun disappeared behind.

Mrs. Giles stood from the bench. 'I should be getting along.'

He walked her down the side of the house and out the gate. Though the sky was still bright, the streetlamps had begun to flicker on. Farther up the street a neighbor watered her lawn.

'Thank you for the tea.'

'Not at all,' he said.

'It wasn't bad news just now, I hope.'

'No, no,' he said. 'Just a friend calling.'

'That's good, then.' She hesitated by the low brick wall that separated their front gardens. 'Owen, there was just one thing I wanted to mention. In my sitting room, the desk over in the corner, in the top drawer there. I've put a letter in. You understand. I wanted to make sure someone would know where to look. Nothing to worry about, of course, nothing dramatic . . . but in the event . . . you see?'

He nodded, and she smiled back at him, her eyes beginning to water. Owen watched her small figure as she turned and passed through her gate, up the steps, and into her house.

He stayed awhile on the sidewalk, gazing onto the common: the expanse of lawn, white goalposts on the football pitch set against the trees. A long shadow, cast by their house and the others along this bit of street, fell over the playing field. He watched it stretching slowly to the chestnut trees, the darkness slowly climbing their trunks, beginning to shade the leaves of the lower branches.

In the house, he found Hillary at the kitchen table, hands folded in her lap. She sat perfectly still, staring into the garden. For a few minutes they remained like that, Owen at the counter, neither of them saying a word. Then his sister got up and passing him as though he weren't there, opened the oven door.

'Right,' she said. 'It's done.'

They ate in the dining room, in the fading light, with the silver and the crystal. Roses, pink and white, stood in a vase at the center of the table. As the plates were already out, Hillary served her chicken marsala on their mother's china. The candles remained unlit in the silver candlesticks.

'He'll be over again,' Owen said. Hillary nodded. They finished their dinner in silence. Afterward, neither had the appetite for the strawberries set out on the polished tray.

'I'll do these,' he said when they'd stacked the dishes on the counter. He squeezed the green liquid detergent into the baking dish and watched it fill with water. 'I could pour you a brandy if you like,' he said over his shoulder. But when he turned he saw his sister had left the room.

He rinsed the bowls and plates and arranged them neatly in the rows of the dishwasher. Under the warm running water, he sponged the wineglasses clean and set them to dry on the rack. When he'd finished, he turned the taps off, and then the kitchen was quiet.

He poured himself a scotch and took a seat at the table. The door to the garden had been left open and in the shadows he could make out the azalea bush and the cluster of rhododendron. Up the lane from where they'd lived as children, there was a manor with elaborate gardens and a moat around the house. An old woman they called Mrs. Montague lived there and she let them play on the rolling lawns and in the labyrinth of the topiary hedge. They would play for hours in the summer, chasing each other along the embankments, pretending to fish in the moat with a stick and string. He won their games of hide-and-go-seek because he never closed his eyes completely, and could see which way she ran. He could still remember the peculiar anger and frustration he used to feel after he followed her to her hiding place and tapped her on the head. He imagined that garden now, the blossoms of its flowers drinking in the cooler night air, the branches of its trees rejuvenating in the darkness.

From the front room, he heard a small sound—a moan let out in little breaths—and realized it was the sound of his sister crying.

He had ruined her life. He knew that now in a way he'd always tried not to know it—with certainty. For years he'd allowed himself to imagine she had forgotten Ben, or at least stopped remembering. He stood up from the table and crossed the room but stopped at the entrance to the hall. What consolation could he give her now?

Standing there, listening to her tears, he remembered the last time he'd heard them, so long ago it seemed like the memory of a former life: a summer morning when she'd returned from university, and they'd walked together over the fields in a brilliant sunshine and come to the oak trees, their green leaves shining, their branches heavy with acorns. She'd wept then for the first time in all the years since their mother had taken herself away. And Owen had been there to comfort her—his turn at last, after all she had done to protect him.

At the sound of his footsteps entering the hall, Hillary went quiet. He stopped again by the door to the front room. Sitting at the breakfast table, reading those letters from America, it wasn't only Ben's affection he'd envied. Being replaced. That was the fear. The one he'd been too weak to master.

Holding on to the banister, he slowly climbed the stairs, his feet pressing against the worn patches of the carpet. They might live in this silence the rest of their lives, he thought.

In his room, he walked to the window and looked again over the common.

When they were little they'd gone to the village on Sundays to hear the minister talk. Of charity and sacrifice. A Norman church with hollows worked into the stones of the floor by centuries of parishioners. He could still hear the congregation singing, *Bring me my bow of burning gold! Bring me my arrows of desire!* Their mother had sung with them. Plaintive voices rising. *And did those feet in ancient time walk upon England's mountains green?* Owen could remember wanting to believe something about it all, if not the words of the Book perhaps the sorrow he heard in the music, the longing of people's song. He hadn't been in a church since his mother's funeral. Over the years, views from the train or the sight of this common in evening had become his religion, absorbing the impulse to imagine larger things.

Looking over it now, he wondered at the neutrality of the grass and the trees and the houses beyond, how in their stillness they neither judged nor forgave. He stared across the playing field a moment longer. And then, calmly, he crossed to the wardrobe and took down the box.

Sitting in the front room, Hillary heard her brother's footsteps overhead and then the sound of his door closing. Her tears had dried and she felt a stony kind of calm, gazing into the wing chair opposite— an old piece of their parents' furniture. Threads showed at the armrests, and along the front edge the ticking had come loose. At first they'd meant to get rid of so many things, the faded rugs, the heavy felt curtains, but their parents' possessions had settled in the house, and then there seemed no point.

In the supermarket checkout line, she sometimes glanced at the cover of a decor magazine, a sunny room with blond wood floors, bright solid colors, a white sheet on a white bed. The longing for it usually lasted only a moment. She knew she'd be a foreigner in such a room.

She sipped the last of her wine and put the glass down on the coffee table. Darkness had fallen now and in the window she saw the reflection of the lamp and the mantel and the bookcase.

'Funny, isn't it? How it happens.' That's all her friend Miriam Franks would ever say if the conversation turned onto the topic of why neither of them had married. Hillary would nod and recall one of the evenings she'd spent with Ben up at the cottage, sitting in the garden, talking of Owen, thinking to herself she could only ever be with someone who understood her brother as well as Ben did.

She switched off the light in the front room and walked to the kitchen. Owen had wiped down the counters, set everything back in its place. For a moment, she thought she might cry again. Her brother had led such a cramped life, losing his friends, scared of what people might know. She'd loved him so fiercely all these years, the fears and hindrances had felt like her own. What good, then, had her love been? she wondered as she pulled the French doors shut.

Upstairs, Owen's light was still on, but she didn't knock or say good night as she usually did. Across the hall in her own room, she closed the door behind her. The little stack of letters lay on her bed. Years ago she had read them, after rummaging for a box at Christmastime. Ben was married by then, as she'd found out when she called. Her anger had lasted a season or two but she had held her tongue, remembering the chances Owen had to leave her and how he never had.

Standing over the bed now, looking down at the pale blue envelopes, she was glad her brother had let go of them at last. Tomorrow they would have supper in the kitchen. He would offer to leave this house, and she would tell him that was the last thing she wanted.

Putting the letters aside, she undressed. When she'd climbed into bed, she reached up and turned the switch of her bedside lamp. For an instant, lying in the sudden darkness, she felt herself there again in the woods, covering her brother's eyes as she gazed up into the giant oak.

THE ANT OF THE SELF

ZZ Packer

'Opportunities,' my father says after I bail him out of jail. He's banging words into the dash as if trying to get them through my thick skull, 'You've got to invest your money if you want opportunities.' It's October of '95, and we're driving around Louisville, Kentucky, in my mother's car. Who knows why he came down here, forty miles south of where he lives, but I don't ask questions that are sure to have too many answers. I just try to get my father, Ray Bivens Jr., back across the river to his place in Indiana. Once we're on the Watterson Expressway, it seems as if we're about to crash into the horizon. The sunset has ignited the bellies of clouds; the mirrored windows of downtown buildings distort the flame-colored city into a funhouse. I can already see that it'll be one of those days when the sunset is extra-brilliant, though without staying power.

My father just got a DUI—again—though that didn't stop him from asking for the keys. When I didn't give them up, he sighed and shook his head as though I withheld keys from him daily. 'C'mon, Spurge,' he'd said. 'The pigs aren't even looking.'

He's the only person I know who still calls cops 'pigs,' a holdover from what he refers to as his Black Panther days, when 'the brothers' raked their globes of hair with black-fisted Afro picks, then left them stuck there like javelins. When, as he tells it, he and Huey P. Newton would meet in basements and wear leather jackets and stick it to whitey. Having given me investment advice, he now watches the world outside the Honda a little too jubilantly. I take the curve around the city, past the backsides of chain restaurants and malls, office parks and the shitty Louisville zoo.

'That's your future,' he says winding down from his rant. 'Sound investments.'

'Maybe you should ask the pigs for your bail money back,' I say. 'We could invest that.'

He doesn't respond; by now he's too busy checking out my mom's new car. Ray Bivens Jr. doesn't own a car. The one he just got his DUI in was borrowed, he'd told me, from a friend.

Now he takes out the Honda's cigarette lighter from its round home, looking into the unlit burner as though staring into the future. He puts the lighter back as if he'd thought about pocketing it but has decided against it. He drums a little syncopation on the dash, then, bored, starts adjusting his seat as though he's on the Concorde. He wants to say something about the car, wants to ask how much it costs and how the hell Mama could afford it, but he doesn't. Instead, out of the blue, voice almost pure, he says, 'Is that my old dress jacket? I loved that thing.'

'It's not yours. Mama bought it. I needed a blazer for debate.' The words come out chilly, but I don't say anything else to warm them up. And I feel a twinge of childishness mentioning my mother, like she's beside me, worrying the jacket hem, smoothing down the sleeves. I make myself feel better by recalling that when I went to post bail, the woman behind the bulletproof glass asked if I was a reporter.

'You keep getting money from debate, we could invest.'

When most people talk about investing, they mean stocks or bonds or mutual funds. What my father means is his friend Splo's cockfighting arena, or some dude who goes door to door selling exercise equipment that does all the exercise for you. He'd invested in a woman who tried selling African cichlids to pet shops, but all she'd done was dye ordinary goldfish so that they looked tropical. 'Didn't you just win some cash?' he asks. 'From debate?'

'Bail,' I say. 'I used it to pay your bail.'

He's quiet for a while. I wait for him to stumble out a thanks. I wait for him to promise to pay me back with money he knows he'll never have. Finally he sighs and says, 'Most investors buy low and sell high. Know why they do that?' With my father there are not only trick questions, but trick answers. Before I can respond, I hear his voice, loud and naked. 'I *axed* you, "Do you know why they do that?"' He's shaking my arm as if trying to wake me. 'You *answer me* when I ask you something.'

I twist my arm from his grasp to show I'm not afraid. We swerve out of our lane. Cars behind us swerve as well, then zoom around us and pull ahead as if we are a rock in a stream.

'Do you know who this *is*?' he says. 'Do you know who you're *talking to*?'

I haven't been talking to anyone, but I keep this to myself.

'I'll tell you who you're talking to—Ray Bivens Junior!'

He used to be this way with Mama. Never hitting, but always grabbing, groping, his halitosis forever in her face. After the divorce he insisted on partial custody. At first all I had to do was take the bus across town. Then, when he couldn't afford an apartment in the city, I had to take the Greyhound into backwoods Indiana. I'd spend Saturday and Sunday so bored I'd work ahead in textbooks, assign myself homework, whatever there was to do while waiting for Ray Bivens Jr. to fart himself awake and take me back to the bus station.

That was how debate started. Every year there was a different topic, and when they made the announcement last year, it was like an Army recruitment campaign, warning students that they'd be expected to dedicate even their weekends to the cause. I rejoiced, thinking that I would never have to visit Ray Bivens Jr. again. And I was good at debate. My brain naturally frowned at illogic. But I don't think for a minute that my teachers liked me because of my logical mind; they liked me because I was quiet and small, and not rowdy like they expected black guys to be. Sometimes, though, the teachers slipped. Once, my history teacher, Mrs. Ampersand, said, 'You stay away from those drugs, Spurgeon, and you'll go far.' That was the kind of thing that could stick in my stomach for days, weeks. I could always think of things to say about a debate topic like U.S.–China diplomatic relations, or deliver a damning rebuttal on prison overcrowding, but it was different with someone like Mrs. Ampersand—all debate logic fell away, and in my head I'd call her a bitch, tell her that the strongest stuff in my mother's house was a bottle of Nyquil.

We've crossed the bridge into Indiana but my father is still going. 'THAT'S RIGHT! YOU'RE TALKING TO RAY BIVENS *JUNIOR!* AND DON'T YOU FORGET IT!'

Outside, autumn is over, and yet it's not quite winter. Indiana farmlands speed past in black and white. Beautiful. Until you remember that the world is supposed to be in color.

Later, calm again, he says, 'Imagine a stock. Let's say the stock is the one I was telling you about, Scudder MidCap. The stock is at fifty bucks. If it's a winner, it doesn't stay at fifty bucks for long. It goes to a hundred let's say, or two hundred. But first it's gotta get to fifty-one, fifty-two, and so on. So a stock *increasing* in price is a good sign. That's when you buy.'

I make sure to tell him thanks for telling me this.

'Doesn't matter what you invest in, either,' Ray Bivens Jr. says. 'That's the beauty. Don't gotta even think about it. That's something you won't hear from an accountant.'

'You mean stockbroker. A stockbroker advises about stocks. Not an accountant.'

His face turns bitter, as though he's about to slap me, but then he thinks the better of it and says, 'So you know who to go to when you get some extra cash.'

'Look. I just told you I don't have any money.' I try to concentrate on looking for gas station signs in the dark.

'You will, Spurgeon,' he says. He puts an arm around me like a prom date, and I can smell his odor from the jail. I don't have to see his face to know exactly how it looks right now. Urgently earnest, a little too sincere. Like a man explaining to his wife why he's late coming home. 'I'll pay back every penny. I mean that.'

'I believe you,' I say, prying his arm from where it rests on my neck.

'You believe me,' he says, 'but do you believe *in* me?' He puts his arm back where it was, like he's some suburban dad, a Little League coach congratulating his charge.

'I believe in you.'

His arm falls away of its own accord as he settles deeper into his car seat with this knowledge, the leather sighing and complaining under him. I take the exit that promises a Citgo, park at a gas pump. You don't usually see insects in this weather, but the garbage can between the diesel and unleaded swarms with flies. The fluorescent lights stutter off and on as I begin pumping gas. I can hear what my mother would say, that my father is a cross I have to bear, that the Good Book says, 'A child shall lead them,' and all that crap, which basically boils down to 'He's *your* father. Your blood, not mine.' Ray Bivens Jr. leans against the car and stretches. Then he cleans the windshield with a squeegee. After that he sniffs and looks around as though he's checking out the scenery. When I'm finished filling the tank he says, 'Hey, Spurgeon. How about breaking off a few bills? You know they frisked me clean in lockdown.'

I give him a twenty and wait in the car. He's in the Citgo for what seems like half an hour. He's in there so long I get out and wipe off the squeegee streaks he left on the windshield. Finally, he comes back with a six-pack of Schlitz and a family-sized bag of Funyuns. 'Listen,' he says, handing me a beer, 'we have to make a quick stop to Jasper.'

Jasper, Indiana, is where his ex-girlfriend Lupita lives.

'I knew it,' I say, and hand back the unopened beer before starting the car. 'You're in trouble.'

He opens the can, looking as though both the Schlitz and I have disappointed him. One of the fluorescent lights overhead blinks out. 'What the hell are you talking about?'

'Why do we have to go to Jasper all of a sudden?'

'If you *shut your mouth* and go to Jasper you'll find out.'

'This is mama's car,' I remind him. 'She wants it back.'

'Why you gotta act like everything I ask you to do is gonna kill you? You my *son*. I tell you to do something, you obey.'

I *do* obey, and hate myself for it, turning the car out to the service road. I try to imagine the worst that can await him in Seymour, figure out what he's running from: men who'll tie him up at gunpoint and demand the twenty dollars that he owes them, policemen waiting at his door, but those thoughts give way to the only thing we'll find in Jasper: Lupita, watching TV, painting her toenails. I've been to Lupita's place twice, but that's more than enough. It's full of birds. Huge blue-and-gold macaws. Yellow-naped Amazons. Rainbow lorikeets who squirt their putrid frugiverous shit on you. Tons of birds, and not in cages either. I don't think my father liked them perching on his shoulders any more than I did, but the birds could land anywhere on Lupita and she'd wear them like jewelry.

Then it occurs to me that this is the only reason he cleaned the windshield. 'You're going to make me drive you and Lupita around so the two of you can get drunk. I knew it.'

'If you don't shut up—'

I don't speak to him, he doesn't speak to me. We pass a billboard that reads, WHEN LIFE GIVES YOU LEMONS, MAKE LEMONADE. I try to think of what my mother will say. She knows I had to get him out of jail, that's why she let me borrow the car. But she wasn't about to pay bail, and she definitely won't want me coming home at midnight, her car smelling of cigarettes and Mad Dog.

My father sees me fuming and says, 'I told you I was going to get your money back, right? Well, there's going to be a march, tomorrow. A million people in Washington, D.C. One. Million. People.'

'No,' I say. 'Dear God, no.'

'Exactly,' he says.

Even though the windows are closed, I feel a breeze pass through me. At one point, I wanted to go to the March; I imagined it would be as historic as King's march on Washington, as historic as the dismantling of the Wall. The men's choir of my mother's church was going, but I didn't want to be trapped on a bus with a bunch of men singing hymns, feeling sorry for me being born with Ray Bivens Jr. for a father. And what's more, I have a debate tournament. I imagine Sarah Vogedes, my debate partner, prepping for our debate on U.S. foreign policy toward China, checking her watch. She'd have to use our second stringers, or perhaps even Derron Ellersby, a basketball player so certain he'd make the NBA that he'd joined the speech and debate team 'to sound smooth for all those postgame interviews.' This was the same Derron Ellersby who ended his rebuttals by pointing at me, saying, 'Little Man over here's going to break it down for ya,' or who'd single me out in the cafeteria, telling his friends, 'Little Man's got skills, yo! Break off some a your skills! ' as if expecting me to carry on a debate with my tuna casserole.

I'd never missed a day of school in my life, and my mother had the framed perfect-attendance certificates to prove it, but the thought of Sarah Vogedes's composed face growing rumpled as Derron agreed with our opponent makes me feel something like bliss; I imagine Derron, index cards scattered in front of him, looking as confused as if he'd been faked out before a lay-up, saying, 'Yo! Sarah V! Where's Little Man? Where he at!'

For once I'm glad Ray Bivens Jr. is scheming so hard he doesn't see me smiling. If he could—if he sensed in *any* way that I might be willing—he'd find a way to call the whole thing off.

'That's in Washington, D.C.,' I remind him, 'nearly seven hundred miles away.'

'I know. But first we're going to Jasper,' he says. 'To get the birds.'

Technically, the birds are my father's, not Lupita's. He bought them when he was convinced that the animals were an Investment. He tried selling them door to door. When that didn't work and he couldn't afford to keep them, Lupita volunteered to take care of them. Lupita knew about birds, she'd said, because she'd once owned a rooster when she was five back in Guatemala.

It is completely dark and the road is revealing its secrets one at a time. I ask, once more, what he plans on doing with these birds.

He tells me he plans on selling them.

'But you couldn't sell them the first time.'

'I didn't have a million potential buyers the first time.'

For a brief moment I'd wanted to go to the March, perhaps even see if Ray Bivens Jr. got something out of it, but no longer. I tell him that I can take him to Jasper, Indiana. I can take him home, even, which was what I was supposed to do in the first place, but that I absolutely cannot, under any circumstances, cut school and miss my debate tournament to drive him to D.C.

'Don't you want your money back?' he says. 'One macaw alone will pay back that bail money three times over.'

'What are a million black men going to do with a bunch of birds? Even if you could sell them, how're you going to get them there?'

'*Would you just drive?*' he says, then sucks his teeth, making a noise that might as well be a curse. He stretches out in his seat, then starts up, explaining things to me as if I'd had a particularly stupefying bout of amnesia: 'You're gonna have Afrocentric folks there. Afrocentrics and Africans, *tons* of Africans. And what do Africans miss most? That's right. The Motherland. And what does the Mother Africa have tons of? Monkeys, lions, and guess what else? *Birds*. Not no street pigeons, but real birds, like the kind I'm selling. Macaws and African grays. Lorikeets and yellow napes and shit.' He might as well have added, *Take that*.

He's so stupid, he's brilliant; so outside of the realm of any rationality that reason stammers and stutters when facing him. I say nothing, nothing at all, just continue on, thinking quickly, but driving slowly. He hits the dash like he's knocking on a door to make me speed up.

Off the interstate, the road turns so narrow and insignificant it could peter out into someone's driveway. The occasional crop of stores along the roadside look closed. We pass through Paoli Peaks and Hoosier National Forest before finally arriving in Jasper.

We pull into Lupita's driveway. In the dark, her lawn ornaments resemble gravestones. Motion-detector floodlights buzz on as my father walks up to the house. Lupita stands on her porch, wielding a shotgun. She's wearing satiny pajamas that show her nipples. Pink curlers droop from her hair like blossoms.

'What do *joo* want?' Her eyes narrow in on him. She slits her eyes even more to see who's in the car with him, straightening herself up a little bit, but when she sees that it's just me, just nerdy ol' Spurgeon, she drops all signs of primping.

I stay in the car. She and my father disappear into the house while I watch the pinwheel lawn daisies spin in the dark. The yelling from inside the house is mostly Lupita: 'I am tired of your blag ass! Enough eez enough!' Then it stops. They've argued their way to the bedroom, where the door slams shut and all is quiet.

But the calm doesn't hold. Lupita breaks out with some beautiful, deadly Spanish threats, and the screen door bangs open. My father comes out clutching cages, each crammed two apiece with birds. I can hear birdseed and little gravelly rocks from the cages spill all over the car interior when he puts them on the backseat. The whole time he doesn't say a word. Looks straight ahead.

He makes another trip into the house, but Lupita doesn't go in with him. He comes back with another cageful of birds.

Lupita follows him for a bit, but she stops halfway from the car. She stands there in her ensemble of sexy pajamas and pink sponge curlers and shotgun.

'Don't get out,' Ray Bivens Jr. says to me. 'We're going to drive off. Slowly.'

I do as my father says and back out of the driveway.

Lupita yells after us, 'Joo are never thinking about maybe what Lupita feels!' For a moment I think she's going to come after us, but all she does is plop down on her porch step, holding her head in her hands.

Once they get used to the rhythm of the road, the birds swap crude, disjointed conversations with one another. The blue-and-gold macaw sings 'Love Me Do,' but recent immigrant that it is, it gets the inflections all wrong. The lorikeet says, repeatedly, 'Where the dickens is my pocket watch?' then does what passes for a man's lewd laugh. If there's a lull, one will say, '*Arriba, 'riba, 'riba!*' and get them all going again.

'Bird crap doesn't have an odor,' my father says. 'That's the paradox of birds.'

'She loved those birds,' I say. 'And you just took them away.'

'They learn best when stressed out,' he says. 'Why do you think they say "*Arriba!*" all the time? They get it from the Mexicans who're all in a rush to get them exported.'

He almost knocks me off kilter with that one, but I stick to the point. 'Don't try to make excuses. You hurt her. And what about the birds? You didn't think to get food, did you?'

'You are a complete pussy, you know that?'

He'd only used that word once before, when I was twelve and refused to fight another boy, and said if I didn't whup that boy the next day that he'd whup me.

'You *need* to go to this March. When you go, check in at the pussy booth and tell 'em you want to exchange yours for a johnson.'

I check the rearview mirror, then cross all lanes of I-65 North until I'm on the shoulder. It's the kind of boldness he'd always wanted me to show to everyone else but him.

'You better have a good reason for stopping,' he says.

'Get out,' I say, as soon as I stop the car. The birds also stop their chatter, and when I turn around they're looking from me to him as though they've placed bets on who will go down in flames.

Ray Bivens Jr. clamps his hand to his forehead in mock dumbfoundedness. 'You ain't heard that before? Don't *tell me* nobody never called you no pussy?'

'Get out, *sir*,' I say.

'Yeah. I'll *get out* all right.' He opens the passenger-side door just as a semi whooshes by, and even I can feel it. He slams the door and traps the cold air with me.

It's late: past midnight. I stop at the next exit to call my mother. She says if I don't get my tail back in her house tonight, she'll skin me alive. I tell her I love her too. She likes to pretend that I'm the man of the house, and says as much when she asks me if I've locked all the doors at night, or tells me to drive her to church so she can show off what a good son she has. But it's times like this when it's clear that the only man of the house is Jesus.

I buy a Ho Ho at the gas station and as I separate the cake part from the creamy insides with my teeth, I think about how Derron would have shrugged Ray Bivens Jr.'s schemes away with a good-hearted hunch of the shoulders. 'Pops is crazy,' he'd say to the mike in an NBA postgame interview, then put his gently clenched fist over his heart like someone accepting an award, 'but I love the guy.'

I get back in the car and the birds squawk and complain at having been left alone. I return to the last exit before heading north again, going slow in the right-hand lane. When I see my father, I pull off to the shoulder, pop open the electronic locks. He acts as though he knew I would come back for him all along. We don't talk for nearly an hour, but everything is completely clear: if I am not a pussy, I will cut school, forget about debate, and go to D.C.

Just outside Clarksburg, West Virginia, I pull over. I can't make it to the exit. Twice I almost nodded off. When I slump onto the steering wheel my father gets out and rouses me enough for us to exchange places, even though he's not supposed to be driving.

I don't know how long I've been asleep, but I wake to the umbrella cockatoo chanting, 'Sexy, sexy!' My eyes adjust to the dim light, first making out the electric glow of the dash panels, and then the scenery beyond the cool of the windows. We are on a small hilly road. It is so dark and so full of conifers I feel like we're traveling through velvet.

Ray Bivens Jr., I can tell, has been waiting for me to wake. At first I think he wants me to take over the wheel, but then I realize he wants company. He raps on the car window and says, 'In ancient Mesopotamia it was hot. There was no glass. What they did have was the wheel—'

The yellow-naped Amazon breaks into the Oscar Mayer wiener jingle before I can ask my father what the hell he's talking about.

'Shut up!' he yells, and at first I sit up, startled, thinking that he's yelling at me. The bird says 'Rawrk!' and starts the jingle over, from the beginning.

He sits through the jingle, and as a reward, there is a peculiar silence that comes after someone speaks. For once in his life, he has had to use patience. 'Here's why windows are called windows,' he says with strained calmness, but the lorikeet interrupts: 'Advil works,' the bird says, 'better than Tylenol.'

My father blindly gropes the backseat for a cage, seizes one, and slams it against another cage. All the birds revolt, screeching and shuffling feathers, sounding like bricks hitting a chain-link fence. One of them says, almost angrily, 'And here's to *you*, Mrs. Robinson!'

But Ray Bivens Jr. raises his voice over the din. 'The Mesopotamians cut out circles, or O's, in their homes to mimic the shape of the wheel, but also to let in the wind,' he yells. 'And there you have it. Your modern-day window. Get it? Wind-o.'

I look to see if he is taking himself seriously. He used to say shit like this when I was little. I could never tell whether he was kidding me or himself. 'You're trying to tell me that the Mesopotamians spoke English? And that they created little O's in their homes to let in the wind?'

'All right. Don't believe me, then.'

We make it into Arlington at seven in the morning, park the car at a garage, and take the Metro into D.C. with the morning commuters. White men with their briefcases and mushroom-colored trenchcoats. White women with fleet haircuts, their chic lipstick darker than blood. The occasional Asian, Hispanic—wearing the same costume but somehow looking nervous about it. More than anything though, we see black men everywhere—groups of black men wearing identical T-shirts with the names of churches and youth groups emblazoned on them. Men in big, loose kente-cloth robes; men in full-on suits with the traditional Nation of Islam bow tie.

My father hands me two cages. He hefts two. While the morning commuters eye us, he breaks down the bird prices loudly, as though we're the only people in the world.

When we get to the Mall, all you can hear from where we stand are African drums, gospel music blaring from the loudspeakers, and someone playing rap with bass so heavy it hurts your heart. Everything has an early-morning smell to it, cold and wet with dew, but already thousands have marked their territory with portable chairs and signs. Voter registration booths are everywhere; vendors balance basketfuls of T-shirts on their heads; D.C. kids nudge us, trying to sell us water for a dollar a cup. The Washington Monument stands in front of us like a big granite pencil, miles away, it seems, and everywhere, everywhere, men shake hands, laugh like they haven't seen one another in years. They make pitches, exchange business cards, and congratulate one another for just getting here. But most of all they speak in passwords: *Keep Strong, Stay Black, Love Your Black Nation.*

The birds are so unnaturally quiet I can't tell if they don't mind being jostled about amid the legs of a million strangers or if they're dying. As we work our way through the masses, Ray Bivens Jr. keeps looking off into the distance in perpetual search for the perfect customer. I try to follow my father, but it's hard to plow through the crowd holding the cages.

'Brother,' one man says, shaking his head at me, 'I don't know if them birds males or not, but they *sho ain't* black!'

I nod in my father's direction and say, 'Looks like you've got a customer.'

He shoots me an annoyed look. 'Let's split up,' he says. 'We'll cover more area if we're spread out.'

'O.K., chief,' I say. But I pretty much stay where I've been.

After a few speeches from Christian ministers, a stiff-looking bow-tied man gives an introduction for Farrakhan and the Nation of Islam. I'm so far back that I have to look at the large-screen TVs, but as Farrakhan takes to the stage, the Fruit of Islam phalanx behind him applauds so violently that their clapping resembles some sort of martial art.

I make my way toward the edge of the crowd to get some air. Though I'm already as far from the main stage as one can be, it still takes me a good half hour to push through the crowd of men, most of them patting me on the back like uncles at a family reunion. Although I've seen a sprinkling of women at the march, some black women cheer as they stand on the other side of Independence Avenue, but others wave placards reading 'Let Us In!' or 'Remember Those You Left Home.' Quite a few whites also stop to look as if to see what this thing is all about, and their hard, nervous hard smiles fit into two categories: the 'Don't mug me!' smile, or the 'Gee, aren't black folks something!' smile. It occurs to me that I can stay here on the sidelines for the entire march. A hush falls over the crowd, then they erupt into whistles and cheering and catcalls, and though I can barely see the large convention screen anymore, people begin chanting, 'Jesse! Jesse!'

I look at the screen and see him clasping hands with Farrakhan, but he doesn't do much more than that. If anything, I'd like the chance to hear him speak in person, purely for speech and debate purposes, but it seems as though the day will be a long one, with major speakers bookended by lesser-known ones.

Now a preacher from a small town takes to the platform. 'Brothers, we have to work it out with each other! How are we going to go back to our wives, our babies' mothers, and tell them that we love *them* if we can't tell our own brothers that we love them?'

At first it sounds like what everyone else has been saying, breaking a cardinal rule of public speaking: One should reiterate, not regurgitate. He reads from a letter written in 1712 by William Lynch, a white slave owner from Virginia. It occurs to me that Farrakhan read from this same letter, the content of which got lost in his nearly three-hour speech. The letter explains how to control slaves by pitting dark ones against light ones, big plantation slaves against small plantation slaves, female slaves against male ones. The preacher ends by telling everyone that freedom is attained only when the ant of the self—that small, blind, crumb-seeking part of ourselves— casts off slavery and its legacy, becoming a huge brave ox.

'Well, well, well!' An elbow nudges me. 'Wasn't that powerful, brother?' A man wearing a fez extends his hand for me to shake.

I shake his hand, but he doesn't let go, as if he's waiting for me to agree with him.

'Powerful!' the fezzed man shouts above the applause.

'Yes,' I say, and turn away from him.

But I can feel him looking at me, staring through me so hard that I'm forced to turn toward him again. 'Powerful,' I say. 'Indeed.'

I must not be convincing enough because the guy looks at me pleadingly and says, '*Feel* this! The *power* here! This is *powerful!*'

I look around for someone to save me from this man, but everyone is cheering and clapping for the next speaker. I decide that my only recourse is to shut the man up with the truth. Maybe then he'll leave me alone. 'Don't get me wrong. I love my Black Nation,' I say, adding the mandatory chest thump, 'but I'm just here because my father made me come.'

The fezzed man screws up his face in the sunlight, features bunched in confusion. He puts his hand to his ear like he's hard of hearing.

'My father!' I yell. 'My father made me come!'

People twenty deep turn around to shoot me annoyed looks. One man looks like he wants to beat the crap out me, but then looks apologetic. I in turn duck my head in apology and murmur, 'Sorry.'

'*Made* you come? *Made you?* This, my brother,' he nearly yells, 'is a day of atonement! You got to cut your father a little slack for caring for your sorry self!'

Everyone's eyes are on me again, but I'll be damned if this man who doesn't even *know me* sides with Ray Bivens Jr. 'I thought the whole point of all this was to take responsibility. Put an end to asking for slack. If you knew my father you'd know that his whole damn life is as slack as a pantsuit from JCPenney ! '

'Hold up, hold up, hold up,' a voice says. The voice comes from a man with a bullet-smooth head, the man who earlier looked as if he wanted to stomp my face into the ground. Now that he's turned toward me, the pistils and stamens of his monstrous Hawaiian flower-print shirt seem to stare at me, and suddenly his face is so close I can smell the mint of his breath.

'You need to learn that responsi*bility* is a two-way street!' The Hawaiian-shirt guy points to my chest. '*You* have to take responsibility and reach out to *him*.'

Now many, many people have turned to look at us, and though I try not to look guilty, people know the Hawaiian-shirted guy is talking to *somebody*, somebody who caused a disturbance. The Phalanx of Islam is on its way, moving in the form of crisp, gray-suited men wearing stern looks and prison muscles. The Hawaiian-shirted guy sees them and waves me away with his hand as though I'm not worth his time. Then, suddenly—despite the Fruit of Islam weaving through the crowd toward us—he decides to have another go at it. 'Let me ask you a question, my brother. Why are you here? You don't seem to *want* to atone—not with your pops, not with anybody.'

Those around me have formed a sideshow of which I seem to be the villain, and they look at me expectantly. The Hawaiian-shirted man folds his arms across his chest and jerks his chin up, daring me to answer him.

'Atoning for one's wrongs is different from apologizing,' I begin. 'One involves words, the other, actions.' I don't want to dignify all this attention with a further response; don't want the four men who are now brisk-walking straight toward me to hurt me; don't want to say anything now that the air around me is silent, listening, now that the sun in my eyes is so hot I feel like crying. I continue, delivering a hurried, jibbering philippic on the nuances between atonement and apology, repentance and remorse. What I'm saying is right and true. Good and important. But I can feel myself getting flustered, can feel the debate judge mouthing *Time's up*, see the disbelief and disappointment in the men's faces, nearly twenty in all, and more turn around to see what the disturbance is about. An Oxford-shirted security guard grabs me by the arm.

'What,' he says, 'seems to be the problem, son?'

'Look,' I say finally to him and anyone else who'll listen, 'I'm not here to atone. I'm here to sell birds.'

I finally spot my father, the cages balanced on his shoulders, when the marchless march is pretty much finished. The sky is moving toward dusk, and though there are still speakers on the podium, you'd stick around to listen only if they were your relatives or something. My father and I get pushed along with other people trying to leave.

I don't bother telling him how security clamped me on the shoulder and sat me down on the curb like a five-year-old and gave me a talking-to, reminding me of the point of the March. I don't tell him how they fed me warm flatbread and hard honey in a hot plastic tent that served as some sort of headquarters, or how they gave me three bean pies, some pamphlets, and a Koran. I know he can tell how pissed off I am. Anyone can.

And he can see I haven't sold any birds, and I see he hasn't either. I wonder if word got around to his section about how security took me out of the crowd for 'safety purposes,' but apparently he doesn't give a shit. Ray Bivens Jr. grabs a passing man by the arm. The man's T-shirt reads: 'Volunteer—Washington D.C.'

'Where's a good bar?' my father asks. 'That's cheap?'

The man raises his eyebrows and says, 'Brotherman, we're trying to keep away from all that poison. At least for one day.' His voice is smooth and kind, that of a guy from the streets who became a counselor, determined to give back to the community. He smiles. 'You think you can make it for one day without the sauce, my brother?'

The bar we end up in is called The Haven, and it's nowhere near where we left the car. Before we left the March, I asked Ray Bivens Jr. how he felt knowing that he'd come nearly seven hundred miles and hadn't sold a single bird. He didn't speak to me on the Metro ride to the bar, not even when the birds started embarrassing us on the subway.

The bartender looks at the birds and shakes his head as if his patrons never cease to amuse him.

Even though he's sitting in the place he loves most, Ray Bivens Jr. still seems mad at me. So do the birds. None of them are speaking, just making noises in their throats as though they're plotting something. I ask the bartender if the birds are safe outside; if someone will steal them.

'Not if it's something that needs feeding,' the bartender says.

'Speaking of feeding,' my father says, 'I'm going to get some Funyuns. Want any?' He says this more to the bartender than to me, but I shake my head though all I've eaten are the bean pies and honey. The bartender spray-guns a 7 Up in a glass for me without my even asking, then resumes conversation with the trio of men at the end of the counter. One man has a goiter. One has processed waves that look like cake frosting. While those two seem to be smiling and arguing at the same time, the third man says nothing, smoking his cigarette as though it's part of his search for enlightenment.

The smoker ashes his cigarette with a pert tap. 'You been at the March, youngblood?'

'Yeah. How'd you know?'

They all laugh, but no one tells me why.

The bartender towels down some beer glasses. 'Anybody here go?' When nobody says anything, he says to me, with a knowing wink, 'These some *shift*less niggers up in here!'

There's general grumbling, and to make them feel less bad about missing the March I say, 'I didn't get all pumped up by the speeches, but in a way I was glad I was there. I think I felt more relieved than anything else.'

'Relieved? What about?' the smoker asks, his voice wise and deep, even though he's just asking a question.

I try to think. 'I don't know. I'm the only black kid in my class. Like a fucking mascot or something,' I say, surprised that I said the f-word out loud, but shaking my head as though I said words like that every day. 'I just get tired of it. You skip it for a day and it feels like a vacation. That's why I was glad.'

There's a round of nodding. Not sympathy, just acknowledgment.

'Man,' the guy with the goiter says, 'I'm happy to hear that. You got the *luxury* of feeling tired. Back in the day, before you were born, couldn't that type of shit *happen*.'

He seems to be saying less than he means, and looks at me, his eyes piercing, his goiter looking like he's swallowed a lightbulb. 'We the ones *fought* for you to be in school with the white folks.' He looks behind him, as if checking if any white people are around, though that's about as likely as Ray Bivens Jr. going sober for good. He lowers his voice so that he almost sounds kind. 'We sent you to go spy on them. See how the hell those white folks make all that money! Now you talking 'bout a *vacation!*'

They all laugh like it's some sort of secret code that got broken.

'You'll be all right, youngblood,' says the smoker. 'You'll be all right.'

Just as I begin to realize that they're humoring me, Ray Bivens Jr. comes blustering in through the door like he lives there. He flashes a wad of money. 'Luck,' he says smiling, 'is sometimes lucky.'

The trio at the bar high-five one another and laugh in anticipation of free drinks.

'Who,' I say, 'did you take that from?'

'*Take?*' He chucks his thumb toward me as if to say, *Get a load of this guy.* He counts out the bills so fast that he can't actually be counting them. 'Sold a bird. Rich white dude. Convenient store. I said, "I got birds." He said, "I got money." Six hundred bones.'

I'm upset, though I don't know why. Six hundred bucks. Who in this neighborhood even *has* six hundred bucks? I lean toward him and whisper, 'I bailed you out of jail, remember.'

'Don't worry,' he says, 'I'll buy you a drink.'

Three hours pass, and my father has beaten all the regulars trying to win money from him at pinochle when a woman appears out of nowhere. Her skin is the color of good scotch. She sits between me and my father, twirls around on her barstool once, and points a red-enameled finger toward the goiter man changing songs on the jukebox. 'Play "Love the One You're With." Isley Brothers.'

'I was going to,' says the Goiter, 'just for you.'

She spins around on the barstool again so that she's facing the bottles lined up on display. 'Farrah,' she says and extends a tiny limp hand in my direction. 'Farrah Falana.'

'That's not,' I say, 'your real name.'

'Yes it is,' she says dreamily. 'Farrah Falana. I was named after that show.'

Now I see that she's going on fifty. She smiles at me with her mouth closed, and for a moment she looks like a beautiful frog.

My father takes a long, admiring look at her seated behind. 'Farrah and Ray,' my father says. 'I like how that sounds.' For a moment, he looks like Billy Dee Williams. The smile is the same, that same slick look.

'I like how it sounds, too,' Farrah says. She actually slides on her barstool and leans toward him, leans so close it looks as if she might kiss him.

'Farrah and Ray,' I say. 'That sounds like a Vegas act.'

'It *does*!' she squeals.

My father and Farrah get drunk while I play an electronic trivia game with the Goiter. He knows more than I gave him credit for, but he's losing to me because he bets all his bonus points whenever he gets a chance. The Goiter and I are on our tenth game when Ray Bivens Jr. taps me on the shoulder. I look over to see him standing very straight and tall, trying not to look drunk.

'You don't love me,' he says sloppily. 'You don't under*stand* me.'

'*You* don't understand you,' I say.

Farrah is still at the bar, and though she's not saying anything, her face goes through a series of exaggerated expressions as if it were she responding to someone's questions. I plunk three quarters in the game machine. 'Your go,' I say to the Goiter.

'Does anybody understand themselves?' he says to me softly, and for a second he looks perfectly lucid. Then he says it louder, for the benefit of the whole bar, with a gravity only the drunk can muster. 'Does *anybody*, I say, under*stand* themselves?'

The men at the bar look at him and decide it's one of their many jokes, and laugh, though my father is staring straight at me, straight through me as though I were nothing but a clear glass of whiskey into which he could see the past and future.

I grip my father's elbow and try to speak with him one on one. 'I'm sorry about what I said at the March.'

'No you ain't.'

'Yes,' I say, 'I am. But you've got to tell me how to understand you.' I feel silly saying it, but he's drunk, and so is everybody else but me.

He lurches back then leans in forward again. 'Tell you? I can't *tell* you.' He drums each word out on the counter, 'That's. Not. What. It's. A-bout. I can *tell* you about Paris, but you won't know 'less you been there. You simply under-*stand*. Or you don't.' He raises an eyebrow in clairvoyant drunkenness before continuing. 'You either take me, or you *don't*.' He throws his hands up, smiling as though he's finally solved some grand equation in a few simple steps.

'Please,' I say, giving up on him. I beckon the Goiter for another game of electronic trivia, but he shakes his head and smiles solemnly, a smile that says he's more weary for me than for himself.

'Let me tel! you something,' Ray Bivens Jr. says, practically spitting in my face, 'Lupita *understands* me. That woman,' he says, suddenly sounding drunk again, '*understands*. She's It.'

Farrah, suddenly sober, smacks him on the shoulder and says, 'What about me? What the fuck about me?'

Another hour later he says, all cool, 'Gimme the keys. Farrah and I are going for a ride.'

I've had many 7 Ups and I've twice asked my father if we could go, told him that we either had to find a motel outside the city or plan on driving back soon. But now he's asking for the keys at nearly three a.m., the car all the way over in Arlington, and even the Metro has stopped running.

'Sir,' I say. 'We need to drive back.'

'I said, Spurgeon, dear son, that Farrah and I are going for a ride. Now give me the keys, dear son.'

A ride means they're going to her place, wherever that is. Him going to her place means I have to find my own place to stay. Giving him the keys not only means he'll be driving illegally, which I no longer care about, but that the car will end up on the other side of the country, stripped for parts.

'No,' I say. 'It's Mama's car.'

'*Mama's car*,' he mimics.

'Sir.'

'*Maaaamaaa's caaaaar!*'

I leave the bar. I'm walking for a good minute before I hear him coming after me. I speed up but don't run. I don't even know how I'm going to get back to the car, but I pick a direction and walk purposefully. I hear the *click click click* of what are surely Farrah's heels, hear her voice screaming something that doesn't make sense, hear his footfalls close in on me, but all I see are the streetlights glowing amber, and the puffs of smoke my breath makes in the October air. All I feel is that someone has spun me around as if for inspection, and that's when I see his face— handsome, hard-edged, not the least bit sloppy from liquor.

Sure. He's hit me before, but this is hard. Not the back of the hand, not with a belt, but punching. A punch meant for my face, but lands on my shoulder, like he's congratulating me, then another hit, this one all knuckles, and my jaw pops open, automatically, like the trunk of a car. I try to close my mouth, try to call time out, but he's ramming into me, not with his fists, but with his head. I try to pry him from where his head butts, inside my stomach, right under my windpipe, but he stays that way, leaning into me, tucked as if fighting against a strong wind, both of us wobbling together like lovers. Finally, I push him away, and wipe what feels like yogurt running from my nose into the raw cut of my lip. I start to lick my lips, thinking that it's all over, when he rushes straight at me and rams me into something that topples over with a toyish metal clank. Sheaves of weekly newspapers fan the ground like spilled cards from a deck. I kick him anywhere my foot will land, shouting at him, so strangely mad that I'm happy, until I finally kick at air, hard, and trip myself. I don't know how long I'm down, how long my eyes are closed, but he's now holding me like a rag doll. 'What the hell are you talking about?' he says as if to shake the answer out of me. 'What the *hell* are you talking about?'

I only now realize what I've been screaming the whole time. 'Wind-o!' I yell at him. 'You and your goddamn "wind-o"! There was never any "wind-o"! And you don't know *shit* about birds! *Arriba! Arriba!*' I say mockingly.

When he grabs my collar, almost lifting me from the ground, I feel as though I'm floating upward, then I feel some part of me drowning. I remember something, something I know will kill my father. My father dodged the draft. They weren't going to get this nigger, was his view of Vietnam. It was the one thing I'd respected him for, and yet somehow I said it, 'You didn't know fucking Huey P. Newton. You never even *went* to Vietnam!'

That does it. I had turned into something ugly, and of all the millions of words I've ever spoken to him in all my life, this is the one that blows him to pieces.

'Vietnam?' he says, once, as if making sure I'd said the word.

I'm quiet. He says the word again, 'Vietnam,' and his eyes somehow look sightless.

I try to pull him back, begging in the only way you can beg without words. I go to put my hand on his shoulder, but a torrent of people, fresh from the March, it seems, has been loosed from a nearby restaurant. They slap one another's backs, smelling of Brut and Old Spice, musk-scented African oils and sweat. I go to put my hand on his shoulder, but already my father has gone.

Ray Bivens Jr. left with the car and Farrah left with someone else. The birds are gone. My blazer is gone. After I have a scotch, the bartender says, 'Look. I can float you the drinks, but who's going to pay for that, youngblood?' He points to one of the bar's smashed windowpanes.

After I pay him, I have no money left for a cab or a bus. The bridge over the Potomac isn't meant for pedestrians, and it takes me half an hour to walk across it. For a long time I'm on New Hampshire Avenue, then for a long time I'm on Georgia. I ask for directions to the train station and someone finally gives them to me.

I wonder if he's right about Lupita. When she sat on the porch and held her head, it seemed she felt more sorry for him than she did for herself; not pity, but sympathy.

I pass by an old-fashioned movie theater whose marquee looks like one giant erection lit in parti-colored lights. People pass by, wondering how to go about mugging me. A well-dressed man asks if I'm a pitcher or a catcher, and I have no idea what he means. I tell myself that it's good that Ray Bivens Jr. and I fought. Most people think that you find something that matters, something that's worth fighting for, and if necessary, you fight. But it must be the fighting, I tell myself, that decides what matters, even if you're left on the sidewalk to discover that what you thought mattered means nothing after all.

'Where do you want to go?' the Amtrak ticket officer asks.

'East,' I say. 'Any train that goes east this time of night.'

'You're in D.C., sir. Any further east and you'll be in the Atlantic.'

Of course I'm not going east anymore. I'd been going east the last day and a half, and it's just now hitting me that I can finally go west. Go home.

After the events of the day, I'm not surprised that I get the snottiest ticket officer of the whole damn railway system. I look into the his gray eyes. 'West, motherfucker.'

The ticket officer stares at me and I stare right back.

The ticket officer sighs. He looks down at his computer, and then at me again. 'Where, pray tell, do you want to go? West, I'm afraid, is a direction, not a destination.'

'Louisville, Kentucky,' I finally say. 'Home.'

He enters something into his computer. Tilts his head. He smiles when he tells me there is no train that goes to Louisville. The closest one is Cincinnati.

I walk away from the counter and sit down, trying to think of how I'm going to pay to get to Cincinnati, then from Cincinnati to Louisville. The only other white person in the station besides the ticket officer is an old woman in a rainbow knit cap. She's having quite an intelligent conversation with herself.

I'll have to call home, ask my mother to give her credit card number to this prick. I start to try to find a phone when a man approaches the ticket counter, his half-asleep son riding on his back. He probably just came from the March. Probably listened to all the poems and speeches about ants and oxen and African drumming, but still had this kid out in the hot sun for hours, then in the cold night for longer. It's almost five o'clock in the morning, and all this little boy wants, I can tell, is some goddamned sleep.

'Hey,' I say to the man. When he doesn't respond, I tap him on the non-kid shoulder. 'It's pretty late to have a kid out. Don't you think?'

He puts his hand up like a traffic cop, but apparently decides I'm harmless and says to me, 'Son. I want you to promise me you'll go clean yourself up. Get something to eat.' He produces a wallet from his back pocket. He hands me a twenty. 'Now, don't go spending it on nothing that'll make you *worse*. Promise me.'

It's not enough to get me where I'm going, but it's just what I need. I sit down on a wooden bench. The old white woman next to me carefully pours imaginary liquid into an imaginary cup. The man with the kid goes up to the ticket officer, who stops staring into space long enough to say, 'May I help *you*, sir?'

'Do y'all still say "All aboard"?'

'Excuse me?' the ticket officer says.

'My son wants to know if y'all say "All aboard." Like in the movies.'

'Yes,' the ticket officer says wearily. 'We *do* say "All aboard." How else would people know to board the train?'

Now the boy jiggles up and down on his father's back, suddenly animated, as if he's riding a pony. The ticket officer sighs, hands grazing the sides of his face as though checking for stubble. Finally he throws his arms up in a 'Sure, what the hell' kind of way, and disappears into the Amtrak offices for what seems like an hour. The father sets the boy down, feet first, onto the ground. An intercom crackles and a voice says:

'All aboard!'

The voice is hearty and successful. The boy jumps up and down with delight. He is the happiest I've seen anyone, ever. And though the urge to weep comes over me, I wait—holding my head in my hands— and it passes.

STARS OF MOTOWN SHINING BRIGHT

Julie Orringer

Lucy waited in her room for Melissa to arrive from Cincinnati. They would drive in Melissa's old Cadillac, that sleek white boat, forty miles east to Royal Oak, where they would spend the night with Jack Jacob. Lucy was fifteen and no longer a virgin. The teen magazine articles pondering the question of whether one was ready to give it up no longer applied to her. She could, at that very moment, be pregnant. Not that she was pregnant. She had been careful, and so had Jack Jacob. Still, there was a possibility. And now she was off to see him again, to spend the night with him in Royal Oak, and it was all right with her parents because he was a boy she'd met in youth group, and because they were staying at his parents' house, and because Melissa would be there too. These friendships were important, her parents had told her. These friendships could last a lifetime.

The trip had been Melissa's idea. She liked road trips and she liked adventures in which she and Lucy did something they could tell everyone about afterward, with lots of dramatic detail. But she didn't know about what had happened between Lucy and Jack. Lucy hadn't told her. It felt too private to talk about over the phone. Maybe if Melissa had lived closer, Lucy would have gone over to her house and whispered it to her in the dark. On the other hand, maybe she wouldn't have. She wasn't sure how Melissa would react. Melissa liked Jack too. She and Jack had even fooled around once at a youth group convention. While everyone else was busy at the Saturday-night dance, Melissa and Jack had snuck away to the high-vaulted sanctuary and made out for half an hour on the floor between two rows of pews. Lucy knew because she'd been there, guarding the door in case any of the youth leaders came along. She remembered trying not to listen but listening anyway. She remembered the bronze Eternal Light flickering in the half-dark. At one point Melissa sat up to twist her hair into a ponytail, and she shot Lucy a self-satisfied smile. Lucy knew what that smile was about: Jack, a senior, liked *her*, Melissa. Not tonight, though.

Things were different now. Lucy was the one Jack wanted, and Melissa would have to live with that.

There was the white Cadillac at last, rolling long and smooth into the driveway. It had once belonged to Melissa's mother, but now it had daisy decals on the hood and a Barbie dangling from a tiny noose on the rearview mirror. Lucy watched Melissa climb out, tall and lank in a short white skirt and sling-back shoes, her hair caught in a high ponytail. There was something about the sheen of her legs, the slowness of her walk, that made Lucy sick with envy.

Lucy went downstairs and tiptoed to the door. Through the peephole she could see Melissa practicing nonchalance, swinging her keys on one finger and moving her hips from side to side as if to music. She tilted her head back, blew a pink gum bubble, and sucked it in as it burst. Lucy opened the door.

Melissa leaned forward coolly and kissed Lucy first on one cheek and then the other, European style. She smelled of nail polish remover and black-cherry lip gloss and beauty salon shampoo. At her feet was a large black shoulder bag stuffed with clothes.

'Where are your parents?' she said.

'Gone,' Lucy said. 'Neighborhood Watch meeting.'

'Good.' Melissa brushed past Lucy and led her upstairs as if this were *her* house, as if she owned Lucy's room and everything in it. She threw her bag on the bed and opened the doors to Lucy's closet, flicking her way through Lucy's shirts and pants and skirts. Every now and then she would extract a garment and regard it with distaste, then replace it on the bar and shove it aside. 'You have no clothes,' she concluded.

'Don't remind me,' Lucy said.

Melissa sat down on the bed, just inches from the place where Lucy had slept with Jack Jacob, and then she opened her overnight bag and pulled out something that looked like a clot of black yarn. When she unrolled it, Lucy saw that it was a crocheted dress with short sleeves and no back.

'I couldn't wear it over here,' Melissa said. 'Your parents would freak.' She peeled off her shirt and skirt and tossed them to Lucy. She was wearing white stockings that ended at the thigh with a band of elastic lace. These too she took off and tossed to Lucy. 'You can wear my clothes if you want,' she said. 'Don't spill anything on them, though.' From her bag she pulled out another pair of stockings, black with lace at the top, and put them on. In stockings, panties, and brassiere she posed in front of Lucy's full-length mirror, bending forward to look at her cleavage. She was the only girl Lucy knew who actually loved her body.

Lucy pulled on the stockings and stretched them up to her thighs. They were a tight fit around the tops. She struggled into Melissa's skirt and shirt. When she looked in the mirror, she thought she hardly looked like herself at all.

'Much better,' Melissa told her. 'Though you should have straightened your hair or pulled it back or something.' She herself was cool and lean in the black crocheted dress, the tops of her stockings and her pale thighs visible through the fabric. 'We don't have time now, though,' she said. 'Do you have your stuff?'

Lucy had packed an overnight bag. In it was a pair of satin pajamas she'd bought without telling her parents. She imagined entering Jack's room in those pajamas, his eyes traveling over her, Melissa looking at her in envy. Was it possible that Melissa could envy her? Maybe when she told her what had happened.

They'd become friends at last year's Regional Convention, when Melissa had told her about the date with Adam Moskovitz. She and Melissa had found themselves sitting next to each other in the synagogue social hall during a long panel discussion about Tikkun Olam, which meant Healing the World. Adam, a senior and the vice president of Midwest Region, had been one of the panelists. Every time he made a point about how important it was to spend time helping out at your local soup kitchen or collecting clothes for Russian immigrants, Melissa would roll her eyes and make a little sarcastic huff. Finally she took Lucy by the sleeve and they went to the ladies' lounge. This was a big Cincinnati-synagogue ladies' lounge, with tailored chintz sofas in a pink-carpeted anteroom. It smelled of rose soap and ammonia, and the plumbing hummed in the walls. Melissa unfolded herself onto a sofa and closed her eyes. Then she told about the date with Adam, how he'd taken her out to a Japanese restaurant and then to his parents' private box at the symphony, where he'd shoved a hand under her skirt and told her he wanted her *right then*. He'd pulled her up against the wall, in a tiny space between the box door and a velvet curtain, and he lifted her skirt and did it, not even using a condom. Melissa cried a little as she told the story, though the way she described the sex itself, with anatomical details and language that sounded like a porno magazine, made Lucy feel as if she were bragging—or lying.

In comparison, Lucy's night with Jack would sound plain and undramatic. She had wanted to do it, first of all. She'd known Jack since she was twelve and had always thought he was nice and not unattractive, though maybe slightly greasy, with his hair gelled back and his dance-club shirts in every color. He was even famous, in a small way: He'd been in a movie, *Streets of Detroit*. In his one scene, Jack, the troubled younger brother, had gotten shot by mistake. Still alive, he lay on the sidewalk looking tragic and vulnerable. The stricken older brother knelt beside him. Jack looked up at him, eyes clouding. *It's not your fault, Tommy*, he said.

The problem was, Melissa had always liked him too. It was obvious she couldn't wait to see him tonight. Lucy had never seen her acting so nervous. As she drove along I-94 toward Detroit, she did not sing with the radio or talk to Lucy. She drove with one hand on the wheel and the other clenched around a small pearl-gray box in her lap. The way she kept opening it just a little and peeking inside seemed calculated to create mystery, so Lucy forced herself not to ask what was in it. Instead, she leaned over and turned up the radio. It was DJ Baby Love, at WLUX.

'The stars are shining bright above Motown tonight,' said DJ Baby Love in his plush baritone, 'and it's Diana Ross with "Ain't No Mountain High Enough."' Lucy sang along, making up lyrics when she didn't know them.

'You're loud,' Melissa said. 'And bad.'

'Yeah, that's right.' Lucy rolled her shoulders and sang with Diana.

'You are so not black.'

'But I'm beautiful,' Lucy said. She tried acting carefree and fifteen, entirely uninterested in Melissa and that pearl-gray box. She had other things to think about, things of greater importance. Somewhere beneath the stars of Motown, Jack was waiting.

That night with Jack, she'd known exactly what was going to happen. They'd gone to see *The Birds* at the Michigan Theater, and they'd shared a bowl of mint chip at the Home Dairy. And then they'd gone back to her house and sat in the driveway in Jack's Continental for what seemed like hours, taking burning swigs from Jack's silver flask. She hated the taste of whatever it was, so most of the time she was just taking pretend swigs, tipping the flask up to her mouth and blocking the liquor with her tongue. She tried acting like she was getting a little drunk. Jack had a hand on her thigh, just in the same place, for a long time. It was early June and cool, the crickets making their shrill dry sound in the box elders beside the driveway. Upstairs the light in her parents' bedroom was still on. Jack told her about California, about the women at the fitness club in Bel Air where he taught Pilates and weight training. A few of the women had offered him money for special favors, which he'd declined to perform. He talked about trying out for sitcoms. He talked about looking for an agent. He talked about living in a shitty bungalow three blocks from the beach, and about going to Compton on Saturday nights with a black friend from Detroit, and almost getting his ass shot off, and consequently having to buy a gun for self-protection. It was a double-action Kel-Tec .32. He had it with him, in fact, and he showed it to her. It was brushed steel, blunt-nosed, small enough almost to disappear in his closed hand. He pulled the slide back to show her a cartridge in the chamber. This gun had no external safety, he said, so she should never touch it unless they were in Detroit some night and she had to protect herself. She'd held guns before, had taken riflery at summer camp, but it frightened her to see this small sleek pistol in his hand, right there in the driveway of her house. She didn't want to touch it. He put it in the glove compartment, and she tried to forget it was there.

She told him about how she was volunteering at a shelter for runaway teen girls and their babies, a place where her parents would never have let her work in a million years. She'd lied to them, saying she was working as a candy striper at the hospital, and her father would drive her downtown and she'd go into the hospital and wait until he drove away before walking to the shelter. She told him about finding packets of crack stashed in diapers, which hadn't actually happened to her but to Lynette, one of the other volunteers. Jack removed his hand from her thigh.

'You're too serious,' he said. 'You should try to act like a fifteen-year-old sometimes.'

'How?'

'You could kiss me,' he said. 'You could climb right onto my lap.'

She laughed. 'Is that what fifteen-year-olds do?'

'Sometimes.'

'And then what would happen?'

'And then I'd take you inside and make love with you. Nice and sweet.'

She said she'd think about it. She was trying to act casual, though really she'd been thinking about it for nearly a month, ever since she'd gotten the postcard saying he was coming back from California for a visit. She'd even taken condoms from the shelter. So she was ready to do it, and here he was. Her parents' light was off now. They'd have to be quiet. She climbed into his lap and kissed him.

Later they went inside and upstairs to her room, where she locked and double-locked the door and got undressed, folding her clothes neatly on a chair as if she were at the doctor's office. She listened for movement from the direction of her parents' room and heard nothing, so she crawled into her bed and waited. She expected it to be painful and brutal, like the unprofessional extraction of a tooth. But when Jack was in bed with her, breathing quiet into her hair, touching her everywhere, getting her to touch him, she forgot to worry about the pain.

When it was over, she felt good. Not a virgin anymore, but better. He kissed her goodnight and went to sleep on the couch downstairs. The next morning he thanked her parents for their hospitality and took Lucy out for pancakes and eggs. As they were leaving the diner, they passed a plant nursery where tiny fir trees stood in a row along a wooden fence. Jack said he wanted to buy one for Lucy to commemorate their night together. She laughed, but he said he was serious, and so they bought the tree and planted it beside a rock garden in Lucy's backyard. The whole time she moved as if through syrup, feeling warm in all her limbs. Now he was planning to leave for California sometime that week. She hadn't thought it would make her sad, but it did.

She'd been waiting to tell Melissa the whole story in person, but now she didn't feel like talking about it at all. How could she describe it, anyway? She didn't want to use the kind of details Melissa had used when she'd talked about Adam Moskovitz, and she didn't want to make it sound romantic, either. But she wanted to talk about it. She wanted to say his name.

'What do you think Jack's doing right now?' she said, trying to sound bored.

'I don't know,' Melissa said, rubbing the pearl-gray box with her thumb. 'Showering, maybe. I'm always asking myself that same question. I'm always like, "I wonder what he's doing right now?" I think about him all the time.'

'You think about him all the time?'

'There's something I should tell you, actually,' Melissa said. 'Something important.' With a serious look, eyes flinty and small, she put a hand on Lucy's arm. 'You have to swear you won't tell anyone about this.'

'What?' Lucy said. Her scalp prickled with sudden cold.

'I mean *swear*. Not your parents, not my parents, not the police. Even if they torture you.'

'Okay, I swear! Just tell me!'

'Jack and I are getting married,' said Melissa. 'We're leaving tomorrow morning to drive out to California, and on the way we're getting married in Vegas. And then we're getting an apartment in LA and he's going to introduce me to this magazine guy he knows. I'm going to get this job working at the magazine. I'll be a model at first, but later on they're going to teach me how to do design and layout.'

Lucy stared. A semi blasted by, rocking the car.

'We don't care what people say about us being too young,' Melissa said. 'We're in love. Plus I have a fake birth certificate saying I'm eighteen.'

'But you can't *marry* him. You're not even going out with him.'

'We are,' Melissa said. 'We hooked up a couple of times before he went out west, and he's been writing to me. We didn't want to broadcast our relationship to the whole world.'

Lucy thought of how he'd gone into her, deliberate and quiet. He'd waited forever, just on the verge. Then she'd raised her hips and they were rocking together.

'It won't be easy at first,' Melissa said. 'But I had to get away from home. I couldn't stand it anymore, with my stepmom treating me like I'm in elementary school. And always making me baby-sit for her own kids, those brats. And acting like she owns my dad. And everyone pretending like *my* mom doesn't exist anymore.' Melissa paused, giving Lucy the dare-you-to-pity-me look that came on whenever she mentioned her mother, who'd left the family three years earlier for a Minneapolis real-estate entrepreneur. 'I can get my GED out there, and when I start learning graphic design I can make some money. This magazine guy Jack knows, he's very artistic. He does films, too. The modeling's just for a while, anyhow, before I get into the design side.'

'What modeling?' Lucy said.

'You know, artistic modeling.'

'You mean nude.'

'It's not *porn*,' Melissa spat. 'Most of it's just partial nudity, and you don't even have to touch anyone. You'd never understand, though. No offense, Lucy, but you're so immature. I never should have told you.'

Outside, trees flashed lean and dark against the distant glow of Detroit. The corn was shoulder-high in the fields, its tassels ghostly silver. 'Ha-ha,' Lucy said. 'Right? You're completely shitting me.'

'I am so not shitting you,' said Melissa. 'I'm so serious I could fucking kill myself for telling you. You'll run home and tell your mom and everything will be ruined.' She stared ahead at the highway.

Lucy couldn't believe it. She kept waiting for Melissa to give her a cross-eyed look and then start laughing. But Melissa was fierce and determined, her face flushed, her hands tight on the steering wheel. 'I knew you'd be a baby about it,' she said. 'But you've got to get your shit together because you're going to help us. That's why you're on this trip.'

'No, it's not,' Lucy said.

'You're going to be our accomplice,' Melissa said. 'We're going to take his car, and you're going to drive this one back to my mom's and leave it in the driveway.'

'Like fuck I am.'

'You have to. It's part of the plan.'

'There's no plan,' Lucy said. 'You're completely lying.'

'I'm not lying,' said Melissa. 'Look.' She opened the pearl-gray box. Lucy took it from her and switched on the dome light. Inside was a plain gold band with a Tiffany-style setting. The diamond was clear and fiery and small enough to be convincing. Lucy took it out and turned it over and over in her fingers, feeling the chill of the gold.

'Okay,' Melissa said. 'Give it back.'

Lucy put the ring back into the box, handed it to Melissa, and turned off the dome light. She looked down at her own hands, which were bare. 'If you're really engaged,' she said, 'why don't you wear your ring?'

'Are you joking? It's not exactly stealth.'

Melissa changed the radio station. On all the presets there were commercials. Lucy wondered what Melissa would do if she grabbed the ring box and threw it out the window.

'He gave me something else, too,' Melissa said, 'but I can't tell you what it is.'

'Why not?'

'Because look at yourself. Everything I tell you, you're like, *Oh, my God!*'

'Fine,' Lucy said. 'I don't care.'

Melissa pulled off the highway toward a gas station, where a red-and-blue sign advertised Icees. She drove up beside a vacant pump and turned to Lucy.

'Do you have any money?' she asked.

'For what?'

'I'll give you a hint: This is a *gas* station, where they sell *gas*.'

'I'm not giving you money.'

'I'm engaged,' Melissa said. 'This can be your engagement present to me.' She grabbed Lucy's purse and fished out a twenty, then went to pump the gas. Lucy watched her as she stood against the gas pump and fiddled with the elastic of her stocking. She did a little hip grind to the bass thrumming from a low-slung Crown Vic. The two boys inside, their hair shaved close and their teeth flashing with gold, watched her like zombies. When the tank was full, Melissa went into the convenience store.

Lucy looked through her purse for quarters. She could call someone from the shelter to come get her—her friend Lynette, maybe. Or she could just grab her bag and hitch a ride home. She imagined herself standing beside the highway in her short white skirt. It seemed like an image from a slasher movie. When she looked through the window, trying to see Melissa inside the store, one of the boys in the Crown Vic waved.

The pearl-gray box was still on the seat where Melissa had left it. Lucy picked it up and shook the ring out onto her palm. Something else was rattling around inside the box, something heavier than the ring. She pried out the velvet insert and a key fell into her lap. It was a Cadillac key but with a round head: a glove compartment key. Turning it over in her hand, she looked toward the convenience store with its racks of chips and magazines. Melissa was nowhere in sight. She fitted the key into the glove compartment lock. It turned, and the compartment fell open. There, on top of the maps and old Midas receipts, was Jack's gun.

Before, in Jack's car, it had frightened her. Now she wanted to hold it in her hand. It was cold and heavy and small enough to fit her palm. The muzzle was clean and oiled, and there was the trigger, a smooth place for an index finger. She pulled back the slide like Jack had showed her. The gun was still loaded. She pointed it into the foot well and said, 'Freeze!'

She could do anything now. Not that she'd *do* anything. But here she was, no longer a virgin, and in her hand she had this gun. They were going to Detroit. They were going to see Jack Jacob. She put the gun back into the glove compartment and waited for Melissa to come out.

The rest of the way to Detroit, Lucy didn't say a word. She knew Melissa wanted her to ask questions, to act interested in what was going to happen, but she refused to do it. Beside her on the Cadillac seat, Melissa tried to act like she didn't care. She sang along with the radio as the suburbs of Detroit rushed by, their shopping malls and car showrooms and soaring Methodist churches glowing alongside the highway. They passed the eighty-foot-high Uniroyal tire and the old New Silver Rolladium of Southfield, with its spotlit fake palm trees and its mural of a freestyle skater in silhouette. Then they pulled off the highway into Royal Oak. The houses there were cramped little castles of white or pink brick, each with its green cropped lawn. Jack's house was a small Tudor in a row of Tudor houses. It was shabbier than the others, somehow—its shutters peeling, its plaster lawn gnome missing the peak of his cap. But the lawn had been mowed recently, and a pair of Jack's grassy sneakers stood beside the door.

'You have to promise you won't do anything stupid,' Melissa said as she killed the motor. 'You've got to stop freaking right now. Think of yourself as my maid of honor. Your job is to help me stay calm before my wedding.'

'Okay,' Lucy said. She felt prickly-skinned and powerful, ready to commit reckless deeds. She'd replaced the key in the pearl-gray box but left the glove compartment unlocked.

They got out of the car with their things and went to the door, and Melissa rang the bell. She made an attempt at door-waiting nonchalance, smacking her gum and twirling the keys, but it didn't last long. After a minute she got up on her toes and tried to look through the tiny sheer-curtained window at the top of the door.

'Where is he?' she said. 'He'd better be here.'

Then he was there, opening the door for them, welcoming them into the living room, with its slipcovered gold couches and its smell of old chicken soup. Melissa jumped at him and he picked her up, swinging her. One of her black shoes fell off. Lucy tried to get him to look at her, but he kept avoiding her eyes. Her stomach lurched and she had to sit down on a couch. A curl of torn plastic bit into her thigh. 'Jesus fucking Christ,' Jack was saying. 'Look at you two.' Lucy adjusted her thigh-highs and crossed her legs. She told herself to relax. She stared at the carpet with its pattern of gold scrolls and turquoise roses, a terrible carpet, perhaps the world's worst.

'Don't sit there,' Jack said. 'Come upstairs. See my room.'

He started up the stairs and Melissa followed. 'Come on,' she called to Lucy.

Lucy went, dragging her overnight bag. She followed Jack and Melissa down the hall, down a strip of olive-colored carpet, past the pictures of Jack's family and Jack himself as a kid with dark eyes and pin-straight black hair. They passed a closed bedroom door. Inside, someone was snoring loudly.

'My mom,' Jack said. 'Out cold.'

In his room, white Christmas lights blinked around the ceiling and Pink Floyd's *Delicate Sound of Thunder* played on the stereo. There was a ratty football-helmet rug half covered by an air mattress, which smelled new, as if purchased for the occasion. The air mattress was made up in black sheets. A TV sat near it on the rug. Beside the TV, on a boy-sized desk, stood a glossy black ice bucket, three glasses, and bottles of gin and peach schnapps and tonic water and vodka. On a bookshelf were some dusty baseball trophies and a framed bar mitzvah certificate. The air was heavy with the smells of vinyl and sandalwood incense.

'The luxury lounge,' Jack said.

Melissa threw her bag onto the floor. 'Let's go out,' she said. 'There must be a party or something.'

'A party?' Jack said. He seemed disappointed.

'It's early. I want to go out. Lucy does too, don't you, Lucy?'

'Sure,' Lucy said. Anything to get away from that room, with its terrible smell and its giant mattress.

'This town's dead,' Jack said. 'The party's right here tonight.'

'I know what we should do!' Melissa said. 'The Silver Rolladium. We passed it on the way here. We *have* to go.'

'I don't skate,' Jack said. 'As a rule.'

'We have to,' Melissa said. 'Please, please. We can leave if it sucks.'

'Jesus Christ,' Jack said, holding the back of his neck with one hand. 'Okay. But just for a little while. I don't want to spend all night there.'

Melissa gave Lucy a look of triumph. Then she took her tiny makeup bag and disappeared into the bathroom, down the hall. Lucy stood on the football-helmet rug and looked at Jack.

'What?' Jack said.

When Lucy didn't respond, he said, 'Let's go downstairs. Let's have a talk.' He took her hand and led her downstairs to the kitchen, where Lucy sat on a yellow stool at the breakfast bar. Jack opened the refrigerator and took out a carton of orange juice. He opened it, sniffed it, put it away. He took out a can of Fanta Grape. 'You want a Fanta Grape?' he said.

Lucy shook her head.

'How about a real drink? I know I could use one.' Jack went into another room and came back with a cut-glass decanter. 'This is Scotch,' he said. 'Is Scotch okay?'

'I don't care,' Lucy said. It was hard to make her voice sound the way she wanted it to, steady and glacier-cold. Maybe a drink would help.

Jack put ice cubes into a glass and poured Lucy an inch of Scotch. He set the glass before her. It smelled like sweetened nail polish remover. She lifted the glass and drank. It was horrible, bitter, burning. She coughed and wiped her mouth.

'Shit,' Jack said. 'That's some drinking.' He took the empty glass and poured some for himself. 'You look hot in that skirt,' he said. 'You really do.'

'Fuck you,' she said.

Jack took a drink of Scotch. 'Lucy,' he said, 'I have to explain a few things.'

'No need. Melissa told me everything.'

'You don't understand, though.'

'What's to understand? You're engaged. Congratulations.'

He gave her a moist smile. 'Let's not worry about all that tonight. We should just have a good time. We know how to have a good time together, don't we?' He put a hand on her arm and rubbed the inside of her wrist with his thumb.

Lucy pulled away. 'I'm going to tell Melissa about last weekend.'

'I don't think that's a good idea.'

'I think it's a fabulous idea.'

'Okay,' Jack said. 'Tell her. I'll say it's not true. Who do you think she's going to believe?' He tilted his head at her and smiled.

Lucy sat back, feeling the heat of the Scotch in her blood. A hum like bees filled her head. Now Melissa was coming down the stairs, crossing one foot in front of the other like a Miss America contestant, singing 'Ready for skating, ready to go roller skating' to the tune of 'Getting to Know You.' In the kitchen she leaned over the bar to give them a look down her shirt. Lucy could see the black bow at the center of her bra.

'Ouch, baby,' Jack said. 'Put those away.'

'Are we going?' said Melissa.

They were.

At the skating rink the air was thick with smoke-machine smoke, and the skaters shot through beams of flashing light. The floor was packed. All the girls were dressed in small tight clothes, their hair done in elaborate braids or ponytails. It was house night, and Lucy could feel the drums at the center of her chest. Jack draped one arm around her shoulders and the other around Melissa's. He steered them through the crowd toward the skate-rental booth, looking as if he were loving this.

'Check out these walls,' he said, and Lucy did. The walls were lined with sparkly black carpet, meant as a crash guard for the skaters. 'It's like a porno movie,' he said. 'It's like we could all just lie down and fuck anywhere, if gravity suddenly went haywire.'

Melissa giggled and gave him a slap on the arm. 'You're so bad,' she said.

They rented skates and put them on. Before Lucy could get the feel of them, Melissa took her by the hand and pulled her out onto the wooden skating floor. Lucy stumbled along, trying to keep her balance. She'd hated skating ever since she was a kid. She'd never wanted those white skates with pink pom-poms like the other kids had. She'd never tried to win the games at skating parties. Now her arms and legs felt numb from the whiskey, and the music was a dull throb inside her head. Jack kept giving her a heavy-lidded look as they skated, a half smile meant to be sexy. She wanted to jab her fingers right into his eyes and watch him double over in pain. The worst part was that when she let her mind go, she was still imagining him apologizing to her, on his knees even, telling her how sorry he was, what an asshole he was, and it was really Lucy he wanted to marry and take to California.

Lucy caught up with Melissa and pulled her toward the girls' room. Melissa was laughing, pushing strands of her ponytail out of her face and adjusting the lace tops of her thigh-highs. They both skidded when their skates hit the girls' room tiles.

'These tights are going to be totally wrecked,' Melissa said, 'but it's worth it.' She leaned against the wall and pulled a crumpled cigarette from her pocket. When she tried to straighten it out, it broke. 'Fuck,' she said. 'Do you have any?'

'No,' Lucy said.

Melissa threw the cigarette away and checked her eyebrows in the mirror. Then she turned to Lucy and smoothed her curls with one cool hand. 'You look like shit. And you smell like whiskey.' She laughed. 'You know what I always thought?' she said, leaning against a sink. 'I thought I could take you and make you into a totally new girl. When I met you at that convention, I said to myself, That girl's kind of pretty but she dresses lame and acts immature. I bet I could make her so cool.'

'I'm not immature,' Lucy said.

'Oh, I know, I know,' Melissa said. 'Your job and all that, doing good deeds for the pregnant teens. Plus I think you lost some weight lately.'

Lucy thought about the gun, about the weight of it in her hand, and the smooth sheen of the barrel, and the arc of the trigger against her index finger. She imagined aiming, squeezing, then the explosion and the peppery smell of gunpowder, like when she used to shoot rifles at summer camp.

'Our friends are *so* going to freak when you tell them,' Melissa said.

'Think about two weeks from now at Nationals! Everyone's going to be like, She did *what*? Oh, my *God*. Her and *Jack*? You have to tell everyone we were seeing each other for months and it was this big secret.'

The restroom door banged open and a group of younger girls skated in. They wore tight glitter jeans and pastel-colored tank tops, and they were all talking about someone named Connie: Connie better get her hands off Trey. Connie didn't know who she was messing with. Connie was going to regret she ever came here. The girls leaned toward the mirror to reapply their lip gloss. Every now and then they glanced at Lucy and Melissa as if to make sure they were paying attention.

'Any of you have a cigarette?' Melissa asked.

'Are you crazy?' Lucy said. 'They're like twelve.'

One of the girls rolled her eyes. 'We're fourteen,' she said.

Another girl opened the door. 'Come on, you guys,' she said. 'It's the couples' skate.' The lights had dimmed, and there was a slow song playing. The younger girls finished putting on their makeup and filed out.

'There's no way those girls are fourteen,' Melissa said.

'I know,' Lucy said. 'It's depressing.' She thought of a girl she'd been tutoring earlier that week at the shelter, a skinny, dark-eyed girl named Tiana Woods. She was trying to pass pre-algebra, but her baby had an ear infection and wouldn't stop crying. The girls in the glitter jeans had looked about Tiana's age. 'Listen to me,' Lucy said. 'Just don't go out to California. I know what I'm talking about.'

Melissa sighed. 'How could you understand?' she said. 'Imagine if your mom had run off with some asshole. Imagine if your dad was married to the world's biggest bitch-on-a-stick, who always tried to treat you like a nine-year-old. Imagine your house feeling like a jail.' She looked at Lucy, her eyes large and dramatic.

Lucy wondered if anyone could feel sorry for Melissa. She'd been to Melissa's house, that iced white cake on a cul-de-sac in Cincinnati. She'd met Melissa's stepmother, a small harried woman with two children of her own. Melissa's stepmother had made a low-fat vegetarian stir-fry for Melissa so she wouldn't have to wreck her diet with manicotti, which was what everyone else was eating that night.

'I guess I can't imagine,' Lucy said.

'Now, here's what's going to happen. I'm going to fix my lipstick, and then I'm going back out there to skate. And then we're going back to Jack's house, and maybe we'll have a few drinks and watch a movie. In the morning Jack and I are going to load my stuff into his car and get on the road, and you're going to drive my car back to my house, and then you're going to take the Greyhound home.' Melissa opened her purse and took out a folded envelope, from which she pulled two twenties and put them into Lucy's hand. 'And you're going to do it so no one sees you, and if they do see you you're going to have sudden total amnesia.'

'And then what?' Lucy said. 'What happens tomorrow night, when your parents start to freak?' She thought about Melissa's father, who'd come to pick her up from youth group conventions—a narrow man in a beige golf shirt and gold glasses, huffing as he carried Melissa's suitcases. Hanging from the rearview mirror of his car was a Lucite photo holder with a picture of Melissa as a kid, playing a tiny violin.

'Are you going to help me?' Melissa said. 'Or are you going to fuck it all up?'

'Let's just go home now,' Lucy said. '*Home* home. Come on.'

Melissa leaned toward the mirror and redid her lipstick. 'Don't fuck it all up, Lucy. I mean that so seriously, you have no idea.'

Lucy went into a stall and sat down. She heard the music swell as Melissa opened the restroom door, and then go quiet again as the door swung closed. She couldn't believe how stupid they all were. She should call Melissa's father right now. She should kick Jack's ass or shoot it off. What was she doing in this roller-rink bathroom? She stared at the back-of-the-door nail salon advertisement, at the gritty tile floor, at the smoked plastic Rollmastr with its eternal roll. All she wanted was to get out of there. She flushed and washed her hands and went to find Melissa.

There she was, on the far side near the railing, holding Jack's hand, leading him out onto the polished floor. He staggered a little at first, but then got his balance and began to skate. The Lurex fibers in his shirt caught the light. Melissa skated beside him, her ponytail swaying. Lucy stepped out onto the rink, meaning to catch up with them, do something, pry them apart, but as she started to skate another girl plowed into her. They both stumbled into the carpeted wall of the rink, trying to keep their balance. High-pitched shrieks of laughter came from the sidelines. There, pointing and calling out, were the younger girls from the restroom. The girl who ran into Lucy took a step back and straightened her pink tank top, her face streaked with tears. Lucy wondered if this was Connie, the Connie who had better watch out. 'It's okay,' she said to the girl. 'We didn't even fall.'

'Fuck you,' the girl said, and skated away.

At Jack's house the volume of his mother's snoring had increased to a roar. Even with the door of Jack's room closed, Lucy could hear her going. She listened to the snore as they sat on a sleeping bag on the air mattress, drinking peach schnapps and watching a soft-core movie called *Wet and Wild West*. Lucy's head felt stuffed with wool. She couldn't take her eyes from the TV. Onscreen, two women in cowboy boots and Western shirts stood naked in a barn, licking each other's breasts and rubbing against each other. They looked bored enough to fall asleep. The sound was turned down low in case Jack's mother woke up, but not so low that they couldn't hear the soundtrack of sighs and moans. Jack had a hand up Melissa's skirt. Lucy could see it moving beneath the fabric. Melissa's eyes were closed and she was breathing fast, but Jack wasn't watching her. He was watching Lucy, giving her a secret smile. He put his other hand on her thigh and made a slow circle with his thumb. Lucy stared at his hand.

'I want to make you both happy,' he said. 'I want to make you both feel good.'

Melissa's eyes snapped open. She looked at Jack's hand on Lucy's thigh. 'What the fuck?' she said.

Jack removed his hand from Lucy's thigh.

'What the fuck, Lucy? Were you going to sit there and let him do that?'

Lucy shrugged. It was a good question.

'Shit, Jack,' Melissa said. 'Can't we go somewhere private?'

'But we're all comfortable here,' Jack said.

'Not me,' said Melissa. She got up and left the room, and Jack followed her. Lucy heard the bathroom door click shut. They were inside together, talking in low voices. Then Melissa began moaning, as if she were performing in the movie herself. Lucy rolled herself into the sleeping bag and closed her eyes. The snores echoed in the hall. Onscreen, the girls climbed coarse-looking ropes. From the bathroom came a series of sharp cries, Melissa's, rising in pitch. Lucy sat up and drank a glass of water with some ice. She knew why she was there that night: She was there because Melissa wanted a spectator. What good was it to elope to California if no one watched it happen, if no one could go to Nationals and spread the news? It would be the most spectacular thing anyone they knew had ever done. And who better to tell everyone than Lucy, that less-than-pretty girl who had no life of her own?

It wasn't just about telling their friends, though; Lucy knew that too. It was about Melissa's family. When her parents had been fighting, they'd been fighting over her: who would get custody, who had hurt her worse. Now, no one was fighting over her. Her mom was happy with the Minnesota businessman. Her dad had his new wife. Melissa was just one of their kids now, a picky teenager worried about her diet.

Lucy pulled herself to her feet. She found Melissa's keys and her own bag of unacceptable clothes, including the satin pajamas she'd bought to tantalize Jack. She went down to the car. Outside everything was dead silent, the small Tudor houses stretching along the curve of the street. She could hear the highway a few blocks away, a constant riverlike hum. The windows of the car were fogged. She opened the door and climbed into the driver's side, then slid the key into the ignition.

She thought about what would happen if she turned the key, if she pulled out into the street, if she drove all the way to Cincinnati and then took the bus home. She thought about what that would mean for Melissa. Melissa would have to go to California. There could be no backing out, after she'd made all those plans and then bragged about them. Lucy wanted to make her do it. She thought about how things would go for Melissa once she was living in Jack's ratty bungalow near the beach. Within weeks they'd hate each other. If they lasted, it would be worse. She imagined Melissa with a crying baby on her hip. Meanwhile, Lucy would have graduated from high school and gone on to college. Maybe Melissa would send a postcard from some miserable town out West. Lucy would spread the word, all right. She couldn't wait to do it.

Then she thought of the girl who'd crashed into her at the skating rink, the girl in the pink tank top who might or might not have been Connie. How Lucy had tried to let the girl know it was okay. How the girl had glared at her and said *fuck you*. That was what happened when girls treated each other the way those girls had treated Connie. They got to the point where they couldn't recognize help, where every other girl seemed like an enemy.

Lucy slid over to the passenger seat and opened the glove compartment. Inside, cool and solid, was the gun. She took it in her hand. It made her feel better just to hold it. What strange power, to be sitting there in a car on a quiet street, sleeping neighbors all around, with a gun in her hand and millions of things to shoot. She opened the door and aimed at a light post, at a bush beside the drainpipe of Jack's house, at the weathervane on the roof. *Bang*, she whispered. *Bang, bang, bang*. She put her hand up under her sweater, pressing the gun flat against her belly. She had to remind herself that it was real, a weapon, a thing that could make someone die. She imagined aiming at the ceiling of Jack's room, the pistol jolt and then plaster falling.

She got out of the car and went up the walk, into the house, and stood in the middle of the living room on the turquoise-rose and gold-scroll carpet. The house was quiet now. Outside, a streetlamp flickered. Squares of yellow light fell through the window and onto the carpet like scattered cards. Lucy climbed the stairs, the gun cocked before her, and edged down the hallway toward the bathroom. The sex noises had stopped. There was just the sound of the shower and of Jack talking. She listened. He was describing a problem he'd been having with his toenails. She could hear Melissa's faint *uh-huh*. They both sounded exhausted.

She went into Jack's room and lay down on the air mattress, holding the gun tight against her chest, beneath her shirt. The porno tape had ended, and the TV screen glowed blue. It had been hours since Lucy had eaten. She wondered what kind of food Jack's mother kept in the house, if there was cereal or a bagel. She would eat lox and cream cheese when she got home, lots of lox, lots of cream cheese, on an everything bagel with capers. Oh, she was tired. Maybe she could just take a little nap.

But down the hall there was the sound of a door opening and closing, and all the muscles in Lucy's back went tight. She pulled the covers over herself, keeping one eye half open. Jack came in, a towel around his waist, his hair wet from the shower. He knelt beside Lucy and touched her face. She breathed in through her nose in a way she hoped suggested deep sleep. There was a soft dull thump, his towel hitting the bedroom floor, and he climbed in beside her, naked. He was saying her name, shivering, pressing himself hard against her thighs.

'Wake up,' he said into her hair. 'Melissa's in the shower. It's our last chance.' He reached under her skirt and wedged a hand between her legs.

She moved away from him, toward the wall, but he followed, trying to move his hand around inside her panties. She jerked away and stood up on the air mattress, bracing herself against the wall. In her other hand, still hidden beneath her shirt, she held the gun.

'Hi,' he said, and gave her a weak smile.

'Get up,' she said. 'Now.'

'Why?' he said.

She pulled the gun from beneath her shirt and pointed it at his head.

His smile fell away. He got to his feet. She could see his thighs contracting as if he meant to jump at her, and she lowered the gun until it pointed at his penis. 'Don't make any fast moves,' she said. 'I could shoot you accidentally.'

'Please tell me it's not loaded.'

'It's loaded,' Lucy said. 'I checked, just like you showed me.' She could shoot him right now. She imagined him lying on the ground, his eyes clouding, saying *It's not your fault.*

Jack's mouth opened. He pointed to a pair of shorts hanging off the back of a chair. 'Okay if I put those on?' he said, trying to smile again.

'No,' she said. 'Just get into the closet.'

He opened the closet door. The closet was crammed with papers, clothes, model cars, letters—hundreds of things. Jack had to climb on top of a crate of laundry in order to fit inside. He crouched in the semi-dark, staring at Lucy. 'It's you I love,' he said. 'I made a mistake.'

'Bullshit,' Lucy said.

'I mean it. I told Melissa everything.'

'Right,' Lucy said. 'After you fucked her.'

'Please, Lucy. Give me the gun.'

Lucy closed the closet door. She took the desk chair and wedged it underneath the doorknob the way she'd seen it done in movies. It seemed to work; he pushed on the door from inside but it didn't open. She wedged the chair in even tighter. 'Stop pushing,' she said, 'or I'll shoot right through this door.'

He stopped pushing.

'You are one greasy motherfucker,' she told him. 'Anyone can see it.'

'But I love you.'

'I'll shoot your ass off,' she said, pointing the gun at the closet door.

'You know, it's dark in here, Lucy. And it smells bad.'

'It's your closet, not mine.'

There was a scream. Melissa stood in the doorway, a towel clutched to her chest.

'Be quiet,' Lucy said, and pointed the gun at her. 'Jack's mom is sleeping.'

'The gun,' she said.

'Get your stuff,' Lucy said. 'Hurry up.'

'Oh, shit, Lucy, don't point that thing at me. I mean it.'

'We're going home,' Lucy told her. 'Get some clothes on.'

'I'm not going home.'

'Yes you are,' Lucy said.

'What are you going to do, shoot me?'

'Is that a dare?'

'This is ridiculous, Lucy.'

'No it isn't. You're getting your stuff, and we're going home.' Lucy picked up Melissa's bag and threw it at her, trying to remember if she'd ever once before told Melissa what to do. It felt clean and right. 'Pack your clothes,' she said. She had to get them out of there, because in another minute she was going to start to freak.

Melissa struggled into her black crocheted dress and high heels. She stuffed the thigh-highs into her overnight bag and looked up at Lucy.

'Stand up,' Lucy said. By this time the gun felt as if it were part of her hand, a magic finger she could point to make things happen. Melissa stood. Lucy took her by the arm and led her out into the hall.

'All right, all right,' Melissa said, twisting her arm away from Lucy. 'You don't have to pinch me like that.'

Jack rattled the closet door again. Lucy let him do it. It was time to go now, down the hall, past the door of Jack's mom's bedroom and the photographs of Jack as a little kid, and then down the stairs to the scroll-and-rose living room and out the front door and into the yard. All along the street the sad Tudor houses were jaundiced with morning sun. Melissa stumbled down the front walk, the black bag bumping against her hip.

'Come on,' Lucy said, and took her around to the passenger side of the car. Lucy got in on the driver's side, throwing their clothes into the back seat. When she started the car, the roar of the engine felt sweet and strong. She pulled out and drove toward the highway, cranking DJ Mellow B on WLUX. He was playing Marvin Gaye, 'What's Going On?' The gun was in Lucy's lap, within plain sight of anyone who wanted to look into the car. She tucked it into the waistband of her skirt. Melissa sat huddled against the passenger-side door and stared through the windshield, unblinking.

The sounds of Motown followed them, the Supremes and the Four Tops and the Marvelettes crooning them all the way onto the open highway. After a few miles Melissa reached for a cigarette and lit it, rolling down the window to blow smoke.

'Jack told me about going to see you,' she said, wiping her nose on her sleeve. 'He told me everything you did.'

Lucy squinted at the road. 'He did?'

'Yeah.' She made a short harsh sound in her throat, half laughter, half disgust, and tapped a bit of ash out the window. 'He said he didn't want any secrets between us. But it sounded more like he was bragging about how great you thought he was.'

'He wasn't so great.'

'God, what an asshole. Who knows who else he would have fucked before we made it to LA?'

'He tried to have sex with me this morning,' Lucy said. 'After he took a shower. That's why I put him in the closet.'

'I'm not surprised,' Melissa said. 'He's got a serious dick problem. He's got hyperdickia.'

'Yeah,' Lucy said. 'He's terminal.'

Melissa put an elbow against the window and stared out at the passing rows of corn. 'I feel sorry for our parents,' she said. 'They have no idea what goes on.'

'At least you're not running away to California.'

'Not this week.'

Five minutes from Lucy's neighborhood, they stopped at a gas station and changed into jeans in the restroom. They fixed their makeup in the mirror and brushed their teeth. Lucy extracted the gun from the waistband of her skirt, where it had pressed painfully against her side. She and Melissa wrapped it in a paper towel and buried it in the garbage can. Silent and exhausted, they drove toward Lucy's house. As they rounded the corner of her street, Lucy could already imagine the way the house would smell when she opened the door: clean and dry, like fresh laundry. She could enter that house and go upstairs. She could take a shower. She could crawl into bed.

When they pulled up in front, her parents were planting flats of marigolds in the flower beds along the driveway. They wore gardening clogs and Michigan visors, and her mother had on her I DIG GARDENING T-shirt. Seeing them made Lucy want to cry with relief. Her mother lifted her trowel and waved.

Lucy touched Melissa's arm. 'Go straight home,' she said.

'I will,' Melissa said. 'I'll call you when I get there.'

Lucy got out of the car and took her bag from the back seat. She slammed the door and watched the long white Cadillac ease away from the curb. After the car had turned the corner, she kissed her mother and father and went upstairs to her room. She threw her overnight bag into the closet. She turned down the covers of her bed, where Jack Jacob had touched her but would never touch her again. Then she went to the bathroom to take a shower, and when she took off her clothes she could still see the outline of the gun, plain as a photograph, against her skin.

LUCKY GIRLS

Nell Freudenberger

I had often imagined meeting Mrs. Chawla, Arun's mother. It would be in a restaurant, and I would be wearing a sophisticated blue suit that my mother had sent me soon after I moved to India, and Mrs. Chawla would not be able to keep herself from admiring it. Of course, in those fantasies Arun was always with me.

As it happened, Mrs. Chawla appeared early one morning, in a car with a driver, unannounced. I was sitting at the kitchen table in my painting shorts, having a cup of tea. There was no time to straighten up the living room or take a shower. I went into the bedroom, where Arun and I had often slept, and put on a dress—wrinkled, but at least it was clean. I put my cup in the sink and set a pot of water on the stove. Then I watched through the window. Mrs. Chawla had got out of the car and was standing with her arms crossed, instructing her driver how to park. The car moved forward, backed up, and then inched forward again.

Mrs. Chawla shaded her eyes to look at the backyard: the laundry line with my clothes hanging on it, the grackles perched on the telephone pole, the pile of soft, rotting bricks. I had a feeling that had come to seem familiar in the eight months since Arun had died, a kind of panic that made me want to stand very still.

The bell rang.

'Hello, Mrs. Chawla,' I said. 'I'm glad you came.' From her handwriting, I had expected someone more imposing. She was several inches shorter than I was, and heavy. Her hair was long and dyed black, with a dramatic white streak in the front; and she was wearing a navy blue salwar-kameez, the trousers of which were tapered at the ankles, in a style that was just becoming fashionable.

'Yes,' she said. 'I've been meaning to. I can't stay long.' She gave me a funny smile, as if I weren't what she had expected, either.

'Will you have some tea?' I offered.

'Do you have tea?' she asked, sounding surprised. She looked at the drawn blinds in the living room. There was a crumpled napkin next to the salt and pepper shakers on the table, where I had eaten dinner the night before, and which I had asked Puja, the servant, to clean. Now that it was summer, cockroaches had started coming out of the walls.

'Please don't go to any trouble,' she said. 'Puja can do it—is she in the kitchen?' Arun had hired Puja to do my cooking and cleaning; when he told me she had worked for his mother, I'd hoped that Mrs. Chawla was making a friendly gesture. In fact, Puja was a terrible housekeeper and a severely limited cook. She lived in a room at the back of the house, with her husband and four little girls; at night I often saw her crouched in the backyard, making chapatis on a pump stove with a low blue flame.

Mrs. Chawla walked confidently toward the kitchen, calling Puja in a proprietary voice, and I realized that Arun's mother had been in my house before. She could have come any number of times, in the afternoons, when I taught art at the primary school or went out shopping in Khan Market. Puja would have let her in without hesitation.

When Mrs. Chawla reappeared, she scrutinized the chairs, before choosing to sit on the sofa. She smiled, revealing a narrow space between her teeth. 'Where exactly are you from?' she asked.

'My father lives in Boston, but my mother is in California now,' I told her.

'Ah,' said Mrs. Chawla softly, as if that explained everything. 'An American family. That must make it difficult to decide where to return to.'

I had no plans to return, as I should have explained. 'It rules out Boston and California,' I said instead.

Mrs. Chawla didn't smile.

My brother, I added, was getting married in Boston in July.

'And you like the bride?' she asked.

'Oh,' I said. 'I only met her once.' I could feel the next question coming, and then a thing happened that often happens to me with people who make me nervous.

'What's her name?' Mrs. Chawla asked.

Her name, which I knew perfectly well, slipped into some temporarily unrecoverable place. 'Actually, I don't remember,' I said.

Mrs. Chawla looked at me, puzzled. 'How strange,' she said.

Puja brought the tea. She knelt on the floor and began placing things, item by item, on the coffee table: spoons, cups, saucers, milk, sugar, and a small plate of Indian sweets that Mrs. Chawla must have brought with her. The tea, it seemed, was no longer my hospitable gesture.

'How is she doing?' Mrs. Chawla asked, nodding at Puja.

'She's wonderful,' I lied. Now that Arun wasn't here to tell her what to do, the house was getting dirtier and dirtier.

Puja's little girls were watching us from the kitchen doorway. When Mrs. Chawla saw them, she said suddenly, 'Girls,' and repeated it sharply in Hindi. 'I have told her that if she has another baby'—Mrs. Chawla paused and looked at Puja—'*Bas!* Enough, I'm sending her back to Orissa.' She turned back to me. 'That's east India,' she informed me, as if I had never seen a map of the subcontinent. 'The people there are tribals. Did you know that? Puja is a tribal. These people have nothing, you know, except floods and cyclones. Now they're having terrible floods— have you seen them on television? Thousands of people are sick, and there isn't enough drinking water. I tell her that, and what do you think she says?'

Puja knew only a few words of English. She seemed to be smiling at her feet, which were bare, extremely small, and decorated with silver toe rings.

'She says she needs another child because she wants to have a boy,' Mrs. Chawla said. 'Stupid girl.' Puja giggled. 'Stupid,' evidently, was one of the English words she did know. Then Mrs. Chawla said something else, in Hindi, and Puja stopped giggling and left the room.

'Did you understand?' Mrs. Chawla asked me.

'A little,' I said. 'You said she was a woman with girls?'

'Very good,' said Mrs. Chawla. 'I said she was the kind of unfortunate woman who has only girls.'

'Oh,' I said.

Mrs. Chawla eyed me craftily. 'You think I'm cruel to them.'

'No,' I said. I was used to this kind of frankness from Indian women of Mrs. Chawla's age and station, and I liked it.

Mrs. Chawla looked as though she were going to say something else, but just then the electricity went out.

'I'm sorry,' I said. 'It usually comes on again in a second.'

'This is a good area, a government area,' she said approvingly. 'Did you know that?'

I had been living on Pandara Road for almost five years, a fact that
Mrs. Chawla knew, so I didn't say anything. The lights came on about
halfway, low and flickering, and the fans spun jusr enough to move the
air. Often this happened at night, when I was sitting in the living room,
pretending to read.

Mrs. Chawla put her hand on my arm. 'The point is—what's wrong
with girls?'

'Nothing,' I said.

'Then . . . good,' Mrs. Chawla said. 'You can help me teach her.' She
leaned back, and the cheap wicker sofa creaked. I had bought it because
Arun thought wicker was cool. I didn't know why a sofa needed to be
cool, and now cockroaches were living in the little wicker spaces. I said
a short, fervent prayer that Mrs. Chawla wouldn't see a cockroach. Puja
started to pour the milk in my tea, but Mrs. Chawla stopped her. 'Let
the lady do it herself,' she said, in English, and then turned to me. 'She's
never seen a woman like you, living so well on her own.'

When I met Arun, I was wearing borrowed clothes. It was my first time
in India and I was visiting Gita Banerjee, the most glamorous friend I
had made in college. My parents had bought the ticket for me—'To see
the world,' my father had written on a card, 'before you come home
and settle down.' I was twenty-two.

A few nights after I arrived in Delhi, the Banerjees had a party. Gita's
father had once been some kind of ambassador, and the entire
extended family seemed constantly to be entertaining important
visitors in their extravagant houses. Gita's younger sisters thought it
would be fun for me to wear Indian clothes, and they spent a long time
dressing me up in a dark pink sari with a matching blouse underneath.
I was wearing glass bracelets, and my hair was braided like theirs—
they even painted my hands with mendhi, which left intricate brown
patterns across my palms. We spent so much time making me look like
them that no one had a chance to teach me to walk in the sari, which
turned out to be more difficult than I had imagined, like finding
yourself in the street wearing only a bath towel.

After a while, I left the party. I had meant to go back upstairs to my
room, but I opened the wrong door by mistake and there was a man
sitting on a bed, in the light of a small reading lamp. He had taken off
his jacket, and the sleeves of his white shirt were rolled up.

'I'm sorry,' I said, and started to back out of the room.

'Hello,' he said. 'Are you hiding, too?'

I laughed.

'You're Gita's friend, the college graduate,' Arun said.

'I was Gita's roommate,' I said. 'Do you know Gita?'

'Since she was born.' He stood up and shook my hand. 'Uncle Arun,' he said. There was a bottle of imported whiskey on the table, and he asked me if I wanted a drink.

I did, but I wondered if that would be inappropriate. I had noticed that although there was wine downstairs at the party (which Gita and I had liberally sampled), most of the women weren't drinking. 'Is that OK?' I asked. 'I mean, in India?'

This was the first time Arun really looked at me. His eyes were green, like a Kashmiri's. 'I think it's up to you,' he said. 'Even in India.'

Arun was twenty-three years older than Gita and me. He was tall, with broader shoulders than most Indian men I had met, and he had a trimmed black beard with some gray in it. I couldn't help staring at his hands as he poured my drink—the long, thin muscles of his fingers, and a raised white scar, straight as an incision, across the top of his left wrist.

He asked if I was enjoying my visit. I admitted that I hadn't been out much, but that I liked the parts of Delhi I had seen.

Arun smiled. 'You want to go to Agra, of course.'

'Not just Agra.' I wanted to sound as if I knew more about India than that.

'Do you know what the Taj Mahal looks like?' Arun asked.

'Of course.'

He leaned forward. 'Did you know that the emperor meant to build another one across the river?'

I nodded, although I hadn't even known that there was a river. I had always pictured it in the desert, surrounded by raked yellow sand. 'He built it for his wife, right?'

'Mumtaz,' said Arun. 'But what you see is only half his plan. There was going to be another one for him, exactly the same but in black marble.'

I thought he was teasing me. 'I don't believe you,' I said.

'But when he died they simply buried him next to her—his grave is the only thing that isn't perfectly symmetrical.' Arun smiled slightly. 'He had a vision. They ruined it.'

We were quiet for a minute.

'Can I ask you something?' he said.

I wondered stupidly if he was going to kiss me. I had never kissed a man with a beard.

'Why did you come to India?'

'I wanted to see where Gita was from.'

Arun sipped his whiskey, as if he were waiting for more. 'So if she'd been from Paris you might have gone there instead?'

'But I've been to Paris.'

Arun laughed. 'You're just like these diplomats' children,' he said. 'World-weary at twenty.'

'Oh, yes,' I said, indicating my clothes. 'Very cosmopolitan.'

'I wasn't going to ask.'

'You don't like them.' I pouted. I was already a little drunk.

'They're nice clothes,' he said. 'I just don't like Western girls in Indian clothes, but I'm perhaps behind the times.'

'Why?'

Arun paused. 'Because clothes mean something here. Historically. And when you wear them it's for romance, glamour—you don't mean anything.'

I stared at the patterns on my hands. Suddenly, it seemed as if Gita's sisters had played a practical joke on me, like dressing up a cat or a dog.

'I've offended you,' Arun said sadly.

'No, you haven't.'

'I'm always offending women. I don't know how to behave around them.'

'Making fun of their clothes isn't the best strategy,' I told him.

Arun smiled. 'Have another drink. Prove we're still friends.'

'I think I'm extremely drunk already,' I said.

Arun seemed to consider this. 'You're extremely pretty,' he said. 'Even in Indian clothes. And since we don't want anything to happen to you, maybe I should take you back down to the party.'

To this day, I remember that as the most thrilling thing anyone has ever said to me.

I am not extremely pretty, a fact that Mrs. Chawla noticed right away. The second time she visited, I was sitting in my studio, in front of a canvas, staring out the window at Puja's children, who were playing hide-and-seek, running in and out between the rows of hanging laundry. The studio was a prefabricated one-room structure, which I used because the rooms in the house were too dark. There was a single bed where I used to sleep if I was working late. Now I slept here all the time.

Mrs. Chawla must have rung the doorbell and, not finding anyone, walked around to the back. Or maybe she was accustomed to coming in through the garden. I looked up and there she was, directly in front of me, peering in the window. It took me a few seconds to realize that she couldn't see through the screen at this time of day. I was wearing my painting shorts again.

'Just a minute,' I called, and then changed my mind. I had no reason to pretend.

Mrs. Chawla was dressed in moss green, and her hair was braided down her back like a girl's. She looked at the paints spread out on the table, at the straw mats on the floor, and the bed with a mosquito net, a foreigner's thing. Then she looked up at the fan, which was dusty, with a black layer of grease on one side of the blades. She sighed and sat down at my table. 'You're not sleeping here, are you?'

'Sometimes. I like it out here.'

Mrs. Chawla looked shocked. 'But he never slept here?'

'Mrs. Chawla . . .' I began. I could hear the milkman calling from his bicycle.

'I mean, I could see why you would want to sleep here now, if the two of you used to—if that was the bed where you slept, as it were.'

'It's not really any of your business,' I said.

Mrs. Chawla ignored me. 'What I do not understand'—she paused, as if we were thinking aloud together, collaborating on a difficult puzzle—'is how he could stand to stay somewhere so dirty. He was always so particular, and his house—the house where he lived, I mean—was immaculate. '

'Leave if it bothers you,' I said.

'Ah!' said Mrs. Chawla. 'I see what he meant. You're not beautiful, but you're strong-willed. That's appealing for a man like Arun, who always got exactly what he wanted.' She lowered her voice, as if she were telling me a secret. 'I used to think we might have spoiled him.'

'Yes. If he hadn't had all of these people coddling him, he might have learned how to make a decision,' I said, surprising myself.

Mrs. Chawla put her palms in the air and shrugged theatrically. 'But would any of us have been happy with his decisions? Do you think you would have been?' She smiled. 'It's a Catch-22 situation.' She stood up. 'This afternoon I have to go see Laxmi and the boys. She's upset, you know, that I am visiting you.'

I pretended to start painting.

'She doesn't understand why you're still here,' Mrs. Chawla told me. 'I'm sure she'll ask me.'

I wondered if finding the answer to this question—why I was still here—was the purpose of Mrs. Chawla's visit.

'Maybe she should come ask me herself.' I hadn't meant to say it, only think it, but it didn't matter. I didn't expect to see Mrs. Chawla again.

She gave a short, barking laugh. 'You seem quiet,' she said. 'But you're sharp.'

After Mrs. Chawla was gone, I realized that I had wanted her to look at the painting, which was the view out my window, with the laundry and the drying okra plants against the main house. It wasn't especially good—I was going to scrape it away and use the canvas again—but I didn't think Mrs. Chawla would have known that. She would have seen the perspective and the colors, and the way I had reproduced the backyard of her son's second home, and she would have known that I wasn't a phony. At the same time, it annoyed me that I should care what she thought.

That first trip to India had been at the invitation of Gita's family, the Banerjees, and they went out of their way to insure that I saw nothing I would not see in New York. We went to a restaurant in Defence Colony, the elite shopping enclave, and to the Lodi Gardens, where women in salwar-kameez and running shoes promenaded briskly down designated exercise paths. Gita had compared it to Central Park, but Central Park didn't have ancient stone architecture. Great ruined domes, purple in the last bit of light, appeared to float above the wet grass. When I asked what period the ruins dated from, Mrs. Banerjee laughed and said that she had no idea.

The only real tourist attraction I saw, on an overplanned excursion in the care of the Banerjees' driver, was an old Mughal fort, the Purana Qila, one chipped blue tile of which Gita forced me to take when we found it lying on the grass. No one else wants it, she said, picking it up and secreting it in her jacket. I protested but was privately pleased— it might be my only souvenir. Then, one morning, Arun showed up for breakfast and announced that he was taking Gita and me on an overnight trip to Agra, to see the Taj Mahal.

As soon as we were on the train, Gita took over her mother's role, commandeering an extra seat from an old man in a Nehru jacket and then, hours before we were hungry, spreading out an elaborate lunch that the Banerjees' cook had prepared. The first-class cars were air-conditioned to a luxurious, wintry temperature, and my arms, in the thin blouse I had chosen, were covered with goose bumps. But when Arun said that we should sit between the cars, where the men went to smoke and where you could see the green country streaming past, Gita looked at him as if he had suggested that we paint our faces and sing in the aisle for change.

'Arun is constitutionally a bachelor,' she told me after he left the compartment.

'I thought he was married.' I still don't remember how I knew this; I may have just assumed it.

'Oh, he's married now, but he waited forever.' Gita looked at me. 'Living that long by yourself, you develop habits.' I knew she wasn't talking about smoking on trains, but I didn't particularly feel like being warned.

Gita and Arun agreed that I had to see the monument for the first time at sunrise, from the gate, and so we spent our first day in Agra trying *not* to see the Taj Mahal. It wasn't easy. The parapets of the Agra Fort opened, in an orderly progression of cusped arches, onto view after view of the tomb. There was little else besides the monument: men beating clothes on the riverbank, water buffalo in the mud, the river itself, skittering into the flat, tan distance and sending silver flashes into the smog like a child playing with a mirror.

'Don't look,' Arun said, coming up behind me. 'Careful,' he gasped, as we passed the arrow slots along the steep red stairs.

That night, we ate in a restaurant Arun knew, avoiding the rooftop tourist cafés, strung with colored lights, that all boasted a 'Taj view.' It was the middle of the summer, and the number of tourists was relatively low. Arun had suggested that we stay in one of the cheap hotels near the monument instead of the colonial palace near the airport where Gita's mother had reserved rooms: 'This way, we can stumble out of bed and be standing in front of the Taj.'

Because of our sunrise engagement, Gita and I went to bed at ten. I had expected that we would stay up talking, but after a few minutes I could hear her quiet breathing. The room had an air cooler, which made a fierce grating sound and did nothing else. I tried to lie absolutely still, but I was already sweating when the power went out. The fan clicked to a slow halt, and the rectangles of light from outside, my only orientation, disappeared in a dark so heavy that it was like a soft cloth in my mouth.

After a few minutes my eyes had still not adjusted to the dark, and I was now sweating uncontrollably. I got up and walked toward the door, my hands in front of me, hesitating for a moment before going out. There was a breeze. Some buildings nearby must have had generators, and the faint, reassuring sound of a television came from the street. A few auto-rickshaws sat outside the hotel gate; you could see the tiny lights hanging from the dashboards, like clusters of lantern fish.

Beyond the patio was a kind of thick Indian garden familiar to me now: overgrown and ripe-smelling, where you might be afraid of stepping on something rotting in the grass. I had been standing at the edge of the garden for several minutes before I saw the smoke. On a hammock suspended between two low, knotted trees, Gita's uncle was smoking a cigarette.

'Hello,' he said.

'The fan went off,' I said. I put one foot on top of the other, as if that would conceal the fact that I was standing outside in a camisole and shorts. I tried to think of a polite way of excusing myself, to go back inside. 'Can I have a cigarette?' I asked instead.

Arun got up and lit one for me.

'This is another of those things I shouldn't be doing in India,' I said.

'What do you mean?' Arun asked.

'Well, I mean, Indian women don't really smoke,' I said.

'Are you trying to blend in?'

'No,' I said. 'I mean, not especially.'

I smoked the cigarette down to the filter. The roots of my hair were wet, but Arun didn't seem to be suffering from the heat at all. He had taken off his blue oxford shirt, which was draped over the railing, and he was wearing a dark blue T-shirt. Something hung from an almost invisible silver chain around his neck. I am surprised today by what I did. I was, in general, very shy.

'What is this?' I stepped close to Arun and took the tiny amulet in my hand.

'It was a gift from my wife.'

I let go of the amulet. 'I think I might take a shower,' I told him. Arun didn't say anything, but as I turned away he grabbed my wrist.

'I'm sorry,' he said.

'Sorry for what?'

'I'm afraid I can't stand that, listening to the shower.'

'The walls are very thick. I don't think you'll hear it.'

Arun was stern. 'I refuse to let you wake my niece, with your profligate American water use. I insist that if you are going to shower in the middle of the night you use the one in my room.'

Although he was teasing me, he let me know that it would be silly for me to pretend that this wasn't exactly what I wanted.

In his room, Arun lit a fat white utility candle. The things he'd brought with him—a notebook, an extra shirt, a toothbrush, a flask— were laid out on the bed, as if he were preparing for some kind of emergency. He looked at me directly, with a sudden focused intensity. It was a quality of attention I hadn't experienced before, an ability he had to suggest that everything that had gone before had led to this precise moment. There was something almost desperate about the sex—it was like skydiving in a dream. I had no illusions about being in control.

'You seemed to be enjoying yourself,' he said afterward.

'I was.' I said it so quickly that I was embarrassed.

'You might make more noise next time,' Arun said, as if he were suggesting a book for me to read or someone I really should try ro meet.

The alarm went off at five. In the room next door, Gita's would be ringing as well.

'What do I do?'

He was lying on his back, with one hand on my hip. 'She's probably not even awake,' he said. 'Go back now.'

'What do I tell her?' I was panicking.

'Tell her the fan went off,' he said. 'Nobody's up yet.'

In fact, many people are awake in India at five. The waiter from the hotel restaurant, the rickshaw drivers, and a hopeful-looking beggar at the gate all saw me leave Arun's room and dash barefoot back to mine. I opened the door slowly, being careful with the noisy key. It was an unnecessary precaution. Gita was sitting fully clothed on the bed, the guidebook in her lap.

'The fan . . .' I began. I didn't think that she was going to believe me.

'We missed it! We have to go back to Delhi, and you missed it.'

'What?'

Gita looked at me as if I were a total idiot. 'The Taj.'

'It's only five.' I wondered if this was some kind of punishment. 'We can still go,' I said, but Gita was shaking her head. Neither she nor Arun had bothered to read the guidebook, and, like theaters and hairdressers in America, the Taj Mahal was closed on Mondays.

We spent the morning before our train left looking at the Taj as best we could. We even went to one of the rooftop restaurants and ordered Cokes.

'It's nicer, in a way,' Arun said. 'You have to pay more attention.'

Arun liked to say that our lives are composed of accidents. I remember the profound appeal of this idea then, when I fell in love with him, and three years later, when I went to India for no reason other than that Arun, with whom I had been corresponding all that time, had asked me to.

After I moved to India, Gita and I continued to see each other, but we never talked about Arun. The rest of her family were not so welcoming. I thought that the reason they never invited me to their home was out of a kind of prejudice. They did not like the combination of Arun and me. Their taste was conservative; and I thought they believed that people, like the drapes and the sofa, should match.

It is embarrassing to admit that I simply didn't consider Arun's wife. I had only the vaguest impression of Laxmi: a mental image of a woman's back as she put the children to bed in the vivid hours of the early evening, while Arun was with me. They lived in Defence Colony, in a house I knew only as the background of a photograph that he carried in his wallet. It showed two boys holding each other in an affectionate headlock in front of a new white Ambassador, barely reaching the top of the sunlit silver grille. Although the photograph was clearly worn, I somehow failed to understand that it had been taken years ago. It never occurred to me that those two boys were now young men, almost in university.

Not long after Arun helped me find the house on Pandara Road, his mother wrote me. 'You must be curious about my son's wife, Laxmi,' she began. 'You are very young, but Laxmi is still ten years younger than Arun. He was lucky, to wait so long and still find a girl like that. (Laxmi is the goddess of wealth and good fortune, you may not know.) She is as beautiful as a goddess as well. In America, I know women want to be skinny, so that you can see the bones. Laxmi is the kind of woman Indian men like: plump and round. She does not need to wear kohl, because of the thickness of her lashes. Her lips are like the inside of a plum.' She closed with what I understood to be a warning. 'We do not know each other, but, if you will allow me to be frank, I would say that to a man it is the issue of will that is most important. Laxmi is devoted to my son and, if he asked, she would do anything.'

All day, I thought about not showing the letter to Arun. But as soon as I heard the front door open I was up and in the hall with the evidence in my hand.

He walked past me to the table where I kept the Scotch and poured himself a drink. He took off his jacket, transferring the letter from hand to hand, and sat down with it. He read it through, and then patted the space next to him on the couch, as if this were a funny thing we could share.

'Lips like the inside of a plum,' he said. 'My mother is a terrible writer.'

But I didn't think Mrs. Chawla was a terrible writer. The words she chose had made another person appear in the room, where before there had been only Arun and me. Mrs. Chawla had started a competition, and she seemed to relish the prospect of being a spectator.

'It's sick,' I told Arun.

He thought I was talking about Laxmi. 'She would not do anything for me,' he said. 'She's not particularly happy with me at the moment.' He took a sip of his Scotch. 'At any moment,' he corrected himself.

He didn't understand, but it didn't matter. Mrs. Chawla hadn't addressed the letter to him. That evening, I unbuttoned my blouse in the living room and held his hand and slipped it underneath my bra, like a high school girl, and climbed on top of him with my skirt around my waist. We had sex on the sofa, with only the screen door between us and the people outside. 'Look at me,' I said, and he looked, but already I was talking to two women: Laxmi, in a tight blouse that stopped just beneath her breasts, her stomach behind gauze, her bitten lips; and Mrs. Chawla, who had brought her into my house.

Until that point, I had been pretending at adulthood; I felt now that I had crossed a divide. I was dating a married man, I had told a friend in a long letter, because I wasn't sure I wanted to get married. I was twenty-five, and it seemed to me that there were two kinds of marriage. One hits a crisis and decisively fails. The other weathers the crisis, with both parties insistently declaring they have been made stronger: I couldn't imagine living with that kind of compromise. Secretly, I was hoping that in a few years Arun would remove the obstacles and arrive with his things on the doorstep of the house that would be, from then on, not just for me.

When Arun died, my family said, 'Come home.' My mother said it first— half invitation and half formality, because of course everyone assumed I would be coming home. But I procrastinated. I didn't like to think that I had spent five years in India entirely because of a man. Then, after several months, my father called. I don't think he had ever said Arun's name, and it was difficult for him. He said it was hard to deal with a friend's death alone, and he talked about when his father had died. I thanked him and said that I wasn't alone, that I had friends in Delhi.

In fact, I didn't have so many friends, although there always seemed to be people aound. I often had lunch with Gita and her colleagues, and in the afternoons I shared a rickshaw with the other teachers who lived in my neighborhood. At home in the compound there was sometimes an audience when I painted: the boys who came from across the road with their cricket bats to stand at my door, and the girls who followed them. I always left the door open.

One day, I noticed Puja's daughters standing just outside, with a girl named Pinky, who was in my class at the school.

'Why don't you bring the girls inside?' I asked Pinky. Her English was good, but she looked confused.

'Ma'am,' she struggled. 'Because, ma'am—'

'Please bring them inside,' I said.

Pinky smiled broadly and brought the children into the studio, carrying Ruma, the youngest, and leading one of her sisters by the hand. Ruma whined to be put down and immediately emptied a bowl of dirt onto the floor. Pinky looked at me with the sympathy of a much older friend.

But after a while it got quiet. I was making so much progress that I didn't hear the girls arguing on the floor or, a few minutes later, the sound of the gate in the yard. It was Mrs. Chawla's third visit.

'That's a good likeness,' she said. She was standing alone in the doorway. I noticed Puja hovering nervously a few feet behind her. You could see that she wanted to collect her children but was afraid to make a move with Mrs. Chawla there.

'It's just a sketch,' I said. 'I'm going to make a painting.'

Mrs. Chawla came in and leaned over the canvas, studying it. 'And then what will you do with it when it's finished?'

'I don't know,' I said. I could feel the pulse in my right hand, which was holding the pencil.

Mrs. Chawla straightened up and looked at me. 'Do you think you could paint the Sultan of Oman?'

I thought I might have misheard.

'You can make a good living, just from that—if you know the right import-export man.'

'How many paintings of the Sultan of Oman do they need?' I asked carefully.

'One for every family,' Mrs. Chawla said. 'And you can charge whatever you want. They have so much money that they would burn it for fuel, if they didn't have so much fuel.'

I laughed, and Mrs. Chawla smiled. It occurred to me that we were having a moment of understanding, and the need for Arun opened, all of a sudden, like a cut.

Puja chose that moment to duck in and scoop up her children, and abruptly Mrs. Chawla whirled around and slapped her, hard, across the face. Mrs. Chawla started speaking Hindi, very fast, so that it was impossible for me to follow. Puja's face was blank, and Ruma began to wail. When Mrs. Chawla was finished, she turned back to me, continuing our conversation as if I were not only uncomprehending but blind as well.

'Of course,' she said, 'it gets easier.'

'What? '

'Painting the sultan. You could start with a photograph, and then you might not even need a photograph after a while.'

'Mrs. Chawla,' I said, 'what did you say to her?'

'To whom?

'To Puja,' I said. 'Just now.'

Mrs. Chawla looked out the window, where we could see Puja hurrying across the yard, an awkward S shape with one child on her hip. I thought she wasn't going to answer me. I was suddenly dizzy and a bit nauseated.

'Mrs. Chawla? I know I need to learn more Hindi.'

She put her hand on my shoulder, almost tenderly. 'Why would you do that? It isn't necessary.' She sighed. 'I only asked her please not to bring the children into the house.'

'But I asked them to come,' I said. 'I *told* them to.'

Mrs. Chawla looked from the unmade bed to the empty water bottles on the table, through the open door to the bathroom, where my towel was lying on the gray cement floor.

'That is why your house is so dirty,' she observed.

A few days later, a young woman appeared with a note from Mrs. Chawla. Her name was Lata. According to the note, she did not have to be paid. She had been working for a friend of Mrs. Chawla's who no longer needed her, and she wanted a place to sleep until a more permanent situation could be found. The exchange seemed more than fair, and I said yes, although I hardly needed another servant.

Lata had fair skin and arched eyebrows; she was lively and tall, and wore a salwar-kameez rather than a sari. I disliked her right away. I felt she was laughing at me, the way girls will laugh at an older woman behind their hands. She was, however, an excellent cook, and the house started to look better immediately. She didn't speak much English, but her Hindi was simple and clear, so even I could understand her.

Lata had noticed the cockroach problem, too. One morning, there was a white line, drawn in chalk across the back doorway. When I went into the kitchen, I saw another line ringing the drain in the floor. A small red-and-yellow box had been left on the counter, with instructions in Hindi and English: 'For the prevention of vermin within the home. These insects will not dare to cross the powerful line. Highest quality poison but not harmful to humans.' Inside was a white stick, like the kind of thick chalk children use to draw on the sidewalk.

I made coffee, and then went into my bedroom, where I found Lata crouched on the floor in front of the armoire, the door wide open to reveal my things inside.

She jumped up, and then smoothed her hair. 'Madam,' she said breathlessly. 'You have such beautiful clothes.'

I was aware that I should have reprimanded her, but somehow I let too much time elapse, and in my hesitation she rushed out of the room. The clothes swung gently from their hangers. They had been mostly purchased in Delhi, and were neither beautiful in the Indian sense nor exotic in the American one. Nothing seemed to be missing, and glancing through them I couldn't see what Lata had been looking for.

That night, she stood just outside my yard, laughing with a boy, and for the first time since Arun died I thought about going into the house to sleep. But when I stood up to leave I was uncomfortable at the prospect of walking past Lata and her suitor, and I stayed where I was, fighting off the familiar panic. If only I could stay still long enough, I felt I might turn myself into an object, something solid and inanimate, like the chair or the unreliable air-conditioner.

Arun's death was unnecessary and stupid. It was an insect-borne hemorrhagic fever called DHF, or dengue. Arun died of a mosquito bite, at an emergency clinic in the Golf Links, in a part of town I had never seen. Like almost all the bad news that I received in India, word of the illness arrived in a blue envelope from Mrs. Chawla. 'I will leave pleasantries for happier times,' she began. 'My son is sick. You may think that you know what that feels like. I do not know you so I will not judge. But I do know that I, who have no daughters, would not presume to know about them. I ask you not to see him, as it would upset the family, who are with him all the time.'

I read Mrs. Chawla's letter again and again, like a page in a high school science textbook. I put the letter in a drawer and made a deal with myself: I wouldn't see him, and, in exchange, he would be all right. Then I revised the terms: I didn't need to see him, because of course he was going to be all right. And if he wasn't, I thought that Mrs. Chawla would tell me. My day was now structured around the delivery of the mail and the sounds of people approaching the house. Mrs. Chawla didn't call; and I didn't know; and for me the hours before Arun's death were no different from the ones immediately after them.

I hadn't planned to return to America for my brother's wedding, and then at the last minute I decided I would go. I told Lata that I wanted her to help me prepare a lunch for Gita and her friends before I left, and she insisted that we go all the way to Defence Colony for the groceries. On the morning of our outing she dressed carefully, in ironed clothes and a pair of gold earrings that I had never seen before.

I didn'r realize why I had agreed to drive so far out of my way until I was in the auto with Lata. By the time we got to the market, I was disgusted with myself, and still I couldn't turn around. I wouldn't let Lara buy meat, because the legs of lamb, marbled with white fat and twisting in the open air, made me queasy. She sulked for a while before becoming enchanted by a small, dark vegetable market that sold a species of fancy Chinese lettuce and miniature round green eggplants. While she shopped, I stood in the shade of the awning and watched the street. It wasn't that I believed I would be able to recognize Arun's wife from Mrs. Chawla's description, but I thought we might know each other by some other identifying mark or smell, the way a bitch can recognize her puppies, even after they have been taken away.

The market was U-shaped, and though Lata was carrying most of the groceries, she insisted on walking all the way around to the other end, and then out to the road. She wanted, she said, to find the same driver who had brought us.

'If he'd wanted to take us back, he would have stayed with us,' I said. I raised my arm, and there were instantly three rickshaw drivers in front of us, fighting among themselves.

'We can take a taxi,' Lata said urgently. The thought of a taxi, particularly an air-conditioned one, was appealing and I gave in. 'This way,' Lata told me, pointing in the direction of the taxi rank, and I followed her. It was the route she had originally wanted to take, down a shady street and out of the market. Here the houses had prominent alarm systems and the walls were very high, so only the second stories were visible.

'It's pretty,' I told Lata.

'It's rich,' she said, which was perhaps more accurate. We turned a corner, to get out to the main road, and almost collided with two teenage boys fixing a motorbike. Or pretending to fix a motorbike; they had the tools out on the sidewalk, but they didn't appear to know what to do with them. Lata stepped into the street to avoid the tools, and the boys stared at me.

When I went out in public, I wore a skirt that touched my ankles and a shirt with sleeves, no matter what the weather was. Inevitably, I was dressed more conservatively than the young women who wore Western clothes in this kind of area. These boys, who made no effort to conceal their interest, made me feel dowdy and conspicuously white.

Lata looked at me sideways, with quick, excited glances. When we were about halfway down the block, one of the boys gave a long, low whistle. With their tools and their expensive motorbike, they obviously belonged to the neighborhood. About a minute later, there was the sound of the motor, and then they were behind us, following very slowly.

'Lata,' I said sharply. 'Do you know those boys?'

Lata giggled. 'Madam, they want to look at you.'

'It's very impolite,' I told her.

The boys came closer, and Lata glanced at them over her shoulder, teasingly. I turned around and stared, the way I would stare at a child who was talking in class until he became self-conscious and stopped. But it didn't work. The boys had longish hair that fell in their eyes and thick, curved lips; they were wearing T-shirts and cargo pants that looked as if they had been bought abroad. The one driving was maybe sixteen or seventeen, and the other was a couple of years younger.

'What are you doing?' I said, as icily as possible.

'What are you doing?' the driver asked. His accent was British in its forbidding crispness.

'What are *you* doing?' the other repeated, falsetto.

The older one smirked. Then he leaned forward, pursed his lips as if he were going to kiss me, and spat, very neatly, hitting the top of my foot, in its open sandal. He revved the engine. The younger boy, who had been looking on with a kind of enchanted shock, whooped loudly and over the sound of the motor he shouted, 'Whore!' Then they arced out into the busy street, banking so sharply that their cuffs dragged on the ground, and disappeared into the traffic.

It astonished me that I had not recognized them before.

Lata bent down and was wiping my foot with a handkerchief, sobbing. 'Madam,' she said. 'Madam, I do not know. I am sorry.' Her cheeks, when she looked up at me, were wet.

'Which house is it?' I asked her.

Lata got up and led me back the way we had come, to the driveway where the boys had been repairing the bike. I rang the bell. I also ran my fingers very lightly over the numbers, where you would enter the code every day, if you lived there. Then I stepped off the curb and walked back out into the middle of the road, until I had the best view of the upstairs windows. I turned around slowly, and pretty soon Laxmi came down.

Was she a goddess, as everyone said? She was certainly very beautiful. Her *chuni* had bits of silver thread woven into the cloth, and she was wearing pearls in her ears. Her hair was hanging down her back, and her eyes, with their celebrated lashes, were deep-set and dark.

Lata set the groceries down and hurried through the gate without looking at me, like a citizen seeking asylum in an embassy. Laxmi waited until we had heard the door to the house open and shut.

'I don't want to talk to you,' she said.

'I wanted to thank you for the loan of your servant.'

She said nothing.

'She was helpful,' I added. 'I hope it wasn't difficult for you without her.'

Laxmi seemed to consider this. 'It was,' she said finally. 'But I thought you might need her more than I did.'

I was ashamed. Laxmi looked confused, and it seemed suddenly touching that she had engineered this moment, wanting to see me for herself. She began to close the gate.

'Thank you,' I said, and she stopped.

She pushed her hair behind her ear, almost flirtatiously. 'I have my sons,' she said casually. 'And you have no one.'

I did not cry until I returned to the compound and got to my room. Then, standing in front of the mirror, covering my breasts, I cried. I cried in the shower, and after I got out and dried my face the tears kept coming. For hours, they wouldn't stop; the second I wiped them away there were more. And then I was calm. It was five-thirty, exactly the time when I might have heard Arun's car coming around the circle. The compound was so quiet that I thought I could hear the cockroaches rustling in the walls.

I wanted to see Mrs. Chawla before I left India; I thought about calling first but didn't, and I was shown into the living room by a servant. I waited a long time, looking in a floor-to-ceiling glass cabinet crowded with mementos: a medal on a green and orange ribbon; a collection of ceramic animals—a deer, a Chinese carp, a giraffe; and an image of the monkey god Hanuman, opening his chest to reveal the faces of Ram and Sita in the place where his heart should be.

'You've come to tell me you're leaving,' Mrs. Chawla said. She stood in the doorway, with her hair hanging down on either side of her face. She didn't want to have a conversation, or even, it seemed, come into the room.

I had planned to tell her that I'd confirmed my ticket. 'I don't know,' I said instead. 'I'm afraid I may not be able to leave.'

'Why?'

'I don't know. I like it here.'

She was incredulous. 'What? The heat, the brownouts? These people, coming from the country all the time with their filthy children?'

'Maybe.'

She shook her head. 'It always looks better from the other side.'

'I'm not on the other side. I'm here.'

'You're not charming, but you're stubborn,' Mrs. Chawla said. 'You're like me—like a daughter of mine would be.'

'Luckily you have no daughter,' I said.

Mrs. Chawla looked surprised. She ran one finger across the top of a small, spotless table. 'When is your brother getting married?'

'Friday.'

'The bride—what's her name—will be very disappointed.'

'Very,' I said.

'It will be a crime to miss that wedding.'

'Mrs. Chawla?'

'You're going to regret it your whole life.'

'I should have been there when Arun died,' I said.

There was a brightness in her voice when she answered, a gold wire of fury.

'You didn't belong there,' she said. 'Nobody would've known what you were.'

On the evening my brother got married, I watched a BBC news report of a dead buffalo that had been polluting the wells of three villages in Gujarat. There were shots of the dry, cracked ground, and the children with flies at the corners of their eyes, and the old people who wouldn't look at the camera. Then you saw the buffalo, a dramatic black shape in the dun-colored water. The reporters must not have wanted to get close, but there was a teenage boy who walked down to the brown river with a stick. He grinned at the camera and waved, and then poked the buffalo three times in the stomach. I had assumed that it was recently dead, because of the shininess of its black coat, and was surprised to see that once the explosion of black flies had risen off the corpse, there were large white spots, especially on the head, where the bones had already been picked clean.

After the news, I went into the bedroom and lay down. I thought about the people in a tent in my parents' backyard, proposing toasts. When I imagined myself there, I was afraid of something new—not just of being lonely but of what I would be lonely for.

Once, when Laxmi took the children to visit her parents in Calcutta, Arun spent four nights with me. On one of those nights, as we were lying in bed, I heard a bird outside, making a sound I recognized: a long swoop and then a two-note trill. I had thought that a nightingale lived in our compound and had asked Arun about it. He'd said it might be a mockingbird or a myna, but he would have to hear it to know.

'Arun,' I whispered. I put my hand on his shoulder. 'Arun, listen.' I was afraid it wouldn't come again, but it did; far away. Then it was closer, and then it was right outside our window, in the dusty leaves of the mango tree.

Arun rolled over, and I could see his eyes in the dark. He was laughing.

'What?' I asked. He kissed my forehead and pulled me on top of him.

'Why are you laughing?'

'It's the night-watchman bird,' Arun said solemnly. 'Sh-h-h, or he'll report us to headquarters.'

Since then, I'd often heard the night watchman whistling, and once or twice I'd seen him on his bicycle, a skinny young man in an olive green civil servant's uniform, with a wooden stick against his hip.

I tried to picture Arun's face, but I couldn't—the image wouldn't stay clear. I could picture the compound, though: the women walking in pairs to the green-tiled vegetable shop across the road, the mango tree, a red cricket ball that had rolled underneath my hedge months ago and now looked like some kind of exotic bloom. Was it Arun, or India? Or was it that, for me, Arun was India?

It was six o'clock, and I recognized the whiskey-colored light on the white sheets: Arun pinning my wrists down with his hands, holding me tight beneath him so I couldn't move. It was not like with other people; he took it seriously, as if these were necessary things we were doing. Those evenings—Arun's car in front of the house, everyone knowing we were there—the whole world was in our room: tiny inscrutable figures moving in a pattern across our sheets.

And then the light was gone, and the windows were long and green, the walls steep. I sat up, and, in that moment, when my feet touched the cool cement, I had such an immediate sense of what had been blotted out: a white slice of dome, like an eye behind a half-closed lid—the unexpected view of something everyone in the world has seen a thousand times.

ACKNOWLEDGEMENTS

'The Toughest Indian in the World' from *The Toughest Indian in the World* by Sherman Alexie. Copyright © 2000 by Sherman Alexie. Reprinted in the UK and the US by permission of Grove/Atlantic, Inc.

'Me and Miss Mandible' from *Come Back, Dr. Caligari* by Donald Barthelme. Copyright © 1961, 1962, 1963, 1964 by Donald Barthelme. Reprinted in the UK by permission of SLL/Sterling Lord Literistic, Inc. Reprinted in the US by permission of Little, Brown and Co., Inc.

'Ancient History', copyright © 1987, from *The Stories of Richard Bausch* by Richard Bausch. Copyright © 2003 by Richard Bausch. Reprinted by permission of HarperCollins Publishers.

'The Rabbit Hole as Likely Explanation' from *Follies: New Stories* by Ann Beattie. Copyright © 2005 by Irony & Pity, Inc. Reprinted by permission of Scribner, an imprint of Simon & Schuster Adult Publishing Group.

'The Miracle at Ballinspittle' from *If the River was Whiskey* by T. Coraghessan Boyle. Copyright © 1989 by T. Coraghessan Boyle. Reprinted in the UK by permission of Granta Books. Reprinted in the US by permission of Viking Penguin, a division of Penguin Group (USA) Inc.

'Mr. Green' from *A Good Scent from a Strange Mountain* by Robert Olen Butler. Copyright © 1992 by Robert Olen Butler. Originally published in the *Hudson Review*. Reprinted by permission of Henry Holt and Company, LLC.

'Blue Boy' from *A Stranger in this World* by Kevin Canty. Copyright © 1994 by Kevin Canty. Originally published in the *Missouri Review*. Reprinted in the UK by permission of the Denise Shannon Literary Agency, Inc. Reprinted in the US by permission of Doubleday, a division of Random House, Inc.

'Errand' from *Where I'm Calling From*. Copyright © 1976, 1977, 1981,

1983, 1986, 1987, 1988 by Raymond Carver. Reprinted in the UK by permission of Tess Gallagher. Reprinted in the US by permission of Grove/Atlantic, Inc.

'Reunion' from *The Stories of John Cheever* by John Cheever. Copyright © 1978 by John Cheever. Reprinted in the UK and US by permission of the Wylie Agency.

'Aurora' from *Drown* by Junot Díaz. Copyright © 1996 by Junot Díaz. Reprinted in the UK by permission of Faber & Faber Ltd. Reprinted in the US by permission of Riverhead Books, an imprint of Penguin Group (USA) Inc.

'Killings' from *Finding a Girl in America* by Andre Dubus. Copyright © 1980 by Andre Dubus. Reprinted in the UK and US by permission of David R. Godine, Publisher, Inc.

'The Palatski Man' from *Childhood and Other Neighbourhoods: Stories* by Stuart Dybek. Copyright © 1980 by Stuart Dybek. Reprinted in the UK and US by permission of International Creative Management Inc.

'The Custodian' from *Under the 82nd Airborne* by Deborah Eisenberg. Copyright © 1992 by Deborah Eisenberg. Reprinted in the UK and US by permission of Farrar, Straus and Giroux, LLC.

'The Tumblers' from *For the Relief of Unbearable Urges* by Nathan Englander. Copyright © 1999 by Nathan Englander. Reprinted in the UK by permission of Faber & Faber Ltd. Reprinted in the US by permission of Alfred A. Knopf, a division of Random House, Inc.

'The Plague of Doves' by Louise Erdrich. Copyright © by Louise Erdrich. First published in the *New Yorker*. Reprinted in the UK and US by permission of the Wylie Agency.

'Grit' from *Poachers* by Tom Franklin. Copyright © 1999 by Tom Franklin. Reprinted in the UK by permission of HarperCollins Publishers Ltd. Reprinted in the US by permission of HarperCollins Publishers, William Morrow.

the UK by permission of author. Reprinted in the US by permission of Houghton Mifflin Company.

'Anthropology' from *Interesting Women* by Andrea Lee. Copyright © 2002 by Andrea Lee. Reprinted in the UK by permission of International Creative Management Inc. Reprinted in the US by permission of HarperCollins Publishers Ltd.

'Nothing to Ask For' from *The Music Room: A Novel*, by Dennis McFarland. Copyright © 1990 by Dennis McFarland. Reprinted in the UK by permission of Brandt & Hochman Literary Agents, Inc. Reprinted in the US by permission of Henry Holt and Company, LLC.

'People Like That Are the Only People Here: Canonical Babbling in Peed Onk' from *Birds of America* by Lorrie Moore. Copyright © 1998 by Lorrie Moore. Reprinted in the UK by permission of the author c/o Rogers, Coleridge & White Ltd., 20 Powis Mews, London W11 1JN. Reprinted in the US by permission of Alfred A. Knopf, a division of Random House, Inc.

'The Management of Grief' from *The Middleman and Other Stories* by Bharati Mukherjee. Copyright © 1998 by Bharati Mukherjee. Reprinted in the UK and US by permission of Grove/Atlantic, Inc.

'Where *Is* Here?' from *Where is Here? Stories by Joyce Carol Oates* by Joyce Carol Oates. Copyright © 1992 by the *Ontario Review*, Inc. Reprinted in the UK by permission of John Hawkins & Associates, Inc. Reprinted in the US by permission of HarperCollins Publishers, Ecco Press.

'The Artificial Nigger' from *A Good Man is Hard to Find: Stories* by Flannery O'Connor. Copyright © 1948, 1953, 1954, 1955 by Flannery O'Connor; copyright © renewed 1976, 1981, 1982, 1983 by Regina O'Connor. All rights reserved. Reprinted in the UK by permission of the Mary Flannery O'Connor Charitable Trust. Reprinted in the US by permission of Harcourt, Inc.

'Stars of Motown Shining Bright' from *How to Breathe Underwater* by Julie Orringer. Copyright © 2003 by Julie Orringer. Reprinted in the UK by permission of Penguin Books Ltd. Reprinted in the US by permission of Alfred A. Knopf, a division of Random House, Inc.

'The Ant of the Self' from *Drinking Coffee Elsewhere* by ZZ Packer. Copyright © 2003 by ZZ Packer. Reprinted in the UK by permission of Canongate Books Ltd, 14 High Street, Edinburgh, EH1 1TE. Reprinted in the US by permission of Riverhead Books, an imprint of Penguin Group (USA) Inc.

'Friends' from *The Collected Stories* by Grace Paley. Copyright © 1994 by Grace Paley. Reprinted in the UK by permission of the author. Reprinted in the US by permission of Farrar, Straus and Giroux, LLC.

'The Half-Skinned Steer' from *Close Range: Wyoming Stories* by Annie Proulx. Copyright © 1999 by Dead Line, Ltd. All rights reserved. Reprinted in the UK by kind permission of the artist and the Sayle Literary Agency. Reprinted in the US by permission of Scribner, an imprint of Simon & Schuster Adult Publishing Group.

'CivilWarLand in Bad Decline' from *CivilWarLand in Bad Decline* by George Saunders. Copyright © 1996 by George Saunders. Reprinted in the UK by permission of George Saunders c/o Rogers, Coleridge & White Ltd., 20 Powis Mews, London W11 1JN. Reprinted in the US by permission of Random House, Inc.

'Ship Island: The Story of a Mermaid' from *The Stories of Elizabeth Spencer* by Elizabeth Spencer. Copyright © 1964 by Elizabeth Spencer. Originally published in the *New Yorker*. Reprinted in the UK and US by permission of McIntosh & Otis, Inc.

'Helping' from *Bear and His Daughter* by Robert Stone. Copyright © 1997 by Robert Stone. All rights reserved. Reprinted in the UK by permission of Bloomsbury Publishing, PLC. Reprinted in the US by permission of Houghton Mifflin Company.

'Natural Color' from *Licks of Love: Short Stories and a Sequel, 'Rabbit Remembered'* by John Updike. Copyright © 2000 by John Updike.

Reprinted in the UK and US by permission of Alfred A. Knopf, a division of Random House, Inc.

'Ladies in Spring' from *The Bride of the Innisfallen and Other Stories* by Eudora Welty. Copyright © 1954 and renewed 1982 by Eudora Welty. Originally published in *Sewanee*, Winter 1954. Reprinted in the UK by permission of Russell & Volkening as agents for the author. Reprinted in the US by permission of Harcourt, Inc

'The Farm', from *Taking Care* by Joy Williams. Copyright © 1972, 1973, 1974, 1976, 1977, 1980, 1981, 1982 by Joy Williams. Reprinted in the UK by permission of International Creative Management Inc. Reprinted in the US by permission of Random House, Inc.

'Firelight' from *The Night in Question* by Tobias Wolff. Copyright © 1996 by Tobias Wolff. Reprinted in the UK and US by permission of International Creative Management Inc.

'Two Dogs' by Steve Yarbrough. Copyright © 2000 by Steve Yarbrough. Reprinted in the UK by permission of International Creative Management Inc. Reprinted in the US by permission of the author and John LeBow Candia, NH: 2000. Printed in an edition of two hundred copies, with only one hundred and seventy-six copies for sale.

'Oh, Joseph, I'm So Tired' from *The Collected Stories of Richard Yates* by Richard Yates. Copyright © 2001 by the Estate of Richard Yates. Reprinted in the UK by permission of Methuen Publishing Ltd. Reprinted in the US by permission of Henry Holt and Company, LLC.